# The FBI Inspector

# The FBI Inspector

**Jay Dubya**

www.bookstandpublishing.com

Published by
Bookstand Publishing
Pasadena, CA  91101
4407_12



ISBN 978-1-63498-317-4

# For Ginger

# Other Books by Jay Dubya

*Pieces of Eight*
*Pieces of Eight, Part II*
*Pieces of Eight, Part III*
*Pieces of Eight, Part IV*
*Nine New Novellas*
*Nine New Novellas, Part II*
*Nine New Novellas, Part III*
*Nine New Novellas, Part IV*
*Black Leather and Blue Denim, A '50s Novel*
*The Great Teen Fruit War, A 1960 Novel*
*Frat' Brats, A '60s Novel*
*Ron Coyote, Man of La Mangia*
*So Ya' Wanna' Be A Teacher!*
*The Wholly Book of Genesis*
*The Wholly Book of Exodus*
*The Wholly Book of Doo-Doo-Rot-on-Me*
*Mauled Maimed Mangled Mutilated Mythology*
*Fractured Frazzled Folk Fables and Fairy Farces*
*Fractured Frazzled Folk Fables and Fairy Farces, Part II*
*Thirteen Sick Tasteless Classics*
*Thirteen Sick Tasteless Classics, Part II*
*Thirteen Sick Tasteless Classics, Part III*
*Thirteen Sick Tasteless Classics, Part IV*
*Thirteen Sick Tasteless Classics, Part V*
*RAM: Random Articles and Manuscripts*
*One Baker's Dozen*
*Two Baker's Dozen*
*UFO: Utterly Fantastic Occurrences*
*Shakespeare: Slammed, Smeared, Savaged and Slaughtered*
*Shakespeare: S, S, S, and S, Part II*
*Snake Eyes and Boxcars*
*Snake Eyes and Boxcars, Part II*
*Suite 16*
*O. Henry: Obscenely and Outrageously Obliterated*
*Twain: Tattered, Trounced, Tortured and Traumatized*
*Poe: Pelted, Pounded, Pummeled and Pulverized*
*London: Lashed, Lacerated, Lampooned and Lambasted*
*Hawthorne: Hazed Hooked Hammered and Hijacked*
*Hawthorne Hacked, Shakespeare Sacked & Thurber Thwacked*
*Time Travel Tales*

## Young Adult Fantasy Novels

# Contents

# Description

The twenty-six imaginative novellas presented in *The FBI Inspector* are works of pure fiction. The stories' themes deal with various types of crime and criminal motivation. Any character resemblance to anyone living on Planet Earth is positively coincidental. In addition, any fictional setting or scenario is also coincidental.

# "Mt. Rushmore"

On Columbus Day, October 12<sup>th</sup>, 2015 a well-rested FBI Inspector Joe Giralo thought he would use the holiday to have an early morning visit with his old friend Jerry Gares, a retired school system assistant superintendent living with his wife Irene in Burlington City, New Jersey. While enjoying a pleasant reunion, precisely at 11 a.m., Chief Giralo was the recipient of an urgent phone call from DC headquarters; a directive that would involve his immediate participation and assignment. After apologizing to his Burlington City hosts for a need for his sudden departure, the Chief swiftly hopped into his gray Chevy Suburban, fired-up the engine, and without further hesitation, motored southeast on Route 541 with the notion of Hammonton, New Jersey being his ultimate destination.

Realizing that his treasured gas-guzzling vehicle needed fuel while cruising through downtown Medford, the FBI Boss decided to stop and fill his gas tank at an Exxon station where the on-a-mission gentleman could conveniently kill two birds with one stone by simultaneously making a planned cell phone call to his always-dependable and available agent, Sal Velardi.

"Sal, I'm sorry to interrupt your mini-vacation, but an important issue just came up that obviously needs to be addressed," the excited Chief mildly apologized. "I'm now in Medford on 541 heading toward 206. I'd like to meet you, Arty and Dan in about forty-five minutes for an impromptu lunch at the Pic-A-Lilli. I'll discuss the pertinent details with you three accomplished detectives at our familiar corner table; you know, the one behind the center stone fireplace."

Agent Velardi instantly remembered that his mentor had on Friday disclosed that on Columbus Day Inspector Giralo would be in Burlington City visiting his buddy Jerry Gares, so in order to extend the Monday conversation and learn more particulars about the local FBI team's most recent federal crime case, the ordinarily diplomatic agent proceeded to comment about his boss's long-time educator acquaintance.

"How did you and Dr. Gares become friends?" Velardi asked, aware that he had heard the boring narrative a least a dozen times. "Wasn't it at a wedding?"

"Yes Salvatore," confirmed Joe Giralo, now relishing a more jovial mood. "In 1998, I was pals with Professor Bill Burns and his wife Fran, both of Camden Community College. In the 1970s, Jerry and Irene Gares and Bill and Fran Burns lived near each other in

Burlington City where both fellas' had incidentally begun their teaching careers in nearby Burlington Township," the Chief articulated. "When Bill's son got married in 1998, Gina and I sat with Irene and Jerry at the same table, the fancy reception being at the Avalon Yacht Club down the Jersey Shore."

"Wasn't your chum Professor Burns a little eccentric? I believe I remember you telling me such."

"Yes, Salvatore," reluctantly admitted Inspector Giralo. "Jerry and I along with our wives had been passengers on the last 'Love Boat' cruise out of New York down to Hamilton in Bermuda. Bill and Fran Burns were merrily vacationing in London at the time," the Boss supplemented. "Burns had promised me a month before that he and his wife would fly from Heathrow to Bermuda to stop-in and have a drink. The itinerant pair took a taxi to a restaurant and met Jerry, me and our wives there, had two drinks at the bar, and then after the very short rendezvous, returned back to the Bermuda Airport by taxi to then fly-off to 'Philly. Now, if *that* irregular instance I've just mentioned isn't demonstrating eccentric behavior, I don't know exactly what is!"

"Bill Burns had kept his promise!" Agent Velardi exclaimed, feigning enthusiasm for the hackneyed tale. "Yes indeed! An honest man always honors his word. But didn't you once tell me that he's on almost every U.S. terrorist list?"

"There were or are a dozen or so scoundrels named 'William Burns' that had been closely associated with the Northern Ireland IRA, so naturally, my pal Bill Burns was always detained for specific questioning when flying in and out of various airports; especially in the U.S. Unfortunately, having a common Irish name such as 'William Burns' could sometimes be a detriment, let alone an inconvenience to its bearer! And Salvatore, I know how you think. Please don't tell me, just to be funny, that your personal IRA is almost bankrupt!"

Agent Velardi was not deterred by his superior's shrewd resistance. "And furthermore, Chief. Didn't Jerry Gares play the large double bass fiddle in a rock and roll band to earn extra money for college? That's gotta' be one of *your* pet stories, too!"

"Yes," Inspector Giralo affirmed, seizing the new-found opportunity to verbally expound on his subordinate's intentional coy introduction. "Back in the early '60s, most rock and roll bands used the double bass fiddle several years before bass guitars took over producing *that* special low background sound. One fine afternoon, Jerry Gares was surprised to get an emergency call from the local union hall. The bass fiddle player for Bill Haley and his Comets became ill during an extended playing engagement in Philadelphia, so my friend Gares was suddenly appointed to play on stage with the famous band at Palumbo's Restaurant in South 'Philly. Even if it sounds fairly redundant," Giralo paused and emphasized, "I just love telling *this* totally terrific story. That chance to play 'Rock around the Clock' with the Comets must've been a truly thrilling experience for an ambitious college freshman! I can't believe I've never told you about Gares and his connection with Bill Haley!"

"Yes, Boss. Palumbo's was a big venue way back then. It was always advertised on TV and the radio. Stars like Frank Sinatra, Rosemary Clooney and Jimmy Durante often sang and entertained there," Sal Velardi melodramatically contributed to the lackluster dialogue. "If I recall, the entire place was really big, located somewhere near the Italian Market on Ninth Street. It burned to the ground in 1994. The dirty laundry 'Philly newspapers maintained that arson was the possible cause. Wasn't Jefferson president at the time?"

"And listen to this one, Sal," garrulous Joe Giralo resumed his Jerry Gares' story litany while ignoring Velardi's cynicism. "Last December my Burlington friend wanted to show me the fantastic red and white poinsettia array displayed inside St. Mary Episcopal Church where Dr. Gares is a venerable deacon. Jerry nonchalantly opened the side door with his key, which then much to *his* embarrassment, had automatically triggered the building's burglar alarm. Cops in patrol cars frantically descended onto the premises from all directions, and it was a good thing that Dr. Gares was well-known in the community and had taught several of the officers when they were in high school. Salvatore, could you imagine the devastating tabloid-type headlines all over Southern Jersey? 'Famous FBI Inspector and Assistant School Superintendent Are Arrested Breaking into Historic Church'! My reputation would've been sullied if not completely ruined!"

But wanting to discover more facts about his new FBI assignment, Agent Velardi determined that he should deftly switch the subject from Dr. Gares' unique personal escapades to government criminal investigation business. "Boss; did you receive the important call from DC headquarters while at Jerry's house?"

"Indeed," Giralo verified over his cell phone loosely wedged between his right shoulder and chin as the Inspector fumbled his chubby fingers inside his wallet to locate the exact denominations to pay the impatient gas station attendant thirty-five dollars in cash. "And thanks to modern-day computer applications' technology," Giralo pontificated, "I was able to skillfully transfer the received DC dispatch from my hand-held device right into Jerry's desktop printer. I now have four copies of the vital information; three of which I'll distribute to you, Dan and Arty around noon at the Pic-A-Lilli."

"We all like the terrific spicy hot wings the 'Pic' has to offer," Agent Velardi attested. "They're absolutely my favorite item on the whole menu. Around noon is a good time to go there, too. In late afternoon, the rowdy pineys arrive along with the rambunctious Harley Hog motorcycle gangs. The bearded and tattooed bikers predictably pull into the Pic's parking lot like ruthless Hells Angels, and soon the four of us would feel like we're eating our delicious meals inside a small sardine can surrounded by ruthless savages."

"Okay, Salvatore; enough of your ludicrous oratory. Let's 'Shake, Rattle and Roll'!" answered Inspector Giralo as he carefully pulled-out of the Medford Exxon Station onto County Road 541.

"See You Later Alligator," Velardi cleverly replied while alluding-to another Bill Haley oldies' rock and roll hit.

"After While, Anaconda!" joked the inimitable Chief as Giralo deliberately twisted certain Haley song lyrics to selfishly accommodate *his* own unorthodox sense of humor.

* * * * * * * * * * * *

Inspector Giralo drove his gray Suburban from Route 541 onto Route 206 at Indian Mills. A mile southbound and positioned on the left was the landmark Pic-A-Lilli Inn, a quaint rustic tavern tucked into a section of the Wharton State Forest, which was often frequented by backwoods pineys and raucous motorcycle gangs. Waiting for their boss at the establishment's entrance were loyal FBI agents Sal Velardi, Art Orsi and Dan Blachford.

After conducting their regular and informal perfunctory greeting, the four comrades-in-law entered the cozy bar area and were promptly escorted to their designated corner dining-room table situated behind the central rectangular stone fireplace.

"Boss, was this bistro named after that tourist attraction across the pond in London?" Agent Velardi quipped. "I don't see any expensive portraits of Queen Elizabeth or William Shakespeare adorning the walls. All I see hanging around this big room are deer and bear head trophies mounted by taxidermists!"

"Don't be ridiculous, Salvatore! Remember Men, we're supposed to be professionals quietly venturing-out in public," politely chastised the all-too serious leader. "Sometimes Sal; I don't know whether you're pulling my leg or suffering from a severe case of constipation of the brain. The world-famous Piccadilly Circus theater district is what you're referring to in London. Furthermore, I understand that the

4

term 'Pic-A-Lilli' pertains to a certain early 1930s Pine Barrens' method of pickled food processing where vegetables were preserved in jars before refrigeration became a much-convenient necessity."

"You have the knowledge and sagacity of a saint!" Sal Velardi praised and guiltily countered.

"I can't be a saint!" Giralo reprimanded in a contrived angry tone of voice. "In order to be a saint, one must first be dead!"

While his eyes were randomly studying the extensive menu, Inspector Giralo monotonously explained to his yawning companions how a wealthy Philadelphia tycoon named Joseph Wharton had founded a renowned business college in the Quaker City and that the motivated entrepreneur had riskily purchased thousands of land acres in the South Jersey Pine Barrens because over five trillion gallons of pristine fresh water exists under the coniferous forests.

"What did Mr. Wharton intend to use all of that water for?" Art Orsi inquired. "Isn't the forest now protected by conservation laws?"

"Yes, it is, Arty," Giralo replied while casually examining the dessert section of the huge menu. "But back in the late 1800s and early 1900s, city water was often polluted, so Joseph Wharton figured that he could profitably have fresh water pumped from the Pine Barrens across the Delaware into 'Philly and across the Hudson into New York. However, when fresh water was obtained from reservoirs in the Poconos and from large lakes above the Big Apple because of new technologies that had been developed, Mr. Wharton abandoned his grandiose scheme of massive water redistribution."

After a pretty blonde waitress jotted-down the four orders of red-hot spicy chicken wings and accompanying cold mugs of draught beer, Inspector Giralo reached into his oak tag folder and disseminated identical sheets of typed paper to his very curious FBI team.

"I figured we should evaluate this data before our hands get greasy from the messy hot wings," the Chief constructively suggested. "Now let's use our cerebrums and fully coordinate our limited mental abilities. Please silently read your copies of this seemingly harmless email that had been adroitly intercepted by the NSA and then forwarded to our DC headquarters, which then relayed the message to me while I had been visiting over at Jerry Gares' home. Confidentially, it's the strange missive's subject matter along with its general composition that has made the guys down in DC quite suspicious and concerned about the item's general content. Notice Men that the letter's grammar, punctuation and vocabulary are rather sophisticated, obviously suggesting that both the writer and the recipient must be college educated."

July 4th, 2015

 Dear Ferris,

As you know, I really love viewing '50s and '60s TV reruns with my favorite variety program being "The Ed Sullivan Show." Most of the classic shows I watch are featured on the cable TVLand network. I highly recommend that you watch them too, because in our last phone conversation, you had stated that you totally love '50s and '60s movies. Obviously, we have plenty in common.

Now Ferris, I've compiled a quality list of my all-time favorite '50s and '60s TV shows, so here they are.

1. Gunsmoke
2. Bonanza
3. Tales of Wells Fargo
4. Beat the Clock
5. Truth or Consequences
6. Lassie
7. Science Fiction Theater
8. The Cisco Kid
9. Dragnet
10. Naked City
11. Peter Gunn
12. The Guiding Light
13. Maverick
14. American Bandstand
15. The Rifleman
16. Hogan's Heroes
17. Jeopardy
18. Mr. Peepers
19. Dennis the Menace
20. Whirlybirds
21. Have Gun, Will Travel
22. The Twilight Zone
23. Sea Hunt
24. Hawaiian Eye
25. 77 Sunset Strip
26. General Hospital
27. The Beverly Hillbillies
28. Ironsides
29. The Fugitive
30. Twelve O' Clock High

31.   Lost in Space
32.   Hawaii Five-O
33.   The F.B.I.
34.   The Outer Limits
35.   The Asphalt Jungle
36.   Route 66
37.   Flipper
38.   Big City Detective
39.   You Asked for It
40.   The Life of Riley

I hope Ferris that you'll be able to appreciate these wonderful '50s and '60s TV shows and enjoy them as much as I do.

Your friend,
James


"Now Men, what do you make of this rather peculiar e-mail?" Inspector Giralo asked. "And Salvatore, please don't ask me if Ferris is a big wheel carnival owner! Now as an illustration of what I actually mean, the idea of 'Flipper' might be relating to a pinball machine manufacturing company. Truly Guys; let's methodically brainstorm this challenge and then construct some relevant, plausible hypothesis about what this dubious correspondence possibly entails. For example, is anything noteworthy in the e-mail being repeated, other than the very evident '50s and '60s TV theme?"

"Well, Boss, numbers 24 and 32 are somewhat related. If you'll notice, Hawaii is indicated twice: once for 'Hawaiian Eye' and a second time for 'Hawaii Five-O'," Agent Velardi indicated.

"That 'Hawaii parallel you've just cited could be a factor in narrowing-down and unlocking the essential key to this oddball puzzle, if indeed it is a puzzle," Joe Giralo commended. "Now here's some basic arithmetic. What numbers go into both 24 and 32?" Giralo rhetorically asked. "The logical answers would be 2, 4 and 8, with 2 being represented as the lowest common denominator."

"I think the key factor is number 4 because then we would have a nice round ten numbers, or comparable TV shows to tinker with," Art Orsi conjectured and expressed. "Ten of the given shows would then be 'hot items', while the other 30 would simply be thrown-into the mix as mere dummy references. If that were the case, the ten items would be #4 Beat the Clock, #8 The Cisco Kid, #12 The Guiding Light, #16 Hogan's Heroes, #20 Whirlybirds, #24 Hawaiian Eye, #28 Ironsides, #32 Hawaii Five-O, #36 Route 66 and finally, #40…."

"The Life of Riley!" Velardi, Blachford and Giralo all uttered in unison, with their instinctive astonishment getting the attention of distracted patrons seated at nearby tables.

"And Number 40 is divisible by 2, 4 and 8!" Art Orsi whispered across the table.

"What do you make of these ten shows that Arty's isolated?" Velardi asked his now-worried colleagues. "I still think that the key to the overall solution is the Number 4. Do you suppose the ten separated shows point to ten prospective singled-out targets? My government issued hand computer shows no recent bombs being exploded in Hawaii or at any other places referenced in the ten show titles."

"This might sound far-fetched, but I think that 'Beat the Clock' might refer to Big Ben over outside Westminster Abbey in London; perhaps a dangerous bomb being planted inside the British Parliament," Joe Giralo wildly speculated and stated. "Yes Fellas'; perhaps a contemporary Guy Fawkes scenario is being set into motion! And the 'Cisco Kid' could pertain to a destructive event scheduled to occur somewhere in San Francisco. And the 'Guiding Light' could allude to any lighthouse detonation along the East or West Coast. And 'Hogan's Heroes' could associate with..."

"Could be any large sub' shop in America because submarines are called 'heroes' in New York, but are otherwise classified as 'hoagies' in 'Philly," Sal Velardi communicated. "And 'Whirlybirds' could be an explosion being created inside any U.S. or foreign helicopter factory. And 'Ironsides' might be as a target that famous War of 1812 battleship the *USS Constitution*, also known as *Old Ironsides,* now docked in Boston Harbor. And of course, good old 'Route 66'..."

"Had originated in Chicago which would make every bank and skyscraper in the Windy City vulnerable," Blachford instantly recognized and shared. "And last but possibly not least, 'The Life of Riley' could be our beloved bureaucratic FBI superior down at DC headquarters...."

"Matt Riley!" Velardi, Orsi and Giralo all exclaimed in chorus, again getting the prompt attention of the other two tables of Pic-A-Lilli diners seated in the general proximity.

"I think I've just lost my appetite!" ordinarily voracious Joe Giralo complained, just as the attractive blonde waitress approached their corner table with an enormous tray holding four large bowls of spicy hot wings along with four frosted mugs of beer.

* * * * * * * * * * * *

8

On Tuesday, Wednesday and Thursday, Inspector Giralo and his three tenacious investigators diligently worked on other intriguing FBI cases besides the perplexing "e-mail Oldies TV Shows' caper", which might have incredibly been in Dan Blachford's humble opinion "an elaborate hoax". All the while, Sal Velardi, Art Orsi and "the Chief" were mutually worried that the revered Matt Riley's life might be in grave jeopardy.

On Thursday evening, the Boss conducted a telephone conference call with his "Three Magnificent Musketeers" and then verbally concluded, "I think that Arty was right in his assumption that the Number 4 is the correct key to identifying prospective target locations. I believe that the 'key to the key' was in the first sentence where the email author James claimed that 'The Ed Sullivan Show' was his favorite. Notice Gentlemen," Giralo persuasively summarized. "There are exactly 4 words in the TV title described in the opening statement."

At 9 a.m. on Friday, Velardi, Orsi and Blachford faithfully arrived at 600 Arch Street in Philadelphia. After exiting the elevator, the threesome strolled into the eighth-floor office of their erudite Chief, who as usual was preoccupied drinking a cup of Maxwell House coffee while avidly reading the early morning front-page headlines of the *Philadelphia Inquirer*.

"Newspaper circulation is diminishing because of the rise of cable news 24/7 coverage and because of efficient Internet search engines like Google and Yahoo," Giralo prefaced. "Now Fellas', I want to cut to the chase in regard to this scary Matt Riley predicament. Yesterday, I received from the wonks over at NSA a second e-mail that apparently corresponds to the subject matter of the first one we had reviewed on Monday at the Pic-A-Lilli. Remember, however; no outstanding crimes or extensive vandalisms have been committed as of yet. Now this second electronic communication is in the form of a direct response from Ferris addressed to James," the FBI official disclosed. "Notice that Ferris, like James, also appears to be a well-educated college student proficient in good grammar and skilled in accomplished writing ability."

Giralo then distributed copies of the second related e-mail to his eager-and-curious G-squad, and next advised the trio to quietly read and analyze the dispatch's '50s and '60s motion picture elements.

July 25, 2015

Dear James,

Please recognize that I totally love all ten of the '50s and '60s films I'm writing to you about. And in regard to your e-mail, I plan on watching the TVLand cable network that you had recommended and catch some of the early shows that have apparently captured your interest. Now, here are ten of my cinema classics.

1.   West Side Story
2.   Cape Fear
3.   The Music Man
4.   Some Like It Hot
5.   On the Waterfront
6.   Rebel without a Cause
7.   Niagara
8.   East of Eden
9.   The War of the Worlds
10.  Bus Stop

And James, here's a pleasant reminder. Be patriotic. Don't forget to vote on Election Day. It's your civic duty and democratic responsibility. Parents should leave no child sleeping, and if necessary, voters should take their infants and toddlers to the polls.

Your college pal,
Ferris


Several minutes elapsed when the portly official seated behind the colossal oak desk asked, "Now Arty, what do you make of these ten splendid cinema productions?"

"Well, Boss," Agent Orsi stammered, stalling for precious time. "Marilyn Monroe had starred in three of the movies: Some Like It Hot, Niagara and Bus Stop. And James Dean starred in Rebel without a Cause and East of Eden. That's about all that my beleaguered brain can decipher right now!"

"Forgive Agent Orsi's disheveled mind," Agent Velardi chuckled. "But at Arty's college admissions' office, there were administrators Dean James, Dean Martin, and Dean Jerry Lewis!"

"Salvatore, this is a very top priority matter we're discussing, and I sincerely caution you to tone-down your absurd humor and gear-up your faulty self-discipline!" politely admonished the Inspector. "Now

Dan; what pearls of wisdom have you derived from interpreting this second sugar-coated e-mail?"

"Well, Boss; unlike the first e-mail from James to Ferris, this one, I think, indicates ten places that are to be attacked starting on Tuesday, November 3rd, Election Day. For example, a War of the Worlds might be ignited between Western and Eastern Civilizations, or perhaps between Islam and Christianity. And fishing piers could be blown-up at Cape Fear, North Carolina. And any big-name Music Man performing on stage might be assassinated on *that* date. And the reference Bus Stop might be an allusion to major chaos being caused at New York's Port Authority Bus Terminal. And East of Eden could be unexpected conflict arising east of Iraq, where Eden was supposedly located in Biblical times. And naturally," Blachford elucidated, "Rebel without a Cause could mean...."

"The famous planetarium near Los Angeles featured in the classic movie's second and last scenes," Hollywood film buff Velardi finished. "And Marlon Brando had starred in the black and white film On the Waterfront, which implies that the entire New York City docks could be at risk. And Some Like It Hot could suggest...."

"A nuclear-type dirty bomb being evilly detonated somewhere over Manhattan; perhaps over Times Square!" Agent Orsi imagined and declared. "And Guys; the obliteration of Niagara Falls would send the entire U.S. economy into sudden turmoil!"

"Say Inspector," Agent Velardi piped-up. "What do you think about the mentioning of West Side Story? It's listed as #1 on the very weird movie list?"

Joe Giralo then amazed his three federal gumshoes by candidly disclosing that his gut instinct was the imaginative deduction that the Dakota Building on New York's Upper West Side had been the home of John Lennon and Yoko Ono, and that the nearby Strawberry Fields Monument, currently regarded as a part of Central Park, was a benign tribute to the Beatles 1966 hit tune 'Strawberry Fields Forever'. "I think that the Dakota in the Upper West Side is the pertinent key to this second e-mail being solved, since West Side Story is #1 on the ten items shown. And furthermore, Gentlemen," Giralo surmised and glibly orated. "Mt. Rushmore is not a national monument dedicated to skilled football fullbacks! It's virtually a sacred American historic shrine!"

"Are you saying that Mt. Rushmore in South Dakota is going to be exploded on Election Day?" Sal Velardi asked in astonishment. "Who in Heaven's name is ever going to believe that?"

"Salvatore; I'm saying that the second e-mail in the exact one-to-ten order sent from Ferris to James spells-out the first ten sites to be besieged, while on the other hand, the first e-mail sent from James to Ferris maps-out targets that will eventually be attacked in the future," the Inspector firmly conveyed to his shocked three-man audience.

"Well then, Boss. Who are James and Ferris?" Agent Orsi wanted to know. "I presume that those two names are aliases!"

"My assiduous research has narrowed-down their exact names," the Chief somberly remarked. "According to reliable FBI records, James is Jamil Mustafa, and Ferris is Faris Safar, both radicalized graduate students at a prestigious New York University. It appears that James and Ferris have announced an upcoming jihad against Americans and American institutions, particularly against Hollywood and against New York TV shows, which in their' warped judgment, generate sin, sex and excessive freedom, all of which are anathema to their strict militant religious convictions!"

"And how does Matt Riley fit into your exotic equation?" Sal Velardi demanded. "Your ethereal theory sounds borderline fantasy, you know!"

"For your information, Salvatore," Inspector Giralo imperatively commented, "reputable Matt Riley is slated to be present at Mt. Rushmore in South Dakota on Tuesday, November 3rd to receive the highly coveted Good Citizenship Award from the very influential American Christian Benevolent Association!"

"So, if that's true, then what is the meaning of the weird phrase 'no child sleeping' that had been authored at the end of the second e-mail?" asked a still-amazed and mentally frazzled Dan Blachford. "Those three innocent words don't translate into jihadist propaganda to me!"

"It means in elementary code language that Matt Riley is not to be *kid-napped* but instead either assassinated or killed in a violent horrific Mt. Rushmore explosion!" Chief Giralo grimly answered. "Are you Men naïve and blind to the simple truth? The second list was the reverse of the first, with Riley being the last TV show and with West Side Story being the first oldies' movie. Fellas'; we're facing a formidable internal enemy that brazenly-and-furtively threatens us all! Don't you idealistic Guys get the whole enchilada? Federal, state and local law enforcement officers are all rapidly becoming a national endangered species! But first we have to save our immediate superior Matt Riley from being violently killed at Mt. Rushmore!"

# "A Concerted Effort"

At noon on Friday, July 26th, 2013 a rather fatigued FBI Inspector Joe Giralo summoned his three prime agents, Salvatore Velardi, Arthur Orsi and Dan Blachford into his eighth-floor office inside the all-too-familiar 600 Arch Street Federal Building, Philadelphia, Pennsylvania. As usual, the curious entrants found their illustrious superior sitting rather stationary behind his Canadian oak desk with his brown eyes seemingly transfixed, his pupils scanning the *Philadelphia Inquirer's* "above the crease" morning headlines, his ever-vigilant mind being keenly engrossed in much more serious crime matters than *those* trivial news' stories his alert cerebral processes were intensely evaluating.

"Greetings, Men!" the Chief nonchalantly acknowledged, lowering the slightly wrinkled newspaper below eye level. "Glad you three somewhat experienced sleuths were in the building when my secretary had summoned you' dynamos from your cramped cubicles. We've got some important business to attend to, but first of all," Inspector Giralo predictably deviated, "I want to know how you men are going to spend this upcoming weekend. The weatherman predicts it's gonna' be a real scorcher, so remember to stay hydrated and seek shade when outside!"

"I'll be taking my wife and kids in the SUV to Six Flags Great Adventure up in Jackson," Sal Velardi politely informed. "The fantastic venue's gotten some neat new thrill rides, some of them being roller coasters, and the giant park's only an hour and a half drive north from Hammonton.  I know it's going to be a sweltering day all over the East Coast," Agent Velardi rapidly prattled, "but before we know it, it'll be winter again and I'll be out shopping for a freshly-cut Christmas tree. I suppose I'm basically biased, but I would describe myself as a summer enthusiast. Fall and springtime are fine, but in all honesty, I find cold weather and snow to be absolutely abominable."

"Abominable as in Snowman!" chuckled Inspector Giralo before turning his attention to Agent Orsi. "And please tell me Arty, what about you?" the Chief imperatively asked. "Do you plan-on staying in air-conditioned comfort inside your Hammonton, New Jersey home, or are you and your clan bravely venturing-out into the torrid outdoors?"

"Tomorrow I'm ambitiously taking the family out to historic Batsto Village and showing my' sometimes-lethargic kids what human life was like during colonial times," Agent Orsi indicated.

"Once anyone sees how people had to struggle and toil performing their ordinary daily drudgery without having the luxury of various appliances and machines, anyone, including my occasionally phlegmatic kids, could then appreciate what it must've been like living without the modern conveniences we all take for granted nowadays. And then of course," Agent Orsi garrulously elaborated, "on Sunday it's always church and next an afternoon patio chicken and beef barbecue, and before I'll know it," the speaker emphasized and paused his mediocre narrative, "I'll be back here with you guys in 'Philly fighting dangerous Interstate Crime with a passion!"

Next, Dan Blachford calmly related to his distinguished audience of three that he and his spouse Bing had booked an expensive motel suite for two days up in New Hope, Pennsylvania for the expressed purpose of strolling around the popular tourist town and visiting the myriad craft and antique stores on Saturday, and then on Sunday afternoon, stopping at famous Washington's Crossing in Bucks County on the return trip to Hammonton. "How about you Chief?" self-conscious Blachford boldly inquired, somewhat out-of-character. "How do *you* intend occupying yourself over this July weekend? I'll bet you're going deep sea fishing out of that dilapidated Wildwood marina, you know, the one where your decrepit boat is currently moored!"

"Wrong, Dan!" the Boss loudly exclaimed, Giralo's tone feigning being offended by his underling's critical remark. "Tonight, I'll be taking Gina and our daughters down the Parkway to Cape May. The ferry to Lewes leaves at 7:30 and we've already reserved a space aboard for my Chevy Suburban to squeeze into. One year, I think it was 2006 if my memory serves me correctly," Joe Giralo communicated, "I had missed the last boat out of Cape May and had to drive a full seven hours to wind-up down in Ocean City, Maryland, which happens to be *our* R & R destination this weekend. I really got a tin ear from my wife and kids, and I never want to go through that kind of verbal trauma again if I can help it!"

"Are you staying again at the Holiday Inn near the 64th Street Bridge?" Agent Orsi wanted to know. "You always brag about that sensational Reflections Restaurant, which you insist is a wonderful mainstay right there on the premises!"

"Yes, Arty, and besides Reflections, I also enjoy dining at Phillip's Seafood Restaurant on 24th Street and at the steak-oriented Embers, not too far away on the Coastal Highway. And also, there's always the boardwalk where I love munching on Thrashers French Fries along with Fisher's Caramel Popcorn and then enjoying a frosted mug of beer inside the off-boardwalk Cork Bar," the Chief fondly related. "The resort's one of my favorite summer getaways and confidentially Men, in late August I hope to navigate my sleek boat down the coast from Wildwood to Captain Bill Bunting's Marina on the Ocean City, Maryland back-bay. And I gotta' admit, the kids really love playing pinball and games-for-prizes inside Marty's Playland and the neighboring Sportland Arcade too, both attractions located down at the south end of the boardwalk. And if I get brave enough, I'll climb aboard..."

"The ever-exciting Zipper Ride at Trimpers Amusements down near the Inlet Jetty," Dan Blachford very capably finished the Inspector's declarative sentence. "You always claim that you desire tumbling around inside your own revolving and rotating Zipper compartment, but you never seem to develop the necessary audacity to ever attempt the challenging adventure. And Boss, don't forget to tell us how you're going to enter the Ocean City White Marlin Fishing Tournament this year, just like you've predicted and *not* done the last three spectacular summers!"

Chief Giralo wisely and temporarily ignored Agent Blachford's extraordinarily excessive banter, the FBI boss's perceptive mind now focusing on much more urgent matters that required the veteran group's indispensable services. Almost in a hypnotic state of mind, Inspector Giralo slowly commenced introducing the vital topic of conversation to his illustrious trio.

"Crabs in a bushel!" Giralo deliberately uttered, almost to himself while again pensively thinking about Phillips Seafood Restaurant in Ocean City, Maryland. "Criminals of all ilks are just like clumsy crabs in a bushel, climbing all over each other trying to escape *our* tenacious clutches and never ever gaining their freedom, which translated into layman's terms means either jail or penitentiary time behind vertical steel bars. If only the doomed evil geniuses would direct their God-given talents to pursuing constructive goals," Giralo speculated and disclosed. "Then they'd ultimately wind-up being much richer and much more successful than they are, futilely advocating a miserable life of engaging in felony after felony. But most short-sighted ruthless law violators don't ever realize the stupidity of their ill-fated endeavors until the impetuous scoundrels are permanently locked behind inescapable prison cell bars."

"We've impatiently listened to and heard from your talkative lips very similar remarks on many monotonous occasions," criticized Agent Velardi, "so please Inspector, in plain commonplace English, explain to us the essential nature of our next assignment. I must confess, at times you have a definite propensity for being vague, mysterious and totally nebulous!"

The slightly insulted Inspector meticulously opened the top drawer of his massive desk and then carefully distributed sets of typed copies, each sample indicating a comprehensive list of recent burglaries that had occurred inside the secluded mansions of prominent and wealthy citizens, all residing in or near various major cities across the country. After allowing several quiet moments of intense visual examination along with keen scrutiny, Chief Giralo requested that Agent Velardi should read the specific locations where April twilight break-ins and daring evening thefts had been committed.

"Let's see now," pallid-faced Agent Velardi stated while carefully glancing-down at his smooth hand-held photocopy. "Here's the data. April 4th, Columbus, Ohio; April 6th, Malvern, just outside 'Philly; April 8th, West Chester, situated north of New York City; April 9th, Rockville, Maryland, just outside DC; April 11th, Louisville, Kentucky and next is April 13th, Oak Lawn, a prosperous suburb just outside Chicago."

"Yes, indeed," interrupted astute Inspector Giralo. "In each incident, millionaires, or should I say *multimillionaires*, had been cleverly targeted and their property imaginatively preyed-upon when no one was home. In each reported instance, the mansions' alarm systems had somehow been deactivated, and in some more complex situations," the Boss emphasized, "the electric power lines going into the exclusive suburban houses had been expertly cut, thus effectively disabling the precautionary hookups linked to different alarm companies and police stations."

"I'm not finished revealing my numerous April break-ins," Agent Velardi insisted, somewhat peeved. "April 18th, Cambridge, Massachusetts, just outside, Boston; April 20th, Uncasville, Connecticut; April 24th, Hillside, New Jersey near Newark; April 26th, Pittsburgh, Pennsylvania, and April 28th and 30th, expensive suburban estates near St. Paul, Minnesota and Kansas City, Missouri respectively."

"And in each case," an inordinately puzzled Inspector Joe Giralo summarized, "silverware, jewelry, cash, watches, mink coats along with other assorted valuables had been shrewdly heisted with the homes' alarms and electricity being neutralized. We're dealing with very skilled villains here, probably more than two teams of devious culprits, all of whom are rather proficient craftsmen at the lucrative art of initiating and completing creative grand larcenies."

Then, Agent Arthur Orsi anxiously read the itemized selections from his May hand-held list, with the following particular cities and their parallel dates being included: "May 1st, Tulsa, Oklahoma; May 2nd, Beverly Hills, California; May 3rd, Little Rock, Arkansas; May

4th, New Orleans, Louisiana; May 5th, Oakland, California; May 8th, San Jose, California; May 11th, Las Vegas, Nevada; May 15th, Anaheim, California; May 20th, Tacoma, Washington; May 22nd, San Jose, California; May 25th, Los Angeles; May 26th, Las Vegas again; May 28th, Anaheim, California again, and finally, May 31st, Oak Brook, Illinois, just outside Chicago."

"Did you Fine Men notice that several burglaries had occurred in or around Chicago, one on April 13th and the other on May 31st?" Inspector Giralo plausibly mentioned. "And Las Vegas had been hit on May 11th and on May 26th, probably by the same malevolent gang of thugs. And lastly Fellas', Anaheim had been victimized on May 15th and on May 28th, with Los Angles being zeroed-in on May 2nd and May 25th! And yes," normally introspective Giralo recollected and orally conveyed, "San Jose has two closely-related dates, May 8th and May 22nd. This scattered information, or should I say, 'irregular pattern sequence', might somehow be germane to *our* eventually solving this rather perplexing mind-boggling mansion theft conundrum! Now, are these dual dates and metropolitan places I've just cited mere coincidences? Or are they random geographic repetitions, or exactly what?"

Without any responses or pertinent interpretations being successfully elicited, the stern-faced Boss then instructed Agent Blachford to read from his typed paper, the names of June house robberies that had happened in separate cities and states, the lengthy recitation sounding something akin to a Homeric catalog being thoroughly described in the ancient *Iliad*. "June 1st, Denver; June 3rd, Chicago; June 4th, Dallas; June 5th, Houston; June 7th, Tampa; June 8th, Ft. Lauderdale; June 10th, Atlanta; June 12th, Detroit; June 12th, Boston, June 14th, Shaker Heights, near Cleveland; June 18th, 'Philly; June 19th, Albany; June 21st, Boston and 'Philly, both hit again; June 24th, Charlotte, North Carolina; June 26th, Des Moines, Iowa; June 29th, Spokane, Washington and finally Boss, June 30th, in Portland, Oregon."

"Kindly notice my Fine Law Enforcers that the Boston area had been hit twice in June and that Chicago had been singled-out on June 3rd just like it had been earmarked on April 13th and May 31st. And let's not forget 'Philly being vulnerable several times right here in our own backyard! Now Fellas', seriously contemplate *this* rather challenging idea. What particular common significance might these corresponding dates and cities have? Think Men, think! Usually there's a simple elementary explanation that'll enable us to decode this massive skein of Interstate mansion robberies. But first, just like in basic mathematics, *we* must initially discover the lowest common denominator!"

"Truthfully Chief, we're positively stymied and overwhelmed by these brazen felonies!" Agent Salvatore Velardi all-too-candidly answered. "If we were now meeting in Missouri, you might realistically conclude that we're all presently clueless in St. Louis! Where in the world is Uncasville? Could *that* Connecticut town be the all-too-elusive Missing Link we're searching for? Why don't *you* read the July dates Boss while *we* study them and look for a magic Rosetta-type Stone! Maybe some obscure pieces to this terribly disturbing jigsaw could then be magically deciphered and finally intelligently discerned."

Chief Giralo cleared his throat and then reluctantly participated in the extensive 'reading dates and accompanying cities' marathon' by identifying July 3rd, Los Angeles, again; July 5th, La Jolla, just north of San Diego; July 6th, Sacramento, California; and also July 6th, Louisville, Kentucky; July 7th, Milwaukee, Wisconsin; July 9th, Shaker Heights, found on a map just outside Cleveland; July 16th, Langhorne, Pennsylvania, just north of Philadelphia; July 18th, Uncasville, Connecticut (for the second time); July 19th, Boston; July 22nd, Washington DC; July 23rd, Pittsburgh for the second time and the next city and date, Thursday, July 25th, Bethel, upstate New York. "That completes my list!" the Inspector indicated.

"Well, Boss, I'm more-than-fairly confused, still blindly searching for *that* all-too-evasive Square One," Agent Orsi apologetically remarked. "For instance, there must be more than one squad of felons involved in this complicated caper because some cities are chosen for house burglaries on the same date in distinct-but-diverse localities as others being hit. I believe it's pretty-darned hazardous being a wealthy citizen in the United States today, even when rich folks are warily living inside gated communities having hired security guards!"

"Well, Fellas', the brass down in Washington has assigned *us* the distinct responsibility of unlocking this baffling case, but first we must determine if these are independent larcenies or if they're all actually ingeniously connected," Chief Giralo firmly articulated. "Until further notification, put this untidy riddle on the back burner; that is, for the time-being, while my DC colleague Matt Riley and I meticulously gather more pertinent details. Just remember during *this* initial analysis, the individual crimes we've just reviewed have all been enacted at night, and the selected manor-houses are usually those of extremely rich suburban heirs, heiresses, businessmen or businesswomen. Hopefully Guys," the Boss concluded in a raspy, hoarse tone of voice, "some salient facts will gradually surface for *us*

18

to base practical theories upon. For now," Chief Giralo concluded with a forced smile appearing upon his chubby countenance. "I suggest that the three of you Dick Tracy impostors keep your powder dry and concentrate on enthusiastically enjoying your summer weekend with your fine families!"

* * * * * * * * * * * *

Strangely enough, unexpectedly, the plethora of national mansion break-ins ceased between July 26th and September 17th, but then quite inexplicably, the countrywide epidemic flared-up again with major mansion thefts quickly occurring in Minneapolis on September 18th, in Chicago on September 20th, in Detroit on September 21st and in Lincoln, Nebraska on Friday, October 4th. That particular fall evening at precisely 8 p.m. Agent Sal Velardi received an emergency cell phone call from his greatly concerned-but-methodical federal boss.

"Salvatore, I've already called Arty and Dan earlier tonight," inscrutable Inspector Giralo began the peculiar dialogue. "Cancel all of your weekend plans. Tomorrow morning," the Chief continued his explicit directions, "Dan, Arty and I will be restively waiting inside my gray Chevy Suburban at your Peach Street driveway at 4 am sharp, so be ready to fly United Airlines out to Denver. I recommend that you should be waiting with enough clothes in your shabby luggage for a special three-day assignment. I don't want to have to blow my noisy automobile horn and wake-up your already-paranoid neighbors from their deep slumbers! Do you comprehend these simple instructions? Be ready tomorrow morning, Saturday, October 5th at 4 a.m. sharp!"

"What's up on such short notice?" Agent Velardi immediately desired learning. "Does this latest adventure involve the enigmatic rekindling of the bewildering Interstate grand larcenies' ring being conducted at the homes of America's richest and most prominent citizens? Give me the juicy details Boss!"

"Yes, Salvatore," Chief Giralo forcefully verified. "I believe that my good DC pal Matt Riley and I have finally figured-out what's been going on. Washington has already booked *us* rooms at a Denver Ramada Inn, that is, with suppers and breakfasts along with First Class air transportation all included. If my conjecture on this delicate suburban mansion burglary matter is generally correct," Giralo quite characteristically rambled on, "benevolent Uncle Sam is gonna' generously pick-up the tab for all *our* accumulative expenses. But if my grandiose theory proves to be wrong, then the four of us will be traveling First Class to and from gorgeous Colorado for three whole days at *my* personal treat!"

"Well then, Boss, don't keep me in painful suspense any longer!" Agent Velardi strongly demanded. "What's the genesis of all of the mansion robberies popping-up all over the country? I won't be able to sleep soundly until my limited brain comprehends the actual elements comprising this most bizarre series of inventive crimes!"

"Well, my dear Salvatore, as you might fathom and already suspect, knowledgeable crooks don't rob the shacks and shanties of American paupers," Chief Giralo rationally replied. "Now our friend Arty guesses that militant Islamic jihadists are the rogues behind this intricate slew of mansion thefts because Arab fundamentalists instinctively despise certain aspects of American life, specifically the use of alcohol, tobacco and the practice of loose morals, all certain freedoms guaranteed by our more-than-liberal *U.S. Constitution*. On the other-hand Sal," Chief Giralo expounded and then paused to inhale more precious oxygen, "our more-than-brilliant acquaintance Daniel Blachford hypothesizes that homegrown American religious fanatics, all motivated by their abnormal zeal, are in truth the vile perpetrators engendering all of the stealing mayhem going rampant all across the nation, and all of the nasty evolving pandemonium happening for the exact same reasons. The fervent Religious Right loons truly abhor the use of drugs, tobacco, beer and liquor along with loathing extra-marital or premarital sex, just like the warped Arab fanatics do! Now tell me Salvatore, what's your gut feeling about the identity of the brazen punks precipitating in all of the grandiose metropolitan felonies?"

"Your last statement just gave me a wild reckless idea Boss. I reckon that it's the old Rock and Roll mantra that's instigating all of the frenetic national chaos, you know, the famous commentary that the music's all about drugs, sex and Rock and Roll," a now-inspired Agent Velardi verbally shared. "If you remember Boss, during the early 1970s, Rock and Roll advocates absolutely loathed the emergence of disco as a rival source of popular musical entertainment. Could it be that some hip-hop or rap proponents, who fully resent classic Rock and Roll, are generating all of the national turmoil in an effort to eliminate the popular music, hurting the well-to-do people that have benefited from it? Or perhaps it's just the opposite in disguise. Rock and Roll disciples are creating all of the harmful criminal activity aimed at aristocratic American moguls who like and profit by rap and hip hop!"

"Now Sal; you, Arty or Dan might be right in your separate assumptions, or then conversely, all three of you aspiring federal

20

detectives might also be simultaneously wrong," Chief Giralo firmly qualified. "My notorious instinct however suggests to me that you dear Salvatore are closer to the truth than are your two off-base comrades."

"Here you go again wildly vociferating your annoying drivel," Agent Velardi loudly complained. "As is your bothersome habit Boss, you're providing *me* with general useful information that instantly translates into being totally useless and meaningless. Please be more laconic and concise in your rhetoric. In a thousand words or less, what does Rock and Roll have to do with this rather intriguing nationwide crime wave?"

"Tell me Salvatore, I'm quite aware of the fact that you're a big Rock and Roll fan, savoring vintage music mostly from the '70s. What unique concerts have you attended this year at the Wells Fargo Center over in South 'Philly?"

"Well, let's see," Agent Velardi inelegantly responded, scratching his head to activate his hazy memory of recent dates and corresponding events. "On April 4th Kathy and I saw Fleetwood Mac; on June 18th Dan and I relished the Rolling Stones' Show, and on Tuesday, July 16th Arty and I enjoyed the Eagles band performing. In my humble estimation, I frankly believe that their incredible song 'Hotel California' along with Queen's incomparable 'Bohemian Rhapsody' are undeniably, without a doubt, the two greatest rock and roll compositions ever produced. But Boss," Agent Velardi expressed, "I'm still clumsily staggering in the dark about this entire problematic ever-growing mansion-raiding dilemma. Why are the four of us traveling First Class out to Denver? Are we taking-up gold or silver prospecting?"

"Well, Salvatore, tomorrow we're flying-out to Denver to see the next Eagles concert taking place at the Pepsi Center!" Inspector Giralo solemnly stated and then indulgently laughed. "Yes Salvatore, you're gonna' get to again listen in person to Don Henley, Glenn Frey, Joe Walsh and Timothy B. Schmit harmonize the superb lyrics to 'Hotel California'!"

* * * * * * * * * * * *

At 4 a.m. on Saturday, October 5th dependable Chief Joe Giralo picked-up bleary-eyed Salvatore Velardi outside his Peach Street residence, and the new passenger awkwardly loaded his two antiquated pieces of weather-worn black luggage into the Chevy Suburban's rear compartment, and soon the newcomer joined yawning Dan Blachford in the back seat. Five minutes later, the gray automobile was passing through somnolent downtown Hammonton, and in another five minutes the Chief's enormous vehicle was entering the EZ-Pass Lane to the westbound Atlantic City Expressway. But instead of discussing the present all-too-secret assignment, the predictably chatty FBI Inspector commenced academically pontificating about the Earth's tremendous elliptical orbit around the sun.

"It's quite astounding to me," Giralo capably prefaced his rather weird monologue, "that the Earth is approximately 93 million miles from our nearest star, the sun. Now Guys, assuming that our planet has an oval orbit around Old Sol, and knowing that *Pi* is an estimated three and a quarter diameters in length, and since the distance between the Earth and the sun is a 93 million mile radius, or about one-half of a diameter," the longwinded Boss boringly lectured to his very disinterested three-member sleepy audience, "*this* basic arithmetical fact means that a hundred and eighty-six million miles is the actual rough diameter of the Earth's orbit, and we must now take *that* outrageous number and times it by three and a quarter to find the general circumference of the Earth's full orbit. Can you imagine *this* astonishing concept Men?" Giralo rhetorically asked. "The profound idea that once every Earth Year *we* travel an unbelievable distance of approximately five hundred and sixty million miles through the blackness of outer space. To me, *that* colossal astronomical annual space voyage is terribly incomprehensible, let alone insanely remarkable! Yes, indeed Fellas', our beloved Earth is analogous to being a most excellent self-sustaining spaceship with around seven billion lucky humans riding aboard!"

Ignoring the intense snoring emanating from the two occupants resting their weary bones in the vehicle's rear seat and also paying no attention to the incessant yawning of Agent Orsi riding "shotgun", the sometimes-encyclopedic Inspector loquaciously proceeded with his non-fascinating 4 am professorial exposition, all the while pretending that his three companions were all fascinated with his erratic rhetoric.

"And furthermore Fellas'," Joe Giralo confidently resumed his undesired non-solicited oration, "I find it quite spellbinding that the Earth never wobbles or shimmies while dually rotating twenty-four thousand miles a day and also concurrently revolving around the sun at a tremendous rate of speed that none of us mortal inhabitants either sense or feel, and incredibly, nothing falls off of shelves, tables or mantelpieces, except maybe during disastrous earthquakes, of course. And essentially, the entire annual orbiting process can be defined and described by science, but still, the whole 560-million-mile journey distance factor both eclipses and dwarfs the ability of humans to fully

22

understand or appreciate the omnipotent forces dominating the Universe."

The gray Suburban soon exited the Atlantic City Expressway and the huge vehicle was now swiftly heading west on the Route 42 Freeway in the direction of the Walt Whitman Bridge, the architectural wonder spanning the Delaware River from Camden into South Philadelphia. While Giralo's three-man investigative contingent uncomfortably dozed, Inspector Giralo navigated his cherished SUV south on I-95, and fifteen minutes later his means of transportation zipped into the airport's high-rise parking garage. The drowsy passengers were then rudely awakened by a shrill whistle blast from their Boss's lips, and minutes later the quartet was presenting their government credentials at the United Air check-in area and soon obtaining their boarding tickets from courteous personnel standing behind the un-crowded "Express" counter. An hour and a half wait inside the airline's VIP Lounge elapsed rapidly, and a half hour later the giant Denver-bound jet was zooming-down the take-off runway and then gracefully gliding into the red dawn sky.

Little conversation ensued among the four federal "First Class" passengers during the routine four-hour flight, which experienced some minor atmospheric turbulence over Central Kansas. That evening the rejuvenated G-men enjoyed the fabulous Eagles sold-out concert at the Pepsi Center, and enraptured Salvatore Velardi was in his glory watching the talented band performing their classic radio hits for the second time in three months.

But after returning in their rented Ford Explorer to their separate rooms at the cozy Denver Ramada Inn, nary a word had been exchanged relative to the very frustrating and beleaguering "Aristocratic Home Purloining and Pilfering Case."

* * * * * * * * * * * * *


The accommodations at the aforementioned Ramada Hotel were better-than-average with Inspector Joe Giralo staying in a King Suite and Agents Velardi, Orsi and Blachford occupying separate regular-sized rooms just a floor below. An on-site restaurant had a more-than adequate steak and seafood menu, and the 1150 East Colfax Avenue facility was conveniently located near the Rocky Mountain city's bustling Historic District.

On Sunday morning, a now-energized Chief Joe Giralo summoned his dedicated team to his King Suite to enjoy delicious room service breakfasts in private so that "the Boss" could confidentially review recent developments that were closely associated with the "national metropolitan mansion larcenies." After the morning bacon, eggs, toast and coffee meals had been consumed, Agent Velardi decided that it was time for Orsi, Blachford and himself to acquire some relevant answers that *their* clandestine superior knew, but had, as usual, deftly kept isolated from the three mutually disappointed subordinates' knowledge.

"Well, Boss, what kind of remote academics are you going to editorialize about this morning?" Agent Velardi courageously inquired. "The splendid Rings of Saturn? What about the immense Red Spot that exists on Jupiter? Or how about the abundance of Earth-threatening solar flares?"

"Salvatore, please learn to be more diplomatic," Chief Giralo gently reprimanded. "When you aren't being frivolous and facetious, you're either being horribly cynical or grossly sarcastic! I suggest that we all be gentlemen and gingerly ease into the problem at hand by first thoroughly reviewing last night's Eagles' concert!"

"It was somewhere between stellar and supreme!" Sal Velardi euphorically replied. "The band's set-list was the same as the one that had been played in 'Philly back on July 16th, but no matter how often you hear the group perform live," the rock concert fan ecstatically elucidated, "they never let their audience down. I even had the opportunity to hear Joe Walsh sing and play 'Rocky Mountain Way' right here in beautiful Denver, situated in the glorious Rocky Mountains."

"I totally agree with Sal's accurate assessment!" Art Orsi promptly chimed-in. "My favorite songs last night were 'Hotel California', 'Take It Easy,' 'Heartache Tonight' and 'Lyin' Eyes', in that order. Thanks for treating us Boss, but I would've paid good American bucks out of my own wallet if I had to, just to see the Eagles doing their thing on stage!"

"That band was truly exceptional!" Dan Blachford amiably concurred. "Not only do they have fabulous harmony, they also write their own lyrics and music, are especially versatile at playing a variety of instruments, and last but not least, the Eagles know exactly how to stimulate their audience and masterfully achieve a concert-ending crescendo! They're at the top of their game and most certainly, now are the cream of the crop in the country rock field! In my humble opinion, Don Henley and Glenn Frey rule!"

"I liked the Eagles too!" confirmed an impressed Inspector Giralo. "Their quality music is indeed classic country rock and has endured since the early 1970s. But I have to admit, I'm glad that I don't have to cover all of the mounting expenses from this strange sidebar trip like I had previously been fearing! My bet with Matt Riley has paid-off handsomely!"

"Do you mean that the looters have been captured? How were they apprehended?" Agent Velardi emotionally asked. "Without being too sanctimonious Boss, kindly provide *us three* pawns with all of the necessary details! I'm glad that the press and the other mass media outlets haven't yet connected all of the random dots to the various mansion felonies!"

Chief Giralo sat erect in his soft black leather chair and clearly mentioned that in the past, savvy crooks would read the local newspaper obituaries, and while the affected families were preoccupied mourning at the town funeral parlor, at church, or at the nearest cemetery, the wily and unscrupulous thieves, knowing that the weeping relatives would be absent from *their* homes, would break-into the dwellings and aggressively purloin the domiciles' valuables. "Of course, newspapers and undertakers finally got wind of *that* rather embarrassing scenario and quickly stopped publishing the street addresses of the deceased souls."

"But what do newspaper obituaries have to do with the myriad mansion larcenies being boldly conducted from coast to coast?" a now-confused and exceedingly addled Agent Orsi interrogated his esteemed mentor. "Tell us some pertinent background before we toss our aspirins away and require the use of powerful sedatives and tranquilizers!"

Inspector Joe Giralo objectively related that the principal key which had unlocked the "mystery's chains" was the fact that Salvatore Velardi had wholeheartedly savored (at Philadelphia's Wells Fargo Center) a Fleetwood Mac concert on April 6th, a Rolling Stones concert on June 18th and an Eagles concert on July 16th. "Yes Salvatore, those three nondescript dates eventually led Matt Riley and me to cleverly solving this rather arduous and tedious case. But first off, as is the norm, the crude-but-essential fundamentals had to be identified and expeditiously explored!"

"Okay, Boss, get off of your rapid ascending escalator and please retreat all the way back to step one on the ground floor," Dan Blachford entreated. "Did you recently have a secret séance session with Sir Arthur Conan Doyle's ghost, or what? Please slowly get to the foundational Rock and Roll theme and then perhaps the entire cryptogram's structure can miraculously materialize somewhere inside *our* thick dense craniums! Remember Boss, over the years you've taught us everything we don't know!" Agent Blachford satirically quipped.

The very tolerant FBI department head next cited that the Rolling Stones' concert tour had extended from May 2nd, 2013 in Los Angeles to June 18th and then again to June 21st in Philadelphia; the Fleetwood Mac touring schedule had started on April 4th in Columbus, Ohio and eventually finished on July 6th in Sacramento, California at the Sleepy Train Arena, and finally, the current Eagles' show dates had begun with much fanfare on July 7th in Louisville, Kentucky at the KFC-YUM Center and would finally wind-up on November 11th in sunny Orlando, Florida.

"But Chief, what do the Rolling Stones, Fleetwood Mac, and now the Eagles performing *here* in Denver last night have to do with the price of rice in Communist Red China?" Art Orsi vehemently requested. "Tell us the vital facts, or someone please get *me* a suitable Houdini-type straitjacket before I absolutely go berserk."

"I think you three Guys have to go back to reviewing Detective Work 101!" chided a now-animated Inspector Giralo. "The four mansion robbery teams now in police custody had traveled all over the country using the three different concert guide agendas as their primary strategy source. Don't you Fellas' get it? The Beverly Hills' mansion had been plundered on May 2nd, the same night that the Stones were performing at the Staples Center in downtown Los Angeles. The Columbus, Ohio mansion burglary had occurred on April 4th, opening night for Fleetwood Mac at the city's Nationwide Center. And on July 16th, the Eagles were presenting their History Tour Show at the 'Philly Wells Fargo Center and...'"

"And the suburban Main Line mansion had been marauded and ransacked by one of the nefarious, on-the-prowl, assigned hit squads," Sal Velardi realized and instantaneously communicated. "I see the general Big Picture now. The rich homeowners would obviously buy the most expensive tickets to see the various concerts and then carelessly leave their manor-houses vacated and consequently exposed to the roaming bands of thieves. But *who* is the silent money-man behind the scenes directing the hired accomplices so that the depraved stooges could handily enact their dastardly deeds?"

"Here's the full rub without any pestering TV commercial interruptions!" Chief Giralo promised, now exhibiting a broad smile. "The brain behind the rash of mansion heists is none other than Louie 'the Louse' Lamonica, a businessman-turned-thug who has definite Mafia ties. Lamonica had owned Beach-Cactus Sales, a formerly prosperous company that had monopolized a dozen gift and souvenir stores in Las Vegas and a dozen more situated on the Atlantic City Boardwalk. But 'the Louse' always loved to gamble heavily, and being influenced by the alluring casinos in Vegas and in AC, the addicted crook, over the past decade, had accumulated enormous debts, mostly owed to no-nonsense Philadelphia and South Jersey Cosa Nostra dons. This numbskull Lamonica quickly lost his formerly thriving retail business empire, had additional IRS debt-crisis problems, ultimately declared bankruptcy, and then the troubled man felt compelled to pay-off his extensive Mafia bills or else lose his life, the obsessed idiot next...”

“Resorted to a life of crime targeting the homes of vulnerable well-to-do American capitalists,” Agent Blachford instantly recognized and offered. “This pathetic knucklehead Louie the Louse probably would fence the stolen goods for cash to pay-off the formidable loan-sharking Mafia dons. So, Lamonica really didn’t have any animosity towards wealthy people. Instead, his sole motive for stealing from them was done out of necessity to save his own life from the merciless mob syndicate. But Boss,” Blachford continued. “*We* now understand how this Lamonica jerk had organized the three rock groups’ concert schedules with the intent of having suburban estates and manor- homes specifically designated to be raided by *his* highly competent hit squads, but how did Lamonica and his lawless henchmen know which specific rich people would be going to the Rolling Stones, to the Fleetwood Mac and to the scheduled Eagles’ concerts?”

Chief Giralo felt obligated to contribute more material information. “Lamonica had a greedy brother-in-law named Darren Fields, a gullible-but-avaricious jealous fool who incidentally had been employed at United Express Federal-Delivery Services, which naturally delivers high-priced venue tickets for outfits such as StubHub, Absolute Entertainment, Vivid Show Tickets and other similar national ducat distribution organizations. This slippery creep Darren Fields would, for example, notify Louie Lamonica when someone with big bucks had purchased five or more rock concert tickets, each at an exorbitant cost of five hundred dollars, or more. Six, or as many as eight potential victims living near a specific city were zeroed-in on, and thanks to info’ gleaned by Mr. Fields, the traveling hit team dispatched to the targeted concert area would stake out the selected property, and if no one was home that evening, then the villains would...”

“Would egregiously cut the electricity or deactivate the security alarm systems and enter the rich dupe’s palace with impunity, steal as many jewels and gems as possible, and then easily abandon the selected mansion unscathed,” Velardi declared. “Holy Hannibal in Honolulu! This diabolical mastermind Lamonica was pretty cunning and stealthy after all!”

"But something else that's puzzling me needs immediate clarification," Agent Orsi observed and assertively remarked. "How did you know what mansion in suburban Denver would be hit last night without taking the proverbial shot in the dark? Did you wiretap Lamonica's phones?"

"This is where Matt Riley and I adroitly combined our career-long FBI expertise," Chief Giralo bragged and non-modestly exaggerated. "The Bureau down in DC had wisely purchased twenty tickets for the Eagles' October 5th concert here at the Pepsi Center, had rented a vacant furnished mansion in suburban Denver for one month, had established viable daily post office delivery to the given address, and had paid a premium price of $10,000.00 for the twenty front row Eagles' tickets. After the tempting bait had been thrown into the water, it didn't take Darren Fields too long to relay the new-found information to all-too-desperate Mr. Louie Lamonica, who then sent his "A-Team" out on its Denver area mission. In case someone would be home at 350 Valley Drive, then the determined crooks would change course and seek-out the second highlighted mansion on their carefully assembled 'rich guy hit list'."

"And our alert agents were just waiting for the unaware culprits to break-in!" realized and stated Arthur Orsi. "The overconfident perpetrators had to be very surprised at being outwitted! What a fantastic set-up!"

"And if I hadn't boasted that I had seen the Rolling Stones, Fleetwood Mac and the Eagles on different occasions at the Wells Fargo Center," Sal Velardi proudly mentioned, seeking well-deserved credit for his vital role in solving the prodigious national crime wave, "then Boss, you might still be helplessly floundering around like a maniac inside Square Number One!"

"Not exactly Salvatore!" Inspector Giralo objected and hastily exclaimed. "The real initial clue came into focus when no robberies had been committed between July 26th and September 18th, the same time interval when the Eagles were on vacation and *not* touring around the United States. For you see Sal, the sophisticated computers installed at FBI headquarters down in DC had efficiently analyzed the relevant statistical data, including coincidental concert venues that precisely matched-up with the individual robbery dates along with the corresponding city performance dates of the Rolling Stones, of Fleetwood Mac and of *your* inimitable and highly revered Eagles. Now if the Eagles could only play superlative professional football," Inspector Giralo jested to his much-relieved admiring employees, "then good old Philadelphia will finally have another well-deserved Super Bowl championship team!"

# "Business before Pleasure"

The late-model gray Chevy Suburban pulled out of the I-95 Chesapeake House parking area and rapidly re-entered congested southbound traffic heading toward metropolitan Baltimore. FBI Inspector Joe Giralo was behind the wheel, and his very serious passengers were agents Art Orsi and Dan Blachford seated in the rear and Agent Sal Velardi riding shotgun alongside the driver. Four bags of golf clubs and eight pieces of luggage had been conspicuously stored inside the large vehicle's rear compartment.

"Well Chief, you had promised that after having breakfast at the Chesapeake Rest Stop, you would divulge the true essence of this combination business and pleasure excursion," Agent Velardi diplomatically prefaced his inquiry. "And if our very capable director Chief Riley at our DC headquarters is the mastermind of this new mystery adventure, I'll maintain that, as usual, it's business before pleasure, or more specifically, business disguised as pleasure! Would my speculative assessment of the situation be correct?"

"Very perceptive observation Salvatore!" Inspector Giralo casually commended Agent Velardi as the other two loyal investigative associates Orsi and Blachford gave their undivided attention to the front-seat conversation. "Gentlemen, after getting to the Baltimore Beltway, we'll then be heading west on Route 40 in the direction of Frederick. Then using my trusty GPS navigation, I plan on eventually getting onto scenic Skyline Drive at Front Royal, Virginia. We'll feast our eyes on the picturesque Shenandoah Valley, stop at a few highway overlooks, and just around Luray, we'll next travel west through the majestic Blue Ridge Mountains until we reach Interstate 81. And incidentally," the grim-faced Inspector further revealed, "our top-secret destination happens to be the famous Greenbriar Lodge Plaza Hotel appropriately located near gorgeous White Sulphur Springs, West Virginia. As you all know very well," the driver continued his lengthy narrative, "that very exclusive place has a renowned championship golf course, but according to very explicit instructions from Riley's Office, only two of us at a time will be playing daily at the nearby Hickory Golf Green Course, commonly known to knowledgeable duffers as 'The Links'. It's a historic nine-hole Par 37, and it was the first functional golf course in America to ever sponsor championship competition!"

"Why can't we play a few challenging rounds at the Greenbriar Lodge Plaza property?" Dan Blachford inquired from the back seat.

"Have we been forbidden to do so from omnipotent Riley's instructions?"

"Yes Dan, apparently two of us are to strategically stay inside our well-appointed suite while the other two of us will be preoccupied a mile or so away exploring the fairways and greens at The Links," Inspector Giralo indicated. "Evidently, Riley fears that it would be entirely too dangerous on the Greenbriar Lodge Plaza grounds for all four of his highly trained government personnel. I believe the four of us will be watching our share of soap operas, woman talk shows and cable TV movies. And we've also been instructed to use room service as often as possible!"

"Exactly how far away is the Greenbriar Lodge Plaza from your home in Hammonton?" Agent Arthur Orsi asked the all-too-focused driver. "And what's so secret about this special activity we've been assigned? I need certainty and clarity in my mind and quite frankly," the twenty-year FBI veteran honestly admitted, "I just can't stand excessive suspense in my life! I'll leave *that* particular feature to Hollywood film studios!"

"Well Art, according to Map Quest on the Internet," Joe Giralo politely answered, "the classic vacation resort is approximately four hundred and eighty miles from my Jersey residence, about a nine-hour drive. But since we'll be cautiously taking a scenic roundabout route, then the trip will require about...."

"About ten total hours," Sal Velardi courteously interrupted his immediate superior. "But Joe, what's so uniquely perilous about this new exploit? I mean truthfully, golf seems to be a rather innocent and peaceful preoccupation."

Inspector Giralo cleared his throat and then very carefully uttered his lucid explanation. "Guys, I'll level with you about most that I've learned from Chief Riley's Washington Office. There's been some rather serious Internet chatter that's been slickly cloaked in encrypted messages. Much to Riley's satisfaction, our skillful Cryptology Department has recently intercepted and deciphered what constitutes significant domestic threats. The name 'Operation Greenbriar' has surfaced among certain terror group communications along with their disclosing of the designated summer dates August 7th to August 14th. In all his great wisdom," Joe Giralo summarized, "Riley has sternly warned me to have two of us alternately out playing the greens at 1 Montague Drive, Oakhurst Links while the remaining two of us are patiently doing surveillance and stationed inside our handsome West Virginia Wing hotel suite. And if and when something abnormal or drastic happens," Giralo hypothesized and genuinely stressed, "the agents doing due-diligent reconnaissance inside the suite are to cell phone the other two of us trekking out at The Links, and then the lucky players will promptly contact *this* very noteworthy confidential phone number. Such action will send a dependable response team into instant reaction!"

Inspector Giralo then reached into his shirt pocket and distributed three copies of the clandestine phone number to his subordinates and quickly requested that his trio of dedicated colleagues memorize the prescribed eleven digits and then rip-up the numerical information before arriving at their exclusive hotel paradise. The driver next articulated that the government operation might be either a massive false alarm or it could actually represent the initiation of a mammoth counter-espionage/terror plot operation, which extensively involved major coordinated police/military deployment.

From meandering I-81 the light gray Chevy Suburban soon progressed southward, and later the vehicle's four occupants were motoring on I-64 in the direction of U.S. 60. The determined agents' verbal exchanges again centered around their' highly-anticipated dramatic interaction with the incomparable landmark Greenbriar Lodge Plaza Hotel.

"Confidentially Men, we're masquerading as the Board of Directors of the Jersey Universal Construction Corporation," Joe Giralo informed his all-too-inquisitive riders, "so I want the three of you acting extremely professional while convincingly impersonating top Wall Street executives in quest of excellent gourmet dinners, the ultimate in golfing experience and finally, some much-deserved rest and relaxation."

"Tell us more about our destination," Agent Orsi insisted. "It's got quite an excellent reputation if it's the same place I'm thinking about."

"I've found-out via Google that the luxurious hotel has 751 swanky guest rooms and suites, has nine terrific restaurants, sports a splendid tournament-caliber golf course, has three distinct coffee shops, possesses a marvelous health club, contains a quality casino and also boasts of a heated indoor pool worthy of European royalty. But allow me to emphasize," Inspector Giralo austerely expressed and then paused, "outside of us taking turns dining later in the week at the fancy ritzy restaurants in sets of two, we are to at all times during daylight hours be assigned as a pair of agents confined inside the West Virginia Wing suite and the corresponding duo positioned out at The Links on Montague Drive. Is that perfectly clear?"

"And I presume that Riley's efficient office secretaries had made our arrangements for our suite reservations, all on the government dime," Sal Velardi deducted and related. "Too bad I can't get a full body massage after we arrive on the job. My decrepit, deteriorating back is aching like you can't imagine! My vertebrae feel like I've been lying in a coffin for a full century!"

"Wasn't the hotel a surreptitious U.S. Government compound during the late '50s and early '60s Cold War era?" Art Orsi verbalized, deliberately ignoring Agent Velardi's futile attempt at sit-down comedy. "I remember reading something fascinating about that fairly interesting fact a couple of months ago."

"You have rather enviable reading comprehension skills," the normally no-nonsense driver humorously remarked, a trifle out of character. "When the West Virginia Wing had been shrewdly added in the 1950s, a spectacular underground 'Bunker' was also furtively constructed directly underneath the surface architecture, thus effectively concealing the Bunker's true purpose. There is enough space in the hidden labyrinth to accommodate at least a thousand people for months on end. Powerful subterranean generators could easily operate the sophisticated ventilation system along with the necessary sanitation waste facilities."

"Now I recall the magazine article I had read! The enormous Bunker was built to be a safe haven for the White House executive branch, for the Congress and for the Supreme Court to all hold meetings underground if Washington DC were to be destroyed by a foreign enemy, namely the Soviet Union, during a hostile nuclear attack," Agent Orsi eloquently contributed to the discussion. "I mean, the Senate and the House of Representatives' members would alone amount to around five hundred people to feed, to sleep and to provide adequate shelter. And if my erratic memory serves me correctly, during the 1950s, many households had their own fallout shelters, the apprehensive homeowners fearing radiation fallout from widespread atomic warfare!"

"Yes Art, and in addition, four large meeting rooms were designed and fabricated to accommodate the three separate branches of the federal government," Inspector Giralo conveyed to his still-alert three passengers. "But as I've already told you three amateur geniuses, the popular tourist-attraction Bunker will be off-limits to us. We're going to be strictly confined to The Links and to our West Virginia Wing suite until some obvious anomaly occurs," Giralo keenly reiterated. "And please don't forget! Seven hundred to a thousand other business executives will be holding various conferences and occasionally reveling at the hotel while we're conscientiously performing our stealthy FBI sleuth and gumshoe work!"

"Those seven hundred to a thousand other hotel guests aren't FBI agents too!" Agent Velardi joked.

"Say, there's the Greenbriar Lodge Plaza just ahead," Dan Blachford declared with relative enthusiasm as he excitedly pointed his right index finger. "Just look at those magnificent white columns and the fantastic garden flowers and shrub landscaping treatments near the main entrance. This place is quite impressive indeed. No wonder why it's classified and advertised as a 5 Star resort. Say Boss, please refresh my faulty memory. What was the name of the company we're supposed to be representing?"

"The Jersey Universal Construction Corporation," Inspector Giralo angrily commented, shaking his head in absolute disgust. "And may I remind you Dan, along with your two distinguished comrades, you Blachford are supposed to be the company Treasurer, Art, you're the Secretary, Sal, you're the business's President, and of course Gentlemen, I'm the revered Corporate CEO should anyone at the hotel ask our identities. It's very important that we all know our various company roles while we specialize in objectively keeping our eyes and ears open and our hyperactive mouths very scrupulously sealed!"

* * * * * * * * * * * *

After registering at the hotel's main lobby desk, the four federal men, accompanied by two friendly bellhops, took an elevator to their West Virginia Wing third-floor suite, which consisted of a spacious parlor area, two beautifully decorated bedrooms, plush green drapes and matching mint-colored carpets, and last but not least, a rather sensational window view of the ageless Allegheny Mountains. Under ordinary circumstances, the tasteful suite would have been a sensual pleasure to behold.

The accommodating Greenbriar Lodge Plaza bellhops were each rewarded with ten-dollar "expense account" tips, and next the cooperative and grateful resort employees exited the comfortable living quarters and soon, the weary travelers began unpacking their suitcases and methodically placing their clothing items into bureau drawers inside the two separate bedrooms. Agent Velardi was awarded "the privilege" (by his boss's authoritative decree) to share the first bedroom with Inspector Giralo. After those perfunctory tasks had been accomplished, the four government men ordered steak and potato dinners via room service. All was peaceful and tranquil with the outside world.

"We're basically stuck in a week-long Twilight Zone alternating between this fabulous suite and The Links Golf Course, which to the average person would be similar to being sandwiched somewhere between Heaven and Nirvana," skeptical Dan Blachford orally evaluated. "None of us will ever be able to stroll around the East and West Terrace sectors or for that matter, even venture-out to the Presidents' Cottage Museum. It states in this informative brochure that twenty-six U.S. Presidents have stayed here at one time or another, the most notable latest one being Dwight David Eisenhower. And even though all four of us live within driving distance of Atlantic City, we can't even try some entertainment gambling in the hotel's casino. I should've joined the IRS or the NSA like my mother wanted me to do."

"When you're on assignment," a somewhat-peeved Inspector Giralo explained the obvious, "you're on company duty twenty-four hours. That's the Bureau's principal rule that I must enforce and it's the standard 24/7 policy that *you* must obey. And unfortunately," the Boss continued, "for you Dan, the casino is seldom jam-packed because it's only available to regular guests staying at the hotel. No outside FBI visitors are allowed!"

"And it describes in *this* pamphlet I'm holding how this resort was originally built near a sulfur water spring that had been believed by locals to relieve agonizing pain associated with severe arthritis and rheumatism," Agent Orsi chimed-in. "Actually, the place was known as White Sulphur Springs for the first hundred and twenty-five years of its existence. But in 1858, a hotel was erected on the property, and during the Civil War the resort had been occupied by both Confederate and Union forces. But soon after the War Between the States, the popular hotel reopened for business. But in 1910, the property was then acquired by the...."

"By the Chesapeake and Ohio Railroad," added and embellished Agent Sal Velardi, who had been reading from the same pamphlet as Agent Art Orsi. "The structure was given the name Greenbriar Lodge Hotel and the original appellation has survived from 1913 right up to the present. And as you might be aware, the Chesapeake and Ohio is now CSX Corporation. In fact, there were several CSX executives down in the lobby when we were applying our alias John Hancocks to the traditional Registration Guest Book."

"Wow! An appellation in the Appalachians!" Arthur Orsi enthusiastically jested. "What wild irony!"

"Say Inspector," Dan Blachford butted-in. "Besides the fact that the noble Duke of Windsor, the wealthy Kennedy Clan and illustrious movie stars like Bing Crosby have vacationed here, what new pertinent details can you tell us about the Bunker from your elaborate Internet research. Just the thought of its basic purpose is both creepy and intriguing. I mean, the 1950s must've been very scary times all throughout America."

Joe Giralo gulped-down the remaining ounces of his delicious hot coffee and then typically grunted to intentionally gain everyone's attention. "In case of a nuclear holocaust, the Bunker was created under the West Virginia Wing as a clever emergency shelter to house the United States government officials. I had read that the Bunker contained radio and TV studios that could have broadcast explicit instructions and programs across the country to citizens that might have been still able to receive radio wave transmissions. Also," Inspector Giralo proceeded with his exposition, "patriotic flags and random familiar Washington backdrops were in the background, all designed to inspire a feeling of national pride and unity should a nuclear attack be initiated by the then Evil Empire, Soviet Russia. And incredibly Fellas', there were eighteen underground dormitories in the Bunker that could phenomenally sleep sixty people each. Give me a calculator, and I'll do the essential math."

"Precisely one thousand and eighty people," arithmetic wizard Art Orsi piped-up. "It was a pretty colossal engineering achievement. That's almost as many folks as the number of students now attending Hammonton High School."

"And each of the underground dormitories had accessible shower areas along with myriad toilets and an accompanying small lounge sector," Joe Giralo continued his general dissertation to his captive audience. "And there was even a hospital clinic situated inside the premises, the area having twelve beds manned by a staff of competent military physicians and reliable nurses. The entire enterprise was quite an amazing undertaking for the relatively primitive medical and scientific technologies that prevailed over a half-century ago. And here's one more relevant item that I failed to mention. The gigantic blueprint had the government code name Project Greek Island."

"Pretty extraordinary!" Agent Sal Velardi blustered. "But let's be totally candid here. The ugly downside of this strange mission is that none of us will be able to tour the Bunker. I feel like I'm being deprived of witnessing the vestiges of a huge part of 1950s Cold War History. Let's face it. The Cuban Missile Crisis during the Kennedy Administration could've swiftly led to total worldwide human devastation."

"And the world is no safer today with plenty of terrorists, jihadists, along with drug and gun smuggling cartels running rampant all over the globe, including South, Central and most importantly, North America," the Boss reminded his all-too-garrulous underlings.

"Our numerous duties and heavy responsibilities are being seriously challenged every single day!"

"And what about the exceptional championship golf course that we're prevented from playing," Dan Blachford mildly protested. "I believe this place is on the official PGA tour. I'm willing to bet a week's salary on it!"

"Yes Dan, you can keep your hard-earned money. The big tournament is held in early July right here on the ground's well-manicured Old White Course, which the hotel depicts as being somewhere between impeccable and immaculate," Inspector Giralo solemnly verified. "I guess that even a super resort such as this one has to once in a while engage in some nice, self-serving propaganda from time-to-time."

Before retiring to their separate bedrooms for the night, the four restive government men watched the local West Virginia evening news in the suite's handsome parlor, and during the ever-boring television commercials, the G-men conversed in an impromptu manner about the country's porous southern borders, about the perils of illegal immigration "coyote criminal activities," about militant hate groups abounding in the United States of America, about the ineffectiveness of Congress and finally, about the general decline of morality throughout the nation.

In the end, Inspector Joseph Giralo reviewed the vital ground rules for the agents' stay at the glorious Five Star Greenbriar Lodge Plaza Hotel, and the proud boss accentuated for all mission participants to always be on the same page. "I'm requesting that each man now states his individual role, duty and responsibility during the proposed enactment of "Operation Greenbriar Lodge Plaza Hotel. Our response to any developing dilemma must be fast, decisive and efficacious!"

* * * * * * * * * * * *

The agents' first four days at the acclaimed Greenbriar Lodge Plaza Hotel were fortuitously without incident or consequence. The relentless FBI men alternated in sets of two, a pair occupying the attractive third floor West Virginia Wing suite while the other duo engaged in morning and afternoon rounds of golf on the 9 Hole Links. Evenings were spent watching television, engaging in pleasant dialogue, playing poker and blackjack, and when feeling less energetic or being downright ambitious, reading several contemporary action/adventure novels that Agent Sal Velardi had brought along to neutralize the risk of ensuing boredom.

The three lower rank agents were observably thrilled when Inspector Joe Giralo imperatively announced early Thursday morning that *that* evening Art Orsi, Sal Velardi and Dan Blachford would be permitted to enjoy swallowing-down sumptuous suppers in the grand facility's main dining hall.

Friday morning, Agents Orsi and Blachford were scheduled to remain in the comfortable third floor suite while Joe Giralo and Sal Velardi rode in the gray Suburban over to Montague Drive to engage in their now-familiar repetitious golf course routine. Everything in the Universe seemed relatively copacetic until Inspector Giralo insisted on taking a Mulligan after topping his ball off the tee on his first wooden club swing.

"Don't feel bad Inspector!" Agent Velardi mockingly encouraged. "There's two acceptable ways to play golf. There's the fairway and then there's the unethical way!"

"You're more on the ridiculous side of hilarious than are either Art Orsi or Dan Blachford," the irritated Boss quickly chided and replied. "Learn to implement some common sense, which evidently today is not-too-common! At least your fellow agents, Salvatore, know how to exercise discretion in what they think and then say. Sometimes it's best and most advisable Sal to simply keep your ultra-critical thoughts exclusively to yourself!"

"Sorry Boss! We're all human!" Agent Velardi apologetically maintained. "Sometimes my valiant confederate Agent Orsi will miss the ball off the tee and almost violently corkscrew himself into the surrounding turf. And when not making a huge divet, sometimes Agent Blachford will smack the ball into the nearby woods or he'll inadvertently endanger unaware golfers putting for birdies on nearby greens. And once Dandy Dan crushed a ball so hard that it smashed directly through the large pane window at the Buena Vista Country Club back in South Jersey!"

"Well, Salvatore, I shot a seven on the first hole and those double pond water hazards tended to intimidate me," the befuddled Inspector begrudgingly retorted. "That lousy misfortune completely wrecked any chance of me ever arriving at a Par 4!"

"I'm not trying to pander to you, but quite frankly, you're much better at performing complex detective work than you are at imitating either Sam Snead or Tiger Woods!" Agent Velardi praised and then chuckled. "And furthermore Boss, we both shot lackluster eights on the 322-yard Par 5. But don't feel too depressed!" Velardi recommended. "At the clubhouse on Tuesday morning, I overheard several amused guys say that one Mississippi fella' several years back incredibly shot a 28 on #2. Based on *that* pretty remarkable statistic,"

Agent Velardi conjectured and rather persuasively expressed, "I'll wholeheartedly confess Boss that we're both having an outstanding day out here on The Links!"

"And the third tee we're now approaching is quite difficult even though it's only 102 yards to the pin," Inspector Giralo assessed and concluded. "That pond over to the right of the green is an awesome detriment and the sand traps are a bit deceiving. Maybe it's time for us to take-up the leisure-time sport of tennis, or even more propitious and beneficial yet, when we return to Jersey we ought to just become burned-out couch potatoes, sleepily watching the Masters at Augusta on our big screen den televisions!"

"That 52 I had shot Tuesday on this Par 37 nine-hole course was truly rather abominable, and confidentially Boss, I've always considered myself a sixteen handicap on typical Par 72s back home," Sal Velardi defensively elucidated. "That usual performance would be comparable to an eight handicap on this abbreviated course, and using *that* certain infallible metric," the agent continued his weird justification, "a round of 45 should be my average on *this* course. And carrying these heavy golf bags around in the hot summer sun is sort of an encumbrance all by itself. As you know, I'd much prefer zooming around the course in an electric cart, even with *you* in control sitting behind the wheel, Inspector. In all due respect Boss, you awkwardly drive a golf cart around as if you're carelessly piloting a bulky ponderous Chevy Suburban on a snake-like rural country road! Say Boss, why do they call some golf courses 'Links'?" Velardi inquired of his well-educated superior.

"Because Salvatore," Giralo said without any hesitation, "in the beginning days of the sport, most golf courses were built along bays and seas. The holes were positioned back-to-back just like the links in a chain, thus the origin, or should I say 'etymology' of the English nomenclature 'Links'!"

Just then Inspector Giralo's cell phone rang, and quickly forgetting his trivial quarrel with Agent Velardi, an expression of seriousness immediately was exhibited upon the Boss's facial features. On the line was Dan Blachford, and the distressed agent sounded as if he and Art Orsi were encountering imminent duress.

"Inspector!" Dan Blachford loudly gasped. "There was just an urgent call from the lobby desk, and the frightened employee stated that all guests in the hotel are to evacuate their rooms and report with dispatch to the downstairs Cold War Bunker. We've also been informed by management that some sort of bomb threat or some kind of security breach has necessitated this spontaneous action. Sorry Boss, but I must soon have to terminate this conversation!"

"There's a definite aberration in progress!" Joe Giralo determined and asserted. "If it's demanded of you Dan, both you and Art are to surrender your cell phones to any intruding radical perpetrators. They mustn't suspect that you're on duty FBI men! Whatever you do, don't resist or offer any struggle while attempting to defend yourselves. What's *that* terrible background noise I hear? Is there someone pounding on the door with their fists?"

"Yes, and they're demanding that we open the portal right this second!" Agent Blachford whispered into his cell phone. "And Art and I are looking out the window and there is a caravan of Avis, Hertz and Budget box trucks parked out front. And there are squads of what looks like armed Mexican bandits and Arab jihadists toting an array of rocket propelled grenades and AK-47s. The maniacs are hopping out of the backs of those box trucks, and Boss, they're presently storming into the building's main and side entrances like a herd of savages! The entire place is under siege. We're right in the middle of a ruthless terrorist attack! Boss, I've never been so scared in all my life! Everything sounds like pandemonium out there in the corridor! I think Art's hyperventilating in an advanced panic mode!"

"Dan, you and Art are to cooperate with the villains, er, I mean hostile insurgents!" the FBI Boss constructively suggested. "Open the damned door before the fanatics break it down, barge in and then wickedly do you two physical harm! Do you read me Blachford! Give yourselves up without any violence!"

Boisterous shouting, obnoxious chaos, remote gunshots and overwhelming confusion dominated the other end of the line as yells of "Allah Akbar" blasted-out from Inspector Giralo's trusty cell phone. And then quite predictably, the electronic transmission went dead as the fierce motivated invaders took full control of the third-floor suite and next roughly confiscated the agents' apparently nondescript communication devices.

Inspector Giralo did not waste any time hesitating about initiating his next move. He instinctively pressed the memorized numbers of the secret alarm code into his cell phone, and then exercising full concentration, "the Boss" adroitly pushed the object's "Send" button. "Counteroperation Greenbriar Lodge Plaza Hotel" had successfully been launched.

"Now Sal!" unfazed Joe Giralo urgently commanded his momentarily paralyzed companion, "it's time for us to return to the besieged hotel and personally witness the upcoming battle unfold. Let's just hope that all of the Greenbriar's terrified visitors and guests have been safely escorted into the establishment's protective underground Bunker. I hope and pray that Dan and Art's lives are not at-this-moment in jeopardy!"

* * * * * * * * * * * *

Time was indeed of the essence. The austere-minded Inspector and his affable golfing partner speedily cut across a fairway and next quickly hastened to the Oakhurst Links half-empty asphalt parking lot. Upon reaching the dusty Chevy Suburban, the on-a-mission men anxiously deposited their heavy golf bags into the rear storage space. Surprisingly, Inspector Joe Giralo's cell phone again rang, and the muffled voice of flustered Agent Dan Blachford was discernible on the other end.

"Boss, I'm down here in a remote corner of the underground Bunker with at least a thousand other hotel guests. I'm crammed between an IBM executive, a Bank of America director and two panic-stricken guys from Alcoa!"

"Tell me Dan, is everyone now safe and sound inside the Bunker?" the FBI chieftain desired knowing.

"Yes, I do think we've all now been barricaded, inside," Dan Blachford nervously answered. "And the stinking terrorists have pilfered my cell phone along with my expensive Rolex watch that my wife had given me for our twentieth wedding anniversary. Boss, I'm now calling you from my miniature cell phone that I had hidden and stored in the hollow heel of my right shoe," the rattled agent rambled on. "The rambunctious marauders never once suspected for one iota that either Art Orsi or I are undercover G-men. And Boss, the vicious, reprehensible riffraff also heisted Art's wallet and cash as well as mine too!" totally frustrated Dan Blachford communicated and complained. "It's pretty darned scary being a helpless victim, that's for sure! But it's a good thing we didn't take our pistols and holsters along on this trip or else Art and I would probably be floating inside some huge black crucible's boiling hot water just about now!"

"Never mind the monotonous minutia!" Inspector Giralo adamantly rankled. "Hang-up immediately Dan! I gotta' call Army Colonel Bob Bauers right this second! He happens to be the head coordinator of this intensely complicated operation!" Click.

The very efficient FBI Investigator had Robert Bauers on his cell phone's speed dial, and upon making the prompt connection, Joe Giralo calmly advised the Colonel of the vital information that *he* had recently gleaned from hostage Agent Dan Blachford. "That's right Colonel. Everyone of importance is now locked inside the Bunker. That includes all the hotel guests, too! You can send your combat teams into the battle arena. Good luck accomplishing your imminent engagement, Sir!" Click.

On the short drive from The Oakhurst Links back to the embattled Greenbriar Lodge Plaza Hotel, Inspector Giralo thoroughly explained to Agent Velardi the major confrontation that was about to transpire both around and inside the popular resort, the comprehensive explanation occurring just as a swarm of Apache attack helicopters zoomed by, maneuvering a mere hundred feet or so above the commonplace Chevy Suburban.

According to the Inspector's very detailed litany, a diverse thousand-man conglomeration consisting of lethal military commandos, Delta Force, Navy Seals, expert Army snipers, along with experienced state and local SWAT squads, had been assembled to counteract the in-progress brazen terrorist attack upon a highly treasured iconic American landmark. Back-up helicopter units coming from as far away as Roanoke, Virginia had already been dispatched to the intensifying and very fluid scene of battle.

"The random accumulative chatter that's been received and interpreted from the most militant Jihadist websites has presented the stark scenario that the Arab and Iranian terrorists, who had reportedly crossed the Rio Grande from the El Paso and Brownsville, Texas areas into the United States, have maliciously planned to raid the Greenbriar Lodge Plaza Hotel, gain full control of the enormous facility, and then make an international political statement by dramatically dying in an Alamo-type shootout with our various law enforcement agencies," Inspector Giralo shared.

"And Boss, what about their criminal Mexican accomplices?" Sal Velardi curiously asked. "How do those evil felons fit into the rather egregious scheme of things?"

"The demented Arab and Iranian jihadists plan to become crusading martyrs, deliberately sacrificing their lives to Allah inside the hotel, but in the process, they had owed the formidable Mexican drug and gun smugglers a rather colossal debt for assisting them entering into the country and then soon getting the vile crusaders furtively transported from Texas up here to West Virginia," the Inspector verbally conveyed to his loyal cohort. "And Sal, the money, the jewelry and the other valuables that had been purloined from the thousand sequestered hotel guests sealed down inside the emergency Bunker would be used to pay off the Mexican criminals, who would gratefully stash their newly acquired plunder inside several of the rented box trucks and then speed away to local safe houses with their very valuable stolen loot."

"Wow!" exclaimed an astounded and excited Agent Velardi as another intimidating wave of descending Apache helicopters zipped-by above. "And Dan's prized Rolex watch represented a minor part of the thieves' tremendous payoff! If he loses it during this thrilling mission, I'll never hear the end of it! And tell me Boss," the thoroughly impressed agent switched his thinking, "where are these thousand or so American commandos coming from?"

"Many of the Apache helicopter units had been stationed at the Greenbriar County Airport. Another strategic staging area, where the Delta Force and Navy Seals are originating from, is the town of Lewisburg, situated about fifteen minutes in a chopper flight from here. And the quick response SWAT teams were being camped at another town named Caldwell, located directly between Lewisburg and White Sulphur Springs."

"Do you mean to tell me that you knew all of this secret information and never shared it with Dan, with Art or with me?" objected Agent Velardi. "What kind of Boss are you?"

"I figured that the less info' you mischievous fellas' knew, the better off you three lower-level sleuths would be, that is, having much less data to think and worry about!" Inspector Giralo confided as his gray Suburban suddenly arrived at the renowned hotel's entrance. "Now Sal, I've been specifically instructed by Colonel Bauers to stay in the car until this full-scale battle terminates. His Delta Force unit will conduct the full operation!"

"Holy cow pastures Boss! There's a whole slew of dead bloody bodies strewn all throughout the front flower and shrub treatment areas!" shocked Agent Velardi panted and vociferated. "Mostly Mexican coyotes I presume, with several Arab and Iranian holy war warriors scattered around in between the other corpses! And notice that a half-dozen choppers have already landed on the hotel's roofs, and look around Boss," Velardi resumed his graphic description, "at least a dozen more have converged and landed all around the esteemed edifice! And just look at all of the empty military jeeps and troop transport trucks surrounding the blocked Avis, Hertz and Budget box getaway vehicles!"

A blazing battle royal ensued on all floors of the revered hotel as the Greenbriar Lodge Plaza was indeed horribly transformed into a modern-day Alamo. Forty-five minutes of close combat elapsed with perpetual gunfire rounds being gradually diminished, both in scope and sequence. Finally, all sounds of a variety of weapons being shot had ceased, and then a face that Inspector Joe Giralo immediately recognized appeared on the scene.

Colonel Robert Bauers exited his command-and-control jeep, slowly approached the now-grimy parked Chevy Suburban, and the Delta Force leader merrily shook hands with an old acquaintance, venerable Inspector Joe Giralo, who was still sitting stationary behind the steering wheel. All the while, rambunctious Agent Sal Velardi looked-on in sheer admiration.

"Congratulations Joe! I'll have to recommend to Matt Riley that *you* ought to be promoted at the Bureau. Your strategic involvement in this remarkable grand hotel siege will definitely be much appreciated and honored by the President!"

Inspector Giralo abruptly turned to Agent Velardi and matter-of-factly said, "Now your' good pal Dan will be able to retrieve his coveted Rolex from one of those rented box trucks! And it's a good thing that we were able to plant several of our elite personnel into the Mexican and terrorist organizations and suggest to them that the hotel guests be held as hostages in the Bunker. Pardon my oversight Colonel Bauers. I'd like to introduce you to Agent Salvatore Velardi, one of my most trusted men, who incidentally had been highly instrumental in contributing to the overall success of this very intricate quasi-military operation!"

"From the outset Colonel, I never once imagined the great magnitude of this immense operation!" Agent Velardi marveled and expressed. "I'm quite awed by it all! Your military strategy was outstanding!"

"And just think," Colonel Bauers declared and then momentarily hesitated to contemplate recent reality, "I nominally estimate that perhaps, conservatively speaking, two-to-three million dollars of extensive damage has been inflicted upon this noble queen venue of American resorts. This exquisite hotel was the perfect opportunity for *us* to get five hundred or so zealous enemies congregated into a small area to be systematically killed en-masse. Regrettably, there're plenty of doors that have been smashed, numerous walls riddled with bullet holes, ornate chandeliers demolished, and there's also scads of carpets smeared and stained with blood and flesh tissue. And that's not counting the multiple grenade explosions *we* had used to save American lives! But now, this historic structure will serve as a fine inspiration of national patriotism for all future visitors to amply value and appreciate! This magnificent grand hotel has been traditionally regarded as a tourist Mecca for well over a hundred years," Colonel Bauers emotionally emphasized, his fervent words meandering out of his normally stoic disposition lane, "and right now it sort of really looks like a morbid Middle East Mecca, especially with all of these lifeless dishonorable Arab and Iranian corpses lying around!"

"It looks like August of 2011 will be a calendar month for posterity to remember," Agent Velardi blurted-out. "Thank goodness the evil terrorist plot has been eliminated."

"Indeed!" Inspector Giralo concurred. "Salvatore, you've just spoken the bloody truth!" the Chief accurately concluded as his keen eyes surveyed the extensive human carnage strewn about the popular resort's violated grounds.

# "Missions Accomplished"

The lengthy five and a half-hour March 14th United Airlines flight from Philadelphia International Airport to San Diego's Charles Lindbergh Field was both smooth and enjoyable, except for a thirty-minute interval of minimal atmospheric turbulence over Nevada. Astute FBI Inspector Joe Giralo, accompanied by his loyal team of Agents Salvatore Velardi, Arthur Orsi and Dan Blachford, had been dispatched west to specifically investigate a very disturbing rash of violent explosions whereby eighteen unoccupied Catholic churches in three separate states had been destroyed or severely damaged by powerful dynamite detonations.

After retrieving their assorted luggage pieces from one of the airport's rotating baggage carousels, Chief Giralo took swift command of the operation and soon rented a comfortable *Ford Expedition* from Avis, and predictably, Sal Velardi was assigned the responsibility of driving the SUV and its fatigued passengers north up *Interstate 5* to where reservations for a pair of two-bedroom suites had been made at the La Jolla Marriott, situated on beautiful Village Drive not-too-far from the campus of *San Diego State University,* and also around two miles from coastal and scenic Torrey Pines Road.

"Say Chief," Sal Velardi announced from behind the steering wheel. "Many classic golf tournaments have been played just down the road from the Marriott at historic Torrey Pines. And here's a proletarian suggestion!" the chattering driver embellished his monologue. "There's a Denny's Restaurant in the vicinity further down on the way to *La Jolla,* which according to a colorful brochure I had casually read at the airport, means 'the jewel' when translated from Spanish into English."

"And what about the all-too-crowded Interstate Highways?" Agent Art Orsi eagerly chimed-in. "Everything in regard to motoring directions out here on the West Coast is that you have to take 'the 5' to travel up toward L.A., or you have to get onto 'the 15' to venture over toward San Bernardino or 'the 10' will get you heading in the direction of Palm Springs or Palm Desert. Back in Philly' and Jersey, equally congested interstate thoroughfares are just basically referred to as I-95 or I-80!"

"And they sure have some strange ecology habits out here in environmentally friendly California," Dan Blachford chipped-in, sitting erect in the back seat across from Agent Orsi and also directly behind stoic-faced Inspector Joe Giralo. "I was just speaking with a transplanted New Jersey gentleman at the luggage carousel, and he told me that the bridge spanning from San Diego over to Coronado Island doesn't require a toll if you have one or more passengers riding in your automobile. Car-pooling is definitely encouraged out here in the Golden State," Blachford continued his prattling. "A driver only has to pay the bridge toll if he or she is alone in the vehicle!"

"Boss," Agent Velardi respectfully addressed Inspector Giralo. "Will we be given some free time off during this caper to visit the famous Hotel Coronado? I've never had the pleasure of experiencing it since this is my first time in the area."

"Only if we're able to first solve this abominable series of horrendous church bombings," Chief Giralo bluntly answered. "After we check into the Marriott, I've made 6 pm reservations for four at the Chart House on the Prospect Street promenade down in gorgeous La Jolla. But Men, I've stayed at the luxurious Hotel Del on three occasions, twice on week-long vacations with my wife and two daughters, and then a third time on government business back in 1990. Now for the benefit of killing some time, what do you know Sal about *that* highly acclaimed tourist trap other than the popular notorious legend that several rooms at the Del are believed by some superstitious guests to be haunted with rather annoying, obnoxious ghosts!"

"Well, I know that the Hotel Del Coronado is a huge, white, wooden, Victorian structure featuring a fabulous red roof," Sal Velardi intelligently replied. "The place has several impressive spires, the largest one is located on top of the tremendous banquet and reception room. And I would be very remiss if I didn't mention that many Hollywood actors and actresses along with a plethora of multimillionaires have over the decades proudly vacationed there."

"Yes, the Del Coronado would be way-too-expensive for us to stay on this extended assignment. While organizing *my* final trip evaluation," the team leader assessed and then cleared his raspy throat, "it came down to a tough choice between the San Diego Sea Lodge nestled on the Pacific Coast or the very reputable La Jolla Marriott. As you're all well-aware, especially in this nasty tight economy, we have to be exceptionally frugal when it comes to spending the taxpayers' hard-earned dollars, and quite frankly, I didn't want to see you three fledgling sleuths constantly being distracted by curvaceous women out on the sandy beach, the alluring dolls all wearing skimpy bikinis. But back on subject, when the Del had opened its doors to the public in 1888," Chief Giralo authoritatively stated to his three-member captive audience, "it was the biggest resort hotel in the entire world. Despite its present noble age, the dignified seven-floor edifice is still one of the highest regarded hotels on all the continents. I remember especially relishing tremendous dining feasts at the resort's 1500 Ocean and Sheerwater restaurants. If we can break this top-secret church bombing case wide open, I promise to buy, with money out of my own wallet, yes Men, I'll generously treat the three of you' voracious chow-hounds to extravagant surf-and-turf dinners at one of the Del's very exclusive restaurants."

"I understand that much of the hotel's landscaping rivals that of a European palace's botanical garden," Agent Art Orsi contributed to the ongoing SUV conversation. "And I had read in a flight magazine on the airplane that Chinese laborers had been brought-in from San Francisco and subsequently relocated down here to semi-tropical Coronado Island in order to construct the original hotel main building."

"Yes, and the Del was the first hotel to ever have electricity," Chief Giralo articulated before squirming about to achieve a better riding position in his front passenger-side bucket seat. "Thomas Edison himself had arrived on the premises to inspect the final product and to conduct a comprehensive safety analysis. And Sal," Giralo then expounded. "You were right about powerful politicians and renowned celebrities frequenting the fantastic place: Presidents William McKinley, Woodrow Wilson, and also silent film stars Rudolph Valentino and Charlie Chaplin, just to name a few dignitaries! Even Richard Nixon, J.F.K., Jimmy Carter, Ronald Reagan and George W. Bush have stayed at the one-of-a-kind national treasure. Yes, and if I accurately recollect, L. Frank Baum, the distinguished author of the *Wizard of Oz,* well Guys, he had produced a good deal of his most creative literature at the totally inspirational Hotel del Coronado, and oh yes, finally Men," knowledgeable and long-winded Inspector Joe Giralo characteristically and incessantly declared. "At least a dozen classic movies have been filmed at the Del including *Some Like It Hot* starring Jack Lemmon, Marilyn Monroe and Tony Curtis."

"Well, Chief, I strongly recommend that we'd better get this bizarre church bombing investigation completed early in the week so that the four of us can spend a pleasant day ambling around at the San Diego Zoo in Balboa Park, after of course," Dan Blachford paused and then qualified, "we journey over to Coronado Island and tour the prestigious hotel's grand lobby and all-the-while appreciate the many terrific amenities the place has to offer! And let's not rule-out a sidebar visit to Sea World too!"

Agent Sal Velardi adroitly steered the rented black SUV off of "the 5's" typical traffic congestion and then navigated onto La Jolla

Village Drive. After registering for two already-reserved fourth floor suites at the Marriott's main lobby desk, three ambitious, uniformed bellboys escorted the four New Jersey men to an empty elevator, which soon quickly ascended to the designated fourth floor. After tipping the cheerful accommodating hotel help, the quartet of federal employees spent the next three hours unpacking suitcases, hastily placing clothes into very clean bureau drawers, resting on comfortable emerald-green chairs and matching cloth sofas, and then later, washing-up in preparation for delicious steak and seafood combination dinners at the Chart House on La Jolla's picturesque waterfront. An hour before sunset, the four hungry FBI detectives were finally being seated at a fine table having a picturesque Pacific Ocean view by a very pretty tanned blonde hostess.

"Boss, while you and Sal were especially preoccupied relaxing on that Prospect Street bench just before we were summoned into the restaurant," Art Orsi smartly remarked to his immediate supervisor while the hungry group was busy consuming their various appetizers inside the Chart House's main dining room. "Dan and I strolled around the corner and we were lucky to observe a family of contented seals lazily basking upon enormous rocks out in the harbor. You don't see that type of extraordinary spectacle too often back in Atlantic City or Wildwood!"

"Did the docile creatures have long floppy ears?" Chief Giralo inquired and academically challenged before chewing and swallowing another morsel of luscious crab meat cocktail.

"Why no!" Arthur Orsi mildly exclaimed with a suddenly observable florid face. "There weren't any long floppy ears!"

"Well then, Arty," sagacious Inspector Joe Giralo verbally supplemented and elaborated. "Those particular animals that you and Dan had not-so-keenly witnessed dozing-off in the setting sun were actually lethargic sea lions and not phlegmatic ocean seals. Sea lions don't have long floppy ears like seals do!"

"Holy crustaceans!" Agent Orsi laughed as a skinny male waiter gently laid a sumptuous-looking combination plate of lobster and crab meat between the famished agent's silverware table settings. "If I'm ever fortunate enough to be promoted to the high rank of FBI Inspector, I only hope that I'll be half as erudite about certain esoteric matters as you are Chief!"

"Before my cluttered overtaxed mind forgets Sal," Joe Giralo confidently related to his favorite chauffeur, "tomorrow morning I want you to take 'the 5' down to San Diego. Here's the address of our local FBI bureau: 9797 Aero Drive," the mission coordinator disclosed as he handed Agent Velardi an official business card.

"Enter the street and number coordinates you've just been given into the SUV's GPS system and then navigate your way to the appropriate location. And don't forget to take Art and Dan along with you on your vital information-gathering escapade!"

"Well Boss, exactly what's the nature of our secret assignment?" Sal Velardi anxiously asked. "As you might already know, I have a special penchant for finding-out pertinent background details in relation to cracking-open extremely complicated crime wave riddles!"

"While you had inadvertently abandoned me on the Prospect Street sidewalk bench and were totally enamored with shopping for several cheap La Jolla souvenirs in three alluring novelty shops," Chief Giralo lightly admonished his sometimes-aberrant subordinate, "and while Art and Dan were around back mistaking despondent sea lions for depressed seals, I wisely utilized my government-issue cell phone and cleverly contacted old reliable Matt Riley back in Washington."

"And exactly what did that wily federal savant have to reveal that's remotely relevant to this incredible West Coast church bombing scenario?" Velardi asked.

"Here's the scoop, Guys!" Inspector Giralo lowly whispered towards the center of the round restaurant table. "Sal, you're to compile an adequate portfolio on the six malicious California church explosions. And Art, you're to glean sufficient info' on the half dozen parallel Arizona incidents. And finally, Dan," the Boss instructed, "your challenging task is to obtain all the essential data that you can muster pertaining to the six very distressing New Mexico church felonies!"

"Tell me Joe, er I mean Inspector," instantly embarrassed Sal Velardi awkwardly corrected his own deviant departure from common courtesy and standard FBI etiquette. "Have the horrible explosions occurred in all three states on the exact same dates?"

"Yes Sal, the same time at noon on the exact same dates, a full Monday apart, each set of three blasts happening at the exact same time," Chief Giralo indicated and confirmed. "That ongoing established pattern means that we only have until next Monday the 19th to satisfactorily figure-out the nuts and bolts to this most perplexing chain of disastrous church desecrations!"

"And tomorrow's already Thursday the 15th!" Agent Velardi contemplated and then gasped. "I'm no Alexander-the-Great by any stretch of the imagination, but this narrow five-day time-frame simply means that we have only a fraction of a week's precious days to unravel this very complex Gordian Knot!"

"That's right Sal!" Inspector Giralo promptly acknowledged. "And Men, if humanly possible, I want to keep the level of church destruction at a minimum. Several more sacrilegious bombings and I'll have to shamefully retire from the FBI as both an absolute disgrace and as a dishonorable failure! For my reputation's sake, please pray for a large miracle Fellas'!"

* * * * * * * * * * * *

At 9 a.m. sharp on Friday, March 16<sup>th,</sup> 2012, the four dedicated FBI men met as planned in the fourth floor Marriott suite currently shared by Inspector Joe Giralo and Agent Salvatore Velardi. Following their determined leader's explicit directions, the three investigators had brought along a wealth of recently obtained information neatly and carefully arranged inside their individual oak tag folders.

"Well Chief," Art Orsi began as the four men formally sat around a mahogany coffee table in the suite's tastefully decorated living room area. "What's your clever theory about who's wickedly committing these atrocious Catholic church bombings?"

"Actually Art, presently I don't know the identities of the individual culprits, but generally speaking," Inspector Giralo elucidated and then momentarily hesitated, "I suspect that we're dealing with a string of hate crimes here, yes indeed, hate crimes directed against the Catholic religion, all being deplorably enacted in three separate states. Now then Gentlemen, I'm inclined to believe that rather than us chasing-down crazed international terrorists, we're concerned with bringing to justice a batch of demented home-grown anarchists, probably zealous fanatics that greatly despise the church's dogmatic teachings, particularly in the areas of abortion, gay rights and also so-called women's *reproductive rights,* which obviously have nothing remotely to do with the normal process of female reproduction. Instead, the practice of reproduction rights conversely prevents reproduction from happening! The all-too-convenient politically correct phraseology is a modern-day euphemism for the use of contraception and for the employment of common birth control methods."

"So therefore, Boss, you hypothesize that radical pro-choice advocates, militant gay and lesbian marriage villains, along with crazed feminists are the central instigators of all of these contemptuous church attacks that appear to be deliberate and not random or copy-cat criminal activities!" Dan Blachford deduced and concluded.

"Exactly Dan," Chief Giralo tersely agreed. "There's nothing at all superficial about these extremely heinous church bombings! Usually though, humans are creatures of habit in their daily behavior patterns. But as a rule, crooks tend to give themselves away when the morally corrupt fools attempt becoming too sophisticated, and then the overconfident perpetrators think that they're uncommonly shrewd and soon audaciously deviate from their standard-but-effective M. O.'s, while interestingly enough, during *their* mania, attempting to send the state and federal authorities onto the wrong trail. That's the crucial tipping point when the cocky erroneous thugs are most vulnerable to being apprehended and then Gentlemen, ultimately being promptly indicted and convicted in like fashion."

"Your novel theory about the haughty nature of the criminal mindset is quite plausible," Agent Velardi commended his highly admired tutor and mentor. "Now Boss, with your permission, may I now begin my formal presentation about the mendacious California church explosions."

"Yes Salvatore, you may commence. But try being as succinct as possible," Giralo sternly insisted. "Conciseness and brevity should be this discussion's principal objectives!"

"Okay then," Agent Velardi almost neurotically replied as he slowly opened his oak tag folder containing his research that had been carefully obtained at 9797 Aero Drive. "As everyone's quite well-aware, six disgusting church bombings have occurred at seven-day intervals, each one on a consecutive Monday. This evolutionary pattern obviously suggests that the next human-caused California catastrophe will occur next Monday, March Nineteenth. No magical crystal ball is needed to prognosticate *that* bone-chilling prediction!"

"That mundane conclusion is both plausible and rational!" Chief Giralo assessed and expressed. "But please Sal, let's meticulously review the six abhorrent California church detonations in their precise chronological order."

"The first demolition regrettably happened right here in San Diego, the second one up in Carmel, the third destruction over in Monterrey County, the fourth in San Gabriel, the fifth in San Luis Obispo County and finally," Velardi vociferated before inhaling an abundance of fresh oxygen to resume his important exposition, "the sixth germane tragedy occurred just last Monday at noon, March 12th up in San Francisco."

"Excellent information gathering," Chief Giralo complimented. "But Sal, you neglected to provide *us* the names of the old Spanish missions that are located nearest to the specific targeted Catholic churches that have been under siege!"

"Chief, I didn't consider *those* remote, minute facts that you had just alluded to as being material to this first stage of our investigation," Agent Velardi quite defensively answered. "And I sincerely apologize for the gross oversight!"

"Art and Dan, do you two contemporary Dick Tracy impersonators have in your possession the names of the nearest missions to the destroyed churches over in Arizona and New Mexico respectively?" Chief Joe Giralo politely-but-directly reprimanded the suddenly surprised duo. "What about the original erection dates of the nearest missions to those affected parochial churches? Precisely, in what years had the nearest missions been established?"

"Why no Boss!" Orsi and Blachford simultaneously chorused, showing signs of instant humiliation.

"Well then, my illustrious trio of professional crime fighters, I want *those* particular vital construction facts available to me by 9 am, tomorrow," Joe Giralo imperatively commanded. "How can I ever make any valid interpretations about this insidious crime wave if I'm given totally mediocre and incomplete backgrounds to the eighteen unscrupulous nihilistic acts, all apparently performed by obsessed political ideologues!"

"Well Chief, what remarkable pearls of wisdom has *your* singular research obtained?" Agent Arthur Orsi intrepidly requested knowing. "Personally, I need to learn some enlightening guidance because right now, my mind is a little stifled by a lack of solid evidence in regard to the vexing Arizona crime spree that's gone way beyond acts of mere vandalism!"

Chief Joe Giralo patiently explained to his now-mortified men that originally, a series of twenty-one California coastal Spanish missions had been founded by Father Junipero Serra of the Franciscan Order. However, the Catholic missions that had been constructed in Arizona and in New Mexico had been established a century earlier by members of the rival Jesuit Order.

"The Jesuit missions outside California are much older than the Franciscan ones that were logically situated along the Pacific Coast," Giralo convincingly lectured with little body animation. "The Spanish were expressly motivated to explore the New World as a result of what history books describe as the Three G's: a quest for *gold,* the avaricious pursuit based on the fabled Indian tale of the lost city of El Dorado; secondly, there was the consuming desire of adventurous explorers and conquistadors like Balboa and Coronado to attain personal *glory,* and thirdly, there was the religious need for devout Spanish missionaries to spread the *gospel* and then successfully convert the various indigenous coastal Indian tribes to Christianity."

"Well, please educate me some more about local history. What labor force had built all of the various western missions?" Dan Blachford curiously inquired. "Each one, just like the venerable Alamo over in San Antonio, Texas is a unique architectural monument having its own distinct design and local personality."

"Great question Dan!" Inspector Giralo enthusiastically praised. "Local Indian populations had labored and toiled in the hot sun to obediently build the wonderful missions, that is," the Chief resumed his scholarly narrative, "that is *after* the tribes had been converted to Catholicism. But Men, when you show-up here with your newly compiled documentation tomorrow, Saturday morning, March 17th, better known as St. Patrick's Day, please have with you the exact dates that the missions in your assigned states had been built. But finally, Gentlemen, I want you to include, or should I say *exclude,* one vital thing in your reports."

"And exactly what's *that* salient item that we have to *exclude?*" Sal Velardi queried his mentor, the agent's confused mind presently addled with a lack of clarity.

"I desire for you three Fellas' on Saturday to *not* include any Franciscan or Jesuit mission that's presently in ruins," Chief Giralo decisively stipulated. "I only want the three of you to acquire the names of the original missions that are still standing and operating in California, in Arizona and in New Mexico. Can I be any more lucid about *that* very elementary specification?"

"Easier said than done," Sal Velardi reflexively complained. "But with Monday's March 19th deadline rapidly approaching, I assure you' Boss, your rather peculiar demands will be satisfied! Well then Guys, I suppose that it's back to the old drawing board! I'll drive *us* back over to the FBI Office on Aero Drive."

"Good then!" Chief Giralo rather blandly exclaimed. "I'll contact Matt Riley later today to synchronize a potential raid with Colonel Bob Bauers of Delta Force being in charge of logistical operations. All we have to do is winnow-down our present all-too-wide path of detective scrutiny and then incisively devise a probable time and place scenario so that Bauers and his competent commando units can swiftly collar or kill the Catholic-loathing anarchists who are recklessly participating in this all-too-sensational, horrible skein of reprehensible home-grown terror acts."

* * * * * * * * * * * *

On Tuesday morning, March 20th a much-relieved Inspector Joe Giralo entertained his three FBI associates with a delectable room service breakfast inside his deluxe fourth floor La Jolla Marriott suite. The three mentally out-of-sync agents were totally dumbfounded at exactly how their rather unorthodox boss had magically unraveled the very difficult hate crime California church bombing crime spree. The veteran FBI detective was immensely savoring every moment of his seemingly vague and obscure verbal rendition recounting recent events. Much to *his* great satisfaction, the abundant suspense existing within *his* all-too-curious agents' hyperactive minds was definitely escalating.

"Yes Men, my close friend Colonel Bob Bauers and his elite Delta Force storm-troopers easily made mincemeat and chopped liver out of the dozen clumsy domestic anarchists causing all of the troubling church havoc out here in sunny California. Confidentially," Inspector Giralo concisely disclosed, "three of the egregious home-grown terrorists had been seriously wounded during the brief military encounter."

"Then you were correct in your assumption that gay and lesbian political militants, abortion rights' radicals and a bevy of truculent woman's rights' fanatics were conspiring and collaborating to eliminate the chosen churches one by one because the crazed nihilists stridently opposed the Catholic religion's moral teachings about certain civil rights issues," Sal Velardi aptly summarized. "Evidently, *their* totally evil purpose represented a contemporary war of the First Ten Amendments versus the written-in-stone Ten Commandments of the Old Testament prophet Moses! Book of Exodus I do believe!"

"Very well put!" Joe Giralo congratulated his main crime-fighting apostle. "And Sal, when I was a kid, I had the distinct pleasure of attending St. Joseph Elementary School on North Third Street in metropolitan downtown Hammonton," Inspector Giralo esoterically mentioned, deliberately stressing every single syllable. "Yes indeed, Salvatore, that's how in my youth I knew from redundant classroom memorization that March 19th was always St. Joseph's Day, traditionally two days following St. Patrick's! Without exception, the school's ultra-strict nuns and priests had the ever-fearful student body attend mass on those two highly-revered March religious holidays!"

"What on Earth are you talking about!" a fully frustrated Arthur Orsi staunchly protested. "Boss, please stop being so darned evasive, elusive, vague and facetious!"

"Okay now, my totally confused investigative Gentlemen, let's academically review *our* formerly bewildering case one illuminating step at a time. But please remember, your stellar gumshoe research over at the San Diego FBI Office actually had been the magnificent springboard that got me thinking about how dangerous ruthless crooks have a certain propensity for outsmarting themselves when they foolishly attempt being tricky by accidentally wandering away from their ordinary habits and methods! And Guys, that's precisely how I had managed to dynamically exploit their vulnerability."

"But the other two anarchy squads patrolling over in Arizona and New Mexico did yesterday, Monday, March 19th, successfully dynamite two more churches!" Dan Blachford profoundly objected. "Please tell me why those two empty houses of worship had to be sacrificed!"

"Well Dan, Matt Riley was getting a lot of verbal static from powerful bishops and cardinals, and the Bureau was also receiving pressure from the persistent TV media about the widespread rash of church calamities being chronicled in local newspapers, but to simplify matters," Joe Giralo audaciously defended his erudite strategy, "in the end I was more certain where the next California attack would happen than I was about where the next surreptitious hate-crime church blowups intended for Arizona and New Mexico would occur."

"Well Chief, my exhausted mind's still in an absolute quandary about how you've miraculously cracked-open this rather oddball case!" Sal Velardi all-too-honestly maintained. "I'm going to again review for benefit of the assembled group sitting here my personal discoveries about the *disparate* California church explosions and then *you* can cast much-needed illumination upon the most recent St. Joseph Day Delta Force invasion!"

Velardi then once more orally conveyed to his three comrades that the first California church debacle had occurred in San Diego, the second in Carmel, the third in Monterey County, the fourth in San Gabriel, the fifth in San Luis Obispo County and the sixth calamity in San Francisco. "Now kindly tell us in plain unvarnished English lexicon Chief, how does all of this seemingly marble-cake data I've just divulged correlate into a feasible FBI detective-oriented explanation?"

"As you know, Salvatore, I'm quite experienced at deciphering hidden meanings that are often furtively disguised inside certain given facts," Giralo affirmatively and arcanely revealed. "Now Sal, here's a nondescript map I've printed off the Internet showing the exact timeframe order that Franciscan Padre Junipero Serra had founded his original twenty-one California missions. Notice that the six places of worship that you had just identified, all situated in six separate counties, correspond perfectly with the first six original missions in exact chronological order. The San Diego mission was the first one built by Father Serra's Indians, its name being San Diego de Alcala as accurately recorded on this Internet map reproduction. The present Catholic Church located nearest the first established mission was the first one to be targeted. And the second church that had been destroyed up in Carmel was the closest one to Father Serra's second founded mission, San Carlos Borromeo de Carmelo!"

"How fantastically unbelievable! I now see the full magnitude of your brilliant methodology!" Agent Velardi marveled and exclaimed. "The Monterrey County Church that had been disrespectfully burned to a cinder was located near the third mission shown on *your* duplicated map, its name being San Antonio de Padua, located not-too-distant from the world-famous Hearst Mansion; and the fourth church that had been dynamited was in San Gabriel over in Los Angeles County, and it was conveniently positioned near the San Gabriel Archangel mission; and in a similar fashion, the fifth selected church that went-up in flames was close to the San Luis Obispo de Tolosa Mission up north in San Luis Obispo County; and finally Boss, the sixth church conflagration was not far from the San Francisco de Asis Delores, which had been the sixth mission erected in the northern city by the bay possessing the same San Francisco name."

"But what about the Jesuit missions along with the related diabolical church shenanigans' occurring in Arizona?" Art Orsi asked and then momentarily ceased speaking with his mouth temporarily agape. "How was *that* hellish skullduggery masterminded by yet-to-be-caught Anarchist Team B?"

"Well Art, I've already cited where criminals often foul themselves up by endeavoring to be too wily and then idiotically deviating from their regular routines," Chief Giralo prudently reviewed. "Well Guys, that's where creativity usually back-fires! If you think about the ugly crime-wave series involving each Arizona church incineration, the separate incidents follow a definite *reverse pattern* to that which had been demonstrated in the aforementioned California mission scheme. Instead of going from oldest to newest," Giralo persuasively emphasized, "the applied Arizona criminal strategy constituted a major backward approach going from a church situated near the newest Jesuit mission, then the second one slated for elimination being close to the second newest mission, and so on, and so on!"

"Well Chief, what about the New Mexico churches that were set ablaze from violent dynamite blasts?" Dan Blachford wondered and asked. "How about them?"

"The demolished churches located close to the chosen New Mexico Jesuit missions were deviously arranged and selected in an extremely deceptive, staggered pattern, actually a unique *alternating pattern,* Dan!" Joe Giralo very judiciously communicated. "The first burnt-to-a-crisp New Mexico church being situated near the oldest mission, the second modern-day church being constructed near the newest mission, the third targeted church being near the second oldest New Mexico mission, and in regard to the fourth designated Catholic house of worship, its specific geography was in close proximity to the second newest mission, and so on and so on!"

"This entire sordid sequence of parallel malicious events, all developing simultaneously in three separate states at precise seven-day intervals is without a doubt mind-boggling!" opined Agent Velardi. "I conjecture that intense, in-house, rough, no-nonsense interrogations of the captured California A-Team radicals will eventually lead to the apprehension of the equally wretched Arizona and New Mexico anarchists. But Chief, how in God's name did you know about the seventh California scheduled attack being treacherously planned for the esteemed San Juan Capistrano Mission?"

"That's where my wonderful Catholic grammar school intuition, or should I pragmatically say 'my strict parochial school educational indoctrination' dramatically kicked-in!" the now-jubilant Inspector Giralo smiled and then consequentially chuckled. "I figured that the miserable vindictive anarchists were quite ready to branch-out of their normal practice for just one auspicious day, and subsequently, carelessly abandon their vile church destruction tactics in order to abruptly shock the public by eliminating the renowned landmark San Juan Capistrano Mission. They just couldn't resist the overwhelming temptation to make a dramatic public statement!"

"So, you had Matt Riley confer with Colonel Bob Bauers and have his ever-vigilant Delta Force units stationed all around the historic Capistrano Mission," Art Orsi surmised and concluded. "But how does the St. Joseph's Day March 19th jargon fit-in as a significant factor into your imaginative mental equation?"

"Here's the marvelous formula Arty! On St. Joseph's Day, March 19th of each year," Chief Giralo nonchalantly prefaced his superb discourse, "squadrons of swallows, yes, very tiny birds, habitually wing their way back to Southern California to roost for half a year at the San Juan Capistrano Mission. In fact, Art, there's an old song commemorating the annual phenomenon that's appropriately titled 'When the Swallows Come Back to Capistrano'! And quite amazingly," Inspector Giralo exhaled, fully enjoying every wonderful second, "on October 23rd of each year, which traditionally on the Catholic Calendar is designated as the 'Day of San Juan', the itinerant swallows obediently depart Capistrano, only to again faithfully return the following St. Joseph Day, March 19th!"

"And so Boss," Sal Velardi excitedly fathomed and generalized, "you had perceptively theorized that the California A Team anarchists would for one time only, imaginatively abandon their fanatical church implosions and stupidly concentrate on a much more colossal and tremendously more shocking violent act of discriminate terror, that is, heinously detonating the famous Capistrano Mission and killing-off most of the swallows in the process, just to make a brazen-but-potent ideological statement to the totally appalled world! I now see and comprehend Boss that incomparable San Juan Capistrano had been the seventh site founded by Father Junipero Serra that's prominently listed on *your* chronological order historical mission map!"

"And now *we* know why the local Major League baseball team is named the San Diego Padres!" Art Orsi declared.

"And why the team up in Anaheim is called the California Angels!" Dan Blachford laughed and related.

"What an outrageously preposterous, fundamentally deranged, maniacal conspiracy!" Art Orsi angrily determined. "And the entire outlandish fiasco was ignorantly based on a diabolical animosity for the Catholic Church's inflexible moral doctrines!"

"That's basically right, Arty," Joe Giralo gleefully verified. "The mendacious villains in all three states were radical, heterogeneous, home-grown anarchists who absolutely despised American History, Western Civilization and the U.S, Constitution in general, and the Catholic religion in particular!"

"And Chief, if it weren't for your notable wisdom," Dan Blachford opined to his eminent team captain, "the dastardly dissidents might've eventually advanced to eradicating epic cathedrals and basilicas! Maybe even initiating repulsively hideous crimes like blowing-up the Vatican!"

"Now I truly believe that you three inimitable geniuses have finally pieced-together the entire puzzle that's no longer an enormous perplexing mystery," Inspector Giralo stated with an artificial lugubrious expression upon his countenance. "So therefore, Gentlemen, contrary to my ordinarily parsimonious nature, I feel extremely obligated to honor my sacred pledge, and so consequently, as a direct result of my former irresponsible rhetoric," the enthralled FBI Chief very politely proceeded, "I feel quite compelled to treat the three of you rather fascinating amateur sleuths to a fabulous well-deserved five-course surf and turf supper inside the beautiful Hotel del Coronado's incomparable Sheerwater dining facility! In the final analysis Gentlemen," self-satisfied Inspector Joe Giralo haughtily snickered, "dining ambiance just can't get any better than that!"

# "Multiple Choice"

As veteran Agents Salvatore Velardi, Arthur Orsi and Dan Blachford entered Philadelphia FBI headquarters at 600 Arch Street, the three black-suited government detectives had been casually discussing the amusing notion that their distinguished boss Chief Inspector Joe Giralo was indeed one hundred percent psychic. But as the chatty trio would soon discover, the astonishing and confounding "Multiple Choice Case" would become a perplexing development that would virtually confirm their speculative suspicions about their boss's seemingly uncanny, paranormal abilities.

Chief Giralo was preoccupied sitting upon his black swivel chair behind his impressive Canadian oak desk, but instead of reading the early morning edition of the *Philadelphia Inquirer* as was his habit, "the Boss" was engrossed in studying certain words printed upon fresh computer paper. Meditative Joe Giralo instantly abandoned his introspection to acknowledge the expected appearance of his illustrious, investigative trio.

"Glad to see that you three non-Musketeer sleuths could make our scheduled Friday morning appointment," the Chief greeted his commuting work staff. "Tell me Salvatore. How was the Eagles concert down at the Wells Fargo Center, I believe?"

"It was absolutely spectacular!" Agent Velardi spontaneously exclaimed. "Don Henley did a terrific job singing 'Hotel California' and 'Dirty Laundry' and Glenn Frey was sensational doing 'Take It Easy' and 'Tequila Sunrise'. The three-hour show was fantastically great. Even Kathy now is an enthusiastic Eagles' fan!"

"Isn't Joe Walsh in that group too?" Joe Giralo asked, his timely query delving deep into his impeccable memory.

"Yes, indeed," Agent Velardi indicated. "Joe Walsh is regarded as the comedian of the band, and just like Don Henley and Glenn Frey, the guy has a well-established solo career too. I especially like his rendition of 'Life's Been Good' along with his performance of 'Rocky Mountain Way'. And the fourth member of the Eagles, a fella' named Timothy B. Schmit also sings a few solo hits of his own."

"The Wells Fargo Center has a super-tremendous sound system," interrupted Agent Arthur Orsi. "In April, Carol and I had gotten tickets to a Fleetwood Mac concert and I have to admit that the show was truly exceptional. Stevie Nicks still has a sexy voice, and Lindsey Buckingham is perhaps the best electric guitarist ever. And John McVie on bass guitar really jams, especially with two particular songs, 'The Chain' and 'Go Your Own Way'. And of course," Agent Orsi prattled, "Mick Fleetwood is one of the premier drummers in all of rock and roll, going way back to Bill Haley and the Comets in 1954."

"And how about you Dan?" the amused Chief inquired of Agent Blachford. "Have you and Bing lately attended any sensational rock concerts at the Wells Fargo Center?"

"No, Inspector; my wife and I had spent last weekend relaxing on the beach and walking the boardwalk down in Ocean City, Maryland," Agent Blachford answered. "We enjoyed the tasty Thrasher's French fries, had a few great meals in the Holiday Inn's Reflections Restaurant, and we also experienced smooth seventeen-mile rides across Delaware Bay on the Cape May-Lewes Ferry. But tonight, Bing and I plan on going to the July 16th carnival in downtown Hammonton. The colorful ritual is become an annual tradition that my wife and I have come to honor each and every summer."

Wily Chief Giralo then intentionally bemused and confused his three crime-fighting disciples by asking the frequent office visitors when was the last time they had taken a 'Multiple Choice' objective question test. Agents Velardi, Orsi and Blachford seemed momentarily bewildered by their boss's rather peculiar inquiry.

"In Mr. Tom Curley's Western Civilization class, I believe, my junior year at Hammonton High School," Sal Velardi remembered and firmly articulated. "If I recall, Mr. Curley loved presenting labyrinth-length multiple choice questions, constantly telling his lethargic pupils that it was too formidable for him to read and grade alternative-type essay test items."

Next, Art Orsi chimed-in to add his commentary to the new-found oddball conversation. "Mr. Bill Heston's tests on Herman Melville's classic novel 'Moby Dick' and on William Shakespeare's tragic play 'Romeo and Juliet' were somewhere between horrendous and abominable for an unmotivated senior like me to take and pass," the all-too-honest agent recalled and guiltily reported. "How I ever graduated from Hammonton High School was truly a minor miracle. I almost had to petition the New Jersey Commissioner of Education in order to successfully make it out of *that* renowned institution of scholarly endeavor."

"Indeed, Boss, I had found Mr. Gordon Strycula's American History tests to be quite atrocious," Dan Blachford attested without direct solicitation. "The guy's enigmatic multiple-choice questions were virtually indecipherable, and by the time I got done reading the introduction to a test item, my total mind would be swimming in a foggy nebulous quandary. If I recall, there was a controversial issue always floating around the high school; whose arduous tests were more difficult, Mr. Curley's or Mr. Strycula's!"

"Fellas', I just have to mention that I also had the distinct pleasure of attending Hammonton High a full decade before you three Einsteins had ever evolved out of kindergarten," Inspector Giralo incisively driveled. "So naturally, I had been exposed to teachers who had become retired prior to your undistinguished high school careers. But honestly, Mr. Neil Pastore's Chemistry multiple choice exams' were predictably quite challenging, and also, Mr. Jimmy DeFiccio's arduous French tests had often made me wish I had taken Spanish or Italian as foreign languages instead."

"Forgive my burgeoning ignorance," a slightly vexed Sal Velardi piped-in, "but what's all of this crazy nonsense about high school academic multiple-choice tests?" the inquisitive agent abruptly asked his often-vague and evasive federal government mentor. "As the Eagles allude to in the famous song 'Already Gone', 'I can see the stars but never see the light'."

"Well, Gentlemen. Now that we've supposedly discussed positively nothing in regard to our all-important FBI workload," Inspector Giralo mildly chided his three subordinates as "the Boss" slowly opened his top desk drawer and gingerly removed three duplicate pages ditto to the one existing before his eyes, "I wish to share something rather bizarre with you' notorious gumshoes. Three weeks ago, I had received *this* unusual item via certified mail, and at first inspection, I had erroneously evaluated it to be a weird joke originating from a jealous prankster who despises government bureaucracy. But now as a result of recent current events, there's strong evidence to the contrary, the accumulating facts suggesting otherwise."

Joe Giralo then methodically distributed the three previously concealed identical papers to his more-than-curious underlings, requesting that the agents read and then render their individual opinions about the rather strange scenario being reviewed. The three investigators intensely and silently read the language and soon anxiously contemplated the five-item quiz selections, each loyal detective having a very serious expression appearing upon his face.

# "Multiple Choice Quiz"

Figure-out the U.S. Cities

1.

A)   Buccaneers but not Pirates
B)   trouble brewing
C)   Marty Robbins saloon fight
D)   Lost Wages
E)   all of the above

2.

A)   KO
B)   Spanish for "that"
C)   mountain water tumbling, (hive-see-sea)
D)   BA, BA black sheep
E)   all of the above

3.

A)   AC/DC
B)   small diamond
C)   bashful girl
D)   elephants and marauders
E)   all of the above

4.

A)   hall of fame rocks
B)   Bulls and Bears
C)   metropolis in the fast lane
D)   Rice-A-Roni miners
E)   all of the above

5.

A)   arachnids in Virginia
B)   small fruit city
C)   remittances and payments
D)   evaders and heavenly creatures
E)   all of the above

Good luck Inspector,
The Puzzler

Chief Giralo perceptively examined the pensive expressions registered upon his agents' faces, allowed thirty additional seconds for document analysis and then imperatively informed his addle-minded men that "the Puzzler" was not just a mere clever practical joker but conversely, the treacherous, anonymous rogue actually represented a major threat to both corporate and government security and that in the short span of two July weeks, the complicated case that was being described had quickly escalated from a minor nuisance caper into an urgent FBI matter, its essence uniquely characterized by the new-found issue's awesome, paramount significance.

"Well, Guys. What do you make out of this fairly unorthodox riddle?" the Chief frankly asked. "I'll meticulously walk you through the first two sets. Now here's a definite starting point. You might want to discard your history and English teachers' multiple-choice tests and exclusively concentrate on Mr. Charles Galinas's seventh grade Geography class quizzes."

"In my humble estimation, it reads like complete and utter jabberwocky. It's total illogical gibberish to me!" Agent Velardi assessed and stated. "Run us through the first two answer groups Boss, and then Dan, Arty and I could possibly pick-up the style of thought being exhibited."

"Okay, Salvatore; but please stay focused on the fact that we're dealing with certain American cities here and nothing else," the Boss emphasized. "Now deciphering the first set of prompts, 'Buccaneers but not Pirates' means Tampa and not Pittsburgh; and next, 'trouble brewing' refers to Milwaukee and not St. Louis in terms of early month July events that I'll soon explain in full detail, and then Marty Robbins' fictional saloon fight comes from the classic rock and roll song 'El Paso', and finally, 'Lost Wages' is a fairly awkward play on words for...."

"I get the pattern now!" reflexively boomed Agent Velardi. "Las Vegas, Nevada!"

Demonstrating splendid self-control, stoic Inspector Joe Giralo ignored Sal Velardi's excessive display of exuberance and proceeded to analyze the second set of tricky answers. The Boss decided to deflate Velardi's fantasy bubble by asking his main apostle what the abbreviation 'KO' meant.

"Could it be 'knock-out' pertaining to the sport of boxing?" Agent Velardi guessed, his emotions swiftly changing from giddiness to obvious uncertainty.

"Well now," Chief Giralo seriously lectured. "I'm a longtime stockholder of Coca-Cola Company, and the soft drink outfit's New York Stock Exchange ticker-tape symbol is 'KO'. As you know, the company's based in Atlanta. But don't feel too bad Sal. I've been busy dismantling *this* disturbing dilemma, or should I say 'conundrum' for two whole weeks now and have a better handle on its elements than you do at the moment," the Chief explained. "But here's a constructive hint to guide you along the illuminated Path of Knowledge. The whole second set of favorable responses all concern major U.S. Corporations."

Seeing that his three extremely befuddled agents were not adequate Wall Street stock market experts, Inspector Giralo continued elaborating on his rather astounding multiple-choice quiz determinations. "And incidentally Fellas', the common Spanish word for 'that' is 'eso', which relating to the popular Fortune 500 Corporations' standard index, magically converts into Esso, which exists in Europe as a separate entity but had been renamed in the U.S. as the appellation EXXON on the NYSE several decades ago. And very shrewdly, 'mountain water tumbling, hive-see-sea' could only signify the letters 'BCC', or Boise-Cascade Corporation, its international headquarters located out west in Idaho. And BA, BA black sheep automatically switches into...."

"BA is Boeing Aircraft out in Seattle, Washington," Agent Arthur Orsi recognized and immediately vociferated. "My great goodness! We're dealing with an evil genius villain here, whoever this crazed Puzzler happens to be!"

Next, during the creative information sharing, Sal Velardi accurately interpreted the third contrived set of clever items. "In the second series of choices, I'll conjecture that 'AC/DC' is not the legendary acid rock band, but I'll say that the decoded translation probably means Atlantic City and Washington DC, since the general theme being applied here is American cities. And naturally, next on the list, 'a small diamond' would be Little Rock and in the next intriguing example, 'a bashful girl' would be..."

"Cheyenne, Wyoming," Agent Orsi realized and spontaneously contributed. "But Chief, how about this mystery of 'elephants and marauders?'"

"That same mystification had stymied me for a few hours, but then I theorized that the right answer would have to be Oakland, California, because the Oakland A's mascot symbol is an 'elephant', and the noun 'marauders' is an appropriate synonym of the word 'Raiders'. Now we're finally cooking with gas Men; our combined efforts shrewdly connecting all of the myriad geography, sports and economic dots. Our initiative is beginning to organize into a lucid plausible pattern."

Agent Orsi then volunteered to unravel the fourth multiple choice's possible answers. "Now I think that my mind is less cluttered and more honed-in to the exact thought process that's needed. First of all, 'hall of fame rocks' must associate with the city of Cleveland, where the Rock and Roll Hall of Fame is flourishing. And next Boss, 'Bulls and Bears' either refers to Wall Street in New York or to Chicago, the professional basketball team being the Bulls and the corresponding Windy City football team being the Bears."

"Excellent observations given, Arty!" Chief Giralo generously commended. "Newly derived information clearly supports your Chicago basketball and football hypothesis. And what about the odd vernacular 'metropolis in the fast lane'?"

"It's not that cryptic anymore!" gushed Arthur Orsi. "That's without a doubt referring to Rapid City, South Dakota." After glancing-down at *his* sample test paper, the suddenly enlightened agent then confidently declared, "Rice-A-Roni miners is indeed pertinent to San Francisco, since the old Rice-A-Roni TV commercial jingle maintained that the delicious food product was 'the San Francisco Treat', and the miners prompt that was provided obviously has to do with the historic California Gold Rush of 1849, hence, the pro' football team, the San Francisco 49ers!"

"Fantastic employment of the Associative Law of Thinking!" Joe Giralo praised and congratulated Agent Orsi. "You're well on your way to achieving the title of Freshman Psychic! And finally, Dan, try your luck at decoding the fourth set of the Puzzler's fairly remarkable quiz."

Dan Blachford was not to be denied earning relevant kudos from his Boss after disclosing that the esoteric phrase 'arachnids in Virginia' 'more-than-likely' meant the Richmond University Spiders, that the allusion 'small fruit city, tiny pop drink' was analogous to Minneapolis, Minnesota, that 'remittances and payments' apparently materially applied to Billings, Montana and finally, that the nomenclature 'evaders and heavenly creatures' dealt specifically with the National League Los Angeles Dodgers and the rival American League California Angels baseball teams."

But after Dan Blachford's brilliant deductions had been uttered, Agent Velardi required much-needed clarification from the coy FBI official seated behind the prodigious oak desk. "But Boss, although this outlandish Puzzler 'City Test' is quite fascinating and interesting, how do these weird play-on-words involve the element of crime in any way, shape or form?"

"Sal, have you noticed anything unique about the four choices provided in each set?"

"Well Boss; now that you've mentioned it," Velardi reluctantly replied, removing some summer sweat deposits from his brow. "In every set, each disguised city is situated in a separate geographic time zone. For example, in Set One, Tampa is in the Eastern Time Zone, Milwaukee is in the Central Time Region, El Paso is the only major Texas city located in Mountain Time, and Las Vegas is thriving in the Pacific Time Zone."

"Have you keenly observed any other noteworthy pattern?" the well-prepared Boss wanted to know.

"Yes, indeed, Chief!" Agent Velardi proudly shared and replied. "I'm quite certain that the correct response that's relevant in all five zany and absurd questions happens to be, in each case, Choice E, 'All of the Above'!"

"Tremendous cognition, Salvatore!" lauded Inspector Giralo. "Now permit me to identify and describe the fundamental FBI problem here which Matt Riley down there at DC headquarters insists that *we* professionally resolve. This pathetically devious culprit, who is inconveniently known to us as 'the Puzzler', has maliciously hacked into various corporate, federal and state government computer systems, and the dangerous felon has also wickedly pilfered invaluable company patent secrets along with top-CIA and State Department highly classified methods of operation. This wanton criminal must be apprehended immediately and his defiant brazenness brought to justice! Do you three skilled detectives now fathom the full magnitude of *our* latest assignment?" the on-a-mission Chief rhetorically asked. "We'll meet again as soon as I acquire more pertinent background info' on this truly complex and quite embarrassing iniquity-in-progress! Our country's reputation along with the health of our great American economy remains in dire jeopardy until this pesky Puzzler villain is promptly arrested and expeditiously incarcerated!"

* * * * * * * * * * * *

A week later in July via e-mail, Inspector Joe Giralo hastily summoned his three agents to a breakfast meeting in the rear dining room of the Red Barn Restaurant, Route 206, Hammonton, New Jersey. G-men Velardi, Orsi and Blachford were all eager to learn more corroborative data about the sinister and unscrupulous mastermind known only to FBI law enforcement officials as "The Puzzler." After the Red Barn's proprietor Evelyn jotted-down the four customers' standard orders, the normally jovial Boss abandoned his ordinary preliminary small-talk remarks and impetuously delved right into the vital subject matter at hand.

"I suspect that this slippery Puzzler fellow has furtively organized a team of dedicated personnel, all deftly working for the prevaricator inside each of the four principal U.S. Time Zones," the Chief austerely declared in characteristic formal fashion. "I suspect that *his* employees must be sophisticated computer hackers that have profound animosity for the American capitalistic economy and also great disdain for the current massive U.S. Government bureaucracy."

"Is that why you've arranged this unscheduled morning conference?" Agent Velardi audaciously questioned. "What other germane information did Matt Riley and you manage to glean?"

Chief Giralo then opened a commonplace oak-tag folder and proceeded to distribute three of the four typed copies that had been contained within the newly obtained grammar school object. Much to the three agents' sheer surprise, the impudent Puzzler had sent their revered boss a second multiple choice test, which the adamant Inspector advised the conscientious agents to solemnly read and interpret.

## "Second Multiple Choice Test"

1. The most popular black and white TV female singing group.
   A)    the McGuire Sisters
   B)    the Andrews Sisters
   C)    the Lennon Sisters
   D)    the Sisters of Mercy
   E)    none of the above
2. Where would you rather not play a game of bridge?
   A)    Dodger Stadium
   B)    at a Golden Gate
   C)    island West of San Diego
   D)    Chesapeake Bay
   E)    none of the above
3. Who was the worst U.S. President?
   A)    Gerald Ford
   B)    Grover Cleveland
   C)    James Madison
   D)    Andrew Jackson
   E)    none of the above

4.  Most dangerous animal species is:
  A)    elephants in Alabama
  B)    birds in Maryland
  C)    rams in California and Missouri
  D)    bruins in Illinois
  E)    none of the above
5.  Name the city
  A)    red stockings
  B)    Bengals but not Tigers
  C)    Lone Star dudes, no ranch dressing
  D)    Is your nickname 'Gino'?
  E)    'none' of the above

After several minutes of silent meditation, Chief Giralo sternly asked his team of astute agents exactly what they imagined the second multiple choice test meant. Sal Velardi was the first to provide an erudite response.

"It stands to reason in item Number One," the senior government squad member pointed-out, "the McGuire Sisters and the Andrews Sisters sang mostly on radio shows in the early and late 1940s, the Lennon Sisters were mainstay feature artists on the Lawrence Welk Show in the '50s and color TV 60s, and the Sisters of Mercy choice was a trick selection possessing no merit whatsoever. Therefore," Agent Velardi deduced, "the only correct answer has to be 'E', 'None of the above'."

"Magnificent comprehension, Sal!" commented Inspector Giralo. "There is a McGuire Air Force Base near Fort Dix just outside Trenton and there's also an Andrews Air Base outside Washington. Both McGuire and Andrews were nefarious canards specially designed to set us off searching for clues in the wrong direction. And now Arty, what do you make of the quiz's second item?"

"Well, Boss; four bridges are rather coyly referenced: Dodger Stadium in L.A. became the future home of the Brooklyn Dodgers, so subsequently, we have the Brooklyn Bridge, and secondly, the incomparable Golden Gate is out west in the neighborhood of San Francisco. Thirdly, the Coronado Bridge connects San Diego with Coronado Island, and finally, the Chesapeake Bay Bridge had been constructed near Annapolis, Maryland, connecting the state's Eastern Shore to the mainland. I've driven over *that* lengthy span many times while going back and forth from Jersey to DC."

"Exactly, Arty, but what is the only satisfactory answer to item Number Two?" interrogated a grim-faced Giralo.

"Why would anyone desire playing a game of bridge atop any of those four already mentioned architectural wonders?" Orsi volleyed back. "Just like in quiz Item One, the best answer is indubitably 'E', 'None of the above'."

"Too bad we aren't at the 16th of July Carnival or else Arty, you would've won an authentic miniature-sized kewpie doll or perhaps a rusty Dewey Button!" Joe Giralo very clearly enunciated. "And Dan," the Boss beckoned to Agent Blachford. "Tell us in a short oral paragraph what you've derived from quiz item Number Three."

Dan Blachford maintained that question three involving United States' Presidents was also "a repulsive red herring mess" with Gerald Ford possibly mischievously referring to Ford Motor Company outside Detroit, with Grover Cleveland pertaining to the home of the baseball Cleveland Indians and the football Browns, with James Madison possibly alluding to Madison, Wisconsin, and lastly, with Andrew Jackson associating with Jackson, Mississippi. "I'm inclined to agree with Sal and Art and unequivocally state with total confidence that the correct choice is 'E', 'None of the above'."

"Admirable evaluation, Danny Boy!" exclaimed the Chief Inspector. "You're developing a masterful *psychic* acumen for skillfully deciphering annoying cryptograms!"

"And consistent with everything else we're discussing with this second Puzzler quiz," Agent Velardi awkwardly butted-in, "a definite relationship pattern that's in stark contrast to the first multiple choice test has been materializing. For instance, in item Number Four, elephants in Alabama refers to the University in Tuscaloosa (tusks are looser), birds in Maryland would rationally be the Baltimore Orioles, rams in California and Missouri would be the Los Angeles Rams football team, which later became the St. Louis Rams, and ultimately, bruins in Illinois would ostensibly be the hapless Chicago Cubs. And here's my stellar deduction from this second quiz riddle. All of the items in Question Four are bogus illegitimate allusions, each one having little or no merit. And so Boss, Number Four is another plain and simple 'E', '*None* of the above'. In the first peculiar Puzzler test, the right response was always '*All* of the above'."

"Fabulous scrutiny and marvelous Socratic deduction rendered!" Joe Giralo verbally lavished. "And in the final irrelevant item, 'red stockings' would suggest the Boston Red Sox, 'Bengals and not Tigers' could mean the Cincinnati football team and not the Detroit baseball squad, 'Lone Star dudes without 'ranch dressing' probably denotes the Dallas Cowboys, and the nickname 'Gino' would easily synchronize with Eugene, Oregon. Gentlemen, this entire second

Puzzler scenario that I had also received via U.S. certified mail obviously constitutes a grotesque exercise in futility."

"So Chief, tell us. Why have *you* called us so early this morning to join you for breakfast at the Red Barn?" Sal Velardi bristled and demanded learning. "Was your' sagacious purpose to have the three of us amply appreciate the true merits of a very disgusting Puzzler wild goose chase?"

Inspector Giralo then opened and again reached into his cheap, nondescript oak-tag folder and next carefully removed four copies of a recent e-mail he had received at midnight from the diabolical Puzzler. Agents Velardi, Orsi and Blachford all sat there with their mouths agape, and the three listeners prudently read the electronically dispatched letter.

FBI Inspector Joseph Giralo,

Greetings there, you incompetent Government Bozo! By now you've finally determined that the second set of multiple-choice questions has been deceitfully and adroitly assembled by me, your new-found formidable adversary, the inimitable Puzzler. Now Mr. Bureaucrat, to set you back on the right trail, you clumsy inept Dunce, I've just concocted a simple little joke for you to genuinely ponder. I now have you over a barrel Inspector, but unfortunately, not a barrel tumbling over cascading Niagara Falls.

Ask me if I'm an orange.

"Are you an orange?"

Yes, I am. Now ask me if I'm an apple?

"Are you an apple?"

How can I be an apple if

I'm an orange!

Have a good one Inspector, and please don't strain your minuscule brain from the rigors of thought overload!

Your Relentless Nemesis, the Ubiquitous Puzzler

"Besides being egregiously insulted, what can you conclude Boss from this ludicrous blabber?" Agent Velardi wondered and asked. "This insolent Puzzler jerk is playing advanced mind games with *us* while demonically denigrating *you*!"

"Yes, Salvatore, but it's my objective opinion that the rotten scoundrel has now gotten to be too arrogant and too cocky for his own good, and I know from decades of experience that *that* sort of overconfidence usually means that he's about to trip himself up big time! The master of disaster will soon become the engineer of his own demise!"

"How Boss?" a perplexed Arthur Orsi injected into the dialogue. "Could you possibly be more explicit?"

"Well, Arty, it's my educated gut hunch that the term 'orange' in the e-mail might be referring to William and Mary of Orange of England, and that possibly the William and Mary University campus in Williamsburg, or maybe *that* entire area of Virginia including Historic Williamsburg along with Busch Gardens Amusement Park has been ruthlessly targeted for mischievous computer hacking. Or perhaps the computer system at the Williamsburg Bridge connecting Manhattan and Brooklyn might also have been selected for its general vulnerability."

"What's the Puzzler's motive?"Blachford insisted on knowing. "Has this clown nothing better to do with his time?"

"I don't believe that the condescending rascal is planning on blackmailing or extorting ransom money out of Uncle Sam in exchange for his purloined classified computer files," Chief Giralo maintained. "The insidious Puzzler's far too smart to pursue *that* risky avenue! Instead, I think he'll attempt selling the illegally acquired confidential information to either the Chinese or Russian governments! But it's always the sin of hubris that eventually brings these haughty punks down to Earth!"

"So, what's our next strategic move, Chief?" Agent Velardi requested finding-out. "Where are we three FBI pawns to be assigned on the government chessboard to perform our due diligence?"

"You, Salvatore, will be dispatched down to Williamsburg, Virginia to engage in some necessary surveillance work; and you Arty," Chief Giralo paused to inhale a much-needed deep breath; "your temporary job will be to stay on reconnaissance duty around the parallel Williamsburg and Brooklyn Bridges. And finally, Dan," the now-inspired Inspector stated to Agent Blachford, "your vital role in this crucial mission will be to keep your vigilant eyes on the James Fenimore Cooper House at 457 High Street over in Burlington, New Jersey. That's all the productive business I have to offer and share for now Gentlemen! Oh terrific! Here comes ever-reliable Evelyn with our delectable breakfast orders!"

Bewildered and beleaguered Agents Velardi, Orsi and Blachford simultaneously and incredulously shrugged their broad shoulders, the awed trio staring at each other with blank expressions registered upon their pallid countenances, the "out of the loop" threesome surmising that their inscrutable superior was either becoming senile or was again experiencing one of his inexplicable psychic moments.

* * * * * * * * * * * *

At noon on Sunday, July 29th, 2012 Agents Velardi, Orsi and Blachford were individually notified by their eminent superior that a summary teleconference session would be occurring at precise 3 pm to "unofficially wrap-up" the intricate high-priority "Puzzler Multiple- Choice Test Case." The always-ready trio had been instructed by a cell phone voice mail message to arrive at respective government video facilities in Williamsburg, in Manhattan and in Trenton in order to actively participate in the Boss's urgently scheduled "group communication".

"Sal, what did you discover while curiously sleuthing-around down there in Williamsburg?" Inspector Joe Giralo inquired with the Inspector's solemn face vividly displayed upon the three agents' video screens. "Was there anything extraordinary or irregular you had noticed or witnessed?"

"No, Boss. Everything was tranquil in and around historic Williamsburg and also in and around nearby Busch Gardens," Agent Velardi verbally conveyed. "I'm afraid that my uneventful week-long presence down here in Tidewater, Virginia has been an exorbitant waste of taxpayers' money. I even got tired from riding the park's exciting roller coasters over and over again!"

"And how about you Arty?" Chief Giralo resumed his informal audio/video roll call. "Did you detect anything out of the usual occurring near the Williamsburg and Brooklyn Bridges? Are any new trees growing over there in Brooklyn?"

"Negative, Boss," Agent Orsi glumly answered in a melancholy, disappointed tone of voice. "The action on both sides of the East River was slim, not even qualifying to be described as mediocre! I'd have learned more just staying home and watching morning and afternoon soap operas with my wife! My true ambition in life is to be more than a lethargic couch potato or an ambitious Lazy Boy cucumber!"

"And tell me, Dan. Did anything exciting or dramatic transpire this morning on your critical assignment over there in Burlington, New Jersey at 457 High Street?"

"Why yes!" Agent Blachford jubilantly exclaimed. "But the boisterous commotion was not happening inside or outside the James Fenimore Cooper House. Your fearless pal Colonel Bob Bauers magically showed-up on the scene and swiftly led a Delta Force commando raid into a brick residence across the street, the designated house situated at 474 High Street. And the well-trained military team was accompanied by a well-armed New Jersey SWAT squad. Together the units easily arrested a short thin fellow and quickly escorted the suspect out to a parked unmarked black police vehicle, which then rapidly sped away, dark tinted windows and all!"

Instead of explaining the crux of the sudden 'suspect apprehension', Joe Giralo then boringly and monotonously elucidated about how Burlington, New Jersey was a historic town, that General Ulysses S. Grant had *had* his family live there on Wood Street for safety reasons during the culmination of the Civil War, and how the small city was also a welcomed place called home to famous Revolutionary War era novelist James Fenimore Cooper, celebrated author of classic American literature works such as *Leatherstocking Tales* and *The Last of the Mohicans*.

"But Boss, you've lost me somewhere in transit!" Sal Velardi nervously interrupted his all-too-garrulous mentor. "What factor does James Fenimore Cooper along with his former 457 High Street home have to do with finding and taking the elusive Puzzler, I presume, into government custody? How did you ever narrow-down the computer thug's location to Burlington, New Jersey?"

"I had theorized from the Puzzler's e-mail riddle that his true identity would either have something to do with Williamsburg, Virginia because of the very deliberate 'orange' allusion, or his operating base would have something to do with a 'barrel'. And because of my ever-dwindling annual budget, I didn't have enough men available to also send to Niagara Falls, to Cooper Hospital down in Camden or to Cooperstown, New York, the traditional home of the Baseball Hall of Fame. Incidentally Sal," Inspector Giralo paused and then orally deviated, deliberately extending his most prolific monologue. "Cooperstown, New York had been named after James Fenimore's religious father, William Cooper. The aspiring novelist had lived most of his life in his native Cooperstown. Actually Men," Giralo elaborated, *"that* unique relationship of 'Cooper' with 'Cooperstown' happened to be the vital first step leading to *our* putting the cuffs on a certain Mr. Thomas Cask, otherwise recently known to FBI law enforcement as 'The Puzzler'."

"But Chief," a very frustrated and animated Arthur Orsi remarked, "what does this elusive trouble-making character Thomas Cask have to do with the James Fenimore Cooper House? Your nebulous accounting makes me feel dumber than a full sack of heavy rocks!"

"It pays to know and be influenced by American literature. That's how I'm aware of the works of James Fenimore Cooper and his early American hero, Natty Bumppo. I also owe my so-called psychic ability to Mr. Edgar Allan Poe's dark story, 'The Cask of Amontillado'," the well-rounded Inspector communicated to his still-stunned audience of three. "As you might know, Amontillado is a rare

Italian wine, and a *cask* is not exactly a hogshead, but rather it's a sort of tightly sealed barrel used for storing and keeping wine until it's ready for consumption!"

"Now you've really stimulated my interest!" Agent Blachford aggressively stated. "But how did you ever equate the idea of a wine cask with James Fenimore Cooper and this repugnant electronic computer file thief, Thomas Cask!"

"That's quite elementary Dr. Watson!" Inspector Giralo replied, poorly imitating the legendary Sherlock Holmes. "As you know, I absolutely love etymology, the academic study of the origin of words. In colonial times, a *cooper* was a barrel maker, just like a tallow chandler was a soap and candle craftsman. Hence," the long-winded Inspector continued his comprehensive video lecture, "the existence today of last names like Carpenter, Chandler and Cooper certainly populate our home telephone books. And when the self-indulgent Puzzler mentioned 'having me over a barrel' in his last tricky communication, my hungry mind instantly connected the word 'barrel' with the word 'cooper' with the word 'cask'. And when I instinctively executed a computer search of former federal employees' names, I soon uncovered that...."

"That this slick computer hacker, the pernicious Puzzler, had been a disgruntled former NSA employee who had become infected with vindictiveness because the jerk had been fired from his government job," hypothesized and offered Agent Velardi.

"Exactly, Salvatore!" verified Joe Giralo. "And then this avaricious and inventive criminal Thomas Edison Cask, alias the now-jailed Puzzler, effectively recruited other disenfranchised former government and corporate computer systems' experts, all hired to practice their illicit acts in the four separate U.S. Time Zones."

"Phenomenal and staggering, both in scope and sequence!" marveled and expressed Agent Orsi. "But Boss, I can't neglect citing my suspicion that you're at least partially psychic!"

"Truthfully Fellas'," Inspector Giralo courteously and modestly replied via the closed-circuit network video screens, "if I'm at all psychic in this particular FBI Puzzler episode, I owe it all to the venerable Edgar Allan Poe, to the illuminating James Fenimore Cooper, and finally, I owe it to my tough-minded high school English teacher who made me suffer through excessive grueling research on common word etymologies, Mr. Tom Alvino!"

# "May 27<sup>th</sup>, 2012"

The top brass at Washington FBI headquarters had assigned relentless Inspector Joe Giralo to the historic Balsams Resort in somnolent Dixville Notch, New Hampshire. The hotel would serve as the essential location where "the Boss" could supervise his strategic operations, which incidentally also involved his most trusted agents, Salvatore Velardi, Arthur Orsi and Dan Blachford.

Over the past week the loyal trio had been individually dispatched to distinct sections of the United States in order to gather very important undercover investigative information. On May 27th, 2012 the now-very-relaxed Chief Inspector amiably greeted his three arriving subordinates inside the famous New England resort's Tavern Restaurant.

"Glad you three accomplished sleuths could finally make it up here to the Balsams for a late lunch extravaganza," sometimes garrulous Joe Giralo merrily stated, showing a broad smile. "Originally, I had been slated to establish my incognito operational base at the Beacon Resort over in Lincoln, but our ever-vigilant boss Matt Riley at DC headquarters moved me an hour and a half north up here to the Balsams because this exclusive resort is temporarily closed to the public for the whole summer. The new owners are renovating the entire main and adjacent buildings."

"Thanks, Boss for the swell three and a half-hour limo' ride from the Manchester Airport to way up here near the Canadian border," Agent Velardi rather cynically answered. "But actually, the ride was more comfortable than traveling up here to super-tranquil Dixville Notch on moose back! Too bad this fine Victorian resort is also closed for boating, fishing and golf!"

"Yes," Agent Art Orsi confirmed. "Sal flew into Manchester from Buffalo, Dan flew in from Vegas and I came in commercial early this morning from Rapid City, South Dakota via Cincinnati. After we ate a quick breakfast at the airport," Agent Orsi thoroughly reported, "your special black limousine picked us up and now here we are, clandestinely meeting at your secret New Hampshire hideout somewhere north of the White Mountains."

"Doesn't this closed-for-repair hotel have some sort of political significance?" Agent Dan Blachford spontaneously asked. "I know I've often heard Dixville Notch mentioned on TV newscasts, but quite candidly Guys, I can't recollect the exact significance."

"Well Dan," Inspector Joe Giralo exhaled after gulping down several ounces of tasty regular coffee, "this famous hotel is where the first votes are cast just after midnight in each national Presidential Election. In fact, the voting room is situated upstairs just past the main dining room and can be found right behind where the attractive second floor corridor lounge ends. I believe that only a dozen or so local citizens actually participate in the much-publicized voting process," the all-too-knowledgeable speaker elaborated. "But as I've already stated, the unique political matter does generate widespread attention across the entire nation. And Guys, the new Balsams' owners were quick to agree to us having our hastily arranged conference right here in the Tavern Restaurant, which has been kept open for the sole purpose of accommodating us and our culinary needs."

"Riley probably intimidated the new proprietors by threatening to have his pals over at the IRS scrutinize their past tax returns. But as usual Boss, and with all due respect," Agent Velardi carefully qualified his words, "Art, Dan and I are again totally confused about what this complicated case in all about. I mean Boss, we've successfully completed our separate surveillance responsibilities, and then we conscientiously reported our confidential observations exclusively to you via encrypted computer messages. But still, all three of us remain basically clueless about the big picture. We've all surmised that we're involved in identifying the central culprits of some surreptitious home-grown terror network," Sal Velardi confided off-the-record. "But as to *us* being familiar with any particular relevant details, the hazy fog floating around inside our three noggins is as thick as Campbell's tomato soup!"

"Ha, ha, ha!" Inspector Giralo indulgently laughed. "Don't worry about the minutia my dear Salvatore. Colonel Bob Bauers of Delta Force should be arriving at the Balsams in about an hour to clarify all of your abundant mental vagueness. In the meantime, for me to attempt mitigating your general consternation," Joe Giralo amply chuckled, "I'll gladly disseminate to you vexed Gentlemen some rather pertinent background. I suppose that during the past week you three illustrious Einsteins have been assiduously functioning in the chrysalis stage of our present law enforcement probe."

"Please speak standard vernacular English, Boss," Agent Art Orsi sincerely requested. "What on Earth is the chrysalis stage? Have Madonna and Lady GaGa ever performed on it?"

"Don't be *fazed* by the chrysalis *phase,*" Giralo joked. "In elementary biology, *that* development is the vital stage of the metamorphosis process. It's when a slow-moving caterpillar amazingly enters a chrysalis, or a small pouch inside a cocoon, and then in time, the creature miraculously transforms into a magnificent butterfly, which then instinctively breaks-out of its protective chrysalis shell and soon marvelously flies away in quest of a new existence."

"Truthfully Boss, Art, Dan and I always feel like we're sort of individually incarcerated into three designated restricted areas, that is, we're kind of like mindless guinea pig hostages expected to hibernate inside FBI-designed cocoons too, just like those in-transition caterpillars you had just mentioned," an exasperated Sal Velardi evaluated and respectfully declared. "Now Boss, we're aware of some aspects of what's been occurring across the terror network spectrum, but frankly, we're cognizant of only a fraction of what you and *our* DC mastermind Matt Riley already know! Now please connect some of the remaining dots!"

"Okay you three totally befuddled federal malcontents," a somewhat-amused Inspector Joe Giralo politely replied. "Why don't you review what you've witnessed over the course of the last week and then I'll genuinely try educating you zany wanna' be Mike Hammer detectives on the true merits of your invaluable contributions to cracking this potentially catastrophic conspiracy crisis wide open. Let's start with you Arty."

Agent Arthur Orsi cleared his throat and then quickly reported that he had followed an itinerant Egyptian named Karim Chalthoum from the Rapid City, South Dakota Airport across regional prairie land to a remote makeshift campsite outside the town of Fairburn. Using powerful binoculars and reliable night vision spy goggles, the experienced FBI veteran had diligently recorded in his notes that a dozen box trucks had delivered certain camouflaged equipment and assorted large heavy boxes, and that the unidentified big and small items had been immediately transferred onto two large flatbed trucks. And next, the various packages were swiftly transported; soon, everything was deposited alongside the secluded and well-concealed wilderness retreat.

"You did well, Arty," Chief Giralo calmly commended. "Your intensive stake-out has led to the capture and arrest of four extremely dangerous Egyptian-born terrorists: jihadists Karim Chalthoum, Mustafa Sawalhi, Ahmad Wadi and Hassan Massri. I'm convinced that these four desperate enemy combatants had been receiving their instructions directly from internationally infamous Ayman Zawahiri, the overzealous Egyptian who has taken Osama bin Laden's place as the formidable inspirational leader of al Qaeda. Now Dan," Chief Giralo next addressed nervous Agent Blachford. "Let's hear what indispensable evidence you've recently gleaned out there in Vegas. I understand that you were able to acquire valuable information without encountering any apparent aggravating snafus!"

Quite-puzzled Dan Blachford aptly described a similar scenario to the one that had been orally conveyed by still-mentally-disheveled Agent Arthur Orsi. The incessant crime-fighter had vigorously trailed a Pakistan-born American transplant possessing the I.D. of Monsin Bhatti from McCarran International Airport's United Airlines Terminal to the bustling hotel New York, New York. And then three days later, with the assistance of the Las Vegas Police Department's helicopter patrol unit, Blachford had followed the suspected malicious villain from the Vegas Strip to the vicinity of an isolated desert cabin that was surrounded by giant saguaro cactus, the ramshackle structure being five miles outside the corporate limits of Henderson. As in the previous episode graphically depicted by Agent Art Orsi, Blachford had alertly observed several different box trucks delivering undisclosed covered objects to the desolate terrorist base at nighttime, and the secret cargo had been cunningly loaded onto awaiting flatbed units, which then hauled the separate shipments away from the narrow asphalt access road and subsequently, re-located the goods nearer to the desert cabin.

"As you three fine Men readily know," Chief Joe Giralo assessed and prudently articulated, "there exists much animosity towards America in much of the Middle East, and in particular, Pakistan is a principal country expressly accountable for perpetuating fierce hostility towards the United States and its rather unassuming citizens. Indeed, al Qaeda and the Taliban skillfully harbor this ever-present rancor towards Uncle Sam, and Pakistan itself provides the unscrupulous insurgents with a safe haven to conduct lethal raids upon American troops presently stationed in neighboring Afghanistan. But Dan, because of your noteworthy Nevada desert perseverance," the renowned FBI Inspector congratulated the still-somewhat-bewildered Agent Blachford, "our dedicated field men along with commandos dispatched from Colonel Bob Bauers' Delta Force team have promptly apprehended Pakistanis' Monsin Bhatti, Yasir Remani, Bilah Rizvi and Ayaz Shah."

It was now the completely-addled Agent Salvatore Velardi's turn to communicate his salient discoveries to the assembled "debriefing conference" members. The flustered crime-stopper orally shared that Saudi Arabian radical Abu Al Reshedi had impatiently obtained his luggage from the rotating American Airlines carousel inside the Buffalo Airport and that the ever-alert defender of justice then had competently tailed Reshedi to an abandoned bungalow located in a shallow ravine on the outskirts of a rural town halfway between Buffalo and Rochester. Again, similar to suspicious parallel nocturnal events that had coincidentally transpired in South Dakota and in

Nevada, a series of unmarked box trucks had stealthily delivered unrecognizable items in sealed boxes along with cloaked heavy machinery to the dilapidated half-collapsed shanty.

"Allow me to generously compliment you Sir Salvatore on accomplishing some exceptionally excellent detective work!"

Inspector Joe Giralo proudly praised. "Your intuitive talent for pursuing dastardly criminals is nothing short of superb! Because of your dedicated service," the esteemed Boss haughtily editorialized, "homegrown Saudi terrorists Abu Al Reshedi, Tariq Al Subaiee, Yousef Al Juhani and Saad Al Dosary have all been effectively collared and are now presumably imprisoned! And don't forget Sal," the internationally famous Chief provided his standard addendum. "Osama bin Laden was also a Saudi as were the vile perpetrators responsible for the colossal 9-11 Twin Towers' tragedy!"

"But Chief!" indignantly balked and squawked Sal Velardi. "Art, Dan and I are still like lazy caterpillars asleep inside our lousy cocoons. Please give us the big picture so that we can adequately erase the thick mystery associated with our most current FBI reconnaissance."

"Ha, ha, ha! This is all-too-rich for my hungry cerebrum to fully appreciate!" Joe Giralo enigmatically exclaimed. "Confidentially Sal, I too had been baffled by this unusual case until *your* targeted man, this Saudi desperado Abu Al Reshedi had led *you* Salvatore to a small town situated between Buffalo and Rochester. Then the complete labyrinth of disconnected, disparate facts suddenly became marvelously all-too-discernible to my sensitive mind's ever-acute comprehension!"

"Stop speaking all of this exotic esoteric gibberish Boss and kindly tell me exactly what your nebulous nomenclature means before I go absolutely insane and become a fanatical terrorist myself!" Agent Velardi angrily rankled. "Needless to say, Chief, I positively despise silly riddles along with absurd, redundant, verbal cryptograms!"

"Fundamentally, it's all a matter of simple history and grammar school geography!" Chief Giralo admirably divulged. "Now Sal, as you've already informed us in your coded e-mails, the town in New York State where you had followed this mendacious jerk Abu Al Reshedi was called Medina, conveniently positioned almost midway between Buffalo and Rochester. Yes, my fine-feathered Friends, Medina happened to be the decisive key that had magically unlocked this whole Pandora's Box!"

"Medina?" Sal Velardi incredulously asked. "Is she a new obnoxious nauseating rock singer?"

"No Salvatore," Chief Giralo reflexively indicated with another grin evident upon his lips. "Medina is not only a town in upstate New York. It's also known as the sacred city of the prophet Mohammad over in western Saudi Arabia. Next to Mecca, Medina is the second holiest city in the Islam faith. In fact, according to my meticulous and fastidious research," the wily Inspector authoritatively and casually pontificated, "Islam's three oldest mosques had been constructed in Medina, which had been established by Mohammad in the year 622 on the Muslim Calendar. Indeed Gentlemen, much of the Quran had been composed in Medina, and just like Mecca, entrance into the Holy City is limited to Muslims only! And most certainly Fellas'," erudite Chief Giralo continued lecturing his long-winded narrative, "Mohammad had become more militant in his religious attitudes upon arriving in Medina from Mecca. And finally, Guys," Joe Giralo predictably expounded, "an American town with the appellation *Medina* would naturally appear to be fascinating, if not enticing to an ambitious Saudi terrorist because Medina had also been the Arabian city where the Prophet Mohammad had been buried!"

"Wow!" the now-enlightened Agent Salvatore Velardi finally realized and orally reacted. "How tremendously interesting! I honestly gotta' grant it to you Chief! It sure pays to be well-versed in basic world history and grammar school geography!"

* * * * * * * * * * * *

The Balsams' skeleton crew consisted of one chef, one waiter and one housemaid, all especially assigned to service the demands of Chief Joe Giralo and his three omnivorous agents. The abbreviated staff was most accommodating, thanks to the persuasive urging of FBI Boss Matt Riley and *his* influential colleagues, who had made several imperative government requests upon the prestigious hotel's new management. After mouth-watering pie and cake desserts had been devoured along with huge mugs brimming with delicious hot coffee, Inspector Giralo continued with his expert analysis of the FBI team's most recent crime adventure.

"Now Salvatore, given the essential clue of Medina," the Boss loquaciously prefaced his post-lunch remarks, "the nefarious Abu Al Reshedi and his three Saudi comrades were cruelly planning on firing a pair of Iranian Fateh missiles from Medina, New York; the first one directly into the gigantic water cascade commonly known as the great Canadian Horseshoe Falls, and the second one into the adjacent American Falls, together commonly called Niagara Falls, the pair obviously situated not-too-far from Buffalo, around seventeen or so miles away, according to MapQuest data on my laptop. Such a brazen horrific act, that is, deliberately destroying a major national landmark like Niagara Falls," Inspector Giralo stressed to his stunned colleagues, "would definitely send people all across America into a terror panic of monumental proportions!"

"Holy Houdini!" exclaimed Agent Arthur Orsi. "They'd be out to launch while everyone else would be out to lunch!"

"And most certainly, the heinous misdeed was evidently scheduled for execution tomorrow, Monday, May 28th, Memorial Day!" gasped parch-mouthed Salvatore Velardi. "The demonic Saudi jihadists absolutely desired to sabotage one of America's most revered holidays by committing a terribly despicable act of war! How deranged! How outrageously atrocious can a wickedly determined enemy get?"

"That's why good' must always discriminate against evil!" Joe Giralo attested and concluded. "As long as there is good, there will also be evil abounding in this unpredictable world!"

"The entire Niagara River area would've probably been drastically devastated by massive flooding!" semi-shocked Sal Velardi uttered in disbelief. "And just think Boss. I had recently read in an edition of *National Geographic* that the Falls and the entire Hudson River Valley had been carved out by Mother Nature when the enormous mile-high glacier had eventually retreated from what is now New York City back into the Arctic polar region, a mere ten thousand or so years ago!"

"And furthermore, Arty," Inspector Joe Giralo emphatically spoke to Agent Orsi while intentionally ignoring Sal Velardi's fairly irrelevant geological comment. "Your excursions out to Rapid City and to Fairburn, South Dakota were not-too-far from the white-stone visages of eminent George Washington, Abraham Lincoln, Thomas Jefferson and good old Theodore Roosevelt, all prominently displayed on the facade of Mt. Rushmore. It seems that our advanced intel' squad had intercepted enemy e-mails that had alluded to Mr. Karim Chalthoum and his three Egyptian accomplices firing another two imported Fateh missiles smack-dab into the treasured national landmark, diabolically blowing the top of Mt. Rushmore to smithereens. How bitterly ugly could *that* kind of stark, harsh reality get?"

"How totally abominable!" Agent Orsi bellowed and concurred. "Those Iranian Fateh missiles aren't just any ordinary, lackluster rockets, that's for sure. Those souped-up missiles have sophisticated GPS guidance systems that are much more accurate than those aboard any mediocre, randomly fired rockets."

"Yes, Arty," verified Inspector Giralo, "and our dependable, anonymous, collaborative sources theorize that the designated Niagara Falls' missiles and also the Mt. Rushmore Fateh missiles had been smuggled into the United States piece by piece from neighboring Canada, all via a porous Northern Border."

"But what about the surreptitious supplies delivered to the desert campsite outside Henderson, Nevada?" Dan Blachford inquisitively inquired. "Was that oddball, distant situation a prospective missile launch site, too?"

"Very perceptive insight, Dan!" the Chief bluntly replied. "Monsin Bhatti and his three Pakistani cohorts had configured modified versions of the deadly Fateh missiles that they planned on aiming at Lake Mead and at nearby Hoover Dam. Could you imagine the national chaos that would have prevailed if the four crazed lunatic terrorists had succeeded in simultaneously blowing-up Niagara Falls, Mt. Rushmore and Hoover Dam on Memorial Day, May 28th, 2012? Those three calamitous events would have been the second terrible day to 'live in infamy' as Franklin Roosevelt had so precisely described the violent unwarranted Japanese sneak-attack on Pearl Harbor on December 7th, 1941!"

"And quite incredibly Chief, we owe it all to *your* impeccable familiarity with Medina!" Sal Velardi respectfully marveled and admitted. "I fully understand that those Fateh missiles are extraordinarily accurate from within a range of one hundred miles. Say Fellas', what's that whirling sound I hear outside!"

"It's Colonel Bob Bauers arriving to brief us on exactly what had developed in Medina, New York, in Fairburn, South Dakota and in Henderson, Nevada!" Chief Joe Giralo ascertained. "That's the sound of chopper blades rotating!"

Five minutes later, the irrepressible Colonel Bob Bauers sauntered into the Balsams' Tavern Restaurant wearing his traditional polished combat boots, and the inimitable American patriot immediately saluted the four almost-hypnotized men seated at their round table. Then without hesitation or delay, the highly decorated military soldier spoke to Chief Giralo and his three confederates in an impressively strong baritone voice.

"The New Hampshire Air National Guard had sent a helicopter from the Pease Air Base over in Portsmouth and the very capable pilot met me at the Manchester Airport," Colonel Bauers sternly revealed. "Then we flew north, had a refueling in Berlin and before I knew it, we had arrived at this world-class Balsams Hotel up here in good old historic Dixville Notch. Since this place is currently undergoing mammoth renovations," Colonel Bauers noted, "it was quite convenient for us five to secretly rendezvous here!"

"What's happened to the three respective conspiracy groups in New York State, in South Dakota and in Nevada?" Sal Velardi intrepidly asked the austere Delta Force officer. "If the on-a-mission terrorists have been corralled, then most certainly, the President should declare this wonderful day May 27th as a fabulous national holiday!"

Then Agent Art Orsi had the audacity to ask the prominent Commander a very direct question. "In all honesty Colonel, it is rumored at FBI headquarters that whenever wanton home-grown or foreign terrorists are apprehended here in the United States, and if Iranian Fateh missiles are involved in enacting *their* hideous schemes, then Delta Force operatives will enthusiastically strap the terrorists to the aforementioned missiles and then deliberately propel the destructive objects off their mobile launch pads through the atmosphere, hurtling wildly into the hinterlands, thus fantastically terrorizing the victimized terrorists all the way to their appointed deaths. Now please tell me Colonel. Is this outrageous scuttlebutt I've recently heard true or false?"

Colonel Bauers paused for a pregnant moment and then after reorganizing his scruples, the well-disciplined veteran soldier cleverly initiated his rather shrewd verbal response. "Well Art, er, I meant to say Agent Orsi," the military guru quite adroitly corrected himself. "It's my sincere opinion that we owe these demented crusading enemies of the United States no ethical courtesy whatsoever, nor should the homegrown or foreign terrorists that are caught red-handed in the act deserve any legal due process either."

"But Colonel, please don't evade my question!" Agent Orsi diplomatically insisted. "Does Delta Force actually harness apprehended terrorists to *their* own Fateh missiles, or don't they? Wouldn't *that* vindictive act be a glaing violation of the United States Constitution? Give it to us straight, in common everyday vernacular."

"Well now, as you four distinguished Gentlemen very well-know, the American media, comprised mostly of ultra-liberal newspaper and TV journalists, often masquerade as enemy combatants' sympathizers and as lily-white Muslim apologists! So, in answer to your very serious question Agent Orsi," Colonel Bauers eloquently expressed with a broad frown firmly exhibited upon his grim countenance, "Delta Force does indeed have its deep dark secrets pertaining to the special destiny of captured enemy combatants. Now, please consider this sage advice, you four loyal FBI Savants. I wholeheartedly suggest that you forget all about the merits of enhanced interrogation methods employed by virtue of regular water-boarding procedure! And as far as tethering the arrested disgruntled ignoramuses to mediocre Fateh rockets goes," Colonel Bauers keenly vociferated without even blinking an eye, "all that I can confidentially convey to you all-too-curious federal government bureaucrats is that you'll never read about the ultimate fate of these twelve captured evil-minded conspirators in the daily newspapers or in the weekly magazines!"

# "Too Much Monkey Business"

Inspector Joe Giralo cautiously drove his huge, gray Chevy Suburban north from Route 54 and then across Route 30 onto New Jersey State Highway 206. Seated in the front passenger seat was true-blue FBI Agent Salvatore Velardi, with dependable Agent Arthur Orsi seated directly behind the grim-faced driver and conscientious Agent Dan Blachford occupying the rear seat behind Agent Velardi. The four government men had promptly departed the Hammonton, New Jersey Third Street Carnival Grounds, but as usual, only the very shrewd Inspector was acquainted in-depth with all of the vital circumstances associated with the team's mission-in-progress.

"I'll tell you, Boss, I don't like the way that certain local traditions are rapidly being dismantled, piece-by-piece," opinionated Agent Salvatore Velardi commented. "Take the annual 16th of July Mt. Carmel Festival for instance. For over a century the town church sponsoring the event had been known as St. Joseph, but now with parish consolidations being the vogue," the overzealous passenger riding shotgun elaborated, "the diocese has changed the church's name from St. Joseph to St. Mary of Mt. Carmel. I don't want to sound sacrilegious or anything," Velardi diplomatically qualified. "But it's as if venerable St. Joseph has had a gender surgery performed and is now transformed into his New Testament Biblical wife, St. Mary. But let me emphasize that it had been the Camden Diocesan Bishop who had mandated the gender name change and not me! Now Boss, as I said, I fully realize that the changing of names was sort of done out of being politically correct, or should I more accurately say, out of 'religiously correct' necessity!"

"But the local Catholic elementary and high school are still called St. Joseph," reminded don't-rock-the-boat Agent Arthur Orsi. "The controversial name-change to St. Mary of Mt. Carmel had been judiciously decided because the three Hammonton churches, St. Anthony of Padua, St. Martin de Porres and St. Joseph have now been incorporated into one entity. Obviously, the Bishop didn't want to be perceived favoring the name St. Joseph Church over the other two town parishes."

"Well Guys, at least the identity of the Mt. Carmel Beer Garden that's situated at the rear of the carnival grounds hasn't been altered one iota," Agent Dan Blachford merrily contributed to the general conversation. "Say Boss, why did you use your cell phone and yank Sal, Art and me out of the crowded beer garden so suddenly? I was just finishing-up gobbling-down a terribly delicious pepper and sausage sandwich!"

"Well frankly, my loyal Confederates," Chief Giralo keenly prefaced, "as you can plainly see on my state-of-the-art government issue GPS tracking device, we're in hot pursuit of a white van that's seven miles ahead of us, somewhere in the vicinity of Atsion Lake. Pretty soon our designated suspects will be passing by that notorious den of iniquity, the ever-popular Pic-A-Lilli Inn, the rather unique pinelands' Mecca for area motorcycle gangs and rowdy Wharton State Forest hunters and pineys. I must admit Gentlemen," Joe Giralo pontificated, "this super-advanced 2007 dashboard GPS map is a major improvement over James Bond 60s' tracking technology. It's rather impressive, to say the least! Thank goodness the Bureau's top brass guys sitting behind *their* big desks down in Washington have dramatically increased our budget expenditures."

"Look Boss, I don't wish to be sounding too impertinent or too blatantly disrespectful," Agent Velardi boldly verbalized, "but most of the time you make Art, Dan and me feel like we're three hapless incompetent buffoons. We're quite familiar with specific fragments of the overall colossal puzzle we're involved in, but only you and Matt Riley down there at DC headquarters are knowledgeable of the entire big-portrait scenario. In my unsolicited judgment, it just isn't fair! Well, quite realistically Chief, *that* happens to be my exclusive personal conclusion!"

"On the contrary Salvatore," Inspector Giralo answered as the light gray Suburban sped by the landmark Red Barn Farm Market and Restaurant situated on the left. "I must confess, you three professional crime-fighters are a tad more sagacious than Moe, Larry and Curly ever were. I've never especially referred to you three potential geniuses as clumsy Stooges; now have I ever?"

"No Sir, but always being out of the loop does not enhance our' faltering self-esteem," Agent Orsi intrepidly stated in support of Agent Velardi's brazen allegation. "And please don't give us your standard enigmatic reply, your predictable cavalier response reiterating the strange notion that 'the true accurate picture is commonly developed in the photographer's dark room'."

"Okay Fellas'," Joe Giralo gleefully chuckled, "I'll fill you in on several essential details, but as is my normal habit, I can't divulge anything that's based on mere speculation. Honestly, in a few days Matt Riley and I will have all of the principal facts logically organized in neat fashion, and at *that* time I hope to reveal the whole amazing situation to you three amateur sleuths over a delectable spaghetti and meatball supper at the Maplewood Inn, of course, at my generous expense and treat. But first Sal," Joe Giralo pragmatically stipulated, "please kindly review for us' how you had successfully executed *your* very important assignment in regard to this complicated investigation."

After assiduously scribbling-down the aforementioned possible dinner engagement date of Monday night, July 16th, 2007 into his trusty notepad, Agent Velardi reviewed and reported that he had followed suspect Anthony Sullivan's black Lexus SUV from the 400 block Arch Street Holiday Inn in Old City Philadelphia across the Ben Franklin Bridge into Camden and then all-the-way up the New Jersey Turnpike into downtown Manhattan.

"Just like you, Boss, I also had used the modernized James Bond-type homing device, placing the sensitive signal mechanism in a concealed area under the SUV's rear bumper. It's the same sort of sophisticated electronic transmitter that you're presently using to pursue at a distance *that* white paneled van up 206!"

"Excellent field work Sal!" congratulated Inspector Giralo. "Notice that the van is now in the vicinity of the Red Lion Circle as we're whizzing past the bustling Pic-A-Lilli Inn. Now then," the renowned FBI Chief wanted to know, "exactly where in New York City did this obviously unscrupulous, charlatan person-of-interest Anthony Sullivan unwittingly lead you?"

"To 10 West 47th Street, and that's where I soon linked-up with my pal Dan here, who had been nonchalantly staking-out the vicinity according to *your* precise instructions," Salvatore Velardi enthusiastically shared. "Dan had been stealthily following another possible perpetrator named. . ."

"Jamie Miduri," Agent Blachford articulated with relative certainty from the back seat. "Then this Miduri jerk and his probable accomplice Anthony Sullivan proceeded to journey north in Miduri's white van, which incidentally we're now following. It's a good thing that I had smartly attached a suitable GPS tracking apparatus to the under-frame of Jamie Miduri's rather mediocre-looking mode of transportation! I then tailed the vehicle from Manhattan all the way up to Yonkers."

"And who in Yonkers did Anthony Sullivan and Jamie Miduri visit?" Chief Giralo very seriously asked.

"A man named Michael Farren," Agent Orsi confidently declared from the Chevy Suburban's rear. "The three men had a half-hour conference inside Farren's Yonkers row-house, which I had been diligently observing for a full week! Then the three of *us* in three separate cars trailed the white van over to Flatbush Avenue in Brooklyn; that is, until elusive suspects Anthony Sullivan and Jamie

Miduri anxiously entered the Farro Plush Toy Company's sole manufacturing facility!"

"What do *you* have to say about those incidental developments that Art had just mentioned Chief?" Agent Velardi inquired of inimitable Inspector Giralo. "A prospective Irish crook with the appellation Sullivan hanging-out with a suspected Italian thug having the surname Miduri?"

Unperturbed and introspective Chief Joe Giralo intentionally ignored his inquisitive subordinate's interrogative and quickly pointed to his indispensable GPS. "Look Fellas'. The white van is now turning off 206 onto Woodlane and heading due west toward Burlington City, and I conjecture that it'll be crossing the Burlington-Bristol Bridge in around twenty minutes or so, and soon venturing into Bucks County Pennsylvania, again foolishly making *their* fairly complex caper a federal crime occurring across state lines. It certainly warrants our FBI attention," Joe Giralo confirmed. "Now which of you three budding Einsteins can tell me where the infamous white van had traveled to after leaving the Farro Plush Toy Company over in Brooklyn?"

Sal Velardi thoroughly explained to his immediate superior that two large boxes had been carefully loaded into the white van's interior and that the itinerant vehicle had then been driven from Flatbush Avenue across the Brooklyn Bridge and next through the congested Lincoln Tunnel into New Jersey. The unassuming driver navigated onto the New Jersey Turnpike, and after proceeding seventy miles south, veered-off onto the Exit 7 ramp at Bordentown. Then the van driver motored down Route 206, ironically stopping at the Hammonton Carnival Grounds on the French Street side.

"All three of us had followed the white van down the Turnpike in our identical black autos, of course at a safe distance, since we could conveniently monitor the mobile suspects with our various GPS tracking equipment," loquacious Sal Velardi indicated and embellished. "Naturally Boss, Dan's car was first since he was able to easily huntdown the villain's rather ugly means of transportation with *his* awesome upgraded GPS!"

Just as the gray Suburban was approaching the EZ-Pass toll of the two-lane Burlington-Bristol Bridge, Agent Velardi had the courage to ask his mentor a very relevant question. "Where do you suppose *their* final destination is?"

"24 Dahlia Lane in the Dogwood Hollow section of Levittown, Pennsylvania," the seemingly omniscient Chief firmly announced with a stern expression upon his countenance. "In Dogwood Hollow, all the streets begin with the letter D. According to my reliable GPS readout," Inspector Giralo added, "you have Dogwood Drive being the circumference of the whole housing section. Inside the oval you have streets bearing the names Daffodil Lane, Dewberry Lane, Disk Lane, Daisy Lane, Darkleaf Lane, Deepgreen Lane, Deerfield Lane and oh yes, how could I forget? Finally, there's good old Dahlia Lane!"

"But how do you know this obscure information about 24 Dahlia Lane?" objected an astonished-but-frustrated Sal Velardi. "Are you inherently psychic or clairvoyant, a true crime-solving wizard, or what?"

Just then Chief Joe Giralo totally befuddled his three nebulous-minded colleagues by turning-off the low-volume background news' transmission being broadcast on Sirius XM Radio and next inserting an old Chuck Berry stereo music disc into the appropriate dashboard slot, deliberately surprising his already stunned men because prior to *that* exceptional moment, the nationally acclaimed Inspector had always preferred listening to classical renditions when driving.

"Here's a definite clue that should satisfactorily lead you three marvelous savants out of your very vexing mental labyrinths!" Chief Giralo critically vociferated in his typical arcane-language manner, which was obviously designed to fully confuse his three exasperated disciples. "I strongly suggest that *you* listen closely to the catchy song's lyrics to be able to comprehensively decipher this wonderfully perplexing riddle."

The 1956 smash-hit "Too Much Monkey Business" was loudly played and upon the tune's completion, the erudite driver instantly shutoff the radio speakers. "Now then, you fledgling Jack Webbs, what fine clue have you just learned from this remarkable, up-tempo rock and roll classic?"

"Well Boss," Agent Velardi spoke-up, "Chuck Berry sang 'Been to Yokohama, been fightin' in the war'. Does this mystery adventure we're now on have anything to do with Japan?"

"Not even close!" Chief Giralo replied with a prodigious grin evident upon his face. "What say you, Art?"

"Chuck Berry sang 'Army bunk, Army chow, Army clothes, Army car'!" Agent Orsi recollected and mentioned. "Is your friend Colonel Bob Bauers of Delta Force somehow involved in the execution of this extremely intricate operation?"

"Great guess Arty, but you aren't even in left field with your hypothesis! In fact, you're entirely out of the stadium! Now please Dan, give us *your* educated evaluation of the all-too-apparent significance of the song 'Too Much Monkey Business'!"

"Is some local academic institution in imminent jeopardy?" Blachford deducted and orally summarized. "The unique words 'Same thing every day, getting up, goin' to school' seem to imply and support *that* particular school building assumption of mine!"

"Wrong again!" Inspector Giralo exclaimed and indulgently laughed as his gray Suburban exited Route 413, zipped under the ancient, rusty Pennsylvania Railroad Bridge and then swiftly turned right onto dual highway Route 13, heading north toward Levittown. "But if my fuzzy memory serves me correctly, I recall that cover versions of 'Too Much Monkey Business' had been later recorded by both the Beatles and the Hollies. Pardon me for switching gears but by now Guys," the more-than-clever Chief stated, "the dilapidated white van is slowly cruising around Dogwood Hollow, its occupants meticulously casing the unfamiliar D Street environment in search of 24 Dahlia Lane."

"Boss, I don't want to appear impolite or obnoxious," Sal Velardi guiltily remarked. "But how the heck do you know that the white van is going to stop outside 24 Dahlia Lane? Are you Edgar Cayce reincarnated?"

"Because Salvatore, for the last forty-one miles the van had been following an innocent family riding in a dark blue Ford Explorer all the way from the Third Street Carnival Grounds in Hammonton, New Jersey to 24 Dahlia Lane, Levittown, Pennsylvania!" Joe Giralo adamantly narrated, adding new confusing information, much to his passengers' general bewilderment. "How plain and simple can I actually describe it to you? I mean Sal, I learned *those* valuable nuggets of info' from the targeted family that had been munching sweet junk food at the carnival's all-too-popular cotton candy stand. And furthermore, Gentlemen, the key element to *our* seemingly weird jigsaw puzzle can be found in the song's outstanding title, 'Too Much Monkey Business'."

The Chevy Suburban was gently steered to the right off of Route 13 and soon was crossing the busy north-south thoroughfare and heading west on Haines Road, in seconds, the vehicle moving past the dried-up Delaware Canal and quickly motoring past the adjacent Windsor Pharmacy.

"That's the Junewood section on our left with its numerous J Streets and there's Kenwood on the right with its corresponding K's," Joe Giralo routinely uttered to his still semi-shocked car audience. And after readily passing the James Buchanan Elementary School on the right, Chief Giralo succinctly declared, "Farmbrook is next on *your* side Sal and now we're coming near Dogwood Hollow with the entrance to Dogwood Drive on our immediate left. I recommend that you have your handguns available for swift action just in case there's an unexpected snag in the forthcoming SWAT-team raid!"

Agent Sal Velardi was about to aggressively challenge his Boss's mental sanity when the highly-focused driver adroitly halted his gray Chevy Suburban along the right-side Daffodil Lane curb, which coincidentally paralleled Dahlia Lane. The illustrious Chief Inspector then advised his three addled passengers to remain silent while they would view between houses an assigned elite Bucks County SWAT unit decisively moving-in to apprehend the unwary occupants of the now-parked Dahlia Lane white van.

"Ha, ha, ha! Mission accomplished!" gushed and roared Inspector Giralo, much to the consternation of his trio of companions. "As I've already promised, I'll provide all of the juicy data to you three mesmerized Dick Tracy wannabes' on Monday night at the Maplewood Inn, that is, after I confer with Matt Riley down in Washington and wrap-up my latest investigative report. By the way," now-jovial Joe Giralo elucidated, "by Monday evening I'll be familiar with all of the salient bits and pieces that have yet to be recognized. Of course, Fellas', a splendid four-course Italian dinner will be *your* special treat, my way of commemorating another FBI job well-done! Just remember these dynamic words Men! 'Too Much Monkey Business'! Ha, ha, ha!"

* * * * * * * * * * * *

On Monday night, July 16th the four refreshed FBI men met at the Route 30 Maplewood Inn's front bar and were soon escorted by the accommodating owner Jim Italiano to a secluded back dining room where the government detectives could conduct their important private discussion pertaining to recent FBI events. After crab meat cocktail appetizers and spaghetti and meatball main course suppers had been ordered, Salvatore Velardi, Arthur Orsi and Dan Blachford's deep desire to fully fathom all of the prominent details of the 'Too Much Monkey Business' escapade was finally addressed by their often-evasive superior.

"Okay now Guys, to satisfy your intense curiosity, first up, please review for me the names of the dastardly culprits you three had been relentlessly trailing. Matt Riley has given me the official government 'okay' to divulge the mechanics of this most secret case to you rather extraordinary potential rocket scientists! I'll attempt to make it brief so that we can enjoy the fabulous 16th of July fireworks at 9 p.m. tonight with our families over at the town carnival grounds."

"The punk in the black Lexus SUV, Anthony Sullivan!" Agent Velardi reflexively exclaimed.

"Jamie Miduri, the Manhattan-based idiot with the lackluster white van having grimy New York license plates!" Agent Blachford orally conveyed.

"Michael Farren, the sinister Yonkers row-house dude!" Agent Orsi incisively communicated. "And allow me to reiterate that the dull, white, decrepit van in need of a Maaco paint job eventually led us to Flatbush Avenue over in Brooklyn, stopping at the Farro Plush Toy Manufacturing Company."

The courteous waitress delivered the scrumptious-looking crab meat cocktail appetizers to the the men's table and without asking his agents for their additional culinary preferences, Inspector Giralo promptly ordered four bottles of Coor's Light beer along with four large slices of carrot cake to be consumed for dessert. After the experienced amiable waitress departed the virtually empty back dining room and re-entered the establishment's kitchen, Chief Joe Giralo eloquently articulated his rather astounding revelations.

"Well Guys, thanks to our ever-vigilant Washington agents' nimble ability to infiltrate certain radical home-grown terrorist organizations here in the USA," the group leader suavely began his stark exposition, "we've determined that Anthony Sullivan's real name is Antwan Sulimoni, that Jamie Miduri was born Jamal Madari and that Michael Farren happened to enter this chaotic world as one Malic Faraj. Those three diabolical crazies are all Saudi Arabians by ancestry. And as far as Farro Plush Toy Manufacturing Company is concerned," the Chief very forcefully enunciated, "the shell firm is owned by a not-so-stellar individual named Omar Farrahkan, a very dangerous Egyptian bombmaker now-residing in Brooklyn. I was sure that one of you brilliant investigators would've finally seen the particular nomenclature relationship between the similar-sounding words 'Farro' and 'Pharaoh' and between the names Farrahkan and the Farro Plush Toy Manufacturing Company. And in the final interpretation Gentlemen," Joe Giralo continued his fascinating disclosure, "this home-grown jihadist Omar Farrahkan had his bomb-making laboratory in the basement situated below the stuffed animal toy company, a very convenient front to effectively launder pilfered money for the expressed acquisition of cell phone IED detonations, the powerful ingredients constituting plastic putty-like explosives such as C-4 and Semtex, and the like! This ruthless fellow Farrahkan was a highly-skilled artist at producing high-quality weapons of mass destruction."

"Holy heavenly Houdini!" bellowed an almost-delirious Sal Velardi. "And what integral roles did Antwan, Jamal and Malic play in this very preposterous enemy enterprise? I presume that the three Arab devils were co-conspirators directly dealing with this avowed treacherous terrorist Omar Farrahkan!"

"Precisely, Sal!" Joe Giralo commended and verified. "Here's the entire big-picture explanation. Antwan Sulimoni traveled from 'Philly to Manhattan to obtain stolen diamonds from Jamal Madari, a dishonorable employee at the New York Diamond Exchange, located at 10 West 47th Street in midtown New York. Madari then visited a wealthy black-market fence named Malic Faraj at the crook's modest Yonkers row-house, one of six residences positioned all over the U.S. that are owned by the extremely corrupt middle-man stolen-goods' specialist. The pilfered diamonds would be traded for cash to buy additional explosives that the formidable Saudis and their demonic Egyptian counterpart Farrahkan were clandestinely seeking to obtain."

Just then the very affable Maplewood Inn waitress brought to the table a loaf of soft Italian bread on a cutting board along with a full bowl of fresh vegetable salad and a handsome-looking cut-glass set of oil and vinegar cruets. When the attractive brunette hastily left the rear "overflow room" to attend to the needs of regular patrons sitting in the main dining area, Inspector Giralo re-commenced his rather mindboggling monologue.

"As I had alluded to earlier, this mastermind criminal Omar Farrahkan, alias Mr. Oliver Farro, was illegally manufacturing C-4 and Semtex, two distinct varieties of plastic explosives, and our very expert Washington DC intel' team had recently learned that the demented Egyptian maniac and his equally warped Saudi comrades planned to blow-up the Empire State Building, since it's now quite difficult to heist a 737 airplane and pilot it into a New York skyscraper as had been done to the Twin Tower World Trade Buildings on that infamous morning, September 11th! Matt Riley and I had believed that the conspirators' Empire State Building attack would soon occur on a work day when the popular edifice would be fully occupied with office workers and tourists."

"And I'll bet that this lunatic Omar Farrahkan of Farro Plush Toy Company, that Jamal Madari and that Malic Faraj all maintained recently rented offices on different floors of the Empire State Building!" marveled and expressed Agent Arthur Orsi. "How absolutely psychologically deranged those four totally wicked homegrown terrorists must be!"

"Exactly!" Joe Giralo affirmatively answered. "But fortunately, our astute-minded undercover team members soon discovered that the

IRS had been investigating Farro Plush Toy Company for income tax evasion so nefarious Omar Farrahkan had to temporarily hide his newfound purloined diamond cache in a remote safe place and out of sheer necessity, the nutcase jihadist had his acquaintance Jamal Madari transport two enormous stuffed baby monkeys all the way from Brooklyn to the traveling carnival down in our hometown, Hammonton, NJ. What a phenomenal-but-fortuitous coincidence!"

The veteran waitress, accompanied by a young male restaurant employee then carefully carried the four spaghetti and meatball entrees to the men's back-room table. The FBI agents gradually resumed their confidential dialogue after being again left alone.

"Well then, Chief," flustered Sal Velardi declared after finally regaining his mental equilibrium. "How did that oddball 24 Dahlia Lane, Levittown excursion and the subsequent criminal arrests fit neatly into your exceptional investigative equation?"

Inspector Giralo momentarily paused, inhaled a deep breath, cleared his throat and then expounded that the ubiquitous white van had delivered two mammoth boxes of stuffed baby monkeys to the basketball shooting game located on the French Street side of the town carnival grounds. The basketball-oriented game had been operated by another Saudi, a lower echelon fellow named Sammy Astaire, whose native name was Samir Asir. The low-ranking Asir had made a crucial mistake in recklessly hiring a mentally challenged American carny bearing the name Frank Dawson. From documented on-the-scene FBI interviews, Dawson had been asked to manage the basketball shooting game while Samir Asir had been preoccupied at the Mt. Carmel Society's Beer Garden enjoying a fine platter of terrific Italian food.

"But Boss, what about the targeted family residing at 24 Dahlia Lane?" Dan Blachford insisted on learning. "How do they fill into the weird scheme of events?"

"Well Dan, a middle-class couple, Bob and Sarah Abbott of 24 Dahlia Lane, along with their two daughters Sierra, age sixteen and Lindsey, age ten, were in Hammonton visiting cousins Charles and Marie Sceia of Fernwood Drive," Chief Giralo academically disclosed. "I found-out just yesterday that Sierra Abbott is a remarkable star athlete, and more specifically, the young lady's an accomplished girls' basketball player at Levittown's Harry S. Truman High School. At least thirty colleges are offering the talented junior scholarships, since Sierra has a fifty-two percent three-point shooting average along with an enviable ninety-three percent free throw shooting reputation!"

"Let me hypothesize the rest," Agent Sal Velardi volunteered his personal assessment. "Sierra had beaten the odds and easily made three consecutive baskets, and so Frank Dawson was compelled to award her the immense baby monkey prize containing the recently transported stolen diamonds!"

"Almost a home run, but no cigar!" mildly reprimanded an animated Chief Giralo. "After Sierra had sunk three straight free throws, she requested the top prize; the first fantastic stuffed monkey that was on display. But then her younger sister Lindsey yelled that she wanted one too, and at the urging of Bob and Sarah Abbott, mentally-challenged Frank Dawson broke-down and consented to their request to allow Sierra to shoot again. Incredibly, Sierra Abbott made three more free throws and at the doting parents' demand," Chief Giralo clarified, "Dawson entered the concession's rear stock area, turned the huge box upside down, thus ignoring the warning instruction scribbled on the top ordering employees to not open the package. Next, this illiterate, itinerant carny named Francis Dawson eagerly opened the box and then inadvertently presented the second giant stuffed monkey to thoroughly delighted ten-year-old Lindsey Abbott. But honestly, Sierra Abbott swishing six straight foul shots at a carnival game of chance is indeed positively surreal!"

"Positively unbelievable! What exactly happened next?" asked totally intrigued Art Orsi.

"That evening the Abbotts drove back to Levittown not knowing that they were being pursued by desperate terrorists endeavoring to regain possession of their pouch of heisted diamonds that had been sewn inside the gargantuan second baby monkey. However, athletically talented Sierra Abbott needed to return to Pennsylvania because the future court hoops' star had just been hired as a summer basketball camp counselor. As a result of *that* development, that evening Bob and Sarah Abbott had to reluctantly travel back to 24 Dahlia Lane. In conclusion," the incomparable Inspector Giralo lectured, "you fine Men must fully understand and appreciate that in the final analysis, most human matters and most people events are basically determined by chance, by circumstance or by uncanny coincidence! And that's precisely how Jamal Madari and Samir Asir had been collared outside 24 Dahlia Lane. Now my stouthearted Companions," Inspector Joe Giralo snickered, "let's indulge and eat to our souls' content so that we can later tonight enjoy the spectacular July 16th fireworks' extravaganza!"

Agent Salvatore Velardi instinctively raised his brown Coor's Light bottle, extended it toward the center of the table and then humorously exclaimed in an exaggerated-but-exhilarated voice, "Too Much Monkey Business! Long live Chuck Berry!"

The other three ecstatic diners seated comfortably at the round Maplewood Inn table lifted their separate cold brown bottles in unison and ambitiously joined the proposed toast, an admirable salute dedicated to the celebrated, sensational 1950s rock and roll recording artist and his "Monkey Business" smash hit.

# "Swarming Killer Bees"

Of all the baffling crime scenarios that have both challenged and intrigued FBI Inspector Joe Giralo, none has ever been more mysterious and bewildering than the difficult case of the "Swarming Killer Bees," which all amazingly transpired in April of 2012. Accompanied by his squad of loyal agents consisting of FBI men Salvatore Velardi, Arthur Orsi and Dan Blachford, Giralo and his trio of dedicated government investigators have once again relentlessly sought-out specific answers to what had constituted a very sinister and perplexing crime puzzle.

Fatigued Inspector Joe Giralo was on a week-long spring vacation away from his grueling investigative responsibilities, and the revered sleuth was presently engaged in performing some perfunctory family grocery shopping chores for his wife Gina, who was on an academic field trip with her older daughter's middle school class to the Franklin Institute over in Philadelphia. While casually ambling with a squeaky-wheeled cart inside the Hammonton, New Jersey Wal*Mart dairy aisle, the now-domesticated husband abruptly stopped to choose between a half gallon of vanilla fudge or a similar container of butter pecan ice cream. The famed inspector's cell phone rang and Giralo immediately read and recognized the caller I.D. to be that of his trusty assistant, mercurial-tempered and garrulous Agent Salvatore Velardi.

"Hi Sal! What's up?" the call's recipient asked. "I told you not to get in touch with me about FBI business matters during my brief hiatus unless the message was somewhere between crucial and urgent! Where are you right this minute Sal?"

"I'm soon leaving Bagliani's Italian Market here on Twelfth Street after I pick-up a watermelon and some fresh lunch meat for my wife," Velardi quickly complained, feigning a degree of bland aggravation. "She claims the melon's too heavy for her to lift and transport from the store and then deposit inside her car while also trying to stay alive inside the chaotic Bagliani's parking lot. Then, after I successfully deliver the perfect ripe watermelon to my laundry room sink counter," the thoroughly flustered agent continued his exaggerated explanation, "I'm immediately off to Cherry Hill to meet-up with Orsi and Blachford to continue our gumshoe work in the complex ongoing Warren and Anastasia interstate drug smuggling operation."

"Well, Sal. I already know all about the intricate probe that's delving into the burgeoning local drug trafficking crime spree," Inspector Giralo rankled. "Please don't say that you're callin' me about how to exactly select a ripe watermelon! But just for the general record, I always look for a yellow spot on the bottom, an accompanying black withered stem and a hollow sound when the dark green item's being gently thumped!"

"Well, Boss," Agent Velardi respectfully replied. "Even though *this* most recent oddball story I'm about to share doesn't cross state lines, it's all quite uniquely interesting to say the least. Here's the scoop! An adult female named Jennifer Carlson of Medford, New Jersey has just early this morning been egregiously attacked and killed by a dangerous swarm of fanatical bees while innocently walking alone in the Laurel Hill Cemetery over in Burlington Township. This type of blatant nature-gone-wild animal instinct aggression is rather inordinate indeed, wouldn't you tend to agree?"

"Indeed, yes Sal; it most certainly is," Giralo conjectured and then concurred. "An indiscriminate random attack you say? What species of bees? Has *that* essential fact been determined yet?"

"Yes, Boss. The stingers that have been removed from the victim's body by the Burlington County Coroner indicate that the invading creatures happened to be formidable African Killer Bees. But according to the most up-to-date info'," Agent Velardi complemented his personal analysis, "*that* particular kind of lethal bee hasn't yet gotten north of Oklahoma, let alone an insect invasion being able to geographically travel up here to Jersey and consequently cause extreme havoc and panic among the local population!"

"From your graphic description Sal, it could be a rogue colony specifically and deliberately harvested by a demented South Jersey beekeeper, the crazed enthusiast having the necessary skill to develop a demonic hive and then unleashing the insects for revenge on some unassuming mortal target," Inspector Giralo evaluated and surmised. "This regrettable event you've just mentioned could evolve into a fairly big case if it becomes a distinct pattern also showing-up in other places like Delaware, New York or Pennsylvania. As of now though, Sal, it sounds like a singular weird-but-sensational incident and nothing more, pretty similar to the analogous classic journalism cliché 'man-bites-dog' example that's prevalent and often cited by editors in the newspaper publishing industry!"

"Okay, Chief. I'll do some preliminary background research on this poor Burlington Township woman Jennifer Carlson to determine if she had had in her past any lunatic enemies that would stoop to such nefarious illicit activity, that is," Velardi scrupulously qualified to his immediate federal government superior, "my professional services performed with your expressed permission to begin initiating an unofficial inquiry."

"As usual, you have my total approval to proceed," Chief Giralo typically consented. "Say, Sal; my weary mind's now in a quandary! Tell me. What flavor of ice cream do you prefer? I'm at Wal*Mart attempting to select between vanilla fudge and butter pecan!"

"Definitely vanilla fudge, without a single doubt," Agent Velardi automatically declared. "Confidentially Boss, I prefer the Turkey Hill brand. Now please inform me. Where will your exciting travels take you after your nondescript Wal*Mart excursion? Are you off to Siberia, or perhaps Death Valley?"

"After I deliver the ice cream to the kitchen freezer compartment and the other grocery items to the refrigerator and the pantry," Joe Giralo revealed, "I'll be off to Oak Grove Cemetery where the family mausoleum is finally finishing-up construction. I mean Sal, I don't plan on dying soon, but truthfully, I want *that* major project fully completed so that my heirs will have a place to eventually bury my human remains. The impressive granite edifice can contain six bodies and it's only costing me a hundred and fifty thousand bucks to build!"

"Oak Grove's a nice cemetery for a pair of morbid romantics like us to rest in peace," Velardi reluctantly commented. "It's got plenty of tall, shady oak and elm trees and the ancient graveyard has both history and character. In fact, Boss, I prefer Oak Grove to Hammonton's Greenmount Cemetery over on First Road. Oak Grove dates back to the Civil War era, even before the town was incorporated, I do believe. I suppose I'll soon have to acknowledge the inevitable, also!"

"Try to stay on the green side of the dirt for as long as possible," Joe Giralo jested. "It's usually a lot warner there!"

"I think I'll purchase six or eight grave plots over there on the Old Forks Road side while there's still a good selection from which to choose. Maybe someday I'll be able to afford *your* kind of macabre investment, that is, if I'm ever promoted to the rank of Inspector; that is of course, after you retire from service Boss," Velardi anxiously emphasized. "Then I'll be able to legally save enough dough to arrange for my own dignified family stone mausoleum."

"I'll recommend *you* for a decent promotion when I gracefully retire in twenty-three years," Joe Giralo promised with a very evident sarcastic chuckle terminating his humor-oriented remark. "Get back to me after you meet-up with Orsi and Blachford over in Cherry Hill. Quite frankly Sal, thanks to your alert reporting, I've certainly become more than a trifle curious about the fate of this unfortunate lady Jennifer Carlson."

After returning home with his assorted food packages and then methodically inserting the acquired products into the correct kitchen cabinets and refrigerator compartments, Inspector Giralo carefully prepared a cup of instant coffee, removed two white powdered doughnuts from a cupboard box and then promptly sat-down at the Canadian oak oval table to indulge in his late morning brunch. 'My age is catching-up with me. I really need this time off,' the serious-minded crime-fighter considered, 'but I also realize that I truly love my meritorious FBI career. I wonder if Salvatore has successfully excavated any additional clues pertaining to the untimely strange death of Jennifer Carlson!'

Just then the land-line phone rang, and Agent Art Orsi's voice was discernible on the other end of the line. "Guess what Boss?" the caller rhetorically asked. "Dan Blachford and I are over here at the recently remodeled Cherry Hill Mall. We're gonna' meet Sal at Maggiano's Little Italy Restaurant for a spaghetti and meatball lunch at around 1 p.m. and we'll be discussing the complicated Warren and Anastasia drug smuggling syndicate," Orsi swiftly elaborated, predictably and characteristically pausing to catch his breath. "Anyway, Boss; Dan and I know all about the Jennifer Carlson killer bee tragedy over in Burlington Township, but there's been an associated bizarre case that's just been reported on the area police bulletin wires; the new extraordinary situation occurring just forty miles southeast of Cherry Hill over in Vineland."

"Another inexplicable killer bee attack?" a now-fascinated Inspector Giralo hypothesized and assertively asked. "Give me the precise details Art!"

"Sorry to interrupt your well-deserved time-off, Boss! But this incredible news I'm currently divulging isn't any frivolous routine stuff either!" Orsi assessed and remarked. "An elderly fellow named Jerome Esposito has just been assaulted and violently killed by a vicious swarm of angry bees over in Sacred Heart Catholic Cemetery in Vineland. Hundreds of bites have been detected all over his lifeless body. Apparently, Mr. Esposito had been doing some spring exercise strolling and before he knew it, the victimized fellow was covered head-to-toe with belligerent killer bees, which obviously, as you're well-aware, are not indigenous to South Jersey!"

"Yes, and if the deadly killer bees populate all regions of South Jersey," Chief Giralo logically theorized and contributed, "then they'll soon eliminate all native honey bees while they're instinctively in pursuit of territorial conquest! Arty, I want you, Dan and Sal to see if there're any significant connection between Jennifer Carlson and this new victim, Jerome Esposito. Get back to me with any pertinent discovery or better yet, contact me with any other vital information that you might obtain. One wild bee attack, in itself, is important!

Two brutal invasions in the same day! That's absolutely something more than simply being dramatically coincidental!"

"Okay, Boss. I'm no Arabian genie escaped from a bottle," Agent Orsi imaginatively responded from his cell phone, "but I'll see what kind of magical research I can organize."

"Alright Arty," Joe Giralo objectively comprehended. "I'll go onto Google and learn some more significant info' about radical bee behavior. Entomology is one science where my basic knowledge is rather limited!"

"You're concerned about studying the origin of words?" Agent Orsi incredulously questioned.

"No, Arty! I said 'Entomology' and not 'Etymology'. Entomology happens to represent the study of insects!"

* * * * * * * * * * * * *

The following morning Inspector Joe Giralo was savoring a hardy breakfast while anonymously seated at the counter of the Silver Coin Diner situated on Hammonton's Route 30, the White Horse Pike. The man's consumption of delectable bacon and eggs was rudely interrupted by a cell phone call from Agent Dan Blachford, who had been secretly stationed on crime-watch surveillance in Cherry Hill with his trustworthy colleagues, Arthur Orsi and Salvatore Velardi.

"Boss, we've got some more pretty bad killer bee news to report!" an overworked Agent Blachford prefaced with woeful rhetoric. "Two additional African bee attacks have occurred early this morning in separate parts of South Jersey. The first gruesome bombardment happened inside the normally tranquil Haddonfield Baptist Cemetery. The victim has been identified as a female named Lisa Serappa."

"Well, Dan," Joe Giralo calmly stated in declarative terms. "At least these rambunctious killer bees don't discriminate. Yesterday, that fellow Jerome Esposito had been savagely brutalized inside a Vineland Catholic Cemetery, Sacred Heart I believe, and today this newly-discovered woman Lisa Serappa has met her demise in a Haddonfield Baptist graveyard. Tell me," the sagacious crime crusader resumed his inquisitive narrative, "describe the second ferocious swarming assault Dan! These very voracious, volatile flying insects don't seem to ever gender differentiate between men and women, regardless of whether the terrorized person that's being targeted is a devout Catholic or a Godfearing Protestant!"

"The fourth horrendous mutilation has just come across the closed-circuit FBI network wire," Blachford almost-hysterically answered. "The latest New Jersey casualty is, or should I say 'was' an independent minded, backwoods' piney, actually a neurotic paranoid loner named Joseph Frederico, who incidentally was horribly attacked by a frenetic swarm while attempting to illegally shoot a squirrel inside Holy Cross Cemetery over in Mays Landing. There was one eyewitness to the ghastly debacle, a completely shocked guy who had observed the grisly onslaught from afar, a now-petrified cemetery caretaker, Stephen Prince!"

"This entire phenomenon is as incongruous as a bill in Congress!" Chief Giralo marveled and commented. "Thanks Dan, for providing the very thorough and efficient update!"

"Boss!" Agent Blachford then very optimistically exclaimed, his excited voice competing with the dissonant din prevailing inside the hectic and crowded Silver Coin Diner. "This very evening local police, a competent Camden County SWAT team and *your* three FBI men will be raiding the homes of Henry Warren and Antonio Anastasia. We now have sufficient evidence to convict those drug-smuggling thugs in a federal courtroom and we're now in the process of obtaining a judge's search warrant. Guess where the notorious scoundrels live?" the on-a-mission agent wildly asked. "They both are neighbors over here in Cherry Hill, frolicking around on Chapel Avenue! Pretty righteous, ethical, moral and religious fellows, wouldn't you agree! Of all the ironic absurdity! Warren and Anastasia both nonchalantly residing side-by-side on Chapel Avenue!"

"Dan, getting back to this rather confusing killer bee swarming mystery," Chief Joe Giralo objectively insisted, "if any more scurrilous attacks occur, especially outside New Jersey, let me know immediately! I'll instantly contact Matt Riley down in Washington and get his direct permission to launch a comprehensive investigation into this enormously perplexing killer bee problem. In the meantime," Giralo bluntly summarized, "I plan on learning as much data as I possibly can about the peculiar mannerisms of these dreadful, lethal hostile insects!"

"And Boss," Dan Blachford emotionally indicated. "Orsi and Velardi are presently preoccupied doing fundamental research on any unique relationships existing between the four, deceased human prey: Jennifer Carlson of Burlington Township, Jerome Esposito of Vineland, Lisa Serappa over in swanky, upscale Haddonfield and Joseph Frederico found dead over in the Atlantic County Seat, Mays Landing."

"My formerly latent curiosity has now been strongly stimulated," usually stoic Joe Giralo confessed. "I'm just as inspired and motivated as you are Dan to professionally get to the bottom of this totally confounding enigma! If you derive any key connections between the four-dead people and the prolific killer bees," the FBI supervisor imperatively instructed, "get on the horn and fill me in about the relevant details! Take care Dan and use your trained discretion when dealing with those armed and dangerous Mafia punks! And be awfully careful when dealing with the whole ruthless Cherry Hill mob syndicate!" Click.

* * * * * * * * * * * *

That Thursday afternoon in April, Inspector Joe Giralo was quite active surfing the Internet and aggressively studying the various characteristics of bees in general and of African killer bees in particular. From his intensive academic inquiry the conscientious FBI official now fully fathomed that ordinary bee swarming constituted a distinctly natural method of facilitating the insects' regular reproduction cycle, which is predictably demonstrated among honey bees and killer bees alike. A traveling bee caravan is usually in quest of a new colony home. A new royal queen leaves the previous hive and then is escorted and accompanied to a secondary location by industrious worker bees. A swarm might involve up to ten thousand bees that are exceedingly loyal to the in-transition new queen, and the old queen is left behind with perhaps just 40% of the original beehive population. And also, the mass migration to a new physical environment usually occurs in the spring during the months of April through early June.

'This entire frustrating examination is quite odd! Definitely an anomaly, but certainly not an exercise in futility,' the esteemed FBI Inspector concluded. 'Bee swarms usually *are,* under everyday circumstances, not regarded as dangerous, that is, unless the entire colony feels threatened, trespassed upon, or suddenly invaded. There're only a few soldier bees in the new transitory brood on hand to defend the single-minded on-the-move bee swarm,' Joe Giralo meticulously considered. 'I've also learned that individual bees have little chance of survival on their own. They must be a contributing part of a productive colony in order to feel safe and integrated, all the while sharing mutual food gathering responsibilities for the new queen and her young. And in my superficial cursory analysis, I've also discovered that loyal scouts wander out to explore new-found nectar sources besides also endeavoring to find a desirable safe place for the moving swarm to permanently re-locate! But contrary to what I had previously surmised,' Giralo aptly conjectured, 'swarming bees are not wild and dangerous during the initial stages of new colony development! However, if the queen perishes, the remainder of the colony is then placed in automatic jeopardy, the now-vulnerable swarm would be losing its central purpose for social existence!'

Just then the den phone rang, and the now bee-enamored FBI Chief Joseph Giralo hastily picked-up the telecommunication device from its vertical cradle. "Hi, Arty. Congratulations on your successful Cherry Hill Mafia raid last night! Those two wicked crooks Warren and Anastasia deserve twenty-year incarcerations apiece. Now tell me, have Sal, Dan and you unearthed anything significant with the inexplicable bee killing pattern? As I've often reiterated to you and your dependable cohorts, first intensively search for clues. And if you don't find anything tangible Arty, then stubbornly *search* again! That's precisely why *this* intricate, illustrious methodology that I'm at the moment carefully reviewing for you is just what happens to be ingeniously called *re-search!*

"Here's some salient news' flash information that's recently been made available to us from headquarters!" Agent Orsi hesitated and then proudly communicated. "New Jersey has company! Two freshly fierce bee attacks have just transpired around noon in other nearby East Coast states!"

"Okay Art, you've successfully gotten my cerebrum activated!" Giralo sternly answered. "But needless to say, this extremely nebulous bee-stalking scenario greatly defies scientific plausibility! Bees usually only swarm and fly around in a several-mile radius from their original colony, their primary focus being to create a new base of operation. These disturbing killing incidents are at least ten-to-fifty miles apart, so therefore," the experienced FBI Chief dubiously speculated and profoundly articulated, "the separate attacking killer bee hordes must come from a variety of swarming colonies throughout the Delaware Valley. And besides *that* very obvious common fact Art, I've just read from reliable sources that swarming bees are ordinarily docile and basically harmless if left undisturbed!"

"Wow Boss!" Agent Orsi loudly replied with great admiration. "I'm becoming as skeptical as that ancient cynic Diogenes. All of these fantastic angry bee incidents are indubitably contrary to normal bee conduct. Anyway, I'll get back on subject, Chief. Around noon today over in Smyrna, Delaware's Glenwood Cemetery, a fella' by the name of Franklin Metz, pardon the forthcoming pun-like expression Boss, but while the designated victim Mr. Metz was merrily ambling about the grounds and then planting pansies in his family's grave plot section," Orsi expounded and then inhaled sufficient oxygen to continue his lengthy report, "the deadly killer insects made a straight *bee-line* and swiftly eliminated poor oblivious Franklin Metz from the face of the Earth! The pugnacious militant killer bees mystically acted in a spectacular frenzy, almost as if the ravaging vengeful swarm possessed a single evil mind!"

"Just like subterranean ants, bees need to cooperate and protect a central queen in order for the collaborative colony to thrive! And please enlighten me Art, what about the parallel abominable incursion to the one that had occurred in Delaware?" Giralo inquisitively queried. "Exactly where did *that* other devastating onslaught happen? And how come all of these atrocious attacks have coincidentally taken place in different town cemeteries?"

"Well Boss, the sixth seemingly demonic surprise bee barrage happened over in West Chester, Pennsylvania inside the normally serene St. Agnes Cemetery. A prominent local small-time politician named Harold Porter was unexpectedly and perversely besieged, beleaguered and soon efficiently terminated by an incensed bee swarm while the unfortunate guy was simply standing there meditating at a deceased relative's stone monument!"

"Alright Art, I've heard enough supporting evidence about this outrageous in-progress bee dilemma! I'll dial-up Matt Riley down in DC and get the go-ahead to conduct a full-scale investigation into this extraordinary interstate bee-killing skein."

"Fine with me!" Agent Orsi respectfully concurred. "Sal's been piecing together some exceptional fragments related to this rather fantastic African bee case, and by noon tomorrow we promise to fully disclose the entire tremendously unbelievable crime landscape to you! This weird killer bee investigation is sort of like putting together an immensely insane jigsaw puzzle!"

"Maybe if we could somehow intercept one of these migrating swarms, then a licensed beekeeper could be employed who could effectively isolate the queen and then adroitly capture the entire insect gang. Then our sage experts over at the lab' could examine the individual specimens within a controlled experimental environment to then determine the exact causes influencing *their* consistent, aberrant, destructive deportment. Keep up the good work Art! I want to praise your high spirit, enacted all for the good of the order!" Chief Giralo complimented and encouraged. "But more importantly Arty; please keep the faith!"

"This killer bee thing goes way beyond religion Boss!" Agent Orsi opined. "I now do honestly believe that we have to hire the services of a well-trained professional exorcist!" Click.


* * * * * * * * * * *

Saturday morning Gina Giralo was traveling in her late-model SUV twelve miles east out of Hammonton on *Route 30* heading to Schuster's Shoes in Berlin, her immediate mission being to purchase summer boardwalk and beach footwear for the family's two daughters. Joe Giralo prudently utilized the coveted, rare free time to engage-in additional research on the subject of mass bee societal habits within a hive or active swarm.

'Bees don't have motives to kill people like humans do,' the Inspector reasonable contemplated. 'They merely act out of genetically programmed instinct, that is, unless they're somehow trained to attack and kill unsuspecting humans by some heinous-minded mortal. And what's so marvelously remarkable about honey bee behavior is that the busy creatures actually accidentally pick-up pollen on their legs while exploring for sources of nectar, thus unintentionally pollinating area fruit and vegetable crops as the busy insects are simultaneously preoccupied gathering food while maneuvering from flower-to-flower, their existential purpose being to produce sufficient honey to keep the colony or hive members productive and to keep the constantly hungry queen fertile! Besides being potentially dangerous when provoked, these buzzing insects are truly vital to the world of agriculture!'

Just then the Chief's cell phone rang and the stammering voice of Agent Salvatore Velardi was instantly recognizable to *his* distinguished FBI superior. Joe Giralo listened intently to his anxious employee's new-found revelations. "Boss, yesterday Art, Dan and I burned the midnight oil over at the 'Philly' Office, and this morning we've finally gotten all our ducks in a row," Velardi quite nervously asserted and affirmed. "What I have to disclose to you is absolutely astounding!"

"Okay Sal, compose yourself and start again at square one," Joe Giralo patiently advised. "I sincerely suggest that you take five deep breaths and then relate to me your new evidence!"

"Boss, all substantial clues linking the six dead killer bee victims point directly to a certain New Jersey beekeeper named Oliver Norton, who lived in the village of Elwood over to the east of Hammonton over in Mullica Township," Velardi orally conveyed via the cell phone transmission. "But imagine this! This suspicious character Oliver Norton in the past had supplied area blueberry, peach and vegetable farmers with honeybees each spring so that the growers could crosspollinate their annual crops. But the most staggering aspect about this lone-wolf man identified as Oliver Norton is that this beekeeper person-of-interest had died a year ago and that his tombstone and attendant grave are in Oak Grove Cemetery. Norton's final resting place is situated about twenty gravestones off the Old Forks Road entrance, just across from Hammonton High School!"

"I believe I've noticed *that* impressive-but-plain Norton gravestone more than once," Chief Giralo recollected and verbally acknowledged. "Yes, I know exactly where it is because I've just had the family mausoleum constructed on the opposite side of the cemetery's thick oak tree canopy. Everything's been finished on the expensive project except the name 'Giralo' being inscribed onto the granite space just below the structure's pinnacle."

"Yes Boss," Agent Velardi reflexively and courteously replied. "According to the latest online cemetery map, the large Norton gravestone is around ten plots west of the very unique Jason St. John marker. But Boss, wait until I divulge how all six morbid deaths are connected in regard to this formerly cantankerous, deceased Elwood beekeeper named Oliver Norton!"

"I think I have to sit down in a sturdy chair before you continue your dramatic exposition," Inspector Giralo firmly stated. "My ancient mind can only handle one uncanny alien iota at a time!"

"Okay Chief. I have my notes all prepared on paper in exact chronological order," Sal Velardi vociferated. "Jennifer Carlson, the first victim attacked by killer bees inside the Laurel Hill Cemetery over in Burlington Township, was once married to Oliver Norton but the estranged pair became divorced in 1985. And the second deceased individual, Jerome Esposito, who had met his fate in Vineland's Sacred Heart Cemetery, was once a business partner of this now-dead beekeeper Oliver Norton. According to Atlantic County records, the two men mutually owned a hundred acres of land just off the Egg Harbor Interchange on the Atlantic City Expressway. The overall deal went sour when apparently Esposito fraudulently cheated Norton out of a percentage of the sale's profit. Hence, a feasible motive has been established and verified through valid government deed documentation."

"But if Oliver Norton is currently residing in spirit form in the undefined afterlife," Joe Giralo deducted and verbally shared, "how could he ever train killer bees in April of 2012 AD to enact revenge on his purported Earthly Enemies? Several hidden factors to this mendaciously arcane equation must be missing!"

"And the third killer bee victim, Lisa Serappa, who came face-to-face with her ultimate destiny in Haddonfield's Baptist Cemetery, well Chief, the scorned woman once had sued Oliver Norton and she actually won a case of sexual harassment against the deceased beekeeper way back in 1992," a perspiring Agent Velardi divulged. "Source records from the court proceedings show that Lisa Serappa refused to date this obnoxious philanderer Oliver Norton when he had awkwardly proposed the not-so-romantic idea while visiting the woman's father's Camden County blueberry farm over in Blue Anchor. And in relation to the fourth corpse, Joseph Frederico, who had been mauled by antagonized flying bees over at the Holy Cross Cemetery in Mays Landing," Agent Velardi rather ambitiously disseminated, "well Chief, this Frederico guy had in April of 1997 deliberately shot Oliver Norton in the left leg after the despicable beekeeper had trespassed onto the territorial piney's land, the remote property being not-too-far from the backwoodsman's dilapidated cabin situated on the south bank of the Mullica River."

"All of these interesting factual events make perfect rational sense under ordinary circumstances," the befuddled FBI inspector reluctantly admitted. "But the resolute key detail confirming that this suspected perpetrator Oliver Norton has been dead for a year adds a dimension of hazy confusion to my already cynical clouded mind. Say Sal, what about the dual out-of-state Delaware and Pennsylvania cadavers! Obviously, scientific clinical autopsies have to be performed by coroner examiners!"

"Well Chief, Franklin Metz, who had been viciously enveloped by killer bees over in the Glenwood Cemetery in Smyrna, Delaware," Agent Velardi eagerly expressed and then paused, "that dead man was once Oliver Norton's brother-in-law. According to a Camden County police report, Metz had severely beaten-up Oliver Norton in 1997 at a bar over in Winslow Township, the loud dispute and subsequent violent altercation resulting over certain stock investments that had terribly gone south! And as far as Harold Porter being mauled by barbaric-like bees over in West Chester's St. Agnes Cemetery is concerned," Sal Velardi cautiously mentioned to his boss, "Porter had moved from Hammonton west to Pennsylvania in September of 2007. It seems that before living in Hammonton, this itinerant fellow Harold Porter had resided in Elwood. Yes indeed, Harold Porter was an incompatible neighbor of volatile Oliver Norton. Well Chief, this guy Porter had legitimately defeated Norton for a political seat on the Mullica Township Council. After Oliver Norton became bellicose and exhibited a plethora of nasty threats to Mr. Porter over the span of four consecutive years, Mr. Harold Porter became totally intimidated with the constant physical encounters and soon abruptly abandoned Elwood for the tranquil, passive atmosphere of West Chester, Pennsylvania."

"Listen Sal, I must wholeheartedly commend you, Art and Dan for doing an excellent job in compiling a sophisticated history of Oliver Norton's biographical background," Chief Giralo politely lauded, "but this ugly epidemic of killer bee felonies positively transcends history, geography, science and just about any other standard academic discipline too. Indeed, regular conventional wisdom seems to have been made ludicrously irrelevant by virtue of the accumulative evidence that has been so impeccably gleaned by you, Art and Dan."

"What's our next step Boss?" Sal Velardi curiously inquired. "Should the four of us venture over to Ancora State Hospital and undergo a comprehensive battery of psychiatric evaluations?"

"Don't be so blatantly ridiculous or so foolishly facetious when describing serious criminal cases," Inspector Giralo mildly reprimanded and demanded. "I intend to drive over to Oak Grove Cemetery, take a perceptive gander at the large Oliver Norton headstone, and then I'll check-out my newly fabricated granite mausoleum on the cemetery's north side. I need the mental luxury of Oak Grove's special solitude to be able to genuinely assess the myriad strange facets of this radically labyrinth-like case!"

"Good luck and God speed!" Agent Sal Velardi candidly declared, carefully arranging his nomenclature so as not to offend his austere no-nonsense boss. "I hope and trust that there's a soon-to-be-found magic silver bullet that'll shed much-needed illumination upon this totally aggravating killer bee mystery."

Chief Giralo slowly exited his two-story colonial home's laundry room, entered his musty garage and cautiously climbed inside his late-model gray Chevy Suburban. The car's remote control reliably raised the garage door, and the G-man behind the wheel gingerly backed his automobile out onto his asphalt driveway and then electronically lowered the dark blue exit portal.

Soon the rejuvenated FBI detective was turning left off of Orchard Street and next taking Tilton west to a familiar right onto Fairview Avenue. A left turn onto Fourth Street was soon negotiated, and after passing the Warren E. Sooy Elementary School, the huge Suburban was next steered right onto Walnut Street, which a mile later ended precisely at Old Forks Road. Across from Hammonton High School, the intensely focused Inspector turned left into stately and majestic Oak Grove Cemetery. After passing the noticeably distinctive Jason St. John monument, ten graves down the lane from the deceased sea captain's faded, dull blue monument was a very outstanding-but-plain gray headstone, the huge ominous object bearing the prominent appellation "Norton".

Upon halting his vehicle, Chief Giralo was astonished to perceive a colossal migratory bee colony resting directly upon Oliver Norton's massive granite gravestone, the listless swarm enveloping the total gray area surrounding the very visible engraved surname. The almost paralyzed veteran FBI guru stared in wonder at the bewildering silent spectacle, indeed a rather disconcerting visualization that his' awestruck eyes had been witnessing.

'This whole grotesque phenomenon is absolutely surreal!' pallid faced Giralo imagined and then gasped. 'I'm going to swiftly evacuate this frightening section of Oak Grove and speed over to the safe haven area of my newly constructed mausoleum. Everything's done *there* with the mere exception of the inscription of the family name to be etched just below the apex!'

Just after the now-paranoid FBI Chief removed his right foot from the brake pedal and began applying soft pressure to the accelerator, the killer bee swarm slowly rose from the massive Norton tombstone and as if governed by a single mental impulse, the entire colony, concealing its protected regal queen, flew north in unison, buzzing directly through the dense oak tree canopy, systematically migrating in the direction of the newly-erected Giralo mausoleum.

Upon arriving at *his* now-eerie destination, the Chief Inspector was both flabbergasted and dumfounded to observe the colossal killer bee colony occupying the two vertical parallel pillars existing alongside the stone structure's recently installed glass door entrance. And much to Joe Giralo's overwhelming alarm and dismay, an assortment of specialized killer bees formed and accurately spelled the surname "G-I-R-A-L-O" upon the formerly blank block of granite positioned just below the tomb's A-frame gray slate roof.

'That does it!' ordinarily non-superstitious Inspector Joe Giralo quickly determined. 'I must honor this repugnant paranormal omen that's somehow mercilessly haunting me from the sordid depths of Hell! I hereby surrender to my diabolical satanic deceased enemy, the undeniably demonic Mr. Oliver Norton! I have neither the desire, nor the wherewithal, or the courageous will to do battle with *this* devilish, supernatural, black spirit! Discretion dictates that I should not tamper with what I can't readily comprehend!' Inspector Giralo fearfully realized.

'Finally, Inspector Giralo gained control of his rational senses. 'It's best to avoid confrontation with Satan's appointed evil representative. I must cease and desist from any futile mission that guarantees a losing crusade against the invisible world's superior-yet-unknown diabolical forces. I seek an immediate truce with this implacable Devil's Disciple, a vile demon whose black soul formerly existed in human flesh as the vengeful and vindictive area beekeeper, Oliver Norton!'

# "Boardwalk Mania"

At 9 a.m. sharp on Monday July 16th, 2012 veteran FBI Inspector Joe Giralo summoned his team of steadfast agents consisting of Salvatore Velardi, Arthur Orsi and Dan Blachford into his third-floor office inside the Federal Building at 600 Arch Street, Philadelphia, Pennsylvania. Immediately, the three standing agents curiously detected an element of urgency evident in their mercurial-tempered boss's raspy voice. But according to standard conversation protocol, small-talk had to precede the more important crime business discussion to follow.

"Today's the 16th of July back home in Hammonton," Chief Giralo solemnly prefaced his intended more serious comments. "The carnival has arrived in *our* New Jersey town and the folks are celebrating the Feast of Our Lady of Mt. Carmel. But much to my total dismay Fellas', each year the religious procession is getting smaller and smaller!"

"I always stop at the Assumption Food Stand and buy a pepper and sausage sandwich and a cold *Coke* to wash it down," Sal Velardi reminded everyone about his legendary enormous appetite. "For some obscure reason those pepper and sausage sandwiches always taste better at the carnival than they do when prepared at home. I think it's quite like buttered popcorn that always tastes better at a movie theater than the microwave variety does when being eaten at home while watching a pay-for-view cable TV movie! And then before leaving the carnival refreshment area," Agent Velardi continued his bland commentary, "I habitually consume two slices of pizza, a plate of French fries and some sticky cotton candy for dessert!"

"I prefer swallowing-down the delicious pepper and eggs sandwiches that are served at the jam-packed Mt. Carmel Society Beer Garden that's conveniently situated at the rear of the carnival grounds," Art Orsi felt inspired to opine. "And I really savor lots of fried onions to sample as a delectable side dish!"

"Well, now that we're all stranded on the same general subject, usually I tramp around the carnival grounds with my wife, making two quick rotations of all the rides and attractions," Dan Blachford contributed to the ongoing trite dialogue. "But over the years I've learned not to wear sandals because of the carnival grounds' rough gravel surface. But Guys, just like the Chief, I'm also afraid that small-town festivals and carnivals are rapidly becoming a lost tradition. I mean, giant amusement parks like Six Flags Great Adventure up in Jackson, Dorney Park over in Allentown and

Hershey Park out in Pennsylvania Dutch Country are now the popular attractions that are slowly-but-surely easily eliminating small town traveling carnivals." "And I know plenty of friends in Hammonton who take their wives and kids on summer vacations to Busch Gardens down in Williamsburg and to Kings Dominion in northern Virginia," Sal Velardi orally volunteered. "Big business seems to be dominating every phase of our daily lives and it's a downright shame that lots of good Americana is being lost in the ugly process. Regrettably, old honored customs are gradually becoming irrelevant and obsolete, thanks mostly to modern technology."

"But new traditions are constantly being created to replace the ones that are diminishing into oblivion," feisty Art Orsi challenged. "For instance, Hammonton has recently started a successful blueberry festival in late June that's almost now as big as the mid-July Mt. Carmel Feast. In fact, last year's one-day blueberry shindig drew twenty-five thousand eager visitors!"

"It's too bad that the blueberry harvest season lasts just eight short weeks," Dan Blachford honestly stated. "That's the one local South Jersey crop that I wish lasted all year long. And as we all fully know, Hammonton's moniker is that it's the Blueberry Capital of the World with over eight thousand cultivated acres being farmed to give the town undisputed bragging rights to *that* coveted title."

"Boss, is this why you've really called us into your office?" respectfully interrogated all-too-practical Agent Sal Velardi. "Do you want us to solely think about town carnivals, colossal theme amusement parks, religious processions and the Hammonton Blueberry Festival? I don't believe so! From years of personal past experience, *we* know you much better than that!"

"No Fellas'!" Inspector Giralo candidly admitted as he opened a Manila folder and then meticulously removed its printed paper contents. "Please get out your notepads and your ball-point pens to jot-down some fairly pertinent information I'm going to communicate."

The men immediately obeyed their fearless leader's particular instruction and were now ready to scribble-down vital new-found facts and details. Seeing that his conscientious investigators were alert and listening attentively, Inspector Joe Giralo referred to his hand-held confidential government documents and began speaking in a monotonous drone, his deep voice reading from the printed sheets while occasionally peering-up at his three very competent agents' grim-looking faces.

"Look, Guys. It now seems that illustrious Matt Riley down at Washington headquarters is understandably concerned about a series of boardwalk merchant disappearances up and down the East Coast, the onerous events occurring over the span of the last thirty-five years," the internationally famous esteemed FBI sleuth commenced his official narrative. "Now Men, the latest missing businessman has been definitely identified as Manny Hammerstein, who had owned several very profitable boardwalk gift shops down in Ocean City, Maryland. But unfortunately, Guys, Hammerstein's body was never found, even though he's been gone from his profitable store for two whole weeks now."

"Well, logically, Boss," Sal Velardi courteously interrupted; "if this guy Hammerstein's corpse was never discovered, how does Matt Riley know who the heck the victim was if there's no sign of any dead body? How do we know that Manny Hammerstein just didn't run away from a nagging wife?"

"Good rational question!" Joe Giralo reluctantly commended while still sitting in his very comfortable black leather swivel chair that was positioned directly behind his expensive Canadian oak desk. "First of all Salvatore, the Ocean City Police were completely baffled when Hammerstein's devoted seventy-year-old wife Rebecca frantically declared him missing-in-action. Second of all, Manny Hammerstein's fishing boat was located five miles out in the *Atlantic* with no one aboard. And third and most significantly, traces of Hammerstein's blood had been isolated and gleaned from the abandoned boat's starboard railing. When compared with corresponding evidence obtained from Mr. Hammerstein's medical records," Chief Giralo sanctimoniously summarized, "the correlated DNA boat samples matched perfectly with the victim's past hospital blood tests!"

"Then, can *we* plausibly deduce that the dead man had been killed on board by fairly careless amateur criminals?" surmised and verbally concluded Agent Orsi. "Their non-thorough methods seem to be both awkward and clumsy!"

"Not exactly as elementary as you might think Arty!" Chief Giralo objectively answered. "Apparently, mild-mannered senior citizen Manny Hammerstein's blood stains discovered on his boat's railing were a result of an accidental cut the avid fisherman had received several hours before him being rubbed-out, ironically while the targeted merchant/angler was deep sea fishing."

"Well, Chief. What do *you* suppose actually happened?" Dan Blachford cautiously inquired. "This minor mystery is quickly transforming into to a rather major conundrum!"

"Now quite obviously, someone strongly desired to have Manny Hammerstein's Ocean City, Maryland lucrative boardwalk existence permanently eradicated!" Joe Giralo reasonably determined and orally conveyed to his three-man committee. "I suspect that his well-equipped boat probably had responded to a distress horn signal falsely given by another nearby approaching boat. Then without warning, I theorize that a gang of villainous thugs speedily boarded Mr. Hammerstein's craft and the vile punks probably knocked him out with a blackjack or with some other heavy blunt object. Next, I conjecture that poor Manny was swiftly taken aboard the felons' escape boat, which probably then headed north to the infamous Baltimore Canyon, twenty-miles or so off the Rehoboth Beach, Delaware coast. That infamous deep ocean trench is a common dropping-off point for recently killed murder victims."

"I see!" Sal Velardi suavely exclaimed, nodding his head in absolute concurrence. "No doubt Hammerstein was ruthlessly chained to a huge cement slab and then wickedly thrown overboard, left to sink to the bottom, becoming instant fish fodder! I only hope that the poor man had already been dead before being mercilessly hurled-down to Davy Jones's locker!"

Then erudite Inspector Giralo graphically described three other associated cases of vanishing boardwalk merchants: Isaac Eichberg of Coney Island, New York in 1981, Obadiah Dorfman of Virginia Beach, Virginia in 1992 and Tobin Kessler of Myrtle Beach, South Carolina in 2003. "At first impression Gentlemen, I had erroneously theorized that these other suspected felonies were hate crimes in progress because all four missing victims were shrewd Jewish boardwalk businessmen."

"Well, according to *their* first and last names, aren't they all of Hebrew descent?" Sal Velardi asked with an element of certainty exhibited in his tone of voice. "And incidentally Boss, Coney Island, Virginia Beach and Myrtle Beach are all out of *our* territorial jurisdiction! So why are these other three guys Eichberg, Dorfman and Kessler deserving of *our* scrutiny?"

"Very keen observation indeed, Salvatore!" Chief Giralo promptly congratulated and praised his astute principal disciple. "I imagine that our Manhattan office will professionally examine the Isaac Eichberg Coney Island matter, our Richmond office will intensively study the Obadiah Dorfman Virginia Beach scenario, and I believe that our on-the-ball FBI Charleston office will thoroughly analyze the 2003 disappearance of Mr. Tobin Kessler down in sunny Myrtle Beach, South Carolina!"

"Then, we only have to be involved with helping the Ocean City, Maryland Police unravel the very troubling Manny Hammerstein suspected murder riddle," Art Orsi prematurely decided and declared.

"That special task shouldn't be too difficult for the four of us to systematically evaluate and eventually solve!"

Always vigilant Chief Giralo then again read from his detailed papers and chronologically disclosed to his investigative team that other similar strange boardwalk merchant disappearances had occurred over the course of the last three and a half decades and that the designated victims were not all Jewish by nationality or religion. Inspector Giralo reviewed that in 1994 Zachary Greenspan had vanished from Asbury Park, New Jersey, in 1987 Nabil Al-Karachi and Khalid Al-Razi were reported as missing from the Rehoboth Beach, Delaware boardwalk scene, in 1997 Gabriel Eckstein seemed to have evaporated into thin air from the Wildwood, New Jersey boardwalk oceanfront, in 2008 Phineas Tannenbaum was last seen inside his amusement arcade on the Ocean City, New Jersey board promenade, and finally in 2010 Taziq Anwar and Hussein Zuabi no longer were visible proprietors selling souvenirs and colorful summer apparel inventory inside their Seaside Heights, New Jersey boardwalk tee shirt, merchandise and beachwear emporium.

"This diabolical crime wave now sounds like some weird American extension of the ongoing Israeli-Palestinian West Bank conflict," Dan Blachford ascertained and somewhat sagaciously remarked. "Could this very fascinating development be some sort of Arab-Jew conflict, a terrible Mid-East war of attrition going on, yes, happening right here on American soil? Er, I really meant to say *on American beaches!*"

"That special responsibility is for you three eminent men to genuinely hypothesize and then ultimately prove!" Joe Giralo imperatively communicated to his ambitious government crimefighters. "But it's not simply Arabs versus Jews. In 1983 a Seaside Heights game operator named Robert Ryan had suddenly disappeared from sight, in 2001 a hamburger stand entrepreneur named Jack Thomas rang his Ocean City, Maryland cash register for the final time, and also Men, in 2006 a Wildwood/Cape May popcorn and French fry vendor named Mickey Santora deposited his last daily receipts inside the local beach bank."

"Well then, tell me what's *our* specific official assignments?" indispensable Art Orsi impatiently demanded learning. "I can't stand attempting to cope with too much excessive drama and suspense! Frankly, I prefer peace, harmony and tranquility!"

"Copy-down these relevant details I'm about to relate on your separate notepads!" Inspector Giralo directed his loyal subordinates. "My very capable secretary Sue Johnson has already made your individual two-week room reservations. Now Sal, your vital job is to snoop around the Asbury Park and Seaside Heights boardwalks and if I may add, your' more-than-adequate two-week-long late July accommodations will be at the Aztec Ocean Resort, 901 Boardwalk, Seaside Heights."

Inspector Giralo then drank several ounces of warm coffee from his frequently used desk mug and next proceeded to deliver his additional declarations. "Art, you're to do your typical gumshoe patrols, but this time ambling around on the Ocean City, New Jersey, Wildwood and Cape May boardwalks. I've verified that Mrs. Johnson has gotten you into the Days Inn Motor Lodge, which is not-too-far from the Wildwood Convention Hall where *we* often attend fall oldies rock and roll shows!"

"I know exactly where the place is!" Agent Orsi automatically acknowledged and bellowed. "The Days Inn is at the end of Rio Grande Avenue right near the beach," the excited fellow elaborated. "Yes, Rio Grande is really Route 47 going into Wildwood! It's not too far from the Crusader Motor Lodge where I had taken my family for a week's hiatus just last September."

"And Dan," Inspector Giralo continued his duty roster while deliberately ignoring Agent Orsi's almost-delirious histrionics. "I want you to take the Cape-May-Lewes Ferry from Jersey over to Delaware. The pleasant hour and fifteen-minute bay crossing cuts around sixty miles of driving from the lengthy trip that I'm presently proposing to you, a decent ramble down to Ocean City, Maryland to exclusively work with the town's police detectives on the perplexing Manny Hammerstein case. You have a two-week reservation at the ultra-deluxe Holiday Inn on 64th Street," the highly revered Inspector expounded. "As you're well-aware Dan, I've spent several rather enjoyable family jaunts down to that terrific resort town. I think you'll find the inn's Reflections Restaurant, much to your overall satisfaction, that is, after gorging your hungry stomach with Thrasher's French Fries, Lombardi's Pizza, Alaska Stand hotdogs, Dollie's Popcorn and finally, Bull on the Beach beef sandwiches, all of those wonderful eating establishments situated up on the crowded boardwalk."

"Any more pertinent instructions?" a rather impatient Agent Velardi anxiously asked.

"And last but not least, Men," Joe Giralo characteristically smiled and commanded, "stay away from the angry vacationers who had been effectively bumped-from their original room reservations. Just like we often do with airplane flights," the Chief explained, "prospective airline passengers can become extremely hostile when unexpectedly moved from first class seats into coach. Well, the same phenomenon can happen at an exclusive lodge when unappreciative guests become very belligerent after learning that their two-bedroom suite has been changed into a small single bedroom efficiency without an exotic ocean view!"

"Any other important central items you have to relay to us?" a now-peeved Agent Velardi repeated to his all-too-garrulous immediate superior. "I know from past practice you're not telling us all that you've accumulated in your preliminary research about these tremendously strange boardwalk merchant disappearances. Quite truthfully Boss, sometimes you treat us like we're brainless baby cave mushrooms. You keep us in the dark and then predictably feed us a lot of trivial fecal matter!"

"Well, Salvatore, while you're industriously gathering information on foot patrol over on the Seaside Heights and Asbury Park boardwalks," the wily Philadelphia FBI Inspector reiterated, "don't go meandering over to Manhattan and take the Brooklyn-bound subway out to Coney Island as you had often done with teenage friends in your self-proclaimed glorious youth. I'm pretty cognizant of the fact that you had been enamored with the boardwalk Parachute Ride along with the famous Cyclone wooden roller coaster, both amusement venues still being very much in existence! And I also recall you having a mammoth propensity for consuming those tasty Nathan's hotdogs."

"And what about Dan and me?" Arthur Orsi instinctively asked, realizing that he too would soon be loquaciously admonished.

"Arty, I don't want you hanging-out at Shriver's Candy Store on the Ocean City, New Jersey boardwalk, and when gleaning your background information down in Wildwood, keep your distance from the Mariner's Landing water-slide park and also maintain separation from the rather alluring roller coaster thrill rides operating on the various Morey Piers."

"And what about me?" Dan Blachford asked. "Am I chopped liver, always being treated last?"

"And finally, Dan. I want you to stay focused on your essential two-week-long summer mission and keep *your* distance from the scary Zipper Ride and the notorious Haunted House excursion at Trimper's Amusements on the south end of the Ocean City, Maryland boardwalk, which are, if my memory serves me correctly, both situated near the inlet jetty," omniscient Inspector Joe Giralo uttered with feigned sincerity. "Now Men, in the final analysis, I want the three of you Mike Hammers to be again standing in my office on Wednesday, August 1st at 9 a.m. sharp to comprehensively review everything germane that needs to be explored in regard to this bewildering boardwalk crime spree that's oddly occurred over the years in all of these different states. And also, Dan, don't forget to check-out all possible leads at Rehoboth Beach, too!"

* * * * * * * * * * * *

At 9 a.m. on August 1ˢᵗ dedicated Agents Sal Velardi, Art Orsi and Dan Blachford again stood in FBI Chief Joe Giralo's Arch Street office to enthusiastically deliver their most recent well-documented investigative reports. Their very accomplished mentor was in good spirits as he cordially greeted his team of concerned subordinates.

"As you know Men, detective work is based on the sound principles of the scientific method, an approach that's employed daily by laboratory researchers around the world," Inspector Giralo academically prefaced his standard lecture. "And the great literary master Edgar Allan Poe had imaginatively transferred the idea of the scientific method into the present crime-solving procedure when the genius had creatively authored the first detective stories involving Inspector Auguste Dupin, who had dynamically cracked-open the very difficult cases of 'The Murders in the Rue Morgue' and 'The Purloined Letter', two classic tales that are among my favorites in American literature. Now Salvatore, do you recall the five basic steps associated with the scientific method as noteworthy and applicable to everyday FBI detective work."

"Well, yes, Chief," Agent Velardi confidently replied and then momentarily paused, gathering his recollection. "First there's the act of making a valid observation, which then is followed by the practice of fundamental objective experimentation."

"That analysis is precisely correct!" interrupted the always-alert Boss, casually sitting behind his enormous Canadian oak desk. "Over the course of the past two weeks, you three terrific gumshoes have been dispatched to different boardwalk communities to make observations and to gather pertinent details. That assiduous endeavor certainly covers the first two stages of the scientific method as it pertains to standard police work as accurately outlined and prescribed almost two centuries ago by the inimitable Edgar Allan Poe!"

"And if I fully remember, the third essential step is making a clever hypothesis, the fourth facet is to verify or prove the relevant hypothesis in the form of finding significant clues, perhaps a dead body, maybe fingerprints or perhaps even obtaining a decent confession from a key suspect," Agent Velardi proudly articulated. "And the fifth and final phase of the scientific method of reasoning as it applies to police investigation is making reliable consistent conclusions that are supported by appropriate facts and not by mere assumptions or faulty first impressions. Do I now get a free value meal at Burger King?"

"Excellent presentation, Salvatore!" Joe Giralo complimented his loyal underling. "As you three all-too-diligent workaholics can plainly determine, being *your* immediate supervisor, my involvement with the scientific method is represented in stages three through five while your direct connection is evident in steps one and two!"

"Chief," Art Orsi piped-up, "in all due respect, the fabled Greek Sphinx standing on a mountain cliff outside the city of Thebes, well Boss, that female monster's crazy riddles that she offered to Oedipus actually made more straight sense than your obscure FBI rhetoric does. How come Sal, Dan and I typically know all the facts in a new case but have no definite clues about the genuine motives of the criminals committing the deplorable crimes? It just seems that the hypothesis advantage that you and your DC comrade Matt Riley enjoy over *us* is way too awesome for *me* to ever fathom! In every case study scenario, Sal, Dan and I get to see less than half of the total puzzle! On the other hand, you and your comrade Matt Riley get to view the entire cross-section!"

Inspector Giralo grinned from ear-to-ear like a pleased shark possessing a satisfied appetite and then specifically asked his three agents to describe what they had respectively learned while prowling around the popular Seaside Heights, Wildwood and Ocean City, Maryland boardwalks. Sal Velardi responsively disclosed that likeable merchants Elijah Friedman, Jonas Goldberg and Mohamed Ba' Albaki had *also* been missing from the Seaside Heights Boardwalk since the genesis year 1978 and that Hezikiah Rosen, Malik Wasti and American Fred Kaminski had also vanished over the same thirty-four-year span from the ancient Asbury Park boards.

"Well, *that* diverse last name pattern undeniably demonstrates that the problem's not exclusively Arabs versus Jews," Joe Giralo persuasively stated. "And remember Guys, everyone with the exception of Manny Hammerstein had been reported as a missing person with no indication whatsoever of any murder ever being committed. Now Arty, what's actually happened down there in Wildwood, in Cape May and in Ocean City, New Jersey since 1978, the auspicious year when this entire grotesque kidnapping evolution began developing?"

Agent Orsi declared that boardwalk store-owners having the names Thaddeus Herzog, Solomon Levin, Saul Kaufmann, Jamal bin Haji, Kareem Al Shahrani, Alex Murphy and Joseph Miller had, over the duration of the last thirty-four years, been listed as vanishing from the business world in those three separate-but-popular South Jersey beach municipalities.

"And what wildly inexplicable, clandestine boardwalk activities have simultaneously evolved down in Delaware and Maryland?" Giralo next asked Dan Blachford.

"Well Boss; businessmen Simon Epstein, Ruben Weinberg, Jacob Garfunkel, Rashaad Ta' Anari, Philip Turner and Thomas Spencer had disappeared in Ocean City, Maryland since 1978 and also, Yasser Raboud, Akeem Assad, Efraim Schwartz, Ebenezer Lieberman, Aaron Cohen, John Palmer and Henry Kelly had all mysteriously vanished from Rehoboth Beach in the last quarter century! Exactly what's going on here Chief? What's your esoteric hypothesis? I mean, we've interviewed dozens of fearful and apprehensive acquaintances of the suspected kidnapping victims in three separate states and no one had a remote clue as to what has become of the aforementioned missing merchants!"

"Okay then, you rank amateur Einsteins," Joe Giralo mildly chided and addressed his now-confused apostles. "Missing-in-action boardwalk proprietors have been individually reported to local authorities in Coney Island, in Virginia Beach, in Myrtle Beach, in Asbury Park, in Seaside Heights, in Ocean City, New Jersey, in Wildwood, in Cape May, in Rehoboth Beach, Delaware and finally, in Ocean City Maryland?"

"Boss, we've already established those very elementary, redundant facts!" frustrated Sal Velardi vigorously reminded his highly regarded superior. "Honestly now, you haven't shared with us anything that we didn't already know!"

"Okay then, my fine colleague, Agent Salvatore," Inspector Giralo amiably-but-sarcastically agreed. "Think very hard now using your entire cerebral capacity. Which New Jersey beach resort *hasn't* reported any missing boardwalk proprietors? I'll give you a powerful hint! It was once known as the Queen of Resorts that featured magnificent, elegant boardwalk hotels!"

"Why Atlantic City!" Dan Blachford realized and exuberantly exclaimed. "Yes! Atlantic City! Casino gambling was introduced for the purpose of rejuvenating the aging resort back to its Pre-Depression glory days!"

"Exactly!" the virtually all-knowing Philadelphia FBI Boss confirmed. "And as a noteworthy parallel relationship, that is, coincidentally speaking, casino gambling had become a reality in Atlantic City on May 26th, 1978, the event being a direct result of a New Jersey public referendum conducted on the voting ballot in 1976. Yes Guys, it all came to fruition on *that* marvelous late spring day in

1978. That's precisely the year when Resorts International ushered in the new legal gambling era and opened its posh doors to enthralled table and slot machine bettors. And then in 1983, the three-floor Playboy Casino opened for business and after *that* hasty enterprise ran into overwhelming financial difficulties, the Playboy project was taken over by a new corporate entity and renamed the 'Atlantis', which soon lost its operating license and consequently went belly-up," Inspector Giralo verbally reviewed.

"Is that so?" Agent Orsi challenged. "You're simply describing meaningless past history to us. I mean Boss: Oz really gave nothing to the Tin Man, that he didn't already have!"

"Please allow me to continue," Inspector Giralo suavely declared. "A while later, investment mogul Donald Trump converted the former casino building into a hotel property named 'Trump Regency', but without a viable casino to support it, the doomed Trump Regency enterprise declared bankruptcy in 1985. The Playboy Atlantis-Regency structure was located near the old Boardwalk Convention Hall where the popular Miss America pageants had been originally held. In fact, the old Playboy boardwalk grounds are now owned by a condominium speculator/developer."

"I've attended several big stage concerts at the Boardwalk Convention Hall, the most recent ones being given by Fleetwood Mac and Elton John," Sal Velardi instinctively remarked. "I think Stevie Nicks is the greatest!"

"Anyway, Men," Chief Giralo proceeded with his exposition, paying little attention to Agent Velardi's singular rock music preferences, "other A.C. casinos have gone totally defunct besides the ill-fated Playboy and the also humbled Atlantis. Another venture had been established in 1980, the Sands, formerly the Brighton. That misadventure eventually went the way of the dinosaur, but remarkably, the operation lasted until 1998. The place was recently purchased by the Pinnacle Corporation, but the new Pinnacle Casino Hotel never materialized. So, as you conscientious Men can feasibly determine, success in the highly competitive casino industry is not necessarily guaranteed!"

"But formidable Donald Trump did eventually get good traction in the new Atlantic City casino market," Art Orsi contributed to the mini-conference. "The Donald boldly opened the Trump Plaza and later unveiled the gaudy Taj Mahal up on the north end of the boardwalk, and let's not forget about the Trump Marina constructed near historic Gardner's Basin, over near Brigantine."

"And don't neglect mentioning the classy Borgata over in the Marina District, and let's not fail to include the swanky Revel up on the boardwalk, and let's also throw into the mix the four related sister hotel casinos: Harrahs, the Showboat, Caesar's World and of course, Bally's. And as a footnote Boss," knowledgeable Agent Orsi expanded his loquacious discourse, "the Trump Marina has now morphed into the new elegant Golden Nugget."

"And let's not neglect to mention the Tropicana and the Atlantic City Hilton, formerly known as the 'Grand'," Agent Dan Blachford vociferated. "But Chief, what-on-earth does Atlantic City casino gambling have to do with the disappearance of all these apparently vulnerable boardwalk merchants in other East Coast beach resort towns? It just doesn't add up!"

"That's precisely where *my* modest genius has surreptitiously entered into the complicated mystery equation," Inspector Joe Giralo unabashedly boasted. "And I owe the entire non-sophisticated simple answer to *me* thinking about my wife's second cousin!"

"What!" Agent Velardi vehemently balked. "You gotta' be kidding me! Say what Boss?"

"Yes, Sal; my wife's bad-luck second cousin Mark Martino and two other Hammonton losers in 1977 opened a risky boardwalk amusement arcade at Missouri Avenue and the Atlantic City Boardwalk called Wheel and Deal. Summer arcade addicts would stroll-in and play electronic poker machines and boardwalk wheel games to accumulate coupons and win displayed prizes."

"So, what does this lackluster Wheel and Deal amusement center have to do with all of these inexplicable human disappearances on a plethora of boardwalks along the East Coast?" bewildered Sal Velardi intrepidly protested. "Art's right-on-target with his patented cynicism Boss! You do treat *us* like we're baby cave mushrooms."

"But Salvatore, this rather annoying missing persons' dilemma has truly *mushroomed* into a fantastically colossal kidnapping/murder mystery!" the very venerable Inspector casually insisted. "Think strategically about the general given circumstances. It's all quite elementary, you see. We have an unusual mathematical equation here, a rather peculiar arithmetical formula having *two* lowest common denominators!"

"So far, Chief, *your* completely weird explanation is as clear as Egyptian hieroglyphics, and your obtuse interpretations are about as lucid as Babylonian cuneiform scribbling," distressed Art Orsi strenuously attested. "And for good measure Boss, throw-in an abundant measure of indecipherable Indian Sanskrit too!"

Unfazed Inspector Joe Giralo ignored Agent Arthur Orsi's verbal vernacular and then haughtily resumed his insightful dissertation. "First of all, Men, the missing-in-action boardwalk merchants from

Coney Island down to Myrtle Beach have all disappeared after 1978, the indisputable year that Atlantic City casino gambling went into effect. Secondly and more importantly, I was on the right track when I thought about my wife's second cousin and his two naïve partners losing their business lease when their shrewd profit-oriented landlord sold the entire Missouri Avenue block to Caesar's World! And that's exactly what seriously compelled me to make my extremely astute scientific method theory!"

"Which is?" an irritated florid-faced Dan Blachford angrily asked. "Quite frankly Boss, you've been about as clear as muddy Louisiana bayou swamp water so far this morning!"

Inspector Joe Giralo nonchalantly explained to his impetuous crew that after casino gambling had been officially and legally approved in 1976, entire blocks on the Atlantic City Boardwalk were quickly purchased and effectively gobbled-up by large corporations. And naturally, while in pursuit of once-in-a-lifetime windfall profits, avaricious boardwalk landlords were quickly motivated to terminate leases with former small business owners, who suddenly felt alienated and abandoned, ostensibly needing new places to earn a living. "For instance," Chief Giralo finished, "the 2012 Revel opening caused at least a dozen displaced merchants to actively seek new boardwalk opportunities elsewhere!"

"I now see the merit of your impeccable reasoning," Sal Velardi perceptively acknowledged. "So as a result, the distraught, displaced merchants from Atlantic City needed new frontiers to conduct their various business specialties; new alluring destinations like Seaside Heights and Rehoboth Beach were aggressively pursued. These were new beaches where the evicted boardwalk entrepreneurs from Atlantic City might already have had hard-working family and friends running various amusement arcades, food joints, gift shops, candy emporiums and beach tee shirt stores!"

"Exactly, Fellas', but here's the most salient part *I've* forgotten to present!" a now adamant Joe Giralo deliberately emphasized. "These aggravated, displaced merchants always ran cash businesses where they could skim twenty-five thousand dollars or more each summer from the IRS's scrutiny. Hence, they could approach greedy landlords at other beach resorts, offer them, let's say, a handsome sum of one hundred thousand bucks under the table to successfully evict former tenants, and then as a proposed rental bonus, promise to provide the delighted, compliant landlords an additional twenty-five-thousand-dollar summer surplus payment, which would be over-and-above the past amount that the former merchant/tenant had been paying."

"How could these itinerant former Atlantic City boardwalk businessmen afford to do this?" Arthur Orsi marveled and inquired. "It doesn't seem economically feasible for them to work for practically nothing! I'm no rocket scientist, and I know that!"

"Very profoundly true, Arty!" Inspector Giralo readily concurred. "Boardwalk store summer rentals have traditionally been exceptionally exorbitant, virtually out of sight! Back in 1977 the going rate on major boardwalks was a thousand dollars a front foot. A meager twenty-five-foot frontage meant a hefty twenty-five thousand rental fee. Today, it's on the average two thousand bucks a front foot. Now if a greedy landlord gets an unexpected offer from a displaced Atlantic City boardwalk merchant for three thousand bucks a foot, the in-jeopardy of losing his store merchant might hire a Mafia hit squad to rub-out the eager newcomer for let's say, a handsome hundred grand for a permanent personal elimination expense!"

"Wow!" expressed a very impressed Dan Blachford. "These poor people that own boardwalk businesses probably have to work from Memorial Day to Labor Day just to cover their enormous rental leases, their escalating merchandise expenditures along with their various employees' salaries, not to mention all of the pressure-related taxes and license fees. So Boss, that's why these affected East Coast beach resorts are attempting to extend their seasons from April to November with enticing promotions and attractive spring and autumn festival tourist packages!"

Then Chief Inspector Joe Giralo shocked his already-astounded agents by revealing that just that same early August 1st morning, he and relentless Matt Riley down in DC had brilliantly figured-out the entire "boardwalk killing and murder spree debacle."

"Just two days ago, a former IRS agent came clean," Joe Giralo informed his still-astonished detective trio. "It seems that the IRS revenue guy had a guilty conscience after he had egregiously violated his federal duty in addition to his solemn government oath. It appears that this rogue IRS agent had accepted a large bribe from notorious Mafia affiliate Carmine Campanella, who as you probably know, owns a slew of boardwalk businesses ranging from Seaside Heights down to Ocean City, Maryland. This disreputable punk Campanella had paid the IRS fellow a hundred thousand dollar bribe to go into the amusement arcades of three competitors and harass them with a federal *gaming tax* attached onto their former games of skill, claiming that the electronic poker machines were now games of chance subject to federal gaming laws, that when applied retroactively for a dozen or more years, upon let's say thirty individual machines," Chief Giralo expounded and then resumed, "would amount to a substantial fine of over a hundred thousand bucks plus accumulated back interest and associated penalties, all owed to *our* most excellent benefactor, good old Uncle Sam!"

"And please allow me to guess the rest," Sal Velardi euphorically interrupted his immediate superior. "One of the arcade guys knew about this demonic thug Carmine Campanella doing the dirty behind-the-scene bribe because Campanella's similar boardwalk arcades were not assessed and taxed by the corrupt IRS guy. But what about the killing of Manny Hammerstein off the Ocean City, Maryland shore along with the attendant disappearances of the other legitimate shore merchants up and down the East Coast?"

"Well Salvatore," Chief Giralo answered with a stern expression upon his stoic-looking visage, "one of the overtaxed arcade owners turned State's Evidence and has voluntarily entered into the Witness Protection Program. This brave amusement games' operator knew all about Carmine Campanella being instrumental in rubbing-out Manny Hammerstein and then stupidly leaving the victim's fishing boat adrift in the *Atlantic*. The arcade gentleman's documented testimony indicates on this official transcript I've just received from DC headquarters that Campanella would have his two bodyguard hit men 'rub-out' a predetermined victim for the nominal sum of $150,000.00 per professional hit."

"Holy Hades!" Art Orsi's voice emotionally boomed. "Has this dangerous Mafia-connected boardwalk crook you've identified as Carmine Campanella been arrested?"

"Ha, ha, ha!" indulgently laughed Inspector Giralo. "Yes indeed. Campanella has been taken into custody. The slippery culprit was captured earlier this morning over in Barcelona, Spain trying to reboard the Royal Caribbean Cruise Lines *Voyager of the Sea,* which had been docked in the city's deep harbor. Campanella and his two diabolical henchmen were heading for scheduled vacation tours in Tuscany, in Rome and then along the fabled Amalfi Coast. How magically ironic! This whole exploit has culminated in a weird geographic paradox! Just imagine Men! The Royal Caribbean doing business in the Mediterranean! Ha, ha, ha!"

Agents Salvatore Velardi, Arthur Orsi and Dan Blachford stared at each other incredulously in total astonishment. Finally, the FBI Inspector's main agent gathered the essential wherewithal to utter a summary comment.

"Boss, your keen ability to solve intricate, complex federal crimes is absolutely phenomenal!" Agent Velardi earnestly announced his well-intended kudos. "And just to randomly think, you did it all without ever soliciting the services of your very close Delta Force friend, Colonel Bob Bauers!"

"Not exactly!" Inspector Giralo facetiously answered and then hardily chuckled. "Sorry to terribly disappoint you my dear Salvatore; for you see, quite coincidentally, Colonel Bob Bauers had been attending a rather boring NATO conference over in Barcelona. But then, my loyal friend's unrivaled military expertise had been enlisted and soon swiftly utilized by Interpol, and so Colonel Bauers both coordinated and later assisted in the well-executed arrest of this lunatic narcissistic ingrate Carmine Campanella along with the vile scoundrel's two despicable Mafia hit men, Louie "the Lance" Lanciano and Denny "the Decapitator" DeLareto. And for all of *our* exemplary scientific method expertise Men," the FBI Chief admirably concluded, "I wholeheartedly say, 'Long live the memory of Edgar Allan Poe along with my favorite fictional hero, the magnificent French Inspector, Auguste Dupin'!"

# "Four Tickets to Paradise"

FBI Inspector Joe Giralo impatiently sat behind his solid oak desk inside his eight floor Arch Street office scanning the above-the-fold front-page headlines appearing in the Thursday, June 27th edition of the *Philadelphia Inquirer*. The prominent federal sleuth was wondering why his normally reliable trio of crack agents consisting of Sal Velardi, Arthur Orsi and Dan Blachford had been fifteen minutes late for their' scheduled noon appointment.

Then at fifteen minutes past twelve, the three government men cautiously ambled into the Chief's walnut-paneled office, their guilty heads crestfallen for being tardy a full quarter hour. Demonstrating noteworthy integrity, Agent Sal Velardi promptly volunteered taking full responsibility for the obvious conference delay.

"Boss, I've contracted this miserable sinus congestion and felt it necessary to visit Dr. Nurkiewicz this morning for him to prescribe some antibiotics to alleviate my terribly distressful symptoms," Agent Velardi prefaced his excusable explanation. "And since the three of us daily commute together from downtown Hammonton to 'Philly via the Lindenwold High Speed Train, Arty and Dan were also regrettably detained because I had been feeling ill and listless!"

"And we just missed by two minutes the next train leaving out of the Lindenwold Station," Agent Orsi constructively added to the believable account, "so we had to wait a full half hour for the next one to depart. To tell you the truth Boss, the whole wicked experience was really pretty frustrating!"

"And then there was a ten-minute delay with track maintenance work going on at the Ferry Avenue Station platform over in Camden. Otherwise, Boss," Agent Dan Blachford frankly stated. "We would've only been five minutes late, considering that we still had to walk several crowded blocks from the Eighth and Market Subway Station over here to Arch Street."

Accepting his men's genuine narratives, Chief Giralo smiled, indicating his fond approbation for his three loyal subordinates' general honesty. And as was *their* usual habit, picayune small-talk had to precede the important FBI business at hand.

"Ah yes, Salvatore. You had mentioned Dr. Stephen Nurkiewicz," Chief Giralo recollected and declared before slowly scratching his left ear. "He's a fine family physician, and actually, also a good personal friend of mine. His wife Marian loves horses, so the affable doctor recently purchased quality pastureland five miles west of Hammonton over in Waterford Township, and now my medical friend has seven stallions and four mares to feed, groom and stable. How the energetic fellow is able to accomplish practicing his demanding profession while simultaneously accommodating the needs of a thriving horse farm is rather remarkable indeed."

"Yes, Boss, and this morning during my annual physical examination, I learned that Dr. Nurkiewicz also has a tremendous fascination with Tuscany over there in Italy," Agent Velardi further contributed to the academic dialogue. "All that the guy ever talked about while he took my blood pressure and viewed my irritated throat was Pisa along with its famous Leaning Tower, Siena, Florence, Tuscany's beautiful rolling hills' landscape, and also a majestic medieval town called San Gimi..."

"San Gimignano," Inspector Giralo impressively finished, deftly retrieving the tidbit of knowledge from his brain's extensive memory base. "San Gimignano is known as the Manhattan of Tuscany because of its many medieval towers that remotely resemble modern skyscrapers. I've been to that wonderful hilltop paradise twice and plan to return a third time with Gina and my two daughters. On a good day, you could look-down from above the clouds and see the verdant valley below. It's really a small high-walled town going back to the Middle Ages when wars between city states and various regions were quite commonplace, but if you were to go to San Gimignano today," Joe Giralo informed and emphasized, "it's just like exiting a time machine and being thrust six hundred years into the past. You'd think you were back in the Italian pre-Renaissance days from the archaic appearance of the buildings along with the narrow cobblestone streets."

Growing bored with Chief Giralo's exceptional comprehension of Tuscany and of Dr. Stephen Nurkiewicz's ongoing Waterford Township equestrian enterprise, Agent Arthur Orsi had the profound audacity to ask his scholarly mentor the true purpose for the day's hastily-arranged noon-time meeting. Equally as curious as their courageous partner, Agents Sal Velardi and Dan Blachford stared at their distinguished superior, who was comfortably seated upon his black swivel-chair behind his splendid solid oak desk.

"Well, my lugubrious-looking Disciples, I suppose it's time to get down to brass tacks, so to speak," Chief Giralo admitted before methodically scratching his right ear. "Matt Riley's veteran team down in DC recently intercepted an interesting e-mail that might surreptitiously contain some dastardly terrorist plot elements. On the surface, everything described appears to be quite innocent and fairly innocuous, but I challenge you three relatively competent Fellas' to search for anything suspicious that might be suggesting tricky embedded code language. Now, here are three separate copies of the original e-mail that I've myself comprehensively read at least a half-dozen times. Incidentally dear Gentlemen," Chief Joe Giralo editorialized, "the original letter had been keenly translated from Arabic into standard English by Riley's crackerjack armchair research guys down there in Washington. Please notice that the initial e-mail is dated Monday, June 6th, 2013."

With the dreaded idea of international terrorism in mind, the three astute FBI agents silently read the dispatch's language while their Boss carefully observed the candid expressions that had been exhibited upon their individual faces.

Jamal,

May the spirit of the Prophet bless and keep you! As you well know, I'll be busy touring Italy in July and early August, and I'm spending the first two weeks visiting friends and relatives in Rome, where I'm rather looking forward to marveling at the Trevi Fountain, the Pantheon, the Forum, the Appian Way and the Colosseum. And if I have time dear Jamal, I wish to appreciate seeing the barren grassy site where the Circus Maximus races had once taken place, which is now (I understand) an open field situated next to the massive Colosseum, the present empty land being an oval gravel track showing where the exciting Roman chariot contests had been conducted.

And during those first two weeks, I hope that I might have time to tour Pompeii, Capri, Sorrento and the Amalfi Drive too, down near Naples, the city where wonderful pizza had been invented. My uncle has a motorbike that I can borrow and use to speed from Rome down to Naples and then Pompeii, and I hope I'll arrive there long before sleeping Mt. Vesuvius decides to explode its top again.

And then dear Jamal, I next plan to travel to Florence and enjoy a relaxing week or so there. As you might know, Florence is on the Arno River in the Tuscany Region, and I have a kind cousin living there who has offered me free room and board during my intended stay.

And next on my private itinerary, I'll be zipping-off to scenic Venice to tour the Doge Palace, the Grand Canal, to walk the Rialto and next meander around the resort known as Lido Island. An aunt on my father's side has generously offered to give me lodging and food, so how could I resist or complain about such fantastic Arab hospitality? And as a side trip, if I lose interest in Venice, I might even shoot over to the La Scala Opera House in Milan.

And finally, my dear Jamal, at the designated witching hour on Friday, August 9th, with the benevolent grace of Allah, I hope to meetup with you, Malik and Abdul in Sicily at the same hotel we had stayed when we were mere kids.

And so, Jamal, the four of us will again rendezvous in Sicily early on Friday, August 9th to joyfully reminisce old times and achievements, but especially to honor the serious intentions of the glorious Prophet.

In Allah's Great Name,
Tariq


After closely scrutinizing and attempting to logically interpret and decipher any hidden meanings, the three perplexed agents raised their eyes and peered incredulously at the countenance of their very stellar First-in-Command.

"Now Men, I hate to break some negative news to you but you'll have to abandon your extended Independence Day Holiday by meeting again in this very office at 9 a.m. sharp on Friday, July 5th. I want to review any further meaningful developments that might have occurred in regard to this intercepted e-mail between now and then."

"Any more pertinent instructions to cover, Chief?" a now-rejuvenated Sal Velardi conscientiously asked. "I've always known you to be admirably thorough and efficient."

"Well Sal, yes, I do have several specific elementary assignments to convey," Inspector Giralo judiciously expressed. "I'd like you to study the Rome references that were quite evident in the translated email. And Arty, you're to report on the Florence terminology. And finally, Dan," Joe Giralo continued with his dissemination of definite assignments, "I want you to look into the various Venice allusions. I don't expect you three amateur interrogators to become notorious lexicographers or etymologists overnight, but perhaps one of you three Sam Spade imitators will ingeniously come-up with some amazing viable hypothesis."

"Italy? Isn't *that* domain more CIA territory than an FBI frontier?" Sal Velardi deductively inquired.

"Yes, Salvatore, but some of the obscure nomenclature represented in *that* strange sugarcoated e-mail might incidentally pertain to targeted locations existing right here in the good old USA," Chief Giralo sagely clarified. "When dealing with repugnant, unscrupulous anonymous jihadists, we have to stay at least three paces ahead of them or otherwise risk putting ourselves or our unwary patriotic citizens into life-or-death jeopardy!"

* * * * * * * * * * * *

At 9 a.m. on Friday, July 5th Inspector Joe Giralo was deeply immersed in introspective thought when his perceptive eyes recognized the entrance of his three loyal agents into his all-too-familiar Arch Street office. As usual, a copy of the *Philadelphia Inquirer's* early morning edition had been spread-open upon the motivated Chief's enormous oakwood desk.

"Let's cut right to the chase Fellas'," the FBI official imperatively declared. "I think that we're gradually latching onto something huge and bizarre in terms of potential consequences. It's a  a rather grave matter that requires our full attention and utmost scrutiny. Now Sal, without you being too sanctimonious or professorial, what cursory details have you diligently learned, or should I say, 'discovered', about the Eternal City, Rome?"

"You know, Chief. I regret relating that my intensive research could only glean the regular commonplace stuff," Agent Velardi reluctantly admitted. "In every Internet website I had the opportunity to explore, the Circus Maximus had been the scene of thrilling chariot races explicitly held for the amusement of Rome's citizens back then, and the chariot race scene in the classic movie *Ben Hur* was actually based on the dimensions of the Roman Circus Maximus, even though *that* fictional contest between benevolent Ben Hur and the dastardly Messala depicted in the 1955 film was happening in Antioch, which was a part of the former Persian Empire."

"Well, Sal, what about the Pantheon and the Forum?" Inspector Giralo replied without a moment's hesitation. "What did you dig-up about those special sightseeing traps?"

"The magnificent Pantheon is a large mostly circular structure and it's probably the only building from the halcyon days of the Roman Empire whose architecture remains virtually intact and not in partial ruins. It originally was the Empire's official temple to all of the Roman gods like Jupiter, Mars, Neptune and Mercury, but now the splendid edifice is also a functioning Catholic church, even though the marble statues of the pagan Roman gods still stand inside."

"Isn't there something rather unique about the Pantheon's ceiling?" Agent Art Orsi chimed-in. "If my faulty memory serves me correctly, I think there's a giant hole in the center, allowing amounts of rainwater to drop inside."

"You're absolutely right Art, and your faulty memory has been temporarily exonerated," Agent Velardi politely-but-satirically answered. "The fresh rainwater falls through the ornate ceiling down upon the marble slates and then flows into holes bored into the floor and finally cascades down to a cistern below. And the ceiling itself is an engineering masterpiece because it's several feet in thickness at the bottom of the dome and then narrows-down to only inches wide towards the top. If not intelligently designed in such a mathematical fashion," Salvatore Velardi seriously stressed, "then the entire roof would collapse from too much weight!"

"Very fascinating and intriguing description indeed," Inspector Giralo commended, "but still Sal, your generic report has nothing to do with a suspected terror crime being cunningly planned or perhaps being boldly perpetrated. Now Gentlemen, I had neglected to mention to you that Gina and I have often stayed at the Visconti Palace on four distinct visits to Rome, the stellar hotel being conveniently located only several blocks from the Tiber River. Now Sal, please resume your almost irrelevant academic presentation. I'll persevere and listen to your unsophisticated drivel only because, as you know, I value minuscule trivia almost as much as I place a high premium on macro-management strategies!"

Next, momentarily befuddled Agent Velardi proceeded to explain to his audience of three that the ancient Forum had been the principal marketplace where citizens gathered to watch military parades to commemorate major triumphs and conquests and that the Forum also had many small temples for worshiping purposes, and in addition, the historic area had been the location of the Roman Senate where Julius Caesar had been savagely assassinated by Brutus and *his* political colleagues. "And by the Appian Way, Guys," Agent Velardi awkwardly joked, "the historic road was..."

"The first important cobblestone highway south of Rome where the proud legions ostentatiously and victoriously marched into the city," Inspector Giralo vociferated, showing a rare degree of petulance and intolerance in his strong tone of voice. "And naturally Sal, the Colosseum obviously had been the site of brutal gladiator fights to the death along with Nero mercilessly having early Christians confronted and attacked by vicious hungry lions. And if you carefully examine the characteristic bricks appearing inside the wall facades of the Colosseum and inside other Roman constructions like the aqueducts, for example," the Boss impressively elaborated, "the bricks utilized back then are a little longer and about half as wide as the ones we use today, and those same building blocks employed by the Roman legions became the architectural standard for arches and for large buildings erected throughout the entire Empire!"

"Gee Boss! You know just as much about Italy as Dr. Stephen Nurkiewicz does!" Agent Velardi facetiously praised his esteemed colleague, much to the Chief's ever-mounting chagrin. "No wonder why you two bookworms are close buddies!"

After a moment of strained silence, Inspector Giralo gradually diminished the excessive frown fixed upon his visage, and soon the FBI guru requested that Agent Arthur Orsi expound upon what basic information *he* had assiduously gathered about the cultural capital of Italy, Florence.

"Well, Boss, Florence is situated on the Arno River, and the city's regarded as the political capital of Tuscany," Orsi gingerly commented. "A very famous colossal-sized church with an orange-tiled rounded dome is obviously called the Duomo, and Florentine art abounds everywhere, along with Michelangelo statues including the fifteen-foot-tall *David* that's on exhibit there in a museum called the, I have it here in my notes," Agent Orsi indicated, anxiously fumbling through several typed sheets, "yes, the museum is called the..."

The Inspector prided himself on trumping his subordinates at every possible opportunity. "The Degli Uffizi is only several short blocks from the medieval Ponte Vecchio, a truly archaic 'old bridge' crossing the Arno River, the exquisite span having retail shops and several stories of homes situated across its entire breadth. The Degli Uffizi and the Ponte Vecchio are landmark attractions for the burgeoning Florentine tourist trade," Joe Giralo aptly lectured. "In fact, Arty, my wife has frequently shopped for incomparable leather goods and apparel at the Misuri Boutique in beautiful Santa Croce Piazza, the square situated midway between the enormous Duomo and the Hotel Mediterraneo where we had been staying."

The three dumbfounded agents stood still as marble pillars with their mouths agape, entirely overwhelmed with their erudite Boss's comprehensive acquaintance with the emblematic intricacies of both Rome and Florence. After a tense moment featuring complete quiet, the on-a-mission FBI leader insisted that Agent Dan Blachford reveal his accumulative data about picturesque Venice.

"Well, Inspector, the extraordinary Doge Palace in St. Mark's Square is an absolute must see for eager tourists, and of course, the Doge was the all-powerful Duke of Venice," Blachford cautiously disclosed. "And if you walk beneath the mammoth arch in St. Mark's Square, the one with the large overhead blueish-tinted clock, the path leads directly to a series of maze-like slate-laden alleys with dozens-upon-dozens of swanky retail shops, the intertwining trails zigzagging all the way to the Rialto, which is....”

“About a mile and a half phenomenal stroll from St. Mark’s Square to the Rialto Pier where water taxis transport visitors to their various hotel destinations,” Chief Giralo adroitly finished Dan Blachford’s statement. “Gina and I have trekked the labyrinth of slate alleys from the Doge Palace and the tall bell-tower known as the Campanile all the way to the Rialto Pier, and if it weren't for certain sign shingles with arrows reading ‘Rialto Pier’ tacked onto various buildings at critical intersections, a visitor could spend hours trying to find his or her way out of the series of bewildering connecting alley-ways. Incidentally,” Giralo personally informed, “my wife and I have stayed at the Hotel Bellini on the Grand Canal on three separate occasions, and truthfully, we positively loved Venice for its lack of cars, trucks and motorbikes polluting the atmosphere. Mobility is primarily done by passenger water taxi transportation and by gondolas!”

After Agent Blachford next monotonously spoke about the Lido Island resort and about the world-famous Murano Glass Factory, Chief Joe Giralo expressed that it was finally time for him to exercise his inimitable detective skills. The distinguished Department Head then read an excerpt from that morning’s edition of the *Philadelphia Inquirer,* the brief recitation being very deliberately delivered in order to give his dedicated proteges a vital clue that would help them more easily unravel the sinister criminal/terrorist mystery currently being meticulously investigated by the FBI’s Washington Bureau.

“Fellas’, it describes in this inconspicuous Page 47 news article that the Trevi Cinema near Rome's famed Trevi Fountain had experienced a minor bomb detonation just yesterday, July 4th, *our* Independence Day. Fortunately, no one in the vicinity had been killed or injured in the small theater explosion.”

“What does the theater explosion have to do with the simple e-mail letter that DC had intercepted?” Sal Velardi impetuously asked. “Oh, now I get it! The Trevi Fountain had been cited in the seemingly commonplace e-mail along with Rome’s Circus Maximus, the Pantheon, the Forum, the Colosseum and the Appian Way!”

“Exactly, Salvatore!” confirmed and verified Joe Giralo. “When I was a kid, my parents often visited relatives in Baltimore. My cousins and I once saw that movie *Ben Hur* at the *Hippodrome Theater* on BelAir Road, and for argument’s sake, a Hippodrome is another name for a type-of Circus Maximus. Therefore Men,” Giralo quite methodically prattled-on, “I maintain that any theater or venue bearing the appellation Circus, Hippodrome, Forum, Appian Way,

Pantheon or Colosseum as part of its business name is *now* vulnerable to subsequent terrorist bomb attacks that could be much more potent than the minor one that went-off yesterday at the Trevi Cinema."

"That means that anything with 'Palace' in its name like Caesar's Palace in Las Vegas or the Emperors' Ancient Palace ruins in Rome might also be possible terrorist targets!" Agent Velardi marveled and exclaimed. "But tell me Boss, without verbally eviscerating or excoriating me in my kind friends' presence, what about the Pantheon and the Appian Way?"

"Well, Sal; I want you to understand that I've now delved pretty deeply into this whole complicated matter," the Boss artfully divulged to his now-incredulous listening trio. "The Pantheon was once a three-thousand-seat movie theater in Detroit that had been demolished back in 1962, but there are many soft-target venues around the world bearing the name 'Pantheon'. And as far as the Colosseum is concerned," Giralo rationally continued with his rather creative exposition, "numerous auditoriums around the world have *that* particular popular designation on their' marquees. And there's even a spectacular Appian Way entertainment center in Lexington, Kentucky too! Now naturally Fellas', the FBI can't possibly protect the myriad 'name scenarios' that have been imaginatively alluded to and identified in the acquired e-mail, all of which might be subjected to dangerous terrorist activity!"

And then Agent Orsi realized and orally shared that the names Florentine, Tuscany and Arno were theater venues *he* had been familiar with in his non-sensational youth. And next, Agent Dan Blachford contributed that the representations Palace, Rialto, Lido and the Grand (Canal) were common names often chosen for assorted American movie theaters and arenas. The intensified discussion was more-than-adequately summarized by certain additional impeccable comments originating from the lips of the 'Philly team's extremely capable leader, the knowledgeable Chief Inspector.

"And Guys," Joe Giralo expounded. "Let's not forget including other theater titles like the Pompeii, Capri, Amalfi, Sorrento and last-but-not-least, the La Scala. I mean, according to my research, there's even a well-patronized La Scala movie theater in Bangkok, Thailand!"

"But Boss," a now totally addled Agent Velardi impulsively interrupted, "other than the minor explosion yesterday at the Trevi Cinema, how do you know that the intercepted e-mail is genuine jihadist chatter? It might be a diversionary ruse or canard?"

"Well, Sal," Joe Giralo answered rather dramatically. "Anyone who goes to Rome would first want to visit the Vatican and the nearby Vatican Museum, wouldn't they? And furthermore Arty," the FBI Chieftain eloquently pontificated. "Anyone touring Florence would naturally desire visiting and later stating in a personal e-mail all about the fabulous Duomo and the very excellent Santa Croce Church too, wouldn't they?"

And before anyone listening could ever render an oral response, the Boss then extended his very lucid narrative. "And also, Dan, the intercepted and translated e-mail fails to mention St. Mark's Square and St. Mark's Cathedral in Venice! Why?" the determined speaker rhetorically asked. "Because jihadists are still conducting an ongoing crusade against Christianity and also against Western Civilization a full seven hundred years after the fact, that's precisely why! There are over a billion Muslims in the world, and if only one percent are militant radicals, then that's over ten million of them putting Western Civilization in jeopardy, not counting the millions and millions of volatile sympathizers in *their* midst!"

After a lengthy interval of four-way mutual contemplation, an emotionally beleaguered Agent Velardi felt compelled to ask a rather necessary question, which he nervously addressed to his FBI superior. "When do you suppose the next attack will occur?"

"I believe that the July 4th Trevi Cinema incident had been deliberately designed to be a minor explosion, a sort of Page 47 news story that would be a definite signal for individual terror cells around the world to be ready for upcoming planned violent action! But now, I think that we still have until August 8th to tediously figure-out and remedy this rather difficult conundrum, and we must use *that* essential month-long time-span to adequately protect our vulnerable American citizens from imminent harm!"

"How can you be so confident that nothing significant will be developing between now and August 8th?" Agent Blachford skeptically wanted to know. "That part of your strange theory seems mostly illogical to me!"

"Because Dan; the Muslims blessed Ramadan occurs on the ninth month of the Islamic Lunar Calendar where devout Arabs all over the world abstain from food, drink and physical pleasures during the daylight hours. During Ramadan, Muslims must practice self-sacrifice, and they generally do not engage in random acts of aggression while being individually penitent," Chief Joe Giralo convincingly maintained. "And this year being 2013, Ramadan will be celebrated between Monday, July 8th and Wednesday, August 7th. That's the basic reason why I've hypothesized that we're probably safe until August 8th."

"And the Trevi Cinema small bomb blast is reported as a trivial event in the newspapers today, Friday, July 5th, just three days before the commencement of Holy Ramadan!" a now-enlightened Agent Arthur Orsi fathomed. "There's much merit in your fantastic theory Boss, and it's no longer totally incredible conjecture! We have a full month to successfully identify and thwart these nefarious, diabolical instigators, whoever and wherever they may be!" Orsi concurred. "I too now believe that the Trevi Cinema occurrence was a mere test, or perhaps a tacit signal devised to activate dormant terror cells mendaciously networked around the world, the evil scheme having the sadistic intention of destroying soft venues like the targeted entertainment facilities with familiar names like Rialto, Lido and Colosseum! But why?"

"Because militant conservative Muslims absolutely loathe the entertainment industry," authoritatively replied Inspector Joe Giralo. "Arab terrorists think that American and European movies display things that *their* narrow-minded religious beliefs regard as being reprehensible and evil: sex, alcohol, women's liberation and finally, an excess of freedom!"

"Wow, Inspector!" Sal Velardi exuberantly complimented. "Honestly now, my sensitive brain's about to explode from it absorbing too much overloaded information! Listening to you is worse than hearing Dr. Stephen Nurkiewicz relentlessly articulating about Tuscany!"

"Now Men, we'll meet again on Thursday, August 8th in my office at noon," grim-faced Chief Joe Giralo very seriously and sternly communicated while totally ignoring Agent Velardi's heartfelt-but-unsolicited testimony. "By then Fellas', I'm quite optimistic that Matt Riley and I should have this knotted terrorist mess entirely analyzed, resolved and permanently eradicated! Until then, go about exploring your regular FBI cases."

"Any final instructions before we leave, Boss?" Agent Velardi curiously asked. "My already damaged cerebrum can only tolerate approximately one more devastating paragraph!"

"Yes, Salvatore!" Joe Giralo confidently replied. "I want you three well-trained geniuses to do some preliminary Greek mythology background checks into the topics of Scylla and Charybdis, Circe on the Island of Calypso. And finally, obtain some rudimentary knowledge on the minor Olympian god Prometheus, who incidentally was one of the deposed Titans, just like doomed Atlas was!"

The three pallid-faced recipients of the rather peculiar instructions stared blankly at each other, raised their eyebrows in mutual astonishment, and then slowly exited the walnut-paneled 8<sup>th</sup> floor FBI office in single file.

* * * * * * * * * * * *

Noontime on Thursday, August 8th had eventually arrived on the 2013 calendar, the anticipated date signifying that Ramadan had been concluded and fortunately for the Federal Bureau of Investigation, no major national or international catastrophes had occurred in the interim. Inspector Joe Giralo routinely folded and placed his copy of the *Philadelphia Inquirer* upon his oak desk and the wily sleuth shrewdly peered at his three somewhat-bewildered agents.

"Well, Sal, have you found-out anything noteworthy concerning the dual dangers of Scylla and Charybdis?" Giralo asked with evident concern. "It's terribly paramount and crucial to the conclusion of this jihadist terror ring investigation. And please Sal, there's a clear difference between being trite and being contrite."

"Yes, Boss. In Homer's epic poem the *Odyssey,* the legendary hero Odysseus had to navigate his ship nearer to Scylla, a horrible carnivorous monster who stood on a rocky cliff and feasted on several of the ancient sailors trying to vigorously row through the narrow channel, the gruesome deed being implemented after the lawless creature reached-down and mercilessly plucked the few frightened mariners from their sitting positions. The reason that the boat had been sailing that close to Scylla was because of the existence on the opposite side of the strait of Charybdis, a giant maelstrom that would swiftly and easily suck the entire ship and crew down to the bottom of the narrow channel."

"And so, Sal; in our English vernacular, the cliché, or should I say 'the idiomatic expression' 'to go between Scylla and Charybdis' actually means to choose the lesser of two lethal killers, or between two deadly evils, and in Odysseus's perilous circumstance," the much 'lesser' danger was the dreadful human-eating monster, Scylla."

Then the inspired Inspector's focus instantly switched to Arthur Orsi, the Boss's primary purpose being to quiz the conscientious agent on the mythological character Circe. Much to the Chief's satisfaction, the new-found mythology student was well-prepared to accurately answer his teacher's entreaties.

"Well, Supreme Investigator, again in Homer's *Odyssey*," Agent Orsi began his prepared response, "Circe lived on an island somewhere in the Mediterranean or Ionian Sea that's identified simply as Calypso. The deceitful goddess was in reality a heinous *witch* who coyly offered Odysseus the gift of immortality, but only if

138

he were to abandon his crew and live with her forever on Calypso. Odysseus valiantly refused the gorgeous witch's tempting proposition, so to keep the itinerant Greek king stationary on the island with her, the enticing Circe then wickedly transformed his crewmen into squealing pigs."

"Very good assessment!" Inspector Giralo promptly commended, giving Agent Orsi a sarcastic mock applause. "And now courteously inform me Agent Blachford. What about the minor Greek god Prometheus? How did he lose being regarded as being fully accepted by Zeus and the other Olympians!"

"According to what specific mythology passages I had read," Dan Blachford diplomatically answered, "the Titans had ruled Heaven and Earth in the beginning of time. Then there was a wild rebellion led by Zeus, and soon the Olympians overthrew the yoke of the Titans and banished each of them to different hideous places, some of the deposed giants being assigned to perform very repetitious tasks. For example, the Titan known as Atlas had to hold the heavy sky on his shoulders to keep it permanently separated from the Earth for all eternity."

"Magnificent!" congratulated Inspector Giralo with an element of cynicism drenching his gravelly inflection. "And Dan, was the minor god Prometheus immediately banished from grace just like sentenced Atlas had been?"

"Not exactly!" Blachford reflexively replied. "The Titan had been a favorite of the Olympians and was allowed to live on top of Mt. Olympus with Zeus and *his* divine family. But then Prometheus felt sorry for mankind and compassionately taught humans how to make and control fire. Since the art of fire-making was a precious secret of the gods," the FBI agent verbally indicated, "Prometheus had obviously committed an unforgivable taboo. As a draconian-type punishment, vindictive Zeus had the noble Prometheus chained to the summit of volcanic Mt. Etna, which as we all know, is in Sicily near the coast. Every morning a huge eagle would land on Prometheus's chest and the famished vulture would voraciously peck-away at Prometheus's pure heart."

Sal Velardi was growing increasingly aggravated with the abundance of remote encyclopedia information being reviewed and the flustered agent then bravely demanded knowing why Scylla and Charybdis, Circe and Prometheus were so weirdly connected to an ongoing 2013 FBI terror plot investigation. Inspector Giralo was more-than-willing to oblige his restive questioner and quickly commenced thoroughly explaining the integral rudiments of the combination FBI/CIA international probe.

"First of all, Men; we aren't dealing with a bunch of Arab weasels or pinheads here. We're involved with ruthless, repulsive, pernicious and fanatical scumbag vermin. Now Guys, the coded e-mail we've all read countless times stated that entertainment places like a Colosseum, a Rialto, an Arno Theater, a Lido Cinema and a Forum Arena might soon become designated terrorist bombing targets. But after studying the letter's content again and again," Giralo esoterically revealed, "during my investigation I've managed to uncover another vital clue in the e-mail that's fundamentally cracked this totally bizarre case wide open."

"And exactly what enigmatic clue was that?" Agent Orsi wondered and asked. "I mean Boss, we've all read the seemingly harmless e-mail document dozens of times!"

"The sly e-mail author Tariq had informed his comrade Jamal that the pair would meet-up with Malik and Abdul at the 'witching hour' on August 8th in Sicily. Don't you Men see the grave veracity cunningly disguised in those particular words? Thank goodness I was forced to read the *Odyssey* for an oral book report when I had been an ordinary, nondescript junior attending Hammonton High School," Joe Giralo disclosed. "Just as you had academically shared Arty, in Greek Mythology Circe had been a lonely goddess/witch living on the Island of Calypso. And the giant maelstrom known as Charybdis and the voracious hill creature known as Scylla were reputed in ancient times to be geographically situated between the boot of Italy and the island of Sicily, where large sea whirlpools are still known to occur today. And the Titan Prometheus was believed to be shackled to the top of Mt. Etna, a huge volcanic mountain located near Taormina, which is often referred to in modern times as the 'Riviera of Sicily'."

Heightened consternation still governed the baffled minds of the three listening agents. Then intrigued Salvatore Velardi garnished sufficient audacity to further inquire into the Chief Inspector's ever-challenging mental riddle. Joe Giralo then completely unraveled the entire "easy-to-fathom" scenario.

"Now Men; I've had the pleasure of vacationing at the Hotel Villa Schuler with my wife and daughters several times in semi-tropical Taormina, Sicily. And consequently, I'm quite familiar with the general area. There's a Greek amphitheater still intact there, surviving from ancient times, and the brazen terrorists may have been egregiously plotting to eliminate some unsuspecting tourists at the treasured amphitheater site should we, that is, the FBI and the CIA, had not directly intervened into *their* devious plan."

"What does them staying at an exotic Sicilian hotel several years ago have to do with us solving this totally complex e-mail message and then with the FBI systematically capturing and next taking the principal malicious characters to justice?" inquisitive Agent Orsi demanded. "And please Boss, kindly cease being so darned vague, nebulous elusive and evasive!"

"Okay, Arty," chuckled the now good-humored Chief. "Thirty-three granite steps up from the elegant Hotel Villa Schuler is Umberto Street, a narrow-slated lane having a variety of gelati, fancy pastry and various pizza establishments, along with some ritzy and exclusive clothing emporiums. In addition, there are some cheap souvenir stores with overpriced merchandise mixed-in, too. Anyway Men, in the center of the ever-crowded Umberto Street pedestrian walk is the classic Hotel Circe, and that's precisely where I reckoned the four radicalized Arabs would be staying before initiating their terror cell havoc all over the world. I suspected that their devious rendezvous would be happening just after the termination of Ramadan."

"Truly amazing and astounding!" Dan Blachford exclaimed. "Boss, you're as smart as Eliot Ness and J. Edgar Hoover put together. I'll never again question or defy your supreme sagacity!"

Not being quite as enamored with the Chief Inspector's enviable acumen as his two comrades had been, Sal Velardi begged for additional clarification. "But Joe, er, I mean Inspector, how can we apprehend these four adamant terrorists and skillfully catch the vile villains in the act?"

"Don't worry or panic, Sal. That's already been achieved and taken care of, thanks to the collaboration of Matt Riley, the CIA, the Mafia and the U.S. Government, along with the always-dependable aid of Uncle Sam's wonderfully-generous taxpayers."

"Could you kindly elaborate on *that* sophomoric commentary before I need to swallow-down a dozen heavy-duty aspirins?" Art Orsi stubbornly insisted. "My expanding headache feels like it's now becoming watermelon-sized!"

Joe Giralo then related to his overzealous disciples that a good percentage of the Italian population of the town of Hammonton, New Jersey had originated from three mountain villages not far from the cities of Messina and Taormina, the singular places being Gesso, Serro and Calvaruso, the site of a famous Catholic Church shrine, Ecce Homo. "My grandfather originated from Calvaruso, Sicily and...."

"My ancestors came from Gesso," Sal Velardi recalled and enthusiastically interrupted. "But how do the Mafia and the U.S. Government along with its overburdened taxpayers get included as factors in *your* oddball equation?"

Inspector Joe Giralo cleared his raspy-voiced throat and then step-by-step explained that numerous Mafia families also live in the Hammonton-Vineland-Philadelphia geographic triangle and that ironically, they are often genetically related to ordinary Sicilian clans living in those exact same three U.S. East Coast areas. But the Boss's forthcoming concluding remarks were so outrageous that their mere utterance almost completely floored his three already-shocked underlings.

"The Arabs have a saying: 'The enemy of my enemy is my friend!' Well, Men, I was forced to choose between Scylla and Charybdis, and naturally, I chose the lesser of the two evils, the Mafia over the Arab terrorists. Under my calculated advice and persuasion, the FBI then agreed to team-up with local American and also certain Sicilian Mafia dons and make the despicable terrorists the ruthless mob's main adversary. The Hammonton thugs knew the Cosa Nostra goons over in 'Philly, who then soon contacted their bloodthirsty greedy counterparts over in Palermo, Sicily. Needing American cash," Chief Giralo coyly continued, "the Palermo hit-men quickly hired a huge helicopter, had their men stay at the Hotel Circe on Umberto Street, immediately kidnapped Jamal, Tariq, Malik and Abdul and then coincidentally, just when Mt. Etna was violently erupting, *our* hired Sicilian Mafia helpers tied the four hostages up and flew the nasty villains directly over the active volcano. The screaming terrorist creeps were then individually tossed alive into the center of the boiling lava pit, their naked bodies probably vaporizing in mere seconds. No expensive trial, no costly prison time, and no relentless, extravagant Justice Department court appeals for us to worry about, either."

"Holy smokes!" Sal Velardi inadvertently hollered in utter exhilaration. "And what did the fantastic operation cost in terms of dollars and cents?"

"Well, it seems that much of the Hammonton, Vineland and 'Philly Mafia families had immigrated to the USA in the early 1900s from the now-impoverished Sicilian towns of Gesso, Serro and Calvaruso, just like *our* indigent ancestors had. So as a special favor to the Sicilian Mafia for their indispensable services as demonstrated in this truly exceptional case," Chief Giralo informatively expressed, "five million bucks was immediately wired to the very efficient Palermo thugs while coincidentally, thirty million greenbacks would be shared and equally distributed to rehabilitate the dilapidated, decaying infrastructures of Gesso, Serro and Calvaruso, whose water and sewer systems are in dire need of repair and renewal, and whose streets and municipal buildings urgently require renovation!"

142

"And Jimmy Hoffa's body will be discovered long before anyone ever finds a trace of Tariq, Jamal, Abdul and Malik," comprehended and uttered Agent Velardi. "But Boss, please tell me, what about the network of until-now dormant terror cells that are still actively operating out there?"

"The hired Mafia guys beat the living-daylights out of the four captives before climbing aboard the massive rented helicopter, and the abused Arab punks eventually coughed-up the names of all of their contacts in the U.S. and in Europe. Other associated names have been carefully obtained from the four creeps recently confiscated laptop computers, and multiple search warrant arrests are currently being implemented all over the globe as I speak."

"Is there anything else of significance remaining to this incredibly exceptional tale, Boss?" Agent Dan Blachford curiously asked. "Your staggering revelations have made me pretty hungry, and I could swallow-down a few delicious cheeseburgers along with a large cold *Coke* right now without ever feeling any nagging guilt whatsoever!"

Inspector Joe Giralo adroitly ignored Agent Dan Blachford's meaningless prattle. "Say Fellas', did you Guys know that the word 'volcano' is actually derived from the Roman god Vulcan, the fearsome deity who had been assigned by Jupiter (Zeus) to chain poor Prometheus to the top of snow-clad Mt. Etna? And just remember Men," Chief Giralo finished his summary with a very apparent eyewink, "it was the avaricious *witch* Circe who had instructed Odysseus that he had to sail his ravaged warship between the formidable obstacles of Scylla and Charybdis in order to return to his wife and son on the Greek island of Ithaca!"

"Until now," Agent Velardi answered in a semi-defiant voice, "I neither knew nor cared one iota about either Greek or Roman Mythology! Now Mighty Inspector, because of your strong influence, I most surely intend to read as much as I possibly can on the wholly fascinating subject!"

"Chief, sometimes I think you're psychic the way you almost miraculously come-up with what seems to be preposterous solutions to fantastically challenging problems!" Agent Orsi decided and praised. "Are you clairvoyant, or what?"

"What on the surface seems to be astounding psychic ability is really the capacity for me to conscientiously cobble-together seemingly unrelated facts into what results in an acceptable and workable method of plausible resolution," Inspector Joe Giralo brilliantly remarked. "That's about the best that I can express to you Guys the whole 'ordinary' theory-development process that to *you* initially seems 'extraordinary'! Each isolated fact is a separate dot, and I somehow just have a certain uncanny knack which enables me to skillfully connect the formerly unrelated dots."

"Well, anyway Chief," inspired Sal Velardi uttered with a broad grin, "Tariq, Jamal, Abdul and Malik have gotten themselves four quick tickets to Paradise. Say Boss. Was your close friend Colonel Bob Bauers of Delta Force involved in supervising the imaginative-and-expensive Mt. Etna terrorist disposal caper?"

Verbose Inspector Joe Giralo demonstratively snickered. Then the master detective casually shook his bald head and next overtly laughed to fully exhibit his spontaneous high spirits. "No Salvatore. Actually, and ironically, *my* good pal Colonel Bob is in Hammonton today playing golf at Frog Rock Country Club with *our* very good mutual friend, Dr. Stephen Nurkiewicz!"

# "Texas High Noon"

The three and a half-hour Continental Airlines flight from Philadelphia, Pennsylvania to Houston, Texas was quite smooth and comfortable, and then the secondary briefer air excursion via the same airlines from Houston down to Brownsville was quite pleasurable despite the general fatigue experienced by the four traveling FBI companions. The entourage was en route to an October week-long federal crime prevention conference at the South Padre Island Convention Centre Hall.

After renting a white *Ford Expedition* at the diminutive Brownsville Texas Airport, the four government agents were soon motoring the twenty-five miles north along the Gulf Coast from Brownsville up to semitropical South Padre Island. Non-business "shop conversation" merrily ensued and abundantly flourished between the combination driver/team captain, Inspector Joe Giralo and his trio of very capable law enforcement subordinates, FBI Agents Salvatore Velardi, Arthur Orsi and Dan Blachford. The latter pair had been occupying the deluxe SUV's spacious back seat.

"It's a good thing I had the foresight to reserve this large *Ford Expedition* from AVIS a week ago," Inspector Giralo loudly opined. "It was the only SUV available from the AVIS lot back at the tiny Brownsville Airport."

"Check-out all of the oil refineries and oil rig repair facilities along this Texas coastal highway," Agent Sal Velardi commented. "I never imagined that those ocean-worthy oil rigs were so gigantic up close. I suppose that everything requires some maintenance and repair, even these huge monstrous oil drilling platforms."

"This highway is low-lying and must flood-out occasionally," Agent Art Orsi observed and stated from the rear. "Say Guys, just listen to the names of some of these parallel streets in South Padre: Retama, Mesquite, Acapulco, Campeche and Esperanza. Sounds like a definite Mexican influence to me. And according to this map I'm holding," Agent Orsi expounded, "the island has three major north south highways: Laguna Boulevard on the bay side, Padre Boulevard up the island center and then Gulf Boulevard situated closest to the alluring Gulf of Mexico."

"I'm more interested in good restaurants serving delectable food dishes than in commonplace street names," Agent Dan Blachford contributed to the casual ongoing four-way dialogue. "According to this informative local cuisine guide, Ted's Restaurant at 5717 Padre Boulevard has tremendous breakfast meals. And then there's other unique eateries such as Louie's Backyard located on the bay, the Sea Ranch Restaurant to be found at the southern tip of the island, Scampi's, Amberjacks and Blackbeards towards the middle of the island, and if we really want some simply scrumptious Italian food," Blachford characteristically embellished, "we can always cross over the causeway to Port Isabel and gobble-down some tasty pasta at either Gabriella's or Marcello's! I gotta' add that this terrific eatery selection must also include the attractive restaurants inside the Pearl, the accommodating hotel where we"ll be staying when not attending the various Convention Hall conference sessions."

"And if we want to go casual or do supper less expensive," Sal Velardi chimed-in while recollecting his beforehand studying of various local dining establishments, "there's always the infamous Dirty Al's Marina next to the Sea Ranch and if we really get desperate, there're several area Whataburgers, Texas's big answer to Burger King and McDonald's."

"We're lucky it's October and not March or April down here in South Padre," Inspector Joe Giralo nonchalantly related after his right front tire made hard contact with a massive highway pothole. "Those hormone-driven college kids invade the island from all over the country. South Padre is sort of the new Fort Lauderdale during the annual rites of spring 'Animal House' celebrations."

For the next several miles, the three weary passengers politely listened to the driver's reminiscences of what circumstances were like when the Inspector had first joined the FBI ranks back in 1974. "In the beginning, computer data bases were few and far in between," venerable Inspector Joe Giralo vaguely recalled, "and hand-held communication devices and cell phones were mere science fiction stuff that appeared in fantasy magazines and also on the original episodes of *Star Trek*. The first computers were a form of calculators, designed for computing or determining sums in addition, products in multiplication and quotients in arithmetical division. And because of certain space-age fantastic advances in computer software technology and in Internet communications, criminals are much easier to track down nowadays, most of the cowardly fools stupidly bragging about and inadvertently confessing their gross felonies on Internet social media. Google, Yahoo, Facebook and Twitter have made it much easier to find and arrest criminals."

"I really think it's now siesta time!" Agent Velardi complained.

"I know I'm boring you fellas', so I'll intentionally bore you three amateur sleuths even more by speaking briefly about my wife, who incidentally this morning accidentally backed into several pylons in the town chain store's parking lot. A thousand-dollar expense, and that's a very mild conservative estimate. Thank goodness I have a low three-hundred-dollar insurance deductible applicable on the two-family vehicles."

"Women, you can't live with them and you can't live without them!" Agent Art Orsi philosophized and blandly articulated. "I had spoken with my wife via cell phone when we were waiting in a lounge area for our connection flight from Houston down here to Brownsville. Well anyway," Orsi gladly pontificated, "Carol was out walking our white miniature poodle Murray down at Hammonton Lake Park when seven or eight angry Canadian geese suddenly popped out of a fern growth clump, and the large creatures began wildly squawking, thrashing and quarreling incessantly."

"Maybe there was a snapper turtle trying to attack one of them," Inspector Giralo conjectured and commented as he unsuccessfully swerved and rumbled over another huge, obscured pothole. "Everything's immense down here in Texas, including the oil rig platforms, the hamburgers and the potholes!" the driver jested in defense of his suspect driving skills.

"Well anyway," Art Orsi continued with his fairly intriguing narrative. "Carol picked-up Murray and high-tailed it to her car. It's bad enough when you're assaulted by muggers and thugs, but apparently now my wife has to worry about squads of belligerent Canadian geese and invisible antagonistic snapper turtles that might wildly vex her daily routines!"

"Well, yesterday my wife received an e-mail from a cousin who lives in Baltimore," Dan Blachford declared, thinking that he also had a decent spouse story to disclose. "The e-mail stated that her cousin' along with her cousin's family were vacationing in London when they were maliciously robbed, mugged and stranded without any I.D.s or important passport credentials, which were also heisted. My better half was about to wire the cousin two thousand dollars to cover air transportation for five back to the States. It's a good thing she had called and told me about the strange situation, which I immediately recognized as a vile Internet e-mail scam. Boss," Agent Dan Blachford specifically addressed Inspector Giralo, "This felonious international wiring of money has generated an intolerable number of crafty cons and hoaxes upon the unassuming public, and many honest, trustworthy and unwary victims are being harmfully swindled out of millions of greenbacks daily!"

"That was quite some story involving your good-hearted wife almost being taken advantage of!" Agent Sal Velardi indicated to Blachford from the front passenger-side bucket seat. "But believe me.

I have a pretty exceptional recent wife story that totally reeks with government bureaucracy!"

"Don't keep us in suspense!" Art Orsi implored, fighting-off the onslaught of drowsiness. "Tell us an even more spectacular wife tale before we violently rumble over another gargantuan pothole!"
"Yesterday my beloved spouse had to go for jury duty in Atlantic City," Agent Velardi prefaced his spectacular tale. "As you know, in Atlantic County criminal cases are held in tranquil Mays Landing, and civil cases are tried at the Atlantic City Courthouse, which unfortunately borders rather dangerous high-crime neighborhoods."

"That's precisely right!" Agent Orsi quickly interrupted and acknowledged. "A juror could easily get mugged walking the five perilous blocks from the assigned high-rise parking lot on New York Avenue to the courthouse on North Carolina Avenue. And the human environment is definitely not the best! I've done *that* precarious trek on two occasions myself!"

"Regardless of the obvious, Art!" a somewhat perturbed Agent Velardi forcefully short-circuited his impetuous colleague. "My wife is sitting there in the crowded Atlantic City Courthouse jury selection room among a group of one hundred and twenty prospective jurors. Thirty names are called and twenty-three candidates are eventually rejected for various reasons after they had been generally interviewed by the assigned judge. Finally, after the next twelve random lottery names had been completed, the eighth jurist was finally accepted, much to the relief of my wife and the remaining prospective citizens sitting obediently inside the congested courtroom!"

"So, tell me Sal; what's so extraordinary about *that* basic situation!" Dan Blachford challenged Velardi. "Your beautiful wife was an exemplary, courageous typical citizen for braving a hazardous five-block trek through an unsavory neighborhood only to be inconvenienced for around four hours of bureaucracy to then learn that she won't again be called for jury duty for the next three years! What's so dramatically unusual about that?"

"You're absolutely right about the bureaucracy aspect of the judicial process!" Agent Sal Velardi promptly agreed. "We do indeed live in a litigious-oriented culture! But then my faithful wife had to silently sit there with full knowledge that she would be rejected for jury duty because of various real conflict factors. First of all, the lawsuit involved an auto' accident at the intersection of the White Horse Pike and Pleasant Mills Road at the all-too-familiar Hammonton Lake highway bend. My wife's older brother had been involved in a similar auto' collision at that exact same place several years ago."

"Okay, is that all?" Inspector Joe Giralo gruffly replied, showing only mild empathy for his agent's rather mediocre revelation. "If the accident being reviewed happened in the town of Hammonton, the courthouse clerk should've realized that no one from Hammonton, including your wife, should ever be eligible for placement on the jury and inconveniently called to Atlantic City in the first place, only to eventually be dismissed by the judge!"

"Well, no Boss! I mean, there is plenty more to this weird scenario," Velardi proceeded with narrating his graphic description. "The aggressive plaintiff doing the suing was once a lackluster student of *our* daughter, who as you know teaches fifth grade at the Hammonton Elementary School, so *that* additional element represents a new conflict of interest right there. And also," Agent Velardi enthusiastically elaborated, "the father of the attorney representing the plaintiff had once been a lawyer on my wife's father's behalf. Is that new development a totally bizarre coincidence or what?"

"Is there anything else of relevance to report?" a somewhat irritated Joe Giralo requested fathoming, solely out of general courtesy. "Remember Gentlemen, to genuinely clarify and balance matters, we're all indispensable parts of the widespread town, county, state, and ever-burgeoning federal bureaucracies. Quite confidentially Men, I find being a meager minuscule cog inside the enormous government wheel rather repugnant and personally insulting!"

"Listen Chief," Agent Sal Velardi intoned, much to the chagrin and dismay of his three fully exhausted traveling companions, "yes Sir, there is another salient dynamic to be introduced here. The defendant accused of slamming her vehicle into the rear of the plaintiff's automobile happened to be a party-animal distant cousin of my wife, so *that* very relevant familial relationship certainly would've also disqualified *her* from participating on the jury panel. And to top it all off," Velardi firmly finished, "the defendant's lawyer had been attending several night graduate classes with my wife at Rowan University, over in Glassboro!"

"Thanks for keeping me slightly awake for the past five minutes!" Dan Blachford grumpily expressed to Sal Velardi. "Say, that must have been Port Isabel we just motored through. And that steep elevation in the road ahead must be the Queen Isabella Causeway! Holy cow! We're going a mile and a half over the Laguna Madre directly into the heart of South Padre Island. Just look at how gorgeous the placid blue-green bay water appears down there!"

"And did you catch the docked shrimp fishing fleet on the right and the Pirate Cove Fishing Pier on the left, not to mention the impressive Port Isabel lighthouse," the suddenly energized driver orally conveyed to his rejuvenated audience. "This small port along with nearby South Padre Island is often referred to as the Shrimp Capital of the United States."

"I can't wait to sink my teeth into a juicy well-done steak, let's say at Blackbeard's Restaurant or at Louie's Backyard Buffet!" Agent Art Orsi directly suggested.

"I'll even settle for a giant two-handed meal at the nearest Whataburger!" Agent Sal Velardi concluded and shared. "I think it takes two hands to handle a Whopper, but it must require four appendages to lift a colossal-sized Whataburger from one of the joint's tables up to your mouth!"

* * * * * * * * * * * *

The FBI agents' two fifth floor rooms at the Pearl Hotel were quite cheerful in appearance and were more than adequate to accommodate their basic needs. The initial three days were rather humdrum and nondescript in nature with all four convention participants attending various educational seminars and associated conferences on such difficult topics as Border Security, Internet Pornography and Interstate Illegal Trafficking, Internet Illicit Gambling and Vice, and finally, A Comprehensive Analysis of Across State Lines' Drugs, along with Kidnapping and Prostitution Violations. Early on Thursday morning, the four-member team was enjoying a peaceful eclectic breakfast at Ted's Restaurant on north Padre Island Boulevard.

"I hope we have some free time to visit the Sea Turtle Rescue Aquarium tanks sometime later this week," Agent Dan Blachford proposed. "At the site, they have giant sea turtles being expertly rehabilitated after losing an essential appendage to hungry sea predators, along with a variety of other injured turtles from other species that are also being salvaged from the Gulf."

"And I have a strong desire to spend a half-day at the famous Schlitterbahn Beach Waterpark that's really not too far from the Pearl," Agent Salvatore Velardi chipped-in and vociferated. "It's widely promoted as one of the major water-slide parks in the whole United States. I know from watching a deluge of local TV advertisements that the venue's a tremendous hit with the Spring Break college crowd!"

"We do have all Sunday to ourselves after the federal convention closes," Inspector Giralo answered. "And since it's our special free time allotted all to ourselves, I won't even have to be granted permission from Chief Riley's office back in DC. So, allow me to allay your innermost fears, Sal. I won't prevent you from exploring your addictive need for juvenile splish-splash entertainment! But while you're frantically cavorting-around at the waterpark and hanging-out with twelve and fourteen-year-old acne-faced kids, I'll either be snoozing in my hotel room or exploring the Turtle Rescue Clinic with Dan and Arty."

After paying their group bill and giving the gorgeous Mexican waitress a well-deserved ten-dollar tip, the four G-men, now possessing satisfied appetites, re-entered the white *Expedition* SUV and immediately headed south in the direction of the modern-architecture Convention Hall Centre. A rare moment of silence was swiftly interrupted by Agent Arthur Orsi, who was presently acquiring some significant New Jersey information from the classified FBI closed-circuit data base.

"Boss, here's some extremely disturbing news from the Garden State," astonished Agent Orsi began verbally sharing his recently obtained knowledge. "An adult female was out jogging in Somerville up in North Jersey when both her and her car mysteriously disappeared. There's been no trace of Mrs. Carolyn Simmons since Tuesday afternoon. And in a second peculiar incident, Ms. Martha Zimmerman and her SUV are missing from the Harrahs Parking garage in Atlantic City."

"These women are very vulnerable to being attacked, especially when walking or exercising alone while on some sort of daily or weekly schedule cycle," Inspector Giralo evaluated and emphasized from his standard stationary position behind the steering wheel. "Most women can easily be overpowered by a weapon-toting male villain out there, the weasel taking his bitter enmity toward the world out on an unsuspecting female target!"

"And Boss, there's much more to this ugly developing trend," Agent Orsi excitedly replied. "Up in the Middletown, New Jersey Shopping Center a woman by the name of Jennifer Carlson was apparently kidnapped and she's disappeared along with her late model black Mercedes. And also, up in the Mt. Calvary Cemetery in Asbury Park, a victim named Denise Jenkins is missing-in-action since Wednesday along with her 2010 Ford Thunderbird. There's a definite heinous pattern being demonstrated here!"

"Perhaps Riley will send us back early to the Garden State to help solve this recent sinister crime wave," Inspector Giralo speculated and related. "As I've mentioned, these women don't realize it, but they're vulnerable, especially with the economy being depressed like it is and a lack of prosperity existing virtually everywhere. And I gotta' admit," the Inspector generalized, "women jogging or speed-walking alone in cemeteries are really susceptible to being mugged, raped, robbed or kidnapped. The culprits know that the ladies are usually wearing earphones while doing their daily graveyard strolls and that they're also carrying their keys to their locked cars with them. When the woman approaches her parked vehicle, then...."

"Then, the dastardly criminal comes out from behind a huge stone mausoleum and viciously attacks the gullible female before she even knows what's been occurring. She's knocked-out, probably with a blackjack or wooden pistol handle and then mercilessly dragged inside her compromised vehicle. Of course, the barbaric robber has already gotten her easily accessible car keys. He can now pilfer the vehicle, unload it for cash at a Mafia chop-shop, sell the woman into sex slavery and then quite obviously, easily steal all of her pocketbook money," Agent Blachford stated.

"Oh no, Inspector! Here's the latest in this terrible skein of devastating events!" Art Orsi exclaimed as he closely examined new FBI news flashing onto his laptop computer screen. "An unwary Waterford woman named Marilyn Passarella has disappeared from inside the Hammonton Oak Grove Cemetery at 7 a.m. Eastern Time, just last Friday morning. Again, there's no sign of her anywhere. It's as if alien space invaders have cruelly abducted the middle-aged lady and unscrupulously purloined her red 2012 Cadillac sedan in the process."

"Great bunions!" Inspector Joe Giralo instinctively yelled. "I just bought eight burial plots in Oak Grove Cemetery last month as an investment. "And women should be extremely careful when either entering or exiting their vehicles in cemeteries, in high rise-parking garages, in shopping center and mall parking lots, and also in innocent-looking city and town scenic parks. I strongly recommend Guys that we all soon call our endangered wives and advise them to not walk, jog or shop alone until these nefarious fiends committing the despicable atrocities have been apprehended, interrogated and incarcerated by the appropriate authorities."

* * * * * * * * * * * *

After enjoying solid nutritious breakfasts of bacon, eggs, toast and coffee on that early October 2013 Saturday morning, the four visiting FBI agents sat outside on comfortable chairs on the Pearl's balmy patio deck and predictably engaged in typical tourist general conversation. Agent Salvatore Velardi, the possessor of a huge culinary appetite, commented on one of the hotel's most outstanding features.

"Just look at that Palpapa Bar and Grill sitting there in the middle of that enticing outdoor swimming pool," Velardi pointed-out. "Hotel guests simply swim over to a circular raised concrete seat and sit in waist-deep water around the bar. They then eat delicious grilled hamburgers and drink a variety of savory tropical cocktails including my favorite, semi-frozen pina coladas. It's sort of like a nifty aquatic Whataburger that's especially designed for aristocratic guests."

"Sal, I know you're my only man who brought along a bathing suit on this particular business/education excursion," Inspector Giralo reminded his underling disciple. "But this evening we're going to feast at the hotel's Beachside Bar and Grill and partake of terrific stunning views of the Gulf of Mexico from inside! Expensive appetizers and desserts will be included as my treat!"

After returning to their fifth-floor rooms to prepare for the slated Saturday morning seminars, the impending Power Point discussions concentrating on Mexican Gun Smuggling and on Modern Day Money Counterfeiting, ten minutes later agents Blachford and Orsi knocked loudly on Inspector Giralo and Agent Velardi's hotel room door.

"Boss, there's been a flagrant rash of female abduction incidents over in Florida," Art Orsi anxiously revealed. "I've jotted-down the pertinent details the old-fashion way; right here on my trusty notepad. Five ladies have disappeared while performing similar daily routines just like the victimized females up in Jersey. One wife vanished while in Indian Harbour's principal shopping center, that is, according to the husband who had planned to meet her there and was in cell phone contact with his spouse just three minutes earlier. Another inexplicable disappearance was in Arcadia's Morgan Park, the third suspected kidnapping was in the Ocean Center Parking Garage in Daytona Beach, the fourth apparent felony was outside Jupiter's Driftwood Plaza Mall, and finally," exhaled an exasperated out-of-breath Agent Arthur Orsi, "the fifth comparable crime occurred in Hollywood at the tranquil Queen of Heaven Cemetery!"

"That's right, Arty!" Inspector Giralo instantly verified. "There's a Hollywood, Florida in addition to the more famous Hollywood, California. And again Fellas', these major brazen muggings and thefts have been systematically executed in designated cemeteries, in diverse parking garages, in quiet parks and in various crowded shopping center mall parking zones."

"And Boss," an equally charged-up Dan Blachford spoke, "I've just thought of something that might be uniquely relevant to this weird riddle. The five horrendous events in New Jersey happened in five separate communities, and the five violations in Florida also occurred in five distinct municipalities. This number five business might be more than just an interesting coincidence!"

"Dan might've discovered some material evidence that links these diabolical illicit acts that are oddly transpiring in different states!" Sal Velardi hypothesized and remarked. "Here's some new information currently coming into FBI Headquarters from five affected towns and cities in sunny California."

"This whole scenario is becoming more fascinating and confounding by the second!" Joe Giralo assessed and concluded. "Hurry-up Guys with the new pertinent data being received!"

"Again, just like in the bewildering New Jersey and Florida examples, five communities have been afflicted in different sections of the Golden State," Velardi announced as he intensely studied the new-found language appearing upon his special government-issue laptop. "One targeted woman regrettably vanished while supposedly power-walking in the Davis Central Park. A second selected female vanished into thin air in Modesto's Vintage Faire Mall. And another unlucky young woman met her unexpected fate at Inglewood Park Cemetery. The fourth bull's eye victim had just exited her *Nissan Maxima* at the Garden Walk Parking Garage in Anaheim and finally, the fifth felony misdeed can be traced to the San Francisco Bay area, Alameda County, the hostile abduction happening inside the Mt. Eden Cemetery in the community of Haywood."

"Again, five towns geographically remote from each other, but all located in a separate state," Art Orsi confirmed and gasped. "This whole grotesque pattern is developing into quite a difficult perplexing dilemma!"

"Men, I still want the three of you to attend those monotonous seminars being conducted over at the Convention Centre," Joe Giralo imperatively instructed his loyal subordinates. "In the meantime, I have two essential things I plan to do up here in this isolated room. First, I want to get in touch with Riley up in Washington concerning this intricate, national crime wave. Secondly, I desire doing some preliminary work on deciphering Art's new 'conundrum', which if I remember accurately, the curious term 'conundrum' being a sophisticated word frequently used by Sherlock Holmes when speaking to his rather clumsy associate in serious crime fighting, Dr. Watson!"

"Okay Chief!" Sal Velardi automatically concurred. "My brain is in a total shambles' state trying to figure-out this enormous enigma. I'll be thinking about all of the relevant facts while pretending to be listening to a battery of bureaucratic presentations over at the Convention Hall Centre."

"Sal, please try using your cerebrum and not your cerebellum!" humorously advised the sometimes-haughty Inspector Giralo. "We fragile humans can never achieve becoming too sagacious when being both influenced and controlled by an overactive medulla oblongata!"

* * * * * * * * * * * *

Later that momentous Saturday afternoon, Agents Velardi, Orsi and Blachford arrived back from the FBI conferences and landed at the aforementioned Pearl Hotel. The ambitious-but-fatigued threesome immediately proceeded directly to Inspector Giralo and S. V.'s assigned room.

"Have you been communicating with Chief Riley?" Dan Blachford spontaneously wanted to ascertain.

"Yes, but first," insisted Giralo while exhibiting a prodigious, stern expression on his stellar Italian countenance, "I believe that I now have this entire female abduction crime spree somewhat figured-out. Now Men, here's the dramatic evidence along with the accompanying underlying theory I'll soon endeavor explaining to you. Here are the five first letters of the New Jersey cities and towns I've scribbled onto this sheet of paper during my initial perfunctory observations," the esteemed Inspector commenced his extraordinary verbal exposition. "Now, you three mediocre Gumshoes. I occasionally spend some much-valued leisure time working-out certain scrambled words that appear in the *Atlantic City Press* and *The Philadelphia Inquirer* morning newspapers. I want you three detective geniuses to focus your eyes on the first letters of 'M' for Middletown, 'S' for Somerville, 'A' for Atlantic City, 'H' for Hammonton and 'A' for Asbury Park. Let's see exactly how brilliant you three fellas' are at practicing elementary problem solving!"

"Holy mackerel, Chief!" Sal Velardi impulsively shouted in sheer amazement. "The five letters you've just provided can be used to form the word 'Hamas'."

"Now let's cautiously scrutinize the five first letters taken from the five Florida towns and cities," Giralo directed his apostles like an accomplished classroom teacher cleverly guiding his or her students. "We have the given appellations Indian Harbour, Arcadia, Daytona Beach, Jupiter and finally Hollywood!"

"This is absolutely mind-boggling!" Art Orsi impulsively yelled. "The five letters could be easily rearranged to amazingly spell-out the word 'Jihad'!"

"Now let's carefully analyze the five California towns and cities," calmly directed the head FBI investigator. "We have Davis,

Inglewood, Modesto, Anaheim and Hayward. What related word can be unscrambled from the five disarrayed nouns?"

A full thirty seconds elapsed before Dan Blachford mentally recognized and then exuberantly revealed, "Mahdi!" "What's a Mahdi?" Sal Velardi wondered and asked.

"Well Men; an hour ago I did some comprehensive research on the subject and I've gleaned the following applicable facts," Inspector Giralo pragmatically divulged to his now-captivated audience. "Mahdi refers to a Muslim warrior/prophet formally named Muhammad al Mahdi. The Muslims as you might be aware," Joe Giralo confidently elucidated, "are divided into two sects that often disagree with each other: namely, the Sunni and the Shi'ites. The Shi'ites believe that the Mahdi, commonly also known as the Twelfth Imam, will exit from a sacred well that he has been staying down inside for the past seven hundred or so years, ever since the Great Crusades that had been warred between Christianity and the Muslim faith. The conflict between the Christians and the Muslims, of course, was over which religion would have dominance over Jerusalem and the Holy Lands!"

"Hey, I've heard of the Mahdi," Art Orsi equivocated. "He's a kind of Apocalyptic religious figure who is believed will successfully lead the Muslims against the West at the end of the world! His presumed ultimate supernatural power is worshiped by the Shi'ites, but the Madhi's assumed authority isn't fully accepted by the minority Sunni Muslim element!"

"Exactly true, Arty!" an impressed Inspector Giralo indulgently commended. "According to my' recent research, the Shi'ites believe that the Mahdi is being protected by Allah while being preserved for centuries down inside that sacred well, which the crusading prophet had entered after being inspired by Heaven to do so. Now, the Iranians are Shi'ites just like most of the Iraqis are, but their culture and their history are somewhat dissimilar from the Iraqis. The Iranians speak Farsi and the Iraqis and the Sunni tribes speak Arabic! But unlike the Saudi Arabians, most of the Shi'ite Iranians adamantly believe that the Mahdi will lead them to victory over the Western infidels at the start of Armageddon, that decisive battle signaling the prophesied end of the world!"

Then suddenly, Sal Velardi hollered, "Wait a minute Guys!" as new information was being transmitted into his laptop from the FBI's Washington Headquarters. Everyone stood motionless inside the illuminated room, the three G-men having their mouths agape as Inspector Giralo furiously wrote down the newly obtained data exclusively pertaining to the Lone Star State of Texas.

"Lubbock, South Plains Mall, Odessa, Sunset Memorial Gardens, Amarillo, Parking Garage at Rick Husband Airport, Laredo, Lake Casa Blanca International State Park, Houston, the Galleria Shopping Mall, Brownsville, Riverside Park, Harlingen, Ashland Memorial Park, and finally, El Paso, Sunland Park Shopping Mall!"

"Okay Men, at least we can now discard the all-too-simplified five letter words' theory!" Inspector Giralo quickly determined and communicated. "Let's look at the assorted letters and see if a plausible word can be derived and constructed. We have an 'L' for Lubbock, an 'O' for Odessa, an 'A' for Amarillo, an 'L' for Laredo, an 'H' for Houston, a 'B' for Brownsville, another 'H' for Harlingen and an 'E' for El Paso! Now what esoteric knowledge could you three erudite individuals extrapolate from this simplistic puzzle? The present elusive word evidently has two Ls and two H letters!"

After a full minute's pause, Agent Orsi bellowed-out "Eureka!" in a similar manner that the Greek scientific sage Archimedes must have exclaimed in Syracuse (Sicily) many years back in ancient BC history.

"Boss," Orsi ecstatically prefaced, "if you simply add a letter 'Z' to the cryptic formula, then the word 'Hezbollah' can be readily formed! The scrambled word is *Hezbollah,* but with the 'Z' missing!"

"Quick Dan, research on Google how many towns in Texas have names that begin with the letter Z!" Giralo urgently commanded. "I think we've meticulously found the Rosetta Stone that'll crack open this formerly most confounding affair!"

"Inspector, there are only two very small Texas towns that begin with the letter Z!" Dan Blachford reported. "The tinier one is Zephyr with a diminutive population of around two hundred residents, and the other remote village is Zavalla, having around a thousand or so country native inhabitants."

"Okay, Men. We have little time to squander!" Joe Giralo related. "Dan, you and Art will be dispatched directly to Zephyr while Sal and I will head a quick expedition over to Zavalla! I've already been in touch with our miraculous savant Riley, and he's given his advanced okay for us to leave South Padre immediately should new essential facts surface. And Guys, they certainly have!"

"I guess this means that I won't be partaking of the tremendous water-slide park and viewing the injured Sea Turtle Clinic?" Agent Velardi pretentiously complained.

"Sal, you can wear your zany-looking three-tone bathing suit in Zavalla if you'd like!" Inspector Giralo hardily laughed. "And I'm glad you didn't embarrass us by cannonballing into the hotel pool with that hideous-looking poorly designed swimsuit on!"

$$* * * * * * * * * * * *$$

Inspector Joseph Giralo and Agent Salvatore Velardi hitched a free ride with the Texas Ranger Highway Patrol. A fast cruiser transported them at speeds reaching 100 mph from South Padre Island down to the Brownsville Airport, leaving Agents Blachford and Orsi fully liable for returning the rented white *Ford Expedition* SUV.

Two civilian passengers had been bumped from the scheduled flight, and the irate displaced couple vehemently protested to airline employees, their vociferous cackling objections delivered completely in vain. The non-turbulent one hour and fifteen-minute Continental flight from Brownsville to Houston went without any further turmoil for Giralo and Velardi, with *that* city having the nearest major metropolitan airport to Zavalla, which is located approximately twenty-five miles southeast of Lufkin, population 35,000. At the ever-bustling Houston International Airport the relentless-in-pursuit FBI men impatiently retrieved their baggage from a rotating luggage carousel and then earnestly rented a *Ford Taurus* from AVIS.

On the several-hour speeding ride to Zavalla, Inspector Giralo reviewed a few salient points with his conscientious understudy, whose eager mind was busy absorbing in sponge-like fashion virtually everything the FBI Chief had to say.

"According to all reliable available records," Giralo amiably introducing his standard dissertation style, "I've neglected to mention to you Sal one essential-but-consistent fact. In each separate abduction incident, the time that the crime had been committed was exactly at high noon on a Friday! However, some of the information was not efficiently corroborated and not quickly entered into our thoroughly independent computer data base, and that's why there appeared to be certain time discrepancies as to the exact days of the week the sensational kidnappings had been occurring. And Sal, since this last Texas 'Z' felony had a lot of letters to spell-out the word 'Hezbollah', I conjecture that there must be at least eight Arab or Iranian hit teams in full operation. That's why the 'Z' ninth Texas kidnapping is probably right now in progress!"

"Why do you conclude that this all is so?" Velardi asked, his' mind temporarily swimming in a veritable quandary. "Wait a minute Chief! Your contention means that a number of hit teams have been accountable for enacting the individual atrocities! I now see and fathom your logic! There must be a total of nine hit squads!"

"Precisely, Sal! After studying necessary background knowledge about the Muslim religion," the speeding Inspector orated and then hesitated as he wildly rounded a highway bend, "Friday noon prayers are without a doubt the most sacred. The Muslim faithful are called to prayer by an announcer sporting the title 'muezzin', who proudly stands high in a mosque minaret while chanting and reminding the faithful to pray to Allah from the tower!"

"I see," Velardi understood, nodding his head. "And if no mosque minaret is in the vicinity, then the insular Muslim will turn in the direction of Mecca or Medina, both cities situated somewhere in Saudi-Arabia!"

"I have an imaginative assumption about exactly what's going on here," the FBI Chief intimated. "But I'll reserve my right to relay my thesis to you until after the abominable perpetrators are arrested and summarily sent to prison. I hereby predict Sal that the next attempted kidnapping will happen at noon today at the Hanks Creek Recreational Park in somnolent Zavalla, Texas. Since we'll be arriving there after noontime, Matt Riley has intelligently alerted the Army, and they've cooperated by dispatching a very competent Delta Force Unit led by the legendary commander, my old college friend, Colonel Bob Bauers! But just in case of a judgment error," wily Inspector Joe Giralo qualified, "another Delta Force Team led by Colonel Joe DiFilippo will handle the second military assignment and coordinate efforts with Blachford and Orsi over in Zephyr, which I think is in No Man's Land somewhere in the center of this mammoth state."

Upon reaching their destination, Hanks Creek Recreational Park in Zavalla, Texas, the determined Inspector abruptly stopped his black *Ford Taurus* in a cloud of dust, his vehicle halting next to an Army jeep. The new arrivals to Zavalla were cordially greeted by vociferous Colonel Bauers.

"It was a common saying in the Old West when riding up-front in a pursuing posse, you either make dust or you eat dust!" Joe Giralo jested. "It seems, Bob, that my rental car just made dust!"

"It took you guys longer-than-expected to get here," Colonel Bauers mildly reprimanded. "Anyway Joe; my men along with four Texas Rangers have, with minimal resistance, already apprehended the two suspects, a Middle East fella' with the moniker Muhammed Aarif, and *his* extremely dangerous accomplice, an imported illegal alien terrorist with the name Jamal Abdul Samad. I looked their oddball names up on the Internet and the first guy's name means Praised Knowledgeable and the second guy's appellation means Servant of the Eternal. These are really weird name descriptions for very formidable vermin that have mutually declared jihad on the United States of America!"

"Just as I had shrewdly surmised!" Inspector Giralo stated in an exhilarated manner as he turned his sweating head, now facing an astonished and beleaguered Agent Salvatore Velardi.

"So Boss, kindly tell me, what was your secret theory to which you had confidentially alluded to me about an hour ago?" Velardi both questioned and requested learning.

"The whole enchilada all makes very rational sense now!" Joe Giralo maintained, speaking specifically very loud for both Colonel Bauers and *his* agent to hear. "The two apprehended evil, pathetic Arabs certainly have Sunni names. This vital fact means that by using the terminology 'Hamas', 'Jihad' and 'Madhi', those deplorable, desperate Sunni idiots have futilely tried to cover their tracks, making it look like bellicose Shi'ite Muslims had been responsible for the plethora of terrible crime abductions that have been brutally terrorizing innocent and unassuming American women!"

# "Calendar Man"

FBI Inspector Joe Giralo and his three loyal Agents Salvatore Velardi, Arthur Orsi and Dan Blachford were sitting in the boss's eighth floor office inside 600 Arch Street, downtown Philadelphia eating cold ham, lettuce and tomato sandwiches with mustard on rye bread, and each man alternately drinking the contents of cold cans of Pepsi Cola. Then Agent Velardi proceeded to read aloud the "above the fold" headline from the *Philadelphia Inquirer's* Monday August 3rd, 2009 morning edition's front page.

"Dangerous Serial Killer Suspected in 12th Area Unsolved Murder," Agent Velardi all-too-politely shared. "It says in this lousy article that federal officials are completely baffled and that the Philadelphia Police are clueless about possible suspects. You would think, Boss that the screwed-up reporter would've used better terminology such as 'without any major clues' rather than naively employing the ugly inflammatory description of *us* and the police being clueless. I think that *this* illiterate scribe who had authored this ugly garbage needs to take a summer school refresher course in Journalism, 101."

"This case is absolutely driving me up a wall!" Inspector Giralo expressed to his principal protégé. "Confidentially Salvatore, I've not only been stymied by the lack of evidence; I've been both puzzled and bewildered too! And *you* gotta' be frustrated also by all of the negative publicity we've been receiving from the *critical*, no; make that from the *hypocritical* so-called newspaper correspondents. But I promise you Men," the advocate of law enforcement pledged. "I'm like a tenacious bulldog and I'm not goin' to voluntarily retire until this extremely perplexing case is solved."

"Twelve murders, the last bloody one being just yesterday," Agent Orsi reminded his superior before sipping the last ounce of cola from his can. "And how can the jump-to-conclusions local press hypothesize that the felonies have all been committed by a single lunatic serial killer? This tabloid approach to the truth without providing any motive or evidence has gotta' be the ultimate in bad journalism! It certainly isn't the epitome of Pulitzer Prize investigative reporting, that's for darned sure! It's actually indirect slander of us!"

"I agree with Arty!" Dan Blachford chimed-in. "The press should be our ally and not our enemy."

"Since it's written in the newspaper," the Chief bluntly corrected, "it's more akin to libel than to slander, which of course is verbal and not put into print for public consumption! Libel is a lot easier to prove in a court of law than slander is, but the papers have immunity to being subjected to libel cases as long as they later print retractions. And besides, newspapers are generally protected by the First Amendment!"

"I guess the press does have immunity from libel charges," Agent Velardi confirmed and agreed. "All they gotta' do is publish a correction in the next edition if they libel someone! But I insist that *this* poorly organized article I'm reading is Freedom of the Press gone amok!"

"Yeah Salvatore, I had read *that* column this morning before you had reported for work. The latest victim is a Chinese computer whiz named Liu Huong, who had been living for the past four years up the *Delaware* in Bristol, Bucks County. According to all accounts," Inspector Giralo continued with his thorough exposition, "Mr. Huong was a responsible citizen, a genuine contributor to our great American melting pot society. And the vital statistics' background check that my secretary has performed indicates that Mr. Liu Huong was only twenty-five years old when his life had been prematurely terminated by being savagely stabbed in the back."

"Who might do such a wicked thing?" Agent Orsi asked. "A demented loner?"

"The anonymous criminal must be a real coward, killing his unwary prey by brutally stabbing him in the back seven times. Only a crime of passion could evoke such a violent, premeditated, surprise attack! Based on the documentation," the all-too-garrulous Chief continued his comprehensive analysis, "I believe that the perpetrator and the victim must've known each other! You'd think that *that* info' would automatically lead us in the right direction, but if the killer has no previous criminal record, and if he or she leaves behind no trace of DNA or fingerprint clues, we're futilely pursuing an anonymous phantom possessing a deranged mind."

"But how does that victim/killer familiarity assumption of yours correspond with the other eleven similar homicides on record here in the Delaware Valley?" Agent Blachford plausibly asked his superior. "What is the essential link that would support the popular theory that we're dealing with a crazed serial killer as the poorly written newspaper article maintains? It seems that we're always going back to nebulous Square One when we pursue *that* particular avenue of reasoning! Maybe we educated should start playing checkers and luckily find Square 2!"

"When faced with a tremendous mystery of this magnitude," Joe Giralo obstinately replied, "I often have to depend on my weapon of last resort. Don't ever tell Matt Riley down at DC Headquarters exactly how I've managed to develop such a stellar reputation at felony solving! If you ever divulge to any mortal soul my obscure secret technique at advanced crime investigation, I'll do everything in my power to short-circuit *your* budding investigative careers. Forget the stereotypical gumshoe clue-gathering police business!" the Inspector facetiously threatened. "I'll make sure Dan that you'll be busted-down to the salary of a first year Bureau employee in no time flat!"

"You mean the fact that you're psychic?" laughed Agent Orsi. "Everyone including Matt Riley suspects that possibility!"

"Yeah Boss, where do you' hide your arcane crystal ball and your magical tarot cards?" quipped Agent Blachford. "I suspect inside a secret locker down in the building's basement?"

The three very affable FBI agents were completely shocked upon witnessing their immediate boss nonchalantly opening the top drawer of his desk, removing a standard-sized Ouija Board and then passively addressing his stunned colleagues. "As you can plainly see Fellas', *this* is your average Ouija Board, but over in Italy the natives call it a Luigi Board," the Inspector jested as his somewhat intrigued listeners rolled their eyes in disbelief. "But seriously Men, the unique name is derived from two European words, 'Oui' in French means 'yes' and 'Ja' in German also means 'yes,' so translated into English," Giralo monotonously pontificated, "the unique term 'Ouija' means 'yes-yes', which obviously refers to two successive positive responses to inquisitive-type questions that the board will cooperatively answer. Are you three gregarious geniuses ready to engage in some creative FBI investigative work?"

"This goofy fiasco is totally ridiculous! Immensely absurd!" Agent Velardi defiantly evaluated and articulated. "My older brother Phil and I used to play with a similar board when we were gullible kids. I think that the thing you move around to spell words somehow picks-up vibrations from your subconscious and then transmits the obscure message through the players' fingertips," Velardi stated without the use of a podium. "But you can't convince any of us that this very interesting-but-common game-board of yours uses the scientific method of reasoning in any way!"

The Inspector carefully explained to his rebellious underlings that the revered "Father of the Detective Story," Edgar Allan Poe would have found much merit in the board's ability to glean and render important information that would prove to be relative to any given crime, either felony or misdemeanor. "And even the great creator of the Sherlock Holmes tales, Sir Arthur Conan Doyle, believed very strongly in the power of séances," Giralo maintained.

But dubious FBI Agents Velardi, Orsi and Blachford adamantly remained unimpressed with their higher-ranked comrade's verbal justification for seeking the advice of the aforementioned mystical game-board oracle. "Maybe you can consult the ghosts of Mr. Poe and Mr. Doyle through the Ouija Board and skillfully obtain their supernatural assistance in solving these twelve, very apparent, gruesome serial murders," Agent Orsi boldly challenged, with his two associates nodding their distrustful heads in full agreement.

"Now listen closely and learn something significant!" Inspector Joe Giralo sternly admonished his three doubting subordinates. "This ordinary Ouija Board is really an excellent spirit medium that defies the accepted tenets of human logic and explanation. This here heart-shaped device is called a planchette," the Chief indicated to his rather lethargic audience. "It either gravitates to a 'Yes' or to a 'No' response or it fully spells-out the desired answer to any specific inquiry that might be made. I'm now directing you Salvatore to place most of your eight fat fingers on the opposite side of this nondescript planchette, to closely watch the plastic window in the middle and then alertly help me spell-out the exact responses to my questions by observing the small pin situated below the cheap plastic window. Are you now ready to initiate *our* unorthodox secret method of obscure data gathering?"

"Ya' know Inspector, there's two *'s'* words I positively hate in life: secrets and surprises! I could lose my veteran position with the Bureau if I ever got caught doin' this sort of crazy stuff, and you're jeopardizing your pension too, if I might add," the all-too-skeptical Agent Velardi protested. "You like to test your luck to the limit, don't you? I hope no irresponsible newspaper reporter ever finds out about *this* rather bizarre experiment you're conducting!"

"Salvatore, go shut the door and lock it just to be safe!" Joe Giralo instructed his all-too-wary apprentice. "The same instructions go for your mouth and jaw! Then upon your return to this part of my office, I'll convincingly demonstrate to you three amateur sleuths just how amazing this wonderful, mystical instrument of truth really is! If we hurry, the whole extraordinary demonstration should only take around three minutes to complete."

After Agent Velardi reluctantly rose from his rickety chair and fulfilled his 'maniacal' boss's strange command, the cynical agnostic returned to his squeaky seat, moved it directly across from the Inspector's, and soon, much to the three observers' total fascination, the famous 'Philly FBI crime fighter positioned the Ouija Board upon his desk.

"Now Sal, please place your corpulent fingers on your side of the planchette!" the Inspector ordered the somewhat disgruntled agent. "Be sure to include your index fingers! They're the most vital ones!"

"I still say that this nutcase procedure is wholly preposterous! It's also blatantly weird and ludicrous!" Velardi balked to no avail. "If anyone else on the staff finds-out about this dumb caper we'll all be the laughing stock of the entire city, especially if *Action News* gets wind of this idiotic canard! We four might even be swiftly committed to a mediocre upstate mental institution!"

"Now let's stay perfectly calm as I perform a basic interrogation," Inspector Giralo stated and equivocated, entirely ignoring his exasperated friend's feasible arguments. "Tell me oh supernatural Ouija Board," the Inspector seriously prefaced, "is the anonymous serial killer a male?"

The remarkable other-world communicator immediately moved to "Yes." "Give me the name of the killer of Mr. Liu Huong?" Giralo persisted, despite the muffled giggles of Velardi, Orsi and Blachford.

The incredible omniscient prognosticator amazingly spelled-out the initials "C.L." and then the word "Male"."

"What is the nationality or ethnicity of the killer?" specifically inquired the Chief Inspector.

The phenomenal spiritual cardboard prophet answered and spelled-out underneath the men's fingertips, "Chinese, Taiwanese."

After a second's pause, Inspector Giralo informed his astounded agents that the brief "unorthodox-but-marvelous interrogation" had officially terminated. "Well Salvatore, you've now heard all of the pertinent details we need to know. The killer of Mr. Liu Huong is a male, has the initials C.L. and is of Chinese origin, specifically *his* heritage undeniably coming from the island of Taiwan. Please get-up and unbar the door, even though your birth name happens to be Salvatore and not Katie."

After Orsi and Blachford ceased their muffled laughter, Sal Velardi felt compelled to reply. "Boss, I fear that you oughta' be committed, not committed to catching villains and criminals but committed to a sophisticated mental hospital designated for advanced basket cases like yourself!" indicted Agent Velardi. "I've never been involved in something this utterly outlandish in my entire life! I think my mother was right when she wanted me to attend graduate school and become a nutcase Freudian psychiatrist!"

"Get a grip on reality, Sal!" Joe Giralo imperatively answered. "We just received from the 'powers that be' three essential leads in this most complex serial murder case and all you can do is sulk and criticize! If you three savants had half a brain, you'd call *that* politically correct reporter over at the *Inquirer* on the horn and tell him that we're no longer 'clueless'!"

"Tell me, where do we advance to from here?" Sal Velardi demanded knowing. "What's our next crucial step? Are you going to hire a shaman or a tribal witchdoctor to recklessly advise us?"

"I want you three Einsteins to be here in my office promptly tomorrow morning at nine to review the chronological history of these supposed twelve serial murders," Inspector Giralo austerely directed. "Bring along all of your files as we methodically analyze each victim separately. By then, my dear Gentlemen, I presume I'll have comprehensively cracked most of this hard nut case wide open."

"You *are* indubitably a hard nut case!" jokingly criticized Agent Orsi. "Not even a hungry squirrel knowing karate and judo could ever crack your thick skull open!"

"I resent your cavalier attitude Arty," Joe Giralo affectionately volleyed back. "I don't care if any of you three nimrods have another scheduled appointment or assignment! Be here at nine o'clock tomorrow morning and we'll conscientiously resume our challenging investigation! And let me warn you three Dick Tracy imitators! Stop abusing me with all of your silly unsolicited, unwarranted excoriating rhetoric!"

* * * * * * * * * * * * *

Precisely at 9 a.m. the following morning obedient Agents Velardi, Orsi and Blachford reported to the brightly illuminated Arch Street office with the twelve necessary victims' files in their reliable possession. Inspector Giralo was in a business-like mood and deftly channeled the entire dialogue directly to his main objective while intelligently conferring with his office visitors.

"As you know Fellas', all twelve ugly homicides had been committed with the same sharp knife, which was approximately eight inches long!" the "bipolar" Chief began his customary narrative. "But since we never recovered the murder weapon...."

"We have no direct evidence, no motive and no suspect!" Sal Velardi finished his mentor's introductory remark. "The serial killer is clever enough to wear surgical gloves when executing his malice. We're looking for a sneaky culprit who's capable of stringing together a pattern of very mendacious-type offenses. Now let's briefly review the dozen murder victims."

"Hey, stop pilfering my most important lines!" Joe Giralo objected. "Arty, why don't you go first!"

"First there's Professor William Stevenson, a science scholar of Drexel University who had been brutally stabbed at his Willow Grove home," Agent Orsi very deliberately declared. "But we've checked all his records, and Dr. Stevenson never gave any of his Advanced Chemistry students an academic grade lower than a mediocre C. In fact, most of those conscientious learners who were enrolled in his graduate classes generally received A's and B's."

"That just about eliminates any vindictive student having a grudge after only earning a lowly D or a disgraceful F," the Inspector professionally summarized. "And the college transcripts we've carefully studied show that only seven students in the last five years have gotten a C final average from Dr. Stevenson, and they've all checked-out as being above and beyond suspicion. Well then Arty, who's second on the list?"

"Frankie Martin, a pathetic used car salesman," the well-prepared FBI detective related. "But he had so many avowed enemies that we can't narrow-down the field. Over the years, Mr. Martin's cheated at least two hundred people in sleazy deals according to a plethora of complaints received by the Pennsylvania Better Business Bureau. But I can run a progressive computer crosscheck to see if any dissatisfied C student in Dr. Stevenson's Chemistry seminar had ever purchased an inferior car from the ultra-slippery creep Frankie 'the Con Man' Martin. Now Inspector, third on the list is Jean Crescenzo, a reputable South 'Philly real estate agent."

"According to my research, *that* lady never cheated or defrauded anyone in her entire life," Joe Giralo recollected and commented to his trio of agents. "But just to be certain Arty, run a sweeping cross-check with the clients of Frankie Martin and the benign Dr. William Stevenson's C-average students, anyway. A vital missing link connection has gotta' turn-up somewhere! You might think we're anthropology professors instead of vigilant FBI Men with all of these oddball missing links that have to be separately delved into. As you fully know Fellas', the Devil's skullduggery's hidden somewhere deep in the details!"

"Now Boss, snafu number four is Joseph Davis, a respectable UBS financial adviser," the astute file reader enunciated. "We don't have too much info' to go on here because just like with Jean Crescenzo, this guy Joe Davis seems to have been loved by nearly everyone in his sphere of influence. But I'll check with UBS to see if any of his clients had gotten margin calls on their stock ownership accounts and then I'll run that particular documentation against the data on Dr. Stevenson and against the numerous M.O.'s we have on the unscrupulous Frankie Martin."

"Who's Number 5?" Inspector Giralo phlegmatically asked next-inline Dan Blachford. "I think it's some unsavory broad!"

"It's Diana Jarvis, a gold-digging platinum blonde prostitute who was always cavortin' around town looking for a wealthy sugar daddy. As you know Chief, we've already run crosschecks on all of these people and no outstanding common denominator suspect has ever been identified. But we'll try working the national and local databases again for some remote iota that's thus far evaded *our* keen scrutiny! And Number 6 is James Filmore," Dan Blachford communicated, "who was a rather talkative-but-helpful pharmacist. We'll investigate Mr. Filmore's biography again and see if there's any legal or illegal drug connection with anyone singled-out as being involved with the other eleven murder victims. And Number 7 in this litany of disparate names is one Marcus Johnson, an elementary school principal over in Bensalem in Bucks County, just above the 'Philly border.'"

"Since Liu Huong lived in Bristol, which is also in Bucks County, that coincidental relationship just might be the Rosetta Stone we're searching for in order to decipher this confounding enigma," Inspector Giralo hypothesized and conveyed. "Dan, see if this Marcus Johnson had any arguments with dissatisfied, aggressive parents over their son or daughter's bad grades, or perhaps the agitated parents might be unhappy about a certain disciplinary action, like a school suspension for instance. Now Dan, what about those unfortunate individuals who' happen to be victims Number 8 and 9?"

"Stabbing victim Number 8 is Sean Andersen, a prominent vegetable farmer who owned four hundred productive acres over in Montgomery County," Agent Blachford enumerated. "Andersen was a jovial and likeable guy and never seemed to have any major conflict with anyone. And Number 9 happens to be Duncan Etheridge, a thrice-arrested drug distributor and a remote acquaintance of the small-time rip-off used car salesman, Frankie Martin. Now Guys, *there's* a convenient evil alliance that might just lead to a conviction, but Boss, we still have more intense probing to perform before we discover anything tangible or make any official public allegation."

"That leaves us with murder victims 10 and 11," Inspector Giralo grimaced, wiping his sweaty forehead with a much-maligned handkerchief. "One of them was a lawyer I believe. Salvatore, now that you've simmered-down, why don't you recite from your notes?"

"Yes Chief, her name is Eileen Dunn, a successful attorney that resided and practiced her legal craft in Delaware," Agent Velardi revealed, reading directly from his notes. "Her history was impeccable, but we'll again double analyze her client list. For the record, Eileen Dunn was not a judge or a prosecutor, but she did represent plenty of plaintiffs in civil defense cases not involving criminal activity."

"Who's Number 11? Oh yeah, I remember; it's that anonymous streetwalker that had been mutilated so badly she's not been identified yet," Inspector Giralo ranted without any soapbox to stand upon. "My hunch is that she's probably a drifter from out of the area."

"And of course," Sal Velardi stated before taking-in a healthy deep breath, "Number 12 is Dr. Liu Huong, the distinguished Temple University Cultural Anthropology Associate Professor. Huong was a veritable genius who had earned his doctorate degree at the tender age of twenty-one. I'll run another scan through the computer files and see if there's any correlation or relationship between Dr. William Stevenson of Drexel University and Dr. Liu Huong of Temple. That about concludes our twelve biographical sketches!"

"Okay Fellas', thanks for rehashing this all-too-redundant exercise in futility," the renowned Inspector concluded and opined. "Now listen to me very closely, Men! Be here at precisely noon tomorrow! I hope to have this seemingly complicated case entirely wrapped-up, culminating with the probable arraignment of a Chinese American male of Taiwanese ancestry having the initials C.L., thanks to the illustrious professional advice provided by my trusty Ouija Board."

Agents Velardi, Orsi and Blachford simply stood there with their mouths agape and with their protruding mandibles nearly disjointed from their sockets, each astounded G-man wondering how in the world the inimitable Inspector Joe Giralo could possibly make such a daring, audacious and outrageous prediction.

* * * * * * * * * * * *

The following morning, just before noon, the still-rattled FBI detectives quietly entered the all-too-familiar Arch Street eighth floor office. Amazingly, the dedicated agents were ten minutes early for their assignation with Inspector Joe Giralo, despite their morning involvement in interviewing eyewitnesses at a bank armed robbery crime scene on busy Market Street. The three G-men found their unpredictable boss in a somber and introspective state of mind, showing little emotion while the mentor was intently staring at the wrinkled front page of the *Philadelphia Inquirer*.

"I have to tell you Fellas' that right now my mind is fresh and clear, just like the air during the start of a summer rainstorm," the Inspector strangely greeted his still-bewildered partners in interstate crime fighting. "At this climactic moment I'm going to employ what the academics often call the 'Socratic Method of Reasoning'. It's what *we* accomplished investigators do all the time, but we refer to the exact same intellectual questioning process simply as 'interrogation'. Now then Gentlemen, for the benefit of noteworthy discussion, what do you three precocious individuals think about when I casually mention the Numbers 12 and 13?"

"Actually Boss, with the Number 12 I think of the twelve apostles sitting at the Last Supper including the religious villain Judas Iscariot," Sal Velardi instantly answered. "Or maybe the movie *The Dirty Dozen,* starring Lee Marvin. And with the very interesting Number 13, my encumbered brain either thinks of something being unlucky, or I think of the thirteen original colonies that had bravely rebelled against King George of England because of unfair taxation without representation. That unlucky 13 jerk Judas Iscariot should have..."

"Let me ask you this," curtly interrupted the Inspector, seeing that his impetuous prime apostle's jargon was going-off on a wild, verbal tangent. "In relation to our current complex murder scenario Salvatore, what do the Numbers 12 and 13 actually mean?"

"Well, Chief; the Number 12 pertains to how many victims have already perished at the hands of this demented maniacal killer still on the loose, and the Number 13 points to the prospective next prey of this very treacherous psycho predator! Have you consulted your Ouija Board lately about the anonymous C.L. Taiwanese culprit?"

"When you think of infamous serial killers," Giralo sagely suggested, pointing at Agent Orsi and completely ignoring Agent Velardi's hysterical extraneous rhetoric, "what idea does your brain conjure-up?"

"Well Boss, the crazed zodiac killer that had terrorized the entire Delaware Valley seven years ago comes to mind right away," Agent Orsi reflexively replied. "He was finally caught during a routine traffic stop in Phoenix, Arizona, if my faulty memory is still functioning. Thank goodness that a national dragnet had been in place so that the perverted animal was so easily and accidentally taken into custody."

"Exactly, Arty!" the impressed Inspector praised the on-a-roll agent. "For the past two weeks I've been contemplating the prospect of another crazed zodiac killer on the prowl right here in the Tri-State region. It stands to reason that there are twelve zodiac signs and that there have been twelve stabbing murders. You gotta' admit the truth Fellas'. It's a rather astonishing parallel, isn't it?"

170

"Does this odd coincidence mean that the new copycat zodiac fanatic, if indeed that's what he is, does *this* imaginative assumption of yours mean that the killing cycle is over, now that twelve people have regrettably perished at the whim of *his* warped mind?" Dan Blachford asked. "Why don't you simply use the *Inquirer's* horoscope page instead of the non-supernatural Ouija Board?"

"Either *that* copycat possibility, Danny Boy, or perhaps the hideous pattern might be cyclical and be repeated all over again," the sagacious Inspector responded, presenting a gloom-and-doom model of future psychopathic behavior. "But Gentlemen, I've assiduously put together all of the key facts about the dozen dead victims, and amazingly, none of the items jibed. It's like trying to place together a hundred and twenty weird pieces from twelve different jigsaw puzzles. Now Salvatore, what zodiac sign are you listed under on the daily horoscope page?"

"I'm a Capricorn, sign of the goat, and the range of those born under Capricorn is December 22 to January 19, if I recall correctly. What sign are you' Boss?" Agent Velardi innocently inquired.

"I'm a Libra, born in October, and my birth sign is the scales, meaning that I'm usually fair and normally objective and that I wholeheartedly believe in the balanced administration of justice and law. Now Arty, the theory of an insane zodiac killer in this massive investigation of ours happens to be both simultaneously correct and also erroneous?"

"It sounds like you're talking gibberish just like the crazed guys speakin' total nonsense at the fabled Tower of Babel in the Bible!" Agent Orsi exclaimed and accused. "Your ludicrous comment is totally ambivalent, absolutely preposterous! How could the notion of a pernicious zodiac killer roaming around 'Philly, Delaware, South Jersey and vicinity happen to be both the right and the wrong hypothesis, all at the same time?"

Inspector Giralo patiently explained to his three doubting disciples that the twelve very recognizable signs of the Occidental/Western World Zodiac were completely different than the twelve more obscure signs characteristic of the Oriental World Calendar. "Guys, I've done a lot of exhaustive research on this fascinating horoscope topic the last two weeks. The twelve astrological zodiac signs that *we* easily know like Aquarius and Scorpio are governed by the annual passage of the sun's path through *them* during the day, each of the twelve symbols representing roughly a staggered month's duration. But in regard to the lesser-known Chinese Zodiac Calendar," now-inspired Inspector Giralo academically informed and differentiated, "there are new and very different twelve signs, but they're basically affected by the dominance of the nocturnal moon and not by the sun's yearly passage. In other words, each of the designated twelve Chinese signs returns every twelve years and not every twelve months."

"Very interesting academic analysis from strictly an educational point of view," observed and stated Sal Velardi, "but to sum up my reaction, I still don't get the gist of what you're trying to present. Please be more dynamically descriptive!"

The famous Inspector slowly picked-up his hand-written yellow notepad and read-off certain applicable information. "Listen to this twelve-year pattern Fellas'. Dr. William Stevenson, the Chemistry professor at Drexel University was born in 1948, the Year of the Rat. Twelve months later Frankie Martin, the nefarious used car rip-off artist, was born in 1949, the Year of the Ox. Jean Crescenzo, the honest-to-a-fault real estate broker was born in 1950, the Year of the Tiger. And Joseph Davis, the amiable UBS account executive entered this world in 1951, the Year of the Rabbit."

As Agents Velardi, Orsi and Blachford stood in absolute silence in zombie-like stupors absorbing the cosmic significance of Inspector Giralo's catalog of Chinese zodiac linkages, the speaker suavely added that the prostitute Diana Jarvis from Wilmington, Delaware had been born in 1964, the Year of the Dragon, James Filmore, the chatty pharmacist in 1965, the Year of the Snake, Marcus Johnson, the elementary school principal in 1966, the Year of the Horse, Sean Andersen, the well-to-do Montgomery County farmer in 1967, the Year of the Goat, Duncan Etheridge, the New Jersey based legal and illegal drug pusher in 1980, the Year of the Monkey, Eileen Dunn, the prominent Delaware Attorney in 1981, the Year of the Rooster, the unknown female streetwalker yet to be identified was probably born in 1982, the Year of the Dog. "And finally, young Dr. Liu Huong, the well-liked child-prodigy Cultural Anthropology Associate Professor teaching at Temple University exited his mother's womb in 1983, the Year of the Pig. Liu Huong was only twenty-six years of age," Giralo orally conveyed.

"Holy Hawaiian hyenas!" a stunned Salvatore Velardi realized and impulsively shouted. "The twelve Chinese zodiac signs' cycle is now complete. The next targeted victim in this unbelievably complex pattern might just have been born in 1984, the 'Year of the Rat' ominously occurring again!"

Inspector Giralo commended his alert assistant on *his* new-found grasp and comprehension of the "ever-evolving, most dangerous, imminent situation." The expert federal investigator next discussed some superfluous information to his three astounded colleagues to persuasively demonstrate to the still-dazzled G-men exactly how

172

diversified *his* sophisticated analysis of the vicious "Astral Chinese Zodiac Serial Killer" actually was.

"The Chinese surname, what we here in America call our family or *last name*, usually comes first in *their* culture, with the unique name of the Oriental person, which incidentally is not capitalized, the individual's distinctive name coming *last* when spoken or addressed. Sometimes the mother's maiden name is included before the individual's un-capitalized separate name, out of courtesy or respect. The entire practice is designed to underscore that in old China, the clan along with the family were regarded as being more important to the sustenance of the culture than the individual was," Inspector Giralo lengthily explained. "This ancient 'last name first' tradition made it especially easy for the Red Chinese to implement their brand of Communism, which promotes the *group* existence prevailing over the individual's own personal identity."

"Okay, Boss; allow me to construct something; that is, according to your rather impeccable logic," Agent Art Orsi eloquently stated. "In Mao Tse-tung, Mao is the family name, Tse the mother's maiden name, and the un-capitalized 'tung' would be the man's first name. And with Chiang Kai-shek, the same type of priority sequence is developed, family name first."

"Precisely, Arty, and your sharp observation brings me directly to the most paramount point in this uniquely complicated case that's now become quite fathomable!" the Chief lucidly indicated. "Mao Tse-tung and Chiang Kai-shek were indeed bitter enemies. When the Communist Chinese under Mao took over the mainland, Chiang Kai-shek gathered his army and followers and led them to the island of Formosa, which today is...."

"Is Taiwan!" Dan Blachford screamed, exuberantly verifying his broad knowledge of history and geography. "And *you* claim that this elusive Chinese Zodiac Serial Killer has connections to Taiwan, at least that's what your marvelous supernatural Ouija Board led you to wildly conjecture!"

"Well, Dan," Inspector Giralo elucidated with a wry smile exhibited upon his chubby countenance. "My intriguing encyclopedia and Google research had discovered that the modern Chinese that have immigrated to the States have Americanized their names from the three-part format down to two names, a first and a last. Hence we have folks like Lui Huong and Chen Lee."

"Who is Chen Lee? I've never heard of him!" an astonished Sal Velardi exclaimed. "Is he a distant relative if Bruce Lee?"

"Chen Lee is the diabolical C.L., the Chinese Zodiac Killer," Joe Giralo very deliberately stated with a sparkle gleaming in his eye.

"Dr. Liu Huong was the militant son of a radical Red Chinese Communist, and Huong still had political sympathies towards the current Beijing regime. And conversely," the experienced FBI sleuth disclosed, "Chen Lee absolutely loathes the Red Chinese because *his* father had been a loyal advocate of Chiang-Kai-shek's political philosophy on the island of Formosa, which is now democratically governed Taiwan! And thanks to the deceased Liu Huong's involvement in this unique case," the Chief Inspector added, "an anonymous caller confirmed to me that Huong was having a Bucks County torrid love affair with the wife of our Chinese Serial Killer, Chen Lee! We can accurately call it the Bristol-Bensalem Love Triangle!"

"Great Caesar's Ghost!" Agent Velardi whooped. "We have to get in touch with the Bensalem Police immediately to protect Mrs. Lee from being the 13th murder victim. According to your infallible sense of reasoning, Mrs. Lee had to be born in 1984, the year of the Rat, which would naturally begin the whole Chinese zodiac cycle rotating again, which obviously had been started with Dr. William Stevenson, Victim #1, who like the vulnerable Mrs. Lee, was also probably born in the Year of the Rat."

"Don't worry yourself into a deep coma!" the Boss laughed and assured Agent Velardi. "The very capable Bensalem Police have already apprehended chemist Chen Lee, who incidentally works at Rohm and Haas up in Bristol near the *Delaware*. And Mrs. Jennifer Lee is safe and sound and also quite relieved that her detestable husband has been taken into custody."

"How did you ever manage to solve this extremely intricate murder riddle?" Dan Blachford asked his stellar mentor. "In my humble estimation, you're one and a half neurons short of ascending to the Einstein genius status!"

Inspector Giralo expressed that certain vague hints had gradually turned into clear clues that eventually led to the arrest *that* same morning of villainous Mr. Chen Lee. The Inspector told his men that Drexel University Professor William Stevenson had given Chen Lee a B in *his* Chemistry course, and consequently the "perfectionist" grudge-oriented Taiwanese descendant became so extremely upset that he eventually initiated the Chinese zodiac murder cycle spree. And *that* above-average college B grade led the Boss to Marcus Johnson, the knifed-in-the-back elementary school principal who had threatened to give lunatic Chen Lee's aberrant son a detention if the naughty lad didn't modify his unruly cafeteria behavior.

"The insolent son wasn't even suspended or given a school detention!" Giralo informed Velardi, Orsi and Blachford. "The unruly kid was only sternly threatened with a week's detention, but Chen Lee felt shamed and had to defend his Oriental honor in a terribly perverted manner. Mr. Lee definitely had exhibited the ultimate Alpha-type personality, Chinese-style!"

"Yes Boss, family honor along with the concept of disgrace is definitely a Chinese cultural thing! Were there any other beneficial clues that you had adroitly excavated that went beyond the scope of *our* superficial investigation?" Agent Velardi guiltily asked his very esteemed superior.

"Well Salvatore, Eileen Dunn once represented a client, a scientist from DuPont Chemical Company down in Wilmington, Delaware that had sued our dear Mr. Chen Lee for a minor patent violation," the all-too-thorough Inspector divulged. "But a handsome settlement had been made a week before the civil case ever went to trial."

"How did the mystical Ouija Board come into play as a decisive fact-finding factor?" Agent Velardi demanded knowing. "Maybe you oughta' have a radical gender sex operation and change your name to Madam Zelda!"

"Actually Salvatore, I just used 'the Board' as a foolproof method of capturing your undivided attention on Monday morning," the clever Inspector remarked and then lengthily chuckled. "The all-too-common oracle board was deftly used as a sort of verification mechanism and not as an original means of making any accurate serial killer prediction. Let's just refer to it as a motivational device, and let's simply reckon Sal that *our* anxious finger vibrations identified what I had already known."

"One thing still puzzles me," Agent Orsi sincerely confessed. "If Mrs. Jennifer Lee was so terrified of her husband's rage that she failed to report him to the local authorities, how did you really get the final goods on Lee?"

"That's all fairly elementary my Dear Orsi!" the Inspector replied, frivolously imitating the honorable Sherlock Holmes addressing Dr. Watson. "My dependable brother-in-law Philip Ennis is a terrific Private Investigator who was able to systematically coordinate all of the known facts and then fabricate them into a coherent story. If it weren't for *his* reliable services," Joe Giralo candidly credited and confessed, "I'd still be fooling around with the cardboard Ouija Board, being greatly frustrated and trying to figure-out who the mysterious culprit C.L. was!"

"And all the while I had thought that you were Mike Hammer or Sergeant Joe Friday reincarnated!" Sal Velardi chided with a trace of sarcasm engendered in his hoarse tone of voice. "In reality, all of your brilliant deductions in your more high-profile cases should be attributed to your very talented brother-in-law, Private Eye Philip Ennis! He's probably done plenty of vital investigative work for you during your entire FBI career!"

"True Salvatore, and with *this* latest colorful feather firmly planted in my cap, I can finally retire at *my* discretion with honor from the Bureau!" the veteran Inspector proudly announced. "And I want you three industrious Men to know that in due time, in perhaps three decades or so, I'm going to recommend one of you noble scholars to be my replacement, that is, once I evolve out of this daunting business of being a dutiful-but-exhausted FBI Investigator."

# "Corporate Sabotage"

As Agents Salvatore Velardi, Arthur Orsi and Dan Blachford entered Philadelphia FBI headquarters at 600 Arch Street, the three government men were casually discussing the amusing theory that their boss Chief Inspector Joe Giralo was indeed one hundred percent psychic, or perhaps one hundred percent "psycho." But as the trio would soon discover, the rather astonishing case of "Corporate Sabotage" virtually confirmed their suspicions about their enigmatic boss's seemingly paranormal cerebrum.

"Our distinguished Mentor always reiterates to us that wily criminals, along with avowed terrorists, are people, just like us; and that those same nefarious anarchists tend to think and behave in observable and measurable patterns, just like *we* do," Agent Velardi accurately declared as the 'dynamic threesome' awaited the arrival of the lobby elevator to transport them up to the building's eighth floor. "But truly, the Inspector has the uncanny ability to connect formerly unrelated dots that ultimately lead *us* to solving certain enigmatic developments. He calls his talent 'a simple knack', but I think it's all much more complicated than just that!"

"Yes Sal, I wholly agree with your assessment," Agent Art Orsi confirmed. "I still think the Chief is psychic although he constantly maintains that all he does is cleverly associate parallel situations and then uses the process of deduction inside the ordinary 'scientific method of thinking' in order to amazingly verify his unique theories. If the Chief were born a woman," Agent Orsi awkwardly joked, "I'm sure that his full name would've been Clair Voyant!"

"Ha, ha, ha!" Agent Dan Blachford giddily reacted as the familiar gray metal elevator doors opened. "That's the tenth time you've told that terribly poor joke, but it always catches me off-guard! Of course, Arty, please remember that when we quietly enter *his* solemn office, the Chief will instinctively make us suffer through listening to a barrage of irrelevant small-talk before gradually introducing our ears to the crux of our next assignment."

Upon exiting the elevator at the eighth floor, Agents Velardi, Orsi and Blachford swiftly entered Chief Joe Giralo's brightly illuminated office and immediately noticed their illustrious superior predictably sitting behind his prodigious oak desk and conscientiously examining the front-page newspaper headlines of the *Philadelphia Inquirer.* Raising his balding head, the inimitable Inspector was quite pleased upon realizing that his capable men had punctually arrived to honor their scheduled Friday, June 14th, 2013 briefing.

"Today's Flag Day, but needless to say, *we* FBI fellows must be highly patriotic three-hundred and sixty-five days a year," garrulous Inspector Giralo commenced his narrative. "Now in the interest of unselfish citizen volunteerism, I'm glad that ten years ago I had sponsored you three distinguished Gentlemen into the Hammonton Lions Club, so obviously, I don't have to remind you Guys that on Sunday, June 30th the four of us will be on duty selling a variety of pastries at the annual Blueberry Festival, which this year will take place at the high school campus grounds on Old Forks Road."

"Yes Boss!" respectfully answered Agent Velardi with a contrived smile. "Hammonton, New Jersey is known as the Blueberry Capital of the World with around ten-to-fifteen thousand acres of the lush blue fruit under cultivation. People from over a hundred-mile radius flock to our small agricultural town to anxiously buy crates of blueberries and various food items made from them."

"And honestly, I've become an accomplished expert at selling blueberry strudel, turnovers, pies and muffins," Agent Orsi genially added to the perfunctory dialogue. "And this year we're also including delicious blueberry-frosted doughnuts to our ever-expanding sales' menu! I'll bet that this year we'll sell-out of our yummy items before 2 p.m. And frankly, I hope we do, especially if the thermometer's mercury hits ninety-seven degrees like it did at the sweltering Lions Concession Tent last summer!"

"And I gotta' mention that our civic service is all done for a good cause," Agent Dan Blachford contributed to the mandatory preliminary conversation. "Our club uses the fund-raising money to purchase eyeglasses for needy school kids, to allow for eye exams' for the less fortunate, to proudly help and support other charitable community organizations, and finally, to assist Lions International in achieving its all-important world-wide aide mission. And Boss," Blachford resumed his characteristic drivel, "selling the blueberry pastries is really an easy task. Every year I'm quite willing to participate in such special humanitarian activity."

Agent Velardi alertly recognized that it was now time to get down to essential 'FBI brass tacks', so the dedicated law enforcement official diplomatically requested hearing and learning the true nature of the important Friday, Flag Day official conference. Inspector Joe Giralo instantly accommodated his inquisitive subordinate's alert suggestion and began stating a feasible exposition that was keenly pertinent to the perplexing subject-at-hand.

"I hate sounding like a verbose courtroom trial lawyer," Joe Giralo predictably and generally replied, "but in my limited estimation, every instance of major criminal or terrorist energy first involves the aspect of *opportunity* and secondly, a definitive *motive* to engage in what constitutes malicious felonious conduct. *That* very crucial foundation being firmly established," the long-winded Inspector continued his incessant prattling, "we're presently dealing with a series of diabolical events all remarkably concerning, etymologically speaking, the historical French word for 'shoe'."

"Since a good number of Puerto Ricans and Mexicans live in Hammonton and vicinity, I know for a fact that 'zapato' happens to be the common Spanish terminology for the common English word 'shoe', but kindly educate my ignorance Boss; exactly what is the appropriate French nomenclature for 'shoe'?" Agent Velardi politely requested knowing.

"The French name for shoe is 'sabot', and our English noun 'sabotage' is derived from it," Joe Giralo casually explained to his slightly embarrassed government listeners. "Now then, according to experienced lexicographers, in the eighteen-hundreds, during the height of the Industrial Revolution, French and Dutch factory workers feared that newly manufactured machines would soon replace *their* workforce existence and therefore, the new-found devices would make the dependent employees obsolete and consequently, out of jobs. And so, according to popular belief the worried workers used their shoes, especially hard wooden ones to stop the mechanical gears from rotating; thus deliberately committing the act of sabotage!"

"Okay, thanks for the somewhat informative language lesson," Agent Art Orsi almost cynically commented. "But could you please be more specific about your rather fascinating 'sabotage' allusion. I strongly suspect that your next related statement will pertain to certain industrial explosions that have occurred at monthly intervals at plants and corporate businesses throughout the country! Is my present assessment correct, Boss?"

Chief Joe Giralo inhaled a deep breath and then orally reviewed the sequence of intentional destructive incidents that had recently occurred at various corporate entities across the USA. Strangely enough, the vile events happening on the first day of each month, with each devastating episode directly involving the elements of heinous human opportunity coupled with wicked human motive. The Inspector's audience of three listened attentively to his very methodical and meticulous oral commentary, which had been carefully outlined, typed and documented on two printed pages.

"Frankly, Fellas', I'm more than a trifle bewildered, or should I say baffled by this skein of apparent random acts of violence, which incidentally have killed over six dozen innocent people and have injured or hospitalized four hundred other American workers," Joe

Giralo sadly shared and reported. "Just this month there was that terrible hotel explosion in downtown Baltimore, and in May, the horrific Wall Street stock exchange detonation. And then in April, if you recall," Chief Giralo emphasized, "we had the tragic..."

"Wisconsin meat packing plant detonation," Agent Velardi recollected and excitedly mentioned. "But I can't seem to remember the March disaster that had transpired."

"In March, there was the enormous catastrophe with the blowing-up of the crowded casino down in New Orleans," Chief Giralo completed Agent Sal Velardi's unfinished sentence, thus refreshing the federal detective's faltering memory. "And back in early February, the enormous steel mill in Western Pennsylvania had nearly been demolished, crippling it to half of its former daily production. What unbridled brazen audacity!"

"And oh yes," Agent Art Orsi anxiously piped-up. "Back in January a large insurance firm had been barbarically dynamited in the Big Apple, and that's precisely when the FBI began coordinating our investigative efforts with those of the beleaguered New York City police authorities."

"Your brain cells appear to be commendably functioning today Arty," congratulated a rather impressed Chief Giralo. "And Fellas', be mindful that each despicable event had taken place in or around large U.S. Metropolitan areas, which the unscrupulous antagonists evidently now think are strategic soft targets. And in December of last year, an important electric utility grid had been seriously sabotaged and damaged out in Central Indiana."

"Do you suppose that radical environmental activist groups are responsible for these contemptible, evil deeds?" Agent Velardi theorized and asked. "What about disgruntled Socialists or perhaps demented Communists who absolutely despise the fabulous success of American free enterprise, better known to *them* in their twisted vernacular, 'imperial capitalism'?"

"Your shrewd speculation is meritorious indeed," Joe Giralo complimented. "And yes, Salvatore, your admirable conjecture warrants our immediate exploration. But let's stay mainly focused here while we're still in our cursory initial analysis stage. Back in November, mass casualties had again been inflicted when a large internationally connected Pittsburgh bank had been virtually rocked from its very foundation, which therefore leads the FBI to conclude that pure, plain terrorism is directly involved in the enactment of *that* particular calamity."

After a moment of silence, the four puzzled G-men then thoroughly discussed the rather gruesome October Boston,

180

Massachusetts telecommunications' center detonation, along with the early September insurance health care complex conflagration, which coincidentally also had occurred in downtown Boston."

"Perhaps there's a very well-structured and well-coordinated terror network carelessly operating with total impunity up there in Bean Town," audacious Agent Daniel Blachford logically hypothesized and contributed. "Two gigantic explosions, both terrible disasters having occurred within a month's duration at two separate-but-key Boston financial institutions. Does *that* totally unique fact tell us anything relevant or what?"

"And let's not forget that in August of last year," Agent Orsi imprudently interrupted, "a huge department store had been partially crumbled down in Tampa, Florida. And when all of this indecipherable craziness began occurring back in July, Boston had again been affected with a large commercial structure being instantaneously put out of operation due to a series of nasty explosions that would've made Mr. Alfred Nobel regret that he had ever invented dynamite! What's your sage opinion Boss?"

The ever-vigilant Chief Inspector reflected for a full half-minute and then cited a very salient observation which his perceptive mind had been objectively assessing and evaluating. "Now Guys, I'm beginning to identify a certain plausible systematic pattern in this extraordinary evolution of man-made disasters. Besides the American economy being savagely targeted," perceptive Inspector Giralo qualified and persuasively remarked, "I've also detected something peculiarly sinister that's quite evident in the last two months' developments, namely, June and May."

"What are they?" Blachford requested knowing. "My present recollection is vague."

"First of all, I had neglected to state that besides the enormous hotel explosion in Baltimore, there was the shocking Silicon Valley computer chip company catastrophe on the very same day. And besides the recent May New York City stock exchange explosion, during *that* exact same day the hyperactive and dangerous Boston-area villains had again initiated widespread havoc by setting-off bombs at a large open-air park rock concert. This treacherous sequence of lethal, monthly destruction now compels me to believe that we're going-up against a network of determined and deadly terrorists whose principal goal is, metaphorically speaking, to evilly bring the flourishing American economy to its knees."

"Well, Inspector, please give us some direct instructions on how we should proceed from here?" now-motivated Agent Salvatore Velardi imperatively insisted. "The economic pillars of American business cannot afford to be further attacked by these mysterious, pernicious enemies, either foreign or home-grown terrorists, or by any hybrid combination of both! Should we be sent-up to Boston to thoroughly investigate the matter?"

"Men, be in my office at noon a week from today, that is, on Friday June 21st," Chief Giralo sternly commanded his now-addled underlings. "In the meantime, perform some comprehensive research on what has just been related and reviewed, and I presume, of course, you'll all loyally execute *that* order in addition to diligently pursuing your other more mundane regular assignments. And also, Gentlemen," Inspector Joe Giralo summarized, "adequately rest-up for the purpose of selling your delectable strudel, your turnovers, your pies and your doughnuts at the Lions Stand during the upcoming June 30th Hammonton Blueberry Festival!"

* * * * * * * * * * * *

At noon the following Friday Inspector Joe Giralo's three loyal associates passively strolled into their boss's all-too-familiar eighth floor office, the 'in the dark' trio finding their stellar mentor sitting erect behind his impressive Canadian oak desk and as expected, carefully reading the early morning edition of the *Philadelphia Inquirer*. The unperturbed Chief glanced-up with his dark brown eyes tacitly acknowledging the presence of disciples Velardi, Orsi and Blachford. Soon a benign smile formed upon the boss's large lips.

"I'm glad you Fellas' aren't out deep-sea fishing from our favorite Cape May marina," Joe Giralo greeted the faithful-and-frequent arrivals to 600 Arch Street. "But don't be supremely surprised if I decide to send you zany mavericks on an FBI 'fishing expedition' within the next several weeks to assist me in solving this complex corporate sabotage conundrum that's also been cruelly riddling my staunch federal colleague Matt Riley along with his active team of crackerjack investigators down at DC headquarters."

"Stop being so darned facetious about *this* very troubling mystery!" Sal Velardi audaciously exclaimed. "And for the record, you keep your boat over at Chestnut Neck Marina at the mouth of the Mullica River, just north of Atlantic City. And Boss, Art, Dan and myself only accompany you into the *Atlantic* because we simply love becoming nauseously seasick. Your flimsy floating tub, or should I say 'sleek fishing boat', has an exceptional propensity for always finding and then challenging the biggest, wildest, most powerful ocean waves out there! I believe that the three of *us* chronic victims are truly vulnerable gluttons for punishment!"

182

"Well then, Salvatore, it's now time for you to stop imitating befuddled Dr. Watson and to commence thinking like the incomparable Private Detective Sherlock Holmes. Let's cease being so frivolous and begin talking some pertinent shop lingo," Inspector Giralo assertively answered, his heightened voice deftly changing the dialogue's tenor from jovial-to-serious. "We have to assiduously hunt, track-down and capture these clandestine, lunatic, domestic saboteurs and also, we must learn who's secretly financing their almost-satanic hatred for the United States of America. Now, Agent Velardi," the Chief bluntly resumed pontificating, "what is *your* honest synopsis of who's directly responsible for this rash of bombings that's gotten the voracious press along with the entire paranoid citizenry going positively haywire."

"It's my personal theory that someone very wealthy with great accessible resources is egregiously subsidizing these dastardly attacks being rendered upon major corporate enterprises coast-to-coast; most of them being listed either on the New York Stock Exchange or on the alternative NASDAQ over-the-counter market," Agent Velardi attested. "Even the brazen demonic assaults on the companies' subsidiaries appear to be *subsidized.*"

"A cute-but-clumsy play on words," curtly replied the usually introspective Inspector. "But truthfully Salvatore, I don't suspect that a foremost American billionaire like Donald Trump, Warren Buffett or Bill Gates would be involved in deliberately destroying corporate America for *his* own sinister personal gain. If your conjecture holds any merit Sal," the Chief effectively articulated, "rationally speaking, the anonymous behind-the-scenes money person calling all of the abominable shots would not be any traitorous American mogul but instead, the backer would probably be a diabolical foreign entrepreneur intentionally capitalizing on causing the gradual downfall of American capitalism. Now then Arty," pensive Joe Giralo pondered and then spontaneously stated in typical fashion, "what innovative hypothesis have *you* constructively formulated?"

"Actually Boss, now that you've solicited my humble opinion, I believe that this alluded-to unknown main perpetrator has concocted a roster, or should I say 'a list' of various national industries that are conveniently represented on the New York Big Board and on the corresponding NASDAQ Stock Exchange, which as you know consists mostly of more-risky high tech' growth corporations. For example," Agent Orsi nervously elaborated, "we've already had the following industry classifications being deviously singled-out and battered: a mammoth iron and steel factory, a prominent media and broadcasting entity, vulnerable banking and insurance buildings, a famous health care company, an important Central U.S. utility business along with its accompanying indispensable-but-vulnerable electrical grid, a greatly prestigious telecommunications firm, a well-known computer-related company, a very popular Louisiana gambling casino and lastly, a landmark hotel in Baltimore along with a modern department store located in downtown Tampa, Florida."

"And what do *you* make of this comprehensive industry laundry list you've quite patiently organized and compiled?" Joe Giralo directly queried Agent Orsi. "I mean Arty, what specific details do you suppose exist other than the already-established fact that the aforementioned attacked businesses are all listed either on the New York Stock Exchange or on the lesser-trafficked NASDAQ ticker tape?"

"I postulate Inspector that the next brutal attacks will be narrowed-down to one of the remaining flourishing industries that have yet to be targeted," Agent Orsi verbally advanced. "For instance, certain Detroit automotive plants, vital Allegheny coal mining installations, necessary interstate railroads, under-guarded airline manufacturers out in the Seattle area, large chemical producers along with integral East and West Coast oil and gas refineries that have yet to be hit. My gut-hunch sort of somewhat winnows-down the target list of industries that are mendaciously slated for attack on the dangerous-but-anonymous evildoers' totally vile agenda."

"Meritorious speculation exhibited, Arty!" generously praised Inspector Giralo. "Meritorious indeed! Now tell me Dan, what exotic assumption or premise have you *industriously* concocted? Obviously, you have two fairly tough acts to follow, and allow me to remind you Blachford; *this* serious venue I'm now conducting isn't Vaudeville slapstick comedy!"

"Yes Chief, I'll basically endorse what Sal and Arty have just impressively presented," Agent Blachford cautiously prefaced and then briefly hesitated. "But to be terse, I'm more inclined to agree with *your* erudite interpretation of grim reality, and so Inspector, I candidly believe that malignant foreign elements are stealthily instigating this ugly epidemic of callous domestic chaos. My current take on the matter is that some jealous enemy state like, let's say for the sake of argument, an envious oil-rich Arab country or perhaps Russia or China, or possibly maybe a combination of any of those three distinct entities is attempting to author the economic downfall of American capitalism."

"You mean to say, Dan," Joe Giralo interrupted, "that you believe international-type terrorism is at play rather than anarcho-domestic terrorism?"

"I mean to say Boss, at the UN both Russia and China have been perpetually opposing intelligent U.S. Initiatives presented to the Security Council, and those two mischievous countries are constantly endeavoring to rub vinegar into Uncle Sam's eyes with their enormous-sized thumbs!"

"Brilliant depiction Dan!" commended Inspector Giralo. "I'll surely take the testimonies of all three of you veteran sleuths under advisement. Now on Monday Fellas', I plan to drive down to Washington and spend a full week conferring with my knowledgeable superior, the venerable and loquacious Mr. Matt Riley. Our little weeklong research-oriented parley should help *us* unravel this rather perplexing chain of surreptitious corporate destruction. And please don't be overly surprised if before July 1st *we* ultimately have to enlist the invaluable services of Colonel Bob Bauers and his highly-skilled Delta Force commando units!"

"Then judging by your especially bold last statement, you've miraculously acquired some significant leads to this truly puzzling sabotage case," Agent Velardi sagaciously concluded and declared. "Why must Art, Dan and I always feel like we're three useless burned-out light bulbs ready for replacement?"

"Demonstrate the proven virtues of patience and prudence, that's my sacred motto!" Joe Giralo austerely recommended. "Now then Guys, I'll meet you three Dick Tracy impersonators at 7 a.m. sharp on Sunday, June 30th for breakfast inside Mary's Restaurant on Bellevue Avenue in downtown Hammonton. We'll need some excellent nutrition before heading over to the Blueberry Festival's Lions Club Tent, because the weatherman's extended prognostication predicts that it's gonna' be a real scorcher and we're goin' to sizzle like three of Mary's bacon strips over at the high school campus grounds."

"Sounds like we'll be having a delicious brunch just before visiting Purgatory!" Art Orsi humorously opined. "Sorry to butt-in, Inspector!"

"Yes, Arty. Maybe our Mary's Restaurant breakfast seminar will help us 'bring home the bacon'," Sal Velardi jested.

Inspector Giralo deliberately ignored his agents' weak attempts at doing impromptu comedy. "And Guys, by the time we enthusiastically enjoy our tasty coffee, bacon, eggs, home fries and pancakes at Mary's eatery," Joe Giralo vociferously continued his anticipated didactic narrative, "I hereby predict that Matt Riley and I should have this problematic 'Corporate Sabotage Caper' all figured-out and fully resolved. Now, I'll see you three junior detective marvels on the 30th of the month, a mere two hours before we start sweating and selling our blueberry strudel, turnovers, muffins, pies and doughnuts!"

Astonished FBI Agents Salvatore Velardi, Arthur Orsi and Dan Blachford incredulously stared at each other in absolute awe, all three accomplished investigators thoroughly-confounded before slowly leaving the Arch Street premises, the veteran trio believing that either Chief Inspector Joe Giralo was indeed supernaturally and inexplicably "psychic" or that their unique immediate supervisor had flamboyantly gone totally insane.

* * * * * * * * * * * *

On the morning of June 30th, the four unsung FBI officers sat isolated in the rear dining room of Mary's Restaurant on Bellevue Avenue, the cooperative owner sacrificing the overflow dining area so that Inspector Giralo and his ambitious G-men could conveniently converse their ongoing business in private. A pleasant, tanned Sicilian waitress interrupted their introductory business discourse by competently taking their commonplace breakfast orders and then fifteen minutes later, efficiently delivering their individual requests and then adroitly pouring second cups of fresh-brewed coffee.

"Well Men, did I ever tell you that the word 'breakfast' actually means to 'break-the-fast', since we had fasted all night without eating," Giralo typically lectured.

"Thanks plenty, Inspector, for adding tremendously to my empirical knowledge," Agent Velardi replied. "I'm really thrilled that I woke-up this morning so that I could listen to your trite drivel!"

Joe Giralo was not-at-all impressed with his agent's sarcastic remark. "Well, Men, the annual Blueberry Festival has arrived on your Lions' kitchen wall calendars," Inspector Giralo reckoned and quickly smiled. "Remember to stay fully hydrated for the next six hours. From past experience, I advise that we all drink several quarts of water in the interim. The temperature might reach 100 by noon!"

"Boss, June 30th to me means that more corporate explosions are imminent, with tomorrow conspicuously being July 1st," Sal Velardi meaningfully injected into the fresh 'Bureau conversation'. "What, if anything, did you and your compatible *comrade* Matt Riley determine this past week and a half down in good old DC? Did you two crime-fighting geniuses attend a ten-day séance session?"

"Well Salvatore, Matt and I don't believe that any white marble or granite-facade national monuments are presently in dire danger in the nation's capital," the Chief courteously answered. "Riley and I agree that only corporate business properties are currently in jeopardy. But

Salvatore, you weren't too far off-base when you had inadvertently used the particular vernacular *comrade*."

"You mean to say that Dan was right all along and that Russia is furtively behind scheming-up this frustrating wave of industrial sabotage?" Agent Velardi wondered and proposed. "Dan must be acquiring some outstanding psychic abilities from you, Chief!"

"Well, my Good Man," The Savant nonchalantly uttered before gulping-down several ounces of flavorful, steaming-hot java. "I'm delighted to report that last night Colonel Bob Bauers and his elite Delta Force units mutually raided two safe-houses; one had been situated in suburban Boston and another one located on the southern outskirts of St. Louis. For you see, dear Salvatore, the next targeted objectives for the ruthless saboteurs to attempt their intentional destruction would've been legendary Fenway Park along with the fabled Anheuser-Busch Brewery; the pair of wicked, contemplated, insidious acts being consecutively and respectively performed."

"How in Heaven did you ever discover those two landmark targets being deliberately selected?" an astounded Agent Art Orsi demanded knowing. "I must admit Chief, your fantastic crime-methodology is floating somewhere between outlandish and phenomenal!"

"I suggest that you three over-zealous novices avidly read the terrific detective stories authored by the great literary genius Edgar Allan Poe, and then you would subsequently learn the essential thought-evolution process that's often described in exclusive academic circles as *ratiocination*, which, in general, is the very practical investigative technique that had been competently implemented by the wonderful, fictional character Detective Auguste Dupin, a 19th Century marvel whose wonderful law enforcement acumen I relentlessly attempt duplicating."

"Forget the vague college literary references Boss, and for a welcomed change, kindly provide us with some straight-forward language," Agent Blachford angrily insisted, totally out of character. "I'm already excessively fatigued from overwhelming weariness, with my stymied brain incessantly evaluating your litany of nebulous monologues, happening only mere hours before I'm ever toiling in the hot summer sun, diligently vending heat-softened blueberry strudel and disintegrating muffins!"

"First of all, Dan, seven malice-minded saboteurs have been recently killed during the separate Boston and St. Louis Delta Force raids, and another five pugnacious rogues have been captured, and the obedient thugs in custody have already spilled some quality information during enhanced CIA interrogation sessions. And as a matter of fact," the informed Inspector lowly added, "the whole crazy scenario has plenty to do with professional football, with the lowest common denominator being the last twelve Super Bowl winners, and the eleventh and twelfth games simultaneously involving the losing teams also! How clearer and more vivid can I be than that?"

The three extremely-confused agents instantly stopped eating their sumptuous breakfasts, and the flabbergasted trio listened attentively to Inspector Joe Giralo's coy explanation.

"The first potent explosion occurred in early June inside a downtown Baltimore hotel, and using the sophisticated Auguste Dupin style of 'parallel deductive reasoning', I eventually fathomed that last year's Super Bowl winner had been the awesome Baltimore Ravens, the NFL champions beating the San Francisco 49ers by a close score of 34-31. And Fellas', next my fertile mind immediately associated the fact that the second devastating terror blast had occurred on May 1$^{st}$ on the floor of the New York Stock Exchange and that Super Bowl 46 had been coincidentally won by the New York Giants; the Gotham juggernaut surprisingly defeating the seemingly invincible New England Patriots by a score of 21-17, the unforgettable inter-league Super Bowl contest occurring in February of 2012. Do you three contemporary philosophers now adequately comprehend most of this incredible scenario?"

As the three listeners at the round table sat there stunned with their mouths agape, Inspector Giralo continued ingeniously elucidating about the now-rational terror-plot pattern. A reputable Wisconsin meatpacking plant had been bombed on April Fool's Day and ironically, the Green Bay Packers had successfully conquered the tough Pittsburgh Steelers in Super Bowl 45. And next, a busy Louisiana casino had been mercilessly crumbled on March 1$^{st}$ to correspond with the New Orleans Saints celebrating a thrilling 21-17 victory over the Indianapolis Colts in Super Bowl 44, and then in February of 2009, the fearsome Pittsburgh Steelers had edged-out the St. Louis Cardinals in Super Bowl 43, the winning margin being a meager four-point differential.

"I now understand the unique dual evolution of events happening in opposite directions!" exclaimed an amazed Agent Orsi. "Every *month* backwards, in terms of a detrimental bombing, *that* time interval directly correlates with another *year* backwards in regard to specific Super Bowl winners. I presume that the staggering double sequence is consistent with other *monthly* TNT detonations and with past *yearly* Super Bowl champions too."

"True Arty!" unfazed Joe Giralo politely verified. "All the way back to Super Bowl 37 in the year 2003 played at Qualcomm Stadium in San Diego when Tampa Bay had clobbered the Oakland Raiders,

48-21. But then Fellas', I perceptively recognized that a large Tampa department store along with a huge Silicon Valley computer company had dually been attacked and severely damaged, and of course, Silicon Valley is not too far from the Oakland-San Francisco Bay area. Matt Riley and I became very concerned about the progressive, horrible monthly events, especially when I sadly thought about innocent human beings all across the country becoming statistical collateral damage!"

"So Boss, that's how your marvelous brain had narrowed-down tomorrow's July 1st cities to two, Boston and St. Louis, since being an avid football fan myself, I recollect that the New England Patriots had luckily squeezed by the St. Louis Cardinals in the 2002 Super Bowl, the exact score being...."

"New England barely winning, 20-17," Joe Giralo authoritatively revealed, infallibly referring to his accurately typed list that the FBI Chief had been confidently holding in his hands. "But just yesterday, I realized and concluded that it doesn't really matter who wins or who loses because both participating Super Bowl metropolises will now certainly be attacked according to the saboteurs' *revised* assigned schedule. That's precisely when Matt Riley and I wisely notified Colonel Bauers to dispatch his daring commando units to both Boston and St. Louis to await further instructions from the Pentagon, that is, once the lethargic, mentally-challenged Washington bureaucrats gave us the official okay to proceed with our intricate dual Massachusetts and Missouri military interceptions."

"Absurdly incredible!" gasped an exasperated Dan Blachford. "I suddenly feel enlightened and inspired! But now that our cream-of-the-crop Armed Forces have bravely captured or killed the two-city saboteurs, tell us confidentially, Inspector. Who is the degenerate mastermind-financier, the pathetic jerk who's actually behind the disgustingly despicable Super Bowl teams' plot?"

"His ignominious name is Gunther Schmidt," the Chief softly disclosed before imbibing some more tasty hot coffee. "This deranged billionaire had silently accumulated a tremendous fortune working the black markets in East Germany before the Berlin Wall had been knocked-down after the famed President Reagan speech, the dramatic event signaling the collapse of the dreaded Soviet Empire's firm domination over Eastern Europe. This filthy-rich decadent crook Gunther Schmidt possesses great animosity towards American democracy and also towards our American free enterprise system. His utter disdain goes way back to his early days as a card-carrying member of the Communist Party. And so, with *this germane* biographical background, my Fine-Feathered Friends," the long-winded Boss forcefully expounded, "this reclusive-but-wealthy European maniac, this disgustingly paranoid Gunther Schmidt, easily enlisted the support of certain...."

"Of certain fanatical followers still loyal to the mandates of the Communist Manifesto," Agent Velardi realized and expressed. "And those same bellicose dye-in-the-wool Soviet nutcases became Schmidt's devout saboteurs, the felons conducting atrocious demolition operations inside the continental United States while being protected, sheltered and concealed by a vast network of strategically located safehouses; which represented sort of a deplorable, contemporary-style Underground Railroad, designated for criminal-minded East German terrorists; and all of the rather nasty thugs possessing extremely dangerous, evil, Lenin-Stalin-Khrushchev-like, political convictions! How bizarrely reprehensible can it get?"

"But Boss, what ulterior motive other than deeply despising American capitalism did this secretive hermit Gunther Schmidt have?" Art Orsi curiously inquired. "What made all of the venomous acrimony inside this devious madman suddenly erupt like Mt. Vesuvius had done in 79 A.D?"

Inspector Giralo genuinely indicated that he and Matt Riley had discovered that Gunther Schmidt had been investing tens of millions of Euros into gold, platinum and silver stocks, and that if the demented tycoon could wickedly and successfully injure large American corporations listed on the major national stock exchanges, then the avaricious crackpot's substantial gold, platinum and silver holdings would more than quadruple, eventually making Schmidt the wealthiest investor on the entire planet.

"But I don't think that Gunther Schmidt desired seeing another World-wide Great Depression similar to the one that had evolved in the late 1920s and early 1930s," the eminent Chief philosophically purported, "simply because a full-scale global economic debacle would mean the fall of governments along with the rise of horrifying tyrants and dictators akin to last century's Adolph Hitler, Joseph Stalin and Benito Mussolini. This covetous East German fellow, our former nemesis Gunther Schmidt, I strenuously maintain, solely wanted to temporarily bring the world's biggest economies to their knees so that his colossal global gold, platinum and silver investments would soon vastly proliferate."

"But what gave this introverted German tycoon-turned maniac the idea of cleverly matching *monthly* demolitions with *yearly* Super Bowl games, with both distinct phenomena obviously going in opposite reverse chronological patterns?" Agent Velardi intelligently asked. "To me, in my modest estimation, such an incredible strategy seems like sheer contemptuous, evil genius!"

"That's relatively *elementary* to answer, my dear Dr. Watson imitator," the enamored Boss calmly and satirically stated. "Eastern Europeans absolutely love football, but it's not American football I'm referring to. *Their* football is what *we* in the U.S. call 'soccer', and so, it stands to reason that an obscure psychotic criminal like this loon Schmidt would be no different than his East German saboteur counterparts. But when I astutely recognized the unique similarities of the reverse chronological yearly Super Bowl pattern and the correlative reverse-sequence monthly corporate disaster timetable, I then merely equated the two opposite-direction factors to effectively decipher Gunther Schmidt's imaginative-but-devilish pro' football game formula!"

"That was pretty brilliant analysis on your part," Art Orsi commended his mentor. "Are there any other pertinent details?"

"Yes, Arty. Since I have several close relatives living in Baltimore," Inspector Giralo further editorialized, "I was very aware of the Baltimore Ravens being victorious over the San Francisco 49ers in Super Bowl 47 on February 3rd of *this* year. And yes, besides *that* rather particular circumstance," Joe Giralo proudly continued his exceptional revelation, "ironically, my wife and I had vacationed at the targeted downtown Baltimore Hotel, the same place where one of my cousin's sons had gotten married three summers ago, back in tranquil 2010!"

"And certainly, of course, just like with his string of advantageous investments, covetous Gunther Schmidt had also gotten carelessly greedy with his detonations and with his calamitous industrial fires," Dan Blachford rather lucidly declared. "And when the overconfident, rich bully began arrogantly targeting both the winning and losing Super Bowl teams' cities," the savvy agent summarized, "that's what eventually led to his ultimate demise. Money isn't the root cause of all evil! Excessive greed is!"

"Very well put into logical paragraph form, Dan!" complimented an invigorated Inspector Giralo, who reluctantly reached into his pants pocket and then left the attractive brunette waitress a splendid ten-dollar tip. "When Tampa and Oakland had been concurrently hit, I automatically knew that tomorrow, July 1st, both St. Louis and Boston would next be slated for planned, belligerent assaults, with the intended cities simply being innocent participants in the memorable 2002 Super Bowl plot."

"I'm almost lost for words. Someone please tell me, what's this totally crazy world coming to?" befuddled Agent Arthur Orsi rather philosophically asked.

"It's not coming to anything, Arty," Salvatore Velardi euphorically replied. "All the Earth does is continuously revolve in an orbit around the sun every three-hundred and sixty-five days or so! Now finally Boss, it's a good thing that the football game sequential pattern didn't start with Super Bowl 1 way back in 1967. That would've probably made the whole ball of wax much more difficult to identify, dissect and solve. Tell us Chief, is this toxic commodities' creep Gunther Schmidt now in government custody?"

"Affirmative!" Joe Giralo mildly exclaimed and confirmed. "Much to the treacherous fiend's warranted chagrin, Interpol authorities had the neurotic psycho' arrested several hours ago while the villainous high-roller was quietly gambling away a small fortune at the renowned Monte Carlo Casino over in gorgeous, semi-tropical Monaco. I don't believe that this not-used-to-losing maniac Gunther Schmidt is presently happily enjoying his swift and abrupt plummet from grace! The shamed scoundrel's loss is society's wonderful gain! Actually, it's civilization's wonderful gain! Now wouldn't you distinguished nimrods tend to agree?"

"What's our next immediate challenge, Chief?" non-reticent Arthur Orsi inquired. "This last one was pretty dramatic and quite traumatic, too! I think my normally reliable cerebrum has suddenly transformed into a frail and mediocre second cerebellum!"

"Okay Men, now that the Three Stooges' comedy hour has grotesquely commenced, and since *your* rather bad humor has thoroughly contaminated our little esoteric dialogue," Inspector Giralo surmised and divulged with a broad grin displayed upon his fat countenance, "let's head on over to Hammonton High School and sell some mouth-watering baked blueberry products for the town Lions Club while we're all mutually still experiencing silly-but-jovial frames of mind!"

"Inspector, we still think you're psychic!" finished a now-energetic Agent Salvatore Velardi. "You won't be receiving any crystal ball gift from us next Christmas! In all honesty, Chief, *we* don't believe you really need one!"

# "Missing Persons"

On the third Monday morning of September, 2012, veteran FBI Agents Salvatore Velardi, Arthur Orsi and Dan Blachford hastily showed-up on the porch steps of Chief Inspector Joe Giralo's Hammonton New, Jersey 321 Orchard Street home, the curious trio wondering what "the new urgent business" was all about that had been received on such short cell phone notice. The "in the dark" triumvirate was quickly greeted at the front door by their illustrious boss, who invited them inside with a stern expression appearing upon his chubby countenance. The host graciously escorted the new arrivals towards the downstairs' anterior section of his home.

"My wife's taken the daughters out to the Deptford Mall for some clothes shopping, so now we can converse in private without any apprehensions about being overheard or eavesdropped upon," the Chief informed his three loyal associates. "Let's sit around the dining room table. We'll review some important details about the latest area case, but first-off Fellas', it's only just mid-September and the local farm markets over on the White Horse Pike are already selling pumpkins and advertising Halloween hay rides even though there's still another full week left in summer. Why the area fruit and vegetable stands rush the fall season is beyond me. Who in his or her right mind really desires to see dreaded winter snow along with sleet blizzards approaching?" Giralo rhetorically asked. "It goes against reason!"

Seeing that no verbal responses were forthcoming from his temporarily confused crime-fighting disciples, the Boss, as was his peculiar habit in regard to small-talk preceding the vital subject at hand, politely asked his men what each had done the past weekend. Feeling more motivated than his momentarily reticent colleagues, Agent Sal Velardi was the first to provide an apt answer.

"Chief, over the past year, Kathy and I had earned room and meal comps at Harrahs Casino, so my wife and I spent Friday and Saturday nights relaxing in Atlantic City," Agent Velardi amiably reported. "We blew three hundred bucks in the casino, but factoring in the free earned room cost for two nights, along with two breakfasts and two buffets for gratis, I figure that we probably broke even in terms of dollars and cents. But in retrospect, I should've listened to the sage advice of my old senior year English teacher who would often joke, 'I'd rather proctor than gamble'!"

"Well, Inspector," Agent Orsi impetuously next said. "Carol and I drove up to Englewood and stayed at some friends' place. The town has a terrific nature center called Flat Rock Brook, and on Sunday morning the four of us trekked the scenic trails bordering the New Jersey Palisades, and we later viewed the exhibits in the 'Walk in the Woods' environmental building situated on the premises. And the mayor of Englewood, whom we were formally introduced to, happens to have lived down here in Hammonton as a youth and actually attended the local high school back in the 1970s. That surprise was a rather ironic coincidence," Agent Orsi cordially shared. "At least that's what I thought. And needless to say, the congested Turnpike along with the Garden State Parkway traffic on the hundred and ten-mile trip back home was absolutely abominable!"

"Well, Guys, Bing and I drove out to Pennsylvania Amish Country and stayed two nights at Host Farms outside Lancaster," Dan Blachford related. "Some of the leaves on the trees were already turning to brown, orange and yellow hues, making our return drive back to South Jersey most pleasurable. Bing simply loves Pennsylvania Dutch country! What sort of extraordinary adventures did *you* experience this past weekend Boss?"

Joe Giralo cleared his all-too-familiar low hoarse voice and then declared, "Gina and I took the daughters down I-95 to Baltimore and visited the Inner Harbor," the Chief stated. "They have a wonderful enormous aquarium on the city's waterfront, and much to my delight, they even have a huge Phillips Seafood counter conveniently located inside one of the main pavilions. And you Men know how I have a certain weakness for delicious crab meat, lobster, spicy shrimp, scallops and the like!"

"Okay, Inspector; now that the customary preliminary conversation has been adequately exhausted," Agent Velardi courageously remarked, "can you now tell us what's so crucial about having this rare impromptu conclave? Have you been gloriously promoted to the high office of United States Treasurer? Have Arty, Dan and I been promoted to be bona-fide FBI Inspectors ourselves?"

"Stop being so intolerably sarcastic and cynical!" Joe Giralo rebuked his facetious underling. "But at least Salvatore you aren't being apathetic, which as you might know, is only one remarkable letter removed from being pathetic!"

"I think I've heard this same conversation before," Agent Orsi commented. "But since I have amnesia, I can't exactly seem to remember where or when!"

"And if I may add to this ludicrous dialogue, anger is only one letter removed from danger!" Sal Velardi adroitly quipped. "Sometimes Boss, it's quite difficult distinguishing between your jazzy jargon and your goofball gibberish! I'm still trying to figure-out what you mean when you always advise me to experience an Epiphany on the Road to Damascus! Do you think I'm St. Paul reincarnated?"

Inspector Joe Giralo inhaled a large quantity of oxygen to fill his immense lungs, and then the Chief revealed to his anxious associates the essence of the impending dilemma, which had now spread its grotesque tentacles from Hammonton, New Jersey throughout the Delaware Valley into both Pennsylvania and Delaware; thus, the missing persons' phenomenon becoming a matter of intense FBI scrutiny and utmost concern.

"Okay, Men. Here's the latest pertinent information the Bureau has gleaned on the enigmatic missing persons' scenario that's now plaguing the entire region," Joe Giralo articulated. "Matt Riley down at DC headquarters wants me, er, I mean *us*, to get involved immediately. Now also, plenty of prominent Hammonton area citizens have strangely disappeared from the face of the Earth, and as of today, there are other new people disappearing in Plymouth-Meeting, in King of Prussia and in Media, Pennsylvania and also in New Castle, in Dover and in Milford Delaware. Since this is now, I believe, a dastardly Interstate crime network in operation," Giralo continued his general exposition, "and it's incumbent upon us to get to the bottom of all the bizarre havoc being surreptitiously created in the entire Tri-State region."

"Gee, Boss, I hope the *media* doesn't get wind of what's just transpired over in Media!" Agent Velardi jested. "I guess we'll then have to endure a full court press from the press!"

"This is no time for levity!" Joe Giralo reprimanded in a rather austere-but-melancholy tone of voice. "These missing folks in all three states are possibly already dead! Please demonstrate some sincere empathy towards their grieving families!"

"I think I've heard these same mediocre commentaries before and I've now become a foremost expert on recognizing verbal redundancies. Please tell *us* Inspector, what is our immediate role in *this* current investigation that's just surfaced?" Agent Blachford seriously asked. "Are we to abandon our other ongoing cases and exclusively concentrate on *this* very baffling missing persons' dilemma you've just described?"

"No, Dan," Inspector Giralo replied. "I just wanted to give you guys a heads-up on what's been materializing. Tomorrow morning I'm going to be meeting with the Hammonton Chief-of-Police and some of his key men in order to more thoroughly discuss the emerging matter in detail. I'll keep you three alert Gents posted as to what we discover, determine and hypothesize. Until then, I strongly recommend that you keep your powder dry and by all means, be ready for any sudden emergency that'll require our prompt government intervention! Loyal to our duty, Men! Loyal to our duty!"

* * * * * * * * * * * * *

The Hammonton Police Department, along with the New Jersey State Police, had been baffled by the wave of a dozen missing persons mysteriously disappearing from the somnolent South Jersey agricultural community, a town especially noted for being "The Blueberry Capital of the World." Chief-of-Police Michael Falcone had summoned Detective Fred Arico and Patrolman Samuel Galletta to meet with Inspector Joe Giralo in *his* downstairs office inside the newly constructed Hammonton Town Hall, located on the corner of Central Avenue, Third and Vine Street.

The recent "missing persons' portfolio" to be reviewed had now become a popular topic being reported and discussed on Philadelphia and Atlantic City television news broadcasts. Chief Falcone felt personally embarrassed at his department having to solicit outside professional help from the FBI and the State Police to engage in solving the complex case currently under investigation.

"As you know Men," Chief Falcone began addressing Detective Arico and Patrolman Galletta, "we're very fortunate to be able to combine our efforts with Inspector Giralo and be able to use the excellent resources of the FBI. Hammonton has become the focal point of attention throughout the Delaware Valley. One of my major concerns is that I fear the bad publicity which our community is receiving is not good for *our* general reputation," Chief Falcone regretted. "And frankly I'm quite confused. This missing persons' deal goes far beyond the ordinary issuing of traffic tickets and police reports on auto' accidents! That's precisely where Inspector Giralo's singular talents come into play!"

"Thanks, Chief Falcone," Giralo respectfully answered. "It's my distinct pleasure to serve Hammonton. As you and your men well-know, I'm a proud resident of *this* fine community!"

"Perhaps the public can assist us in cracking the complex riddle," Detective Fred Arico constructively suggested. "I meant to say, alert people represent the cornerstone of local law enforcement. Vigilant citizens might just be the key we need to figuring-out this very difficult, pardon the expression if I now use a favorite Sherlock Holmes statement," Detective Arico resumed his opinionated commentary, "This very difficult conundrum."

"Now Detective Arico, what you've just mentioned about citizen participation might be a valuable asset," Joe Giralo interrupted, "and I'm sure that any clue from any origin will be quite welcome."

"This entire matter requires *our* full scrutiny and energy twenty-four hours a day, seven days a week, until we've found all the vital answers we need," the Chief-of-Police emphasized to his two honest cops and to his eminent federal guest. "I do have a certain stake in *this* matter. The timing of it all is absolutely abominable! Only seven months until it's my retirement and pension time, and now I have to endure *this* crazy situation that's rapidly evolving into a major crisis. I'm at wits end! These twelve important missing townspeople couldn't all just have vanished into thin air!"

"We're now receiving reports of well-to-do individuals vanishing in Pennsylvania and Delaware too," Inspector Giralo added. "That's why the brass down in DC has assigned me and my agents to this truly perplexing sequence of missing persons. I'm now convinced that their disappearances are not just merely accidental or coincidental!"

"And as you've just said Inspector, according to our files, the local missing subjects were all stellar members of this community in good standing with the police department," Detective Arico observed and concurred. "Yes, members of the Kiwanis Club, the Lions, the Rotary, the Women's Civic Club, the Exchange Club, the Sons of Italy, you name it! We're all taking a lot of heat over this strange predicament. and that's why the also-bewildered State Police had recommended that the FBI should step in and aid *us* in our law enforcement efforts. In truth, this enormous puzzle sort of makes the Hammonton cops look like we're a pack of incompetent boobs!"

"I've worked on many similar cases and have a specific frame of reference to which I can refer," Joe Giralo confidently remarked. "My gut instinct is to suspect interstate foul play! In the beginning of any of my interrogations, everyone imaginable is a suspect; even everyone who is now present in this office! And then from *that* angle Gentlemen, the all-essential filtering-out process commences!"

The quietest person in the brightly-lit room then felt compelled to speak. "Could it be that the missing twelve Hammonton people have schemed-up a conspiracy just to distract and fool us?" Patrolman Galletta re-actively asked Chief Falcone, Detective Arico and the Inspector. "Doesn't this very exceptional debacle have all the markings of a massive prank in progress? I meant to say," Officer Galletta proceeded with his fanciful monologue, "you don't suppose, Inspector, that a mass murderer is on the prowl and that certain specific names are being checked-off his hit list, one by one, as each additional elimination happens!"

"Nonsense! Totally ridiculous! All of *your* bizarre theories are absolute rubbish!" Chief Michael Falcone vehemently exclaimed, mildly admonishing his junior patrolman. "Hammonton is a decent town of fifteen thousand hard-working ambitious residents! And besides *that* rather-normal scenario, Sam, we haven't had a murder-type felony committed here in over twenty years. But what totally frustrates me the most, Gentlemen, is that there hasn't been a trace of evidence discovered anywhere, not one solitary, minute clue turning-up! Nobody seems to know anything about anything!"

"What about cause, opportunity and motive?" Detective Arico inquired. "Let's start there!"

"Good proposal," Inspector Giralo commended. "Honestly Fred, we could use intelligent fellas' like you in the FBI."

"Extortion doesn't seem to be any motive because no ransom notes have surfaced from any particular source," the Chief-of-Police asserted. "It's a lousy annoying *Kind-Un-Drum* as you've just said, Fred. But much to my regret Inspector," Falcone proceeded, slowly turning towards Giralo, "it's all happened on *our beat!* Now let's review exactly who has disappeared and perhaps we can connect some isolated dots, or maybe establish some relevant links," Chief Falcone indicated to Arico and Galletta while attempting to impress his venerable FBI visitor. "The worst feature of all this nebulous confusion is that just about everybody in Hammonton is somehow related to each other. Our elderly citizens are extremely nervous and quite frankly, they have every right to feel *that* way unless something gives soon in the form of an arrest!"

"I'm slightly apprehensive myself," Giralo admitted. "And I'm supposed to be an esteemed keeper of the peace. Honestly, I don't like the idea of criminals profiling or targeting me in my own town!"

"Certainly, Chief Falcone," Patrolman Sam Galletta confirmed as the rookie cop awkwardly fumbled opening his folder while also paying little heed to Inspector Giralo's standard drivel. "For example, you and I Chief Falcone are cousins, and our wives are second cousins on our mothers' sides! And my second cousins are related to Detective Arico's family, if my defective memory serves me correctly. The townspeople are suffering from excessive anxiety simply because *we* haven't made any apprehensions!" the zany young officer quipped, much to Chief Michael Falcone's ire and much to Inspector Giralo's satisfaction.

After giving Officer Sam Galletta a serious frown (as Detective Fred Arico covered his mouth to avoid overtly laughing), Chief

Falcone sternly admonished his comedic subordinate to show Inspector Giralo that *he* maintained an element of discipline among his staff. "Look here Sam! Our department is in a serious quandary, a complicated, evolving crisis situation! Let's show some professional discretion during this confidential-but-informal meeting! Let's try and be more discreet, even though *that* practical task might be contrary to *your* general nature Mr. Galletta! This is no time to pretend being either Jay Leno or David Letterman! Even Bill O'Reilly is out of your league as a basic humorist!"

Detective Fred Arico then informed the Chief and the Inspector that Patrolman Galletta would review the first six missing persons in the chronological order of their swift disappearances and that *he* would present the final six in the same manner. That chosen approach would be done in order to see if any direct or remote connections existed that could lead to a primary source of evidence or that could constitute the platform for a plausible police theory. The impatient Hammonton Police Department's head honcho then directed the young officer to commence with *his* background analysis.

"Well, Sir; the first victim, er, I mean 'missing person' to vanish was Bernard Norton, who as you know sat, or should I say sits on the Board of Directors of Hammonton Trust Bank. Mr. Norton was on the Parish Council of St. Joseph Church, served in the marines during the *Vietnam War,* and he is unhappily married to the former Susan Parker, a past Hammonton Peach Queen and also a glamour model for local newspaper-print-ads and Philadelphia and Atlantic City glossy cover magazines. Mr. Norton's personal vices are Atlantic City casino gambling junkets and having two known affairs outside his unstable marriage. But for the record," Patrolman Galletta clarified, "Bernard Norton's unfaithful wife Susan is also guilty of those same questionable behaviors, so I guess their unstable marital relationship is, how should I say, is sort of a wash."

Inspector Giralo jotted-down notes as the exchange of words accelerated. "There're no signs of anything illegal being committed, although some of Mr. Norton's activities might be a trifle immoral and unethical," the very beleaguered Chief-of-Police evaluated and ascertained. "But this investigation is not a church or marriage counseling matter; it's a police concern! Now then, who was the second individual to become mysteriously absent from the town proper?"

"Frank Gibson, a rough and tough fruit and produce broker who has his base of operation seventeen miles south of here at the Vineland Produce Auction," Officer Galletta neurotically related. "Mr. Gibson also manages a successful freight company that hauls mostly locally grown vegetables all up and down the Eastern Seaboard from Boston, Massachusetts to Richmond, Virginia. My brother-in-law is a dispatcher for the flourishing trucking company, which I believe has twenty-five tractor-trailers in its fleet. But outside of once being arrested for brawling with another patron outside the Silver Coin Diner and also breaking another customer's nose during a fistfight inside the Silver Fox Tavern," Patrolman Galletta summarized, "Frank Gibson's overall police record is pretty clean. He's definitely not the gangster type capable of performing twelve heinous kidnappings or murders!"

"Yes, Gibson can become rowdy and pugnacious occasionally, especially when intoxicated, but remember," Chief Falcone austerely reminded Officer Galletta while winking in Inspector Giralo's direction. "Gibson's now a prospective victim of foul play and not a perpetrator of minor or major crime, although I can fully understand why someone on a revenge mission might be seeking retribution against the obnoxious instigator. Frank Gibson does have a certain reputation for charging higher commission rates to farmers to sell their fruit and vegetables to chain stores than do other produce brokers in the Hammonton/Vineland area. We'll keep *that* particular fact in mind as we objectively try to piece together the details of this rather challenging investigation and then hopefully, we'll make our assumptions more comprehensive. Now who's next on our agenda?"

"Next, Chief, there's Jack Hines, a prosperous blueberry farmer who often did business with the highly volatile Frank Gibson," Officer Sam Galletta read from his oak tag folder. "As you know, just like Frank Gibson, Jack Hines is divorced, and he's permanently separated from *your* sister-in-law's niece. Jack likes auto' racing and has sponsored pit-stop teams participating in the Dover Classic and the Daytona 500. Outside of two minor speeding tickets on his otherwise impeccable record," Officer Galletta expounded, "some small-town politics are also involved! Although Mr. Jack Hines has committed no serious violations, according to our sketchy documentation, on two different occasions, Hines tried to bribe Officer Hunt and Officer Ambrose with cash to try and quash his citations before the complaints could reach Judge Philips' bench."

"That association between Jack Hines and Frank Gibson is a definite red flag and might be essential later on," the veteran Chief-of-Police concluded and shared. "But nevertheless, unfortunately nothing mentioned thus far would warrant, let alone justify kidnapping, which as you two Gentlemen both know, could represent a federal crime, especially if the victims are transported across state lines. Needless to say, Men," the perplexed Police Department Czar continued his glib spiel, much to the mounting disappointment of Inspector Giralo, "I've spent thirty-six years of dedicated service on the force, and I don't want to see this very irritating rash of disappearances mar my impeccable history of dependability to this very special community. To me," Chief Falcone insisted, "*that* sort of departure would be a shameful exit! Now then Sam, who's next on your' list? And try being a bit briefer! It's almost lunchtime!"

Officer Galletta then revealed that James Olsen, a chronic alcoholic, was the proprietor of a large winery on the White Horse Pike, that Joseph Spinelli, a reputed Casanova, was a skilled surgeon at Kessler Memorial Hospital, and that Thomas Ritter, a shrewd conniving businessman, was also an industrious, wealthy real estate broker and an outstanding charity benefactor. Chief Falcone appeared worried that all of those "high-repute" missing persons that just had been identified were also outstanding citizens of and contributors to the Town of Hammonton.

"What is your assessment, Inspector?" Chief Falcone inquisitively asked. "I need some expert guidance from you!"

"It's too early to say, and any casual perception at this tender juncture would be entirely premature and inconclusive," Joe Giralo coyly replied.

"This is all very overwhelming indeed!" a distressed Michael Falcone uttered to his equally pressured pair of underlings. "Why couldn't *this* entire weird fiasco, er, I meant to say 'development' have had happened in Vineland, in Mays Landing, in Berlin, in Pleasantville or in Egg Harbor City? If we don't bust open this bizarre case soon, more FBI G-men will surely zoom onto our turf, and we'll then be the laughingstock of every town and borough in South Jersey. I think I'll be submitting my resignation within the week if we fail to collar any likely suspects in the interim. But who might the evil villain or villains be? That's the $64,000.00-dollar question!"

"Sometimes one minor bit of obscure knowledge will unravel the entire Gordian Knot," Joe Giralo attested. "Be meticulous and patient and in the end, good things will result!"

"Well now, Chief Falcone and Inspector Giralo, this final statement I'm about to make just about completes my terse presentation," Patrolman Galletta vocalized before taking a deep breath. "James Olsen was having a supposed secret love affair with Joseph Spinelli's wife, and the flirtatious surgeon was cheating on his spouse and having another tryst with Thomas Ritter's promiscuous wife, but since all three men have disappeared like evasive, itinerant space aliens, all vanishing from the Hammonton map. And we can't accuse any of them of anything. Strangely enough," Patrolman

Galletta concluded his comprehensive report, "all three marital cheaters can only now be classified as missing persons and nothing more! I'll now transfer the missing persons' reporting over to Detective Arico."

Chief Falcone then asked Detective Fred Arico to discuss the six remaining names of missing persons whose records were quite neatly organized inside *his* police folder. The accommodating civil servant quickly opened his document records and began his narrative, which was a trifle more sophisticated than was that of Officer Sam Galletta.

"Well Chief and Inspector Giralo, Maria Fischer was, or should I say, *is,* the President of the local Soroptimist Club and is involved in many noteworthy community charities," Detective Arico cited from his comprehensive records. "As you know Chief, she's a millionaire ten-times-over who owns and runs a very financially solvent clothes manufacturing factory on Fairview Avenue, and Ms. Fischer has several flourishing retail-outlet stores in Atlantic City, in Rehoboth Beach, Delaware, in Ocean City, Maryland and on Cape Cod, Massachusetts," Arico candidly added. "It should be cited that Maria Fischer's daughter has had a major drug problem and was once arrested for cocaine and marijuana possession, and her only son had once done some minor vandalism at the local bowling alley, but as far as Maria Fischer is concerned, our principal's record is virtually immaculate. There's no doubt in my mind that...."

"That all of these missing persons identified so far have one specific thing in common," Chief Michael Falcone declared as he rubbed his right ear with his forefinger, deliberately interrupting his favorite detective and preempting Inspector Joe Giralo from making *his* own loquacious dissertation. "They're all, no doubt in my mind, prosperous millionaires, but most remarkably in my mind, most of the missing persons are extravagant egotistical multimillionaires! This fact could be the vital connection we're searching for, and *that* aspect's well-worth delving into! Well Fred, who's next on your short list?"

"I concur with Chief Falcone's lucid evaluation," Giralo chimed-in unexpectedly. "Money and greed are ordinarily the genesis of most large crimes!"

Undeterred, audacious and reliable Fred Arico resumed his elaborate pontification. "Jeffrey Stokes is a successful furniture store operator and also the main influential power member of the Hammonton Democratic Club," the competent detective stated. "Jeffrey's been suspected of being implicated in county loan-sharking pursuits, but we never could get anyone to file a written grievance or testify against him. As has been extensively published in various

South Jersey newspapers," Detective Arico eloquently stated, "Mr. Stokes has amassed considerable connections among important politicians throughout the county and on the state echelon too, and he's believed to be currently circulating a petition for running for a county freeholder seat. Stokes is also a close friend and confidant of several judges sitting on the Superior Court over in the Mays Landing County Seat."

"Jeffrey Stokes does represent a character of interest," Chief Falcone readily acknowledged. "But we must be very careful going forward here. We can't intrude upon his privacy and question his family about his suspected dishonorable relationships and then have the press accuse *us* of being irresponsible by practicing guilt by association. That's all I need is the local ACLU sticking its sharp talons into my ribs right before my earned retirement," the Chief blustered and maintained. "I'll not leave my position in the midst of a firestorm controversy that's guaranteed to fuel massive scuttlebutt in the barbershop and hairdresser gossip mills. I'll only leave my post with honor and accomplishment! Who's the next name in your confidential folder?"

"John DiFrancisco is a builder and real estate developer with a stellar reputation, but he's also president of the town's Republican Club," Detective Fred Arico clearly enunciated. "Naturally one would indeed speculate that a certain distinct political difference of opinion would exist between..."

"Between Jeffrey Stokes and John DiFrancisco," Inspector Giralo immediately recognized and stated, finishing Detective Arico's intended remark. "And if I recall with any degree of accuracy, Mr. DiFrancisco was supposed to build Jeffrey Stokes' new furniture store over on Second Road but the whole deal fell through after the two egomaniacs had a bitter argument that required the intervention of your police department. I'll bookmark *that* past conflict and keep their antagonism toward each other as something pertinent we'll have to examine more in perspective, but still, according to my preliminary research," Giralo persuasively argued, "no criminal activity, not even a picayune misdemeanor could be attributed to either Mr. Jeffrey Stokes or to Mr. John DiFrancisco. But I will express *this* complaint. That creep Stokes once sold me an inferior set of den furniture!"

"Now then, Fred, isn't my old high school sweetheart Barbara DeMarco also a missing person?" Chief Falcone vociferated, endeavoring to pilfer some of Inspector Giralo's on-a-roll thunder. "What information do you have about her, Fred?"

"Yes Chief, as you know, Ms. DeMarco never married. The woman's probably never gotten over being amorously dumped by *you.* She's very creative however, owns three dress shops for women at strategic locations throughout the town and has made several million investing in small-cap technology companies on the major stock exchanges. But outside of her being a vocal Scientologist just like Tom Cruise had been on the Oprah Show," Detective Fred Arico reminded his avid listeners. "Your old flame, Chief Falcone, namely Ms. Barbara DeMarco, has never been *engaged* in anything illicit or nefarious. What do you think about her, Sam?"

"It's too bad Chief that you never married gorgeous Barbara DeMarco!" Patrolman Galletta opined after he had heard Detective Fred Arico mention the key word *engaged.* "Then Chief, you wouldn't have to worry about jeopardizing your pension benefits! You'd have it made in the shade with plenty of available cash to spare, all the way up to the Pearly Gates!"

"Look here, Sam. I'm not a lame duck police administrator, so watch your loose tongue and how it wags!" Chief Falcone scolded his somewhat frivolous subordinate as amused Inspector Giralo sat in his comfortable chair, chuckling. "Any more idiotic comments on your part Sam and you might just find yourself getting splinters in your rear end *engaged* in desk duty instead of merrily cruising town in your shiny new patrol car. Now please continue with your superb briefing Fred. Who's next?"

"Now Chief, as you're fully aware, according to the National Census, Hammonton is the most Italian town in the entire United States, and Officer Galletta, *yours* and my last names all have Italian heritage," Detective Arico keenly observed and communicated. "Over fifty-three percent of the town's population is of Italian origin, mostly Sicilian. Our next missing person is one Guido Renzi, a notorious Atlantic City gambler and card counter who has been banned from three boardwalk casinos. It's rumored all around the community that Guido had inherited five million dollars from his greedy loan-sharking old man and that Renzi's more than tripled his fantastic windfall, which incidentally had never been deposited into any bank and was never ever reported to the IRS."

"Yes, Guido Renzi could definitely be a target of foul play!" Chief Falcone verified as he slowly rubbed his whiskery chin. "And you're positively right, Fred. There're too many Guidos living in Hammonton!"

"Now as you're keenly aware Chief, good old Guido is a confederate of Stephen Messina, your uncle on your mother's side who, as a matter of fact, is a conniving junkyard owner with reputed ties to the Philly' Mafia," Fred Arico insinuated, instantly making the broad smile disappear from Inspector Giralo's face. "This wily maverick Renzi is slippery and slick, and we can't pin anything substantial on him other than suspecting that his closest friend's retail auto' used parts business is a front for the syndicate's stolen goods' fencing operations and also, the mob's drug trafficking activities," Detective Arico elucidated. "But both Renzi and Messina are regarded as respected benefactors to many local charities, and they're both very generous in their contributions and fund-raising benevolence. The congregations of all three Catholic churches in town amply appreciate the donations given by Guido Renzi and by *your* benevolent uncle, Stephen Messina."

"Yes, Fred. Every family in town seems to have its black sheep! Uncle Steve Messina could charm the belly off of a rattlesnake, that's for damned sure!" the Chief-of-Police reluctantly verified. "I've often had to distance myself from *his* unsavory presence! Last summer during the 16th of July Carnival, I had to leave the Mt. Carmel Hall when *he* showed-up, so as not to be seen in public mingling with the unscrupulous Mafia-suspected maniac! And to tell you the truth," Chief Michael Falcone proceeded, "I'd love to wiretap Uncle Steve's myriad phone conversations. But since he's a philanthropist of sorts, the local public foolishly regards *my* Uncle Steve as a kind of area Robin Hood, cheating the general fools out of their money and then mercifully and kindly assisting the poor and the less fortunate with some of the pilfered proceeds. Because of extenuating circumstances, and I hate sounding too much like a modern-day Eliot Ness," Chief Falcone diplomatically qualified, "Steve Messina right now is viewed as an 'untouchable', if you know what I mean. But just remember, Men. Guido Renzi happens to be one of the twelve missing persons and not *his* diabolical pal Steve Messina. Isn't there one more name that you've got itemized inside your packet?"

"Yes, Chief; it's Richard Farinelli, a millionaire produce/package supplier to area peach, blueberry and vegetable growers," Detective Arico carefully stated. "Farinelli's a cunning and mean old buzzard who drives a hard bargain, especially since he's the only fertilizer distributor in Hammonton and vicinity, that's for sure! I could see where someone of Richard Farinelli's determined ilk could've accumulated hard-boiled enemies over the years, but then again, my name's not Kojak or Perry Mason, so perhaps I should keep my unsolicited random conjecturing all to myself!"

"Excellent self-analysis! It's about time you faced reality, Fred, and became aware of your all-too-obvious shortcomings!" Chief Falcone mercilessly chided. "But in the future Detective Arico, think before you open your mouth so that you don't have to apologize afterwards upon revealing your all-too-often silliness! And *that* needed criticism pertains to you too, Officer Galletta! Now then, you two floundering Imbeciles, time is of the essence! Get the heck out of my airconditioned office, stay away from the plethora of coffee and doughnut shops doing business up on the Pike, and last but not least, start finding some big concrete clues to solve this extremely vexing *Kind-Un-Drum!*"

After the two Hammonton cops paced out of the office, Chief Falcone asked Inspector Joe Giralo what the FBI sultan thought about the missing persons' case.

"I think; I think; I think, therefore I am!" Giralo philosophically answered, deliberately quoting the inimitable Rene Descartes.

* * * * * * * * * * * *

Seven miles north of Hammonton, a terrible automobile accident had occurred at the dangerous "S-Curve" above Atsion Lake on *Route 206*, a two-lane highway that is New Jersey's only north-south corridor through the state's center. A brand new dark blue Cadillac driven by millionaire Jason DeLucca had veered off the road and was instantly demolished after smashing into a gigantic pine tree. Jason DeLucca died instantly from multiple injuries sustained in the mishap, and the auto's front-seat passenger, his brother Nicholas, was immediately transported by ambulance to Hammonton's Kessler Memorial Hospital for lacerations' treatment and for overnight observation.

The following morning, a third brother Rocco DeLucca arrived to pick-up the discharged patient, his very fortunate younger brother. After hospital doctors had examined and released "the lucky rider" from the emergency ward, the driver and the survivor had a meaningful conversation.

"You know, Nick," Rocco said as he drove his black Lexus out of Kessler's nearly empty parking lot, "Jason was really the greatest older brother we could have ever had. It's really too bad you guys got into that terrible accident on the way to your meeting destination, the Pic-A-Lilli Inn! In my case, as you well-know Nick, Jason had financed three of my retail businesses that have failed, insisting that I not repay him one lousy penny," Rocco explained to his surviving brother. "And good old Jay; once the great guy had told me that he's goin' to remember both of us in his will along with his wife and three kids. Well, anyway Nick, I honestly hate getting misty-eyed and all that emotional stuff, but Jay's certainly goin' to be missed."

"Come to think of it, the whole accident seemed quite strange!" Nick confided to Rocco. "And it's a good thing I was wearing my seat

206

belt, although Jason's belt didn't matter in his case! After our intended rendezvous with you in the Pic-A-Lilli Inn parking lot, Jay and I were goin' to be on our way to have supper at Izzy's Restaurant over on *541* in Medford. Jay's new Cadillac was in excellent condition, but then we either blew a right front tire on *206* or the wheel became unhinged," Nick sadly told Rocco. "The next thing I knew we had veered off the road at the S-Curve and were barreling straight into the pine-barrens. Then as soon as the air bag inflated, there was an immense impact and I went unconscious," Nicholas recollected and related. "Thank God for the swift actions of the Hammonton Rescue Squad or else I probably would've bled to death en-route to the hospital fifteen minutes later! I suppose you're going to make final arrangements for Jason at the Blake Funeral Home over on Third Street. That's where Mom and Dad had their viewings."

"No, Nick," Rocco replied as the traffic light turned green and the driver stepped on the accelerator, making the turn from Central Avenue onto *Route 30*, the White Horse Pike. "At first I was thinking about having the Franklin Mortuary over on Egg Harbor Road doing the funeral. But then again, I considered that the Melora Funeral Home over on Central Avenue could better accommodate the massive crowd that's goin' to be showing-up to pay their last respects. Last night, I already had contacted Bill Melora and told the cooperative undertaker to get in touch with Andrew Blake, who still has the entrance keys to the family mausoleum."

"That sounds like a good idea!" Nicholas DeLucca agreed with Rocco's recommendation. "Melora has a much bigger parlor viewing room than either Mr. Franklin or Mr. Blake does!"

"But before I take you home and drop you off, we're gonna' head over to Oak Grove Cemetery to check-out the family crypt," Rocco suggested. "The mausoleum might have to be power-washed to get the accumulated algae and green slime off of its façade. We should've never neglected the granite structure for so long, so now we'll have to get the ugly mess cleaned-up before Jay's burial. Sometimes I wish I had more foresight, at least as much as Jay possessed."

As Rocco's black Lexus pulled into the Old Forks Road entrance to shady Oak Grove Cemetery, the man behind the wheel noticed something irregular happening a hundred yards down the asphalt lane, so the alert driver quickly detoured his expensive vehicle onto a side dirt road bordered by a hedgerow of tall pine trees. Nicholas's curiosity had also been stimulated by what *his* eyes had just perceived. Immediately, the driver's unexpected maneuver had energized the recently injured passenger's imagination.

"What's this crazy detour all about?" the bandaged brother demanded knowing. "Did you forget where the family mausoleum is? Chief Falcone would instantly get your butt hauled into the station for reckless driving!"

"Be quiet and stay still!" Rocco commanded from behind the pine tree cover as the older brother pointed to a familiar distant structure situated under a canopy of tall oaks. "Look over there at *our* mausoleum. There's funeral director Andrew Blake and his lazy assistant Phil Ruggeri entering *our* cemetery building without our approval or knowledge."

"Maybe they're just inspecting the crypts to make sure everything's in order," Nicholas theorized and explained. "You have to give Mr. Blake the benefit of the doubt and not have a rush to judgment and accuse him and his helper of trespassing! There's enough craziness goin' on in Hammonton without us making false allegations! Let's sit tight and be cool."

"Yes, perhaps you're right!" Rocco acceded, shrugging his broad shoulders. "Mr. Blake still does have the master entry key since he had conducted Mom and Dad's funerals! But please remember, Nick, Andrew Blake probably already knows that the Melora Funeral Home is going to handle Jason's arrangements. This is all very intriguing! Let's just hold tight and witness what's goin' to happen next!"

Ten minutes later, the pair of diligent observers was shocked at what their keen eyes were beholding. "Oh my God!" Nicholas exclaimed with the windows rolled-up inside the air-conditioned luxury automobile. "Look at that! They're carryin' a body under a black blanket out of the mausoleum, *our* mausoleum! Instead of putting a corpse inside the stone building two days from now, they're taking one out right this minute!"

"This is highly irregular, let alone bizarre! I don't know if this spectacle we're watchin' is body snatchin' or not, but I gotta' report the suspicious incident to the police," Rocco DeLucca declared. "I'll get in touch with my good pal Detective Fred Arico immediately. I'll make sure he'll get to the bottom of this strange incident, and then we'll learn exactly what's going on here!"

* * * * * * * * * * * *

The morning after Jason DeLucca's huge funeral and subsequent burial inside the family's Oak Grove Cemetery mausoleum, Detective Fred Arico and Patrolman Samuel Galletta promptly accompanied Rocco and Nicholas DeLucca into Chief Michael Falcone's Town Hall office. The head Hammonton police official was sitting behind his cluttered desk, and the administrator of justice acted surprised by the appearance of his four unanticipated visitors. The Chief's skeptical mind wondered what *their* purpose was for barging into his sacred bailiwick without any special invitation.

"What could I do for you impulsive Gentlemen?" the Chief-of-Police gruffly asked as Michael Falcone noticed (but did not initially address) the presence of the accompanying DeLucca brothers. "I've already expressed my deepest condolences to you two distinguished Gentlemen last night at the Melora Funeral Home."

"Chief Michael Falcone; it's my unhappy duty to inform you that you're under arrest!" Detective Fred Arico boldly announced. "Thank goodness we're inside Town Hall and we don't have too far to go to transport you to the nearest jail cell."

"What nonsense did you say? How ludicrous can you presumptuous fools be? Don't be ridiculous!" Chief Falcone challenged with defiant indignation apparent in his rather astonished tone of voice. "Are you Nutcases trying to smear my integrity? I hope that this absurd charade is a perverted joke because it's not too-funny! Tell me Detective Arico, on what grounds am I being charged? For me being too courteous and tolerant of Officer Galletta and yourself?"

"Your incarceration is being turned-over to the Atlantic County Prosecutor and you'll soon be taken to the Mays Landing jail for interrogation!" Officer Galletta orally quantified. "You have entirely too much influence with the local judges. and we don't exactly know how far into the town's government the overall corruption extends. The county seat will be a better venue to hear your impending trial. Now then," the determined patrolman continued with his indictment, "thanks to Inspector Joe Giralo's tremendous help, you'll soon be behind steel bars for a long time. Michael Falcone, you have the right to remain silent, and any and all things you say can be held and used as evidence against you! You have a right to an attorney. Do you understand your lawful Miranda Rights?"

"This two stooges' drama-fiasco is absolutely illogical, positively asinine Galletta! Totally preposterous and unwarranted! Put the handcuffs away or else you'll be accused before Town Council of being insubordinate to your superior officer!" Michael Falcone vehemently yelled. "Didn't you hear me, Galletta! Put the cuffs away or else risk your future as a police officer!"

Detective Fred Arico then explained the pertinent details that Rocco and Nicholas DeLucca had witnessed inside Oak Grove Cemetery and what funeral director Andrew Blake and his lethargic assistant Philip Ruggeri had confessed after being fully interrogated at their funeral home. The captured cohorts' separate testimonies had been fully corroborated by statements given by Stephen Messina, which immediately led to the severe charges presented against Police Chief Michael Falcone.

"As soon as my ears heard Rocco and Nick's very strange Oak Grove Cemetery story, I immediately got in touch with Patrolman Galletta and Inspector Giralo," Detective Arico explained the initial chronology of events in an accusatory tone of voice. "Immediately, we confiscated Jason DeLucca's dark blue Cadillac and quickly found that the right front wheel had been expertly tampered with, thus eventually causing the car to swerve off of *Route 206* right into the dense Wharton Tract Forest. And so," Detective Fred Arico continued his explanatory narrative, "I promptly knew right then and there that *we* had a solid and concrete death-by-auto' manslaughter case on our hands!"

"And it seemed mighty peculiar to us Chief that your uncle, the reprehensible and belligerent Stephen Messina, could dispatch a flatbed truck seven-miles north of Hammonton to the S-Curve between Atsion Lake and the Pic-A-Lilli Inn and get it there before any other trucks or flatbeds from nearby *206* gas stations and junkyards could ever arrive on the accident scene and claim the wrecked vehicle! That oddity had to be definitely looked into, especially since Hammonton is in Atlantic County and Atsion is geographically in Burlington County!"

"That unique occurrence could've been just a remote coincidence!" Chief Falcone argued and insisted in a stuttering voice. "How does an odd combination of events possibly implicate me in your wild-goose-chase amateur investigation? I promise you Arico, your job along with your suspect career is in serious jeopardy!"

Detective Fred Arico next calmly explained that the body being removed from the DeLucca Mausoleum in tranquil Oak Grove Cemetery belonged to Richard Farinelli, the wealthy produce/package distributor and fertilizer merchant who happened to be the twelfth and last missing person who had recently disappeared inside Hammonton city limits. Then Officer Galletta provided additional information germane to the alleged grand felony.

"Funeral Director Andrew Blake finally broke-down and told us the missing pieces to the weird puzzle!" the very responsible patrolman articulated. "Mr. Blake's crematoria had broken-down the week before the funeral director believed he would be receiving Jason DeLucca's body for embalming. Blake couldn't cremate Richard Farinelli because of the crematoria malfunction, so Mr. Andrew Blake and his not-too-bright sidekick Philip Ruggeri temporarily housed the package king's embalmed corpse inside the DeLucca Mausoleum because Blake still had the key to the family's cemetery edifice. And when Andrew Blake suddenly realized that the Melora Funeral Home had been chosen to conduct Jason DeLucca's wake and interment, the flustered funeral director had to act fast and…"

"Remove Farinelli's body from the DeLucca family mausoleum before turning the sepulcher's key over to Mr. Melora," the sleuth-like Detective Fred Arico finished the patrolman's accurate testimony. "Further questioning of the implicated suspects Blake and Ruggeri revealed that the first eleven missing persons were all victims that had been heinously murdered and then later intentionally cremated. Mr. Blake had cunningly mixed the victims' ashes in with the ashes of legitimately cremated dearly departed local people, and so the embers of the eleven murder victims are now coincidentally preserved in various urns respectfully situated upon fireplace mantels all over Hammonton! The former missing persons are missing persons no longer."

"But how am I involved in this absurd alleged murder caper you've just awkwardly alluded to?" handcuffed Michael Falcone demanded knowing. "Your flimsy evidence connecting me to these fairly interesting facts is flimsy at best! I know the law! I'm innocent until proven guilty! Your speculative accusations will never stand-up in a court room, county, state, or otherwise!"

"You can no longer intimidate *us* with your bullying and gruffness, so I'll cut right to the chase, Chief! We've already obtained a confession from your unethical uncle, Stephen Messina," Officer Sam Galletta disclosed as Rocco and Nicholas DeLucca attentively listened to the patrolman's remarkable commentary. "Guido Renzi and your despicable relative by marriage, the unscrupulous Stephen Messina, were secondary henchmen working for the formidable Philadelphia Mafia. When the city mob needed to extort some extra highly-desired 'seed money' from a dozen-or-so, readily available Hammonton millionaires in order to expand their' South Jersey criminal operations," Galletta impressively articulated and then paused, "the ruthless Philly' thugs received the exact names and addresses of rich citizens of our fair community from none other than reliable informants Renzi and Messina. "

Detective Fred Arico added to Officer Sam Galletta's accusations. "The rest of the incredible story is now modern Hammonton history! But then soon thereafter, Messina and Renzi got into an argument over money. According to Mr. Andrew Blake, Mr. Stephen Messina had killed Mr. Guido Renzi with a hammer, and under threat of being murdered himself', Blake' had no alternative other than cremating

Renzi soon afterwards. Inspector Giralo helped us in connecting all of those distinct, random dots!"

"But *your* fairy tale insinuations all hint at you two clowns having only circumstantial evidence!" Michael Falcone loudly protested. "You'll never be able to convict me of anything except *your* futilely presenting to the court the usual weak argument of 'guilt by association!' I'll testify that both you Sam, and you Fred, are looking for lucrative promotions at my expense, trying to put feathers in your caps by extorting me! Yes, Fred, you and Sam are both conspiring against me! I'll accuse both of you of impugning and slandering my integrity for your own personal gain!"

"On the contrary, Chief Falcone!" Detective Arico sternly objected. "We've just discovered that Mr. Andrew Blake had owed the Philly' mob over a million dollars in accumulated gambling debts over in Atlantic City. And *your* onerous Uncle Stephen Messina has turned state's evidence and has already entered a convenient plea bargain arrangement with the county prosecutor's office. Your crime-prone uncle is also being considered for admission into the Witness Protection Program because the County Prosecutor has allied with Inspector Giralo and the FBI, and the top lawyer over in Mays Landing wants to go after the ruthless Philly' mob, too!" Arico convincingly indicated. "And as far as *your* direct involvement is concerned...."

"Blood is much thicker than water!" Officer Galletta interrupted Detective Arico. "You knew quite well Chief that all of this perverse, illegal activity, including the heinous twelve murders, was going on while you were covering-up and deliberately ignoring the mess in order to protect your detestable uncle and his despicable mob confederates," Officer Galletta related to his former boss, much to the astonishment and amazement of witnesses Rocco and Nicholas DeLucca. "And furthermore," the conscientious patrolman persisted. "We have on record valid testimony that you Michael Falcone had also received mob hush money to the amount of two-hundred-and-fifty-thousand-dollars, which was derived from the total extortion money being obtained from *other* still-alive-but-fearful Hammonton residents of means, the remaining wealthy individuals who had handed-over their precious dough to save their precious lives," Patrolman Galletta impressively reviewed and indicted. "And those unfortunate individuals that refused to participate in the Philly' mob's lethal extortion scheme caper, they were...."

"They were systematically eliminated, cremated and their charred remains placed into jars along with the ashes of other *normally deceased* members of the community," Detective Arico affirmed.

"But the one thing that broke the entire case wide open was when Mr. Andrew Blake's crematoria oven-device coincidentally became inoperable. That's when Mr. Farinelli's body had to be hidden quickly in the Oak Grove Cemetery mausoleum until Blake would get his undependable cremation mechanism fixed and operable again. And finally, if poor Jason DeLucca hadn't unfortunately died in that devastating automobile accident up on *206*, then...."

"Then Chief Falcone, *your* dormant and stalled police investigation would still be stationary, in neutral gear sitting directly upon Square One!" Rocco DeLucca logically concluded and expressed. "Nick and I had no idea that our older brother's tragic death would spark the beginning of a major crime scene investigation once the police matter emerged from being under Former Chief's Michael Falcone's reprehensible jurisdiction!"

"Thanks to the fantastic service and expertise of FBI Inspector Joe Giralo," Detective Fred Arico summarized and praised, "Mr. Michael Falcone will soon become Inmate Michael Falcone!"

* * * * * * * * * * * *

A full week later, Inspector Joe Giralo met with his loyal agents Salvatore Velardi, Arthur Orsi and Dan Blachford in the back room of Illiano's Italian Restaurant on South Twelfth Street, Hammonton, New Jersey to assess the *solved by accident* "Missing Persons' Case." After ordering pasta dishes from the extensive lunch menu, the four G-men engaged in their informal discussion.

"That was quite spectacular the way you had assisted Detective Arico and Officer Galletta in cracking-open this totally crazy murder skein case," Agent Orsi complimented Joe Giralo. "I'm sure that you and Matt Riley were instrumental in assisting the town law enforcement guys in arresting the iniquitous Michael Falcone along with corrupt funeral director Mr. Andrew Blake and his accomplice, Philip Ruggeri."

"Once the auto accident up at the dangerous *206* S-Curve had occurred," Joe Giralo indicated, "the rest was as easy as apple pie, which ironically, will be my forthcoming dessert! It's quite regrettable that Jason DeLucca had to perish in order for the Hammonton Police Department and me to finally decipher exactly what had been transpiring with unethical Mr. Andrew Blake, with vitriolic Stephen Messina, with shamed Michael Falcone and also, with the vindictive South Philly' mob!"

"Thanks a lot Boss for dispatching me down to Fortescue and to Bivalve on the Delaware Bay," Agent Velardi squawked and balked.

"I didn't appreciate or savor smelling empty clam shells for the past week. The odor was disgustingly nauseous!"

"And Boss, you dispatched me to New Castle, to Dover and to Milford, Delaware for seven uneventful, fruitless days!" Dan Blachford adamantly protested. "Next time, please give me a soft boardwalk assignment in sunny, pleasant Rehoboth Beach!"

"And Inspector," Agent Orsi contributed to the burgeoning complaint litany. "I wound-up wasting a full week's time meandering around in Media, in Plymouth Meeting and in King of Prussia, Pennsylvania. Next time, have me roaming around sampling treats inside the Market Street Gallery Food Court in center city Philly'!"

"Don't forget, kind Gentlemen!" Inspector Giralo nonchalantly answered before taking another bite of his spaghetti and meatball lunch. "You three junior sleuths have gotten paid by the Bureau for basically accomplishing absolutely nothing. What more could you *gifted* Fellas' ever want!"

"We want to know all of the ongoing facts in real time while assisting you in fighting crime!" Agent Velardi stubbornly objected. "That's all that Arty, Dan and I really want! And we want the basic facts pronto, Tonto!"

"Cogito ergo sum!" Inspector Giralo deftly replied in his characteristic raspy voice. "Cogito ergo sum!" the Boss reiterated.

"What did you say?" Dan Blachford asked. "I didn't know that you knew how to speak French!"

"Look it up in a quality Latin-to-English dictionary!" Chief Giralo uttered before swallowing-down several additional morsels of delectable spaghetti. "Cogito ergo sum is actually the true genesis of all essential FBI detective work!"

# "Wolverton Mountain"

Veteran Agents Salvatore Velardi, Arthur Orsi and Dan Blachford stepped into FBI Inspector Joe Giralo's office, loftily situated on the eighth floor of 600 Arch Street, Philadelphia. Each of the conscientious trio was wondering exactly what new investigative matter was of such "urgent and strategic importance", the precise terminology that their reputable Boss had dramatically characterized *their* very next challenging government assignment. As usual, "the Chief" was sitting behind his enormous Canadian oak desk and his brown eyes were carefully examining the front-page articles of the *Philadelphia Inquirer* appearing "above the fold".

"I'm glad that you three easily distracted-but-ambitious junior sleuths have gotten here on time for your scheduled noon appointment, and I'm personally delighted that you're *not* now eating pizza or hoagies down at the crowded Reading Terminal Food Market," the Boss gruffly greeted his loyal subordinates. "I'm also happy to note in my latest report to Matt Riley that you three remarkable gumshoes had easily solved the rather preposterous 'Treasure Map Caper' that had been annoying various local police departments in the Pennsylvania, New Jersey, Delaware tri-state area, which had warranted the indispensable services and intervention of the local FBI. Now Men," Inspector Giralo rambled on. "I'm pleased to inform you three savants that DC headquarters has acknowledged *your* crucial participation in swiftly solving *that* particular, regional dilemma."

"At first, the Treasure Map Case was pretty mind-boggling and not so routine in either scope or sequence," Agent Sal Velardi honestly attested. "If you recall Chief, Treasure Maps had been mailed only to kids of wealthy parents. The first time each targeted kid went and dug in the indicated bonanza location, the thrilled lad would find a fifty-dollar bill deliberately deposited inside a shallowly-buried box. The second time around, after receiving another easy-to-read map, the amused parents would usually, out of sheer curiosity, accompany their beloved offspring to the indicated *new* dig site. After merrily excavating a box containing a hundred-dollar bill, upon returning home, the entertained well-to-do family would discover that...."

"That their opulent home-sweet-home mansion had been broken into and that thousands of dollars-worth of jewelry, silverware, stashed cash and expensive watches had been criminally pilfered. The Treasure Map Caper represented a very clever ruse, a nifty canard designed to get the parents of ten-year-old boys, usually each one an only child, who incidentally has read too many Robert Louis Stevenson' sea adventure stories. Well, my dear Agents," Joe Giralo embellished his monologue. "The shrewd charade was to get the duped adults out of their residences, allowing enough time for the furtive burglaries to be safely and successfully completed!"

"And so, Boss, the wily crooks would audaciously trade a hundred and fifty-dollar legal tender loss in exchange for a multi-thousand-dollar illegal gain," Agent Arthur Orsi very capably summarized. "I've learned over the years that the criminal mind could sometimes also be very creative. It's too bad that nefarious felons don't use their ever-schemin' cerebrums for enacting constructive pursuits that are beneficial to society."

"As you often remind us, Chief," Dan Blachford addressed his well-organized commentary to Inspector Giralo. "Many criminals become too cocky and overconfident. The haughty thugs tend to underestimate the competency of law enforcement, and then the dastardly knaves soon fall into redundant behavior patterns that in the end, lead to their swift apprehension and incarceration."

"True, Dan," Sal Velardi verbally volunteered. "The Treasure Map practice became overused and when it did, it was quite an easy task for us to collar the initially imaginative crooks, especially after an alert suburban mayor had notified us that *his* wannabe' pirate son had received a suspicious-looking Treasure Map in the morning post. In the final analysis," Agent Blachford proudly disclosed, "the cunning crooks turned-out to be mere rank amateurs! The quartet of rogues was easily taken into custody while the idiotic dolts were preoccupied staking-out the astute mayor's ritzy suburban palace!'

"Why did you call us into the city today, Boss?" Agent Orsi boldly asked his immediate superior. "Are you gonna' again oratorically expound on the ethical merits of ancient Greek philosophers Socrates, Plato and Aristotle like you had so monotonously and so tediously done last week?  Your lengthy diatribes work much better than even the best sleeping pills!"

Chief Joe Giralo quickly frowned, and then after regaining his normally placid composure, the inimitable Inspector effectively lectured his three happy-go-lucky associates that the renowned "Socratic Method" of asking relevant questions had eventually become the sturdy foundation of modern-day police interrogation techniques and that the sage Socrates himself was, in truth, a moral philosopher who had been principally interested in the basic distinction between good and evil and between right and wrong. "In simple historical perspective, erudite Socrates was the teacher of

216

Plato, but in the end, the savant had been falsely accused of corrupting the minds of the Athenian youth, and the distinguished master had to drink a poison, hemlock, as his totally unjustified death punishment."

"I really liked the character Socrates in the time-travel movie *Bill and Ted's Excellent Adventure,*" Agent Orsi bizarrely contributed to the rapidly deteriorating conversation. "Particularly, when Bill had humorously demonstrated the lyrics to the Kansas rock and roll song 'Dust in the Wind' by blowing sand from his hand. Despite an obvious language barrier," the FBI speaker elaborated, "the impressed Greek thinker instantly realized that the teen's gesture had been alluding to the frailty of human life on this wonderful planet. The famous teacher Socrates ironically then became Bill's fine student!"

"And Socrates would often tell the tale of the Cave Allegory," Chief Giralo prattled-on while deliberately ignoring Agent Orsi's fairly facetious remarks. "And in this unique 'Cave Story', the great philosopher described a group of common people, the masses, who were representing most of mankind, sitting with their backs to the sun and spending their entire lives in shackles, only witnessing the reflection of the sun's light, the manifestation obviously symbolizing truth, which was really artificial wisdom being reflected off the cave walls situated in front of them; the daily illusion is still being experienced by most of humanity every palpable moment of *their* lackluster lives from womb-to tomb!"

"Just like in the song 'Already Gone' often sung by the Eagles," rock and roll enthusiast Sal Velardi impetuously chimed-in. "The inspiring lyrics go, "Often times it happens, that we live our lives in chains; not ever knowing *we* have the keys!"

"And the Eagles in that same song also sang 'You can see the stars and never see the light'," Agent Dan Blachford added to the oddball discussion, inadvertently fueling Inspector Giralo's mounting chagrin. "And in the song 'Lyin' Eyes', Glenn Frey brilliantly sings the line: 'Every form of refuge has its price'!" the FBI detective finished.

"Enough of your inane, ludicrous frivolity!" the mercurial-tempered Chief Inspector affectionately reprimanded his three presently clownish G-men. "I suppose, Sal, that your next comment will be about Plato being a character who had been shot by the Los Angeles Police in the 1955 movie *Rebel without a Cause* starring James Dean and Natalie Wood, while also featuring Sal Mineo as the confused smart kid, Plato!"

"Well, er, kinda', Boss," Sal Velardi nervously confessed. "In *that* case you've just cited, I would only be practicing the Associative Law of Thinking like you always encourage us to do! I truly believe that imitation is the sincerest form of flattery, wouldn't you agree?"

"For your education and general information Sal," Chief Giralo orally qualified, "the philosopher Plato often told the story of the Ring of Gyges, which was a unique tale where the favored owner possessed the supernatural power to become invisible by simply turning the ring around on his or her finger. Now, the crucial, paramount question is, my dear Salvatore, 'Would the possessor of the wondrous ring do good things or selfish things while having its supernatural power at his or her command?' And furthermore," Giralo strongly articulated, "the Scientific Method of Reasoning that we, as dedicated detectives, owe to Plato's famous pupil, Aristotle, who not only taught academics to the young Alexander the Great of Macedonia, but later in life, well anyway Men," the Boss paused and reflected.

"Was Aristotle famous for anything else besides philosophy?" Blachford asked. "If I remember correctly, the guy was a pretty versatile ancient dude!"

"Yes, Dan," Giralo confirmed. "Later in life the ancient sage Aristotle also was responsible for classifying science into its primary functioning categories: chemistry, physics, astronomy, botany and biology!"

"Okay, Chief. I think you've now satisfactorily exhausted and satisfied the usual mandatory preliminary small-talk aspect of our current meeting," Sal Velardi intrepidly insisted, "so let's cut-out the fat and finally get to the meat of the matter. Why are *we* three accomplished crime-fighters summoned and assembled here at 600 Arch Street on Monday, August 26?"

"Strangely enough Sal, the entire ball-of-wax involves rock and roll music, specifically, mostly familiar oldies' tunes from the '50s and '60s," the Boss surprisingly related. "And furthermore, Agent Velardi, I believe you still remember the several excellent Rock and Roll shows I had generously treated you to a few years back, you know, the ones down at the Wildwood Boardwalk Convention Hall!"

"Oh yes. We had the pleasure of seeing Charlie Gracie doing his classic hit 'You Butterfly', and then there was the truly terrific Chubby Checker performance, and still another time we enjoyed the Frankie Avalon, Fabian and Bobby Rydell's 'Golden Boys Show'! And who could ever forget Ronnie Spector, former lead singer of the Ronettes. The accompanying small orchestra band played the same introduction over and over again for fifteen full minutes before the temperamental diva eventually came out on stage to sing 'Be My Baby'! Say Boss," Agent Velardi continued with his rambling lexicon. "Did you know that Rydell High School in the teen movie *Grease* was actually named after pop singer Bobby Rydell, who incidentally had starred in the film *Bye, Bye Birdie?*"

Chief Giralo wiggled his nose, slowly shrugged his broad shoulders and then judiciously decided that it was finally time to explain the true purpose of the hastily-arranged conference. The Boss related to his motivated Men that modern songs played by radio station DJs often fit into certain classification themes such as Boys' Names, Girls' Names, Colors, Days of the Week and Animals, but a recently intercepted email obtained from the CIA had "the top brass at the Washington FBI Bureau" rather baffled.

Inspector Giralo deftly reached into his top desk drawer and removed copies of the enigmatic electronic communication, handed the vital "photo-documents" to each of his concerned Men, and next asked his three loyal staff members to render "a viable interpretation" of the e-mail after given adequate time to slowly and silently reading the nondescript, ordinary-sounding letter.

August 3, 2013

Dear Mr. Mint Triumph:

I'm having a super time vacationing down here in good old Nassau. The Bahama Islands are wonderfully warm in August. Anyway, I want to thank you for the well-appreciated home-made CD music disc you had sent me last month. I absolutely love '50s, '60s, '70s and early '80s'rock and roll.

After thoroughly listening to all twenty splendid songs, here are my favorite artists arranged from best liked to worst enjoyed. Glen Campbell, Wilbert Harrison, Johnny Rivers, Paper Lace, Bob Seger, Dovells, Manhattan Transfer, Freddie Cannon, Marty Robbins, Elton John, Jan and Dean, Scott McKenzie, Claude King, Harry Belefonte, Gerry and the Pacemakers, The New Vaudeville Band, Big Bopper, Johnny Horton, Bruce Springsteen and Billy Joel.

I can't wait until I receive your next music disc via international courier. Thanks again for so kindly thinking of me.

All the best,
Violet Verdant

"Okay Fellas'. I want you to liberally exercise your superlative detective instincts! What's so peculiar about *this* particular e-mail?" Chief Giralo imperatively asked. "Don't be too shy in offering an opinion; any opinion."

"Nowl Boss, first of all, the given names Mint Triumph and Violet Verdant seem mighty irregular and uncommon," Salvatore Velardi spoke-up "But other than *that* weird first name and surname facet, upon initial inspection, quite candidly, the oddball e-mail's general content seems fairly innocuous."

Inspector Giralo proceeded to explain that apparently "Mint Triumph" was a sophisticated code name for the notorious scoundrel "Victor Grenoff," a wealthy European tycoon now living and doing business in Sofia, Bulgaria.

"Sofia Bulgaria!" Sal Velardi exclaimed in amusement. "I think that *that* doll used to be an exotic, erotic dancer across the river in Camden over at the Aquarius Strip Club on Route 130."

"Stop being so absurd and so ridiculous!" the now-serious Boss admonished. "Open any mediocre encyclopedia and learn some fundamental geography, Salvatore. Sofia is the capital city of Bulgaria, which was formerly a Soviet Block country that had been languishing for decades behind the Iron Curtain. Now, this unscrupulous financier Victor Grenoff, alias Mint Triumph, had made his fantastic fortune in the 1970s bartering purloined goods on the black market, and as a result," Inspector Giralo qualified, "the upwardly mobile social chameleon is now pretending to be a legitimate international corporate mogul. The entrepreneurial Bulgarian is indeed heavily invested in the flourishing wind and solar energy business."

"Okay," Arthur Orsi concurred and conceded, "but what about this oldies' song collector basking down in the Bahamas, this Violet Verdant person? Does she have an alias too?"

"Our reliable data base records confirm that Violet Verdant is really a fanatical female anarchist, Viola Greene, a ruthless female who is now a staunch environmental and clean energy activist; a militant radical 'green rights' advocate', at that!" Chief Giralo assertively informed. "But Matt Riley and I just can't seem to connect these two 'persons of interest' with the string of jewelry store robberies along with the skein of power grid explosions and electric company dynamite blasts that have been occurring in recent weeks."

"Mostly big cities and towns in the U.S.," Agent Orsi recalled and verbally offered. "I've read about the debacles both in the newspapers and in the FBI's confidential files."

"Yes, Arty. Already there's been significant jewelry thefts in New Orleans, in New York, in Chicago, in San Francisco and in Tallahassee, Florida with coincidental power plant explosions violently happening in Allentown and in Bristol Pennsylvania, in Chantilly, France, in Chicago and also most recently, in El Paso, Texas. What the heck kind of evil chain reaction is being clandestinely wrought upon our vital free enterprise economic system? How do we get to Square One in order to advance to Square Two?"

"You've always advised us to look for distinct patterns and sequences," Dan Blachford solemnly declared. "Maybe the series of jewelry store thefts and the corresponding electric plant explosions are somehow maliciously connected. You know Chief, perhaps there's a correlation between the two sets of criminal events?"

"Dan might actually be on to something mammoth in magnitude!" Art Orsi automatically agreed. "Maybe the series of jewelry store smash-and grab-operations are somehow financing the massive acts of sabotage being diabolically performed in this country and also in an specific area of France; Chantilly, I believe."

Just then the desk telephone rang, and it was spontaneously recognized that Matt Riley was calling the Philadelphia FBI office from metropolitan downtown DC. After completing an intense two-minute dialogue, Chief Giralo briskly hung-up, and then gingerly placed his phone into its flat cradle. Next, the perplexed Boss meaningfully stared at his three-man-team with a very grim expression formed upon his chubby, middle-aged countenance.

"Riley just reported that there's been a huge explosion over at the Egg Harbor Power Plant on the Egg Harbor River over in Jersey, the enormous blast happening not far from Ocean City. And also, there's chatter on the government hot-wire that a tremendous diamond heist has been reported by the nearby Atlantic City Police Department. I now wholly believe that your extraordinary hypothesis is correct, Arty! And yours too, Dan!" Giralo genuinely commended appreciative Agents Orsi and Blachford.

"What's the deal on this woman Violet Verdant?" Art Orsi asked. "It's a rather peculiar name simply because a violet is purple and the word *verdant* means green."

"The diamonds and the other precious gems purloined in the various jewelry store hits might be financing the TNT and other dangerous materials being subversively used by the pernicious saboteurs, whom I suspect are extremely radical environmentalists maniacally being led by the formidable and despicable Viola Greene, alias *Violet Verdant*, which is a rather silly appellation, especially when the two names are pronounced out loud. Violet Verdant is essentially a suspicious female I.D. that sounds more like a very poorly designed oxymoron!"

"Boss, you had earlier mentioned that songs often have certain themes like Boys' Names, Girls' Names, Colors, Days of the Week, Animals and so on," Dan Blachford impulsively revealed the nature of his sudden brainstorm. "Well then, what about the names of certain places. I mean cities such as New Orleans, New York, Chicago, San Francisco, Tallahassee and now good old Egg Harbor City over in South Jersey."

"You're a veritable genius Dan!" Joe Giralo lavishly praised the most laconic member of his effective G-man squad. "I now see a definite developing pattern being synchronized here. The jewelry stores are evidently not contrived in any special order, but the power plant explosions, at least the five that have been starkly brought to our attention, well, those affected facilities whose industries have been struck appear to exist in alphabetical order: Allentown, Bristol, Chantilly, Chicago, and also El Paso."

"I've heard of *Weird Science,* but now we have weird Geography!" Agent Velardi marveled and exclaimed. "Coincidentally, each power plant explosion occurs near each jewelry store heist."

"Salvatore, this whole matter is truly *your* strong suit," the Chief clearly emphasized, pounding his right fist upon the hard, flat surface before him. "Do any popular oldies' artists sing any of the songs mentioned in the intercepted e-mail that had been sent from Nassau in the Bahamas to Sofia, Bulgaria?"

"Holy cow herds, Boss!" Sal Velardi boisterously bellowed upon recognizing a definite relationship. "Billy Joel does the number 'Allentown', the Dovells do 'Bristol Stomp', the Big Bopper had recorded 'Chantilly Lace', and if my fuzzy memory serves me accurately, a group called Paper Lace did 'The Night Chicago Died'. And then, Chief, Marty Robbins had performed the big smash 'El Paso', but the recent Egg Harbor power company explosion doesn't seem to mesh with the rest of the evolving big city song pattern!"

"Wait a cotton-pickin' minute, Sal!" normally reticent Dan Blachford impetuously yelled. "What's *that* popular fast-paced Bruce Springsteen song about motorcycles roaring down Highway 9. Highway Nine is in New Jersey, and I know for a fact that it meanders right past the Egg Harbor Power Plant!"

"Yes! True! Eureka!" bellowed a now-euphoric Agent Velardi, inadvertently mimicking the Greek scientist Archimedes. "The catchy lyrics about *Highway 9* are found in the best-selling Springsteen song, 'Born to Run'!"

"Okay, Men. I'm now sufficiently convinced that we're on the right trail!" Inspector Giralo concurred with a healthy sigh of relief. "Tomorrow morning we'll meet at 9 a.m. sharp in the side room at Marcello's Restaurant on Bellevue Avenue in downtown, Hammonton. I want you three, fairly zany Teslas to make a comprehensive list of all twenty recording artists that had been specifically identified in the surreptitious e-mail I had received from Matt Riley, and then thereafter," the Chief carefully proceeded, "I want to know the titles of any songs sung by those same twenty recording stars that deal with a particular city or a particular place. And finally, Men," the rejuvenated Boss concluded his inspirational pontification, "please don't forget to also make a second list of the cities mentioned in the twenty researched tunes, and in your final analysis, meticulously organize the city names into a logical alphabetical order!"

* * * * * * * * * * * *

The following morning, Inspector Joe Giralo and his determined agents conveniently met inside the closed-to-the-public, adjacent room at Marcello's Restaurant in downtown Hammonton, New Jersey for coffee, Italian pastries and some frank discussion about the enigmatic jewelry store smash-and-grab felonies along with the rash of energy installation explosions executed at various strategic settings across the USA. And now, the devastating crises also happening overseas in the vicinity of Chantilly, France, and in Kingston, Jamaica and in Liverpool and Winchester, England, as well.

"That Bruce Springsteen song 'Born to Run' really had us four FBI Guys sniffing our nostrils in the wrong direction," Sal Velardi commented. "But then when it had been mentioned about the Egg Harbor Power Plant being located just outside Atlantic City, immediately, *Highway 9* nicely entered into the difficult equation, and then *we* were able to be more plausible about defining the true reality of our very treacherous new-found enemies, the very ruthless wind and solar panel czar Victor Grenoff, alias Mint Triumph of Sofia, Bulgaria, and his ax-to-grind vindictive accomplice, Viola Greene, stealthily masquerading as Violet Verdant, the female terrorist leisurely sunning herself down in semi-tropical Nassau," the perceptive agent adroitly reviewed and nut-shelled.

"And naturally Boss, plenty of loose money is won and lost in nearby Atlantic City casinos," Agent Blachford contributed to the discussion. "So logically, diamonds, rubies, emeralds and sapphires are always in abundant supply there. Those precious gems are easily available and ready to be stolen in broad daylight during instant surprise-type attacks. Yes, the brazen felonies are being performed by violent smash-and-grab robbers."

"Actually Inspector, there are a few obscure rock and roll bands along with one-hit-wonder recording artists represented and appearing on the twenty songs' list that Sal, Dan and I have so diligently researched and photocopied," Agent Orsi informatively indicated. "For instance, Boss, the New Vaudeville Band, Wilbert Harrison, Scott McKenzie, Paper Lace and finally Claude King, but amazingly, when *those* non-household names were matched-up with their respective familiar song titles," 'Sir Arthur' promptly clarified. "Logically speaking, it all quickly made better sense to us experienced, sage researchers."

"Yes, who in the world was, or *is* this fellow Claude King?" Dan Blachford very honestly inquired. "I'm quite aware of the hit song 'Wolverton Mountain', but I had never heard of an entertainer having the remote name Claude King."

"Last night, I had performed some elementary Google Internet research on the artist Claude King and his main success, 'Wolverton Mountain'," Sal Velardi eagerly communicated. "And this fellow King was a country and western singer, but in 1962, he hit it kinda' big with his catchy tune, 'Wolverton Mountain', which in reality is little more than a tall lackluster hill located in the northwestern corner of Arkansas, near a town named...., yes, here it is; I've jotted it down in my notes," Velardi fumbled his notepad and then announced. "It's an Arkansas town named Morrilton. Columbia Records had produced and marketed Claude King's clever tune to myriad Southern radio stations and to Dixie disc jockeys who were involved in the early Rock and Roll/Country and Western '60s era."

"Yes," added Agent Orsi, capitalizing on the momentary slack in Agent Velardi's biographical presentation. "And just this morning, I had discovered on the Internet that the song 'Wolverton Mountain' had been based on a certain real-life character, a hillbilly recluse named Clifton Clowers, who had incidentally lived on *that* small, unexceptional mountain up in northwestern Arkansas."

"Very interesting info', but fundamentally extraneous to and detached from the parallel jewelry store larcenies and the very damaging corresponding power plant criminal activity," Joe Giralo recounted before indulgently gulping-down a mouthful of Marcello's fresh-brewed coffee. "And Fellas', I also learned during *my* individual computer search analysis that Wolverton is a village or town in England, not too far from London, so having an open mind," the Boss summarized, "I suppose that *this* coincidental connection might also have something germane to do with the targeted British cities of Liverpool and Winchester."

"And Chief," Agent Orsi felt compelled to articulate. "Last night I found-out that the song 'Wolverton Mountain' was later covered and redone in other versions recorded by Dickey Lee and also by Nat King Cole; both in 1962, and later by Bing Crosby in 1965."

"Quite fascinating but otherwise rather immaterial details Arty, and arguably, not-at-all pertinent to *our* proliferating dual crime-wave dilemmas at hand," Joe Giralo evaluated and maintained. "Now Sal, please distribute to us your artist list that had been gleaned from the intercepted e-mail with the city song titles arranged in their original order next to the singers' names. After we thoroughly examine and study your singer/song revised laundry list, we'll then assiduously confer about its content."

"Here guys!" Agent Velardi stated as he slowly disseminated the requested documents to Chief Giralo, to Arthur Orsi and to Dan Blachford. "Let's closely study this original list of singers along with *their* counterpart city song titles and see exactly what can be derived and determined."

| **Artist** | **City and Song Reference** |
|---|---|
| 1. Glen Campbell | Galveston, (Wichita Lineman) |
| 2. Wllbert Harrison | Kansas City |
| 3. Johnny Rivers | Memphis |
| 4. Paper Lace | The Night Chicago Died |
| 5. Bob Seger | Hollywood Nights |
| 6. Dovells | Bristol Stomp |
| 7. Manhattan Transfer | Boy from New York City |
| 8. Freddie Cannon | Tallahassee Lassie |
| 9. Marty Robbins | El Paso |
| 10. Elton John | Philadelphia Freedom |
| 11. Jan and Dean | Little Old Lady from Pasadena |
| 12. Scott McKenzie | Going to San Francisco |
| 13. Claude King | Wolverton Mountain |
| 14. Harry Belefonte | Jamaica Farewell (Kingston) |
| 15. Gerry & Pacemakers | Ferry Cross the Mersey (Liverpool) |
| 16. New Vaudeville Band | Winchester Cathedral |
| 17. Big Bopper | Chantilly Lace |
| 18. Johnny Horton | Battle of New Orleans |
| 19. Bruce Springsteen | Born to Run (N.J. Route 9) |
| 20. Billy Joel | Allentown |

After scrutinizing the original list of twenty singing artists and their respective "Place Songs," persistent Inspector Joe Giralo requested personal observations and reactions from his thoroughly engrossed underlings. "Obviously, Glen Campbell represents a glaring problem for us to consider with two major cities existing in his song titles, Galveston and Wichita," the astute Chief began the agents' "focus group" interpretation.

"And there's a Kansas City, Kansas and also a Kansas City, Missouri too," Arthur Orsi remembered and shared. "That parallel existence could amount to a thorny problem of sorts. And let's not forget in reality that there's a Hollywood, California and also a Hollywood, Florida!"

"And there's a Bristol, Pennsylvania and also a Bristol, England," Dan Blachford noticed and responsibly disclosed. "But since there's already been destructive power plant explosions in Bristol, Pennsylvania, I suspect that the Dovells' 'Bristol Stomp' has successfully eliminated Bristol, England from the designated endangered cities' target list."

"I must admit, Men. Some superb reasoning is now being admirably exhibited!" Inspector Giralo congratulated his illustrious team members. "And let's not forget Victor Grenoff's sinister motive: theoretically, to destroy his competitors' fossil fuel refineries and installations and to vigorously promote wind and solar power throughout the world while simultaneously profiting from his secretive illicit endeavors. And in regard to the desperate anarchist Viola Greene, I presume that *that* wicked *witch* wants to soon rob a well-stocked jewelry store in Wichita! Now Salvatore," Joe Giralo firmly instructed, his graphic speech not missing a syllable. "Please distribute the second list I had asked you to put together, you know, the one having the twenty song titles with cities' names now arranged in strict alphabetical order."

"Okay Boss, here it is!" Agent Velardi cooperatively answered. "I trust that the language typed upon *this* piece of paper will somehow result in enlightening us all!"

The alphabetical list of twenty cities alluded to in the song titles and lyrics were then quietly studied.

1.  Allentown, Pennsylvania
2.  Bristol, Pennsylvania
3.  Chantilly, France
4.  Chicago, Illinois
5.  Egg Harbor, New Jersey (Route 9)
6.  El Paso, Texas
7.  Galveston, Texas (or Wichita Kansas)
8.  Hollywood (California or Florida)
9.  Jamaica Farewell (Kingston)
10. Memphis, Tennessee
11. Mersey (Liverpool, England)
12. New Orleans, Louisiana
13. New York City
14. Pasadena, California
15. Philadelphia, Pennsylvania
16. San Francisco, California
17. Tallahassee, Florida
18. Wichita, Kansas (or Galveston, Texas)
19. Winchester, England
20. Wolverton Mountain (Arkansas)

"Ostensibly Chief," Agent Velardi anxiously stated, "as we all know, the first five cities have already been attacked, at least power plants and refineries operating near them. Allentown, Bristol, Chantilly, Chicago and Egg Harbor, located near Atlantic City; these five specific anarchist targets are no longer in play!"

"And Fellas'," observant Chief Giralo strongly stressed and then momentarily paused his hoarse voice. "After the giant oil refinery outside El Paso had recently been maliciously destroyed in a colossal conflagration, *that* horrifying catastrophe probably means that the next city of interest is either Galveston or Wichita, according to the two Glen Campbell hit 'city songs' provided on the alphabetical list!"

"Great Boss, but which of the pair will it be?" a now-frustrated Agent Orsi demanded knowing a plausible answer. "Use your legendary psychic abilities to intelligently narrow-down the field!"

"Naturally, Arty. Regular alphabetical order would rationally suggest Galveston, but my ordinarily dependable sixth sense gut instinct tells me it's going to be Wichita, instead."

"Designed to intentionally throw our investigation off course?" Dan Blachford asked. "How cruelly cunning and how wickedly deceitful their madness was!"

"Possibly Dan," Chief Giralo replied and soon hesitated. "But let's be practical here. To understand the criminal mind, we must seriously adjust our ordinary thought process and begin thinking like unscrupulous criminals do. The last song appearing in alphabetical order is the classic 'Wolverton Mountain,' which on the U.S. map, in actuality, is geographically closer to Wichita, Kansas than it is to Galveston, Texas."

"But on the revised list, Galveston is indicated next, placed right after El Paso, that is, in true alphabetical order!" a still-skeptical Dan Blachford argued. "Wouldn't *that* Texas city be the now-predictable villains' next patterned target?'"

"Naturally, Dan. All-too-militant Viola Greene and her indoctrinated green-minded subordinate saboteurs know that Texas has plenty of oil refineries and pipelines that are probably *now* under heavy police and federal surveillance, so if the home-grown terrorists have an ounce of intelligence," Joe Giralo conjectured and persuasively insisted. "They'll instinctively deviate from their established methods and foolishly attempt demolishing a facility that's closest to Wolverton Mountain, Arkansas, and Gentlemen," the veteran FBI Inspector confidently revealed, "the most convenient and closest metropolis to Wolverton Mountain on the 'song city list' is Wichita, Kansas."

"Chief, I'll bet that you'll probably promptly notify the Galveston cops and the Texas Rangers about keeping a tight guard on Galveston and its numerous oil and electric plants," Art Orsi stated. "But I'll wager that you're going to have *our* brilliant colleague Matt Riley dispatch Colonel Bob Bauers and his highly-skilled commando units to patrol every major jewelry store and every significant power plant operation in and around *that* next designated city in the State of Kansas, namely Wichita."

"Wow Boss!" Agent Velardi gleefully exclaimed. "Viola Greene will be apprehended just like those moronic Treasure Map culprits had been easily captured over in suburban 'Philly."

"Right Salvatore!" the sagacious FBI Chief readily predicted. "Villainous Victor Grenoff didn't want a traceable paper trail for his cash payments to Viola Greene because the slippery rich European crook was fully aware that the IRS monitors all bank wire transmissions exceeding ten thousand dollars. Then, more than likely," garrulous Inspector Giralo adroitly pontificated, "Grenoff's wily business confederates and his global surrogates in various cities, like Nassau in the Bahamas, paid the ruthless 'save the planet' Ms. Greene off in cash for her hired destructive services. So, I currently surmise that Viola Greene was probably operating on her own accord, but had been forced by realistic circumstances to subsidize her national and international power plant explosions by lowering herself to mundanely robbing diamonds and rubies from retail jewelry stores throughout the USA and other nefariously targeted countries like France, Jamaica and England."

"And soon that other diabolical nemesis of ours, Victor Grenoff, will predictably be arrested and taken into custody by Interpol over in Sofia, Bulgaria," Arthur Orsi concluded and added. "Boss, thanks to you capably teaching the three of us how to connect seemingly unrelated details, Sal, Dan and I are quickly becoming psychic human beings just like you! In fact, Chief, it's *our* genuine conviction that *you* have impressively become the new paradigm in federal crime-fighting all by yourself! Congratulations!"

"Just relax and swallow-down your delicious coffee!" Chief Giralo sternly recommended, feigning a degree of modesty. "I'll readily concede that all three of you wacky wizards are indeed qualified experts on satisfactorily imbibing large quantities of caffeine! You even have me becoming an addict!"

"You'll have to be admitted into the Maxwell House for immediate rehab'!" Agent Orsi jested to his good-natured superior. "Are the Hills Brothers' doctors still practicin' experimental medicine over there?"

"I'll bet that the traitorous and insidious Viola Greene will soon modify and alter her alphabetical list, next starting from Wichita and then possibly proceeding backwards all the way down to Galveston in reverse order, but her futile efforts will all be to no avail," Agent Velardi confidently prognosticated.

"Very true Salvatore," Inspector Joe Giralo verified. "Galveston is probably a planned trigger mechanism to furtively switch to Wichita at the bottom of the alphabetically organized song list. That relevant assumption is more truth than hypothesis!"

"And thanks to Mr. Claude King along with his diminutive 'Wolverton Mountain' lyrics, and also kudos to our collective, ever-maturing psychic and detective talents," Agent Sal Velardi concluded and articulated, "this extremely confounding series of dual jewelry store thefts and industrial sabotage crimes have been magnificently and marvelously cracked wide-open. Say Boss, please pass the coffee pot! I think we've all earned a third cup!"

# "Fishing Expedition"

FBI Agents Salvatore Velardi, Arthur Orsi and Dan Blachford had received orders from their 600 Arch Street, Philadelphia headquarters to proceed immediately to Philadelphia International Airport and fly directly to sunny Paradise Island, just off the coast of Nassau in the Bahamas. The three curious G-men had been speculating and discussing the urgent nature of their emergency assignment during their southern flight, and later that evening, the investigators were reviewing matters while sitting inside one of their three moderate suites at the very impressive tourist-oriented Atlantis Resort. Never before had the illustrious trio ever conducted a federal investigation in the gorgeous Bahamas.

Just when the three agents' intrigue had reached a culminating point, their inimitable boss, Inspector Joe Giralo, rapped his fat knuckles upon the thick door of Agent Velardi's very accommodating and comfortable temporary living quarters.

"Well Chief," Sal Velardi amiably greeted his government superior. "Why are we all meeting here at this excellent tourist resort on such short notice, that is, instead of us ordinarily fighting regional crime back in 'Philly?"

"As usual, you're being more than a trifle rambunctious, not to mention being immensely impulsive and impetuous," the Inspector mildly chided his principal apostate. "Before I identify the specifics of our current re-location, I'd like to learn exactly what you three federal sleuths have sacrificed this coming weekend in order to participate in *this* top-secret FBI enterprise. As usual, let's start the repertoire with you, Salvatore."

"Well, Boss; as you know Kathy and I have subscriptions to the Walnut Street Theater, and we were looking forward to seeing the widely acclaimed play *Wicked*, which really happens to be an extension of the *Wizard of Oz* theme. But now that I'm gallivantin' around down here in semi-tropical Paradise Island," Agent Velardi continued his protest, "my wife had to get Agent Orsi's wife Carol to accompany her to the Saturday night performance, that's incidentally gotten rave reviews from various show-biz' critics."

"And how about you, Arty," Chief Giralo resumed his small-talk prattle. "In two minutes or less, what were your unfulfilled family plans that had to be nixed because of this sudden Paradise Island caper we're about to initiate?"

"Well, as Sal just indicated," Agent Orsi prefaced, "Carol is going to the Walnut Street Theater with Kathy. But in the meantime, my spouse and I had to surrender our intention of driving over to Kennett Square, Pennsylvania and admiring the magnificent wonders of Longwood Gardens, which features many spectacular botanical flower arrangements and eye-pleasing meadows on 1,077 exquisite acres. The many fabulous greenhouse exhibits alone are worth the price of admission. And of course, the scenic drive west from Hammonton to Kennett Square takes about an hour and a half, with traffic and road construction delays permitting."

"I've been to Longwood Gardens many times with Gina," Inspector Giralo related to his well-rested team. And it's perhaps the finest display of flowers anywhere in the entire Delaware Valley. My wife especially loves the thousands of red and white poinsettias that are abundant there every Christmas season. Now Dan," the Chief motioned towards normally reticent Agent Blachford, "what are you and Bing giving-up this coming weekend?"

"Well, Fearless Leader," the FBI employee replied in a mellow tone of voice. "On Saturday morning my wife and I were going to drive from Hammonton up *206* and stroll around the Princeton University campus. Bing had taken several graduate courses at the prestigious Ivy League college, and she desires to nostalgically reunite with the main academic buildings and grounds. And then on Sunday," usually laconic Agent Blachford elaborated, "Bing and I were going to venture down to Cape May and enjoy the annual Wine Festival. Various rock and roll bands perform to several thousand vintage vino enthusiasts, and a general carnival atmosphere prevails. And of course," Blachford added, "the ships of the Cape May-Lewes Ferry are impressively moored in the background of the very popular South Jersey event."

"This Atlantis Resort appears to be rather sensational," Inspector Giralo commented, deliberately attempting to delay conferring about the new serious FBI mission with his loyal assistants. "I've done my due-diligence research, and this place has a fantastic marine habitat having over two hundred ocean species. And over fifty thousand ocean animals overall, all of which can be viewed through thick, protective glass. The resident sea creatures appear swimming around inside a giant aquarium environment. And then there's SCUBA diving and snorkeling lessons and a plethora of other activities along with, according to the descriptive colorful lobby brochures I've perused," Giralo quite characteristically lectured, "a hundred-forty-acre waterpark named Dolphin Cay, which has nine spectacular water-slides and eleven unique water pools. It's too bad Salvatore that we're here at the Atlantis strictly on FBI business and not staying for vacationing or for pleasure."

232

"True Inspector," Agent Velardi anxiously acknowledged. "But please inform us; what is the actual purpose of...."

"And Sal, the only real thing we're going to savor down here at the Atlantis besides delectable room service food," the Boss casually indicated, "is the tasty cuisine available at the Dune Restaurant, at the Mesa Grill, at the Bahamian Club and at the Cafe Martinique."

"We've already visited and toured those four terrific eateries," Sal Velardi diplomatically answered. "However, Boss; we haven't seen nor heard from you in over a week. Where have you been keeping yourself? Have you been maneuvering your coveted ancient fishing yacht in and out of various Wildwood and Cape May marinas?"

"And, oh yes, Salvatore," Giralo recollected and stated, deliberately keeping his main man in well-contrived melodramatic suspense, "I had neglected to mention the resort's splendid Sea Fire Steakhouse along with the equally inviting Casa D' Angelo, specializing in serving delectable Italian dinners! But unfortunately, most of our meals will be provided by routine room service. You can't always have classic restaurant ambiance, you know!"

"But Boss," a now nearly exasperated Agent Orsi interrupted. "Why in the world are the four of us federal professionals presently situated in this attractive hotel suite at this very minute? Please be kind enough to specifically address *that* issue!"

The slightly insulted Inspector then qualified Agent Orsi's depiction by strangely citing that his forty-five foot-long "extremely reliable 1979 fishing vessel" the *Sun-Daze* happened to be a well-equipped Cris-Craft that had cost a handsome three hundred thousand dollars back in the spring of 2,002, and that the sturdy boat possessed a recently renovated galley featuring a slate counter, a functional microwave oven, an adequate stove and a nifty refrigerator.

Joe Giralo proceeded to attempt impressing his fully disinterested audience. "My cherished fishing ship also has a 39-inch flat screen TV that's wall-mounted in the lounge area, has six-foot four-inch head space leading to the Master Stateroom, has a shower in the Captain's Room, and last but not least, has comfortable bunk beds in the smaller Guest Stateroom. And also, my refurbished craft is powered by..."

"By twin diesel Detroits, the awesome inboards generating up to eight hundred and fifty horsepower," Agent Blachford aptly finished the Inspector's often-mentioned declarative sentence. "And you had paid a mere three hundred thousand bucks for the magnificent tub back in April of 2002. Now Boss, we've heard you redundantly brag about the *Sun-Daze* numerous times, as if it's the Royal Caribbean *Voyager of the Sea.* And so Chief, we know that you frequently value being ambiguous, so if you don't wish to reveal to us where you've been all week long, please tell me; when was your arrival time flying non-stop into the Bahamas?"

"I didn't fly to Nassau on a commercial jet airplane," Chief Giralo bluntly responded. "I arrived into port just an hour ago piloting my wonderful *Sun-Daze*."

"What!" Agents Velardi, Orsi and Blachford all exclaimed simultaneously, leaving their parched mouths agape in absolute disbelief.

"You heard me correctly," coy Inspector Giralo nonchalantly emphasized and reiterated. "I navigated my dependable fishing boat south along the Atlantic Coast from Wildwood, and when I finally reached West Palm Beach, I voyaged east from Florida straight toward the Bahamas. And frankly Men, I relished every single second of my peaceful ocean adventure. But in truth," Giralo further explained, "my treasured forty-five-foot-long boat is now in the Atlantis Marina quietly docked next to incredible ships belonging to international billionaires, some of the extraordinary vessels being over two-hundred-foot-long!"

"Okay Boss, you courageously navigated the *Sun-Daze* from Jersey down here to Paradise Island, so why did you do it?" Sal Velardi inquired. "I mean, for Pete's sake, what's this mysterious confidential assignment all about?"

Inspector Giralo casually opened-up his black leather briefcase and handed Agent Velardi a blank piece of computer paper. Showing instant astonishment, the FBI recipient yelled-out, "It's got nothing written, drawn or typed on it!"

"Ha, ha, ha!" Chief Giralo indulgently laughed at his momentarily addled disciple. "It's back to Detective Work 101, dear Salvatore! Ha, ha, ha!"

"I don't appreciate being the object of your bizarre sense of amusement!" the bewildered G-man shakily answered. "Level with us Boss, and I mean without you giving us any of your emblematic nebulosity. What's behind all of the unnecessary levity?"

"It's an old spying trick dating back to colonial times and the American Revolutionary War!" the Boss remarked and then chuckled. "The message I just transferred to you is handwritten in lemon juice. Just light a match under the paper, Salvatore, and the appropriate words will magically appear!"

Feeling quite beleaguered and annoyed, Agent Velardi clumsily lit a match and held the object's heat underneath the empty-worded document. The enigmatic message "Atlantis Resort, Initiate Operation Fishing Expedition," automatically came into focus.

234

"Fishing Expedition!" Art Orsi marveled and hollered-out. "We flew down here to Nassau and you piloted the *Sun-Daze* all the way down the East Coast for *us* to superficially engage in a wild fishing expedition? Is this some kind of obscure impractical joke, or what?"

"Allow me to explain a certain point," a totally humored Inspector Giralo articulated. "In *this* particular instance, the word 'fishing' is spelled P-H-I-S-H-I-NG! Ha, ha, ha, Men! We're taking the *Sun-Daze* on an exploratory 'Phishing Expedition'! Ha, ha, ha!"

The three perplexed G-men stared incredulously at each other, generally astounded at their renowned mentor's rather peculiar "homophonic language." Meanwhile, effervescent Inspector Joe Giralo persisted in fully indulging in his unbridled guffawing.

* * * * * * * * * * * *

That Saturday evening, after devouring delicious surf and turf room service suppers, the four FBI men conducted an impromptu "Phishing Conversation" inside Inspector Joe Giralo's luxury Atlantis suite. As was his distinct habit, the Chief felt it was of paramount importance to first review some irrelevant-but-interesting personal observations, with his mundane oratory being much to the dismay of his three listeners.

"Guys, this splendid resort we're staying at is called Atlantis, an obvious allusion to the presumed Lost Continent that had been destroyed by violent volcanic eruptions and then haplessly slipping into the merciless Atlantic, as aptly reported in the writings of the Greek scholar Plato. According to the ancient historical and mythological renditions," Joe Giralo editorialized, "Atlantis had been the home to a superior unrivaled civilization possessing advanced science and technology. In fact, the...."

"The Atlantic Ocean was named after the legendary Lost Continent, which supposedly existed somewhere beyond the Pillars of Hercules and the eastern entrance to the Mediterranean Sea," finished Agent Velardi, accurately guessing and then completing the garrulous Inspector's all-too-familiar oral presentation. "And as is your grotesque, standard, redundant style, you've told us on more than several occasions Chief that the word Mediterranean means...."

"A Sea situated in 'the middle of the land', specifically meaning between the African, the European and the Middle East continental masses," Agent Orsi contributed to the academic dialogue. "The Greek king Odysseus spent ten whole years trying to get back to his wife, his son and his kingdom in Homer's epic poem the *Odyssey*, which describes in detail the myriad exploits of the brave hero Odysseus, and hence, any long meandering trip is called...."

"An odyssey," Agent Blachford satisfactorily enunciated. "Now Boss, please educate us about this oddball 'phishing expedition' that's goin' to take place a thousand miles from our homes. I'm getting seasick and homesick just pondering it."

Inspector Giralo cleared his raspy throat and then enunciated a short seminar on the particular form of 'phishing' that had been relayed to him by Matt Riley, Head Senior Investigator in the Bureau's DC office. Innocent Internet users had been receiving false e-mail notices from the FBI announcing that the Bureau would stop the customers' browsing activities if the worried surfers didn't pay a hefty fine using their credit cards, quickly sending the wired money to an offshore account located somewhere there in the Bahamas. The wily scam artists would first stealthily steal Internet web addresses from the naïve responders using a fake "Internet phone book" that would be sneakily "embedded in a system network".

"Next, I speculate that the harmful hackers would soon be enabled to mischievously plant users' 'phishing' threats, seemingly originating from the FBI," Inspector Giralo declared. "During the all-too-critical method of phony e-mail transmission, the Bureau's official-looking seal could be prominently displayed on the victims' computer screens. Finally, the targeted dupe would be brashly instructed to immediately wire his or her credit card payment along with his or her Visa or MasterCard number to the despicable, threatening crooks."

Then Salvatore Velardi felt compelled to make a comment. "Over two million e-mail users have been contacted in the last three months, and who knows how many gullible and vulnerable folks have wired the offshore creeps the requested ransom fine money. The afflicted victims instinctively feared that *their* essential computer services wouldn't be terminated," Agent Velardi summarized. "Some felons are imaginative evil geniuses! But like you've always reminded us Boss; the arrogant thieves eventually get themselves caught when they begin to think that they're invincible! We can throw-into the mix them believing that they're infallible and omniscient, too!"

"The web address in the ribbon located at the top of the e-mail page should be green and it ought to read *https* and not simply *http*," Agent Orsi constructively clarified. "If the letter *'s'* is not on the given *http: preface*, it's not originating from a valid, legitimate, authorized source, and the phony message should be either ignored or deleted."

"Good point Arty," Inspector Giralo commended his veteran agent. "However, not every common American is aware of *that* specific *https* green strip e-mail knowledge. The original worm

236

implant will later lead the way for the devious culprits to install additional harmful malware that if undetected or cured," the Boss elucidated, "will ultimately permit the malicious villains to take over a person's computer and perhaps even engage in accomplishing identity theft of private sensitive, confidential information."

"Yes," usually shy Dan Blachford boldly agreed and confirmed. "I believe the e-mail criminals utilize certain Trojan horse virus software to swiftly infect the innocent user's desktop or laptop without him or her ever knowing. This brazen technique allows the evildoers to successfully lock computer systems and then perform unethical scamming and extortion practices, namely, fraudulently claiming that the computer owner has been furtively downloading pornographic material or has been violating government copyright laws by illicitly acquiring pirated movies, books or music. Some people that had met *those* alleged, pretentious criteria nervously wire money to the offshore criminals without any prudent reluctance or any suspicious hesitation ever being exercised."

"Yes, indeed," concurred Inspector Giralo. "The whole FBI e-mail scam being egregiously perpetuated by the insidious impostors attempts scaring unwary victims into paying unwarranted fines for non-existent wrongdoing, because no half-decent citizen desires ever having unwanted confrontations or encounters with the FBI, or with the IRS, as far as *that* type of negative experience goes. I'm telling you directly, Men. The audacious swindlers behind this frustrating Internet crime wave must be expeditiously apprehended!"

Agent Velardi summarized the entire bogus flimflam operation by revealing, "And the fake FBI screen appearing in the unsolicited random phishing e-mails also has certain language threatening the intimidated recipients with ample jail time or with other harsh legal repercussions, that is, if the sender's falsified demands are not satisfied in a punctual manner. I now fathom the entire scenario!"

"Okay Admiral Giralo," Art Orsi jested. "What special roles do Sal, Dan and I have to play in this rather challenging ongoing phishing expedition, which I assume will somehow transpire aboard your less-than-phenomenal *Sun-Daze* fishing yacht. Or Boss, should we now address you as Commodore Giralo instead of Admiral Giralo? And who or what are we pursuing down here on exotic Paradise Island? I positively despise vagueness!"

Inspector Giralo again opened and slowly reached inside his commonplace black leather attache case and then removed another blank piece of computer paper, handing the barren white sheet to a completely puzzled Agent Orsi, who immediately struck a match and gently heated the lit object underneath.

The baffling initials B.B.B. were spontaneously formed from the formerly concealed lemon juice missive, with the scribbled revelation gradually appearing being much to Agent Orsi, Agent Velardi and Agent Blachford's mounting consternation. Silence momentarily dominated the room.

"I don't know who requires more discipline," the enamored Chief haughtily replied. "You Arty, you Dan or possibly you Salvatore! But anyway, in this very fluid investigation, DC headquarters has expertly narrowed-down the principal racketeer as one Bernard Bertram Baxter, better known to international law enforcement as B.B. Baxter. Are there any pertinent questions?"

"I thought that *you* were going to identify the hidden words 'Better Business Bureau'! Salvatore Velardi's voice laughingly boomed. "Inspector, do you think we have to shoot Mr. Baxter with high-powered B.B. guns?"

"Get serious, Salvatore," Joe Giralo admonished. "This is no time for your juvenile levity!"

"Didn't this wrongdoer once work for the government, in the CIA ranks, if my failing memory rightly recalls?" Dan Blachford asked while peering straight into Chief Giralo's eyes. "Yes, come to think of it, I do recollect a rather sinister-minded B.B. Baxter working undercover for the CIA!"

"Affirmative, Daniel!" the Chief exclaimed. "The surreptitious thug speaks Russian, Spanish, Italian and Arabic fluently and, if I might embellish, with perfect native accents, too. But this punk Bernard Bertram Baxter had been a chronic alcoholic who had been fired from the CIA for being too irresponsible and for being too erratic in terms of total job performance. But while unscrupulous B. B. Baxter had been employed by Uncle Sam," Joe Giralo convincingly expounded, "the distrustful conniver had made numerous, illicit foreign contacts while cunningly disguising himself as a double-agent, and that's where the scheming manipulator became acquainted with international crime along with its potential risky rewards and handsome illegal benefits!"

Sal Velardi then survived having a sudden inspirational brainstorm. "Boss, why don't we simply employ the process of reverse psychology and send a creative phishing e-mail to Mr. Bernard Bertram Baxter, whom I suspect is now an extremely dangerous multimillionaire because of his clandestine-but-profitable tax-free Internet scamming businesses. We could sweeten the pie by offering him maybe, five million dollars in an ingenious reverse phishing scam. What do you think, Boss?"

"Salvatore, the Bureau would be wasting its valuable time assigning four significant G-men like *us* to a meager FBI e-mail phishing scam like the one being widely propagated by one of our gadfly nemeses, the diabolical B.B. Baxter. But this felonious phishing expedition of his has led *us* to something even more dramatic, and in actuality, a grave matter of true national security!" Inspector Giralo maintained. "Mr. Baxter is no longer a small fish swimming in a large pond. He's now the dominant killer whale liberally operating in the vast Atlantic!"

"Please Inspector!" begged a now-flustered Agent Velardi. "Stop being so damned indefinite! Divulge to us three humble underlings the true nature of this so-called *fishing* expedition."

"We're going to be stationed aboard the *Sun-Daze* and trail Mr. Baxter's two-hundred-foot-long yacht across this section of the Atlantic by means of sophisticated electronic surveillance."

"And what's the glorious name of B.B. Baxter's opulent cruising yacht?" Art Orsi politely asked. "If I may quote William Shakespeare: To B.B. or not to B.B.! That is the question."

"It's ironically named *'New Clear Fishin','*" Inspector Giralo disclosed with a weak smile showing upon his florid, chubby face. "Yes Fellas', I'm not kidding. The missile vessel belonging to Mr. Bernard Bertram Baxter is officially listed in the International Boat Registry as *'New Clear Fishin'!'*"

Shocked and quite apparently stunned, Agents Velardi, Orsi and Blachford suddenly and keenly comprehended the great magnitude of their latest top-secret government assignment. In their limited minds, their new dangerous exploit now appeared to easily eclipse any typical, picayune Internet phishing scam.

* * * * * * * * * * * *

On Sunday evening, the three relaxed agents again congregated inside Chief Joe Giralo's well-appointed Atlantis suite to listen to the Inspector's monotonous monologue about the ever-evolving and highly complex "Fishing Expedition," which was about to be initiated in perilous pursuit of the newly introduced and very sleek *New Clear Fishin'* yacht.

"As you know, Men," the all-too-serious Boss began his latest pragmatic drivel. "The Bahamas are located here in the West Indies, and in 1492 Columbus thought he had landed the famed Santa Maria off the coast of India; so consequently, the ambitious Italian explorer mistakenly called the natives Indians. And Guys, did you know that Columbus discovering America was not the most significant event occurring in 1492?" Giralo rhetorically asked his totally bored audience of three. "The Spanish had successfully re-conquered their homeland from the occupying Arab Moors in 1492, and *that* exceptional historic event had been regarded as the greatest achievement of *that* auspicious year all throughout post-medieval Europe!"

"Chief, please stop your incessant, verbose, academic jabberwocky and finally get to the relevant truth of our current mission," Agent Velardi nervously implored. "You have this obnoxious, uncanny propensity of relentlessly maximizing immaterial, encyclopedic knowledge that, although strangely interesting, we're all actually already very acquainted with."

The Chief Inspector was not majorly offended or fazed by his neurotic subordinate's most recent accusation. Giralo explained to his impatient trio that the *Sun Daze* would strategically intercept the aforementioned *New Clear Fishin'* in the Atlantic's international waters just north of the Tropic of Cancer. "We'll rendezvous with Mr. Baxter's magnificent yacht precisely at maritime coordinates 24 degrees North Latitude and 78 degrees West Longitude," the Boss calmly uttered to his conscientious G-men. "Just before our coincidental engagement with the treacherous crook, I'll distribute loaded pistols to you three Fellas' to keep our charlatan host along with his three-man crew at bay until vital military help arrives on the scene."

"Whatever floats your boat," Sal Velardi instinctively joked, awkwardly trying to ease the sudden strong tension that his vacillating emotions were feeling. "I promise you, Chief. We'll keep Baxter and his shipmates at *bay* in the *ocean!*"

Not at all rattled by his agent's fairly weird comment, determined Inspector Joe Giralo next competently explained that the Miami FBI had installed special monitoring devices inside the *New Clear Fishin's* engines that would "on remote control command" deactivate and immobilize the yacht in the deep Atlantic.

"Mr. Baxter's expensive vessel will instantaneously and automatically cease to function by use of *our* department's remote control. The high-tech' instruments that had been shrewdly inserted into the yacht's engines during a routine dry-dock maintenance will act in a similar manner to the 'On-Star' feature that's equipped in many automobiles. If a car is stolen," the long-winded Inspector pontificated, "the engine can be shut-off by the utilized 'On-Star' mechanism, so the relative dangers associated with a normal high-speed police car pursuit have been intelligently eliminated. The thief will have just enough time to steer the pilfered vehicle to the side of the highway and stop."

"Pretty remarkable employment of modern technology!" conceded Agent Orsi. "Are *you* going to be operating the stopping mechanism?"

"No Arty," briskly answered Inspector Giralo. "The FBI agents in Miami will capably handle *that* aspect of *our* secret project, or should I say of our 'surprise operation'. The general plan is rather elementary. We'll slowly float-up to the stalled *New Clear Fishin'* in a friendly manner and courteously offer our honest assistance. I'll yell-up to Baxter that I have two expert mechanics aboard who could get his expensive yacht navigating again. When you and Dan hop aboard his ship," Giralo instructed an attentive Agent Orsi, "you'll quickly pull your pistols out of your concealed shoulder holsters and then Sal and I will remove our handguns also, having Baxter and his three deckhands surrounded until additional help from the U.S. military arrives on the scene."

"And how will *we* know when and how to track and follow Baxter's pleasure ship?" Dan Blachford logically questioned. "I'm a trifle confused about *that* particular facet of *our* intricate plan."

"That's easy to understand," Joe Giralo declared. "Several Navy Seals had attached a sonar beeper to the hull of Baxter's yacht back in Miami. All we have to do is observe the screen displaying the beeping beacon on the *Sun-Daze's* instrument panel. The rest should be as easy as taking candy from a baby! I've recently had some practice using the amazing FBI sonar scanner," Chief Giralo vociferated, "and believe me Gentlemen when I affirm that the newly invented apparatus works much better than an ordinary boat fish-finder or a standard sea-depth indicator."

"And where is the *New Clear Fishin's* point of origin and where is its ultimate destination?" asked a now-invigorated Agent Velardi.

"Baxter is scheduled to depart Miami within the next few hours and immediately head out to..."

Just then a loud beeping sound emanated from Inspector Giralo's multifunctional cell phone, which had been in direct electronic communication with the turned-on tracking monitor situated upon the *Sun-Daze's* instrument panel, the real-time transmission signaling that the incomparable *New Clear Fishin'* was just leaving port.

"Chief, shouldn't we proceed directly toward the Atlantis marina and climb aboard the *Sun-Daze?*" excitedly suggested Art Orsi, somewhat mentally disheveled. "It seems that our new-found enemy Mr. Bernard Bertram Baxter has just begun his final voyage."

"That immediate response by us won't be necessary," Inspector Giralo suavely advised, shaking his head sideways. "Mr. Baxter is now on his way to Havana to obtain a nuclear bomb that's the size of an ordinary Volkswagen Beetle. Now confidentially, the nuclear bomb had been shipped via commercial cargo ship from North Korea to Cuba. The bomb is intended to be detonated next week in downtown Miami while deceitfully positioned inside a rented box-truck," Giralo divulged to his almost-mesmerized agents. "Radical Islamic terrorists that had been smuggled by Mexican coyotes via the Rio Grande and then clandestinely transported into Florida will attempt to explode the potent A-bomb, evilly killing tens-of-thousands of innocent Americans. Our logistically important mission, Men, is to swiftly prevent such a horrendous urban catastrophe from ever occurring!"

* * * * * * * * * * * *

Monday evening the four dedicated G-men inconspicuously abandoned the Atlantic Resort Hotel and slept the night inside Inspector Joe Giralo's deep-sea fishing vessel with Agents Art Orsi and Dan Blachford slumbering in the Guest Stateroom's bunk beds and with Sal Velardi and Inspector Giralo dozing in the Master Stateroom's very comfortable queen-size bed.

A bacon' and eggs early breakfast was prepared by the *Sun-Daze's* versatile chef/owner/captain, and at 8:10 am the Boss's cell phone receiver began wildly beeping like a quality Geiger-counter detecting a plenteous cache of radioactive uranium. After eagerly conversing with Matt Riley on *his* indispensable utilitarian cell phone, Inspector Giralo thoroughly shared and disclosed to his dependable crew evolving concurrent developments.

"The cleverly covered A-bomb has just been lowered aboard the *New Clear Fishin's* deck over in Havana Harbor," Chief Giralo verbally commented, "and the vessel soon will be drifting-out of port. And when the luxury ship eventually reaches the prescribed coordinates of 78 degrees West Longitude and 24 degrees North Latitude, that's precisely when...."

"The *Sun-Daze* miraculously approaches the vicinity and we offer to help the pernicious saboteurs getting the enormous yacht running again," Sal Velardi accurately communicated. "And Chief, I won't forget to draw my pistol in unison with you while looking-up to that odious Baxter nutcase and his unsavory henchmen."

"I figure we'll be making contact with Mr. Baxter's yacht in about eight and a half hours, that is, if we maintain full throttle," the Chief predicted and conveyed. "It's a good thing I've brought along a sufficient supply of fuel to allow for the return trip to Nassau. It always pays to think about all possible contingencies in advance!"

Nine hours later, just as the brilliant sun was majestically setting on the western horizon, the four FBI men alertly spotted the *New Clear Fishin'* aimlessly adrift in calm ocean water. Showing no overt sign of suspicion, the innocent-looking *Sun-Daze* gracefully pulled alongside of Bernard Baxter's colossal floating ship, gently stopping on the enormous vessel's starboard side.

Barely glancing at the huge hidden object that had been covered by a black tarpaulin situated upon the colossal yacht's deck, Chief Joe Giralo yelled-up to Bernard Bertram Baxter. "Ahoy there! Do you need any help? Is anyone hurt or injured?"

"No Captain!" Baxter loudly answered, showing embarrassment at his helpless predicament. "We're all just fine! Our engines have oddly cut-out, and we're awaiting assistance. We've already contacted my base in Miami and they're immediately sending-out a team of experts to get my pleasure yacht running again!"

"I have two expert mechanics aboard who'll get your beautiful ship navigating again within the hour, I guarantee it," the unflappable Chief hollered-up, using his hands as an improvised megaphone. "I assure you, Sir. They're among the best in the nautical repair business! The guys really know their stuff!"

After briefly consulting with his three mariner accomplices, Bernard Baxter consented to allowing Art Orsi and Dan Blachford aboard, and no sooner had the fearless pair ascended a side-swivel gangplank that the undaunted FBI duo drew their trusty revolvers from their holsters (the guns being coyly concealed beneath their life vests), and then just as quickly, Inspector Giralo and Agent Sal Velardi did likewise from their *Sun-Daze* deck positions below.

"Is this some sort of sophomoric prank or amateur hoax?" Bernard Baxter belligerently shouted with his lily-white hands raised above his head. "Are you jerks small-time punks, reckless robbers, or are you small-time dolts desperate, masquerading sea smugglers? I'll have you four dunces instantly prosecuted once I get back to Miami!"

"We're the FBI and you're under arrest for trying to sneak an atomic bomb into the United States," Chief Giralo *stern*ly informed from the *Sun-Daze's* aft. "Miami will not become another Hiroshima or Nagasaki, *that* truth I assure you! We've tracked you by satellite all the way from the Florida Coast to Havana and also, we've traced your bomb's progress from North Korea, to Syria, to Cuba! Your diabolical plot has been discovered, Mr. Bernard Bertram Baxter, and soon, much to your imminent dissatisfaction, and much to your permanent disenchantment, I feel compelled to inform you that the highly skilled American military will soon decide what to do with you!"

Before the dishonorable rogue Bernard Bertram Baxter could ever organize and effectively deliver any derogatory expletives, an Army helicopter dispatched from a nearby U.S. Navy destroyer propelled its way across international waters towards the two stationary ships. The noisy chopper swiftly descended from the east. A steel cage containing two captured Islamic jihadists was soon deftly lowered onto the *New Clear Fishin's* polished deck, and marvelously, Inspector Joe Giralo's good friend Colonel Bob Bauers of Delta Force was firmly holding-on to the taut tethering cable while the proud Army Officer was standing erect atop the six-foot-square and seven-foot-high cyclone-fence cage.

After the heavy object had landed upon the varnished deck, the distinguished career officer detached the resilient connecting hook, and next, the highly-decorated Army Colonel adroitly leaped-down from the sturdy cage. After the cable and its accompanying hook had been raised back into the giant helicopter's interior, Colonel Bauers addressed his still-confounded FBI acquaintances.

"These two loud-mouthed, captured al Qaeda affiliates have been handcuffed with masking tape strapped across their foul mouths," Colonel Bauers austerely stated, before meticulously cleaning some dust particles off of his trademark spit-shined combat boots. "Good to see you again Joe!" the fabled military man shouted-down to Chief Giralo, still standing in the *Sun-Daze's* deck. "After your two agents handcuff these four nasty, disgruntled scoundrels, your fine men and I will clamber aboard your reliable fishing boat and then promptly head back to the Bahamas."

"But what's to become of *me!*" petrified Bernard Baxter frantically screamed. "I'm an American citizen! I know my Constitutional rights! I demand a fair trial in front of a sympathetic jury! I know I'll be easily exonerated from any alleged wrongdoing!"

"That's what the heck you think, Idiot-king!" Colonel Bauers abruptly answered. "I believe, Sir, that you've just enjoyed your very last phishing expedition!"

"But you can't leave *us* handcuffed out here, bouncing around like ducks in the middle of the Atlantic!" Baxter indignantly balked. "The United Nations will punish you for your flagrant human rights violation! I'll make sure that they do!"

"We don't need any permission slip from the United Nations, that I can guarantee you! And now, Sir, you have a definite choice to make," Colonel Bauers hardily laughed. "You, Mr. Baxter can either fall overboard and be consumed by voracious, hungry sharks, or on the other hand, you can live a little longer and wear some old ragged clothes stuffed inside Davy Jones's Locker! Ha, ha, ha!"

As handcuffed Bernard Baxter and his' three deplorable hit-men futilely squawked and shrieked for help, no-nonsense Colonel Bob Bauers, followed by Art Orsi and Dan Blachford, stepped down the *New Clear Fishin's* side-swivel walkway and then each man carefully jumped-down upon the *Sun-Daze's* fishing area. Inspector Giralo indulgently smiled and firmly and repetitiously shook his old Army pal's right hand.

"What's to happen to those six mendacious thugs gyrating-about on the gigantic yacht?" Giralo asked his elite, ribbon-ornamented comrade. "Aren't we going to take the vile violators into custody? I'm sure that federal prison time will do them all some good!"

"Well, Inspector," Colonel Bauers replied with an exaggerated wink of his right eye. "As long as there's no nosy media or press around interfering with this delicate operation, the United States military will conveniently dispose of, or should I say 'dispense with' those six collared vermin, including the two formerly formidable caged al Qaeda affiliates! Now, Good Buddy, fire-up your notorious twin engines, and let's evacuate the battle area as soon as possible!"

Five minutes later, two powerful torpedoes were discharged, zipping out of a pair of massive U.S. Navy submarine tubes, and several severe impacts seven seconds later resulted in tremendous explosions that were witnessed only by the five patriotic men riding aboard the nondescript *Sun-Daze*.

"Why didn't the atomic bomb detonate?" Agent Velardi wondered and asked. "How come it didn't explode when the two torpedoes blasted into the yacht's hull?"

"Because Salvatore," Inspector Joe Giralo perceptively realized and ascertained. "The tarpaulin-covered A-bomb aboard the *New Clear Fishin'* was not fully assembled. Don't you comprehend the essence of this rather rudimentary ruse? The needed uranium had been confiscated yesterday from another ship making its sinister way from Mexico to Miami. Without the radioactive material," the Chief stated, "the bomb was hardly dangerous!"

"Well Inspector," Colonel Bauers evaluated with a meek grin exhibited upon his well-tanned countenance, all the while being fully aware of Agents Velardi, Orsi and Blachford's eavesdropping. "Joe, I think it's safe to say 'mission accomplished'. We're now heading back to tranquil Paradise Island while the souls of those six pathetic, iniquitous weasels are simply on a one-way trip to Paradise! Ha, ha, ha! Or should I say, Inspector. On a one-way trip to Hell!"

# "Triple Jeopardy"

Ever vigilant t FBI Inspector Joseph Giralo was quite fatigued from his grueling daily work schedule that involved apprehending major East Coast felony criminals, and now the veteran federal law enforcement official and his wife Gina were anxiously looking forward to a weeklong bus excursion originating from the Senior Tours Bus Terminal on Route 9 in Cape May Court House, New Jersey. Upstate Michigan was the land tour's principal destination and also its culminating tourist experience, the site of the famous and historic Grand Michigan Hotel, which majestically occupies a picturesque ridge on tranquil Mackinac Island. The world-renowned vacation resort is ideally located midway between the mid-western state's Lower and Upper Peninsulas.

After boarding the huge white bus along with the other dozen bleary-eyed, early rising passengers, Joe and Gina were ready to start their great adventure at precisely 5 a.m. on a mild September Saturday morning. The husband and wife sat impatiently in their soft blue seats and watched out the window as Mike the bus driver dutifully loaded the group's luggage into the modern deluxe vehicle's right-side storage compartment. The FBI Inspector seemed rather content coping with his "rooster time existence."

"It's great being a regular non-government civilian for the next seven days. And Hon, you just can't get any bus better than this one anywhere in Jersey," the somewhat relaxed man commented to his devoted spouse. "This is one of those new 'kneeling buses' that has an impressive spiral boarding entrance. I don't know if you had noticed it or not Gina, but the front steps had actually lowered several inches to allow us to conveniently step inside and then move up the aisle more easily. How long until our first rest stop? I could use some hot coffee to wake me up?"

"Well, Hubby; according to the itinerary I'm holding in my hand," Gina Giralo alertly answered, "we'll be stopping at the King-of-Prussia rest stop on the Pennsylvania Turnpike in about three hours. The local bus tour company had to team-up with a couple of other regional operations to fill-up this bus. Other passengers will be picked-up at the Shore Mall just outside Atlantic City, and later at the Wyndham Hotel on Route 73 in Cherry Hill," Mrs. Giralo prattled and informed. "Then it'll be across the Delaware River via the Betsy Ross Bridge to the Neshaminy Mall where the remainder of the group will be picked-up along with our special tour guide."

"This trip looks like a real bargain costing only eleven hundred dollars a person," Joe Giralo reminded his very upbeat traveling mate.

"Where are we staying the first night?"

"At a La Quinta Inn in an Ohio town called Macedonia."

"I hope we don't run into King Philip or his conquest-minded son Alexander-the-Great," Joe jested as he curiously stared through the passenger window and noticed Mike slamming shut the side luggage door. "This might sound stupid, but I've done more than my share of up-front combat with enough local *barbarians* during my thirty-year FBI career. I hope that folks traveling the busy Interstates in Ohio and Michigan don't think we're a part of a traveling high-jacked sequestered jury," the husband facetiously quipped.

"Why do you say that?" Gina asked, anticipating one of her spouse's incessant, ridiculous jokes.

"Because on the side of the bus is painted the words Senior Tours, Cape May Court House," Giralo replied before giggling. "You know me Hon. Always thinking about some aspect of the law and some oddball facet of the American justice system."

At eight a.m. (and on schedule) the bus rumbled into the King-of-Prussia rest area on the Pennsylvania Turnpike, and Joe and Gina stepped-out to enjoy some hot coffee and fresh doughnuts during their half hour stop. In the midst of their light conversation, the wife gave her loyal companion some background on what Senior Tours had planned for the week besides a "glorious three-night stay" at the splendid Grand Michigan Hotel.

"After the first night in Ohio at the La Quinta Inn, we'll be occupied Sunday afternoon viewing the many exhibits at the Ford Museum in Dearborn, just outside Detroit," the excited woman reviewed. "Then right next to the museum is Greenfield Village, a wonderful re-creation of the place where Henry Ford had lived his childhood. I won't go into all the details of what's in the museum or inside the village because I want to see how surprised you'll be when we view them. Our tour guide Julie told me five minutes ago that we'll be on our own for the entire museum and village explorations. Then we'll be staying the night at an area Ramada Inn before heading out to Frankenmuth in the center of Michigan."

"What's Frankenmuth?" the puzzled husband wondered and asked. "It sounds like a gift the Three Wise Men brought to Bethlehem or it might just be a distant relative of Victor Frankenstein. Or perhaps it's a gross mispronunciation of the dangerous monster's *mouth*?"

"No, Silly!" Gina corrected, revealing a cute grin upon her lips. "I read in the informative trip brochure that 'Franken' refers to the

German people that eventually settled in central Michigan and that 'Muth' is a German word meaning courage, so together Frankenmuth means the bravery of the original German settlers. The place is a really neat Bavarian-style town in appearance, and I think you'll actually feel like you're in a Black Forest village rather than meandering around in the middle of a Midwestern State."

"That all sounds pretty terrific and exactly what I need, a nice change of pace from our hectic New Jersey environment," Joe opined. "Now tell me Dear, did you bring along that new deck of cards of yours? I'm even willing to play a game of 'Phase Ten' to pass the night in Macedonia; that is, if there aren't any major baseball or football games on the TV."

Julie promptly sauntered over to the Giralos' rest stop table and announced, "Our bus leaves in five minutes! Mike's already had his standard two cigarettes and an extra-large cup of coffee, so the nicotine and the caffeine will keep him wide-eyed for the next two and a half hours until we reach western Pennsylvania and have a chance to view the beautiful Allegheny Mountains. After another casual rest stop," Julie continued her narrative, "it's then into Ohio, and finally off to rural Macedonia and supper at a Cracker Barrel Restaurant followed by a restful night at the very comfortable La Quinta Inn. And after a decent continental breakfast to be eaten just off the lodge's lobby," Julie concisely expressed, "Sunday morning it's off to Dearborn. Don't forget Folks, except for the nights at the Grand Michigan Hotel, you can only take your two carry-on bags into the several motels where we'll be staying."

"Thanks Julie," Joe replied with a smile. "What does La Quinta mean in English? Is it a number?"

"No, but just like we have different words for 'house' like 'home', 'abode', 'dwelling' and 'residence' in English," the knowledgeable tour guide stated and then paused to further emphasize her point, "La Quinta means 'country house' in Spanish, and it's a synonym for regular words like 'casa' and 'hacienda'."

"Pardon my ignorance when it comes to foreign languages," Joe indulgently laughed as he rose from his red plastic snack area seat. "But even a broken clock is right twice a day! Ha, ha, ha!"

* * * * * * * * * * * *

Late Sunday morning, Mike used his reliable GPS device to leave a very congested Interstate having plenty of new infrastructure construction, and then the man behind the wheel skillfully navigated his ultramodern bus through downtown Detroit, heading west in the direction of Dearborn and the aforementioned Ford Museum and adjacent Greenfield Village. Since the outside temperature was approaching an unseasonably high eighty-degrees, most of the bus entourage, including the smart-thinking Giralos, decided to amble through the village first and then later enjoy the air-conditioning that would be provided inside the immense museum.

Train tickets were purchased at the village's main station and the New Jersey duo stepped aboard the third carriage car of the *Edison*, which was a small refurbished steam locomotive that had been manufactured during the past century. Gina explained to her somewhat interested husband that one of Henry Ford's closest friends was inventor Thomas Alva Edison, so naturally it made perfectly good sense that the train engine appropriately bore *that* particular name.

Most everyone riding the colorfully painted train cars decided to exit at the second depot stop, which amazingly was a full-scale recreation of Michigan's legendary Port Huron Railway Station where incidentally, a young Thomas Edison had become a twelve-year-old "news butcher" on a train owned by the then prominent Grand Trunk Railway. Young Edison was quite ambitious and the lad sold newspapers, candy, peanuts and various sandwiches on a popular rail route that ran from Port Huron all the way down to Detroit.

According to a brochure Gina had been reading, one day young mischievous Tom tried conducting a difficult chemical experiment in the baggage car when a stick of phosphorus accidentally caught on fire. The appalled and angry conductor entered and roughly grabbed the boy, vigorously boxed Edison's tender ears, and then mercilessly kicked the non-penitent youth off the train at the next station. That particular ear abuse led to Edison being nearly deaf, but later in a separate railroad incident, another conductor on a slow-moving train helped Tom clamber aboard by lifting the adolescent up by the ears, thus additionally contributing to Edison's virtual deafness that regrettably accompanied the very famous inventor throughout the remainder of his curiosity-oriented life.

"Last year my class read a short story about the amazing Thomas Edison," elementary school teacher Gina Giralo recalled and related to her somewhat apathetic spouse. "The theme was that Thomas Edison had often said that he didn't mind being almost totally deaf because the lack of sound afforded him the luxury of thinking and concentrating better. Edison really was quite a remarkable man."

"And I remember from a high school science class lecture that Edison had kept plenty of clocks on the walls and tables of his New Jersey laboratory, but none of them ever had the right time," the husband shared. "Soon everyone on his staff working on their various projects forgot all about time and focused their undistracted attention on individual tasks at hand. Perhaps I'll remember to do a similar thing in my FBI office when I get back home."

Greenfield Village was indeed rather spectacular for the first-time visitors to experience. After stepping away from the realistic-looking Port Huron Railway Station, the New Jersey couple stopped their trekking for several minutes and enjoyed listening to the calliope music emanating from an enormous children's amusement carousel house, which was strategically situated towards the center of the spotless clean-street village.

Other delightful surprises were seen and soon entered. One brick building was a facsimile of the original H.J. Heinz office and processing plant, another attractive edifice was a rendition of the Wright Brothers Store in Dayton, Ohio, and also several foundries had been meticulously erected inside Greenfield Village to show the public the tremendous economic "factory progress" that had been made during the great American Industrial Revolution.

And next, the two enamored visitors strolled around the grounds of Henry Ford's birthplace, a handsome white country house with a fine rotating windmill occupying the back yard, the eye-appealing property being quaintly situated next to a replica of Thomas Edison's gray laboratory building in Menlo Park, New Jersey where marvelous inventions such as the phonograph, the light bulb and the motion picture film projector had been conceived during the extraordinarily dynamic early stages of the twentieth century.

But the most truly wonderful aspect of anachronistic-looking Greenfield Village was yet to come. At a booth the Giralos purchased tickets to climb into an authentic, well-maintained Model-T Ford that was still functioning as if it was a brand-new transportation machine. A fleet of fifteen Model-Ts of different designs (ranging through the years 1915-1927) was available to the visiting public. Every Model-T had a chauffeur, and the knowledgeable drivers took captivated tourists on refreshing fifteen-minute rides all throughout the immaculate, cement-paved, wide streets of absolutely incomparable Greenfield Village.

"Nothing at all like this unique attraction exists back in Jersey," Giralo noted to his wife. "I'm not exaggerating when I say that *this* inspirational ride is borderline sensational."

"Yes, Sir. The Model-Ts became obsolete in the late 1920s and the design was then followed by the upgraded more sophisticated Model-A Ford," eavesdropping Ben, the Model-T operator added to the dialogue. "Don't ask me why the early Fords are in reverse alphabetical order because I can't academically answer that question. But it's a known fact that the Model-A definitely came into production right after the Model-T became extinct."

"Regardless of the chronological order," Joe Giralo declared with an air of certainty evident in his tone of voice, "tell me now Ben. Are the buildings here in Greenfield Village all miniature models of the original structures?"

"Actually, many of the main structures are the same size as the originals and have been carefully dismantled and after being specially transported here, they've been gingerly reassembled stone by stone, brick by brick," Ben conveyed to his fascinated audience of two. "It was quite a colossal undertaking to say the least, but just like good old Henry Ford had achieved during his remarkable life-time, the almost impossible engineering feats represented here in Greenfield Village could only be accomplished with extra diligence and perseverance. When you have a chance, be sure to walk through the several large machinery buildings where the theme 'machines making machines' is the key message."

"Positively incredible!" Joe Giralo evaluated and exclaimed, contrary to his normally placid demeanor. "*Special* is the only word I can think of to describe this pretty unbelievable place! Positively incredible!" The Inspector repeated.

After passing through the Main Pavilion's exit turnstiles, Joe and Gina strolled hand-in-hand like two newlyweds over to the nearby Ford Museum, which also offered its appreciative guests many outstanding attractions. And after taking photos' of each other standing in front of the sentimental-in-appearance Oscar Mayer Weinermobile, the rejuvenated pair swallowed-down delicious hot dogs at the adjacent Oscar Mayer food concession.

Other exquisite exhibits were visually enjoyed including a reproduction of a '50s Texaco gas station, an original Golden Arches McDonald's walk-up Restaurant advertising 15cent hamburgers, the actual Rosa Parks bus that was still in mint condition, a walk-in '50s diner, and the historic Presidential limousines of Franklin D. Roosevelt, John F. Kennedy and Ronald Reagan. But besides the giant generators, turbines, tractors, airplanes and powerful steam locomotives occupying strategic spaces, the main highlight of the Ford Museum (for the Giralos) happened to be the nearly two hundred classic American automobiles on display, the array including a vintage white Dusenberg, a terrific-looking Rolls Royce Phantom, a sporty red Jaguar Roadster, a fantastic Bugatti, several memorable Cadillacs and Packards along with a contingent of nostalgic-looking shiny '50s Chevy Corvettes and sporty Ford Thunderbirds.

252

"Did you see the rear seat of F.D.R.'s limo'?" Gina asked. "It had three buttons positioned on a back seat console; one each for NBC, ABC and CBS, the three dominant radio networks of the awesome 1940s' decade!"

"Wow!" Joe Giralo merrily exclaimed, showing his new-found exuberance. "President Roosevelt had a form of push button radio remote control several years before television had ever been invented. I suppose that those three useful network buttons were really high tech' state-of-the-art back in the Big Band art deco days of the 1940s. Glenn Miller really had it right all along. This fabulous out-of-this-world Ford Museum has really gotten me out of my tedious work doldrums and 'In the Mood'."

* * * * * * * * * * * *

Midway into the third day of scenic early fall traveling Mike steered his bus into the town of Frankenmuth, and the weary passengers all checked into their various rooms at the Drury Inn at 260 South Main Street. That evening a tasty chicken and beer supper was enjoyed at the extra-large-sized Bavarian Inn, owned by the same family as the landmark Zehnder's Restaurant situated across the street, which proudly promotes itself as the largest family restaurant in the entire United States. The waiters at the Bavarian Inn wore green feathered hats and knee socks with short pants, traditional German festival apparel known in and around 'Old World' Munich as 'lederhosen', while the pretty waitresses were garbed in attractive cotton dresses that were being referred to as 'dirndl.'

But much to everyone's appreciation, after a delectable pastry/ice cream dessert had been served and consumed, the Jersey tourists re-boarded the dependable bus and Mike drove the now-spirited delegation to the magnificent Bronners Christmas Land on the east end of Frankenmuth. Upon its nighttime arrival, the bus passed up and down a series of parallel lanes that featured a brilliant spectacle of flickering and blinking lit Christmas decorations: angels, elves, Magi, a North Pole setting, Bethlehem manger scenes, Santa Clauses, glistening snowmen, colorful giant boxed gifts, impressive toy soldier guards and the like. The bus's radio was instantly tuned to a certain FM frequency and everyone cheered when the thrilled passengers heard the loud refrains to "We Need a Little Christmas," "Here Comes Santa Claus" and "Frosty the Snowman," with the entire fantastic circuitous lane route requiring three full songs to finally complete.

After a quick breakfast the following morning, the energized group spent several hours walking around downtown Frankenmuth, viewing and taking pictures of the elaborate Glockenspiel Clock situated on the side of the alpine-in-appearance Bavarian Inn, the very splendid time apparatus chiming twelve bongs at noon. And simultaneously, the Giralos and their traveling party were treated to seeing character figures mechanically moving-out one by one from the high-elevated clock and then methodically reenacting a rendition of medieval history's legendary perfect pest exterminator, the classic "Pied Piper of Hamelin." Later that afternoon, Mike again conducted the forty-eight bus travelers to Bronners, the colossal-sized Christmas store that advertised itself as being open for business three hundred and sixty-one days of the calendar year.

"This building is incredibly mammoth, at least ten times as big as anything like it I've seen back in Jersey," Gina observed and stated. "Joe, this place Bronners claims to be the most prodigious Christmas paradise in the whole-wide world, and now I believe that their assertion is without a doubt a hundred percent true."

"Yes, and the only thing saving us from getting lost inside this phenomenal building are the gigantic overhead red and white ceiling signs that tell us what section of the store we're shopping in, ranging from area #1 to area #12. And Gina," Joe Giralo said. "I just got an idea. I think I'll get my office's two secretaries these matching Michigan State and University of Michigan stockings to hang from their fireplace mantels. The two schools are bitter rivals ya' know; especially during football season."

"And about a half an hour ago, I had seen some cute Christmas tree ornaments that I'd like to purchase. They're located over in Section 7," the wife indicated. "I had always thought that the Yankee Candle Christmas Shop we had visited in Connecticut on our last fall bus trip up to the Beacon Resort in New Hampshire was massive, but this whopping place is at least three times as big."

The Giralos lazily spent the remainder of the afternoon sampling various red and white wines (offered in plastic jiggers) at the town's St. Julian's Winery and that evening the couple played two games of 'Phase Ten' in the Drury Inn's 'Card and Recreation Lounge' with another husband/wife twosome they had met on the trip, Jim and Janice Heisler from Buena, a rustic South Jersey borough just south of Hammonton.

And finally, after indulging in a good night's sleep and partaking of the usual continental breakfast, the rested Jerseyites toting their various carry-on bags climbed aboard the long white bus and then settled into their respective seats. Loquacious tour guide Julie Setzer provided her attentive audience with essential background about the Grand Michigan Hotel and picturesque Mackinac Island.

"The name Mackinac has a French pronunciation, and it's really sounded-out as the word *Mackinaw* would be enunciated in English," Julie educated her listeners over the bus's microphone. "Ironically, Mackinaw City is the town from which you'll take your ferry ride three miles across the channel to Mackinac Island, having the exact same pronunciation, but obviously spelled differently. There're three ferry services shuttling people and goods back and forth from Mackinaw City to Mackinac Island: Arnold, Starr Lines and Shepherd's Ferry."

"How far is the island from the famous Mackinac Bridge?" an elderly male senior citizen seated in the back of the bus hollered his question. "My uncle worked on that super five and a half-mile long span way back in the mid-1950s."

"Actually, you'll be able to see the Mackinac Bridge from certain parts of the Grand Michigan Hotel property," Julie communicated over the bus's intercom. "The span is quite an engineering marvel. Now here's something fairly interesting I just thought of. The Michigan people that live on the state's Northern Peninsula are called Oopers, a name given by the residents living on the Lower Peninsula. And the folks living on the Lower Peninsula intentionally gave *them'* that designation 'Oopers,' the local term being a deliberate misspeak of the word 'Uppers'. Conversely," Julie lectured on, "the Upper Peninsula residents refer to their Lower Peninsula Michigan neighbors as 'trolls,' probably referring to the fairy tale The Three Billy Goats Gruff, the children's story having a mean-spirited troll threatening the three crossing goats from below a bridge."

"I think the Mackinac Bridge goes over one of the Great Lakes," a gentleman sitting in the fourth row (right hand side) blurted-out. "Would you know which one?"

"Well, let me see now," Julie politely thought and answered. "The Mackinac Bridge separates Lake Superior on the left and Lake Huron on the right that is, presuming we're facing the Upper Peninsula. Yes, that's correct," the guide clarified. "Facing north, Lake Superior would be on the left and Lake Huron would be on the right."

"Do the locals call *us* tourists anything weird?" an inquisitive-but-vociferous woman in the central section asked Julie. "I mean, *we* at the Jersey Shore call summer tourists 'shoebies' because during the Great Depression, the day-tourists would come into Atlantic City on a train carrying their modest lunches on their laps in shoe boxes."

"Why yes!" Julie quickly acknowledged and laughed. "Tourists are referred to up here as 'fudgies' because there's a variety of at least thirty fudge shops selling their delicious sweet confections to visitors, both in the shops in Mackinaw City and also in the many fudge stores on Main Street on Mackinac Island."

"How will our luggage get from the bus to the Grand Michigan Hotel?" the curious woman's apparently worried husband wanted to know. "I understand that there aren't any cars, trucks or buses allowed on the island."

"You're right!" Julie concurred with a smile. "When the famous Grand Michigan Hotel was built back in the late 1880s, the island's town council passed an ordinance stating that no new-fangled noisy horseless carriages would be allowed. So, from that day forward," Ms. Julie Setzer courteously explained, "the only way around Mackinac Island is by foot, by bicycle or by horse and wagon, with many of the transportation carts looking like colonial-era stage coaches. During the peak summer months, around six hundred horses take people around Main and Market Streets, the island's two chief thoroughfares. The horses are usually arranged in sets of two, but if you want to take a ride to the higher parts of the island, the horses will be in a team of three."

"But you didn't answer my question! How will our luggage get from the bus to the hotel?" the stubborn, impetuous elderly fellow persisted as his perturbed wife gave him a dig into his ribcage with her bony left elbow.

"Dock workers will take the luggage from the bus's storage compartment, put the pieces onto carts and then carefully wheel the carts onto an awaiting Shepherd's Ferry. When the boat makes the three-mile trip across the bay to the island," Julie suavely conveyed to her traveling flock, "several horse-drawn wagons will be loaded with your suitcases and I assure you, then your items will be safely delivered to the hotel, where you'll find your luggage in the hallway just outside your assigned rooms."

"I saw some postcards of a few wonderful houses on Mackinac Island and the homes look like the bread and breakfast places in Cape May," Gina told Julie. "Many of the houses show a lot of external gingerbread designs."

"Yes, even the incomparable Grand Michigan Hotel flaunts a Victorian appearance," Julie Setzer articulated through the bus's overhead speakers. "And the hotel's magnificent front porch overlooks a flower-laden terrace facing down towards the water. The famous porch is over six hundred and fifty feet long, the largest hotel porch in the world. And the Grand Michigan's spacious dining room easily seats seven hundred and fifty guests for supper and breakfast. And Gentlemen," Julie purposely reminded her male passengers, "this next announcement is very important. You *must* wear a suit or formal jacket with a tie if you wish to be seated and eat supper in the resort's extraordinarily elegant main dining room."

"It sure beats enjoying informal dining at Burger King!" vacationing FBI Inspector Joe Giralo whispered into Gina's ear and then characteristically chuckled.

"And now, Folks," the charming tour guide proudly announced, "you'll be seeing the widely acclaimed 1980 movie *Somewhere in Time*, starring Christopher Reeve and Jane Seymour. The film's a classic time-traveling adventure where a young playwright goes back in time to the early 1900s and has a dramatic love affair with an actress of that era who had done stage performances at Mackinac Island's Grand Michigan Hotel. And a lot of the movie's scenes had been filmed on location at the Grand Michigan!"

* * * * * * * * * * * *

The scenic three-mile Shepherd's Ferry ride across the placid channel from Mackinaw City to Mackinac Island was both swift and invigorating for the picture-taking passengers aboard the bus.  A trio of two horse-pulled open-air carriages (capable of seating eighteen passengers each) met the eager tourists at the central Mackinac Island docking terminal. Another three wagons that had been differently designed to specifically convey cargo had six strong workmen diligently loading-up the group's bulky luggage pieces and after everyone was accounted for by Julie, the Giralos and their highly motivated traveling colleagues were soon riding down Main Street enthusiastically viewing its many souvenir shops and casual eating establishments.

"Looks a little like a typical Jersey Shore boardwalk without any evidence of any boardwalk!" Joe instinctively quipped. "Julie was right! There're fudge shops galore here! And there were plenty more too operating over in those tourist-trap shopping centers back in Mackinaw City. If we were to stay on this island paradise for a full month, I'd probably easily weigh seventy-five more pounds than I do right now!"

"Stop being so cynical!" Gina coyly chided her all-too-garrulous husband. "Learn to relax and forget your eminent FBI identity for a few days! Look Joe! The driver's turning the corner at the end of Main Street, and we're now going onto Market! And you just have to admire those stately Victorian mansions up on the high ridge overlooking the water! And just look at the architecture of that church steeple!"

Upon arriving at the regal-looking Grand Michigan Hotel, the New Jersey guests were warmly greeted by an employee/guide who then led the awed group through the well-decorated and extra-large main lobby, through a beautiful green-draped oval-shaped sitting lounge and next directly into the venue's sophisticated entertainment room where orchestra music was played nightly after supper.

Various hotel speakers and guides then addressed the assembled visitors, describing and discussing in detail the myriad amenities available to guests, explaining the "no-tipping policy," lecturing about the exotic botanical gardens surrounding the majestic edifice and finally, a woman greeter enthusiastically elucidated about the hotel's inimitable Paul Bunyan outdoor swimming pool.

When the Giralos' finally reached Room 132, their three pieces of luggage had already been delivered outside their door. Each of the hotel's three hundred and seventy guest rooms had its own sophisticated décor and no two sleeping chambers were identical. And the window view of the property's flowers, shrubs, well-manicured lawns, stately coniferous trees and gardens, along with an abundance of astonishing deciduous tree varieties was indubitably stupendous, and none-the-less, extremely breathtaking.

"Joe, just look at the gorgeous dark green drapes, matching mint-colored wallpaper and accompanying light green, silk-cushioned background above the bed's headboard," Gina marveled and gasped. "And the contrasting green and white table lamps and the thick rich rug match perfectly. I'll bet this place had a separate interior decorator for each room!"

"And besides, the bed's soft, and the mattress seems more-than-adequate. When do we eat supper?" the lesser intrigued spouse desired receiving some feminine response. "My stomach's actively growling for some fine cuisine."

"Joe, did you see the framed caricatures of all the U.S. Presidents hanging along the wall down the first-floor corridor," the wife asked as she zipped open *her* Totes carry-on bag. "And just a couple of doors to our left is the Presidential Suite. I wonder if anyone important or famous is staying in it?"

"Maybe it's the President of Somalia, or perhaps the Yemen Ambassador to Cuba!" Joe pessimistically replied and then characteristically laughed. "I'm famished Honey! Perhaps I won't be so sarcastic after I have the highly publicized five-course dinner!"

The patient wife totally ignored her mate's brazen attempt at demonstrating typical male negativity so she shrewdly decided to change the subject. "Well Honey, what did you think of the movie we had seen on the bus, *Somewhere in Time*?"

"I'd have liked the film a whole lot more if Christopher Reeve had fallen in love with a female in his own 1980s past and not be smitten by Cupid's arrow with an attractive lady in the year 1912," Joe Giralo aptly criticized. "I mean, I think that Jane Seymour is an excellent actress, but quite frankly, I prefer TV reality shows to science fiction fantasy time-travel love stories. I liked Christopher Reeve better when he played Superman."

"Have it your own way without the culinary magic of Burger King!" Gina Giralo wittily retorted. "You probably think that Oscar Mayer hot dogs are the greatest thing going since ancient man invented the fork and knife!"

"Now you're talking!" the FBI official officially on vacation bellowed. "Let's unpack our stuff and then get ready for supper in the main dining room. I can't remember the last time I wore a jacket and tie at a restaurant. Maybe it was a tuxedo at a wedding, but definitely not a suit and tie for dinner!"

"You'll have to start some intensive dieting when we return to Jersey," Gina diplomatically mentioned and predicted. "I don't want you getting diabetes!"

"But really and truly, I have to apologize to you, Honey! The filet mignon on tonight's menu is several levels above either a frankfurter or a charcoal-broiled slab of meat. But honestly Gina, I don't know why they call the round things hamburgers," Joe Giralo awkwardly introduced his next comical remark. "Ham comes from a pig, and steak happens to come from a cow. The round food in a bun should rightfully be called 'steak-burgers' and not hamburgers!"

* * * * * * * * * * * *

The first full serene day on Mackinac Island (for the Giralos) was a rather nondescript pleasant one. After the couple consumed a sumptuous breakfast in the hotel's nearly eight-hundred-seat main dining room, Joe and Gina ventured outside to partake of the early brisk Northern Michigan autumn air. The pair slowly descended wooden steps leading them through the eye-appealing terrace area and then ambled-down to the massive Paul Bunyan Swimming Pool to inspect the many other recreational facilities that were conveniently provided to satisfactorily accommodate the Grand Michigan's thousand or so catered-to, pampered guests.

Julie Setzer was standing outside the hotel's main entrance with her names' checklist clipboard and at precisely ten a.m. three red and yellow painted horse-drawn carriages were ready to take the forty-eight New Jersey tourists on a "horizontal cross island journey" to the

"Carriage House," where fifteen minutes thereafter a fleet of three horse' carriages was available to transport the delegation to the island's higher elevations. There, the tourists could observe marvelous panoramic views of Lake Huron along with snapping impromptu pictures of the natural rock "Arch Formation" located towards the island's summit.

Next on the itinerary was a tour of Fort Mackinac and nearby were the dull, white ramparts that were emblematic of the Governor's Summer Mansion, where James Heisler remarked to the Giralos, "Mitt Romney probably spent many of his youthful years there since his father George was once the Michigan Governor."

The afternoon hours sped-by rather rapidly as the Giralos and the Heislers casually meandered around parallel Main and Market Streets, doing light shopping at the sundry souvenir stores and occasionally munching the irresistible fudge "free samples" randomly being offered on employee-held trays to targeted pedestrians. Pizza and Coca-Colas were purchased at a snack bar, but Gina warned Joe that he was limited to two slices so that the weight-conscious food connoisseur would not spoil his upcoming five-course lobster tail feast back at the hotel.

That evening, after the sumptuous seafood-style dinners were consumed, the remainder of that Tuesday night had the formally dressed Giralos and Heislers sitting on sofas in the expansive color-coordinated lobby and drinking cocktails while listening to an accomplished pianist playing a selection of popular 1940s and '50s melodies. And then after playing three fun-packed games of Phase Ten, the card playing couples retired to their respective first floor rooms for the night. Everything was copacetic with the world, and FBI Inspector Joseph Giralo's mind was finally devoid of solving the plethora of illicit criminal activity habitually plaguing American society.

On Thursday morning, Joe was suffering from a mild case of acid reflux so the ailing epicure thought he would rest-up and recover from his brief malady inside Room 132 while his energized wife accompanied the Heislers on a walking tour of the hotel's majestic gardens, their prime objective being viewing the property's many deciduous trees exhibiting their wondrous red, brown and yellow autumnal hues.

The husband promised Gina that he would be feeling better after a few cups of "Room Service Coffee", and the traveling Inspector also mentioned that she should not worry about his general health during her three-hour absence. Giralo picked-up a copy of the *New York Times* main stories that had been left under the suite's door and feeling his newly acquired lackadaisical disposition, the calm vacationer waited for his pot of coffee to be routinely delivered by room service.

* * * * * * * * * * * *

At nine-thirty a loud frantic rapping upon Room 132's door interrupted Joe Giralo's peaceful coffee consumption. The FBI man opened the portal and the occupant was somewhat astonished to perceive the normally debonair suit-and-tie head hotel manager impatiently standing in the hallway.

"Mr. Giralo," the exasperated hotel executive said all out of breath. "I'm Giles Martin, the Grand Michigan's chief operating officer. May I come in?"

"Why of course!" the surprised Inspector replied, closing the door behind the unexpected visitor's entrance. "Is everything okay? You do appear to be more than a trifle alarmed!"

"I understand that you're an experienced inspector with the FBI. Our desk records indicate *that* much Inspector Giralo, and I've already verified *that* formerly confidential information through our local police department, which incidentally also drastically needs your immediate assistance."

"Mr. Martin, exactly what is wrong?" the now thoroughly interested hotel guest asked. "What matter is of so much paramount importance and concern?"

"A most serious epidemic of colossal proportion has broken-out among the horse population here on Mackinac Island," panic-stricken Giles Martin boisterously disclosed. "Just about all of our six hundred horses are terribly sick with colic and with influenza symptoms and our town veterinarians are going crazy attending to all of the afflicted animals. And besides that," the agitated hotel manager impulsively expounded, "the entire transportation system on the island has been shut down. This is a colossal nightmare dilemma in progress Inspector Giralo, an unimaginable worst-case scenario and its basic origin, or should I say 'its real cause,' *we* certainly find exceptionally baffling. That's why, Inspector Giralo, I'm here to both urgently request and solicit your reputable expertise."

"But Mr. Martin, by your vivid description, I'm not so sure that a genuine FBI crime has actually been committed here on this island," Giralo politely answered. "To be perfectly candid, I'm usually involved with kidnappings, ruthless murders, interstate prostitution and drug smuggling, money counterfeiting along with major assassinations and multiple homicides performed in adjacent neighboring states. Horse epidemics might just be out of my law enforcement background realm, and the infections that you've depicted might just be a result of a rather bizarre-but-rare, widespread contagion that's going on."

"The horses are biting their stomachs in response to the colic and others inside their stables are nauseous and lethargic, apparently suffering from their own flu symptoms," the virtually delirious and animated hotel executive reported. "If you can't help us, truthfully Sir, I don't know who else can!"

"Well, Mr. Martin, what about the hotel's CEO? Is he around for me to interview?"

"He's away attending a national conference at the Greenbrier Resort out in White Sulfur Springs West Virginia, and quite confidentially," Giles Martin pontificated, "I'm afraid to divulge the exact magnitude of the current horse catastrophe to him!" the desperate and now-neurotic man-in-charge of daily operations ranted.

"Well then, what about your Board of Directors? Can I consult with and interview them about this urgent horse matter?"

"Unfortunately, Sir, the Board is spending a week at the Hotel Del Coronado near San Diego where off-the-record, they're doing a little espionage work checking-out *that* facility's various amenities including the food menu," the nervous and distraught hotel administrator reluctantly shared. "They won't be back until next Monday and I'm afraid to contact them about the bad news, but I'm sure they'll soon learn about the calamity from another source!"

"Now Mr. Martin, how about your Corporate President? Is he to be found anywhere in Michigan?"

"This is all indeed very embarrassing for me to endure," the fit-to-be-tied emotionally encumbered hotel executive apprehensively complained. "Our illustrious President is over in Dixville Notch, New Hampshire and he's anonymously staying at the famous Balsams Resort while sizing-up the competition. Is there no compassion or rhyme or reason in this heartless world?"

Just then Giles Martin's cell phone rang three times and the man's anxiety level instantly heightened to its crescendo level. The hotel manager's facial expressions along with his florid complexion suggested to Inspector Joseph Giralo that the executive's secretary on the other end of the line was communicating additional negative news to the completely harried fellow.

"Mr. Giralo; I think I need to swallow-down at least a dozen aspirins. My secretary Ms. Gibson just informed me that the famous small photograph/portrait of Jane Seymour has been stolen from the downstairs Hall of History. And in addition," miserable Giles Martin continued his tale of woe, "I've recently learned that three priceless paintings from the mezzanine level art gallery have also been pilfered and nefariously replaced with authentic-looking counterfeits."

"I usually get involved with counterfeit money distribution, but if there's evidence or suspicion that these valuable heisted paintings have crossed state lines," Inspector Giralo qualified his complicated explanation, "then I'll be obligated to cut my vacation short and get immersed into cracking-open these new-found riddles of yours."

The usually composed and normally unfazed hotel manager's cell phone again rang and the already besieged and flustered Giles Martin hesitated before finally responding to the three rings. Obviously more horrible information was being transmitted to *his* ear because the perplexed man's facial skin was gradually turning from red to purple. After ending the disturbing telephone call, the beleaguered perspiring executive had more catastrophic developments to sadly convey to his now-fascinated listener.

"Oh my God, Inspector Giralo!" the chagrined about-to-go-insane manager screamed while dramatically holding the sides of his head. "Duchess Priscilla from Denmark is staying with her cousin Princess Natasha two doors down from you in the newly renovated Presidential Suite. I feel like fainting and collapsing on the rug, Mr. Giralo. Their cache of diamonds, of sapphire necklaces and of jeweled pendants, along with their emerald and ruby gemstone rings. have suddenly been mysteriously purloined from their exclusive room's safe. What an unprecedented career shattering nightmare I'm experiencing!" the extremely delirious gentleman related to his objective-minded Grand Michigan guest. "This entire sequence of events is absolutely scandalous, not only for me but also for the respectable reputation of this distinguished hotel! It's unprecedented and horrendously devastating upon the long-honored history of *this* truly noble and esteemed establishment!"

"Okay, Mr. Martin; you've now overwhelmingly convinced me to personally and professionally intercede in your crisis!" Inspector Giralo declared. "I'll immediately notify my superiors in Washington of the problems here on the island. I strongly suspect that definite criminal activity is going on here, bizarre occurrences that are evidently on the cusp of being suspiciously pernicious! The events you've just described have to be more than a series of unorthodox coincidences! This complex puzzle now is much greater than a simple case of grand larceny!" Inspector Giralo firmly maintained. "The present circumstances absolutely warrant and justify my pledged Justice Department services! The Duchess and the Princess are both foreign dignitaries that have inadvertently become felony victims. The fact that royal foreign aristocrats have been robbed now makes *your* very unenviable hotel plight into an important federal investigation matter!"

* * * * * * * * * * * *

Much to Giles Martin's utter astonishment, FBI Inspector Joseph Giralo showed-up without an appointment at the hotel director's office early on Friday afternoon, and the man-on-a-mission was bearing some wonderfully propitious news. After being greeted by the somewhat relieved upper echelon executive, the highly skilled federal investigator orally delivered a most stunning exposition.

"Well Mr. Martin, I've cracked your seemingly strange and inexplicable conundrum wide open and I'm happy to tell you that the overall case has been solved."

"Please divulge what you know and how you've managed to achieve your amazing results so quickly," Giles Martin reflexively insisted. "For example, what was the horse sickness hysteria all about? What culprit, or should I say *culprits* were responsible for such a despicably cruel deed?"

"When you had first told me about the unusual colic and influenza epidemic affecting your Mackinac Island work horses, I immediately suspected that some sort of ruse, or should I say some sort of deliberate diversion had been set into motion," the experienced FBI sleuth remarked. "And when you later found-out about the missing Jane Seymour portrait stolen from the Hall of History and about the Duchess and the Princess's cherished jewels being burglarized, then those two separate revelations fully confirmed my theory about a clever cover-up horse malady canard being slyly enacted."

"Before you proceed with your discoveries, did you work alone on this case?" Giles inquired. "That prospect would seem to me to be a relevant part of the mystery riddle."

"Yes, Giles. I must confess that I did have competent assistance," Joe Giralo curtly answered. "FBI command in Washington assigned and dispatched a trio of fine men operating up here in Michigan to help me, Agent Arthur Orsi out of Flint and Salvatore Velardi and Dan Blachford out of Saginaw. The three ambitious agents immediately drove up here to Mackinaw City, conducted comprehensive interviews with the local merchants, most of whom were proprietors and employees of shops on Central Avenue, on Huron Street and in the Mackinaw Crossings shopping mall. Several conversations from trustworthy people at the Sweet Tooth Confectionery Store, at Joann's Fudge Shop, at the Michigan Peddler and at the Mackinac Bay Trading Company provided *us* with key information that then led to the acquisition of essential clues and additional vital evidence. Once that specific knowledge had been gleaned and fed into our sophisticated national police data base computer system," Inspector Joe Giralo attested, "the remainder of the well-conceived plot was quite fairly easy to decipher."

Mr. Giles Martin demanded that Inspector Giralo slow-down his general recollection and precisely state the pertinent facts in their exact chronological order. The cooperative investigator promised to comply with the still-mentally disheveled manager's entreaty.

"Well, as I had already stated Giles," Joe Giralo proceeded with his sage analysis on a more personal basis, "just as I had suspected, the abnormal horse epidemic was basically a creative canard to divert *your* attention from high level felonies that were in the making. Now Giles, I've noticed that most of your summer employees here at the hotel are from Jamaica and the Dominican Republic and a few more from Haiti."

"That is quite true," Giles Martin readily verified. "The hotel annually closes for business in mid-October. Most of the imported summertime help then all return to their native lands while the Island's working horses are transported to various farms in the Upper Peninsula for the winter. Only about five hundred brave souls stay around on Mackinac for the extremely frigid, snow-laden months."

"Anyway Giles, after I learned about the art collection counterfeit replacements and about the replica phony Jane Seymour portrait being exchanged for the original one, along with the snatched jewelry from your royal guests staying in the luxurious Presidential Suite," Inspector Giralo keenly elucidated, "I immediately thought about your employees and about their countries of origin. A background check on various merchants across the bay over in Mackinaw City established that a certain art gallery dealer there by the name of Mortimer Benton had once owned a pawnshop in Montego Bay, Jamaica and that Mortimer's eldest son Clyde..."

"Once was a lower management clerk here at the hotel who had been dismissed two years ago because Clyde Benton had gotten into a heated dispute with my younger brother Ted, *his* immediate boss at the time! We don't tolerate or allow insubordination to occur here! That's our strict company policy!"

"So, Giles, now we have two distinct motives: Aggrieved Clyde Benton wanted his revenge on the hotel management team, and diabolical Mortimer Benton loved the hotel's art collection and ultimately schemed to steal its three most valued canvas treasures," the Inspector plausibly explained. "But don't you see, Giles? It was the missing and substituted for Jane Seymour Portrait that got me hot on Mortimer Benton's trail."

"How did that narrowed-down pursuit come to be?" the still bewildered hotel administrator asked. "There are still several missing components to this rather confusing jigsaw puzzle!"

"Agents Orsi, Velardi and Blachford had discovered over in Mackinaw City that Mortimer Benton was infatuated with *that* very desirable Jane Seymour portrait ever since he had first cinematically viewed in 1982 what later became his passionate obsession, his favorite movie, *Somewhere in Time*. In Mortimer's conniving mind," Inspector Giralo revealed and then paused, "my hypothesis upon initial instinct was that nothing was going to prevent this scheming thug Mortimer Benton from confiscating and possessing that coveted Hall of History object. But then I logically reasoned that the other art masterpieces along with the opulent jewelry would eventually be fenced, the obtained money being used for desperate Mortimer Benton to pay off his huge gambling and loan-sharking debts before the ruthless Detroit Mafia closed-in on their pathetic 'mark'."

"And I guess that since Mortimer Benton once owned a pawnshop in Montego Bay, Jamaica," Giles Martin surmised and expressed, "the slippery conniver, just like his volatile son Clyde, the devious rogue was able to speak Patois, the language often used by the island's natives that had been handed-down from their colonial-era Jamaican slave ancestors, who didn't want *their* vindictive masters to understand what they were plotting or communicating. To the British colonists, the words in Patois all sounded like stupid gibberish."

"And since Clyde and Mortimer Benton both spoke this contrived language Patois pretty fluently," Inspector Giralo eloquently concurred, "the reprehensible Benton thieves were able to bribe and persuade some of your hotel's less loyal employees to temporarily poison the island's horses, to snatch and replace the three expensive art works, to steal the precious jewels from the Duchess's Presidential Suite and finally, to stealthily swipe and switch the authentic Jane Seymour Portrait inside the Hall of History."

"And naturally, a former pawnbroker would have access to unscrupulous trading fences and illicit underworld dealers along with numerous nefarious-minded business connections that would be able to easily dispose of the artwork trove at a handsome profit and to also...."

"To also chop the brilliant diamonds, rubies, emeralds and sapphires down to be dispensed with on the thriving global black market," Joe Giralo clarified. "Now also Giles, I've learned that Mortimer's brother, Nigel Benton owns and operates an import/export business over in Alpena, thanks to the dedicated research of FBI Agents Orsi, Velardi and Blachford. But I still need to dig deeper into Mortimer's strategy in order to excavate more salient facts that will enable me to fully implicate Nigel Benton directly to Mortimer and Clyde's felonious Michigan activities."

"And I must say, *that* imaginative horse epidemic diversionary ploy really had us officials here on the island going on a frustrating wild goose chase, just as it had originally been designed by the unscrupulous perpetrators," Mr. Giles Martin concluded and orally conveyed. "For several days, pandemonium had been rampant all over Mackinac. And oh yes Inspector Giralo, the Chief-of-Police just notified me a half hour ago that a Jamaican room-cleaning maid he's described as a definite 'person of interest' is now under interrogation for her possible participation in the incredible grand larceny, royal jewelry theft caper."

"Yes, and I must admit, even the crafty crooks were surprised when the flu and colic epidemic proved to be more widespread than they had ever anticipated or imagined," the very skilled Inspector nonchalantly verbalized to his most recent admirer. "And to add a new dimension to the confounding ugly mess, another disgruntled former hotel employee named Milo Ransom has confessed to being a secondary co-conspirator in the elaborate crime scenario. Up to yesterday," Giralo informed Martin, "Milo had been employed as a maintenance crewman on Arnold Ferry Services boats. But after Mr. Ransom admitted to smuggling and transporting the jewelry, the original canvas paintings and also the singular Jane Seymour portrait from Mackinac Island back to Mortimer Benton's art gallery in Mackinaw City, I'm obligated to report to you that *our* subordinate villain Milo Ransom is currently out of a job and the adventurous lowlife is now on the local judge's docket and scheduled to be sentenced to a minimum of six months jail time."

"Most remarkable and extraordinary detective work!" Giles Martin sincerely commended his veteran crime-fighting guest. "If it weren't for you coincidentally vacationing here at the Grand Michigan, *we'd* still be struggling with a mammoth mystery on square one!"

Just then the elated manager's land-line phone rang and Ms. Gibson stated over the desk speaker that Inspector Joseph Giralo's boss wished to converse with the new Mackinac Island hero.

"Hello Joe! And may I add congratulations too!" Chief Inspector Matthew Riley praised and complimented over the desk speakerphone for everyone present inside the hotel manager's office to hear. "My reliable sources have informed me that you've become a veritable champion of justice up there in Northern Michigan!"

"All in the line of duty Sir, but quite frankly, I didn't expect all of the wild excitement to transpire in the middle of my late summer vacation! It's all been a little surreal to tell you the candid truth! But the Duchess and Princess's gemstones have been recovered intact, and also the stolen paintings from the hotel's art gallery along with the original Jane Seymour portrait, are all now safely back in the possession of their rightful owners," Joe Giralo respectfully replied. "Honestly Boss, Agents Orsi, Velardi and Blachford did most of the difficult gumshoe groundwork investigation. Everything appears to be back to normal on the Island. But what's up Chief? Anything new developed that I should know about?"

"Well now, Joe," Giralo's no-nonsense, straightlaced superior driveled on. "Since your well-earned Michigan hiatus has been abruptly interrupted with the outlandish Mackinac Island crime spree adventure, I want you to know that I've received special permission to have your vacation at the Grand Michigan Hotel extended for an additional week, expenses all paid for by good old Uncle Sam. Such fine compensation couldn't have happened to a more deserving guy. Nice going Inspector! You have my sincere congratulations! I now only wish that I could be so lucky! I should change my last name from my Irish nationality to Italian!"

"Why that's positively wonderful news, Chief!" the very satisfied Inspector boomed into the telephone speaker. "My wife Gina is enamored with this place and she'll be absolutely thrilled to be relaxing here for another seven days. In fact, my better half and I are seriously thinking about moving up here to Northern Michigan after I retire from government service!"

"And that's not all!" Chief Inspector Matthew Riley expeditiously vociferated. "As an added bonus reward, at noon a week from tomorrow we've arranged for a limo' to pick-up you and Gina at the Mackinaw City central loading pier and then a hired chauffeur will drive the two of you down to a cute German town in central Michigan called Frankenmuth where you'll both be treated to another free and fully paid week at a certain lodge, here it is on a sheet of paper sitting on my cluttered desk," Chief Riley said as he fumbled through some irrelevant letters and associated memos. "It's called the Drury Inn. What do you think about those apples, Joe? Talk about living the 'Life of Riley!' Ha, ha, ha! Pretty neat stuff, huh?"

"Why, er yes, it most certainly is, Chief!" the totally shocked and astounded FBI Inspector uttered. "I'm almost flabbergasted! My Uncle Manfred is from Bavaria, and I can't wait to tell him all about my good fortune, being able to hang out in a German town right here in idyllic Michigan! Thanks a million Chief! I can't wait to relay the good news to my wonderful wife! Another week up here in this green paradise is like a full month relaxing at a desert health spa! Thanks again for the good news Matt!" Click.

The following morning Inspector Giralo was feeling a bit sluggish, suffering from mild indigestion. The Investigator was all alone peacefully sipping his morning coffee inside Room 132 when a loud knocking on his first-floor hotel room door interrupted the gentleman's intense reverie. Deja Vu! Standing in the hallway was the very distressed hotel manager.

"Mr. Giralo, a very terrible horse epidemic has just broken-out on the island!" a perspiring Giles Martin announced. "I've learned through our confidential records kept here at the Grand Michigan that you work for the FBI. It's a very urgent matter I have to tell you about! A serious emergency situation has emerged involving the island's six hundred horses suffering from colic and influenza, and the dire matter must be addressed! May I come in?"

# "Poetic Justice"

Every December 1$^{st}$, FBI Inspector Joe Giralo proudly invites his three loyal agents Salvatore Velardi, Arthur Orsi and Daniel Blachford over to Orchard Street and into his cozy downtown Hammonton, New Jersey home to admire *his* extensive train display and accompanying elaborate village, all spectacularly exhibited on an enormous platform that virtually encompassed the man's entire downstairs "second den."

"I see that you've added several new buildings to complement your intricate Christmas hometown extravaganza," Agent Velardi noted and expressed. "I don't remember *that* dress shop and *that* yogurt and ice cream parlor on the corner ever being in the village last year. You've managed to re-create miniature scale model of downtown Hammonton! Quite impressive indeed!"

"Thanks for the rather exaggerated kudos, Salvatore!" Inspector Giralo genially replied. "Ever since I was a curious toddler, I've been infatuated with model trains. This entire project has taken me seven years to complete, and all of the stores and buildings along Bellevue Avenue, Central Avenue, Horton Street along with Second and Third Street I've diligently assembled with my own two hands. The tedious labor was done right here on the premises, with all the items being assiduously built down in my workshop basement."

"I especially like the work you've done on the Post Office Building, on the newly built Town Hall and also on the adjacent St. Joseph High School structure," Agent Orsi commended. "Your very meticulous, miniature renditions are almost perfect right-down to the basic not-so-familiar details! You could've been a terrific architect if you hadn't gone into the FBI."

"Look here, Arty!" the now-elated Chief exclaimed, pointing with his preferred left index finger. "I even have *your* house erected over on Tilton Street, and over here is Dan's humble place located on Pleasant, and oh yes, here's Sal's handsome residence over on Peach."

"I didn't notice those three novel additions before you brought them to my exact attention," ordinarily pensive Agent Dan Blachford articulated. "I feel quite honored having my nondescript abode represented on your fantastic town exhibition. The craftsmanship is borderline magnificent. And look over there next to Sal's house on Peach Street. You've actually fabricated a tiny duplicate of ..."

"My good neighbor Carmen Martino's silver and green Eagles' bus that I drive over to Philadelphia for Sunday home football games," Agent Velardi recognized and promptly declared. "Twelve other guys from Hammonton make the home game pilgrimages with me across the Delaware to 'the Link'. And of course," Inspector Giralo's loyal disciple continued his addicted prattling, "two of the season-ticket guys that cross the Walt Whitman Bridge with me into Philly' are Arty and Dan, and needless to say, we all enjoy munching on scrumptious barbequed Omaha steaks along with delicious burgers and grilled hot dogs while tailgating with other jolly Eagles' fans two hours before game time."

Suddenly, Chief Joe Giralo's contagious grin transformed into a somber, grim frown, which to his three alert subordinates indicated that the specific dialogue was about to change from standard, casual, folksy levity to serious FBI business that required their immediate addressing and professional problem-solving.

"Salvatore, I know that you've been feeling rather embarrassed lately," the Boss sympathetically indicated. "Please review for Arty and Dan's sake exactly what had transpired on your Peach Street property just a month ago, as a matter of ironic fact, the macabre incident occurring right on Halloween!"

Sal Velardi inhaled a healthy deep breath and then reluctantly related that for essential economic reasons, he had decided to switch his home heating system from oil to gas. The new gas heater had been professionally installed without any snag or snafu, and the subsequent pipe service extending from the street's main gas line to the house had been satisfactorily completed by the always-reliable South Jersey Gas Company. But upon the workmen excavating the old three-hundred-gallon metal oil tank from the property's back yard, a truly gruesome observation had been made by the front-end loader operator, the very stark discovery demanded the immediate services of the New Jersey State Police and the Philadelphia FBI.

"The whole thing was absolutely horrendous besides being totally humiliating for me to personally experience, certainly when happening in a small gossipy town like Hammonton!" Agent Velardi candidly reported. "The talk soon was in every local barbershop and in every hairdresser salon several hours before the disgusting news ever hit the area papers and TV stations. As you Gentlemen are quite aware, I'm very environmentally conscious about the size of my 'carbon footprint', and so I had optimistically changed from using an obsolete oil furnace and then wisely converting to gas heat. When my ancient rusty oil tank was being dug-up and removed," Velardi recalled and reviewed, "a buried male skeleton was found crushed underneath the huge oil tank's circumference. It's a good thing my wife was out grocery shopping when the fragmented remains were found. Kathy would've had a French hemorrhage, even though she's Italian!"

"But Salvatore, just because you're involved in law enforcement, you shouldn't feel guilty or mortified about the rather bizarre occurrence and the resulting negative community scuttlebutt that automatically developed thereafter! The aged oil tank had already been installed a full decade before you ever moved into your Peach Street home," Chief Giralo plausibly clarified. "The former owners of the house, Mr. and Mrs. Thomas Fallucca, both retired schoolteachers, well, the elderly couple had migrated down to Florida where they both have been deceased since 2010. Obviously, the old oil tank and the unearthed anatomy had been placed into the ground ten years before you ever purchased and occupied the dwelling."

"And the Falluccas are no doubt completely innocent of any wrongdoing, and evidently, they probably had nothing to do with the alleged crime that had been committed," Agent Orsi constructively contributed to the conversation. "And furthermore, *you* Sal are simply an unfortunate victim of oddball circumstances, all compounded by unwarranted hearsay community association!"

"Well, Chief," Dan Blachford anxiously chimed-in, "I suppose we'll have to separate our subjective emotions from our objective detective skills and conduct a thorough and efficient investigation into this apparent shocking local felony. As you often reiterate, Boss, when villains consider themselves as being too clever to ever be apprehended, that's precisely when their tender posteriors are most vulnerable to the legendary long arm of the law."

Introspective Inspector Giralo then initiated a lengthy oral litany that entailed the nature and competence of the FBI, that described the benign forces of good ultimately triumphing over the abundance of world and national evil, and finally, the sage's profound words pontificated about how the suspected crime (that had coincidentally been finalized on Agent Velardi's placid estate) needed to be expertly delved-into "for the fate of Salvatore's ultra-sensitive reputation and for his necessary peace of mind."

"Truthfully, Boss," Agent Velardi emphatically stated and soon momentarily hesitated, "I'm looking forward to collaborating with you on cracking-open this premeditated Peach Street burial, and in all sincerity, quite frankly I do believe that it'll be far easier for us four detectives to capture either a phantom Bigfoot or the all-too-elusive Loch Ness Monster than to decipher this very disturbing riddle that had regrettably transpired upon *my* present property over thirty long years ago!"

"You're a noble, positive genius, Salvatore!" Inspector Giralo surprisingly complimented his main assistant. "Your general exquisite verbosity has just provided me with the tangible clue my tortured mind had been frantically searching for. Thanks to you, my brain has formulated a quality hypothesis that's truly worthy of *our* dedicated pursuit! In fact, your acumen might've even afforded me *two* distinct material ideas!"

Led by inquisitive Sal Velardi's perceptive interrogation, the other two listening agents, being somewhat confused by their Boss's characteristic, enigmatic language, requested learning more pertinent information about the dead man's identity. Inspector Giralo was fairly reasonable and obliging about sharing and conveying the newly gleaned confidential FBI data.

"The victim's name is Jake Sacco, formerly of Hammonton, who had been living in Mays Landing prior to encountering his unenviable fate," the solemn-faced Chief disclosed. "Matt Riley and his crackerjack research team down at DC headquarters were able to determine *his* I.D. from certain DNA evidence and then later deftly comparing the acquired info' with existing criminal records, since deceased Mr. Jake "the Snake" Sacco had previously been arrested in Massachusetts, in Colorado, and in California on assorted burglary charges. Any introductory questions Men?"

"Then evidently, this dearly departed crook Jake Sacco was also quite itinerant!" Art Orsi concluded and verbally offered. "Now Boss, I've been hanging around you long enough to carefully study and fathom your shrewd analytic methodologies. Exactly what are our specific assignments relative to this nefarious-but-immobilized Jake Sacco fellow?"

"Salvatore, first of all I want *you* to find-out and evaluate every single iota about this dead thug's checkered-past," Inspector Giralo forcefully commanded. "And secondly Arty, I order that you investigate into the multiple home burglaries performed in Cambridge, Massachusetts, in Fort Collins, Colorado and in Palm Springs, California. And finally, Dan," Giralo next austerely instructed Blachford, "see if you can possibly explore some other major crimes besides commonplace burglaries being enacted by our dead, diabolical scoundrel, namely this mysterious cross-country wanderlust, Jake Sacco! Are my stated directions clear enough?"

"Will do, Chief!" Agent Blachford readily agreed and accepted. "This exploit might amount to one of our more exciting adventures! When will we be meeting again to comprehensively discuss the fruits of our individual explorations?"

274

"How about on Wednesday, December 11th for the four of us having breakfast at 9 a.m. sharp? We'll share a booth at the Silver Coin Diner. And by the way Salvatore!" Inspector Giralo added with a contrived smile. "I expect you to drive your white Nissan Murano over to the Silver Coin and not Carmen Martino's silver and green 1981 Ford Philadelphia Eagles fan bus!"

* * * * * * * * * * * *

The four government men informally met inside the foyer of the Route 30 Silver Coin Diner. Inspector Giralo was an acquaintance of "Gus," the establishment's congenial proprietor, who then escorted the federal quartet to a comfortable and secluded green, leather booth in the hectic eatery's back dining room. After the standard bacon, eggs, toast, home fries and coffee breakfasts had been ordered, predictably, casual small-talk and cheerful banter had to be exchanged prior to the veteran FBI officials commencing with their intended discussion about the past biography of deceased and disreputable Jake Sacco.

"Sal, I'm glad to see that you didn't drive up here from town to the White Horse Pike in Carmen Martino's green and silver Eagles bus," Chief Giralo humorously chided. "That enormous tin pig looks a little like a Farm Labor Transport vehicle, you know, what the Mexican crew-leaders use to drive their hard-working pickers to the big area blueberry farms. The crew-leaders have to paint the buses various colors because...."

"Because yellow buses in New Jersey exclusively mean school buses," Art Orsi abruptly interrupted. "Say Sal, do you possess a CDL to drive that two-tone monstrosity to the Sunday home football games? It's really an eyesore because my pupils hurt every time I glance at the archaic menace chugging by!"

"Yes, I had to obtain a Commercial Driver's License from the Motor Vehicle Department," blushing Salvatore Velardi reluctantly admitted. "And it's even good to use across the Walt Whitman Bridge in Pennsylvania too! But Boss," Velardi blandly stated, switching his attention from Orsi to Joe Giralo. "I want *you* to know that I don't also have a New Jersey farm crew-leader's license. Perhaps when I retire from the FBI, I'll apply for one of those babies, too!"

"Say, Senor Inspector," Dan Blachford butted-in, desiring to change the subject to something less ludicrous than an Eagles fan bus. "Sal, Art and I still believe that you have a particular propensity for being psychic. Could you elaborate on *that* shared speculation of ours?"

"It's more an understanding of the criminal mind and the alluded-to talent has less to do with the utilization of any noteworthy ESP phenomenon," Chief Giralo modestly lectured. "Actually, what you three students of justice interpret as being 'Psychic', I understand as being 'psycho'. Take the 1960 Alfred Hitchcock movie for example, you know, the film starring Anthony Perkins and Janet Leigh happening at the sinister Bates Motel. The depraved killer was mentally disturbed; demented, so to speak. And the gullible blonde female shower victim, who was soon brutally stabbed, perceived Mr. Norman Bates's twisted personality as simply being odd, peculiar and a trifle weird. Thus, she wound-up being terribly murdered by a cold-blooded maniac, never realizing until it was too late that young Mr. Bates had the emotional wherewithal to enact such a heinous act of despicable violence!"

After the courteous and accommodating auburn-hair diner waitress delivered the men's remaining food and beverage orders, gradually the topic of interest evolved from 1960 cinema fiction into the 1970s and 1980s activities of Jake Sacco in Massachusetts, in Colorado and in California. Inspector Giralo asked Agent Velardi to expound on *his* appointed aspect of the investigation.

"Well, Chief; according to the police and FBI files I had accessed, this fellow Jake Sacco had a unique method of operation, which was basically behaving like a common everyday thief in all three states," the senior agent revealed. "First of all, the deceased was an adept locksmith who had graduated from a home instruction course under a mail-order education supplied by the National Locksmith Academy. A year after legitimately receiving his diploma," Agent Velardi accurately declared, "our un-illustrious criminal worked with the Diebold Company, conscientiously inspecting and repairing safes and vaults at various Massachusetts' banks. But after turning to a life of redundant illicit acts, Mr. Jake Sacco's new, devious pattern was to follow mail delivery vehicles around on rural road routes, especially ones featuring residences having long-winding tree-shaded driveways set-off from the road. Many unwary and unassuming homeowners would nonchalantly amble out to their mailboxes to retrieve their daily mail, exiting their electronic garage doors and then incidentally leaving the portals leading into the houses open. And then this scheming malicious felon having the name Jake Sacco..."

"Would pull into the person's driveway and politely ask the targeted dupe for directions," Art Orsi surmised and contributed. "Then the vile perpetrator would probably pull-out a gun or a knife and tell the startled person to enter the house. Naturally, the alarmed resident would comply with the sudden threatening command."

"Exactly," Agent Velardi concurred with Agent Orsi's random conjecture. "And after tying-up and gagging the still-stunned victim, our nasty Mr. Sacco would rob the house at his leisure, and perhaps with the aid of an accomplice, proceed to steal the victim's car keys and easily pilfer the homeowner's auto' from the open garage. This relatively creative technique had been employed in all three aforementioned states, and after executing a dozen or so larcenies in each one, eventually, Sacco finally settled-down in Mays Landing."

A moment of silence was sharply broken when Inspector Giralo felt inspired to make a specific, lengthy inquiry that was advanced in the form of a declarative statement followed by an exclamatory sentence. "This rather fascinating punk Jake Sacco had been deliberately eliminated and consequently buried under the heavy oil tank in Sal's backyard; the devious goon being furtively terminated from existence, Mafia style! Surely, our Mr. Dead Locksmith must've been engaged in some other surreptitious crimes that were much-more-risky than him performing mere home robberies via open garage doors! Tell me, is my current assumption correct Dan?"

"Yes, and your insightful comment Chief has directly led to *my* segment of *our* now-complicated, multi-state federal investigation," Blachford suavely and diplomatically answered. "I've discovered that this tricky creep Jake Sacco came into contact with the dreaded National Mafia Network and the greedy, neurotic jerk began pilfering jewelry and cash from various millionaires' luxurious mansions in Cambridge, Massachusetts, in Fort Collins, Colorado and in Palm Springs, California. Using his versatile locksmith skills," Blachford continued his pertinent narrative, "cunning Jake "the Snake" deftly manufactured a variety of keys used to gain easy entrance into any designated home or business. The determined trespasser even learned how to dismantle and deactivate burglar alarms, either silent ones or otherwise, and the brazen intruder also was remarkably adroit at neutralizing sophisticated house video cameras along with special home connections to local police stations."

The four government men then conversed about how Jake "the Snake" Sacco needed to wear thin plastic or rubber gloves while purloining expensive items from selected mansions in order to stealthily avoid leaving any trace of fingerprint residue, and the four sleuths also considered and related how the slippery felon had to deal with electronic sensors on garage doors that were specifically designed to stop the remote-control objects from fully descending when detecting an obstacle or human form nearby or underneath. Thus, the targeted portal would remain only half-closed to motorist or pedestrian scrutiny from the nearby street or highway.

"In the case of typical electronic garage door sensors," Sal Velardi reckoned and orally offered, "I suspect that Mr. Sacco, being an accomplished scheming locksmith, the wily culprit would simply manufacture a house key and then, being able to lock the front or side door, the astute rogue could slickly abandon the selected mansion unscathed and undetected; that is, if he and a helper didn't plan on also thieving the best available car from the garage."

"But why did the almighty Mafia have Jake Sacco suddenly disappear from the face of the Earth?" Art Orsi wondered and asked. "Did the small-potatoes' locksmith betray any big 'Philly or New York City Dons? I mean Fellas', loyalty to evil practices, and to the awesome Mob Bosses, and to their formidable Cosa Nostra Lieutenants is what keeps absolute discipline alive among the syndicate's ranks! Any noticeable deviation leads to severe reprisal, and ultimately, even a painful death by execution! Jake Sacco must've known how dangerous it is to fool around with Sicilian fire!"

"Arty, stop your annoying plagiarizing! That's precisely Part II of my intensive Case Summary," Dan Blachford impetuously insisted. "This dead punk Jake Sacco had a reputation for being a Casanova, a habit which turned-out to be *his* principal Achilles Heel. After becoming romantically connected with three separate debutantes in Massachusetts, in Colorado and in California respectively, our dear Mr. Sacco quickly and independently fled those triple locations, his progress swiftly leaving behind three female corpses. Jake was thrice arrested for the brutal murders, but the district attorneys in all three states were unable to convict the clever felon, simply for the lack of non-circumstantial crime scene evidence. Thus," Agent Blachford concluded his graphic revelation, "our man Jake was labeled by local and state authorities as being 'a person of interest' for nearly thirty years until his recent skeletal discovery deep inside Sal's new lawn pit. But the athletic thug's female victims were all found lying dead inside their homes with all of the doors and windows locked, and now we've learned precisely how the three murdered women had been egregiously eradicated with *their* house keys discovered inside their mansions! Obviously, Mr. Sacco easily duplicated the master keys!"

"Chief, do you think that the vindictive Cosa Nostra guys are really the ones that had our subject murdered?" Art Orsi requested knowing. "This entire Peach Street episode has the markings of gangland activity, no doubt about it! Messing with the mob will more than put someone in jeopardy. It'll send the recipient to a premature grave in Salvatore's backyard cemetery!"

"Well, Arty. I would respond to your sagacious Mafia theory by saying both 'yes and no'," Inspector Giralo very coyly replied. "I had told Salvatore that either Bigfoot or the Loch Ness Monster had given me a definite hunch to further assess events. I've already acknowledged to you my original suspicion about the title Loch Ness Monster, my initial reasoning alluding to the Locksmith Academy and then your mentioning that Jake Sacco had been functioning as an experienced house robber and locksmith."

"Now Boss, what is the second obscure hypothesis that the terms Bigfoot and Loch Ness Monster had elicited your dynamic mind to create?" Agent Blachford boldly questioned his immediate superior. "How are those *two* science-fiction-type nomenclatures even again remotely germane to our present investigation?"

Chief Giralo slowly swallowed-down the last ounce of his tasty coffee and then quite clearly announced, "Gentlemen, this dastardly-but-crafty dead villain Jake "the Snake" Sacco even was able to construct his own .38 caliber bullets to cruelly kill his' three unfortunate rich love-mates. Now Men, your next important bit of homework is to thoroughly read and fully comprehend the classic poem 'Lochinvar,' authored by the distinguished Sir Walter Scott. Now I'm fully confident that *that* piece of popular poetic literature will automatically steer us in the direction of Mr. Sacco's unscrupulous criminal motive, of his advantageous criminal opportunity and of the mob's eventual lethal retribution."

"Logically, maniacal Jake Sacco lived by the pistol and probably, the fiend also died by the pistol. In my estimation, *that* assumption is the real poetic justice, either with or without 'Lochinvar' ever coming into play. Now then, Boss, when will we meet again?" Sal Velardi asked his well-respected mentor. "I hope our next scheduled conclave doesn't interfere with the upcoming Eagles game!"

"We'll meet in my Arch Street office at 9 a.m. on Wednesday, December 18th," Inspector Joe Giralo conveyed, recording the specific date and time into his trusty handheld computer. "By then I predict that Matt Riley and I should have this entire ancient murder case successfully wrapped-up and documented."

Agents Sal Velardi, Art Orsi and Dan Blachford could only simultaneously sit there inside their Silver Coin Diner green leather booth, instinctively shrugging their broad shoulders and mutually staring blankly and incredulously at one another in total disbelief.

* * * * * * * * * * * *

At 9 a.m. on Wednesday, December 18th, 2013 a rather fatigued FBI Inspector Joe Giralo seemed abnormally unprepared to eagerly commiserate with his three prime Quaker City agents, Salvatore

Velardi, Arthur Orsi and Dan Blachford, who had punctually arrived inside the Chief's eighth floor office, situated inside the all-too-mundane 600 Arch Street Federal Building, downtown Philadelphia, Pennsylvania.

As usual, the curious entrants found their all-too-conspicuous administrator sitting rather comfortably behind his prodigious Canadian oak desk with his large brown eyes seemingly in a self-induced daze. Giralo's pupils were vaguely scanning the *Philadelphia Inquirer's* morning headlines. The Inspector's ever-vigilant mind was keenly immersed in the process of genuinely contemplating much more challenging crime scenarios than *those* lackluster newspaper stories his enviable cerebrum had been evaluating.

"Hi Boss," Agent Velardi politely greeted his revered superior, methodically breaking Inspector Giralo's deep dual concentration. "How about lunch later today at Maggiano's Little Italy over on Filbert Street; you know, the popular fancy restaurant across from the Reading Train Terminal Food Market."

"It sure beats brunch at the corner Dunkin' Donuts!" Agent Orsi opined. "And Boss, the Maggiano's four-cheese ravioli entree is vintage Sicilian. I'd recommend the delectable meal to anyone, even to non-Italians like Blachford here!"

"I prefer good old spaghetti and meatballs," vociferated an already hungry Dan Blachford. "And may I also suggest the traditional Maggiano's family-style salad bowl. That tempting delight is enough to gratify all four of our enormous appetites!"

"Okay, Gentlemen," Chief Giralo cooperatively agreed with his always-famished, three-member panel. "I'll wholeheartedly endorse Salvatore's sensational recommendation, that is, only if we also enjoy consuming the home-baked luscious cheesecake and fresh-brewed coffee for dessert."

Satisfied that the customary preliminary small-talk had been adequately dispensed with, Chief Giralo maintained that his three underlings should academically explain the essence and the meaning of Sir Walter Scott's romantic poem, "Lochinvar".

Sal Velardi related that Lochinvar had been a young ambitious cavalier who decided to intrepidly enter the castle of a powerful queen and king and boldly demand permission to marry the kingdom's beloved royal princess.

Next, Art Orsi noted that the king and queen were extremely appalled at the obnoxious suitor's urgent request, the unsolicited declaration coming from a bold, insolent, wet-behind-the-ears, quixotic knight. And then Dan Blachford aptly summarized the story's culmination by citing that young Lochinvar had avariciously gathered-up the beautiful princess and next, the merry couple, in a wild frenzy, escaped from the ornate throne room seconds before any summoned guards could ever thwart *their* exciting elopement.

"And so, Fellas', "Chief Giralo remarked and then paused. "This callow-but-stubborn knight Lord Lochinvar was indeed a sort of medieval gigolo, much like our more contemporary amorous Don Juan, the deceased Jake Sacco had been three decades ago. That rather glaring similarity between the two connivers appears to be a most intriguing parallel being represented here!"

"All right, Boss. I get the significant connections," Sal Velardi ascertained. "Loch Ness Monster, locksmith, Lochinvar! But why did the Mafia rub-out Jake the Snake? Did the itinerant gigolo accidentally double-cross somebody big?"

"For the past several weeks, Matt Riley and I have intensely examined the matter and our combined effort finally figured-out the true scope and sequence of meaningful events," Joe Giralo confided. "This amorous-minded gigolo/rogue Jake Sacco had been secretly courting the daughter of a wealthy South Jersey oil baron, Mr. Pasquale Rinaldi, whose prosperous energy-supply company had been centrally based down in Cape May Court House, just outside of Stone Harbor. Anyway," vociferous Joe Giralo resumed his impressive monologue, "the wealthy Mr. Rinaldi didn't savor the ugly notion of a common proletarian flirting with his favorite daughter, and so good old Pasquale, who had certain strong Mafia associations with the ruthless 'Philly' syndicate, conveniently had dear Mr. Sacco erased right off the planet and propelled directly into the hereafter. And much to my satisfaction, the Washington FBI had no difficulty in pinpointing the South Jersey financier of the mob hit by virtue of...."

"By virtue of the Rinaldi Oil Company insignia that had been painted onto the bulky oil tank recently excavated from my own backyard!" Agent Velardi realized and loudly exclaimed. "I now recall seeing the grimy corporate logo on the oil tank's side but thought nothing of it at the time that the metal container was being removed!"

"Do we now arrest and prosecute Mr. Pasquale Rinaldi for authorizing and subsidizing the murder of Jake Sacco?" Art Orsi asked. "I must confess Boss that I do have more than a little mercy and empathy for the venerable, elderly aristocrat."

"Such a law enforcement response is completely unnecessary," Joe Giralo respectfully advised. "Mr. Pasquale Rinaldi and his wife Ethel both passed away in 2007, and the pair are buried in the Cape May Court House Cemetery. And so, Men," the Boss elucidated with a wide grin, "we can't hold our deceased oil baron suspect responsible for the wicked murder of Jake Sacco, which constituted a rather grisly act surgically performed nearly thirty years ago."

"The mob's hit-men that had committed the barbaric crime are probably also dead too! And thanks to Sir Walter Scott's marvelous poetry," Sal Velardi expressed, "unlike the very lucky Dark Ages' rascal Knight Lochinvar, our ill-fated Jake Sacco, along with the very rich Pasquale Rinaldi, did not in the end get off *scot-free* from Next World *heavenly* poetic justice!"

"Sal's right, Boss," Art Orsi enunciated, wholeheartedly verifying Agent Velardi's keen observation. "With Jake Sacco and Pasquale Rinaldi both dead, it's all sort of like a basic mathematical equation where no common denominator exists after both main factors have been efficiently canceled-out!"

"Einstein couldn't have said it any better," commended Agent Blachford. "The whole formerly complex case is now reduced to a simple veritable wash! Sometimes I think that the four of us are more-clever than we actually believe we are!"

"But Salvatore, without your knowledge, another perplexing dilemma has recently surfaced in the interim," Inspector Giralo informed his momentarily-euphoric assistant. "This new debacle directly concerns your admirable Philadelphia Eagles bus neighbor, Mr. Carmen Martino."

"What about Carmen?" Sal Velardi asked with instant anxiety. "Is my good friend injured or hospitalized?"

"Carmen's perfectly okay! Your highly-valued football game amigo had recently contacted South Jersey Gas," the amused Inspector calmly answered. "But your good pal heard that you had switched your home heating system from oil to gas, so Carmen soon contacted South Jersey Gas and had his own line installed and attached to his new cellar heater."

"So, what's so incredible or extraordinary about *that* rather mundane information?" a perturbed Agent Velardi cynically responded. "Imitation is the sincerest form of flattery, isn't it?"

"Yeah, Boss! Let's just focus on relishing our Italian feast over at Maggiano's!" Art Orsi logically suggested. "I relish pasta even more than I relish ballpark hot dogs!"

"I wholeheartedly endorse Art's very intelligent culinary proposal one hundred percent!" Agent Blachford uttered. "Even though I'm a mixture of British and Irish genetics, it's almost time for me gobbling-down some tasty, Italian appetizers!"

"Maybe so!" Chief Giralo indulgently laughed. "But astonishingly enough my dear Salvatore, another anonymous skeleton has since been discovered, the fresh skull and bones being entrenched beneath the newer Rinaldi Oil Company tank just excavated on your affable neighbor Mr. Carmen Martino's Peach Street backyard. Yes indeed, Agent Velardi. It looks like we're all back to the proverbial drawing board and all-too-familiar Square One again!"

# "The Multi-Faceted Diamond Caper"

On Wednesday morning, September 18th, 2013 FBI Inspector Joe Giralo patiently sat behind his solid oak desk inside his 600 Arch Street eighth floor office and silently listened to animated Agents Salvatore Velardi, Arthur Orsi and Daniel Blachford discuss the Philadelphia Phillies versus Miami Marlins National League baseball game that the three G-men had attended the evening before at Citizens Bank Park. The sports-fanatical trio was thrilled that the previously hapless home team had won the close contest by a score of 6-4 and that the new interim club manager Ryne Sandberg had then achieved a respectable record of eighteen wins against thirteen losses ever since taking over the squad's helm from former beloved manager, the very likeable Charlie Manuel.

"Looks like dependable Roy Halladay is making a major comeback, giving-up only one run and four hits in his fifth start following his return from right shoulder surgery," fan Sal Velardi observed and stated. "This season is basically shot, but if 'Doc' comes back next year in good health as the club's ace starter, he, Cole Hamels and Cliff Lee will make a really formidable pitching rotation."

"But also recovering from leg problems, my favorite player Chase Utley emerged as the hero of last night's game, hitting a clutch homer and driving in four vital RBIs," Art Orsi melodramatically added to the general baseball euphoria. "According to the left field scoreboard, that fifth inning three-run smash into the right field bleachers traveled 404 feet. If first baseman Ryan Howard rebounds next year in tip-top shape from his foot injury, and if *my* man Utley avoids being hurt again, the Fightin' Phils will definitely be Eastern Division contenders in 2014, I guarantee it!"

"That mighty blast was Utley's 217th homer of his Big-League career," Dan Blachford contributed to the unrealistic dialogue. "But I caution you Guys that Doc Halladay's fastball had only a maximum velocity of eighty-eight miles per hour on the official radar gun, but on the positive side," "Dandy Dan" emphasized, "Jonathan Papelbon was able to close-out the Phils' victory by allowing only a scratch single in the 9th. Remarkably, it was the durable closer's twenty-eighth save of the season. That ninth inning guy's been tremendous ever since the Phils' acquired him from the Red Sox."

"I thought that the best part of the game was the terrific 'Philly cheesesteaks and giant pretzels we swallowed-down after participating in the seventh inning stretch," Agent Velardi recalled and blathered. "And those TastyKake Butterscotch Krimpets you bought down in the stadium concourse Dan really made it a great evening! Tell us Chief. did Philly' have those giant pretzels and savory TastyKakes when Richie Ashburn, Del Ennis, Robin Roberts and the other 1950s Whiz Kids were playing baseball in Shibe Park, later better known as Connie Mack Stadium?"

Ignoring Sal Velardi's bothersome sarcastic drivel, formerly reticent Chief Joe Giralo decided to incorporate some academic aspects into the mediocre conversation, and so the knowledgeable Boss suavely lectured his three subordinates, communicating that the stellar hurler Roy "Doc" Halladay's nickname actually was a gabby sportscaster's allusion to John Henry "Doc" Holliday, a notorious American Wild West gambler, dentist and lethal gunfighter. Most of his short life, Holliday suffered with and eventually died from a severe chronic tuberculosis condition, with the tough quick-draw's womb-to-tomb longevity lasting only from 1851-1887."

"Historically speaking," Inspector Giralo boringly proceeded and prattled, "the original Doc Holliday was a close friend of lawman Wyatt Earp heir association was often depicted in old '50s nightly black and white TV cowboy shows, and the invincible pair were involved in the classic 'Gunfight at the O.K. Corral' that had occurred in legendary Tombstone, Arizona. Now if the Phillies had another effective pitcher named Wyatt Earp," Inspector Giralo facetiously joked, "then *that* unimaginative sportscaster's play-on-names' coincidence between John Henry 'Doc' Holliday and Roy 'Doc' Halladay would really be a....."

"Er, Boss," Agent Velardi very politely interrupted his encyclopedic federal superior. "I'm sure you didn't call this special meeting for the purpose of evaluating the Phillies' baseball prospects for next summer. What's on *our* agenda today? Are you taking us to the airport to vacation in sunny St. Thomas? I think that tropical Aruba or balmy Bermuda would be very nice, too!"

"That type of extended excursion to any of those majestic islands would be more than adequate," Art Orsi chimed-in. "Strolling the Ocean City, Wildwood and Atlantic City boardwalks with my family for the past four months has become monotonous and redundant!"

"I hope we don't have to travel south and work with Matt Riley and his overly ambitious true-blue employees down in DC headquarters," normally sedate Dan Blachford all-too-honestly opined. "Truthfully Guys, I had labored diligently in *that* totally stressful, bureaucratic environment the first three years of my FBI career, and yes, quite frankly Gentlemen, my memories aren't exactly super-fond ones whenever I recall me being perpetually hazed as a novice detective."

Growing intolerant of Dan Blachford's exaggerated sulking and unwarranted peeving, Inspector Giralo discreetly elected getting to the crux of the matter, offering an introduction that cited a series of aggravating diamond heists adroitly executed in assorted cities across the USA. Local police jurisdictions, state authorities, along with the ordinarily competent Federal Bureau of Investigation had all been incredibly stymied by the lack of tangible clues available to the beleaguered and puzzled investigators.

"In April and May of this year," the Chief enunciated while carefully examining and slowly reading from a hand-held sheet of paper, "costly diamond thefts had been made in Atlanta, Miami, Cincinnati, New York, Cleveland, San Francisco, Phoenix, Miami again, Washington DC and Boston. The guys down in DC are extremely baffled, with my pal Matt Riley being especially embarrassed that the Friday, May 24th gem heist had occurred on his sacred home turf!"

"Miami was hit twice," Sal Velardi observed and confidently remarked as the alert agent scribbled-down the new pertinent information in his nearly-full notepad. "I theorize that *that* particular Miami repetition might prove to be significant."

"Maybe the perpetrators like warm weather," contributed Agent Orsi. "It's relatively hot in April and in May down in Miami, out West in Phoenix, down south in Atlanta, Georgia and sometimes over in Cincinnati. But on the other hand, San Francisco is either cold or cool during those two early spring months, and Boston, Cleveland, New York and Washington can be either cool or mild, depending on the Jet Stream's seasonal path!"

"The fact that only large cities are targeted is uniquely peculiar!" Dan Blachford rationally expressed. "We all know that there're many suburban malls and wealthy rural communities that have well-stocked jewelry stores. This oddball random pattern that's already been established does represent a sort of enigma."

Taking all of his agents' reactions into consideration, the frustrated Chief then enumerated the cities that had been designated for diamond thefts during June and July of 2013. The list being reviewed read like a contemporary Homeric catalog: Milwaukee on June 8th, Minneapolis, on June 12th, Denver on June 26th, San Diego on June 25th, Los Angeles on June 27th, Pittsburgh on July 3rd, New York on July 19th, St. Louis on July 25th and finally, Detroit, occurring on July 28th.

"Notice again, Guys, that New York had a huge gemstone larceny occur for a second time, just like Miami has had," Agent Velardi commented and then recorded onto his trusty handheld notebook. "The crooks involved in this national crime-wave must be enamored with Florida sunshine and with Big Apple Broadway plays, being especially fond of Times Square, the Empire State Building and the Statue of Liberty, too!"

"The fact that San Diego and Los Angeles are geographically in close proximity and the reality that Pittsburgh and Detroit are only within several hundred miles of each other might be fundamentally relevant," Art Orsi reckoned and shared. "But I still can't understand why America' suburbia has been excluded from the pattern, if not ignored or neglected in this abominable rash of interstate felonies."

"There's little or no rhyme or reason to this implausible series of diamond pilfering," Dan Blachford assessed and concluded. "Other than New York and Miami being plundered twice each, my jumbled mind is swimming in a complete quandary."

"Well, Fellas'," the equally befuddled veteran Boss vociferated. "Here's the remainder of the metropolitan areas that have been victimized in August and then up to September 13th. We have Washington DC on Friday, August 9th, and Guys, this second District of Columbia hit has Matt Riley and his team totally infuriated," Joe Giralo added with a broad grimace exhibited upon his florid countenance. "And then Wednesday, August 14th in Atlanta again, Tuesday August 27th in Manhattan for the third time, Sunday September 1st in Chicago, and finally, Friday September 13th in our Nation's Capital for the third time. That third heist naturally has the DC boys fit to be tied!"

"There must be some obscure method to this out-of-control madness," a thoroughly-addled Sal Velardi evaluated and voiced. "This colossal conundrum is far worse than sitting through the entire disappointing 2013 Phillies' season as a lousy depressed centerfield, grandstand patron!"

"Wait a Philadelphia minute!" a now-motivated Agent Orsi enthusiastically exclaimed. "Boss; have *you* also perceptively discerned that none of the August and September crime dates had been performed on a Monday or a Thursday?"

Chief Giralo closely scrutinized his comprehensive Phillies' calendar list and then convincingly uttered, "Arty, what you've just mentioned about August and September is partially accurate and correct. You're absolutely right about Mondays being eliminated, but according to *this* infallible documentation I'm now referring to, a prodigious diamond theft had occurred in Los Angeles on *Thursday,*

June 27th and in St. Louis on *Thursday,* July 25th. But Arty," the Inspector paused and smiled, "I must commend your general acumen. Your keen mental dynamics concerning Mondays just might be valuably instrumental in cracking-open this very vexing mystery."

"Maybe the ambitious villains involved in the DC heists are really and truly infatuated with the Washington Monument, the Lincoln Memorial, the U.S. Capitol Building, the White House and the Smithsonian," Agent Orsi awkwardly jested. "We might have some patriotic felons on our hands; indeed, a collection of advanced citizen thugs who can't get enough of American history!"

"This is no time for preposterous amusement Arty," Dan Blachford rankled and reprimanded. "The very reputation of the Bureau is at stake here. These brazen diamond thieves are blatantly acting with impunity and making a grotesque mockery of our justice system."

"We know that we have a determined gang of diamond fanatics scouring every big city jewelry store and corporate gem exchange," Sal Velardi verbally summarized. "Boss, what do you think of these bewildering circumstances? You've remained rather laconic these last five minutes and from past experience, I just know that your brain is hypothesizing something major."

"Believe it or not Salvatore, your loose tongue has just given me a rather brilliant idea. Instead, you should make *my* last statement into *two* rather brilliant ideas. I want to see you three Geniuses in my office at noon on Tuesday, September 24th. Yes, Sal. I think that you're an erudite genius without you ever seriously ever contemplating that special notion!"

"Boss, to tell you the truth," Sal Velardi then hesitated to contemplate an adequate, clever response. "Right now, you've made me feel like a resurrected Neanderthal Man!"

* * * * * * * * * * * *

Tuesday, September 24th quickly arrived on the 2013 calendar and the three dedicated agents once again stepped from the 600 Arch Street elevator and promptly ambled across the eighth-floor corridor into Inspector Joe Giralo's walnut-wood paneled office. The three visitors were still somewhat emotionally distressed because the faltering Phillies had lost the past Sunday's afternoon baseball game played against the equally dismal New York Mets.

"Another ugly and pathetic Phils' defeat registered into the baseball annals," Agent Velardi pessimistically recounted his personal grief. "I really feel disenchanted about the team's inferior performance, and I'm seriously weighing whether or not I'm going to moronically purchase season tickets for next year."

"Well, the Eagles are off to a fairly decent start with new coach Chip Kelly," Agent Orsi ascertained and spieled. "I must admit: hope springs eternal during the beginning of football season just like it also does in the Phillies spring training camp down in Clearwater."

"Why are you looking so glum and pale Dan?" Chief Giralo asked Blachford. "Did your ferocious pet Doberman die after eating contaminated cat food?"

"No, Boss," the seemingly disgruntled agent lethargically replied. "My wife's kitchen stove went haywire on Friday, and besides *that* irritating bummer, our overhead microwave needed rehab' too, so being good American consumers, Bing and I motored down to Appliances Plus in Vineland, and during our productive shopping spree we shelled-out two thousand bucks for a new GE range and accompanying overhead quick serve oven."

"Sounds like you negotiated a pretty thrifty bargain," Sal Velardi butted-in. "So why are you so melancholy and miserable if you and Bing got such a swell deal?"

"Well," Blachford indignantly answered. "When the aggressive salesman described the two products, he made it sound as if the devices were easy to install. 'Just rip-out the old range and the old overhead microwave and insert the new ones and next, simply plug them in,' the clerk claimed to us. But in reality, after the range and the accompanying microwave were delivered to Pleasant Street, it didn't work-out *that* way because...."

"Because Dan, originally you and Bing had had a custom-built remodeled kitchen professionally installed fifteen years ago," Art Orsi piped-up, "and I surmise that the diagonal space situated behind the stove and the area located behind the elevated microwave frame had to also be expertly modified in order to accommodate the newly obtained units."

Sporting a profound frown, Dan Blachford then painfully explained that it was soon required for him to enlist the capable skills of Hammonton builder David Noto to re-structure the dual stove and microwave areas, and next the talented builder had to commission the services of tile guru David Paretti to reconfigure the ceramic tile surrounding the original 'special range'. "But in addition," Blachford regretfully added, "Noto had to summon his company electrician Mark Vaccarella to re-wire the new appliances to my electric circuits down in the cellar. The unanticipated supplemental labor eventually cost almost as much as the two new Appliances Plus ovens did!"

Realizing that more than enough valuable time had been wasted on commentaries about the Phillies, about the Eagles and about Agent Blachford's ultra-modern kitchen replacements, Inspector Giralo refocused the group's consultation on the ongoing skein of big city diamond thefts.

"Meanwhile Sal and Art, while you two Savants were attending Phillies and Eagles games and while you, Dan, were preoccupied clumsily solving your kitchen appliance dilemma, I've been preoccupied racking my brains out about this continuous coast-to-coast precious gemstone caper," Giralo reminded his wayward disciples.

"And exactly what did your splendid problem-solving efforts achieve?" Sal Velardi cynically inquired. "That the Phillies Phanatic has buried the missing jewels in the Citizens Bank Park baseball diamond!"

"Believe it or not, Salvatore, your anemic attempt at ridiculous humor is not too far off base!" the Chief chuckled. "You were close but earned no cigar or brass ring! Do you remember during our last session when *you* had remarked that the diamond thief must've been a fanatic?"

"Why yes, but not the Phillies Phanatic!" Agent Velardi responded incredulously. "It was just an innocent utterance at the time, and nothing more!"

"Matt Riley and I now happen to believe that our anonymous diamond thief might very well be an avid Philadelphia Phillies fan who travels around the country picking-up stolen diamonds and then casually driving to other cities and selling the gemstones to Mafia and Cosa Nostra syndicates elsewhere. Quite possibly," Chief Giralo expounded on his surprise exposition, "our nameless subject might also be illicitly trading the purloined jewels for drugs in order to then barter the contraband for laundered legal tender."

"Your most fascinating theory rationally accounts for why no diamond heists had been committed on Mondays," Agent Orsi admirably marveled and verbalized. "But if that's the case, Chief, if our unidentified suspect is a dye-in-the-wool Phillies fan, why haven't any related crimes happened right here in 'Philly?"

Joe Giralo then opened and slowly reached into his massive oak desk's center drawer and removed four copies of the 2013 Phillies baseball schedule, which the Mentor distributed, and then instructing his stunned agents to intensely peruse the new information. "After examining the cities and related game dates Sal," the revered federal supervisor directed, "what American League teams are *not* on the Phillies Major League agenda?"

"Let's analyze this intriguing information for a minute," Agent Velardi requested. "Okay Guys, the Phillies this year have played every American League team except the Baltimore Orioles, the Kansas City Royals, the Oakland Athletics, the Seattle Mariners, the Tampa Bay Rays, the Texas Rangers, the Toronto Blue Jays, the Houston Astros and finally, according to the schedule, the always formidable New York Yankees."

"But the Phils' have played American League teams the Kansas City Royals, the Cleveland Indians, the Boston Red Sox and the Chicago White Sox at home in Citizens Bank Park," Joe Giralo recited, reading from his list.

"But the Phillies have played the Boston Red Sox up in Fenway Park on May 27th and May 28th," Sal Velardi divulged, "and they've also played another American League club you've just mentioned in an *away* series, the Cleveland Indians at Progressive Field on Tuesday, April 30th and on Wednesday, May 1st."

Art Orsi was inspired to remark that New York had already been hit with enormous diamond thefts and that Oakland was situated across the bay from neighboring San Francisco, which had already also been targeted for gemstone robbery.

"True, Arty," Dan Blachford recognized and verified, "but besides the New York Yankees, who incidentally are categorized in the American League, the rival cross-town New York Mets are in the National League, so consequently, this is why the Phillies would visit the Mets in Shea Stadium more than once a summer, and also, *that* glaring detail possibly explains why the incognito Phillies fan/jewel courier would do business in New York City more than once a baseball season, and this is also why...."

"Why Miami, Washington and Atlanta have experienced immense multiple diamond thefts," Sal Velardi gasped in astonishment, "apparently because those three baseball bastions are stationed in the National League's Eastern Division. And obviously, the Phillies would visit the Marlins, the Nationals and the Braves for series' games more than once a summer, as would the unidentified person of interest, this phantom, itinerant avid Phillies fan."

Chief Joe Giralo again glanced-down and studied the Phillies schedule held between his chunky hands and his firm voice asked his three still-confused agents the significance of the following terminology: "Progressive Field, Fenway Park, Target Field and Coamerica Park."

After a half-minute of tense silence, Agent Blachford offered a suitable answer. "Progressive Park is where the Phillies had played the Cleveland Indians; Fenway Park is where the Fightins' later went-up against the Boston Red Sox; Target Field is the newly constructed home of the less-than-devastating Minnesota Twins, whom the Phils' also played horribly against in mid-June, and last-but-not-least, Comerica Park is where the lackluster Phils' had a terrible series against the juggernaut Detroit Tigers in late July, but most importantly Boss," Blachford orally conveyed. "It's an undeniable fact that all four *away* opponents were American League teams."

"Wow!" exclaimed a suddenly enlightened Art Orsi. "According to the 2013 schedule, as we've already mentioned, the Phillies have played some other American League teams like the Chicago White Sox and the Kansas City Royals, but *those* other inter-league games were at home and not on the road. All of the accumulative evidence is now lending heavy credence to the Chief's outstanding guess that the main perpetrator we're wildly seeking is indeed also a bona fide Philadelphia Phillies fan!"

"Now, the big picture all makes perfect sense!" Sal Velardi bellowed. "Notice on your schedules that sometimes there are weeklong intervals between diamond heists and that other times, the individual thefts are separated only by being several days apart. When the insular robberies are weeks apart...."

"The Phillies are coincidentally playing *home games* with Mondays off," Agent Orsi acknowledged and insisted. "But when the jewel felonies are only mere days apart...."

"Then understandably, the Phillies are playing *away games* in either National League or in American League cities with Mondays still off-days, too!" an almost out-of-breath Dan Blachford excitedly blurted-out. "This ever-evolving baseball scenario is absolutely amazing! Boss, if you aren't ESP psychic, then you must be a genuine genius in disguise!"

"Matt Riley and I are still ironing-out the specific details of this rather challenging investigation," Chief Giralo calmly informed his three impressed confederates in law enforcement. "Next Monday morning, September 30th, we'll meet again in my office and confer about this case's most recent developments."

* * * * * * * * * * * *

The three blithe-spirited FBI agents eagerly returned to the Federal Building at 600 Arch Street to honor their pre-arranged September 30th rendezvous with Chief Inspector Joe Giralo, who contrary to his widespread, parsimonious disposition, cordially greeted his award-winning team into his sacred bailiwick, and next treating the rambunctious trio to freshly-brewed coffee along with a variety of tempting TastyKake Butterscotch Krimpets, complemented by nine chocolate cupcakes and four small packages of TastyKake apple pies stacked on three individual trays.

"My junk food diet sure beats ingesting sea gulls or bagels (bay gulls)," bantered jovial Sal Velardi. "I'm glad I came in to work today. I don't regard eating sweet snacks as drudgery or as punishment."

"I wouldn't even desert these desserts out in the desert," Agent Orsi' added, ineptly entertaining only himself. "Now Fellas'. I'll gladly honor the erudite person who had invented 'p-i-e' just as much as I value the ancient Einstein who proficiently studied the esoteric composition of a circle and then accidentally also discovered 'pi'."

"Enough frivolous quips from you, you equivocating, prevaricating wannabe' comedian!" rebuked Dan Blachford in Orsi's physical direction. "Let's confine all of the slapstick foolishness to the obsolete Vaudeville stage, and let's limit all of the zany clown antics and semantics to Ringling Brothers, Barnum and Bailey."

"Say, Boss," Sal Velardi articulated, desiring to change the totally ludicrous conversation from utter stupidity to more mature FBI concerns. "What new info' have you gleaned on the scurrilous Phillies fan turned Mafia' messenger. We all know how the fearsome Cosa Nostra crooks along with dreaded al Qaeda terrorists are world-famous, or should I say *world infamous* for mendaciously killing the hired messenger!"

"That's positively true!" Dan Blachford confirmed. "The al Qaeda network is afraid of being monitored by their use of cell phones, so the vile anarchists solely utilize scouts and messengers to transfer letters and documents. Even in our daily lives, just about everyone residing in America is worried about privacy and about secret NSA electronic surveillance."

"Both the Mafia and al Qaeda are renowned all over the globe for doing deleterious and detrimental things to other doomed-by-decree human beings," Joe Giralo concurred. "But to be perfectly candid, we can't have disorganized law enforcement fighting organized crime, or we can't allow the existence of organized terrorists, either. It's all just gotta' happen in reverse in order for Jeffersonian democracy to survive and flourish in the 21st Century!"

"Listen, Boss. Today you sound like the incompetent captain of a ship that can't cant," Art Orsi stupidly joked. "I'd honestly like to hear from you more crime-solving activity and less crime-fighting philosophy!"

The Boss, being in an extraordinarily favorable mood, next elaborated on how the evasive 'diamond culprit's I.D.' could probably be isolated by a national computer bank search, for the 'phantom' more-than-likely every year purchased a brand-new car with cold cash, since the mysterious 'person of interest' would naturally compile many odometer miles each summer while driving from city to city all across the nation.

And then, Supervisor Giralo again effectively baffled his dumbfounded listeners by boldly pontificating that the anonymous transgressor probably conducted his year-round delivery enterprise by also being a fervent Philadelphia Eagles, Philadelphia Flyers and Philadelphia 76ers on-the-road fan.

"Inspector. Please don't keep us wallowing in suspense!" Sal Velardi demanded. "Who is this pernicious felon who immediately needs the cuffs slapped on his avaricious wrists?"

"After narrowing-down our nationwide dragnet search, we eventually honed-down to a slick individual named Melvin Michael Mitchell, who truly and actually *is* a robust Phillies fan!"

"Sounds like the audacious knucklehead should've worked for the *3-M Corporation* rather than being employed as a meager Mafia courier exchanging diamonds for illegal drugs and under-the-table untaxed cash," punster Art Orsi summarized.

"And ironically," Chief Giralo proceeded with his all-too-familiar litany while deftly ignoring Agent Orsi's totally ridiculous language, "our boys from the Bureau's Atlanta Office just successfully nabbed Mr. Mitchell."

"In the Turner Field parking lot?" Agent Velardi speculated and curiously asked. "That's where the Phillies wound-up their disastrous season yesterday, weakly losing to the Braves, 12-5."

"Correct," Chief Giralo readily affirmed. "Mr. Melvin Michael Mitchell was apprehended while exiting a 2013 red Lexus sedan having a suitcase containing a whopping $850,000.00 cash snugly deposited in the trunk. No doubt Mr. Mitchell shrewdly regarded his risky assignments as being too dangerous for him to be traveling through airport security checks, so the devious crook nonchalantly drove from city to city, specifically from Phillies away game to the next slated away game. And here's some true FBI serendipity for you Glorious Guys to savor. Mr. Melvin Michael Mitchell lives in New Castle. As you Guys might know, Delaware is also known as 'the Diamond State'!"

"And this slimy snake Mitchell even got to see the Phillies play the National League Arizona Diamondbacks out west in Phoenix!" Agent Orsi related and then guffawed.

"We still think that you're psychic Boss!" Agent Blachford opined. "You're a veritable ESP genius!"

"Fellas', I'm about as psychic as the phony ancient Oracle of Delphi was in the time of Socrates," Inspector Giralo maintained. "But in essence Men, it was the combined idea of the mischievous Phillies Phanatic coupled with the innocent reference to a 'baseball diamond' that got me whimsically thinking about a hardcore Phillies *fanatic* enthusiast who had been guiltlessly engaging in villainous criminal activity."

"Well, Boss," hollered-out an almost delirious Agent Orsi. "It's too bad that this FBI investigation couldn't have happened twenty years in the future!"

"Why's that, Arty?" Inspector Giralo wondered and asked. "Stop speaking in riddles! Why two decades from now?"

"Because of the idea of a Baseball Diamond, Boss," Agent Orsi explained. "Phillies fanatical fan Mr. Melvin Michael Mitchell's thrilling arrest made outside Turner Field could've simultaneously occurred on *your* sparkling Diamond Jubilee Wedding Anniversary!"

# "The Perplexing Pie Picture Puzzle"

On a pleasant seventy-five-degree Friday afternoon in late May of 2014, FBI Inspector Joe Giralo was seated and somberly commiserating with his loyal Agent Sal Velardi inside the 19th Hole Clubhouse at the public Buena Vista Country Club, the recreational accommodation situated ten miles southeast of somnolent Hammonton, New Jersey. The rather quiet conversation centered-around the Chief's rare sub-par golf outing. After the affable bartender delivered several frosted mugs of beer to the duffers' square table, the disappointed G-men continued their woeful conversation.

"Sometimes Salvatore, I think you're better off than I am because you don't take your golf game too seriously," Joe Giralo began his pessimistic litany. "Eighteen holes of mediocre golf can be a very humbling and frustrating experience to a dedicated player."

"You're absolutely right, Boss," agreeable Agent Velardi reluctantly verified. "I shoot in the low 80s. If it gets any hotter, I don't play. But all joking aside," the Chief's zany government associate prattled. "I'm usually either looking for a diamond in the rough or a Titleist in the rough. On the fairways or on the greens, my luck is not blessed by St. Andrew; that's for darned sure!"

"Well, bless my soul, Salvatore. You've just told me several old, obnoxious, very mediocre jokes. You'd better watch yourself. You might actually be committing wholesale plagiarism from a struggling low-rank amateur comedian! But now getting back to today's distressful reality, I unfortunately shot four strokes over my established twelve-over-par handicap," the peeved Chief complained. "And the four par-five holes my effort encountered today really destroyed my regular game. You know, my Friend; several years ago, I got two holes in one on this course but after twenty-seven years, I've never been able to get an eagle. And please don't tell me that you wear two pair of pants when playing golf, just in case you get a hole in one, because that's another one of your leprous, repetitious wisecracks that absolutely tortures my sensitive eardrums."

"A three on a par five is exceptionally difficult to achieve," Agent Velardi sincerely admitted and confirmed. "Not even Tiger Woods or Phil Mickelson is an expert at hitting eagles. There's a certain amount of Divine Luck involved, that's for certain. But if you ever shot an eagle Boss," the subordinate jested, "I promise I won't report you to the National Wildlife Association or the equally powerful Environmental Protection Agency."

"I still can't get over shooting a detestable 88 on a par 72," the veteran player explained. "And today's disappointment comes after I had a score of 78 in my last outing. Golf is an unpredictable game that deviously defies a veteran player's daily improvement. This sport can humble you in a hurry if you take it too seriously!"

Sensing Inspector Giralo's general and lengthy melancholy mood, Agent Velardi slowly sipped his cold beer and then casually mentioned to his dejected mentor that numerous black bears have been recently sighted meandering around in the Hammonton, Batsto, Winslow Township and Waterford areas.

"Well, Sal, the blueberry farmers have been reporting that their crops are running two whole weeks behind schedule because of the severe winter we've all suffered through here in South Jersey, so there aren't too many ripe wild huckleberries in the local forests and woods. So, lacking *that* particular aspect of their food supply, the rarely seen black bears...."

"Are leaving their natural habitats in desperation and looking for any available edibles in random trash cans situated in neighborhood backyards," the Devil-may-care agent orally finished his master's statement. "Up until last week I had believed that dangerous bears were exclusively a North Jersey phenomenon. And furthermore Boss,"

Velardi voluntarily vociferated, "I just can't wait for the start of the all-too-short eight-week blueberry season. Dukes and Blue Crop are my favorite varieties followed by Bluettas. I buy them a flat at a time over at Atlantic Blueberry. And I gotta' confess, twelve pints don't last too long in my household!"

The pair of fatigued men then commenced discussing the still-existing, negative, after-effects of 2012 Hurricane Sandy, which had ravaged the New Jersey shore in Ocean City, in Atlantic City, in Pt. Pleasant and in Seaside Heights almost two years before. The original dull communication suddenly turned more upbeat in nature by next focusing upon where the two men would be traveling with their families over the weekend.

"I'll be heading down to Cape May with Gina and my two daughters," Chief Giralo indicated with a brief smile upon his porky countenance. "We'll be staying at the historic Congress Hall, just off the beach. My wife and I plan to stroll around and admire the classic Victorian architecture of the many bed and breakfast guest homes and visit several old tourist-trap mansions in the downtown area," Giralo disclosed, "while in the meantime the girls will be busy swimming in the hotel's pool. How about you, Salvatore?"

"Kathy, me and the kids will be taking the Lindenwold High Speed Line train into 'Philly," Velardi revealed. "We'll get-off at Eighth and Market and catch a cab to the Franklin Institute. A brand-new astronomy show will be featured in the Fels Planetarium, and some new educational hands-on exhibits involving the functions of the human brain will be open, too. Of course," Agent Velardi qualified, "I'll also be quite preoccupied eagerly swallowing-down a savory 'Philly cheesesteak and a warm soft pretzel being sold by hawking street vendors. Say Boss, all afternoon you seem to be distracted by something dominating your mind. Is it the four par three holes where you shot fives and uncharacteristically bogeyed on the $5^{th}$, $8^{th}$, $16^{th}$ and $17^{th}$ greens?"

"Very astute observation! That might be part of my temporary emotional depression," Inspector Giralo honestly commended and acknowledged. "Yes indeed. Shooting a three on a par five hole is a definite challenge for even the best golf pro. But actually, my Good Man; just yesterday I received something quite unusual in the mail."

"What was it?" a suddenly curious Agent Velardi asked. "A one-way plane ticket to either Baghdad or Tehran? How about a bloody horse's hoof stuffed inside a shoe box! What about King Tut's petrified right thumb, instead?"

"Listen Sal," Chief Giralo very firmly insisted. "Tonight, Gina is taking the girls to a rehearsal for their dance group's recital being staged in two weeks. Here's the plan! Get in touch with Arty and Dan, and I want all three of you promising sleuths inside my place at 7 p.m. on the nose. This peculiar item that I've gotten is somewhere between bizarre and puzzling. Show-up at my place with the guys at seven this evening and you'll fathom exactly what I mean."

* * * * * * * * * * * *

The front porch light was illuminated at 321 East Orchard Street when the three punctual FBI agents arrived in separate black government cars at precisely 7 p.m. Inspector Giralo cordially greeted his subordinates at the entrance and invited them through the foyer into the spacious home's dining room. After sitting at opposite sides of the oval conference table, the three anxious visitors awaited vocal declarations from their often cryptic superior, who was now seated next to Agent Velardi.

Finally, breaking the room's tense silent atmosphere, Agent Velardi felt compelled to render a harmless inquiry. "What's up Boss?"

"The word 'up' could either be an adverb or a preposition, depending on how it's used in a sentence," the Federal Administrator facetiously quipped. "If you say 'the balloon is drifting up, in that case 'up' is definitely an adverb modifying the verb phrase 'is drifting'. And if you say the cat climbed up the tree, then 'up' is a preposition initially positioned in an adverbial prepositional phrase, which would distinctly be modifying the action verb 'climbed'."

"Sorry I had accidentally asked such a thoroughly naked question," Agent Velardi sarcastically replied with a weak smile expressed upon his lips. "I should've known better from past conversations that I've had with a knowledgeable, expert grammarian such as yourself! I suspect that in your youth you probably were a lackluster private in the French Foreign Legion before you eventually transferred to London and miraculously evolved into an English Major!"

Diplomatically changing the subject, and also resenting being verbally challenged, Chief Giralo coyly asked his three underlings, "I trust that you Fellas' are gonna' volunteer for the upcoming St. Anthony Church Chicken Barbecue two weekends from now. Father Tom called me from the rectory up on *206* and said he needs some ambitious cooks and also a few competent counter servers. Salvatore, I believe you'll be in charge of the soda and beer responsibility; Arty, you'll handle the combined baked beans and French fries' department, and Dan, I designate that you'll be the parish's official cashier. And of course, Fellas'," Joe Giralo emphasized, grinned and then paused. "I'll be on duty meandering around and keenly supervising all the minute details of the entire operation."

"And if a mob of angry traveling clowns' attacks any of us," Agent Orsi jested, "my sage advice is to go for the juggler."

Realizing that mediocre comedy time had obviously run its course, the Federal Official grunted, cleared his throat and then closely studied the happy-go-lucky faces of his three dependable G-men. The cardboard back side of a fairly large, flat, circular, cardboard sheet had inconspicuously occupied the center of the dining room table, and without any apparent hesitation, the Chief Inspector grabbed the object with his two hands and gently turned it over, face-up. Looks of consternation suddenly appeared upon the surprised visages of the Investigator's three intrigued guests.

The three-feet in diameter configuration situated upon the table was a sort of pie graph having a circumference of sixteen curved, pasted triangular sections, all individually pointing to the round object's center. Four particular colors were deliberately presented in sequence in each of the four quadrants, consecutively repeating the outstanding hues of blue, red, yellow and brown. After analyzing the extraordinarily odd color display, being observant, Sal Velardi garnered sufficient courage to make a remotely relevant statement.

"Boss, being curious, at first, I theorized that this weird artwork was a clock, but then I quickly recognized that there were more than twelve hours being represented. I automatically concluded that the strange notion of a sixteen-hour day is absolutely preposterous, and in reality, fundamentally illogical."

Another loquacious agent sitting at the table then felt compelled to speak. "Well Chief, I originally thought that the unusual item was a two-dimensional model of the type of wheels-of-chance you ordinarily see spinning on the Wildwood and Seaside Heights boardwalks," Agent Art Orsi shared, "but then I noticed that the sixteen colors were blank without any associated numbers being provided. This thing you're showing us Boss is both rather irritating and perplexing! But I'm quite eager to find-out more about it."

"The four repeating colors in the accompanying quadrants must indicate or symbolize something rather obscure," a baffled Agent Blachford offered, "but exactly what *that* factor is in this ridiculous riddle remains a complete mystery that's really annoying my very limited mind."

Inspector Giralo then had a fleeting moment of positive inspiration. The notorious crime-solving guru methodically removed a black magic marker from his cotton shirt pocket, lifted-off the cap and then carefully labeled the pie chart's various color elements ranging from Number '1' to Number '16'.

"Now finally, the oddball chart possesses an aura of arithmetical plausibility," Joe Giralo evaluated and uttered. "But what really agitates my delicate psyche is *this* lousy typed note that had accompanied this bothersome enigma that had unexpectedly arrived on my front porch via U.S. mail at nine this morning. Does anyone have any idea with what we're dealing with here?"

"That weird pie chart reminds me of my extremely boring high school geometry class in which I was lucky to pass with a D. Where was the thing shipped from anyway?" Sal Velardi asked. "From what Post Office did it originate?"

"It had been mailed from the Trenton Post Office, but which facility in the State's Capital can't be traced or identified," Inspector Giralo regrettably divulged. "A person can obtain a similar carton from any post office, put the appropriate postage on the package and then hand it to any mail carrier who is inadvertently stopped at a traffic light while sitting in his or her delivery truck. The preoccupied driver probably only checked to see that adequate postage was on the standard carton and never checked for a return address, which if given, could've easily been a false wild-goose-chase residence. Then the traffic light might have changed, and the mail truck zoomed off!"

Seeing that his accomplished colleagues were just as beleaguered and dumbfounded as he was, Inspector Giralo then read a taunting memo' that had been stealthily inserted inside the folded-up, triangle-laden, sixteen-section round design. The three avid listeners sat virtually mesmerized as their illustrious superior slowly read the disturbing missive.

Treasured Toledo Tomfool Tumorbrain:

Today will be tedious, Tomfool. Tomorrow you'll be tattered, tortured, trounced and traumatized.

Tzar Tantalus Tease

"Apparently this new-found treacherous jokester has a certain infatuation with the letter T," Agent Velardi readily determined. "And the ludicrous salutation 'Treasured Toledo' undoubtedly is a lame way of saying 'Holy Toledo'."

"Yes, Salvatore," Inspector Giralo incidentally concurred. "And the closing I.D. is ostensibly plagued with several unique etymologies. Tsar, for instance, is a Russian corruption of Czar; a derivation of the Roman 'Caesar'. And in the realm of ancient Greek Mythology," the contemplative Boss further editorialized, "Tantalus had been a wealthy king who had offended the gods. His eternal punishment in Hades was to be chained while standing inside a huge vat of water. When thirsty Tantalus would bend over to drink, the water would quickly funnel out of the tub," Inspector Giralo explained. "Then amazingly, delicious fruit would appear on overhead branches, and when the hungry victim would desperately reach up, the apples, peaches and bananas would vanish as a volume of fresh water would predictably surge into the vat.

Consequently, our English word 'tantalize' has its origin..."

"From the name Tantalus, meaning to deeply tease," Agent Orsi realized and commented, "but Boss, I'm more impressed with this devious trickster having a psychological fixation with the letter T than I am with your totally pedantic English lesson."

"Oh, mighty Inspector. What's next on the agenda besides the imminent Chicken Church Barbecue over at St. Anthony picnic grounds?" Agent Blachford inquired.

"This scheming culprit reminds me of the elusive Puzzler, but since *that* dangerous nemesis is still isolated behind prison bars," Agent Velardi intelligently reckoned, "this reprehensible Tzar knave can't possibly be him. Perhaps that slippery criminal Thomas Cask apprehended up in Burlington has a twin brother who is just as diabolical as he is.”

“Guys, I suggest that next week you go about your regular routine investigative assignments,” Chief Giralo sternly directed. “In the meantime, if anything untoward or bizarre develops in relation to this demented new tricky twit Tzar Tantalus Tease, then we’ll swiftly meet again to organize a comprehensive attack strategy.”

* * * * * * * * * * * *

Early on Saturday morning, Inspector Joe Giralo received an urgent phone call from a rather frantic Agent Sal Velardi. After calming his almost-hysterical agent down, the ever-rational Boss insisted that the notoriously hyperactive G-man inform him about what the novel emotional pandemonium was all about.

“Chief! We can’t procrastinate!” Velardi boisterously yelled into his cell phone. “At 9 this morning the mailman dropped off four standard post office packages at my home. I opened one up and found the blue, green, yellow and brown pattern of the first quadrant, but it was sort of a convenient overlay with the numbers one-through-four along with certain small-sized related clues cut-out from magazines and Internet displays, which I presume had been run-off on what appears to be computer printer paper.”

“Stop hyperventilating Sal, like you need to be put on hospital life support!” Joe Giralo reprimanded and answered. “Your information sounds quite interesting; I’ll change *that* noteworthy description to ‘fascinating’. Now here’s how we’ll proceed. Get in touch with Arty and Dan right away. We’ll meet at eleven at Joe’s Maplewood for lunch. It’ll be my treat; I promise,” the normally parsimonious Inspector related. “I’ll call Jimmy Italiano right after I get off the horn with you and reserve the restaurant’s back room where the four of us could have some decent privacy in order to review the material that you have, and then we’ll construct some viable plan of operation. We’ll meet first and eat afterwards.”

“Sounds pretty copacetic to me, Boss! I could taste the homemade spaghetti and delectable secret recipe meatballs already!” Agent Velardi jubilantly exclaimed. “This sinister Tzar Tantalus Tease guy is going to great lengths attempting to thwart us. We’ll nab him good once we discover and solve his specific M.O.”

“Yes, Salvatore, but like most cocky overconfident idiots of his inferior ilk, his narcissism along with his basic arrogance will ultimately defeat him. I’ve seen this same-type of oddball scenario enacted before. I imagine that Tzar Tantalus Tease will spend plenty of quality time in a federal penitentiary. Matt Riley down in DC headquarters has meticulously assembled a list of heinous crimes that have recently been executed, and I have a distinct feeling that our mail post tormentor is both the organizer and the perpetrator, possibly wickedly contriving an elaborate, destructive rampage against both the United States government and civilized American society."

"It doesn't get any more complicated than that!" Agent Velardi spontaneously attested. "Boss, Arty, Dan and I will be at Joe's Maplewood up on the Pike promptly at 11 a.m."

"In all your excitement, Salvatore," Chief Giralo cautioned, "don't forget to bring the four sets of numbered blue, red, yellow and brown quadrants that had been delivered to your residence. We have to conscientiously decipher the exact whereabouts of this possibly very formidable evasive fellow, Tzar Tantalus Tease."

* * * * * * * * * * * *

The regular lunch crowd was just arriving at the popular White Horse Pike eatery when the four on-a-mission government law enforcement men met outside in the asphalt parking lot and then nonchalantly sauntered into the bustling dining establishment. Giralo, Velardi, Orsi and Blachford were soon merrily greeted by Jimmy Italiano, the "Maplewood's" congenial proprietor, who then casually escorted the foursome to the unoccupied reserved back room.

After seating themselves at a large square table, Chief Giralo carefully removed and unfolded his circular pie diagram from a brown grocery store shopping bag, and next Agent Velardi followed suit and adroitly opened the four commonplace shipping cartons and then laid the four sets of numbered and pictured quadrants directly upon the Boss's original designed pattern.

"Let's study all aspects of this sophisticated configuration and see what sort of clever hypothesis we can ascertain," Joe Giralo instructed. "Salvatore, you can now adequately describe the principal ingredients from Box #1 evident in quadrant Number One."

"Well now," Agent Velardi stated before drawing-in a deep breath to relax his abundant overzealous enthusiasm, "Blue Triangle One in Quadrant One has a tiny picture of what seems to be Edgar Allan Poe; Red Triangle Number Two has a pair of blithe nuns; Yellow Triangle Number Three has several little, quacky ducks; and Brown Quadrant Number Four has what appears to be two red-robed Catholic Cardinals."

"Nuns are often defined in slang terms as penguins," alert Agent Blachford observed and proudly expressed. 'I think I learned that salient fact from my Aunt Arctica!"

"If you incorporate the literary fact that Edgar Allan Poe had authored the classic poem 'The Raven'," completely focused Chief Giralo conjectured and authoritatively commented, "then we could have four different types of birds being identified: the raven, the penguin, the duck and the cardinal."

"I think you're on to something concrete," Agent Orsi genuinely commended. "I'll describe the four pictures from Sal's Box #2 that are now connected with the somewhat mysterious Second Quadrant. Perhaps additional bird discoveries can be made."

Art Orsi quickly remarked that Blue Triangle One inside Quadrant Two featured a set of blue jays, the Red Triangle that was shown in Quadrant Two depicted 'a cookie'; the Yellow Triangle in Quadrant Two showed amorous falcon love-mates, and the Brown Triangle in the Second Quadrant exhibited a small photo' of a flying pelican.

"Boss," Agent Orsi impulsively declared. "Three bird species are also given here in the Second Quadrant, blue jays, falcons and the pelican. But I'm a trifle confused about the out-of-place cookie drawing."

"Arty," Chief Giralo indulgently laughed. "The cookie hint is actually an Oreo, which sounds almost like 'oriole'. That pertinent understanding ought to mitigate your temporary quandary."

Next, Agent Dan Blachford boldly discussed the four Box #3 representations displayed in the now not-so-arcane Third Quadrant. "The blue portion in Triangle Number Nine has a hawk duo; the red area in Triangle Ten again has two red-robed Catholic Cardinals for the second time; the yellow segment in Triangle Eleven in Quadrant Three has the words 'three-for-five; and lastly, the brown division in Triangle Twelve indicates a rather crude drawing of a futuristic space needle."

"This entire fiasco is astonishingly remarkable!" Chief Giralo bellowed. "Remember Salvatore, the terminology 'three-for-five' we had discussed over at Buena Vista Country Club. You had maintained that the phrase meant your version of an 'eagle', which is indeed a very fabulous predator, just like the aforementioned falcon and hawk happen to be. But where does the space needle clue fit into the general equation?"

"I get it now!" boomed sports fan Salvatore Velardi. "The famous space needle is in Seattle, the city where the Seahawks NFL team plays their home games."

"Good surmising, Sal!" congratulated and praised Inspector Giralo. "The Seattle Space Needle is six hundred feet high and had been constructed for the Seattle World's Fair of 1962," the erudite FBI Chief academically pontificated. "This is grand fun we're having, making basic sense out of sheer nonsense!"

Without any sign of reluctance, Agent Dan Blachford felt obligated to review the compelling facets slyly portrayed in Quadrant Four. "Blue Triangle Number Thirteen has a pair of dinosaurs, and I'm bewildered that Red Triangle Fourteen, Yellow Triangle Fifteen and Brown Triangle Sixteen are essentially blank; each one completely devoid of necessary clues!"

"Well now," perceptively noticed Inspector Giralo. "Dinosaurs are frequently referred to as 'raptors,' the hulking prehistoric creatures being the extinct ancestors of today's birds of prey like the eagle, the falcon and the hawk!"

"Tremendous deduction, oh Great One!" Sal Velardi generously lauded. "And now I think I partially understand the whole general conundrum. The birds on the complicated diagram can synchronize with various professional baseball, football, basketball and ice hockey sports teams in different cities. For example, in Quadrant One we could have the Baltimore Ravens football team, the Pittsburgh Penguins and the Anaheim Ducks ice hockey squads, and also, the St. Louis Cardinals baseball unit."

"And Fellas'," Agent Orsi instinctively hollered, euphorically interrupting his more vociferous comrade, Agent Velardi, "in Quadrant Two we have the Toronto Blue Jays and Baltimore Orioles baseball teams, the Atlanta Falcons football squad and the New Orleans Pelicans NBA basketball players."

"And in Quadrant Three," Agent Blachford assertively contributed to the intensive analysis, "we have the Atlanta Hawks, the St. Louis Cardinals again, the Philadelphia Eagles and the Seattle Seahawks. But Boss, why are the Toronto Raptors the only team shown in Quadrant Four?"

"Because Dan, your eyes ought to examine and scrutinize the pie graph a little more accurately," Chief Giralo advised. "Notice that four of the cities depicted in Quadrants One-through-Three have two separate bird teams. My guess is that Toronto is eliminated because the Raptors already are exhibited in Quadrant Four and the Toronto Blue Jays are already alluded to in Quadrant Two. Therefore," Chief Giralo resumed his stellar monologue, "the remaining cities with two separate already-evident bird teams are Baltimore, Atlanta and perhaps the city of Phoenix, with the Phoenix Cardinals football team being a likely candidate for Red Triangle Two of Quadrant Four. I predict that Phoenix Baltimore, and maybe Atlanta will be the wily conspirators' next selected targets. But I predict that the Phoenix electrical grid is the crafty perpetrator's next designated target."

"Kindly go back to Chapter 1, Page 1," Agent Velardi requested. "You've lost me, Boss! My addled mind is now as clear as extra-muddy water!"

The FBI Official orally conveyed to his somewhat astounded three-man-audience that the ever-wary Washington bureaucrats didn't want the nosy press and TV media to learn about the drastic proliferation of certain nefarious sabotage incidents that had been occurring over the course of the last four months in metropolitan regions all across America. But the Chief Inspector deftly told his flabbergasted men about what the DC FBI brass suspected was the true significance of the intricate blue, red, yellow and brown color coding prevalent on the colorful flat pie graph.

"Blue signifies water treatment plants, and in March and April," Joe Giralo bluntly stated, "guided missiles had been launched into large facilities in Baltimore, in Toronto, in Atlanta and in Toronto again, respectively, causing widespread devastation. And then also during those two difficult months," the Chief patiently announced, "other missiles destroyed red area electrical grids in Pittsburgh, again in Baltimore and then in St. Louis."

"I see," chimed-in Agent Blachford. "Electrical grids had been compromised in Pittsburgh, in Baltimore, in St. Louis and next, according to the Boss's astute speculation, next will be Phoenix!"

"Well then; what about the four triangular yellow zones?" Art Orsi wondered and asked. "I suppose that they had been vulnerable to missile attacks, too!"

"Important radio towers had been targeted and destroyed in Anaheim, in Atlanta, and in Philly'. The unidentified three remaining targets of Quadrant Four have yet to be clearly determined."

"So, what do the Brown Triangles mean in all Four Quadrants?" Dan Blachford politely interrogated his revered fearless leader. "How do you theorize *they* fit into this growing sensational plot?"

"I've concluded that Brown denotes sewage treatment plants," the Chief Inspector instantly disclosed. "And we already know that sewage treatment operations in St. Louis, in New Orleans and in Seattle have all been greatly crippled by rocket detonations."

"And Boss, you now conjecture that this insane person Tzar Tantalus Tease is evilly orchestrating this terrible rash of catastrophic explosions all across the continental U.S.," Agent Orsi quizzed.

"Yes, Arty. As you're well-aware, domestic terrorism is dramatically on the rise," Giralo said with convincing certainty. "But within the next week, I prognosticate that this vindictive lunatic barbarian, namely Tzar Tantalus Tease, along with his malicious accomplices, will be expertly apprehended and brought to justice. And I'm more than relatively inclined to believe that the next impending strike will be enacted in one of the cities shown twice, but my gut conjecture is most probably Phoenix, Arizona!"

"Why do you' say *that* Inspector?" Dan Blachford questioned. "To me, your assumption seems to be a rather remote conjecture."

"Because Dan, in mythology, the Phoenix was a remarkable desert bird that would burn itself up and then be reborn from its ashes," Joe Giralo admirably lectured. "And I believe that these pernicious saboteurs we're about to hunt-down want to obliterate American civilization and wickedly wish to create an anarchistic New World Order from the ashes."

"My throbbing brain is about to disintegrate, and my frivolous mind is frazzled, feeble and it also feels fully frayed and fractured," Agent Velardi exaggerated and alliterated. "Let's take a break, reward ourselves and order some Joe's Maplewood homemade spaghetti and meatball platters. My empty stomach demands digesting some tasty Italian grub immediately!"

"You're truly a marvelous revelation, Salvatore!" Chief Giralo candidly complimented. "How terrifically sublime! How mystically ironic! How supremely coincidental! Yes, my Good Man," the super-elated FBI Chief propitiously added. "You've just given me a fantastic idea! In fact Agent Velardi, you've just afforded me *two* rather incredible ideas!"

* * * * * * * * * * * *

Just after dawn on the Saturday morning of the St. Anthony Chicken Barbecue, Chief Joe Giralo contacted his three trusty agents and told them to head on over to the recently remodeled Canoe Club at Hammonton Lake Park for a hastily scheduled "very important information exchange". The Boss had already arranged to have the upstairs conference room exclusively reserved while the town's gossipy Senior Citizens Club members were busy eating doughnuts and sipping coffee and tea in the capacious facility's downstairs' recreation room.

"This senior citizen hangout is called the Canoe Club because an actual boathouse existed on this lagoon's location in the 1940s and 1950s," Giralo expounded. "Canoes were rented-out and happy paddlers enjoyed gliding along tranquil Hammonton Lake from late spring to mid-fall."

"Thanks for the unsolicited local history lesson," Sal Velardi cynically balked. "But why did you summon us here at 7:30 a.m. on the same day we're supposed to be working in the sweltering heat out on the St. Anthony picnic grounds way across town?"

"I want you three wannabe' FBI inspectors to fathom that, late last night, the radical scoundrel known to us as Tzar Tantalus Tease had been taken into government custody, and the dangerous punk is now in a high-security jail up in Teaneck, Bergen County. Commissioner Matt Riley had the head FBI honchos dispatch my good golfing pal Colonel Bob Bauers along with his elite Delta Force Army Commandos to the exact site where the criminal apprehension had been strategically implemented."

Desiring to learn the specifics of the reported arrest, the three impressed agents pressed their superior for supplemental data pertaining to the apprehension of the new-found deceptive trickster/rogue. The effervescent Boss eagerly accommodated the G-men's request to further comprehend the saga's full story.

"This mendacious thug possesses the birth name Theodore Timothy Thurston, whose alias we presently recognize as Tzar Tantalus Tease. Thurston had been a radical anti-Vietnam War college hippie back in the tumultuous late 1960s. The feckless weasel began his inglorious teaching career at a Toledo high school after eventually graduating from Tulsa University in 1973. Then, thereafter, the disgraceful Mr. Thurston earned a Master's Degree in political science from Towson University and the scoundrel later obtained his doctorate from Temple over in North 'Philly."

"I see that Mr. T. never lost his special infatuation with *that* particular alphabet letter," Agent Orsi accurately generalized. "It's no wonder why this rather eccentric jerk Theodore Timothy Thurston mailed his no-return-address pie graph packages to Hammonton via the Trenton Post Office."

"Well, Guys," Inspector Giralo continued with his extraordinary explanation, "this erratic bozo criminal Mr. T. is still active teaching political science with a definite liberal bias. Over the years the unscrupulous Mr. Thurston had become friendly with other militant '60s era professors instructing their slanted ideology to gullible students in the social studies and science departments at various colleges and universities all across the country."

"And these radical left-wing dissidents all deeply despise American capitalism," Dan Blachford inferred and indicated. "And I presume all of them diabolically want to diminish this great nation by attacking its aging infrastructure in the form of water treatment plants, electrical grids, communications' towers and vital urban waste management facilities."

"But Boss, I don't yet fully understand," a still-perplexed Agent Velardi informally addressed his sagacious superior. "How was I being instrumental in helping to effectively crack-open this very complex FBI Mr. T case?"

Inspector Joe Giralo then elucidated that Professor Theodore Timothy Thurston had invested his life's savings in vacation homes and condominium properties in Toms River, New Jersey, in Titusville, Florida, and also along the Hudson River in Tarrytown, New York. The crazed "America hater" had intentions of flipping the residences and making handsome profits, but then the housing bubble of 2008 had caused the horrible recession, and Mr. Theodore Timothy Thurston then loathed the federal government even more, and like a pathetic loser, blaming his prodigious losses on good old Uncle Sam, Wall Street, and the ever-vacillating and all-too-risky American free enterprise system.

"Well then," Agent Orsi piped-up. "How do the disenfranchised, warped-minded science and humanities' professors mesh into Thurston's prolific animosity toward apple pie, truth, justice and the American way?"

"Those misguided academic clowns amply resent the USA too and the nihilistic morons have always wished to weaken the homeland nationally, thus essentially limiting American military involvement in foreign affairs," Joe Giralo aptly summarized. "This quasi-intellectual lethal snake, namely Professor Thurston, had leased an apartment in the Tacony section of Philadelphia while he was teaching at Temple, but over the weekends the cunning conspirator commuted back and forth between his main bailiwick up in Teaneck to his other place in Tacony, principally to visit his two girlfriends, one hussy up in Tenafly in Bergen County, and his second naughty lady friend residing in Tinicum, just south of Philly'."

"But Chief; you're now drifting into another conversational dimension. You still haven't answered how I had magically motivated you to interpret and then put this exceptional pie chart puzzle all together!" adamantly implored Agent Velardi. "Sometimes you make me feel like an Arctic Eskimo without an igloo, left completely stranded out in the miserable polar cold!"

The amused Boss inhaled a deep breath and resumed his participation in the fairly extensive dialogue. "Salvatore, when you had mentioned that you had an appetite for Italian 'grub' over at the Maplewood Inn, I quickly thought that 'grub' were the wriggling larvae of insects in addition to being American slang for food."

"So, what do insects and human hunger have to do with the dynamics of this all-too-confusing pie chart case?" bewildered Agent Velardi strenuously objected. "At times I think that ancient Indian totem poles and Babylonian cuneiform tablets make more sense than your irrational commentaries do!"

"Salvatore," Chief Giralo mildly chided, "common honey bees are a unique variety of flying insects. During the mating season, male flying insects called 'drones' by instinct accompany the airborne future queen bee to start a new nest or colony."

"I get the big picture now!" Agent Velardi loudly articulated. "The alienated science professor goons were assigned by Professor T to design and build remote-control drones in university towns all over the country, and the loathsome odious plotters probably attached powerful loaded guided missiles to the illicit flying machines. And after the destructive weapons were discharged into the selected urban utility plants, the drones were...."

"Were self-exploded via remote control devices precisely over the inflamed target area after evilly releasing their bombs over chosen infrastructure facilities, thus, in the process, wickedly obliterating most of the convicting physical evidence," Agent Blachford rapidly comprehended and orally rendered. "What a stunning and shocking set of outlandish circumstances!"

"Well now, my Tribal Leader. Where was Professor Thurston finally captured?" Sal Velardi insisted on knowing.

"At Teterboro Airport up in Bergen County," Inspector Giralo enunciated. "He and six of his vile comrades were caught boarding a chartered flight originally slated to take off for Phoenix, but then the plane's destination plan had been cunningly switched to Toronto, Canada where coincidentally, the entire entourage happened to become cowardly draft-dodgers way back in the tumultuous 1960s. The escaping group would've been encountered at Teterboro whether the chartered plane was heading to Phoenix or Toronto. So, as you Gentlemen can now readily determine," the very-garrulous-but-egotistical speaker emphasized, "beneficial insightful knowledge of both etymology and entomology can be absolutely crucial while professionally pursuing advanced detective work!"

"So, this delusional gigolo fanatic Mr. Theodore Timothy Thurston and his craven college colleagues were probably suspicious that the government was getting close on their heels," Dan Blachford concluded and affirmed. "They were hastily heading to Toronto, but not to see Blue Jays or Raptors!"

Just then Mrs. Eleanor Flood entered the Canoe Club's upstairs conference room carrying a tray of assorted fresh doughnuts. "Would any of you like to sample some delicious leftover pastries? I hate to see them go to waste."

"No thanks Eleanor," Chief Giralo courteously answered, much to the total disappointment of hungry Agents Velardi, Orsi and Blachford. "We're about to promptly head over to the St. Anthony picnic grounds for the Annual Chicken Church Barbecue, and I'm sure we'll soon be deluged at the fundraising event with a variety of tempting treats along with a myriad of mouth-watering desserts!"

# "Coarse Code Communication"

At noon on the last day of winter in 2014, FBI Inspector Joe Giralo had summoned his three prime agents, Salvatore Velardi, Arthur Orsi and Dan Blachford into his eighth-floor office inside the relatively nondescript 600 Arch Street Federal Building, Philadelphia, Pennsylvania. The three commuting Hammonton, New Jersey entrants soon discovered their preoccupied supervisor sitting rather comfortably in his soft, black leather swivel chair, which was located behind his huge Canadian oak desk. The Chief's pupils had been intensely focused on the last chapter of a newly purchased Nancy Drew girls' novel. Inspector Giralo's eyes promptly glanced-up and recognized the presence of the all-too-familiar new arrivals.

"Sit down Guys, and make yourselves feel right at home! You know Boys," Chief Giralo prefaced his typically confident salutation as his G-men quickly parked their individual posteriors into three, small black leather office chairs conveniently situated on the opposite side of the impressive oak desk, "this book title was the first novel my wife ever read, and her teacher actually assigned the novel for a sixth-grade book report. This imaginative adventure in my hands inspired Gina so much that I've picked-up a copy at the local Barnes and Noble for my youngest daughter to read."

"Boss," Agent Velardi blurted-out and excitedly stated. "On the drive from Hammonton to the Lindenwold High Speed Line the three of us stopped at the Dunkin' Donuts on Route 30 in Atco. The neurotic guy standing in front of us was acting real belligerent, having a regular counter fit yelling at the shocked cashier, who had accidentally given the petulant jerk the wrong doughnut bag. Then I decided to intervene in the loud mounting argument and…"

"And you whipped-out your FBI badge and threatened to have the antagonistic fellow arrested on the spot," Agent Orsi added. "And as soon as *that* sudden interaction occurred…"

"The out-of-control loudmouth amazingly calmed-down and quickly and objectively evaluated his situation, politely apologized to the distraught freckle-faced girl behind the counter and then speedily left the premises with the correct order in his possession," Agent Blachford accurately finished.

"To tell you the truth, Salvatore, I'm glad you badgered the wise guy instead of coming here and badgering me," slightly embarrassed Joe Giralo jested as the fearless leader self-consciously placed the Nancy Drew novel upon his expensive-looking desk. "And I must commend you three loyal government employees for expertly cracking-open the Tri-State Lottery Fraud Case. I've always argued that people should all have landline answering machines that screen incoming calls, and then the astute residents should habitually ignore the ones that are not originating from trustworthy friends and family."

"You're right on that count, Boss!" Sal Velardi summarily agreed. "Pennsy', Delaware and Jersey were all affected by the commonplace, sophomoric scheme we had investigated. And if I may add, even several gullible Hammonton citizens were caught off-guard and brazenly scammed, and the naïve dupes easily gave the nefarious callers their private bank account numbers so that the non-existent sweepstakes' jackpot money could be fictitiously transferred into the fooled victims' personal checking and savings accounts."

"Yes, Boss," Agent Orsi spoke-up and concurred with Agent Velardi. "The six slippery swindlers are now incarcerated awaiting official federal charges. We had traced their wily scheme to certain phone lines being utilized in the Bahamas, and when the six unwary perpetrators boarded a flight from Nassau to 'Philly, *our* reliable response team corralled the vile villains while the wicked weasels were nonchalantly passing through airport customs. The half-dozen imbeciles were en route to the Quaker City…"

"To attend an international championship soccer game between Bermuda and the Bahamas being played at Citizens Bank Park," Agent Blachford completed his vociferous colleague's lengthy sentence. "It's truly amazing how something remote like a big soccer game could cause regular avid-fan criminals' to forget everything else in their wrongful lives and then get themselves' carelessly arrested. Say Boss," Dan Blachford resumed his constructive commentary, "why have you summoned the three of us to your office? Do ya' want us to read, study and then write Sunday newspaper reviews of archaic Nancy Drew girls' novels?"

Not paying sufficient attention to Dan Blachford's annoying drivel, Inspector Giralo inhaled a deep breath and next divulged to his G-men the following strange narrative, stating that he was a good friend of newly appointed Hammonton Police Chief Ken Mortellite. An anonymous customer shopping at Canal's Liquors in the town's Blueberry Ridge Shopping Center had a few pieces of folded-up computer paper drop-out of his coat pocket before hastily paying his bill. Several minutes later, Anthony Guerere, the store's friendly partner/owner, found the two printed papers and immediately showed the odd-looking documents to off-duty Police Sergeant Ed Slimm, who had been in the establishment purchasing a bag of pretzels along with lottery tickets. Being fairly intrigued with the obvious coarse code communications exhibited on the two sheets, the next morning

314

Sergeant Slimm turned the suspicious information over to Police Chief Mortellite, who had been instantly perplexed by the weird nomenclature, so the top town cop next presented the strangely configured language over to Inspector Joe Giralo for his professional FBI interpretation.

"Wasn't the liquor store patron caught on the business's surveillance cameras?" Sal Velardi asked. "The video evidence should be a no-brainer."

"Yes, but apparently," Joe Giralo carefully qualified his reply, "the over-anxious fellow was not a town resident, and so his face was nonrecognizable to the local authorities. Chief Mortellite speculates that the guy was from somewhere else and was just passing through Hammonton on his way to an unknown destination."

"What about shopping center surveillance cameras outside the liquor store?" Agent Orsi requested knowing. "They're operating 24/7 around the clock."

"Great thinking Arty," congratulated the area FBI head honcho. "The person of interest's license number was identified and his car's toll transponder signals showed that his red 2010 Ford Taurus had entered the New Jersey Turnpike at Exit 7 at Bordentown and then left the highway at Woodbridge Exit 11, where the auto' next traveled northwest along the Garden State Parkway. The vehicle passed through one EZ Pass toll plaza at the I-280 Interchange. That's the last electronic monitoring we could trace of the Ford Taurus, since *that* red car had recently been reported stolen from a Vineland auto repair shop! Here's a distant photo' of the punk entering his Taurus that had been taken from the liquor store's rooftop camera."

"Why that's the same knave who had been harassing the girl at the Atco Dunkin' Donuts!" Agent Velardi exclaimed. "If only I knew then what I know now, I would've gotten the Waterford Township cops to take the nasty knucklehead into custody."

"Well then," inquired Agent Art Orsi, "what's so mysterious about the terminology appearing on the two folded-up sheets of paper? I'm a bit befuddled by it all. What makes you and Chief Mortellite suspicious of anything?"

"The names represented on the two separate sheets are familiar Hammonton first names and surnames, too," the Inspector revealed to his esteemed colleagues. "But the basic problem is that since the obnoxious guy who had inadvertently lost the two pieces of paper inside the liquor store is from out of town, my first reaction question is, 'Why are the litany of names typical Hammonton ones'?"

"Do you mean mostly Italian names found in the local telephone directory?" a surprised Dan Blachford inquired. "As we all know,

Hammonton is 54% Italian, mostly Sicilian, and it's the community with the highest percentage of bona fide Italian population in the entire country!"

Noticing the concern and intrigue that was evident upon his agents' faces, Chief Joe Giralo gingerly opened his desk drawer, reached inside and then distributed four stapled copies of the aforementioned two Xeroxed pages to his now-fascinated investigators, who immediately studied the first series of names on the initial sheet, which instantly suggested to each examiner an unsophisticated coded message.

"Umosella, Quincy, Young, Ulysses, Austin, Ingrid, Granato, Charles, Noto, Kristen, Raffa, Zoe, Ingemi, Edward, Olivo, Larry, Fichetola, Daniel, Carrelli, Aaron.

Testa, Peter, Olivo, Larry, Ingemi, Edward, Carelli, Aaron, Vaccarella, Samuel, Ingemi, Edward, Pagano, Rebecca, Ingemi, Edward, Carrelli, Aaron, Fichetola, Daniel, Watson, Megan, Carrelli, Aaron, Pagano, Rebecca, Noto, Kristen, Xeno, Thomas, Jacobs, Wanda, Carrelli, Aaron, Austin, Ingrid, Quinn, Nick, Carrelli, Aaron, Quinn, Nick, Fichetola, Daniel, Santelli, Ollie, Danks, Hilda, Ingemi, Edward, Quinn, Nick, Pagano, Rebecca, Baglivo, Yolanda, Hiltwine, Barbara, Santelli, Ollie, Santelli, Ollie, Noto, Kristen, Vaccarella, Samuel, Austin, Ingrid, Danks, Hilda, Carrelli, Aaron, Fichetola, Daniel, Vaccarella, Samuel, Ingemi, Edward, Quinn, Nick, Xeno, Thomas.

Pagano, Rebecca, Ingemi, Edward, Carrelli, Aaron, Fichetola, Daniel, Granato, Charles, Danks, Hilda, Carrelli, Aaron, Pagano, Rebecca, Olivo, Larry, Ingemi, Edward, Vaccarella, Samuel, Olivo, Larry, Young, Ulysses, Xeno, Thomas, Jacobs, Wanda, Austin, Ingrid, Fichetola, Daniel, Morano, Glenn, Ingemi, Edward, Fichetola, Daniel, Santelli, Ollie, Fichetola, Daniel, Morano, Glenn, Vaccarella, Samuel, Santelli, Ollie, Quinn, Nick, Vaccarella, Samuel, Carrelli, Aaron, Olivo, Larry, Austin, Ingrid, Granato, Charles, Ingemi, Edward, Austin, Ingrid, Quinn, Nick, Jacobs, Wanda, Santelli, Ollie, Quinn, Nick, Fichetola, Daniel, Ingemi, Edward, Pagano, Rebecca, Olivo, Larry, Carrelli, Aaron, Quinn, Nick, Fichetola, Daniel, Xeno, Thomas, Santelli, Ollie, Santelli, Ollie.

Lancetta, Xavier, Ingemi, Edward, Pagano, Rebecca, Santelli, Ollie, Lancetta, Xavier, Zucconi, Frank, Pagano, Rebecca, Austin, Ingrid, Fichetola, Daniel, Carrelli, Aaron, Baglivo, Yolanda."

"Please observe, Fellas'," Inspector Giralo firmly indicated, "that the 8.5 X 11-inch paper sheets have been cut-down to 8.5 X 8, meaning that the e-mail source addresses have been deliberately eliminated, both top and bottom. Also, Fellas', the punctuation marks in the body of the memo' signify pauses with one semi-colon and one apostrophe along with two periods present; of course, not counting the period at the text's end."

"This cute little puzzle should be easy as pie for us to decipher," Agent Velardi boldly claimed. "It follows a definite pattern of last name preceding first name, all oddly implemented consecutively throughout the whole message. At initial glance, the sequencing of the first letters of the first names seems to be the more logical method of approach."

"Correct, Sal!" Agent Orsi reflexively verified. "*Q*uincy, *U*lysses, *I*ngrid, *C*harles and *K*risten indeed spell the word 'quick'. The solution key to this simple cryptogram is in the first letters of the first names and not with any distracting letters shown in the corresponding surnames."

"But although the last names pertain to folks now living in Hammonton," Agent Blachford perceptively noted, "the complete names are all fictitious people. For example, I know Pete Santelli and Mike Santelli, but I don't know an Ollie Santelli."

"And I'm well-acquainted with Anthony, Rocky and Ralph Morano, but I'm unaware of any town person named Glenn Morano," Agent Orsi confirmed. "And I also know Bill and Helen Pagano, but certainly no woman named Rebecca Pagano."

"This name riddle ought to constitute no significant intellectual challenge because the vowels 'a, e, i, o, and u' are probably the most commonly used letters," Agent Blachford ascertained. "So then, the most frequently used first names would plausibly correlate to those five repetitious most frequent letters."

"Okay, Men. The e-mail authors must have some definite connection with Hammonton. Your' immediate assignment is to concisely figure-out the hidden message concealed on the first page," Joe Giralo explicitly directed. "But when you get to scrutinizing the all-important second sheet return e-mail, you'll realize that the same Hammonton names are cleverly reversed in familiar ordinary fashion, first names followed by second surnames."

"I can't wait to scribble-down the peculiar particulars of this interesting but rather amateurish coded message. Are there any other pertinent instructions for us to consider Boss?" a now-motivated Agent Velardi wanted to know.

"Yes Salvatore! Watch the Sci-fi and History Channel programs showing Nevada's Area 51 to fully learn the advanced technologies employed in space aliens' UFOs," Inspector Giralo replied and then indulgently laughed. "I believe you'll have to employ some heavy-duty reverse engineering during your message dissecting."

"Real funny, Chief," Velardi indignantly volleyed back. "Anything else of vital relevance you have to recommend?"

"Indeed Salvatore," affirmed the still-chuckling Inspector Joe Giralo. "Tonight, you can cook for yourself a can of hardy alphabet soup on your kitchen stove and then closely examine the floating letters that will surface to the top of your bowl. The vowels and consonants might actually form the exact words you're searching for! When you complete your research, you'll truly be an erudite 'Man of Letters'!"

"When shall we meet again to discuss our findings?" asked a more rational Agent Orsi. "I hope it's at a Bellevue Avenue eatery."

"We'll again gather tomorrow night at 7 p.m. at Marcello's Restaurant," Chief Giralo announced. "I'll call Marco or Tony on the horn and arrange to have the place's side room available for our cozy little FBI conference."

* * * * * * * * * * * *

The four federal men were cordially escorted into the vacant side room of Marcello's Restaurant, 225 Bellevue Avenue, soon ordered a Sicilian pizza and large Cokes, collectively discussed the Phillies mediocre spring training record down in Clearwater, Florida and then after devouring their allotted pizza slices and soft drinks, the foursome finally orally addressed the bizarre coded name list that Inspector Giralo theorized had some indispensable connection to specific crime waves being egregiously conducted in the West, in the Mid-West and also along the East Coast.

"Before I obtain your research findings on the two scrambled e-mails," the Boss began his introductory exposition, "first and foremost, I want to explicitly say that Matt Riley down at DC headquarters and I have surmised that this seemingly innocuous set of loosely encrypted e-mails might be associated with some highly illicit felonious activity that's been maliciously transpiring all over the nation. Now then," Joe Giralo continued his prologue with great emphasis, "I've taken adequate time to have all of the previously noticed Hammonton names re-organized into regular alphabetical order, first names first, and next, alphabetical last names in standard order to make it easier for us to relate to the already-given material being considered."

The on-a-mission Chief next slowly opened his black attache case and meticulously disseminated four copies of the two parallel, separate columned first and surname sections that he had prepared, and the four federal men took several quiet minutes to pensively review, assess and recollect all of the names in strict alphabetical order from A to Z, all twenty-six letters being efficiently covered.

| **Alphabetical Order First Names** | **Alphabetical Order Last Names** |
|---|---|
| 1) Aaron | 1) Austin |
| 2) Barbara | 2) Baglivo |
| 3) Charles | 3) Carrelli |
| 4) Daniel | 4) Danks |
| 5) Edward | 5) Elliott |
| 6) Frank | 6) Fichetola |
| 7) Glenn | 7) Granato |
| 8) Hilda | 8) Hiltwine |
| 9) Ingrid | 9) Ingemi |
| 10) Juliet | 10) Jacobs |
| 11) Kristen | 11) Keenan |
| 12) Larry | 12) Lancetta |
| 13) Megan | 13) Morano |
| 14) Nick | 14) Noto |
| 15) Ollie | 15) Olivo |
| 16) Peter | 16) Pagano |
| 17) Quincy | 17) Quinn |
| 18) Rebecca | 18) Raffa |
| 19) Samuel | 19) Santelli |
| 20) Thomas | 20) Testa |
| 21) Ulysses | 21) Umosella |
| 22) Veronica | 22) Vaccarella |
| 23) Wanda | 23) Watson |
| 24) Xavier | 24) Xeno |
| 25) Yolanda | 25) Young |
| 26) Zoe | 26) Zucconi |

"But Inspector," Agent Velardi anxiously piped-up and inquired. "There's only one full name on this new combination alphabetical list that I'm acquainted with and that's Frank Fichetola. This name listing must be a freak coincidence because Frank is a retired gym teacher and successful high school football coach with an impeccable reputation. As far as I'm inclined to believe, everyone else on the weird, straight-alphabetical list is an imaginary person!"

"Sal's absolutely right Boss!" Art Orsi endorsed his comrade's astute remark. "I'm also familiar with all of the last names on the paper but from experience, I can only relate to Frank Fichetola."

"Ditto!" blustered Dan Blachford. "Frank Fichetola is beyond one iota of suspicion! I'll vouch for his character and integrity any day of the week!"

"Well, Fellas'," Inspector Giralo verbally concluded. "Let's see the hidden messages in the initial e-mail *first name* sample that the forgetful guy at the liquor store had accidentally lost. Sal, why don't you read the result of your findings?"

"Quick Zelda. Please read Mark Twain and O. Henry books I had sent. Charles Lutwidge Dodgson's *Alice in Wonderland* too!" Velardi flawlessly recited.

"Gentlemen, I just fathomed something salient. I conjecture that there's some obscure secret message cloaked inside the seemingly superficial general literary sentence structure," Inspector Giralo cited and affirmed. "Please comprehend that all three given names provided so far are pseudonym substitutes for the alluded-to authors' real birth names. This new coincidental element certainly requires additional contemplation and due diligence on *our* part."

"Three unique pen names!" acknowledged Agent Velardi. "That's pretty extraordinary! If your hairy hypothesis still swimming about in your colossal mind is true Boss, then we could be dealing with something more sinister, more formidable and more surreptitious than we had originally thought!"

"Let's now abandon our dialogue regarding the first e-mail addressed to Zelda. Before we proceed to any further deductions, let's momentarily ponder the exact contents of the second return e-mail that's clandestinely addressed to this guy Zeke," the Chief strongly recommended. "That intelligent process ought to alleviate the amount of clutter currently clogging our limited minds! If you remember," Joe Giralo pontificated, "this time the names are deliberately reversed into ordinary literate order: the first name followed by the second or surname, which realistically should be easier for us to understand and interpret. Now let's make some practical sense out of all this seemingly meaningless gibberish."

The four men diligently gazed-down at their individual copies of the second encrypted e-mail, which read:

"Quincy Umosella, Ulysses Young, Ingrid Austin, Charles Granato, Kristen Noto, Megan Watson, Yolanda Baglivo, Peter Testa, Aaron Carrelli, Larry Olivo, Zoe Raffa, Edward Ingemi, Kristen Noto, Edward Ingemi.

Yolanda Baglivo, Ollie Santelli, Ulysses Young, Rebecca Pagano, Edward Ingemi, Aaron Carrelli, Daniel Fichetola, Frank Zucconi, Rebecca Pagano, Aaron Carrelli, Nick Quinn, Kristen Noto, Larry Olivo, Ingrid Austin, Nick Quinn, Wanda Jacobs, Daniel Fichetola,

Ingrid Austin, Xavier Lancetta, Ollie Santelli, Nick Quinn, Barbara Hiltwine, Ollie Santelli, Ollie Santelli, Kristen Noto, Nick Quinn, Ollie Santelli, Wanda Jacobs, Ingrid Austin, Nick Quinn, Thomas Xeno, Hilda Danks, Edward Ingemi, Megan Watson, Aaron Carrelli, Ingrid Austin, Larry Olivo.

Aaron Carrelli, Nick Quinn, Daniel Fichetola, Rebecca Pagano, Edward Ingemi, Aaron Carrelli, Daniel Fichetola, Larry Olivo, Aaron Carrelli, Ulysses Young, Rebecca Pagano, Aaron Carrelli, Larry Olivo, Edward Ingemi, Edward Ingemi, Hilda Danks, Ollie Santelli, Peter Testa, Edward Ingemi, Samuel Vaccarella, Glenn Morano, Ollie Santelli, Ollie Santelli, Daniel Fichetola, Wanda Jacobs, Ollie Santelli, Rebecca Pagano, Kristen Noto, Thomas Xeno, Hilda Danks, Edward Ingemi, Barbara Hiltwine, Ollie Santelli, Barbara Hiltwine, Barbara Hiltwine, Samuel Vaccarella, Edward Ingemi, Yolanda Baglivo, Thomas Xeno, Wanda Jacobs, Ingrid Austin, Nick Quinn, Samuel Vaccarella, Aaron Carrelli, Nick Quinn, Daniel Fichetola, Samuel Vaccarella, Hilda Danks, Ingrid Austin, Rebecca Pagano, Larry Olivo, Edward Ingemi, Yolanda Baglivo, Juliet Keenan, Aaron Carrelli, Charles Granato, Kristen Noto, Samuel Vaccarella, Ollie Santelli, Nick Quinn, Barbara Hiltwine, Ollie Santelli, Ollie Santelli, Kristen Noto, Thomas Xeno, Ollie Santelli, Ollie Santelli.”

“Boss, now that my strained mind is fully absorbed in analyzing the essence of this totally idiotic, moronic message,” Agent Velardi instinctively communicated, “and quite candidly, I must admit that it’s totally primitive English garbage in both design and substance.”

“Maybe Salvatore, but maybe not,” Joe Giralo wisely cautioned his rambunctious disciple. “Let’s strive to exercise prudent discipline and discretion while systematically attacking the basic issue at hand. For all we know, Zeke and Zelda might realistically be accomplished, dangerous, reprehensible co-conspirators.”

“Can I attempt to volunteer disclosing the nature of the return e-mail’s statement?” Agent Orsi courteously asked during a rare moment of silence. “If you give me the opportunity, Boss, I assure you, my vivid translation won’t disappoint anyone!”

“Okay hot shot,” Joe Giralo cynically remarked to his close friend. “What do you think the return e-mail says? And I only want to hear judicious and plausible answers!”

“Quick pal Zeke. You read Franklin W. Dixon book now in the mail and Laura Lee Hope’s good work *Bobbsey Twins,* and Shirley Jackson’s book, too,” Agent Orsi contributed his keen rendition. “But Boss, I’m completely stymied. What does all of this accumulative nonsensical jargon mean? It sounds so ridiculous, so bewildering that perhaps some silly-headed giddy seventh graders have composed these two preposterous missives."

"The true message Arty means that serious crimes are in progress as we speak," grim-faced Inspector Giralo swiftly determined and expressed. "It's a good thing I learned something academic in my two college literature classes. If you concentrate on the subject at hand, four distinct pen names are provided to us as valuable hints inside the letter clues: Samuel Langhorne Clemens is Mark Twain, William Sydney Porter is O. Henry, Lewis Carroll is Charles Lutwidge Dodgson, Franklin W. Dixon is a conglomeration of many different authors over the decades, the first writer being a fellow named Leslie McFarlane, and finally, Laura Lee Hope is an eccentric gender pseudonym for a fellow named Edward Stratemeyer."

"Why would a man use a female name as his own pen name?" wondered and asked Sal Velardi. "It just doesn't seem logical for a dignified male actively living and writing in the early 20$^{th}$ Century!"

"Probably because the *Bobbsey Twins* book was exclusively written for the enjoyment of girls," Joe Giralo guessed and explained. "And Salvatore, since no reader back then really was aware of the author's true persona, the public presumed that Laura Lee Hope was an authentic reclusive woman author. And Fellas', I remember reading *Silas Marner* in high school penned by George Eliot, who honestly happened to be a proud woman named Mary Ann Evans cautiously living in the pre-Victorian 1800s, which was a highly structured chauvinistic time period when book writing and publishing was almost strictly a man's domain."

"Holy moly!" articulated an impressed Art Orsi. "I had read Franklin W. Dixon's Hardy Boy novels from fifth to eighth grade. My favorite one was *The Secret of the Old Mill,* which incidentally got me' steered in the direction of career law enforcement. But truthfully," Agent Orsi graciously admitted, "I had never known that the writer's pen name was actually a composite of many authors producing Hardy Boys' works over many decades."

"Well then, I'm still a trifle confused!" confessed Dan Blachford. "How does Shirley Jackson fit into the complicated equation? I mean, I'm somewhat familiar with her famous short story 'The Lottery', but other than *that* relationship, what's her special involvement in this bizarre, ever-evolving code-sending scenario?"

"That elusive missing piece to this prolific jigsaw puzzle you've just cited is for us four sleuths to find out," Inspector Joe Giralo confided. "After you determined Lawmen fully finish celebrating the March vernal equinox, we'll assemble again on Thursday night at Bruni's Pizzeria for another extra-thick tomato and cheese pie feast.

I'll call Rick Collini and reserve a table for four in the far back corner. Be there at 6:30 p.m. sharp! I'll also collaborate on the phone with Matt Riley on any emerging developments connected to this rather fairly frustrating e-mail code-cracking case."

"If those two absurd e-mails had been sent from a college fraternity," laughed Sal Velardi, "then the crazy organization's real title should be 'Signa Phi Nothing'!"

"Stop being so repulsively obnoxious and flamboyant, Salvatore!" the mercurial-tempered Chief reprimanded. "I've heard you say *that* stupid asinine quip at least five times before. Now, I want you three ambitious detectives to get very serious about pursuing and exploiting the embedded coded messages that are slickly concealed inside the rudimentary surface-coded messages!"

"We'll strictly focus our collective attention on the given authors that have already been deciphered," Agent Velardi promised. "But this entire oddball enterprise still seems like a stranger-than-fiction misadventure to me!"

* * * * * * * * * * * *

On Thursday evening, at precisely 6:30 p.m., the four Hammonton FBI men informally met in the rear parking lot of Bruni's Pizzeria, 303 12th Street. After casually sauntering into the popular eating establishment via the back-door entrance, the quartet was immediately greeted by Rick Collini, who then deftly listened-to and jotted-down the hungry gentlemen's standard large Cokes and extra-thick double tomato and cheese pie order.

Sitting in the side back corner of the pizzeria with his three hungry colleagues, Sal Velardi insisted that the G-men should endeavor having a dinner at nearby Illiano's and also a breakfast at the Pine Crest Inn over on the Black Horse Pike in neighboring Folsom once the "Coarse Code Communication Case" had become authentic FBI history. "Maybe we can get some essential assistance from your Aunt Chovy," Velardi innocently joked to his eminent Boss, humorously referring to the customary Italian pizza topping.

"That won't be necessary!" Inspector Giralo whispered across the corner round table, restively waiting for a fellow customer receiving a huge carry-out order to pay the cashier and rapidly leave the premises. "Thanks to you Salvatore, and also special kudos to revered Shirley Jackson, to Mark Twain, to O. Henry, to Franklin W. Dixon, to *Alice in Wonderland* and to the *Bobbsey Twins,* too. Matt Riley's accomplished team down in DC and I have creatively integrated our synergies, and we've competently solved the notorious national crime wave that's been operating with impunity for the past half year. Tomorrow' morning *we* head up to North Jersey and we'll participate in a grand arrest to be enacted not far from the George Washington Bridge."

The jaws of Agents Velardi, Orsi and Blachford nearly dropped off their chins when their disbelieving ears had discerned the dramatic information. The trio then aggressively begged their furtive Boss for much-anticipated clarification of the complex matter, which still remained obscure in their separate minds.

"As you Guys know, my family has various relatives buried in all three town cemeteries," the Inspector very oddly answered, "some of them in Oak Grove over on Route 30, some of them in Greenmount on First Road and the others having their revered graves in the adjacent Catholic Cemetery."

"Were you busy yesterday having séances with your dead ancestors?" asked a rather addled Art Orsi. "Please Chief', try to be more coherent and precise in providing your opaque explanation. Your perpetual evasiveness is rapidly being perceived as rather distressful nonsense to the three of us!"

"As I was saying before being so rudely interrupted," Giralo mildly chastised Agent Orsi, "I was driving at a snail's pace around the graveyard asphalt roads when I started noticing and began reading the assorted engraved names etched upon the myriad tombstones: particularly the designations Porter, Dixon, Langhorne, Carroll, Jackson and Lee. Then it all registered and miraculously synthesized as a remarkable flash of pure knowledge igniting inside my thick skull!"

"What did?" demanded Blachford. "Was it raining inside your cerebrum and were you suddenly having a massive brainstorm? Tell us all about this supernatural miracle event! Are you intentionally being devious and facetious?"

Disregarding his alert agent's weak attempt at sit-down comedy, Inspector Giralo proceeded to reveal that when Sal Velardi had mentioned that the guy who had inadvertently left the two folded sheets of names at Canal's Liquors also was the same idiot who had gone ballistic at the shocked girl cashier at the Atco Dunkin' Donuts, then the entire big phenomenal picture incredibly came into focus. The three agents were totally bewildered by Inspector Giralo's vague and fuzzy preamble.

"What big picture!" vehemently exclaimed Agent Velardi, whose boisterous response momentarily got the whole attention of temporarily distracted Rick Collini, who almost had his airborne pizza

324

dough land squarely upon his lowered noggin. "What big picture?" the engrossed agent softly reiterated.

"The punk having the 'counter fit' at Dunkin' Donuts also was the same numbskull at Canal's who was probably buying lottery tickets several minutes before off-duty Sergeant Ed Slimm had been present in the store," Chief Giralo all-too-patiently replied while repeating already known facts. "Then while still riding along very slowly in Greenmount Cemetery, I immediately thought of *counterfeit* bills; the twenty-dollar denomination in particular. And my frenzied mind next focused on its singular image of Andrew Jackson, whose portrait as you know vividly appears on the twenty. The entire mind-boggling, mystical incident compelled my finite brain to suddenly reflect on Shirley Jackson, on her classic novella 'The Lottery", while also thinking about Andrew Jackson."

"My own brain's about to explode right out of my dense cranium and zoom like a dysfunctional rocket right through the ceiling and roof, blasting high into the upper stratosphere!" Agent Orsi graphically exaggerated. "Go back to the beginning Boss and adroitly fill us in on some more elementary details!"

"All U.S. pirates are not from Pittsburgh," symbolically joshed Inspector Giralo. "We're dealing here with going-up against an extensive, national counterfeiting ring. At first the crafty felons were successfully shuttling around low-level contraband such as illicit T-shirts, illegal music CDs, pilfered movie DVDs, and shoddily duplicated Disney toys, with all the imitation products obviously violating established protective U.S. trademark and copyright laws. When their stealthy operations began moving large amounts of merchandise around from state to state, however," the Chief elucidated and paused. "That's when Matt Riley and I became directly involved in apprehending the unscrupulous culprits, who were indiscriminately engaged in performing their nefarious activities. But Riley and I are cooperating in holding the brazen scoundrels responsible for the unauthorized transportation of illegal goods."

"Well, what cities were *their* main distribution bases?" Agent Blachford intrepidly interrogated his Boss. "Please, don't tell me one of them was Jackson, Mississippi?"

"Actually Dan, the extremely active rogues had kept small warehouses in Jackson, Mississippi, in Jackson, Ohio, in Jackson, Tennessee and in Jackson, New Jersey, not far from the Great Adventure Six Flags Amusement Park. I had discovered early in my career that most felons are so cocky and so arrogant in their habits that they eventually end-up destroying themselves by getting caught from blatantly indulging in enacting overconfidence."

"But Chief," Agent Orsi candidly questioned. "That takes care of Shirley Jackson. But what about the *Bobbsey Twins, Alice in Wonderland*, Mark Twain, Franklin W. Dixon and O. Henry?"

Inspector Giralo then embarked on a long-winded, round-about dissertation about how *he,* the master-savant, had earnestly employed the rather common, public school educational "Interdisciplinary Approach" by imaginatively integrating literature and geography. In his impressive discourse, the Chief stressed that he soon had realized that the national counterfeit smuggling syndicate had ambitiously rented a plethora of staging warehouses in Langhorne, Pennsylvania just northeast of Philadelphia, in Carroll, Iowa, in Dixon, Illinois, in Jackson as well as in Ft. Lee, New Jersey, operating a facility located right near the magnificent George Washington Bridge.

"Well Boss; that inspiring disclosure of yours simultaneously takes care of Mark Twain, Lewis Carroll, Franklin W. Dixon, Laura Lee Hope and Shirley Jackson," Sal Velardi finally comprehended and respectfully uttered. "But kindly tell me; what about William Sydney Porter, better known as O. Henry?"

"At first effort, I had avidly researched on Google and found Sydney, Australia and then learned about Sydney, Nova Scotia," Joe Giralo orally conveyed. "But then I objectively reckoned that Sydney, Australia was too far away and that Sydney, Nova Scotia was up in Canada, and that the problem of transporting counterfeit goods across international borders would not be expedient for the principal criminals to ever attempt. So, then I persevered and assiduously found Porterville, California, a town about the size of Hammonton, and *that* targeted West Coast location proved my wild theory to be accurate with seven arrests being made in *Porter*ville just this afternoon."

"Well Chief; what about the ill-tempered hostile nutcase who had left the two sheets of names at the liquor store and who had quarreled with the cute cashier over at the Atco Dunkin' Donuts?" Sal Velardi curiously asked. "No wonder why the distraught bully changed his tune when I flashed my FBI badge in his face!"

"His name is Richard Turner, but the mischievous rascal is only a minor actor in this ongoing melodrama," Chief Giralo shared. "Turner was a mere courier doing small errands and minuscule jobs for the major counterfeiting crooks. Richard Turner drove leased Budget Rental trucks between the already-mentioned various tax-free 'underground economy' warehouses, more than likely the ones located between Langhorne, Pennsylvania, and Millville and Jackson, New Jersey. The boys down in DC were able to relate Millville with Herman Melville from a third sent e-mail. In fact, this nasty messenger Richard Turner had the code name Moby Dick!"

"That leaves one more pertinent factor to be unveiled!" Dan Blachford declared. "Who are the brains behind this aggravating interstate smuggling ring?"

Inspector Giralo inhaled a quantity of oxygen and explained that the appellation "Zeke" was Ezekiel Wilson, a disgruntled former English teacher at Oakcrest High School, situated ten miles southeast of Hammonton in Mays Landing. Wilson was an aspiring author who had ghostwritten a contemporary novel for Fred Dempsey, a creative-minded business instructor at the alluded to high school. But Dempsey possessed inferior writing skills, and the greedy pedagogue only wanted to give Ezekiel Wilson a 20% editing fee for *his* prodigious labor, but the insulted English teacher demanded 50% of the book's sales' profits and royalty rights. So being adamantly defiant, Mr. Ezekiel Wilson spitefully published the book in both their names, but later a local court decision ruled that Mr. Wilson was guilty of gross plagiarism.

"What happened next?" Art Orsi asked. "Did the ongoing conflict escalate?"

"The school system eventually fired Ezekiel Wilson on grounds of attempting illegal publishing fraud," Joe Giralo shared with his now-enamored comrades. "And the frustrated writer was also cited for being a chronic alcoholic, especially being observed several times by school supervisors 'under the influence' while slurring his words when teaching Shakespeare and Cervantes."

"One more item remains to be resolved," Sal Velardi maintained.

"Who was this Zelda person? Was she an accomplice?"

"Zelda Zenobia is a legal immigrant who had migrated to America in the late 1980s," the Chief answered. "Zelda was a former gypsy of Hungarian and Greek descent, and the attractive woman in 2006 became shamed Ezekiel Wilson's romantic girlfriend and also his entrepreneurial partner in executing insidious crime. Tomorrow morning, we'll head on up to Ft. Lee on the banks of the Hudson to nab both Zeke and Zelda doing their' harmful mischief in their newly constructed contraband bailiwick!"

"Hey Guys, sorry for the brief delay! Here's your piping-hot large tomato and cheese extra-thick pizza!" Rick Collini hollered as the conscientious proprietor promptly delivered the recently prepared delectable to the corner table.

"Rick, could I pay you with a hundred-dollar Franklin!" Joe Giralo merrily stated as his three seated FBI agents covered their mouths with raised hands and pretended not to laugh at their haughty Chief's pathetically disguised reference. "It seems Rick, that I'm all out of twenty-dollar Jacksons today!"

# "The Chain Store Solution"

FBI Inspector Joe Giralo was quietly sitting upon his captain's chair at his Orchard Street kitchen nook table in downtown Hammonton, New Jersey and passively sipping his cup of Maxwell House coffee early on Wednesday morning, June 17, 2015. Wife Gina was already out grocery shopping at the local ShopRite up on Route 30, and FBI agents Arthur Orsi and Dan Blachford were away with their spouses wandering-about on separate much-needed vacations. Agent Orsi was spending the week with wife Carol exploring a rustic Virginia Skyline Drive itinerary while relaxing and staying in the vicinity of Luray Caverns. Meanwhile, hard-working Agent Blachford and his wife Bing were in Massachusetts traveling around upon the Cape Cod Peninsula while staying at an attractive motel in Hyannis.

With the normal departure of two of his trusted assistants, Chief Giralo figured he would casually occupy himself at home performing routine-but-tedious government bureaucratic paperwork while still having the time and pleasure of occasionally conversing with his third trusty associate, Agent Salvatore Velardi.

All was evolving in a copacetic manner until the wall phone rang, and the shrill ring automatically disturbed the Inspector's intense scrutiny of the Op/Ed page of the *Atlantic City Press*. Giralo was reluctant to pick-up the phone from its wall fixture, but after studying the distinguished name "Salvatore Velardi" appearing upon the caller I.D. readout, the eminent Inspector decided to break the monotony of silence and cordially engage in regular human communication.

"Boss, there's something urgent I have to tell you about!" Agent Velardi nervously exclaimed. "This morning I…"

"Sal, did you see that atrocious Phillies-Orioles game last night at Camden Yards down there in Baltimore?" Chief Giralo angrily mentioned, momentarily distracting the principal concern of his anxious caller. "It was absolutely abominable. The Phils' lost by an incredible score of 19-3. Their amateurish performance was totally disgraceful and shameful. To tell you the truth, I think I'm gonna' start rooting for the Mets!"

"Inspector, I know you like the Phillies even though the club's having a truly horrible season," Agent Velardi eagerly interrupted, "but this morning I had the shock of my life. I was…"

"And Sal," Chief Giralo calmly uttered, completely ignoring his underling's rather neurotic and mercurial tone of voice. "Guess what? The ugly game was so lopsided and so out-of-control that the Phillies manager deviated from standard procedure and brought-in outfielder

Jeff Francoeur to pitch the seventh and eighth innings. The entire scenario was more than embarrassing! It was a catastrophic fiasco! I only hope that Ryne Sandberg's job isn't in jeopardy. As they sometimes say in the chaotic television world, being in *Jeopardy* is almost as bad as being sacrificed upon the totally lethal *Wheel of Fortune,* ha, ha, ha!"

"Look, Joe! Stop changing *my* damned subject to the hapless Phillies travesty and please listen to me!" Velardi defensively begged. "I was driving…"

"And Salvatore," Joe Giralo nonchalantly resumed his typically annoying prattle. "The Orioles hit a club record eight home runs during the painful massacre. What a nasty sham that hideous contest was, if it can accurately be described as a contest!" Inspector Giralo vehemently complained. "And the Phils' best players Chase Utley and Ryan Howard are having the worse years of their careers in terms of batting. Truthfully Sal, it's all quite horrendous! I feel more than humiliated by last evening's very sad rendition after being a dye-in-the-wool Phillies fan ever since I was a mere six years old!"

"Boss, excuse my present petulance, but I need to tell you something very important that's just developed!" Agent Velardi loudly vociferated in a frustrated voice. "As I was explaining, this morning I had driven…."

"Now Sal," Joe Giralo imperatively stated, re-establishing his notorious authority during the in-progress peculiar dialogue, "as you're well-aware, Camden Yards is right down the street from Baltimore's magnificent Inner Harbor, which features great seafood and also a terrific aquarium. Now I plan on taking Gina and the girls down there when I get some time off from the Bureau the second week in July," Giralo elaborated. "And Salvatore, did you know that right this minute Dan and Bing are probably taking the ferry from Hyannis over to Nantucket Island to visit the Whaling Museum and that Arty and Carol are probably ready to wander around the Shenandoah Valley in search of some sublime tourist adventure. Now then Sal," the Chief continued and then paused, attempting to catch his breath. "Exactly why are you so motivated to buzz me on the horn at 8 a.m. on this lazy Wednesday morning. I told you yesterday that you could sleep late and then rendezvous with me for a noon lunch at the Silver Coin Diner. In fact," the talkative Inspector pontificated. "I have a fairly brilliant idea and will convey it to you. Here's a change in arrangements. Why don't you meet me at the Silver Coin up on the Pike in fifteen minutes and then you can reveal to me this vital matter that seems to be dominating your erratic emotions? And then afterwards, we'll discuss the possibility of Dan and Bing taking noteworthy photos' of the Kennedy Compound up in Hyannis!"

"Okay Boss, but you must be a relative of the late Frank Sinatra! As usual, you win and have it *your way!* And I think it's too bad that you're a century or so too late for being a ludicrous, mediocre Vaudeville stage comedian!" the fully distraught agent speaking on the other end of the line undiplomatically asserted. "As you've just constructively suggested Chief, I'll meet you in the diner's parking lot at precisely 8:30. And frankly, I must confess that I've never been so miserable in all my life! Now Boss, here's my basic problem. I'll be driving my wife's black Nissan Altima simply because my new silver Nissan Murano has just been criminally stolen!"

"Sal, do you have remote control garage doors?"

"You know that I do!" bellowed back Agent Velardi. "What's *that* simple reality got to do with the price of olive oil in Sicily or the amount of exportable tea in China?"

"We'll meet in fifteen minutes at the Silver Coin!" the Inspector's terse-but-vague voice insisted. "I hope you still have an appetite."

* * * * * * * * * * * *

When Inspector Giralo deftly guided his gray Chevy Suburban into the Route 30 1950s art deco-styled Silver Coin Diner, the Boss immediately spotted impatient Sal Velardi parked in his wife's black Nissan Altima. The pair simultaneously emerged from their respective vehicles, shook hands and true-to-habit, the Chief initiated the discussion, and his bothersome prattle again was concentrating on minor, irrelevant details.

"Back in the '60s, this building was then the Scaffidi Diner and conversely, the Midway Diner, which is now the Midway Medical Building down the highway, well anyway, Salvatore," the Inspector proceeded to recollect and communicate his specific immaterial, trivial jargon, "the new owner Gus really jazzed-up this landmark edifice, especially the bathrooms, adorning them with fancy tile floors and exquisite marble walls."

"Gus the Greek really did a splendid job renovating the place for us Italians, all done in our mostly Sicilian town," Agent Velardi keenly quipped. "Kathy and I either eat here or, when we want great Italian cuisine, we go down the road to the Maplewood."

"Yes," Inspector Giralo pleasantly concurred with his still-upset companion. "Both the Silver Coin Diner and the Maplewood Restaurant highly benefit from the heavy traffic coming south from *206;* of course, the hungry motorists and their thirsty passengers are eager to get to the Atlantic City casinos. Now let's step inside this popular establishment so that you can tell me all about your recent automobile purloining conundrum! Say Sal, did I ever tell you that the last time I had vacationed in Hyannis was on Gina's and my second wedding anniversary. We ate at a place called the Priscilla Mullins. I forgot to recommend it to Dan before he ventured north. On second thought, the restaurant might no longer be in business."

The two government officials entered the well-designed retro' building and were promptly escorted by the cute hostess to a remote green leather booth in the diner's rear room. A newly hired brunette waitress, who politely introduced herself as Bianca, quickly poured two cups of freshly-brewed coffee and enthusiastically jotted-down the men's orders of burgers and French fries. After the ambitious waitress departed their booth, the anticipated verbal exchange between the newly-arrived Silver Coin patrons ensued.

"Sal," Inspector Giralo began his non-sensational preface. "Why didn't you inform me right away this morning that your precious car had been so expertly pilfered. Instead, you preferred engaging in impertinent small-talk about the Phillies debacle suffered at the hands of the Orioles down at Camden Yards last night."

"Well Boss," Agent Velardi disappointedly answered, cleverly feigning a courteous apology, "I suppose I had experienced trouble getting to the crux of the matter, which is a rather poor practice that I must ardently learn to correct."

"Well now," Chief Giralo continued his unspectacular oratory, weakly disguised in a subdued and soft narrative. "Things could've been much worse. Always perceive the glass as being half-full, that's what I staunchly maintain! For instance, instead of sulking about your car being hijacked, be happy your house didn't burn-down!"

"You're right about *that* salient observation Boss," the still-upset federal agent bluntly acknowledged, abruptly shrugging his' broad shoulders. "While you were preoccupied watching the Orioles trouncing the feeble Phillies last night, Kathy and I had journeyed east to Harrahs Casino to spend the night. We had planned to do a little gambling and to see a show. When we eventually returned to Hammonton at 7:30 this morning, we vigilantly stopped at A.T. Auto Clinic on Fairview Avenue, and we were instantly met by the owner Louie who…"

"Who had just discovered that your newly serviced SUV had been successfully swiped by some downright greedy crooks," the alert listener concluded and declared. "And of course, Salvatore," Joe Giralo stressed while slowly scratching his right elbow. "Louie over at A.T. Auto had already notified the Hammonton Police about the audacious and inexplicable grand theft auto episode.”

Agent Velardi then further revealed that honest and reliable Louis Tedeschi had sworn that he had never before had a car stolen from (or ever vandalized inside) his open asphalt parking lot in over thirty years of doing business in Hammonton. And the outspoken mechanic wished that the thieves responsible for the illicit heist ought to spend at least twenty years of solitary confinement in austere penitentiary cells as deserved punishment atoning for their brazen felony.

“From your graphic description. Sal,” Joe Giralo assessed and commented, “this’ rather bold-faced crime you’ve just described sounds like a professional Mafia larceny operation to me. Here comes Bianca with our fast-food lunch orders. After we consume our meals, I want to accompany you over to your residence and closely examine your garage doors along with your remote-control access.”

The men eagerly ate their delectable early lunches and then drove their respective vehicles over to Salvatore and Kathy Velardi’s Peach Street home where the black Altima driver soon raised the second garage door by touching the convenient button situated directly below his rear-view mirror. The government men exited their cars and then entered the half-empty garage, now devoid of the much-valued and highly-cherished silver Nissan Murano.

After carefully examining the remote-control mechanism upon the back wall, Inspector Giralo delivered a quite surprising oral statement to his loyal colleague. “Well Salvatore, everything seems to be in order. I’ve developed a unique hypothesis about what probably happened and how your expensive car had been snatched. But I’ll reserve my making any plausible evaluation until the appropriate time; that is, when I’m thoroughly certain of the general extenuating circumstances. Until then,” Inspector Giralo related to his baffled and puzzled associate, “I’ll prudently reserve judgment and keep my off-the-beaten-track theory all to myself. What has on-the-surface appeared to you my dear Salvatore as being a remarkable theft might in actuality only really have been several perceptive felons taking advantage of a tempting opportunity and therefore, daringly enacting a slightly bizarre crime that only required a rather fundamental knowledge of a certain electronic operating device.”

“As usual, I’m entirely perplexed by your all-too-confident, nebulous sagacity,” an astounded Agent Velardi lividly replied. “Sometimes Boss, your rambling language makes both me and my intelligence feel totally inadequate and inferior!”

“Your current dilemma Sal is plagued by the fact that you’re being too *subjective* about your regrettable loss,” Giralo determined and boisterously shared. "And obviously, in your mental condition you can't be *objective,* and quite candidly, you aren't thinking in a true detective mode because you're personally involved in your car loss. In short, you're thinking emotionally instead of rationally."

* * * * * * * * * * * *

For the next several days, Chief Giralo assiduously applied his time doing meticulous Internet and FBI computer work in a dedicated effort to sagely solve Agent Velardi's mysterious car theft. On Saturday morning at ten o'clock, the now-paranoid larceny victim received a call on his cell phone from his enigmatic superior.

"Hi Boss," the aggravated agent lethargically answered. "Are you going to remind me how disgusted you feel ever since the Orioles almost swept the Phillies in the Citizens Park home game series, and how infuriated you are that the Phils' have now lost fifteen of their last twenty games? I'll drive you over to the drug store for some aspirins if you ask me to render that errand for you. Don't feel isolated! I think I need a few miraculous pharmacy tablets to swallow-down, too!"

"Don't forget, Salvatore. Tomorrow is Sunday, June 28th. You, Arty, Dan and I are scheduled to work the Lions Club charity tent at the annual town Blueberry Festival. Rest-up so that you can sell all those delectable muffins, strudel, pies and turnovers!"

"Is that why you've called me?" peevishly protested Velardi. "Here I'm anguishing about my missing SUV and now you have the unsolicited audacity to remind me of trivia that's presently totally irrelevant to me that I already know!"

"Salvatore, I believe I have this new-found stolen SUV case cracked. Meet me at Casciano's Coffee Bar and Sweetery in half an hour. Linda makes the most scrumptious bacon and scrambled egg on warm Italian bread sandwiches I've ever had the pleasure of tasting. In fact," Joe Giralo articulated in his inimitable parlance, "I'm in such an ecstatic mood this beautiful morning that I'll gladly treat you to a hardy lunch!"

* * * * * * * * * * * *

FBI Agent Sal Velardi and Inspector Joe Giralo greeted each other in the town's Vine Street parking lot that was opposite the historic Eagle Theater and with an on-a-mission cadence entered Casciano's Coffee Bar and Sweetery via the eatery's glass back door. Linda Cashan, the business's proprietor, intercepted her friend the Chief

Inspector before he and his agent could ever approach the main counter, and then after a few perfunctory complimentary salutations, the well-mannered lady swiftly escorted the federal patrons to the only table and two accompanying chairs situated outside the front window of the 212 Bellevue Avenue coffee shop. After recording two duplicate orders of the famous bacon and scrambled eggs on warm Italian rolls entrees, the suave owner reentered her place of business to personally prepare the selected coffee and dual food items.

"It's really nice with us detective gurus sitting out here on Route 54 and breathing-in all of the toxic carbon monoxide fumes coming from the eighteen wheelers, most of them originating from Vineland and Bridgeton, hauling freight up to New York," bristled Velardi, just as a massive semi-truck motored by. "Aren't there any better ways on this planet to get asphyxiated? We might as well be sitting inside Mt. Etna and enjoy inhaling the active volcano's lethal methane and carbon monoxide fumes! Boss, you should've been more considerate and creative and should've brought along two vintage World War II gas masks with you?"

"Privacy does at times have its own detrimental consequences," introspectively admitted the Inspector. Seeing that his valued comrade was still distressed about *his* confiscated SUV, Giralo endeavored to change the subject from environmental fossil fuel pollution to Sal Velardi's disastrous casino experience.

"Did you have any good luck playing the slots and tables at Harrahs?' Inspector Giralo asked. "I presume that you and Kathy had stayed overnight at the gaudy tourist trap and had driven back to Hammonton the following morning in the black Altima while Louie Tedeschi was busy servicing your silver Murano that, if I recall, you had purchased back in early January."

"That's generally what happened, including *our* unbelievable bad luck on the casino floor," promptly acknowledged the veteran agent. "Just like Arty down there in Luray and Dan up in Cape Cod, as you know Boss, I too have taken the week off. I figured Kathy and I would rest and enjoy a couple of day trips down the shore to soothe our frazzled nerves. Then this wicked, detestable SUV dilemma occurred, and I gotta' confess that it has really rattled my spirits in a negative manner!"

"Well, Dr. Salvatore. If it'll alleviate your rampant apprehensions," Inspector Giralo uttered just as Linda Cashan was delivering the men's coffee and warm sandwiches. "I've adroitly performed some essential research, and in the process, I've isolated the scoundrel organization along with the dastardly culprit who had committed the unfortunate crime at hand." Agent Velardi was staggered beyond belief upon hearing his erudite Boss's rather startling revelation. The stunned FBI man purposely ceased his incessant chewing and then sternly demanded that his often-surreptitious supervisor fully disclose what *his* extensive research had amazingly uncovered.

"Now Salvatore," Giralo shrewdly cloaked and initiated his explanation. "Tt all happened when I was inside the Hammonton Wal*Mart standing in the outdoor garden department while looking for a comfortable summer porch chair, the same kind that Arty had bought for $35.00. I then inadvertently overheard two Mexicans, apparently crew-leaders in town for the June blueberry picking season, suddenly locating some insect repellent situated upon a high shelf. The first fellow said words to the second one, something like, 'Mira! Aqui! Tu compras eso'!"

"What on Earth are you talking about?" sarcastically criticized the rattled stolen car victim. "I hate to sound too cynical, but your language is borderline insanity! I never studied Spanish in high school, so what in tarnation do those words mean in translation?"

"The *palabras* mean 'Look! Here! Buy this'!" Giralo explained.

"What does a can of insect spray have to do with my pilfered Murano?" grieved Agent Velardi in a gruff, un-politically correct baritone. "In all honesty, I think you're ready for a long incarceration at Ancora State Mental Hospital!"

"Don't be ridiculous!" volleyed-back a mildly insulted Joe Giralo. "I'm deeply serious about my' on-the-money Spanish interpretation. Simply focus on the word 'Aqui', which incidentally is what inspired me to easily unravel *your* seemingly complicated felony. The nomenclature sounds very similar to the phrase 'a key' in English; in fact, my mind instantly focused on your Nissan 'Smart Key'. Now then Salvatore, did you have any visitors or repairmen arriving at your domicile between Monday morning and Wednesday afternoon?"

"Why yes!" Agent Velardi reflexively verified. "My distant cousin Buster Branca, who now owns a small appliance store over in Egg Harbor. He delivered and installed a new washer and dryer in my laundry room; that is, after gingerly removing the old appliances. Now just because Buster was once affiliated with the 'Philly Mafia twenty long years ago," the FBI man adamantly stated, "my reformed relative has done his required jail time and has solemnly promised to lead a straight life after being released by the merciful warden after doing half *his* sentence for exhibiting good prison behavior."

Inspector Giralo then very deliberately divulged to his stubborn colleague that Louie Tedeschi was an honorable and reputable automobile mechanic and had been quickly eliminated as a prime suspect in the extraordinary car larceny caper. The Chief then reminded his competent agent that twenty years prior to *that* current June date, Buster Branca needed money to pay-off colossal mob gambling debts and had savagely robbed a prominent blueberry baron of a twenty-thousand-dollar horde of cash taken from the family safe, the wealthy grower's handsome sum being designated for a Friday afternoon farm worker payday.

"The scared-to-death farmer and the wife were cruelly tied to the mansion's staircase banister; Buster and his fellow thugs had used thick telephone cords, and then the petrified couple's mouths were gagged with dirty handkerchiefs, and next the victimized pair was subsequently threatened at gunpoint," Giralo bluntly related. "My diligent computer research has proficiently detected that *your* unscrupulous and unethical distant cousin Buster Branca has again accumulated enormous gambling debts and as a result, has been specifically targeted to being snuffed-out by the ruthless 'Philly syndicate; that is to say, if those long-term, huge horserace debts are not completely satisfied."

"Well then, how did you ever narrow-down the list of potential suspects to good old Buster Branca?" Agent Velardi incredulously asked his mentor. "There still remain too many unidentified pieces to this fantastically mendacious theft cryptogram! And kindly divulge exactly how this matter of 'a key' directly fits into the whole non-majestic scheme of things."

Inspector Giralo momentarily stared at his companion and next slowly communicated that seven other SUV heists had recently transpired inside other wealthy suburban communities in New Jersey, in Delaware and in the Pennsylvania, which would naturally bring the FBI into the crime-wave equation by virtue of the felons crossing state lines. But the real 'key' had occurred when the thorough-and-efficient Chief had carefully inspected the remote-control buttons inside the two-car garage at 633 Peach Street.

"Salvatore," Giralo attested after gulping-down the last savory bit of his bacon and egg sandwich. "When I had commenced my preliminary investigation inside your garage, I aptly noticed that you have the old-fashioned type of garage door buttons attached onto your composition-board wall. Your remote-control doors can be opened outside by any decent electronic scanning device that runs a series of signals and then easily deciphers your home's special code. Your obsolete operating system lacks the advanced security features of the newer models!"

"So, according to your wholly sophisticated theory," the suddenly enlightened agent determined and enunciated, "my undependable and devious cousin Buster Branca had aptly observed the second set of car keys hanging upon the laundry room wall when he had delivered the new washer and dryer. But how could the unpredictable maniac manage to borrow the reserve set of keys, steal my treasured Murano from Louie's asphalt lot, and then get the new keys back inside my house during my overnight absence at Harrahs Casino? Are you saying that Buster has one of these electronic scanning devices?"

"As you know Salvatore, if your car stays at A.T. Auto Clinic overnight, Louie keeps the original set of keys locked away inside his office safe," Inspector Giralo convincingly revealed and indicated. "Now apparently, Buster Branca was knowledgeable of your mechanic's precautionary 'key' practice too! So, the slippery scoundrel used an advanced electronic scanner to open one of your non-modern garage doors. Branca entered your home and next, the non-reformed gambling addict temporarily acquired your second set of SUV keys. After doing that," Inspector Giralo emphasized, "the cunning knave lowered your garage door with his special scanner and then probably driven by an anonymous friend, the sly duo traveled over to Louie's mechanic shop to illegally obtain your SUV, which Buster probably had perceptively seen parked there earlier in the day. Then the misguided twosome drove from the A.T. Auto Clinic on the Pike and…"

"And my car was probably driven to a Mafia chop-shop over in 'Philly, repainted and then sold at a bargain discount to an unethical used car dealer, who would then legitimately or illegitimately get a new VIN and complementary auto' registration for my Murano's resale. And after again secretly using the electronic scanner, my corrupt cousin next furtively replaced the borrowed second set of keys back onto their hanging hook in my mudroom before swiftly abandoning the premises," G-man Velardi logically comprehended and finally ascertained. "What a preposterously exasperating and reckless criminal enterprise!"

"That just about summarizes the ultimate fate of your lost Murano," Inspector Giralo remarked before sipping the remainder of his flavorful coffee. "I trust you have sufficient gap-insurance to cover the balance of your expensive investment."

"Has Buster been arrested anywhere in the Delaware Valley region?" Salvatore Velardi hesitantly inquired, instinctively gritting his teeth about being naïve when the Peach Street resident should have been more distrustful and vigilant. "The felonious jerk was so arrogant and so stupid that he probably has been involved in various car thefts in three different states and as a result of his previous on-file record, my questionable cousin was particularly vulnerable to astute

FBI detection along with the impudent fool being tracked by Tri-State police department surveillance."

"It's my pleasurable duty to inform you that your infamous cousin will be apprehended Monday afternoon at Philadelphia International Airport," Inspector Giralo chuckled and then broadly grinned. "Buster's returning home on U.S. Air, fully clueless about his inevitable fate. He'll be arriving as an unassuming passenger on a regular flight from Las Vegas, the renowned gambling mecca where the nefarious rogue also owes the West Coast mob some fairly significant debt obligations. It appears that your imbecile cousin keeps robbing Peter to pay Paul without ever figuring-out how to ever become either Peter or Paul!"

"So Boss, you're saying that I've allowed a dumb, moronic cousin of mine to steal my sacred SUV!  To capsulate the whole weird story in a nutshell, my un-illustrious, idiotic cousin had treated my Home-Sweet-Home as if it was an unprotected computer, and the heartless villain had then diabolically *hacked* into my non-secure two-car garage. I can't believe I had been so gullible!"

"Yes Sal," Giralo affirmed, clearing his throat. "And Buster's sinister yet-to-be-identified accomplice foolishly followed Branca and your Murano into 'Philly, dropped it off at a cooperative chop shop, and then the punk helper drove Buster back to your Peach Street home while you and Kathy were still in Atlantic City. Your hoodlum cousin guilefully entered the house by means of your' targeted garage door, and after utilizing the electronic scanning device, the small-time crook deposited the second set of keys back upon the appropriate wall hook, and after accomplishing that simple task, then your unscrupulous kinsman sneakily lowered the garage door, the successful crime culminating with the craven pair merrily hopping into their get-away vehicle and proudly and jubilantly departing your violated property."

"I should've never foolishly told Buster that Kathy and I were going to spend the night at Harrahs Casino!" grumbled Velardi. "I should've known better. As is often said, a person can pick his friends but not his relatives!"

"Of course, Sal, much of my narrative about Buster Branca's activities is still predicated on conjecture," Giralo modestly confirmed. "But in the final analysis, I believe that most of my speculation will prove to be exactly what had occurred while you and Kathy were away thirty miles east in Atlantic City."

Just then, right before the boss's lips could formulate another reasonable anecdote to share, the FBI men's ongoing dialogue was rudely interrupted with the loud rhythm of Inspector Giralo's cell phone, which was soon answered on the second ring.

"Oh hi, Arty. How was your little hiatus down there at Luray Caverns? Isn't that scenic Blue Ridge Drive exceptionally panoramic this time of year? Did you take lots of pictures at the numerous mountain overlooks along the way? Tell me. Are you ready and rested enough to work the Lions Club concession at tomorrow's hectic Blueberry Festival?"

"Forget the all-too-mundane, sanctimonious small-talk," objected an extremely mortified and agitated Agent Arthur Orsi. "I've just pulled into my driveway, raised the garage door with my remote-control device and lo and behold, my wife's new Toyota Camry is gone! Vanished! What a horrible nightmarish calamity!" the disgruntled caller yelled. "Don't antagonize me Boss because right now I feel greatly devastated and completely violated!"

"Mira! Aqui! Tu compras eso!" riddled-back the now-jovial Inspector Giralo in very poor Spanish. "Aqui!" the wily FBI Chief soon intentionally reiterated to his always-trustworthy but now-beleaguered phoning disciple, much to the total befuddlement of already excessively flustered and exploited Agent Arthur Orsi.

"What did you say?" the caller asked. "I must say, Inspector, that your Spanish is atrocious!"

"I said that you shouldn't worry about your dilemma one iota, Arty! Trust in what I am telling you. Your *bueno amigo* Senor Salvatore will professionally explain to you the entire fiasco later this afternoon!"

# "FBI Interstate Interdiction"

On Monday afternoon, June 30, 2014 FBI Inspector Joe Giralo reserved the Golden Galleon Lounge at Hammonton, New Jersey's Frog Rock Country Club for an important and hastily arranged conference with his three loyal government agents: Salvatore Velardi, Arthur Orsi and Dan Blachford. Rocky Colasurdo, affable proprietor of the popular local golf course and also a close friend of "the Chief", was gracious enough to provide the private dining room meeting on short notice. As the four federal arrivals comfortably sat around a circular table, sipping hot coffee and munching on assorted Danish pastries, "the Boss" was monotonously describing what he was planning to do over the upcoming July 4th holiday weekend.

"I'm glad the four of us are taking much-needed weeklong vacations," the talkative, grim-faced supervisor firmly remarked. "I know that Gina is expecting…"

"Yes," agreed Agent Velardi, inadvertently cutting-off his mentor's declarative sentence. "It's a pleasant relief not to have to worry about pursuing vile interstate drug traffickers, sly counterfeiters and wanton kidnappers all over the East Coast. Oh, sorry to interrupt you, Boss. Where did you say you were going this weekend?"

"Well, now that the annual Red, White and Blueberry Festival has been another huge success," Inspector Giralo evaluated and shared, "and yes indeed, I'm also happy that the Lions Club sold-out of our blueberry muffins, strudel and pies, so as I was saying, this weekend I intend to…"

"Professor Giralo," impulsively chimed-in Agent Orsi. "I honestly think that Hammonton made a colossal mistake having over ten thousand people attend this year's Blueberry Festival while also having 1,200 industrious bikers race twice around the entire downtown district in the Atlantic City Triathlon Challenge. Bellevue Avenue looked like the Olympics, and traffic congestion all over town was an absolute pain-in-the-neck for hundreds of disenchanted motorists trying to attend the overcrowded festival."

"Art's right!" Agent Dan Blachford contributed to the impromptu dialogue. "Could you imagine how much stamina the whole marathon event required of the well-trained participants? First, they had to swim over two miles across designated Atlantic City Bay Channel. Then the superb athletes had to compete in a 116-mile bike race, first zipping down the A.C. Expressway, then energetically pedaling twice around Hammonton's perimeter, and next venturing a full thirty miles back to the boardwalk; all of that exhausting physical endurance occurring before finally engaging in a grueling 25K plus run. Er, excuse me Boss," Blachford politely apologized, "but what were you saying before all-too-neurotic Arty so rudely butted-in."

"I was saying that I had rented a week's stay in a terrific beach house at 16th and the Boardwalk for the wife, daughters and me in Ocean City," Chief Giralo divulged. "The nice place is located right where the boardwalk narrows on the south end, and the attractive home has a magnificent view of the ocean and beach from the second-floor open-air front porch. Gina really loves it! And exactly what sort of 4th of July mischief are you preparing for Salvatore?"

"Well, Guys," Agent Velardi prefaced. "I'm taking Kathy and the kids to the House of Blues inside the Showboat Casino, and we're going to see the Huey Lewis and the News Show. I was quite lucky to get decent seat tickets for one obvious reason," the very capable G-man emphasized. "Some folks fear that Hurricane Arthur might veer west and skirt the Jersey Coast, causing Atlantic City to be suddenly evacuated, but the latest weather forecasts indicate that the first tropical storm of the summer season is fortunately heading several hundred miles out to sea."

"I've read where the Showboat is closing its doors on August 31st," Joe Giralo reliably informed his three yawning listeners. "Counting the Atlantic Club and the Revel, that makes three boardwalk casinos going bankrupt and defunct in one year. There's entirely too much competition in the local gambling industry with numerous casinos now open in 'Philly, in Chester and in New York, not to mention the myriad of similar alternative venues thriving out in Las Vegas."

After a moment of rare silence, Agent Orsi felt compelled to reveal his own family's weekend plans. "Well Boss, Carol, the kids and I are traveling down to the other Ocean City, you know, Ocean City, Maryland. Last year we stayed at the Quality Inn at 17th and the Boardwalk, but this year we rented a three-bedroom luxury condo' in the newly constructed Belmont Towers, conveniently situated on Dorchester and the boards."

"I'm glad that the weather bureau named the non-destructive imminent hurricane 'Arthur' after you," Joe Giralo jested to Agent Orsi. "And what about you Dan? Are you driving up to Coney Island to again rival champion Joey Chestnut in the world-famous Nathan's hot-dog-eating contest? Last year the incredible guy swallowed-down forty-nine dogs and buns in a mere ten minutes. I understand the fella' diligently practices all-year-long for the annual July 4th event!"

"No Boss," Agent Blachford replied with a forced smile. "Unlike you three seashore enthusiasts, Bing and I are going to experience a cultural weekend. On Saturday, morning my wife and I will be traveling into 'Philly, and we'll be touring the incomparable Art Museum. We haven't been there in five years and want to see if they've added any new noteworthy exhibits."

"Enough irrelevant discussion of your thoroughly predictable, standard, preliminary conversations!" Agent Velardi courageously protested to his wily superior. "What's this special parley that we're now miserably engaged in all about? I hope it doesn't interfere with me seeing Huey Lewis and the News! If I recall," the worried objector indicated. "I once missed seeing Billy Joel perform at Boardwalk Hall because *you* had assigned me to a lonely swamp surveillance detail out in the vicinity of Ft. Dix!"

The unflappable Chief ignored his flamboyant agent's rebellious diatribe and then slowly removed a commonplace school oak tag folder from his black briefcase and adroitly found four sheets of computer paper. Joe Giralo next distributed printed copies to his three curious underlings, who immediately scrutinized the unique subject matter with bewildered expressions evident upon their suddenly pallid, tense faces.

"Matt Riley down in DC headquarters informed me that this communication enigma had been intercepted by the CIA, assisted by the NSA. Let's see what you three clever sleuths can derive from this most fascinating-but-baffling mathematical statement," the Inspector imperatively suggested. "Quite frankly, I'm relatively baffled by most of the characteristic elementary school arithmetic that, according to the Washington brass, has apparently originated from rather questionable and insidious sources. I'll give you distinguished fellas' a minute or so to keenly concentrate your collective minds on this rather peculiar newfound puzzle."

The four seated men next methodically examined the following strange numbers and accompanying math' functions very closely, their veteran psyches completely engrossed in their current endeavor.

"70 + 55 - 67 + 76 + 95 - 30 + 90 + 55 - 41 + 10 + 5 - 101 + 20 + 75 - 29 + 30 + 45 - 75 + 66 + 395 - 50 - (2 x 347)"

"41-40-70"

"Notice that the seemingly indecipherable array is cunningly presented in sets of three numbers, in each case, two additions are preceding one prominent subtraction," Chief Giralo related. "But like most fundamental operations involved in simple algebra," the Boss boringly lectured, "one should first perform the function identified *inside* the given parenthesis and then pursue solving the remainder of the total problem.”

“But what do you suppose the 41-40-70 business at the bottom means?” Agent Velardi asked. “I see it as being some sort of numerical quagmire.”

“That’s the easiest part, Salvatore!” Chief Giralo confidently explained. “The six numbers you’ve just cited are similar to a closing signature, or indeed comparable to the word ending, or to the last phrase in a letter. If you reverse the six numbers from backward to forward,” the Boss haughtily instructed, “we then have 07/04/14, or the impending July 4th Independence Day! How coincidental can you get?”

“I feel like a victimized mouse trapped inside an incomprehensible maze!” Agent Orsi criticized his often-aloof mentor. “Where’s the nearest exit?”

“Now you’re making the three us feel totally stupid!” Agent Velardi stubbornly complained. “But I’ve just realized something fairly significant. If this is some sort of sinister, malicious plot we’re now studying, we only have four days to correctly figure-out this devious mystery and to then swiftly act. There goes my highly anticipated Huey Lewis House of Blues concert; my future treasured experience is being thrown completely out the open window!”

“Just like Sal, I still feel grossly overwhelmed by all of this’ crazy math’ jargon!” Art Orsi assessed and spoke. “I hope that this frustrating grammar school arithmetic stuff doesn’t sabotage my Ocean City, Maryland family excursion!”

“I’m gonna’ need a calculator to be able to determine a correct answer to the rest of the formula,” Sal Velardi regretfully commented. “Math’ has always been my academic Achilles Heel. I had failed Algebra II and Trigonometry in high school and had to travel by Public Service bus twenty-three miles during two Julys from Hammonton to summer school at Audubon High.”

“I’m done the numbers in my head,” math’ wizard Dan Blachford boasted to his still-preoccupied colleagues, “and I find that *this* particular long set we’re evaluating is really pretty amazingly intriguing, I must say. The final tabulation is....”

Just then Frog Rock Country Club owner’ Rocky Colasurdo and Hammonton Police Lieutenant Kevin Friel briskly entered the Golden Galleon Lounge with flustered looks showing upon their anxious faces.

“Inspector Giralo!” Lieutenant Friel eagerly exclaimed. “Sorry to disturb your in-progress think tank! I was just casually patrolling the Frog Rock parking lot across Boyer Avenue when I observed a

344

definite irregularity in *your* license plate I.D. Most New Jersey plates have a letter followed by two numbers, followed by three letters again; for example, B17-CRS."

"Of all the unmitigated audacity! Do you mean that some brazen felons have clandestinely removed my legitimate license plates in broad daylight and the scumbag weasels have wickedly substituted counterfeit ones in their place?" an infuriated Giralo gruffly interrogated the all-too-calm police officer.

"Not only that!" Rocky Colasurdo bluntly added. "All four of you Gentlemen now have the exact same plate number. Here it is. I've scribbled it down! 41-40-70!"

"Inspector!" Agent Velardi articulated and finally comprehended. "Instead of us being hot on the trail of vicious criminals, it appears that unscrupulous crooks and harmful local thugs are doing expert reconnaissance on us!"

"I suspect that these unsavory individuals chasing us around are not simple mediocre crooks and thugs Salvatore!" Chief Giralo concluded and enunciated. "Here's my gut instinct. I now believe we're dealing with some very formidable and exceptionally dangerous lunatic terrorists!"

* * * * * * * * * * * *

Early on Tuesday morning, July 1st, Inspector Joe Giralo phoned Agent Sal Velardi and requested that his principal disciple meet him for cups of java and a few muffins at Casciano's Coffee Bar and Sweetery, 212 Bellevue Avenue, downtown Hammonton. The pair parked their wives' automobiles near the curb, greeted one another at the front entrance, soon sat at the counter and mutually concurred that the July 4th day of reckoning was rapidly approaching, that the four sets of identical license plates were a deliberate attempt at intimidation, and that the extended mathematical problem provided to them by the CIA and NSA still remained mostly a "merciless, prolific perplexity."

"Linda, please pour us several cups of steaming-fresh hot coffee," Joe Giralo requested of the establishment's cordial owner. "And while I have your attention, Salvatore and I could easily handle two scrumptious blueberry muffins each. I trust that they're not left over from Sunday's festival," The Chief awkwardly joked. "Confidentially Linda, your fresh-baked muffins are a tad better than the swell ones the Lions Club sells at their popular tent concession."

"I'm glad that your second statement clarified your first one," Linda Cashan diplomatically answered. "To promote good business practice, I've always believed that sugar goes a lot farther than vinegar does when interacting in the realm of polite public discourse."

After the conscientious woman behind the counter stepped to the large metal urn to prepare two newly-brewed cups of coffee, Chief Giralo asked Agent Velardi what specific sound observations he had made in regard to the lengthy arithmetical riddle.

"Well now, Boss. Arty, Dan and I have intensively analyzed the weird numerical presentation at my place late last night and after laboriously adding, subtracting and multiplying, we all ascertained the exact same thing. I mean," Agent Velardi genuinely qualified, "the additions, along with the corresponding subtractions all came-out to the number 694, but incredulously, the multiplication item in parenthesis, namely 347 x 2, also came-out to 694. Thus, the entire ridiculous problem cancelled itself out with the only feasible answer oddly being zero."

"Don't you fathom the underlying symbolism?" Inspector Giralo mildly reprimanded his colleague as Linda Cashan promptly brought the newly ordered coffees and muffins to the especially hungry G-men. "The final total reads zero because that figure is an intentional communique signaling to other crazy fanatics that the time period has expired for the dastardly culprits to soon pull their next terrorist act."

"I conjecture that you know more about an ongoing sequence of events than I do," Agent Velardi surmised and declared. "Why don't you please fill-in for me the missing blanks before I recklessly speed over to Ancora State Hospital and adamantly insist to the on-duty psychiatrists that I'm beyond-the-pale paranoid along with being wholly delusional and mentally insane? Boss, you always make me feel like I'm hopelessly lost without a map or compass, somewhere in a vast wilderness, participating in a chaotic-but-futile wild ostrich expedition!"

Inspector Giralo inhaled a deep breath and very meticulously revealed to his beleaguered law enforcement associate that in the last three months vital highway overpasses and key bridge infrastructures across the country have been systematically sabotaged in an inexplicable illogical succession, starting with St. Louis and Philadelphia in April, and next with Chicago and Atlanta in May, the mass destruction was effectively crippling and stifling major transportation hubs in already-congested metropolitan regions.

"Yes, I've read about the 'Philly and Atlanta devastations in the papers," Agent Velardi recollected and disclosed. "I now see where the idea of stealthy terrorism is distinctly connected in this secret FBI probe, possibly the home-grown domestic type, too."

"The latest demolition has happened in late June in downtown Dallas," the Boss quietly uttered so that no other patrons seated inside the eatery could eavesdrop on *their* verbal exchange, "and Salvatore, there's no telling where the next urban disaster will be heinously implemented. Frankly, I'm just about as stymied and as frustrated by these evil events as you are. All we know is that July 4th, 2014 has been specifically targeted without any specific urban I.D. given to successfully interpret the rather baffling equation."

"Where do we go from here?" Agent Velardi candidly asked in a fully confused state of mind. "Truthfully Inspector, I feel like I'm back in sweltering summer school at Audubon High."

"Ah yes; the Camden County town named in honor of John James Audubon, the nineteenth century naturalist and nature lover," pedantic Joe Giralo educationally related, much to his listener's mounting disappointment. "Every time I visit the fantastic bird sanctuaries down in Stone Harbor and Avalon, I think of that renowned man's many contributions to science and to environmental sensitivity. John James Audubon is often referred to as 'the French Woodsman', and the fellow also proved to be an excellent 1800s ornithologist who had carefully documented American birds and systematically listed their indigenous habitats. In fact, Salvatore, while I'm still on the topic," Chief Giralo loquaciously pontificated, "I have a first cousin who happily lives in Audubon."

"Forget this local geography minutia, Chief! All I know is that I absolutely despise advanced math' ever since I flunked Algebra II and Trigonometry," Velardi very seriously lamented. "What's next on our over-crowded agenda? And it better not conflict with this weekend's Huey Lewis gig at the Showboat!"

"Tell Arty and Dan to meet you and me 7 p.m. tomorrow night at DiDonato's Alley Bar and Grille," Chief Giralo sternly directed. "Although we won't have time for ten pins Salvatore, even though I realize that bowling is up your alley, I do believe I'll have some more crucial information from DC headquarters that I surely maintain will positively both enlighten and illuminate you three amateur gumshoes!"

"That's perfectly fine with me," verified fully-motivated Agent Velardi. "Let's capture these elusive felons and put the domestic terrorists inside the nearest prison where they can make fraudulent New Jersey license plates to their hearts' content!"

* * * * * * * * * * * *

On Wednesday evening at 7 p.m. the four famished FBI men consumed delicious turkey club sandwiches and glasses of ice-cold beer at the Route 30 DiDonato's Alley Bar and Grille. Inspector Giralo softly informed his three government detectives that he had earlier conferred with Steve DiDonato and learned that the bowling alley's Party Room was not being used, despite the fact that area league keglers were utilizing all of the recreational facility's twenty-six lanes.

The Chief had auspiciously brought along his personal slide projector and had planned on giving his three interested apostles a serious "Power Point Presentation" to be displayed upon the Party Room's enormous white screen. As the well-focused Boss was setting-up and preparing his expensive equipment, Agent Velardi, as was his bad habit, unintentionally distracted his dedicated leader with some rather bothersome drivel.

"Inspector, why do the guys down at DC headquarters refer to the recently captured international drug smugglers as 'the Moon Goons'? Even the snobbish Scotland Yard blokes who had collaborated on the arrests use the same derogatory terminology as the FBI does."

The more than slightly irritated Chief glanced-up and next peevishly communicated that the drug smugglers had been captured wearing SCUBA gear, and then the agitated Boss further affirmed that the appropriate nomenclature "Moon Goons" had been imaginatively created because the Earth's natural satellite constantly governs our planet's ever-vacillating ocean and sea tides.

"When it's on one side of the Earth, the moon's gravitational pull causes high tides while the great tug in *that* direction affects low tides developing on our sphere's opposite side," the temporarily disgruntled Chief Inspector communicated. "The devious Moon Goon SCUBA diving smugglers would swim their contraband underwater into various U.S. and U.K. ports during high tide, making it more difficult for the local authorities to detect their encroaching presence in deeper water. I must confess Salvatore," the non-reluctant speaker proudly continued his informative litany. "Matt Riley and I had been instrumental in helping to solve the daunting international dilemma; that is, once we had mutually hypothesized the *gravity* of the situation, ha, ha, ha! Okay now Arty, we're ready to roll. Dim the lights."

In several moments time, an obsolete 1950s map appeared projected upon the prodigious white screen. Much to the three seated agents' consternation, the vociferous standing commentator described that the highway map featured the exact pattern of major U.S. roads during and immediately after World War II.

348

"Observe Gentlemen, that the highways going from east to west and then north to south across the United States are configured lowest odd-numbered roadways to higher numbered odd-numbers. For example, Route 1, which still exists today, extends from Maine down to southern Florida."

"I've traveled Route 1 quite frequently driving between Rutgers University in New Brunswick and the College of New Jersey in Trenton," Agent Blachford stated. "I'm fairly familiar with *that* crowded traffic artery."

"And Men," Chief Giralo continued his monologue while using his chubby index finger as an improvised pointer. "Notice that odd-numbered Route 11 meanders north to south between the Canadian Border in upper New York State and gradually heading way down yonder to New Orleans. And over here, observe that U.S. Route 17 parallels Route 1 and hugs the East Coast from Virginia to the lower Atlantic Dixie states; and next, over here, Route 19 descends from the Great Lakes south in the direction of Florida. Please recognize that the odd-numbered U.S. highways are increasing in numerical sequence as our alert attention is directed westward."

"I see it all rather clearly, now!" Sal Velardi mildly exclaimed into the room's dark atmosphere. "Route 23 moves from north to south from Northern Michigan down to Jacksonville, Florida; and in like manner, the ascending odd-number cross-country progression continues all the way to the West Coast where finally U.S. 101 winds its way from Washington State down to San Diego in sunny California."

"But Fearless Leader. Why are we three agents being exposed to this bizarre, sophomoric history and highway geography lesson?" Art Orsi angrily blustered. "Although curiously logical, it all seems so rather mundane and nondescript."

"You'll understand my esoteric premise in around fifteen minutes," the sage Power Point Presenter promised. "You Fellas' need more discipline and self-control! Just kindly exhibit a trifle more courtesy and demonstrate some basic human patience."

Seeing and hearing no objections to his reasonable stipulations, Inspector Giralo then resumed his alien, descriptive oratory. "Now Men, because the old north-south U.S. highways were numbered from 1 to 101 moving from east to west, when President Eisenhower later announced the Interstate Highway Program in the mid-1950s, the new numerical pattern was organized as the exact opposite of the previous one with...."

"With odd-numbered I-95 paralleling Route 1 in the east and I-5 coinciding with shadowing U.S. Route 101 on the West Coast," Agent

Blachford perceptively summarized. "I gotta' admit that the entire schematic was pretty ingenious of President Dwight David Eisenhower! According to your second slide up on the screen, Boss," Dan Blachford accurately concluded, "the odd-number Interstates running north-to-south in between book ends I-95 and I-5 are I-81, I75, I-55, I-35, I-25 through Wyoming, Colorado and New Mexico and finally, I-15 going through Boise, Idaho, Las Vegas, Nevada and southern California."

Joe Giralo next changed the projected image to Slide #3, which aptly authenticated the north-south 1940s and 1950s major roads that had been identified in Slide #1. Everyone closely studied the enlarged second U.S. Highways map for several seconds.

"What does all of this incredibly pretentious lecture mean?" Agent Velardi vehemently protested. "Boss, are you going to require that the three of us take a U.S, Highway Geography exam' in order to prove that we comprehend your current immaterial hypothesis?"

Chief Giralo stoically ignored his agent's annoying petulance and pragmatically proceeded with his extraordinary oral report, enthusiastically showing his addled audience that during the 1940s and 1950s, principal *even-numbered* U.S. highways built east to west like U.S. 6 from Massachusetts to Northern California, U.S. 20 from Boston to Oregon and U.S. 60 from Virginia to Arizona were once recognized as major transcontinental thoroughfares.

"Holy guacamole!" Agent Orsi impulsively yelled. "I see on your third slide, ancient map that U.S. 30 starts in Atlantic City and winds-up in Oregon and that U.S. 40 also begins in Atlantic City but terminates in San Francisco. And now I also grasp that U.S. 50 originates in Ocean City, Maryland and traverses the entire country all the way out to Sacramento. But Boss, I say again; of what essential importance is this ongoing academic consultation?"

"Arty," Chief Giralo placidly related to his impetuous subordinate, "let's now advance to Slide #4. You've learned that the older 1950s *even-numbered* east-to-west highways are arranged lower numbers to the north and then higher numbers to the south. Now with the modern Interstate Highways running east to west, the opposite effect is established with the lower numbers to the south and the accompanying higher numbers to the north: for example, we have I-10 between Jacksonville and Los Angeles, I-20 from Mississippi to Texas; I-40 connecting Wilmington, North Carolina to Southern California; I-70 from Baltimore, Maryland to Utah; I-80 from Bergen County, New Jersey almost straight across the nation to San Francisco, and finally, I-90 from Boston heading out to Seattle, Washington."

"And Chief, famous Route 66 had gone from Chicago westward to distant Santa Monica, California," Dan Blachford comprehended from viewing the enlarged fourth slide screen image. "But that historic highway is only used in certain parts of the mid-west now. I had watched television specials on Route 66, and I sometimes see old reruns of the once popular TV series employing *that* now less-traveled east-west highway."

"But truthfully Boss," a now-vexed Agent Velardi bravely replied. "Precisely how do these combined archaic and modern highway maps co-exist in assisting us mere mortals in solving the very hindering, preposterous math' brainteaser that had been anonymously sent to you? Basically, besides having the self-confidence of a common buffoon, I now feel like I'm a chopped-down tree, totally stumped!"

"Don't get your bowels in an uproar and learn to relax your lightly bruised ego, Salvatore," Inspector Giralo wisely advised. "Matt Riley and I are working intensively on the problem at hand. and we're in the process of ambitiously exploring certain wild theories and assumptions. Although I'm not a betting man, I wager that in the final analysis, Adolph Hitler will give us the needed information that we were so lacking."

After Inspector Joe Giralo nonchalantly turned-on the lights in the DiDonato's Bowling Center's spacious Party Room, Agents Velardi, Orsi and Blachford all featured disbelieving frowns masked upon their respective stunned countenances.

"Gentlemen, I hereby request your presence on Thursday evening at 8 o'clock on the button in the downstairs serving area of Rocco's Town House on North Third Street," Chief Giralo austerely commanded his somewhat-shocked comrades. "Forget for now my left field Fuehrer allusion! I predict that by Thursday night I'll have even more dynamic puzzle pieces for you to digest, new revealing elements that will shine new light on this rather troublesome and irksome highway bugaboo arithmetic case."

* * * * * * * * * * * *

On Thursday evening, all four G-men descended the back stairs of Rocco's Town House and soon were sitting around a square table. Co-owner Dave Ruberton carried-down a large tray loaded with four cold beer drafts, baskets of French fry potatoes along with four deluxe giant hamburgers. After the taste-tempting food had been satisfactorily consumed, the empty plates and related mugs were gathered-up by a sweet blonde waitress and quickly taken upstairs, the assembled quartet finally got "down to brass tacks".

"Now Salvatore," Inspector Giralo imperatively commenced his anticipated exposition. "Have you, Arty and Dan imaginatively decoded the mystical numerical problem yet?"

"Well Boss, we easily realized a definite relationship between specific items like 95 and I-95, like 5 and I-5, and like 66 and Route 66, but we failed to construct the various arithmetic factors into any discernible cohesive pattern."

"Why you have my utmost congratulations, Men!" Joe Giralo answered with an element of cynicism exhibited in his tone of voice. "You've deftly made it to first base."

"Look Boss," Agent Velardi addressed his superior in his own defense. "The nasty people over at the New Jersey Motor Vehicles Department have given me a hard time about obtaining new license plates for my car, so please don't aggravate me any more with your ludicrous propensity for sarcasm. Please put together the pieces of the myriad math' items so that I can sleep lightly for at least two precious hours tonight!"

"Okay Sal, you win this time!" responded Inspector Giralo, feigning a degree of aggravation. "Do you remember when I told you Fellas' that the given numbers were presented in sets of three, two additions followed by a subsequent subtraction?"

After the three investigators nodded their heads in the affirmative, the sagacious Boss indicated that the first series 70 + 55 - 67 actually pertained to St. Louis where I-70, I-55 and U.S. 67 all converge. And then 76 + 95 - U.S. 30 concerned Philadelphia where all three new and old highways coincidentally enter the Quaker City metropolitan area. "And 90 + 55 - 41 relates to Chicago where I-90, I-55 and U.S. 41 all virtually intersect."

"I get the big picture now!" loudly exclaimed Agent Orsi. "Bridges, overpasses and other valuable infrastructure have already been attacked in St. Louis, in Philly' and in Chicago. So therefore, 10 + 5 - U.S. 101 involves the West coast city of...."

"Of Los Angeles where I-10, I-5 and scenic U.S. 101 generally rule most of *that* populous hub's transportation system," Art Orsi theorized and verbally deduced. "And 20 + 75 - 29 must naturally equate with Atlanta because I-20, I-75 and U.S. 29 seem to rendezvous there. And also, 30 + 45 - 75 must mean Dallas, Texas where I-30, I-45 and U.S. 75 seem to meet. And obviously Boss," Agent Orsi elaborated, "I-30 is nowhere near east-west U.S. Route 30, which actually passes right through Hammonton."

"Good detective work Men!" praised Chief Giralo. "You're rapidly becoming sophisticated 'roads scholars'. Now finally Guys, tell me the juxtaposition where the last three numerical factors representing I-66, I-395 and U.S. 50 actually collide?"

"Holy George W.!" excitedly shouted Sal Velardi. "They almost merge in downtown Washington D.C. And I-66 is nowhere near venerable-but-archaic U.S. Route 66. But Guys, all of the historic monuments and memorials, and even the White House and the Capitol Building, are in immediate jeopardy of being demolished on Friday, July 4th! But which one, if not all of them?"

"Don't worry one scintilla, Salvatore!" confided Inspector Giralo. "Once Matt Riley and I had rationally solved the arithmetical conundrum, Colonel Bob Bauers and his elite Delta Force units were instantly dispatched to DC, and the villainous terrorists have been swiftly apprehended at two remote safe houses situated across the Potomac in Alexandria and a third haven in Rockville, Maryland."

"And who was the main instigator, the evil brain behind the entire wicked skein of diabolical operations?" Art Orsi asked. "An al Qaeda affiliate who totally loathes American democracy?"

"No, not a radical Sunni but instead, a militant Shi'ite professor at the University of Tehran," the Boss explained. "Dr. Farid Madani had recruited and structured together a comprehensive network of avid U.S. domestic terrorists. The home-grown fascists were a tight-knit conglomeration of indoctrinated Iranian college students situated on various university campuses spread throughout the United States."

"But Boss," Sal Velardi frantically interrupted. "The month of Ramadan this year is slated for June 28th to July 28th. According to the Muslim religion, violence is not to occur between those sacred dates, so why is Washington DC on July 4th so vulnerable?"

"Because Sal, this demented math' Professor Farid Madani has hired avowed home-grown atheists to conduct his diabolical acts of vile destruction here in America! The treacherous American-born non-Muslim traitors were actually plotting to explode the Smithsonian Natural History Museum into microscopic smithereens while the annual 4th of July patriotic celebration was being conducted on the nearby mall. But during his precise raid on the group's safe houses," Inspector Giralo added, "Colonel Bauers' commando teams have expertly confiscated several tons of dynamite."

* * * * * * * * * * * *

"That's really great news, Boss!" volatile Sal Velardi exuberantly exclaimed. "Now I'll get to see Huey Lewis and the News at the House of Blues, and Arty will be able to vacation down in Ocean City, Maryland, and Dan will venture into Philly' with his wife and obtain some much-needed culture at the city's classic art museum, and last-but-not-least, you'll achieve hanging-out as an average civilian on the family-oriented Ocean City, New Jersey Boardwalk. But Chief, my inquisitive brain's still in a quandary about this one rather disturbing detail. How did Adolph Hitler help you and Matt Riley brilliantly solve this extremely complicated Interstate Interdiction Case?"

Inspector Joe Giralo cleared his throat and then gracefully revealed to his still-stunned agents that on Wednesday morning, he had been driving twelve miles west of Hammonton on U.S. Route 30 passing through the town of Berlin, and his Chevy Suburban was about to enter West Berlin. Suddenly, the crime-solving guru's mind was hit with a very powerful inspiration when Inspector Giralo's ever-active cerebrum had magnificently associated the similar-sounding words 'Audubon' and 'Autobahn'.

"I was driving Gina and my two daughters to the Echelon Mall over in Voorhees for them to purchase some beach apparel at Macy's or Boscov's," Inspector Giralo related and then chuckled. "But then in a terrific cognitive flash, the entire big-picture scenario marvelously registered and soon magically synchronized inside my aging head. During the U.S. Army's stellar World War II march to Berlin, then General Dwight D. Eisenhower became fabulously impressed with the advanced design of the German Autobahn. Soon Hitler and his iniquitous Nazi Air Force repeatedly bombed the superhighway to slow-down the on-a-mission U.S. military from reaching Berlin. So, when Eisenhower became our American President, the newly elected Republican...."

"Proposed that the modernistic Interstate Highway System be built all across America, modeled of course after the state-of-the-art German Autobahn," Agent Sal Velardi immediately realized and effectively articulated. It's absolutely amazing! Adolph Hitler has helped save our American Civilization!"

"What a spectacular bit of mental reasoning you had so instantaneously accomplished Boss, admirably relating the separate ideas of Audubon, Autobahn, Berlin, West Berlin, Dwight David Eisenhower and Adolph Hitler!" Agent Art Orsi wholeheartedly complimented Chief Giralo. "Sometimes I think you're playing hardball in the same league as Einstein, Edison and Tesla!"

"And Sal," Agent Dan Blachford chimed-in with a broad smile evident upon his rosy lips. "You'll now undoubtedly get to visit the Showboat's splendid rock and roll concert in the after*math* of this incredibly outstanding FBI adventure."

354

# "Beauty in the Least"

One of Inspector Joe Giralo's most baffling-but-interesting cases was what his loyal subordinates Agents Sal Velardi, Arthur Orsi and Dan Blachford have often genially referred to as "File 537, Beauty in the Least". The particular gleaned subject matter had gained the FBI's scrutiny when a series of similar horrific crimes had been conducted in various cities across the U.S., with all of the violent episodes dealing with beauty pageant contestants along with well-established cosmetology schools.

On the sunny morning of Tuesday, September 1, 2015 Agent Velardi was comfortably seated behind his ancient desk inside his nondescript Philadelphia office and casually reviewing crime statistic charts when the ever-vigilant G-man received an urgent phone call from his immediate superior.

"Salvatore, I'm now just leaving Dr. Ralph Lanciano's Cherry Hill office," prefaced Inspector Giralo. "You know, Ralph's my trusted ophthalmologist who has taken care of my eyes for the past twenty-seven years. If you recall, his other New Jersey office is on the Pike over in Somerdale. I believe that Arty and Dan are also Ralph's patients. Now that your Lions Club friend Dr. Steve Streitfeld has moved his practice from Hammonton to Mays Landing," Giralo calmly declared, "you'll probably want to switch over to Dr. Lanciano too!" the Boss recommended. "As you get older Sal, you'll learn that optometrists are okay, but sooner or later, you'll need the vital services of a highly-skilled ophthalmologist."

"Did you read a few chapters from a romance novel, or perhaps either peruse through a vampire or zombie sci-fi book while sitting in the waiting room?" Agent Velardi awkwardly joked. "I know your exact habits and propensities, Chief! If you aren't fully absorbed into female mushy, pulp literature, you're actively involved in reading totally off-the-wall, weird space alien stuff!"

"Cut-out the ridiculous comedy-hour humor nonsense," Joe Giralo abruptly chastised. "I've just learned that I'll soon be needing cataracts removed from both eyes. The operations are scheduled for October 6th at Wills Eye Hospital, you know, it's directly across the street from the Walnut Street Theater. Dr. Lanciano's very reputable associate Dr. Penne is going to perform the surgery."

"Is Dr. Penne going to be assisted by Dr. Rigatoni and Dr. Lasagna," Agent Velardi clumsily jested. "If you want to know the truth Boss, just the mere thought of your impending eyes' operation is making me quite hungry for Italian cuisine!"

"Cataracts are no laughing matter!" the caller reprimanded, as Giralo feigned being insulted. "And don't try making another bizarre un-funny pun stating that the Nile River has lived with cataracts for thousands of years. I remember quite vividly that my maternal grandfather had had his cataracts removed back in the early '70s, and I gotta' tell ya', he had to wear heavy bandages over his eyes for several weeks. Medical technology has really significantly advanced in the last half century, and now the delicate procedure has become rather pedestrian in nature for competent doctors to perform."

"You'll then have better super-vision to do your supervision," Velardi jested, laughing at his mediocre double entendre. "Now Boss, why else besides your bothersome cataracts have you contacted me and annoyingly interrupted my intense FBI research?"

"Salvatore, I want you, Arty and Dan to be in my office at 1 p.m. this afternoon," the Boss imperatively insisted. "I have some important details to discuss with you three notorious savants, we'll be reviewing certain facts that are connected with the rash of duplicate beauty pageant sabotages that have been plaguing the country. I think that Matt Riley and his team down in DC are finally excavating some pertinent information that'll allow us to be accurately identifying the prime suspects. I'm not Alexandre Dumas, but it's essential that my *Three Musketeers* be present for the briefing."

"That's terrific news," impressed Agent Velardi promptly acknowledged. "Prime suspects are always more relevant than targeted persons of interest. We'll see you at one this afternoon, I promise. And here's some sage gastronomic advice for you Chief. On your way back to 'Philly, don't stop and eat more than two double hamburgers at that Jersey 5 Guys restaurant you're always bragging about!"

"5 Guys is much better than Martin Luther's appetite," Inspector Giralo quipped back. "If I recollect, the rebellious Protestant Reformation leader had a Diet of Worms!" Click.

* * * * * * * * * * * * *

Inspector Giralo's Philadelphia arrival had been delayed by a massive traffic snarl on the Camden side of the Ben Franklin Bridge, so by the time the Chief had parked his gray Chevy Suburban in a lot adjacent to 600 Arch Street, the time of day had already been 1:12 p.m., a dozen minutes past the meeting time with his three agents that *he* had scheduled. The normally-punctual and slightly-embarrassed Boss quickly stepped into the main lobby elevator and was soon ascending to the all-too-mundane eighth floor. Against his normal authoritarian, demeanor, the FBI Inspector briefly apologized to his three noteworthy underlings who had already been assembled and seated inside the Chief's spacious-but-modestly furnished office.

"The bridge traffic was horrendous," florid-faced Giralo claimed. "And if I didn't have E-Z Pass, it would've taken me five more minutes to get through any of the designated toll booths. And to top-off my challenging day," the sweating federal bureaucrat maintained before breathing-in a substantial quantity of oxygen, "I have a routine dental cleaning appointment back in Hammonton scheduled at four this afternoon."

"How did you successfully cope with your severe highway congestion?" Agent Velardi asked. "Did you listen to the local classical radio station to calm your frayed nerves?"

"No Sal, you'll be delighted to know that I was tuned-in to WOGL-FM, the 'Philly oldies station, and the DJ was playing one of your favorite songs!"

"Sorry, I Ran All the Way Home?" Velardi instinctively replied. "That's truly a fantastic rock and roll hit from 1958 sung by the Impalas. I simply love that upbeat tune and never grow tired of listening to it!"

"No Salvatore, I was actually thinking about 'Rock Around the Clock' by Bill Haley," the Boss contradicted and answered. "My close friend DJ Lou Costello at W-VLT down in Vineland plays the Comets all the time during his morning show. But I have to compliment you, Sal. That other popular '50s song you've just mentioned by the Impalas has just stimulated my formerly dormant investigative mind right out of its mediocre monotony!"

After Giralo had true-to-form enthusiastically discussed the fact that Hammonton and Vineland New Jersey had both been established by an entrepreneurial mid-nineteenth century land developer named Charles K. Landis, Agent Arthur Orsi reckoned that it was time to review the real reason for the hastily called FBI conference.

The room's general atmosphere instantly transformed from joviality to serious individual contemplation. Naturally, Inspector Giralo presided over the session, explaining that he intended to play "two very curious" CDs that the DC Bureau and the NSA had intercepted while performing vital national terrorist surveillance. To Velardi, Orsi and Blachford, the voice pattern on the first recorded CD sounded entirely like foreign-language gibberish.

"Was that erratic message transmitted in Arabic?" Dan Blachford honestly inquired. "It sounded as if it's emblematic of some Middle Eastern dialect."

"Actually, Dan," Chief Giralo clarified before orating one of his typical elucidations. "Those foreign words that your ears had just heard were spoken in Farsi, which is the language that's prevalent in Iran. And so, Sal," the Inspector continued while turning his head toward Agent Velardi. "When you had quoted the lyrics 'I Ran All the Way Home', your' innocent comment suddenly made my brain begin to connect some very separate-but-unique ideas."

"In terms of the Muslim religion, aren't the Iranians mostly Shi'ite?" Agent Orsi contributed to the conversation. "Most of Iran's people are not Sunni, I believe!"

"Yes Arty," Joe Giralo swiftly confirmed. "There are over 1.6 billion Muslims living on this wonderful planet, and as you've knowledgeably cited, they're divided into two major-but-distinct sects: the Sunnis and the Shia. The Muslim world population is mostly Sunni, I estimate around 85% or so. And throughout history, the Sunnis have maintained economic and political power over the suffering Shi'ites, who incidentally, in our modern age, tend to be more radical, militant and belligerent toward Western Civilization than are the Sunnis."

"Wasn't Saddam Hussein a Sunni who had harassed and persecuted the minority Shi'ites living in certain parts of Iraq?" piped-up Dan Blachford. "Tell me, Boss, and please refresh my erratic memory. What Muslim countries are mostly Shia, and which ones are predominantly Sunni?"

After inhaling another very deep breath, the Chief academically expounded upon the fascinating topic introduced by Agent Blachford. Giralo indicated that Iraq was 50% Shia, Bahrain 70% and Iran, which speaks Farsi and not Arabic, was around 90% of the less dominant sect. The Boss summarized his scholarly remarks by reiterating that the people of Iran were predominantly of Persian descent and therefore, the inhabitants spoke Farsi and not Arabic like most other native Sunni and Shi'ite Muslims in the Middle East.

"On the other side of the proverbial coin," Giralo emphasized to his somewhat intrigued audience of three, "Saudi Arabia, Egypt and Pakistan are mostly Sunni. But most definitely," emphasized the famous FBI investigator, "the language that we just heard on that CD had been spoken in Farsi, the native tongue of Iran. And going back to the 700s," the Boss resumed his academic lecture, "there has always been abundant conflict and strife between the poorer Shia and the more prosperous Sunnis. Now Gentlemen, the DC Bureau's team has taken the time and effort to translate the intercepted Farsi monologue into English using a female agent's voice. Listen intently to the more distinguishable information provided on this second CD."

Giralo next adroitly removed the aforementioned Farsi jargon CD from the office player and deftly inserted the easy-to-comprehend second disc, which contained the following communication.

Greetings Sister,

In the long run, the Muslim faith and Sharia law will become victorious here in America. Truthfully, I just can't easily walk away from all of this country's dirty laundry such as rampant prostitution, liquor, pornography and gay marriage. Americans artificially claim that life's been good to them, but in the crowded city and also in the nearby countryside, you and I both painfully suffer from heartache tonight while regrettably witnessing all the blatant sin that evilly surrounds us.

But please remember dear sister, one of these nights, with the help of Allah, our many emotional troubles will be already gone. In the U.S., there is entirely too much intolerable life in the fast lane that must be permanently eliminated.

Take it easy until your next visit to the familiar California hotel where I will be restfully staying at the end of September.

In the Prophet's Name,

Your devoted sister Nazila

"Let's try to defend the principles of freedom and justice, my primitive Musketeers. What rhyme or reason do you interpret from this rather unusual CD encryption obtained from a random, intercepted e-mail? Personally," the fully-inspired Inspector qualified, "my gut instinct tells me that we're attempting to decipher a secret message concealed inside a secret coded message. Regardless, I must admit that this strange letter is both perplexing and captivating."

"I think I understand something solid about the phraseology," Agent Velardi intrepidly volunteered. "The words depicted in the CD recording are all associated with hit songs produced by the country rock band, the Eagles. 'In the Long Run', 'Walk Away', 'Dirty Laundry', 'Life's Been Good', 'In the City' and 'Heartache Tonight' are all Eagles vintage hits. And then…."

Agent Orsi felt motivated to pursue and extend Agent Velardi's astute train of thought. "And Fellas'," the now-excited participant anxiously enunciated. "The songs 'One of These Nights', 'Already Gone', 'Life In the Fast Lane', 'Take It Easy' and 'Hotel California all remarkably complete the fairly imaginative riddle."

"Good articulation Arty!" congratulated and alliterated Chief Giralo. "Now Dan, exert your crime-solving cerebrum and associate the rock band Eagles with the skein of beauty pageant and cosmetology school explosions that've recently threatened the stability of our nation's urban life."

"It all makes perfect rational sense now, that is, from a wanton criminal's mindset; a style of thinking that's been egregiously influenced by a totally warped perspective," Agent Blachford profoundly prefaced. "According to the chronology of events starting in March of this year, there have been beauty contestant kidnappings in Eugene, Oregon, in Atlanta, Georgia, in Galveston, Texas along with a litany of beauty school explosions in Little Rock, Arkansas, in El Paso, Texas and in Seattle, Washington. Obviously," 'Dandy Dan' conjectured and clarified, "if you take the first letter from each of those already mentioned six American cities, you've deliberately and methodically spelled-out the rock band...."

"E-A-G-L-E-S!" marveled and orally concluded Agent Orsi. "The guys and gals down in DC have really organized a superb acquisition of current lethal terrorist activity. I wouldn't be surprised if the captured beauty queen contestants have already been transported to somewhere in the Middle East and have been wickedly sold into slavery or prostitution."

"I gotta' admit, I'm now a true believer in coincidences," Agent Velardi sincerely confessed. "I'm a Philadelphia Eagles season ticket holder. In fact, my wife and I can't wait to attend the first home game at Lincoln Financial Field against the dreaded Cowboys on Sunday, September 20th."

"And ironically, Carol and I have purchased tickets to see the play 'Footloose' at the Eagle Theater on Vine Street in downtown Hammonton," Art Orsi related in a hoarse tone of voice. "The movie was quite excellent and I'm sure the recently produced play will be outstanding too! As you guys very well know," Orsi garrulously elaborated during his impromptu speech, "the Eagle is no longer a commonplace community theater. It's now evolved into an equity theater attracting professional singers and actors, and the town government is donating a considerable sum of money to finance the very positive upgrade."

"And let's not forget the amazing parallel existing between Iran and the catchy lyrics '*I Ran* All the Way Home'," Sal Velardi vociferated to his almost-mesmerized colleagues. "Now Boss, back onto the subject at hand, what do you have to say about all of these absolutely mindboggling, correlative, terroristic circumstances?"

"I say that this Saturday you men should come over to my house at noon for some cold beer and a few grilled hot dogs and burgers," Chief Giralo generously invited his law-enforcement disciples. "We'll enjoy an early old-fashioned backyard Labor Day weekend! I want to show you boys some treasured photos' of my dependable white 1974

Chevy Impala that I faithfully used to commute back and forth between Hammonton and Glassboro State College."

* * * * * * * * * * * *

On Saturday, September 5th the on-a-mission foursome gathered at Inspector Giralo's 321 Orchard Street residence for a special high-calorie hot dog and hamburger Labor Day weekend feast. Wife Gina and the Chief's two daughters were staying the holiday at the family Ocean City, New Jersey rented beach house, and the Inspector's wife was planning to do some essential "late minute" back-to-school shoes' shopping for her two daughters at the convenient and newly renovated Hamilton Mall on Route 322 in Mays Landing.

"Fellas'," Joe Giralo addressed his three-person staff. "Before we indulge in our culinary barbecue delight, I must relate to you how I had once toured a hot dog and sausage processing plant up in North 'Philly, and believe me," the Boss energetically chuckled, "when I tell you about certain graphic facts, you'll then fully understand exactly how those greasy junk foods are produced. I predict that you would never eat another delicious frankfurter, even if you humbly lived for years in Frankfurt, Germany!"

"I suppose that the same axiomatic principle holds true for delectable hamburgers eaten by residents of Hamburg, Germany!" Agent Orsi glibly suggested.

"Not to forget baloney consumers occupying stone dwellings in Bologna, Italy!" Agent Blachford uttered and prolifically laughed. "You don't suppose that every resident living there is full of baloney, do you? Ha, ha, ha!"

"I'm an occasional vegetarian," commented Agent Velardi with a contrived straight face, "so let's also include Limburger cheese savored by the inhabitants of Limburg, Belgium!"

"Enough of your prodigious slapstick food etymologies," Chief Giralo criticized. "Before I fire-up my new grill, I want to play for the benefit of you three geniuses a new set of CDs I've recorded early this morning from a classified Top Secret Voice Dispatch sent from Matt Riley at DC headquarters!"

Inspector Giralo next escorted his three G-men from his screened-in back porch and into his library/study, and after the apprehensive agents were seated in their respective red leather chairs, the unpredictable Boss inserted the new disc into the player's narrow slot. "I'll politely skip the unfathomable Farsi version and instead, I'll play for you the second translated CD rendition narrated in English by the same female FBI employee!"

Dear Sister,

All night long I've been thinking, 'I'm not a problem child doing dirty deeds on a highway to hell like most Americans are.' I've concluded that the United States is certainly an evil dog eat dog country consisting of much lowlife and redneck riff raff.

But thanks to Allah's inspiration, I have a dynamite idea that is rich in high voltage. I promise you Nazila, I refuse to be the jack wallowing at the low-end in this demonic playing card deck. May Allah on High be praised! Soon dear sister, you and I will be back in black living in Tehran!

In the Prophet's name,
Nikoo


"Okay, Comrade Salvatore," Joe Giralo jested and challenged "What happens to be your' keen synopsis of this extraordinary, second intercepted obscure missive."

"This task you've assigned is extremely elementary when the new data on the second English CD is referenced to that appearing on the first one we had heard," Agent Velardi recognized and verified. "Acid rock is not my favorite type of modern music. That being said, instead of the country rock group Eagles, this time around, random AC/DC songs have been utilized on the new CD. For example, I've recognized the titles 'All Night Long', 'Problem Child', 'Dirty Deeds,' as determined in the song 'Dirty Deeds Done Dirt Cheap', 'Highway to Hell' and obviously, last but not least, 'Dog Eat Dog'!"

"And also," euphorically added Agent Orsi, "we have the song 'Riff Raff' and the direct allusion to dynamite, signaling the lyrics to 'TNT' as it equates to 'High Voltage'."

"And finally," offered the usually pensive Agent Blachford, "the song 'The Jack' has been identified on the CD, but I think that the stating of 'Back in Black' and the subsequent terminology suggesting a dual returning to Tehran is indeed most intriguing, of course the unscrupulous perpetrators desiring to wear black apparel while living and being reunited as devout Muslim women in the Iranian capital!"

"But of what importance does the group AC/DC have to do with this overall beauty pageant scenario?" the beleaguered Chief asked his alert agents. "The previous nomenclature 'Eagles' had quite apparently spelled-out the earmarked cities that had had either beauty contest queens kidnapped or had had cosmetology schools attacked with dynamite. In this case," Giralo asserted, "we already know the

362

significance of the letters AC/DC, but we don't know which isolated cities the four given letters connect with!"

"Perhaps it's not four cities, but only two," speculated and verbalized Agent Velardi. "Here's my hypothesis! AC could pertain to Atlantic City, and DC most probably could be the District of Columbia."

"Holy Holocausts!" yelled Agent Orsi. "This problem must be addressed immediately! The Miss America Pageant is only a week away, Sunday night, September 14th at Boardwalk Hall in nearby Atlantic City."

"And this year's Miss New Jersey is from Hammonton," Agent Orsi reminded his associates. "And my wife and her cousin have tickets to attend the event on September 14th! Their lives will be in jeopardy if we don't act quickly!"

"Chief, for Arty's sake. we must act expeditiously!" Agent Blachford demanded with beads of sweat accumulating upon his forehead. "The 2015 Miss America Contest could end in a devastating disaster, one turned into a colossal national TV tragedy."

"This is no sinister hoax we're presently evaluating!" Chief Giralo concurred. "It's an existential threat to Boardwalk Hall and to all of the thousands in attendance! We only have seven days to crack this mystery open and save a multitude of innocent lives."

"Suddenly, because of this imminent danger, I've lost my appetite for grilled hot dogs and hamburgers!" Arthur Orsi exclaimed, exhibiting palpable emotional anguish. "Violent crime seems much more overwhelming, much more realistic, and much more personal when it hits so close to home!"

* * * * * * * * * * * *

On Sunday morning, Inspector Giralo got on the horn and in three separate calls, commanding his sleepy-eyed agents to meet him for lunch at Rocco's Town House, a popular restaurant located at the corner of Third Street and Orchard. "I've already contacted Dave Ruberton about a private eating area where we can confidentially discuss this aggravating Miss America scenario," the worried Chief individually informed his crime-fighting confederates. "Dave will be off-duty tomorrow, but his younger brother Steve will gladly accommodate us. In the last twenty-four hours Matt Riley and I have exhaustively excavated some rather pertinent data concerning the two Iranian ladies and their onerous subversive schemes. I'll share all of this new evidence tomorrow at noon. I even promise to buy the three of you' a round of beers during our little Town House symposium!"

Amiable Steve Ruberton greeted the four federal crusaders at the establishment's oval bar and then led the quartet into the side patio room that featured a greenhouse-type semi-circular glass roof. After being served BLT sandwich and French fry platters along with frosted mugs of cold light beer, Joe Giralo began deluging his now-awake listeners with his inimitable rhetoric.

"Matt Riley's crackerjack FBI terror-watch squad has acquired some very revealing information from the NSA. The newly obtained details have cracked this diabolical Farsi CD e-mail investigation wide open. Where do you men wish for me to begin?"

"First tell us some basic background on Nazila and Nikoo?" Sal Velardi requested. "How are they implicated is this dastardly plot?"

"The biggest mistake the girls had made was thinking that they could disguise their identities by simply using Farsi to exchange emails. By not using false names or pseudonyms, Nazila and Nikoo were relatively easy for the FBI to research because the dastardly duo has been too audacious and too overconfident in their pursuit of revenge against our American way of life," Giralo declared. "The Iranian name Nazila ironically means 'cute and charming', and by the same token," the fully-prepared Chief continued his very thorough exposition, "Nikoo coincidentally means 'beautiful and good' in Farsi. Both females have been under FBI and NSA scrutiny for several years now. Nazila and Nikoo were raised by their immigrant Muslim parents in Melbourne, Florida. Nazila and Nikoo Kalani were born identical twins and in their teens, each had won numerous beauty contests while competing in the Sunshine State."

"Well then," Agent Orsi wondered and asked his self-confident Boss. "What major event had occurred that turned the two girls into avowed beauty queen kidnappers and formidable cosmetology academy anarchists?"

In response, Chief Giralo related that in 1999, both gorgeous girls Nazila and Nikoo had been severely afflicted with first and second degree burns all over their bodies during an early morning family house fire. "The Kalani girls' former beautiful faces were terribly deformed from their ghastly life-changing ordeal, and not even advanced plastic surgery performed in the finest hospitals could ever repair their grotesquely disfigured noses, ears and lips."

"Now I get the big picture!" Dan Blachford blurted. "Because of their new-found ugliness resulting from the home inferno, the Kalani twins eventually became radicalized. Nazila and Nikoo became disenchanted with American culture and with Western standards of beauty. Soon the disgruntled twins abandoned Western values and then seeking social support, regressed back into their militant, Iranian jihadi roots!"

"And the Iranian girls probably want to sabotage the upcoming Miss America Pageant on September 14th at Boardwalk Hall!" Sal Velardi instantly verified. "Boss, what else can you divulge about this insidious plot that could evolve into a gruesome catastrophe?"

"Our sophisticated intelligence corps along with our very competent international reconnaissance units have learned that Nazila and Nikoo have recently chartered two large fishing boats out of Gardner's Basin, situated in the inlet section of Atlantic City; the marina being not too far from Harrahs Casino," Giralo communicated. "We're now monitoring the transportation of two small guided missiles being shipped from Saddle Brook, New Jersey down to AC via several rental trucks. And their malicious plan is to…"

"Shoot the missiles from the Atlantic Ocean directly across the beach into Boardwalk Hall, and in the process, kill as many beauty contest attendees as possible," Art Orsi deduced and gasped. "Bert Parks is probably spinning-around inside his cemetery grave as we speak. And I dread the hideous thought that my wife and her cousin would be among the random innocent victims!"

"What makes you think that Atlantic City will be hit before Washington DC?" Dan Blachford intelligently interrogated his erudite superior. "Explain *that* specific time-line factor to me."

"Because of our department's fastidious homing-in on Farsi chatter being conveyed in coded symbols via selective jihadi e-mail correspondence," Inspector Giralo disclosed. "Thank goodness we were able to get a federal judge's search warrant issued on the Kalani twins. And besides Dan," the Boss resumed his plausible explanation, "the FBI, in conjunction with the Pentagon and the military, has the three largest DC cosmetology schools under tight security in strict regard to unusual sidewalk pedestrian activity along with irregular human behavior."

In his slick summary, Inspector Giralo next shared that after firing the lethal rockets from the Atlantic into the Boardwalk Hall event, the pair would navigate their respective fishing boats twenty-five miles out into the ocean where their crafts would rendezvous with an awaiting Iranian submarine in international waters. The two crazed saboteurs would next climb aboard and the sub' would quickly descend into the depths, leaving the two abandoned chartered boats bouncing-around upon the night ocean waves.

"Is your old pal Colonel Bob Bauers participating in the capture of the Kalani twins?" Sal Velardi shrewdly asked. "I'd like to witness his expert commandos in action!"

"Yes, Sage Salvatore," the clever Inspector affirmatively replied. "A Delta Force attack unit will board the two Gardner Basin boats and systematically apprehend Nazila and Nikoo along with any of their demented criminal henchmen. And the pair of guided missiles will be confiscated and meticulously dismantled before the destructive objects can cause any harm, injury or structural damage. Two well-equipped Coast Guard ships out of Cape May will be obstructing the entrance into the Gardner Marina while Delta Force is courageously conducting its stealthy raid. Any hasty escape will be impossible!"

"And Chief, what about the Iranian submarine brazenly stationed there in deep water off the Jersey Coast?" Blachford demanded knowing. "Will it be part of an international incident?"

"The sub' will be blasted out of the Atlantic if it violates *our* sovereignty by encroaching into the twenty-five-mile international waters' boundary. Otherwise, Dan, in the reality realm, the lurking Iranian sub' will not be able to meet and pick-up the already-captured Kalani twins, and everything will return to business as usual without any serious military consequences or any secondary repercussions ever occurring. And now Gentlemen," Inspector Giralo artfully announced, "the best part' of this fabulous chronicle is that Colonel Bob has personally invited the four of us to observe and appreciate the entire clandestine commando operation from beginning to end. I'm beyond-a-doubt sure that both you' and your two zany colleagues will immediately jump at *that* once-in-a-lifetime golden opportunity!"

"Life is full of incredible coincidences as has been glaringly proven in this particular case," Agent Velardi comprehended and professed. "As another example of precisely what I mean, one of my favorite rock concert DVDs is the phenomenal Eagles *Farewell 1 Tour* performed and filmed in Melbourne, Australia!"

# "The Thirteenth Victim"

On Saturday morning, September 19, 2015, several weeks after the treacherous "Beauty in the Least Case", FBI Inspector Joe Giralo was passively seated in his comfortable den perusing the headlines in the morning edition of the *Press of Atlantic City.* The approaching arrival of the Autumnal Equinox signaling the Northern Hemisphere end of summer had prompted Agent Arthur Orsi and wife Carol to spend the lazy weekend in a plush hotel near Baltimore's popular Inner Harbor and the prospect of fall and winter had compelled Agent Dan Blachford and wife Bing to enjoy a pleasant short hiatus at a quiet and cozy Cape May, New Jersey bed and breakfast. But a sudden 10 a.m. phone call from revered Matt Riley down in Washington DC instantly interrupted the Inspector's tranquil disposition. Reluctantly, the slightly disturbed man of the house slowly picked-up the annoying, loud-ringing phone from its table cradle.

After conversing and conferring for several minutes, the Orchard Street federal official decided to diplomatically terminate the dialogue. "Okay Matt," Joe Giralo sternly agreed. "Arty and Dan are out of town until tomorrow night. I'll head on over to Sal's place on Peach Street and discuss this urgent matter with him. Sometimes Agent Velardi has a terrific brainstorm that brings more clarity to in-progress criminal activity. I'll keep you updated about any important developments that *our* preliminary research discovers." Click.

After gulping-down the remaining ounce of his morning coffee, Inspector Giralo rapidly paced to an adjacent room, rinsed his empty cup under the faucet and placed it inside the kitchen sink. 'Gina's already out shopping in Mays Landing at the Hamilton Mall with Sal's wife Kathy,' the now-focused Inspector remembered, 'so Sal and I can have a private and confidential government business discussion. I'll catch him at home before he drives over to the Silver Coin Diner to have his standard Saturday morning breakfast.'

Soon, Inspector Giralo exited his Orchard Street residence, entered his huge gray Chevy Suburban, fired-up the engine and drove his enormous vehicle the familiar six blocks to Agent Velardi's recently remodeled house. After the Boss's surprise "guest visit" had been acknowledged by *his* subordinate, Joe Giralo was cordially invited inside and then swiftly escorted to the home's breakfast nook where the gentlemen's conversation would be conducted.

"Salvatore, I just received a rather alarming Saturday morning phone call from my superior, or should I say *our* illustrious superior

Matt Riley down in DC," the Chief prefaced his remarks. "As you know, Arty is down in Baltimore and Dan is in Cape May, so that leaves just you and me to contemplate and consider a rash of recent missing person bulletins in the New Jersey, Pennsylvania, Delaware and metropolitan New York City vicinities. These very alarming disappearances may or may not be connected."

"The Inner Harbor waterfront is a really neat venue," Agent Velardi politely verified. "The delicious specialties sold there are especially fabulous, starting with the crabs and spicy shrimp at the Phillips Seafood counter. Or after Arty and Carol visit the nearby spectacular aquarium, some quaint Italian restaurants are within casual walking distance from the Inner Harbor over in Little Italy. I hope Arty gets to tour Fort McHenry before returning to Jersey. If I recollect correctly, that's where…"

"During the War of 1812 against the British, Francis Scott Key had patriotically authored the lyrics to 'The Star-Spangled Banner'," Joe Giralo authoritatively vociferated. "The original flag at Fort McHenry is now a prominent exhibit inside the Smithsonian Institute's American History Museum. Say Sal, did you know that the *Star-Spangled Banner's* melody was actually taken from an old English pub drinking song?"

"How ironic, Chief! You say that our National Anthem is a plagiarism from a now-obscure ordinary British drinking song," Agent Velardi alertly observed and commented. "And you claim that the whole thing had been copied from the British during a major Baltimore Harbor battle against the Redcoats! This is only the fifth time you've told me *that* historical fact!"

After generally evaluating *his* underling's logical assessment, and next wishing to extend Agent Velardi's utter suspense about the impeding FBI investigation, Inspector Giralo switched the subject from Agent Orsi's Maryland escapade to Dan Blachford's Cape May excursion. "And Salvatore, I presume that Dan and Bing will soon become bored staying inside the bed and breakfast and will become motivated to take the ferry from Cape May over to Lewes, Delaware, perhaps as regular foot passengers. The seventeen-mile bay cruise is rather calm during September, and schools of dolphins often accompany the ferry as it makes its scheduled transit across Delaware Bay. Buses at the Lewes terminal efficiently transport tourists to enormous shopping outlets several miles away, or perhaps even shuttle them to Rehoboth Beach where folks could stroll the resort's boardwalk before again boarding a bus and conveniently returning to the Lewes terminal to take the awaiting ferry back to Cape May.," Inspector Giralo prattled. "Sal, did you know that Cape May once billed-itself as 'America's First Resort' and that Presidents Franklin Pierce and Benjamin Harrison preferred vacationing there in the 1800s?"

"No, I wasn't aware of *that* particular, insignificant, historical trivia," Agent Velardi rather dispassionately answered. "But Chief, could you now get back to the subject-at-hand and…."

"Yes," Joe Giralo reflexively stipulated, paying little heed or attention to his frustrated colleague's request. "And just like Cape May, our town of Hammonton has had its own bit of history, too. I mean," the garrulous Inspector paused to ascertain the impact of his mediocre oratory upon his disenchanted listener, "Teddy Roosevelt's whistle-stop Presidential Campaign Train stopped here in the early 1900s on its way to Atlantic City, and also, John Philip Sousa's Marine Band gave a sensational concert in the 1920s. Ya' know Salvatore, I really relish that wonderful marching song *The Stars and Stripes Forever.* And did you know that in her youth, the noted anthropologist Margaret Mead had helped her sociologist mother do vital research on the early Italian immigrants working on Hammonton farms after the turn of the last century? Mead and her pioneering mother had been living in a small house on Fairview Avenue. In many respects," Giralo proudly emphasized, "Hammonton is equally as historical as Cape May is!"

"Now Boss, in all due courtesy, what type of wicked criminal activity has inspired you to make this unexpected trip to Peach Street? Please satisfy my overabundant curiosity! Oh yes, I remember now. It concerns missing persons, I believe!"

Inspector Giralo introspectively glanced-up at a certain religious painting conspicuously hanging above the portal separating the Velardi kitchen area from the abode's dining room. The colorful 'Last Supper' rendition had recently been skillfully attached to the above wall segment by the property's resident/artist.

"I see you've finally finished your challenging creative endeavor," Chief Giralo commended. "The total project required a full month's labor, if I accurately recollect. I must congratulate you, Salvatore! The end result is most appealing indeed!"

"Well, Boss. As you can recall, two months ago I was descending the stairs while stupidly putting a dollar bill in my wallet at the same time. I awkwardly missed a step and speedily tumbled six feet to the ground floor, in the process double-spraining my left ankle. Since I had been incapacitated for five weeks and had to go on disability, Kathy thoughtfully purchased the 'Last Supper' paint-by-numbers product you're now viewing at a hobby shop. My wife desired to keep my mind occupied during my monotonous month-long convalescence. Behold the fruits of my dedicated effort!"

"Rather magnificent, indeed," the somewhat impressed FBI Boss complimented, "but not exactly a da Vinci. Someday, my Good Man, I'm going to teach you how to walk, chew gum and snap your fingers all simultaneously," Giralo jested, entertaining his gigantic ego at Agent Velardi's expense. "You know what I mean, Sal. I'll show you how to successfully perform three unique, concurrent functions instead of just two!"

"Very hilarious, Chief!" Velardi protested and exaggerated, weakly feigning his overall embarrassment. "It was a painful injury caused by a mere moment of lack of concentration. But I really learned my lesson from the terrible experience. I'm now especially careful every time I ascend or descend steps! Now Boss, I'm not a lightbulb, but try illuminating me anyway. What serious FBI matter has brought you to my front doorstep? Or, should I say: what is the magnitude of these missing person reports?"

"As I've already alluded, there has been a rash of East Coast missing person dispatches originating from various police departments over the course of the last month," grim-faced Joe Giralo indicated and revealed. "And yes, Salvatore. It's *our* expressed duty to solve this fairly perplexing riddle. Get in touch with Arty and Dan tomorrow night after the guys come back to Hammonton from their little side-trips. I want to see you' and my other two veteran sleuths in my 'Philly office at noon on Monday. We'll then thoroughly review all of the relevant details that pertain to this rather baffling conundrum. And Sal, I'd like you to comprehensively compile a list of all missing persons that have mysteriously disappeared from American society within a hundred-mile radius of Hammonton. We'll then fully examine and thoroughly interpret all available pertinent information in my office on Monday!"

* * * * * * * * * * * *


Just like clockwork, at 11:55 a.m. true-blue FBI Agents Salvatore Velardi, Arthur Orsi and Dan Blachford stepped into the central lobby elevator inside the federal building at 600 Arch Street, Philadelphia. Recognizing that Inspector Giralo's office had been moved from the third floor to the eighth, G-man Velardi hesitated and almost pressed the "3 Button" instead of the "8" one. A minute later, the loyal trio departed the people transporter and soon presented themselves to Mrs. Alice Jensen, Giralo's new secretary/receptionist, who then granted the three 'expected' government agents' a speedy entrance into the legendary Main Man's prime base of operation.

"Hi Boss," Agent Velardi greeted the pensive-looking individual behind the Canadian oak desk seated inside his black leather swivel chair. "Arty, Dan and I have been busy studying the identities, occupations and towns of twelve missing persons within a hundred-mile radius, just as you had austerely directed us to do."

"Yeah, Chief," contributed a now well-rested Agent Orsi. "We're well-trained human beings with high self-esteem, so please address us as if we aren't three imbecile zombies. Frankly, Dan and I are fully relaxed and we're both quite anxious to get back to the conscientious art and science of federal crime solving!"

"Well, Inspector, I'm back to work after being rejuvenated in breezy Cape May," Dan Blachford next informed. "Bing and I really love that seaside town and its many marvelous houses, most of them featuring splendid Victorian architecture."

"Okay, Men. Let's stop with the traditional introductory statements and the shallow frivolous platitudes," criticized Joe Giralo. "Let's cut the fat out and get to the meat of the matter. Now Salvatore, please describe the first four area people who have rather strangely disappeared from public scrutiny over the course of the last month or so."

Agent Velardi lowly grunted, cleared his throat and then methodically explained that Andy Morgan, a variety store proprietor from West Chester, Pennsylvania; Nate Crowley, a community college professor from Blackwood, New Jersey; James Dempsey, an architect from Yonkers, New York and Jim Reynolds, a building contractor from Freehold, New Jersey had all enigmatically vanished from the face of the Earth.

"Thanks, Sal. You've greatly added to my empirical knowledge," Giralo facetiously added with a contrived frown evident upon his chubby countenance. "Now Arty, what valuable facts can you provide that'll aid us in satisfactorily cracking this extremely bewildering regional missing persons' caper."

"Well, Chief, I'll hereby capably cover victims five through eight," Agent Orsi volunteered and offered. "Number five is John Hawkins, an electrician from New Castle, Delaware. Six is Thad Saunders, a police sergeant from Elkton, Maryland. Seven happens to be Matt Walsh, a newspaper journalist working out of Dover, Delaware, and missing person Number 8 is Pete Sheridan, a computer programmer employed in White Plains, New York."

"Excellent presentation, Arty," lavishly praised the Inspector. "Now kindly notice fellas' that all of the missing humans are males and not females or wandering zombies. Tell me, Dan, why don't you define for us the next four innocent-but-victimized missing individuals you've researched."

Equal to the assigned task, Agent Blachford read from his hand-held paper that Phil Taylor, a prominent stockbroker from Media, Pennsylvania, Simon Heggan, a chemical engineer living in Glassboro, New Jersey, Tom Jacobs, a wealthy plumber from Allentown, Pennsylvania and lastly, Andrew Mason, a gas station owner from Waterford, New Jersey had all somehow been mystically eradicated from known human existence.

"Thank you, Fellas'," Inspector Giralo austerely replied. "You honest men are not mushrooms, so I won't keep you in the dark and feed you an abundance of fecal matter. This morning, I received a call from our distinguished mentor Matt Riley down in DC headquarters, and guess what?" the flamboyant Boss rhetorically asked. "We put our heads together and with our combined talents, Riley and I managed to crack this fairly confusing case wide open!"

"What?" loudly exclaimed Agent Velardi. "Which of you' two geniuses is Albert Einstein, and which guru is the incomparable Leonardo da Vinci?"

"Actually, Salvatore, you aren't too far off in your wild conjecture!" laughed Joe Giralo in his inimitable, hysterical style. "I must admit that it all started with *your* magnificent painting of the Last Supper suspended on the wall between your kitchen and dining room. Sal, if it wasn't for you, Riley and I would've never been able to sagely unravel this bizarre case!"

"I think I need both an IQ Test and a professional Psychological Analysis," flustered Agent Velardi replied. "Truthfully, I'm certainly no Michelangelo by any means, but what might Leonardo da Vinci have to do with your plausibly solving this totally cryptic missing persons' case? Is the phantom mastermind behind these kidnappings named Mona Lisa by any chance?"

Amused by Agent Velardi's humorous response, Inspector Giralo (as was his typical fashion) proceeded to evade the central theme and instead gave a tangential and seemingly immaterial account. The Boss completely bored his audience of three and loquaciously driveled-on about how he and his wife had in the late 1990s been on a Globus Company bus tour across Italy, and how the couple's entourage had visited Milan's Teatro alla Scala opera house and enjoyed the performance of the Barber of Seville, which had been followed the next day by our tourist group's expedition to the Convent of Santa Maria delle Grazie where the famous fresco painting "The Last Supper" was wonderfully exhibited on a full wall.

372

"Another painting titled 'The Crucifixion' by a lesser-known artist than Leonardo da Vinci, a fellow by the name of Giovanni Donato da Montofano was displayed on an opposite wall of the revered convent. It seems that Leonardo was just as secretive as the cunning brains behind this skein of brazen kidnappings, since da Vinci, fearing punishment from the post-medieval Church Inquisitions of *his* time. The Renaissance genius stealthily wrote most of his notes in mirror writing. No one ever deciphered *his* imaginative encryption until someone accidentally viewed his scribbling while looking backwards into a mirror. Now Leonardo's paintings were done in the late 1400s, and actually, Columbus discovering America was not nearly as significant an event as the Spanish defeating the Moors in Central Spain had been at the time, and thus, their valiant crusade saving the existence of what today is specifically known as Western Civilization."

"Excuse my excessive ignorance. Boss," Sal Velardi genuinely insisted. "But exactly what does my amateurish re-creation of Leonardo da Vinci's 'Last Supper' have to do with you' very competently unlocking the essential aspects in this most intricate 'missing persons' crime-wave?"

"None of this outlandish gibberish you're mentioning makes any decent sense," opined a totally befuddled Agent Orsi. "To tell the truth, I should've stayed a few more days at the less complicated and easy-to-understand Inner Harbor."

"Be more definitive Boss," Dan Blachford sincerely urged the often-evasive and facetious federal administrator. "The refreshing Rehoboth Beach Boardwalk was much more fathomable than either you or arcane Matt Riley!"

"Okay, my fine, rational Gentlemen," Joe Giralo related with a rather apparent broad smile showing above his fleshy neck and chin. "I'll begin my precise explanation from Square One!"

* * * * * * * * * * * *

"Now Salvatore, as you had learned in elementary school catechism class, Jesus had presided over the Last Supper, which had been attended in Jerusalem by his twelve apostles, including the notorious traitor Judas Iscariot," Inspector Giralo firmly stated. "And the Last Supper meal was probably financed by Joseph of Arimathea, a wealthy disciple of Christ."

"Boss, was Joseph of Arimathea good at arithmetic and math' as his name suggests?" quipped a disappointed Arthur Orsi.

"Yes," concurred Dan Blachford in a lesser-jovial spirit. "Did he excel in trigonometry too? Now Chief, I really wish you would stop your habitual, frivolous rambling along with your constant, bothersome, didactic propensity for equivocation."

"Besides *those* horrendously bad practices, Inspector, I suspect that you might even be grossly prevaricating, too," chimed-in an agitated Sal Velardi. "Let's get back to the original Last Supper theme in relation to these twelve diabolical kidnappings that have just been established."

Undeterred by his agents' severe objections, Inspector Giralo continued academically explaining the extraordinary background role of Joseph of Arimathea, who was according to most Biblical accounts, believed to be the uncle of the Virgin Mary. "After the Crucifixion, Joseph of Arimathea had gone to Pontius Pilate and had convinced the Roman Governor to give him possession of Christ's body, which was to be then buried in Joseph's tomb."

"But what does the Last Supper painting hanging in my house have to do with these twelve coincidental missing person reports?" frustrated Agent Velardi demanded knowing. "There's a rather mammoth disconnect here if you ask me! It all exceeds my limited comprehension!"

"Salvatore, there's a major difference between being insightful and being inciteful. Now, for the sake of sanity, please read and review the *first names* of the twelve males that have not only been recently kidnapped, but probably also maliciously murdered," Chief Giralo commanded in a very stringent tone of voice. "This unusual conversation we're conducting definitely needs to have more-light and less heat!"

Embarrassed Agent Velardi immediately peered-down at the already referred-to list and recited: "Andy, Nate, James, Jim, John, Thad, Matt, Pete, Phil, Simon, Tom and finally, Andrew again."

"Now if you three men were sophisticated Biblical scholars," Joe Giralo asserted and maintained, "you would astutely realize that the twelve specific names typed upon your duplicated lists coincide with the names of the apostles present at the Last Supper: "Andrew, Nathaniel, James the Elder, James the Younger, John, Thaddeus, Matthew, and Peter, who is also known as Simon Peter, the disciples' banker. Peter was reputed to be a trifle stingy, and our English word par*simon*ious is derived from *his* name."

"What about the remainder of the apostles seated at the Last Supper? Agent Blachford asked. "Who were they?"

"And to round-out the attendees," the solemn-faced FBI Inspector softly communicated, "there is Philip, Simon the Zealot, Thomas, and then as you had pertinently mentioned, back to Andrew again at the top of the list. This repetitious pattern implies that the whole kidnapping/murder scenario is being repeated, and the pattern is obviously using the same apostle first names over again, beginning with 'Andrew'."

"But weren't there twelve apostles at the Last Supper?" argued Arthur Orsi. "What happened to Number Twelve, Judas? Why was he deliberately left out in this perverted kidnapping scheme?"

"Great observation Arty!" Inspector Giralo determined and expounded. "Jesus plus His twelve apostles present at the Last Supper amounts to the Number 13. This sum is precisely why thirteen is often considered by many to be an unlucky number."

"A baker's dozen," grumbled and complained Agent Velardi. "Once I was a customer inside the bakery on Fairview Avenue and asked the clerk for a baker's dozen. I was promptly given a box with twelve doughnuts in it along with a white bag containing number thirteen. Then I was rudely charged for all thirteen doughnuts! But Boss, where is the traitor Judas inside this totally absurd, stranger-than-fiction Biblical/crime equation?"

Inspector Giralo took a deep breath and then divulged that he and Matt Riley had collaborated in performing an intensive FBI computer search and eventually learned that Judas Iscariot in real contemporary life would probably be a woman on record born 'Judith Iscariot'. After converting from Catholicism to Islam, the evil contemptuous woman cleverly changed her name to Alika Icaria. Quite weirdly enough, Alika means 'Love' in Arabic," Inspector Giralo explained. "Judith Iscariot had been born up in the Lehigh Valley near Bethlehem, Pennsylvania and ironically, was later raised in Nazareth, just outside Philly'. Our records confirm that she had converted to Islam at the age of twenty-five and frequently attended a mosque outside Trenton."

"This preposterous story still lacks tremendous clarification," Agent Blachford protested. "Why did this Judith Iscariot felon turn violent and start having men kidnapped and murdered in five different states?"

"At age twenty-three Judith became an apostate to the Catholic religion and quickly left the convent where she had been preparing to become a nun," Chief Giralo disclosed. "She immediately switched her faith to Islam but soon became involved in the profitable underworld economy drug smuggling and heroine distribution network. During her minor crime activities, Ms. Icaria had been arrested twice, once in Jersey and a second time in Pennsy', so that's how her ignominious name had appeared in our FBI database."

"But how did you and Riley trace her name as the targeted kidnapper?" questioned a still-skeptical Arthur Orsi. "In fact, Boss, how do you know that this unscrupulous female, Alika Icaria was a dangerous, wanton murderer?"

"Because all of the twelve kidnapped victims were Catholics and had former illicit drug business dealings with Alika Icaria," the Chief calmly expressed. "Riley and I sensed that there were plenty of double-crossing maneuvers and deals going on between all thirteen people. And early this morning victim Number Twelve, Andrew Morgan was found decapitated inside a farmer's septic tank that was being cleaned-out over in Waterford, New Jersey. The various factors then all neatly added-up: a jaded woman studying to become a nun converts to Islam; Islamic terrorists behead people; Andrew Morgan was kidnapped and then savagely beheaded. Several of the other victims had in the past been associated with drug-related arrests. And amazingly, my oddball hypothesis all began with my eyes keenly peering at Agent Velardi's copycat version of Leonardo da Vinci's fantastic Last Supper."

"Gee, Boss," uttered a fully astounded Arthur Orsi. "I don't think that da Vinci's painting 'The Last Supper' would be nearly as famous today if it had been horribly and originally misnamed 'The Final Dinner'.

# "Holiday Hooligans"

The very interesting English word "Holiday" originally pertained to the specific nomenclature "Holy Day" before secularism became the watchword/monitor of modern times. Before School Winter Break, before School Spring Break, and before Love/Chocolate Gift Day ever existed, religious celebrations of Christmas, of Easter and of St. Valentine Day were revered Christian "Holy Days" appearing on the yearly calendar.

The very interesting English word "Holiday" originally pertained to the specific nomenclature "Holy Day" before secularism became the watchword/monitor of modern times. Before School Winter Break, before School Spring Break and before Love/Chocolate Gift Day ever existed, religious celebrations of Christmas, of Easter and of St. Valentine Day were revered Christian "Holy Days" appearing on the yearly calendar. Chief FBI Inspector Joe Giralo still remains one of those old-fashioned advocates of tradition who wishes that Christmas (and not X-mas) would continue to be a tribute about the birth of Christ and that Easter would not exclusively be about the particular activities of the ever-ubiquitous, egg-distributing, basket-carrying, harebrained, totally juvenile "Holiday Bunny".

At noon, on Monday, December 9, 2019 a rather fatigued FBI Inspector Joe Giralo had summoned his three principal agents, Salvatore Velardi, Arthur Orsi and Dan Blachford into his eighth-floor office situated inside the all-too-familiar 600 Arch Street Federal Building, Philadelphia, Pennsylvania. As usual, the curious entrants found their illustrious superior sitting rather stationary behind his massive Canadian oak desk with his brown eyes seemingly transfixed, their superior's large pupils scanning the Philadelphia Inquirer's "above the crease" morning headlines. The veteran crime-fighter's ever-vigilant mind was apparently keenly engrossed in much more serious illegal matters than those particular trivial news' stories, which his always-alert cerebral processes were then intensely evaluating. Finally, the Boss recognized the presence of his three loyal underlings.

"Greetings, Men!" the Chief rather nonchalantly acknowledged, lowering the slightly wrinkled newspaper below eye level. "Glad you three somewhat-experienced sleuths were performing your regular duties in the building when my secretary had summoned you' illustrious dynamos from your cramped cubicles. We've got some important business to attend to, but first of all," Inspector Giralo predictably deviated, "I want to know how you men had spent the recent Pearl Harbor Day weekend. It's too bad that December 7th isn't declared a national holiday. Now tell me: what did *you* do Sal?"

"Well, Chief, I took my wife and kids to New York where we enjoyed seeing the terrific Christmas Show at Radio City Music Hall," Agent Velardi disclosed. "Kathy really was impressed with the Rockettes' fantastic performance, and the kids really relished the 'March of the Toy Soldiers'."

"And how about you, Arty? How did you and Carol spend Saturday, Pearl Harbor Day?"

"Okay, Chief. My wife and I drove east to Smithville Village, which was well-decorated for the Christmas season," Agent Orsi revealed. "We ate a delicious lunch at the historic Smithville Inn, perused the many gift shops in the quaint village and then anxiously motored over to Harrah's Casino to try our luck in Atlantic City. I lost a hundred bucks playing blackjack, but Carol got lucky on the slots and canceled-out my losses. In all, our Atlantic City gambol to gamble was not especially lucrative, but we did have fun!"

"And Dan, what did you and Bing do on Saturday?" Inspector Giralo inquired as if the master detective were conducting a rather important criminal interrogation.

"My wife and I took a really fascinating South Jersey steam locomotive train ride on the 'Santa Express', which is a seasonal branch of the area Cape May Seashore Line," Agent Blachford suavely articulated. "The unique trip was a fifteen-mile fun excursion from Richland to Tuckahoe. Of course, Santa was a mobile passenger on the slow-moving train, and his presence was enjoyed by the many children who had been escorted by their doting parents. And also," Dan Blachford elaborated, "jolly St. Nicholas was accompanied by a host of Dickens-dressed Victorian carolers, and to add to the pre-winter experience, soft background music was provided by a talented accordion player. We savored the scenic ride back to the Richland boarding station; in fact, just as much as we delighted in taking the parallel rails out to Tuckahoe."

"Well, Boss. Now that you know what we did over the Pearl Harbor weekend," Agent Velardi piped-up, "exactly what sort of caper did you do? Go flying around in a Japanese Zero?"

"If you really want to know, Salvatore," a slightly annoyed Inspector Giralo answered in a feigned, gruff tone of voice, "Gina and I did some preliminary Christmas shopping at the Deptford Mall. Afterwards, my exhausted wife and I consumed a sumptuous filet dinner at the nearby Longhorn Steakhouse."

Sensing that the time for cursory small-talk chatter had expired, Agent Sal Velardi requested to learn about the real reason the three

FBI men had been asked to report to the Inspector's spacious office. Joe Giralo reached into the top drawer of his desk, and his search produced a commonplace oak-tag folder similar to ones in which school children keep their graded English writing compositions.

"Guys, this is perhaps the most bizarre, eccentric, nonsensical case that I've ever been assigned to investigate," Giralo prefaced. "Our ingenious mentor Matt Riley down at D.C. headquarters dispatched an encrypted communique just two hours ago and requested that my team attempt to decipher exactly what is going on."

The Chief quickly distributed copies of the newly transmitted information to his trio of assistants, who then diligently studied the strange contents while their boss provided additional input. "Now Men, these rather insane activities I'm about to describe occur on standard United States holidays. Five nutcases will enter a privately-owned family convenience store," Giralo communicated, "and the queer quintet would be dressed in costumes appropriately related to the particular holiday being celebrated. The five customers would then point their water pistols at the clerk or proprietor behind the counter, and instead of robbing the establishment in question, the five would hand-over a thousand dollars in crisp, unmarked hundred-dollar-bills and then exit the premises and speed-off inside a six-passenger van."

"This is some sort of weird crimewave happening in reverse," an intrigued Agent Arthur Orsi noted. "Instead of performing an armed heist with real guns, the tricky intruders use harmless water pistols and then philanthropically give the dumbfounded owner or clerk a bonanza of a thousand smackers."

"Right, Arty," Chief Giralo affirmed. "I suspect that the ruse is more pernicious than it appears on the simplistic surface. Now Salvatore, I'd like you to read the first three crazy incidents that are described on the printout-sheet I've just disseminated."

"New Year's Day, Tuesday, January 1st, 2019. Five individuals gaudily dressed as mummers enter a Philadelphia deli and hand-over a thousand bucks to the astonished Quaker City female employee that had been standing behind the counter. The outlandish intruders then evacuate the West Philly business and hop into a van driven by another fellow, who is also dressed in pretentious mummer's garb."

After a moment of exhibiting intense hilarity with his government associates, Agent Velardi read to his alert audience of three that on Tuesday, February 12th, 2019, five bearded men dressed as Abraham Lincoln (wearing high stovepipe hats and black suits) entered a novelty store in Las Vegas, Nevada, gave the shocked worker a cool thousand bucks and speedily departed without ever firing their loaded water pistols.

The third absurd, corresponding incident occurred in Atlanta, Georgia on Sunday, St. Patrick's Day, March 17, 2019. Five merry leprechaun imitators, acting in an outlandish and ridiculous manner, presented the fellow manning the cash register with ten "Ben Franklins" and then anxiously evacuated the corner retail store and next, quickly hopped into an awaiting van that soon accelerated out of its temporary parking space.

Agent Dan Blachford was then designated by the Chief to read items four through seven that had been listed on the printout sheet, and subsequently, Agent Arthur Orsi was assigned to read events seven though eleven. Amidst great amusement exhibited by the four men, here are the incredible results that had been identified on the official communique copies that had been sent by Supervisor Matt Riley from FBI D.C. headquarters:

4)    Easter Sunday, April 21, 2019. Five individuals in colorful Easter Bunny apparel intentionally hand a thousand dollars to a petrified Los Angeles store clerk.

5)    Memorial Day, Monday, May 27, 2019. Five men dressed in Army, Navy, Marines, Air Force and Coast Guard garb eagerly point loaded water pistols at an Austin, Texas store employee, and then the impostors gladly hand over a thousand non-counterfeit dollars.

6)    Friday, June 14, 2019, Flag Day. Five men wearing typical Uncle Sam costumes enter a Denver, Colorado convenience store and threaten to shoot water pistols at the astonished husband-and-wife duo standing behind the counter. Instead, the imaginative trespassers generously provide the startled couple with a thousand dollars in cold cash, and then the pseudo-patriotic charlatans rapidly speed-away in a van wildly driven by a sixth Uncle Sam.

"Okay, Arty. It's your turn to review occurrences seven though eleven; that is, if you can cease your incessant laughing," Chief Giralo mildly admonished. "Gentlemen, I realize that *this* matter seems to be lunacy to the tenth power, so please try to control yourselves and act professionally as Agent Orsi adequately describes in detail the remaining peculiar episodes."

7)    "Thursday, July 4, 2019: American Independence Day. Indianapolis, Indiana," still giggling Agent Orsi read out loud. "Five white-wigged gentlemen masquerading as colonial George Washington enter a corner grocery store and deliver a thousand-dollar bonus to the extremely stunned owner."

8)    Saturday, August 3, 2019. El Paso, Texas: Watermelon Day. Five muscular males wearing round straw hats and dressed in blue

denim overalls, that were held-up by immense, thick matching suspenders, threaten to drench the main store clerk with water pistols but instead, voluntarily deliver ten hundred-dollar greenbacks to the astounded manager.

9) Monday, September 2, 2019: Labor Day. Houston, Texas. Five men imaginatively disguised as pregnant women, having large soft pillows stuffed inside their acquired maternity outfits, provide the store proprietor with a handsome thousand dollars in cash.

10) Monday, October 14, 2019: Columbus Day. Pittsburgh, Pennsylvania. Five males dressed as fifteenth century Spanish ship navigators grant a totally surprised candy shop employee a thousand-dollar reward to be immediately placed into the confectionary business's ancient-looking cash register.

11) Thursday, November 28, 2019: Thanksgiving Day. Irvine, California. Five fascinating men disguised as Mayflower Pilgrims hand-over a thousand bucks to the rattled-and-confused elderly convenience store manager.

After the three assembled FBI agents finally stopped their relentless laughter, Chief Joe Giralo insisted that his humored G-Men ask some pertinent questions designed to help solve the outrageous conundrum that had been egregiously puzzling their investigative minds.

"But Chief. If the prospective bandits give away money instead of pilfering it in an unlawful manner, I don't see how any general or specific crime has been committed!" Agent Velardi volunteered his objective conclusion. "The only aspect of a crime I can determine that might involve FBI intervention is that these similar events have transpired in many different states."

"Sal's absolutely, logically correct!" chimed-in Agent Arthur Orsi. "Has criminal behavior gone completely bonkers and off the rails? This entire oddball scenario we've been scrupulously analyzing, and quite frankly, wasting our precious time upon, is preposterously puzzling, to say the least!"

"Well, Chief," Agent Dan Blachford began his evaluative inquiry, "do the clever masqueraders demand anything in return for contributing a thousand clams to store personnel once each monthly holiday, occurring in various cities all across America?"

"Dan, I'm glad you asked *that* very relevant question," Inspector Giralo commended usually reticent Agent Blachford. "Yes, the five holiday-disguised mimickers do make two distinct purchases each time that they enter a different shop each month."

"And exactly what do the idiotic rascals buy?" a very curious Agent Velardi strongly desired learning.

"Apparently, Sal, each of the five prankster-holiday-honoring personages truly possesses a sweet tooth. Every time the candy lovers randomly enter a convenience store on a celebrated holiday, the group habitually purchases two chocolate bars in exchange for a thousand cash bucks: the first being a Pay Day Bar, and the second, a 100 Grand Bar," a somewhat addled Joe Giralo replied. "Now Guys, we'll meet again here in my office a full week from today, Monday, December 16 at noon. I want you three Dick Tracy-types to thoroughly research and report back every single iota you detect about this candy phenomenon that has been discussed so far. Something is definitely amiss in this perplexing sequence of loony holiday fiascos," Inspector Giralo hypothesized and concluded, "and I desire learning precisely what is going on in certain urban convenience stores throughout the country on special calendar holidays!"

* * * * * * * * * * * *

When Agents Salvatore Velardi, Arthur Orsi and Dan Blachford strolled into the first-floor lobby of Philadelphia FBI headquarters at 600 Arch Street at noon on Monday, December 16, the three purpose-minded government officials were casually discussing the amusing theory that their "arcane boss" Chief Inspector Joe Giralo's "uncanny problem-solving ability" was indeed one hundred percent intuitive. The discourse proceeded in the following manner:

"Our distinguished Mentor always reiterates to us that certain wily criminals, along with avowed terrorists, are people, just like us, and that those same nefarious folks tend to think and behave in observable and measurable patterns, just like *we* do," Agent Velardi accurately declared as the 'dynamic trio' awaited the arrival of the lobby elevator to transport them up to the building's eighth floor. "But truly, the Inspector has the extraordinary capacity to connect formerly unrelated dots that then ultimately lead *us* to interpreting certain enigmatic developments. Our boss calls his fantastic talent 'a simple knack', but I think it's all much more complicated than just that! He seems to marvelously discover the critical missing element that literally always tends to confound and elude the three of us!"

"Yes, Sal. I wholeheartedly agree with your depiction," Agent Art Orsi confirmed. "I still think the Chief is more than a tad psychic, although he constantly maintains that all he does is cleverly associate parallel situations. He then uses the process of deduction inside the ordinary 'scientific method of thinking' in order to amazingly verify his authentic theories. I believe that our eminent 'Mentor' is also our diabolical 'Tormentor'."

"Ha, ha, ha!" Agent Dan Blachford cheerfully reacted as the familiar gray metal elevator doors slowly opened. "Of course, Arty, when we quietly enter *his* solemn sanctuary, the Chief will instinctively make us suffer through listening to a barrage of irrelevant small-talk. I hope that you fellas' are better prepared than I am in regard to explaining the ludicrous stunts being enacted by these very baffling holiday masqueraders."

Upon exiting the elevator at the eighth-floor, Agents Velardi, Orsi and Blachford swiftly paced into Chief Joe Giralo's office and immediately noticed their distinguished superior predictably sitting behind his prodigious oak desk and conscientiously examining the front-page newspaper headlines of the morning *Philadelphia Inquirer.* Raising his balding head, the inimitable Inspector was quite pleased upon realizing that his "very capable threesome" had punctually arrived to honor their scheduled Monday, December 16 noon conference with their erudite mentor.

"Hi Boss," usually laconic Dan Blachford greeted. "What does the morning paper have to divulge today? It's really yesterday's news, and soon most daily rags will be obsolete just like the Pony Express, Conestoga wagons and the Morse Code Telegraph. If you really want to get what's developing right this minute," Blachford offered, "you need to rely solely on your trusty hand computer!"

"I got quite bored with the main headlines," somewhat-aggravated Joe Giralo answered, "so I rummaged to page fifteen and read where two altar boys over in Spain had mischievously put marijuana in the church censer. After burning the censer contents, the Catholic priests who were saying Mass were really fuming!"

"That's one way to get Catholic priests *incensed!*" intrepidly joked Agent Arthur Orsi. "But Boss, you're correct in observing that real news is now mixed-in with pathetic tabloid journalism. I actually think that social media is the true culprit that's wholly responsible for *that* grotesque metamorphosis."

"Needless to say, Boss," Agent Velardi facetiously spoke-up before Giralo could respond to Agent Orsi, "the exasperated Spanish priests soon found-out that there was pot in the pot!"

"Fellas', take your seats," Inspector Giralo announced in an almost apologetic tone, feeling a bit guilty for being drawn into the rather inane conversation. "This will be an abbreviated session for us today because I have an upcoming appointment with several highly-motivated rookie recruits that's slated for 12:30."

"An appointment is always better than a disappointment," jested Agent Velardi.

"Salvatore, you'd better watch your ridiculous sense of humor or else you might be replaced by one of the Bureau's neophytes that I'm about to interview," the slightly irritated Chief chastised his main G-Man. "I think that you might actually fit-in better writing off-the-wall satire and parody scripts for Comedy Central. I could be wrong, but you might even work your way up to organizing hilarious dialogue for South Park!"

"Sorry, Boss," the Team Captain candidly indicated. "Sometimes my mouth gets ahead of my brain."

"As I was saying," Giralo proceeded while nodding his head to show that he had tacitly accepted his subordinate's sincere statement of regret, "today I'm dispensing with the regular picayune small-talk about what you three Dr. Watsons had done over the weekend. As for me, I've already completed my holiday gift buying and have erected this year's Christmas tree," Giralo characteristically boasted. "As you dedicated Guys know, I'm a devout miniature-train enthusiast, and I've even gotten my village platform organized early so that the neighborhood kids can appreciate how yesteryear youngsters used to enjoy themselves before this terrible age of sophisticated hand-held computers and annoying video games."

"That's really great Inspector," impatient Agent Orsi half-heartedly appreciated. "But what have you and Matt Riley's stellar committee down in D.C. learned about these conniving holiday mimickers? Honestly, I think we're wandering a trifle off-subject reviewing *your* many mediocre Christmas preparations!"

"Not exactly, Arty. There's an old maxim among newspaper editors that goes, 'Dog bites old man; no story. Old man bites dog; absolutely a frontpage, newsworthy story'," Joe Giralo sternly expressed. "I believe that these bizarre holiday masqueraders are creating a distinct diversion for something more sinister that's happening. Naturally, the moronic media pays attention to the insane, superficial behavior that's in progress while the distracted press obviously usually ignores rather ordinary criminal acts that are simultaneously and deliberately occurring. Now Arty, kindly give me a non-superficial synopsis of what your recent academic research has uncovered."

Agent Orsi coughed and then delivered a formal dissertation about how Pay Day candy bars had originated on the retail market in 1932, but the brand name had then been sold to Consolidated Foods in 1938; however, Consolidated Foods later became the Sara Lee Company. "The very delicious peanut and caramel candy bar production and distribution rights are currently owned by the Hershey Corporation," Art Orsi skillfully communicated.

Agent Dan Blachford then orated a brief summary of the 100 Grand Bar created in 1964, which formerly had the title "Hundred Thousand Dollar Bar" until 1986. "The delectable ingredients are chocolate, chewy caramel and crispy rice," Blachford methodically explained, "and the candy bar was a product of the Nestle Company until last year, but now in 2019, Nestle has merged with another confectionery firm named Ferrera Candy Company."

"This is all well and good," Chief Giralo mentioned, "but we still haven't established the evasive motive for these five, devious knuckleheads oddly dressed in foolish-looking outfits giving store personnel a thousand dollars just for two money-oriented candy bars. Now then, before I dismiss this informal meeting," Giralo meticulously specified, "I have something additional to share that Matt Riley and I regard as rather pertinent evidence for you three gumshoes to constructively examine."

Giralo again opened his impressive oak desk's top drawer, removed the same faded oak-tag folder and cautiously handed his men three photocopies of an "essential incomplete word" that the Boss theorized was most definitely a material clue. "Gentlemen, this brief documentation I believe represents a key factor in cracking-open this up-to-now incredulous Holiday Hooligans case."

"This looks like total gibberish to me," complained and protested Agent Velardi. "Why didn't you hand us the Rosetta Stone or maybe some cryptic Indian Sanskrit message instead?"

"For your intense scrutiny," the Inspector addressed his competent team, "I've taken the liberty to type-in exact chronological order the first letters of the eleven cities that have thus far been frivolously exposed to the abnormal shenanigans of the five disguised suspects, along with their similarly-dressed van driver accomplice."

"I see a definite connection already," Agent Blachford deduced and verbally shared. "There are eleven letters indicated on this piece of paper, and eleven cities have actually been targeted. I conjecture that the twelfth mystery city will be hit on Christmas Day."

"Dan's right," impulsively verified Agent Orsi. "The twelfth impractical intrusion will mischievously occur on Christmas Day, and our challenging task is to figure-out what U.S. city will be the next setting for these obnoxious, six slippery rogues to visit."

"Now study the eleven letters carefully," Giralo advised his fully preoccupied assistants. "There might be some elusive-but-germane hint embedded within the chronological sequence of first letters starting with alphabet item P."

"Listen, Men. I confidently predict that the next candy store exploit will occur with six individuals dressed as Santa Claus on Christmas Day, Wednesday December 25," the overweight man seated behind the oak desk prognosticated. "And I also think that city number twelve will begin with the letter 'H', but it will not again be Houston. We'll meet this coming Saturday at noon inside Andy's Restaurant, Route 54, in Hammonton to further discuss this most fairly sensational case. Until then," Chief Giralo remarked and then smiled, "I strongly recommend that you three crackerjack detectives also actively pursue your regular happy investigations."

* * * * * * * * * * * *

Rural Hammonton and vicinity had for over a century been a prosperous, commercial, agricultural hub for Southern New Jersey. In the 1950s, peaches were the dominant fruit crop. Then in the late '60s, blueberries became the area farmers' money favorite. Now in 2019, raspberries, grapes and blackberries have been gaining a solid economic foothold. To remember and honor the community's vital agrarian past and present, Peach Tree Plaza on Route 30 and Blueberry Crossing Mall on the same four-lane highway respectively refer to the '50s and '60s, and now Raspberry Run Shoppes, located south of town on Route 54, alludes to the state of the present summer produce industry.

Inspector Giralo and his three proficient federal colleagues were scheduled to unite at Andy's Restaurant at Raspberry Run for a pertinent noonday discussion on Saturday, December 21st."

"It was nice for the owners to cooperate and provide an isolated table for us in the back room," Joe Giralo stated as the four hungry patrons sat-down at the reserved round table. "Thanks to my shiny FBI badge, we G-Men always receive top priority when it comes to accommodations and seating arrangements."

An attractive blonde waitress scurried across the brown tile floor and intended to pass-out menus that included breakfast and lunch entrees. "That's all right, Miss," the Inspector pleasantly declared. "Just bring us three cups of hot coffee and three orders of eggs, bacon, home fries and white toast. And please have the chef make the eggs over light!"

"Now Chief," Agent Velardi softly uttered. "Arty, Dan and I have successfully decoded the cryptogram with the letters P-L-A-L-A-D-I-E-H-P-I. You told us that the twelfth missing alphabet letter is a second 'H'. If you rearrange the twelve letters after adding *your* 'H', the city of 'Philadelphia' is formed."

"That easy observation is only a minor coincidence," Giralo plausibly informed Velardi. "The important factor to note is that the second 'H' city is going to be something other than Houston."

"Inspector, I'll wager that it certainly isn't Hammonton," Art Orsi surmised and chuckled. "Inspector, I'm pretty befuddled about this whole silly ordeal. What's *your* esoteric theory about the second 'H' city having a variety of convenience stores that could potentially be harassed by a bevy of asinine St. Nicholas wannabes. The next event, or should I say 'fiasco', will be a dumb, foolish Santa Claus intrusion happening somewhere in an 'H' city on Wednesday, December 25th."

Just after the breakfast orders had been graciously served, Joe Giralo then delved deeply into the crux of the matter. "I conjecture that the redundant 100 Grand candy bar purchase is probably the master key that unlocks this entire freaky holiday costume mystery. Certain criminals are so cocky and haughty that they think they can easily outsmart anyone involved in law enforcement," Giralo maintained. "This ongoing holiday candy bar travesty is merely a cute diversion to draw the press's attention away from a crime-in-progress. Reporters and TV news anchors will stupidly divert *their* so-called 'news stories' from describing crimes to writing disgusting tabloid journalism such as imbecilic leprechauns and Easter bunnies fanatically paying a thousand dollars for one Pay Day candy bar and for one 100 Grand candy-bar that will have been obtained at twelve separate stores in a dozen different metropolises."

"Okay, oh Great Leader," chipped-in a generally bewildered Sal Velardi. "We understand that the press is conveniently distracted. But how do we determine what the second 'H' city will be that'll have some unfortunate store clerk scared to death by these nutcase holiday hooligans on Christmas Day?"

"You're putting the cart before the horse," Giralo responded by uttering an overused, hackneyed cliché. "Now Salvatore, certain expensive automobiles such as Mercedes-Benz CL Class, top-end Cadillac Escalades and Porsche 911s retail at around a hundred thousand dollars each. I speculate that the 100 Grand candy bar is the real decoding mechanism to be utilized here."

"Holy cow! I think you're positively right, Boss," Agent Blachford confirmed after aggressively consulting related data from his indispensable handheld FBI computer. "Now, I believe I understand the entire complicated canard. High-end plush cars have been stolen precisely on the same holiday dates that the weirdo masquerading hooligans had created havoc in all eleven cities that formed most of the letters to the word 'Philadelphia', which if I recall, was the first city existing on the comprehensive FBI list."

After sipping a mouthful of his tasty coffee, inspired Inspector Joe Giralo directed Agent Orsi to research on *his* handheld computer the identities of the next three densely populated U.S. "H cites".

"Huntsville, Alabama is indicated as Number 123, Huntington Beach, California is listed as Number 124, and Hollywood, Florida is not far behind," G-Man Arthur Orsi contributed his valuable input in solving the formerly perplexing holiday hooligan enigma.

"Then it's all settled!" Inspector Giralo sagely proclaimed. "I'll consult with Matt Riley later today, and we'll dispatch three separate FBI squads: one each to Huntsville, to Huntington Beach and to Hollywood, Florida. I'm quite sure than our triple 'H' dragnets, all occurring at high-end car dealerships, will ultimately land us with at least several surprised suspects this coming Christmas Day! The clowns that we will apprehend will surely rat on all of *their* criminal accomplices. Bon Appetit, Gentlemen!"

# About the Author

Jay Dubya is author John Wiessner's pen name and also his initials (J.W.) John is a retired New Jersey public school English teacher and he had taught the subject for thirty-four years. John lives in southern New Jersey with wife Joanne and the couple has three grown sons. John is the creator of fifty-five books.

Jay Dubya has written adult satires *Fractured Frazzled Folk Fables and Fairy Farces* and *FFFF and FF, Part II*. *Black Leather and Blue Denim, A '50s Novel* and its sequel, *The Great Teen Fruit War, A 1960' Novel* and *Frat' Brats, A '60s Novel* are adult-oriented literary endeavors constituting a trilogy.

*Pieces of Eight, Pieces of Eight, Part II, Pieces of Eight Part III* and *Pieces of Eight, Part IV* are' short story/novella collections featuring science fiction, paranormal and humorous plots and themes. *Nine New Novellas* is the companion book to *Nine New Novellas, Part II, Nine New Novellas, Part III* and *Nine New Novellas, Part IV*. And *So Ya' Wanna' Be A Teacher* is a satirical autobiography describing the author's thirty-four-year educational career in American public schools.

*Ron Coyote, Man of La Mangia* is adult humor and the work is an imaginative satire/parody on Miguel Cervantes' Don Quixote, published in 1605. *Mauled Maimed Mangled Mutilated Mythology* is a work that satires twenty-one famous ancient tales. *The Wholly Book of Genesis* and *The Wholly Book of Exodus* are also adult satirical humor. *Thirteen Sick Tasteless Classics, Thirteen Sick Tasteless Classics, Part II, Thirteen Sick Tasteless Classics, Part III* and *Thirteen Sick Tasteless Classics, Part IV* are adult satirical rewrites of famous short fiction.

John has also authored a trilogy of young adult fantasy novels, *Enchanta, Pot of Gold* and *Space Bugs, Earth Invasion*. *The Eighteen Story Gingerbread House* is a new collection of eighteen diverse and creative children's stories.

Jay Dubya likes '50s rock and roll music and he also enjoys pop' songs by the Beach Boys, Fleetwood Mac, the Eagles, the Rolling Stones, ELO, John Mellencamp and by John Fogerty.

# Author Biography

Born in Hammonton, NJ in 1942, John Wiessner had attended St. Joseph School up to and including Grade 5. After his family moved from Hammonton to Levittown, Pa in 1954, John attended St. Mark School in Bristol, Pa. for Grade 6, St. Michael the Archangel School in Levittown for Grades 7 and 8 and then Immaculate Conception School, Levittown, Pa. for Grade 9. Bishop Egan High School, Levittown Pa was John's educational base for Grades 10 and 11, and later in 1960, the aspiring author graduated from Edgewood Regional High, Tansboro, NJ. John then next attended Glassboro State College, where he was an announcer for the school's baseball games and also read the nightly news and sports over WGLS, GSC's radio station.

John Wiessner had been primarily an English teacher in the Hammonton Public School System for 34 years, specializing in the instruction of middle school language arts. Mr. Wiessner was quite active in the Hammonton Education Association, serving in the capacities of Vice-President, building representative and finally, teachers' head negotiator for 7 years. During his lengthy teaching career, John had been nominated into "Who's Who Among American Teachers" three times. He also was quite active giving professional workshops at schools around South Jersey on the subjects of creative writing and the use of movie videos to motivate students to organize their classroom theme compositions.

John Wiessner was very active in community service, being a past President of the Hammonton Lions Club, where he also functioned for many years as the club's Tail-Twister, Vice-President and Liontamer. John had been named Hammonton Lion of the Year in 1979 and in 2009 received the prestigious Melvin Jones Fellow Award, the highest honor a Lion can receive from Lions International.

John also was a successful businessman, starting with being a Philadelphia Bulletin newspaper delivery boy for two years in the late 1950s in Levittown, Pennsylvania. After his family moved back to New Jersey in 1959, John worked at his grandparents and his parents' farm markets, Square Deal Farm (now Ron's Gardens in Hammonton) and Pete's Farm Market in Elm, respectively. He later managed his wife's parents' farm market, White Horse Farms in Elm for three summers.

Also, in a business capacity, for 16 summers starting in 1967 John Wiessner had co-owned Dealers Choice Amusement Arcade on the Ocean City, Maryland boardwalk and also co-owned the New Horizon Tee-Shirt Store for eight summers (1973-'81) on the

Rehoboth Beach, Delaware boardwalk. In addition, "Jay Dubya" was a co-owner of Wheel and Deal Amusement Arcade, Missouri Avenue and Boardwalk, Atlantic City. And then, for 18 summers beginning in 1986, John had been the Field Manager in charge of crew-leaders for Atlantic Blueberry Company (the world's largest cultivated blueberry farm), both the Weymouth and Mays Landing Divisions.

After retiring from teaching in 1999, writing under the pen name Jay Dubya (his initials), John Wiessner became the author of 55 books in the genre Action/Adventure Novels, Sci-Fi/Paranormal Story Collections, Adult Satire, Young Adult Fantasy Novels and Non-Fiction Books. His books exist in hardcover, in paperback and in popular Kindle and Nook e-book formats.

Google: Jay Dubya books